SLOW
BURN

CHERRY
ADAIR

SLOW
BURN

ISBN-13: 978-0-373-77874-4

SLOW BURN

Copyright © 2014 by Harlequin Books S.A.

The publisher acknowledges the copyright holder of the individual works as follows:

SEDUCING MR. RIGHT
Copyright © 2001 by Cherry Wilkinson

TAKE ME
Copyright © 2002 by Cherry Wilkinson

Recycling programs for this product may not exist in your area.

Printed in U.S.A.

www.Harlequin.com

CONTENTS

SEDUCING MR. RIGHT

CHAPTER ONE

THREE THINGS OCCURRED to Catherine Harris as she jerked out of a dead sleep.

One, she was stark naked in Luke Van Buren's bed.

Two, he was about to enter his bedroom.

Three, he wasn't alone. A woman's throaty laughter mingled with Luke's deep baritone in the hallway.

Luke wasn't supposed to be back in San Francisco for a couple more days. Catherine tried not to panic. Suddenly years of planning didn't seem like nearly enough time.

She leaned up on one elbow, squinted into the darkness and remembered she'd thrown her bra over the clock to block the red LCD light. Catherine flopped back on the pillow, several options, none of them viable, flashed through her sleep-fogged brain. Hiding under the bed while bedsprings bounced was too hideous to contemplate. As was the picture of the fire department rescuing her from the ledge outside Luke's bedroom window, twenty-two stories above the street.

She heard a soft thud. A shoe? The sound of her own rapid pulse did nothing to block out the next thump. The swish of clothing. An impatient sigh. A hungry kiss pressed to bare flesh. Framed in the open doorway, barely discernable, was Luke's white shirt, which the woman's hands were rapidly removing. Catherine saw it flutter to the carpet. Heard a click.

Oh, God. His belt buckle?

"Speak up, Catherine," she whispered.

There was the distinct rasp of a zipper.

The sound of a juicy kiss.

"Oh, Luke!" The woman giggled. Then there was more rustling, more heated murmurs, breathy sighs. Catherine's cheeks flamed, blood pounding in her ears. Anticipating the fireworks to come, she felt hysterical laughter bubbling up in her throat.

"Make love to me, Luke. Oh, yes…I adore when you touch me…yes. Mmm. Oh, yes."

Oh, no. Catherine tried to slither out of the way before the woman flopped onto the bed. Too late.

The weight of two full-grown adults squashed the air out of Catherine's lungs. Grunting, she tried to wriggle out from under, but couldn't get any traction on the satin sheets.

The woman rolled to the side, shot to her feet and let out a bloodcurdling scream. With a thump and a curse, Luke landed on the floor beside the bed.

"What in God's name—"

"There's someone in your bed!" the woman shrieked.

Catherine heard Luke get to his feet, then fumble for the switch on the bedside lamp.

Showtime.

She sat up, tucked the slithery sheet under her armpits and tried her best to appear nonchalant. Chances were she looked like the wild woman of Borneo. She hadn't braided her hair before she'd gone to bed; it frothed about her bare shoulders, tickling the tops of her breasts. The bedside light snapped on just as she blew a particularly stubborn hank out of her eyes. As she squinted in the brightness, her gaze clashed with a pair of narrowed gray-green eyes boring a hole into the middle of her forehead.

"Catherine." Luke zipped his pants, then raked his fingers through his disheveled dark hair. His broad, hairy chest expanded with the ragged, frustrated breath he dragged into his lungs.

Reluctantly she tore her gaze from his splendidly naked chest and waited for the dragon to roar. He appeared twice as tall as six foot three, and three times as irritated as he'd been when she'd backed his new sports car into the mailbox years ago.

"I might have known." He plucked her bra off the clock. "Yours?" The black sports bra hung like a limp piece of licorice in his large, well-shaped hand.

Catherine leaned forward just enough to take the bra without losing her grip on the safely tucked sheet. "Thanks." The brush of his fingers sent an electrical charge up her arm. She cleared her throat, then decided to live dangerously and fluttered her eyelashes at him. "Does this mean I have to get dressed now, honey?"

Catherine gave his friend a wide smile, which the woman didn't reciprocate. Drop-dead gorgeous in a little black number hardly wider than a belt, she had long legs and an ample bosom, displayed to advantage in the skimpy dress. Expensive, high-maintenance, honey-colored hair cascaded seductively over one shoulder. Catherine sighed. Another pocket Venus. Without a sense of humor. Figured.

Into the tension-laced atmosphere, Catherine asked brightly, "Is it your birthday?"

"What is she talking about?" the blonde demanded,

hand splayed across her chest to hold up her dress. Keeping her eyes firmly fixed on Catherine, she turned her back so Luke could zip her. The twin lines between her plucked-to-a-fare-thee-well eyebrows would become permanent in short order if she persisted in scowling like that. The woman had the kind of looks that would go rapidly downhill the moment gravity took over, and a slight overbite that made her, in Catherine's opinion, look a little like a hamster she'd once owned. She also had the same mean-eyed look Scamper used to give just before he gnawed her finger.

Narrow-eyed, Luke scrutinized her. "What are you up to?"

Catherine opened her eyes so wide her lashes tickled her eyebrows. "Didn't you bring her home to play, Luke, sweetums?"

"Catherine..." he warned.

She gave him an apologetic little smile, filled with as much sincerity as she could muster, and spoke normally. "I thought you were out of town. Honestly, I wouldn't have—"

"Who the hell is she?" the woman demanded, slipping her dainty feet back into high-heeled mules, her mouth unattractively pouty.

Luke strode to the highboy against the far wall, then glanced over his shoulder. "Cat Harris. Elizabeth Wyrech." He jerked open a drawer, yanked out a sage-green cotton sweater and pulled it over his head. It did wonderful things to his eyes.

"Hi." Catherine didn't offer her hand, for the sheet was in danger of slithering into her lap. "Look, you don't have to run off. Does she, Luke? I mean—"

"Cut it out, Catherine," Luke said, clearly not

amused. "Explain to Elizabeth who you are, then shut up."

Catherine stared at him. "Everything? Are you sure? Doesn't she know you get bored with just one lady in your be—"

"A ménage à trois? This is really sick, Luke." Elizabeth scooped up her purse and held it in front of her like a shield. "I'm calling a cab."

"She's my sister, for God's sake!"

"Oh, really?" No matter how beautiful, the woman had a nasty mind and an ugly sneer. Catherine narrowed her eyes at her. Elizabeth narrowed hers back.

"You have different last names."

"Different mothers," Luke said.

"Different fathers," Catherine said at the same time.

"She's my stepsister!" Luke strode across the room and wrapped his strong fingers around Catherine's clenched jaw. "Siblings. Right, Cat?" His hand moved her head up and down to acknowledge the statement.

"Right." Catherine gave Elizabeth the Wretch a tight smile and pretended that arrow hadn't pierced her heart. "His sister."

"That's even sicker," Elizabeth said coldly before storming out of the bedroom.

Catherine gripped the sheet tighter, a hard knot in her throat. She couldn't drag her eyes away from Luke, and her face flamed hotly enough for her to damn her pale skin. His sister.

From six years old she'd dreamed, wished, prayed he'd accept her as family. When she'd been older that wish had come true. But by then sister was no longer the relationship she craved.

Usually pragmatic and sensible, Catherine had made

a gigantic leap of faith in coming to Luke. This was not an auspicious start to her plan.

"I'll take Liz home and be back in twenty minutes."

"I'll be here." If she didn't take a cowardly leap from the balcony first.

He turned when he got to the door and glanced back. "Don't go to sleep. We're going to talk. Tonight."

Did they have to? She checked his eyes. Absolutely.

"Be dressed when I get back."

"Aye, aye, Captain." Catherine saluted. The satin sheet glided like water over her naked skin, baring one breast.

She froze and stared at Luke.

White-knuckled, he gripped the doorknob.

A beat later he slammed the bedroom door behind him.

I'M IN DEEP, deep trouble here, Luke thought on his circuitous, I-need-more-time-to-think-about-this drive home an hour later. How in heaven's name was he ever going to be able to forget the sight of Cat's bare b— His fingers tightened on the steering wheel. Oh, man…

His dad had married Cat's mother nineteen years ago. So there wasn't a drop of familial blood between them. Thank God. But Luke could never forget what a mean, nasty jerk he'd been to Catherine for years. It had taken even more years before he'd been forced to realize just what his cruelty was costing her, and he'd sworn to himself he would always love and protect her to make up for the years he'd done just the opposite.

The way he now felt didn't negate the promises he'd made.

He'd sworn to his dad, just before he'd died, that he would take care of Catherine. More important, he'd made Cat a promise to be her big brother. He'd assured her he would always be there for her. To protect her, to keep her safe, to have him to depend on, for anything and everything. Luke considered these promises sacrosanct, unshakable and nonnegotiable.

Too bad his libido wasn't as ethical as his brain. He reluctantly turned his decrepit Jaguar into the basement parking lot beneath his building. Just because his feelings had changed dramatically was no reason to disillusion her. He had to remember that to Cat he was no more than her big brother. Her safe, dependable big brother. End of story.

HER FACE STILL hot, Catherine speedily dressed the second the front door closed behind Luke and what's-her-name. Her goal had seemed so simple and straightforward back home in Beaverton. Get Luke to see her as a desirable woman and act on it. Of course, she hadn't planned on him seeing her naked in his bed. At least not yet!

Catherine padded into the living room and flung herself into the squishy black leather chair she'd bought Luke with every penny of her savings when he and their friend Nick had gone off to New York to become architects. The chair smelled like Luke. She snuggled her cheek against the skin-smooth leather and closed her eyes. She'd thought of little else but him for years. She could do this. She *would* do this.

Perhaps it wasn't so bad, after all, that Luke had had a sneak preview....

WEARING JEANS AND one of his old Pratt Institute sweat-shirts, Cat's five-foot-ten frame was curled up in the big black leather armchair in the corner of the living room when Luke returned.

Thank God she's dressed, he thought, *and thank God she's tamed that hair.* Catherine Anne Harris had the reddest, wildest, most touchable hair he'd ever seen. It had a life of its own.

Seeing her naked in his bed with that electrified mane, like living flame gone berserk, had almost given him a coronary. He wasn't quite so tempted to bury his hands in it when she had it scraped back in her usual French braid. And if he concentrated very hard for the next three or four hundred years, he might forget how the light had sculpted, in shadows and high-lights, the satin sheets on Cat's naked body. And the sight of one plump, perfect, pale freckled breast. He stuffed his hands into his pockets and sauntered into the living room.

"Hi." Cat sat up and rubbed sleepy hazel eyes, her cheeks flushed under a generous sprinkling of cinnamon-colored freckles. She pulled her bare feet up and wrapped her arms around her knees. Even her slender toes had cinnamon dots.

There was a short, strained silence. "She seems like a nice woman," Cat commented, offering a hopeful smile. Luke was caught by the humor in her eyes and the lushness of her wide, soft mouth.

He shook his head. "Not particularly." He sat on the edge of the coffee table facing her. Thank God she had no inkling how much it cost him to sit this close and not jump her bones.

Cat frowned. "I don't get it. If you don't like her, what were you doing sleeping with her?"

"A, I hadn't slept with her. Yet. B, I like Elizabeth just fine. C, don't change the subject. Not that you aren't welcome, Catwoman, but what are you doing here?" he asked mildly.

"I thought you'd gone to New York this week." She rested her chin on her bent knees. "What did you tell her?"

"I told her you have a warped sense of the ridiculous, but that basically you're harmless." About as harmless as dropping a centerfold into a maximum-security prison block.

"I was embarrassed. It was awkward for all of us. I guess I made it worse by trying to joke about it. I'm sorry to have put you in an uncomfortable position, Luke. Really. If you want me to call her—"

"There's no need, Cat. Don't worry about it." Elizabeth had the sensitivity of a newt. Anyone else would have seen Catherine's embarrassment. "I came home from New York early."

She wasn't wearing a bra. He could see her full breasts move gently as she shifted. He frowned. "Don't distract me, answer the question. What are you doing here?"

Cat yawned, then rubbed the tip of her nose with her palm. "I was in a rut in Oregon. I needed a change, so here I am."

"You aren't going to stop day trading, are you?" Luke asked, horrified. Self-taught, Cat had become a market wizard. She enjoyed the challenge of figuring out which stocks were about to go up, and buying and selling them on the same day to immediately profit on the stock's rise in value. This enabled Cat to multiply her money many times over the course of a day. Plus she'd been able to do it from home, on her own computer, while she took care of his dad. With her canny knowledge of the stock market, and uncanny intuition, she'd made a bundle of money trading stocks for Luke over the years. If it wasn't for her, he and Nick would never have been able to afford to open their own architectural business so soon. The business was doing well enough to afford them the luxury of owning their own building.

The woman had a mind like a steel trap and the Midas touch. There were several of his dad's old cronies whose money she'd parlayed into small fortunes, just for the fun of it.

"Don't worry. I brought my computer. Your future fortune is still safe in my hands."

"Thank God. You can set up camp at Van Buren and Stratton if you like. There's a spare office on the second floor you can use." The thought of being with Catherine Harris 24/7 terrified him. He wondered where he could find large amounts of saltpeter.

"You don't have to sound so unenthusiastic," Cat laughed. "No, thank you, it would never work. We all know each other too well. You're too much of a slob, and Nick and I would goof around and I'd never get any work done. If you don't mind, I'll work from here for a while."

"Sure." Cat would be here every night when he got home. A curse and a blessing.

"Did I mess up a beautiful relationship?" she asked suddenly.

Luke easily followed the non sequitur. Cat was nothing if not tenacious. "Probably not."

"Will you see her again?"

"More than likely."

"She could have given the situation the benefit of the doubt, you know." Cat nibbled her bottom lip. He wished to hell she wouldn't do that. "A little sense of humor would have gone a long way." She sighed gustily. "Okay, it was stupid, and I'm really, really sorry."

Ah, Cat's innate sense of honor and fair play. "No harm done. Don't worry about it."

"Do you mind if I stay here until I find a place of my own?"

Don't offer, he thought. *Do not, the hell, offer.* "No, not at all. I wouldn't have given you a key if I minded your comings and goings." He paused, then scowled, alarmed that his eyes kept dropping to her chest. "I told you when I came home for the funeral that you'd be welcome anytime. Why didn't you tell me you weren't happy there?"

Cat sighed. "Luke. How old am I?"

"You're…twenty-three?"

"Try twenty-six, I've always been seven years younger than you. How come you never remember?" She shifted back in his chair, clearly uncomfortable under his close scrutiny. She'd always been a prickly little thing. "Life was passing me by. I want to stretch my wings a bit."

"I know, honey." He reached out and covered her hand. Cat had nursed his father for the five years preceding his death eight months ago. Luke had frequently envied Cat and his father's close relationship. Now Luke was all Cat had left. Her flaky mother didn't count.

She flushed and withdrew her hand. "I didn't sacrifice anything. We were father and daughter by choice, not chance, and I loved him. Don't go all big brother on me. It took longer than I thought to get his affairs tied up. I contacted a real estate agent and put the house on the market—" She put up a hand to forestall his usual rhetoric about the estate. "No, Luke, I'm not keeping the house. Besides, my moth—Faith is between husbands at the moment, and she's been broadly hinting she might like to come 'home to rest' for a little while."

"She's run out of money." It wasn't a question. If Faith was between husbands or lovers, it was a given.

Cat's smile broke his heart. "That, too."

He'd like to wring Faith's beautiful neck. "You should buy a nice condo with the money Dad left you."

Those expressive tiger eyes of hers darkened. Ah, hell.

"It's invested. If you don't want me here," she said stiffly, slender shoulders hunched, "just say so. I'll go and stay with Nick."

Nick. Their mutual friend, partner, fellow architect and ladies' man? No way. "Does Nick know about this?"

"Not yet."

At least she'd come to Luke first.

He and Nick had been next-door neighbors, and best friends, when Luke still had a matched set of parents. After the divorce, and his father's remarriage, Nick and Cat had become friends. Luke wasn't jealous of their close relationship anymore, but he was inordinately pleased she'd chosen to come to him instead of going to Nick.

"Hey! *Mi casa es su casa.* Finding an apartment in San Francisco is almost impossible. I was planning to keep the condo for the nights I work late. You might as well live here. In a few months the house should be finished, and I'll be moving out of the city, anyway. Until then we can figure out who gets the bed and who gets the sofa."

Her eyes clouded briefly. "Sure?"

He knew this particular insecurity well, and said casually, "Positive. But on one condition. This time unpack and spread out. Last time you came you kept your stuff in your suitcase stuck in the closet for two weeks. If you're going to live here, live here. Okay?"

"Okay. Thanks." Her shoulders relaxed. "The house is that close to being finished, huh?"

"Yeah, it's coming along great. You can come and help me tomorrow, if you like." He noticed her sleepy eyes and smiled. "Since you had the bed last, why don't you finish the night there? I'll take the sofa. We can work out our sleeping arrangements tomorrow."

"I'm not sleepy. How about hot chocolate?"

"I don't have any."

"Yes, you do. I bought groceries on my way here." She unfurled her long, long legs and stood. Luke rose at the same time, and they came nose-to-nose, inches apart.

He'd forgotten how tall she was. Her mouth was almost on a level with his.

If he bent his knees…

If Cat stood on her toes…

If she had been any other desirable woman, he would have slipped his arms about her slender waist, drawn her against his chest and kissed that soft succulent mouth until they were both gasping for air. He quickly shook off the thought.

He trailed her into his chrome-and-black-glass kitchen, observing the way her hips moved as she padded on bare feet. She had a loose-jointed walk that made Playboy centerfolds look like windup toys.

Luke settled at the small table under the window as Cat heated milk and made their drinks. She knew where everything was because she'd put it there when he'd moved in two years ago.

"Thanks." Luke took the brimming mug she offered. Chocolate-scented steam tantalized his taste buds. He waited until she slid into the other chair before he spoke. "You were stifled in that house with Dad all those years, Cat. I understand you wanting to try something new and exciting. And San Francisco certainly is that. But don't you think it might be a culture shock?"

She'd taken a tentative sip and already wore a chocolate milk mustache. She watched him over the rim of her mug. Transfixed, he watched her pink tongue come out and lick the creamy film off her upper lip. He was going to drop dead from a heart attack at age thirty-three.

Her eyes flickered away, then back again.

"Okay, Cat. What are you up to?"

"Me?" She was all wide-eyed innocence. "Nothing."

"The first time you gave me that look was when you said you weren't running away to join the circus, remember? We found you in the park two blocks away, panhandling for bus fare."

Cat grinned. "I promise, I don't want to join the circus."

The chocolate must have burned the hell out of her throat, but she chugged it down, then cradled the empty mug. She had pretty hands. Slender, no-nonsense, with short, unpolished nails. He wanted them on him.

Luke's heart took up an unexpected arrhythmic beat as he watched her. Despite her mother's influence, Cat had always been a sensible woman. Somehow she'd remained refreshingly innocent. She was what was known as a "good girl." More than likely the last of a dying breed. In spite of her lush, curvy body, she was wholesome. Natural.

Cat gave him a level, serious look. "I came because you're the only man I trust, Luke. I have a problem."

He felt sick. "Do you want him to marry you, or do you want me to punch him out?"

Cat looked at him blankly. "Marry? Punch? Who?"

"Cat, for God's sake! The man who got you pregnant!"

She stared at him as though he'd lost his mind. "I'm a virgin, Luke."

"Well, hell, what does that have to do with anyth— What?"

"Virgin? Unmarried woman? Untouched? Pure?"

"Jesus." His breath gusted out, and it took several moments to get his heartbeat back to comfortable. He scraped his fingers through his hair, feeling ridiculously as if he'd stood perilously close to the edge of an abyss and survived. "Sorry, I tend to get a little carried away," he admitted gruffly.

"I've noticed." Cat's voice was dry. Her mouth wore a small, tentative smile, but her eyes still looked as if she were about to tell him something he didn't want to hear. He'd anticipated the worst and rallied. Relaxing, he leaned back in his chair.

"What do you need help with? Want to come and work out of our office? No problem, I told you we'll find a spot for you—"

She watched him with big, serious eyes. "I don't want you to find me office space, Luke. I want you to find me a husband."

CHAPTER TWO

"WELL, SAY SOMETHING." Catherine tried not to let her nerves show as he sat there gaping.

Even while she'd agonized over doing this, she'd hoped she'd have to go no further than to ask Luke for his help. It would have made life a whole bunch easier if he'd just cut to the chase and declared his undying love for her at the onset.

The Plan hadn't gotten much beyond that. She wanted more, but with Luke's attitude toward permanence, she was realistic enough to know she wasn't going to get it.

Her biggest leap of faith had been to burn her bridges, and take the chance that he wouldn't reject her outright. Again.

Ten years was a long time, she kept reminding herself. They'd both grown up since. She wasn't that naive, impulsive kid anymore. She knew Luke better now. For her plan to work, this seduction was going to have to be his idea. Unfortunately, he was still staring at her, slack-jawed.

"Well?" she said with a shaky breath. "Say something."

"I'm speechless."

"Could you hurry up and get over it?" Catherine pulled a yellow scratch pad and a pen out of the canvas bag she'd slung over the finial of her chair earlier. She concentrated on writing "Prospective Husbands" at the top of the page in neat block letters, more to give Luke time to assimilate what she'd said than the need to make a list. She glanced up. His eyes were squinty.

"What?" she asked innocently.

"What do you mean, you want me to find you a husband? You have a phobic aversion to marriage!"

"No. That's you." *Keep it casual, Catherine.* "I have a phobic aversion to my mother's marriages. What if poor marital judgment is hereditary? My apple might have fallen closer to my mother's tree than I'd like. I just don't trust my own judgment."

"And you'd trust mine? I don't believe in marriage, remember?"

How could she forget? "You'll meet someone someday."

"No," he said unequivocally. "I won't. And frankly, Cat, considering we've both seen your mother in action, I'm surprised that you'd want to make the same mistakes."

"With your help, I won't."

"I don't get it. Why?"

"Because I need someone to take care of, Luke. After Dad died I realized I liked taking care of someone. I love being a homemaker. I know it's politically incorrect not to want a career, but I don't. I enjoy trading stocks on the market, and as long as I have my computer and a phone line, I can do that anywhere. But if I had to stop that tomorrow, I wouldn't care. I guess I'm a throwback, what can I say? I want a husband to love, and to be loved by. Eventually kids. I want a couple of dogs, and a house with a big yard. Is that too much to ask—where are you going?"

"To make more hot chocolate."

"There's still some. Here." She handed him her mug and waited while he poured hot chocolate haphazardly from the pan. Catherine observed the motion of muscles flexing beneath his green sweater. She drew in a deep breath, then held it until her stomach behaved itself. Luke had never made any bones about his intention to remain a bachelor. She remembered him telling her just that, right after his own mother remarried for the third time. Luke didn't believe in promises any more than Catherine did. The difference was she was willing to take the chance. Luke wasn't.

He yanked open a cabinet and grabbed a bottle of something hideously expensive, using more force than necessary. She perked up. Wrenching the cap off, he sloshed liquor into his mug, then slammed the bottle onto the black granite countertop. Even better.

"Are we celebrating?" she asked as he placed both mugs on the table. She plucked napkins out of the holder to mop up the chocolate milk he'd sloshed onto the tabletop.

"What do you think, Catherine?" He strode back to retrieve the liquor bottle, which he slam-dunked onto the table between them. Then, scowling, he threw himself into his chair and raked his fingers through his hair until it stood up like a shark fin.

"Well, I think a celebration is a little premature right now…but sure." She reached out to take the bottle. Luke removed it gently from her grasp. Which was fine with her. If it tasted anything like it smelled, she'd gag. *Come on, Luke,* she silently urged, *let's hear it.*

"Are you out of your mind, Cat?" A vein throbbed in his temple. His eyes had turned a smoky green. "If you have this burning need to take care of something, get a poodle."

"Not quite the same thing, Luke."

Even with that look of total exasperation on his face he was the sexiest man she'd ever laid eyes on. Too sexy for plain Catherine Harris. But she wanted him anyway. Her and about a billion other women. Luke Van Buren was Mr. Confirmed Bachelor Playboy himself. He'd never had to look for female companionship. Anything female would spot him from a hundred feet away and be charmed. He loved women. He treated his girlfriends with care and consideration, and adored them.

As long as he was with them.

Lucas Van Buren epitomized the expression "out of sight, out of mind." Over the years she'd witnessed the ebb and flow of Luke's lady friends. None of the relationships lasted very long. Which didn't bode well for her own future. But if she didn't try, how would she ever know?

Luke was a freewheeling playboy. She valued security and stability above all else. He was a daredevil who considered variety the spice of life. She wanted marriage. He wanted affairs.

She wanted him. He didn't want her.

When she'd first decided to come to San Francisco she'd considered asking Luke to find her a lover, not a husband. Since he wasn't husband material, that would have been closer to the truth. But she'd immediately dismissed that idea. Luke would have choked out a resounding and unequivocal *"N.O."*

"Did being stuck in that house with just Dad for company turn your gray matter into oatmeal?"

"Not that I know of. Look, this is quite simple, Luke. You must know a gazillion single guys. Lots of cultures have marriage brokers. Which, if you think about it, makes perfect sense. Look at the divorce rate when people find mates by random selection. It's up to sixty percent. Our mothers probably had a lot to do with that figure rising."

He splashed more amber liquid into his mug. His knuckles glowed white where he gripped the bottle. He hadn't said a word in minutes.

"You're intelligent. You know me, you care about me. You'll make a perfect marriage broker. Pick a few friends you think would make good husband material and I'll do the rest."

Catherine grabbed the pen, ignored the thud of her heartbeat right under her breastbone, and gave him a perky smile. She set the tip of the pen in the left margin and wrote a large number one. "Any interesting prospects in your address book under *A?*"

HE'D DONE SOMETHING really bad in another life and God was punishing him, Luke thought as he silently opened the bedroom door several sleepless hours later. To get to the bathroom and a cold shower, he had to traverse the bedroom where Cat slept. He'd spent a miserable night on the sofa thinking about her—and her harebrained scheme.

The world was her oyster. She should be enjoying the bliss of singlehood. Besides, how could a woman whose mother had been married, at last count, eight times even consider marriage?

Variety was the spice of life. Why would anyone put all their emotional eggs in one basket? How could one person be everything to another person? It wasn't logical. It wasn't smart. And Cat was usually so sensible, so predictable, so…sane.

Last night she'd been too tired to listen to reason. He'd talk some sense into her today, he decided, as he sneaked into his own sun-washed bedroom on Sunday morning, averting his gaze from the bed—for half a heartbeat.

Sleeping the sleep of the innocent and still wearing his sweatshirt, Cat sprawled diagonally across his California King mattress, sunlight streaming across her smooth bare legs. His fingers itched to slide up the satiny expanse. He wanted to follow his hands with his mouth and taste those freckles.

He sped into the bathroom, closed the door and wilted against it in his relief to have made it this far unscathed.

An icy shower went a long way to making him feel halfway human. When he opened the bathroom door again the first thing he saw was Cat's smiling face. His heart did a ridiculous and wholly inappropriate double axel as she sat up in bed, his bed, to smile at him.

"Good morning." She yawned, stretching like a cat.

"Get your lazy butt out of bed, woman," he told her sternly, digging through the chaos of his drawers for clean underwear while he held on to the towel around his waist with the other hand. "We have things to do and places to go." He'd have to knuckle down and do laundry soon. He looked over his shoulder and raised an eyebrow at her. "Are you awake in there?"

Cat shook her head as if to clear it, then scrambled

over the edge of the bed. "You betcha, Bubba. Give me ten minutes and I'm all yours." She shuffled into the bathroom. The door snicked behind her. He dropped the towel, dragged on underwear over damp skin and waited for the click of the lock.

He waited in vain.

The shower turned on.

He struggled to zip his jeans.

The bedroom smelled like Cat. Soft. Flowery. Permanent. He searched the upper shelves for a sweatshirt. Finding one he'd stuffed in there months ago, he held it up. Not too wrinkled. So he put it on.

"Hey, Luke?" she shouted over the noise of pounding water.

He closed his eyes. "What?"

"Did you come up with some names for me?" The shower turned off. "Hey. What happened to the towe— never mind, found them."

People showered naked every day of the week. He wished to hell Cat wasn't one of them. "We'll talk about it."

"What? I can't hear… That's better." A billow of Cat-scented steam preceded her as she opened the door. "Well, did you?"

"I said…" He clenched his teeth, bending down to tie the laces on his boots. They were on the wrong feet. He removed, then switched them, before tackling the laces. "…we'll talk about it."

She came out of the bathroom wearing one towel around her body, another wrapped turban style about her head. Her face was scrubbed shiny, her skin like fresh cream sprinkled with cinnamon. Her legs went on forever. In his fantasies he joined the dots.

If she was any other woman... But she was Cat. He'd bite off his own foot before he'd hurt her. This was not a woman a man played with. Cat was a keeper.

There wasn't a drop of blood in common between them. Their relationship was a state of mind. One he'd better keep remembering. She thought of him as her *brother,* he reminded himself grimly. Therefore Cat was off-limits. A no-no. Absolutely forbidden fruit.

"I hope it'll be soon, Luke." She pulled the towel from her head. "I'm not getting any younger, you know."

"Who is?" He'd tied the laces too tight, but he walked to the door anyway. When he turned back he managed to look just at her hair. Wet and wild, it tangled around her face and bare shoulders, and lovingly clung, like wet flames, to the upper swell of her—

"Hurry up and dress, will you? It's past ten and my stomach thinks my throat's been cut."

He closed the door gently behind him, feeling as though he'd just escaped something too terrifying to contemplate.

"Oh, my God, Luke, don't take the corners so fast!" Catherine screamed as the Hideous Harley did a faster-than-a-speeding-bullet skim around another corner. Clinging to his waist, she gripped his belt buckle with both hands. The seat felt obscenely wide between her thighs.

"Lean, Cat. Lean."

She leaned, sure her helmet must have brushed the gray asphalt as they cornered at an impossible angle.

Luke hadn't given her time to dry her hair. The moment she'd dressed in jeans and another of his over-size sweatshirts, he'd hustled her down to the parking garage, ignored his well-preserved 1977 Jag, climbed onto his enormous black demon motorcycle, handed her the spare helmet, revved the engine and instructed her to hold on.

If she'd been holding him any tighter, she would have been in front. The speed scared her speechless, no easy feat. Nevertheless, she'd better learn to love the wind tugging her hair from the helmet, biting into her face and making her nose and eyes run. Luke loved his bike.

His house was an hour south of San Francisco, down narrow, windy, stomach-churning coastal roads. Catherine squeezed her eyes shut and buried her icy nose against his leather-clad back, remembering the first time he'd taken her up behind him. She'd been ten. He was seventeen.

He'd only taken her because Dad had insisted she get the first ride on his new bike. She'd been terrified. Luke had been furious at her for being such a baby and had screamed blue murder at her for three blocks. The wind had caused her eyes to tear. And Luke and Dad had had a huge, yelling, door-slamming fight when they got back.

"Loosen up a bit, Catwoman. I can't breathe."

Since Catherine hadn't drawn a proper breath in more than an hour, she ignored his request. He felt warm and solid in her arms. "Are we there yet?" she whined like a five-year-old.

She felt Luke's laugh vibrate through her body like dark, sinfully rich chocolate. Oh, yes. She'd made the right decision coming to San Francisco. Yes, indeedy.

"STOP HERE FOR a sec," Catherine demanded an hour later as the bike turned from the tarred road parallel to the ocean onto the as-yet-unpaved gravel of Luke's new driveway. The fog had burned off, leaving sparkling spring sunshine glinting off the Pacific in the distance. Catherine inhaled the fresh briny air deep into her lungs as she let go of him and flung her leg over the bike the moment he brought it to a stop.

She stood, took off her helmet, then shaded her eyes with one hand against the sun, waiting for her heart to take up its normal rhythm after being glued to Luke for miles.

While the soft whoosh of the ocean sounded behind her, she forced herself to check out his house, as opposed to analyzing which body part felt what from the close encounter of the third kind with Luke's body.

Constructed of weathered redwood, tucked into the surrounding trees on a bluff overlooking a sliver of beach and the vastness of the ocean, the single-story house already had a look of permanence. Wonderfully gnarled, windblown cypress trees dotted the front yard.

"It's going to be magnificent, Luke."

Unaccountably, she felt the sting of tears, and rubbed the end of her nose with her palm. The house had been a goal of his for as long as she could remember. From the second he'd decided he wanted to be an architect, Luke had vowed to build his house from the ground up with his own two hands. A strangely permanent idea for a temporary kind of guy. Catherine wondered if Luke realized how at odds owning a house was with his playboy lifestyle.

While Luke loved the intricate curlicues and elaborate bits and pieces of Victorian houses, he'd explained to her once that he needed the clean, uncluttered lines of more modern architecture to cleanse his palate when he came home.

She noticed the enormous bay window in the living room. A window she'd suggested one rainy winter's night as they'd pored over the first version of his blueprints years ago. She doubted if he suspected how many of her own dreams had been woven into his house plans.

Gravel crunched under his workboots as Luke came up behind her and rested his hands lightly on her shoulders. They stood silently for several moments looking up the slight incline to the house. Catherine was excruciatingly conscious of him behind her. She felt each finger on her shoulders, the warmth of his tall body shielding her back from the hair-ruffling breeze. The air smelled of salt spray and fresh lumber. But most of all it smelled of sun-warmed Luke in leather.

His proximity had already caused her stomach to coil into knots. After an hour of straddling his rangy body she needed to put some distance between them. She stepped out of reach and smiled over her shoulder. "Let's walk the rest of the way so we can get the full ambiance."

Luke grimaced and Catherine grinned. If Luke could ride instead of walk, sit instead of stand or call instead of write, he was a happy man.

"Exercise is good for you. It can't be more than half a mile."

"These are workboots," he told her, "not walking boots. I have to save my energy for bossing you and Nick around."

She shrugged. "Fine. I'll walk. You ride. You should be an interesting-looking specimen once you hit forty. Flabby. Weak. Pasty. Probably sickly. That's okay," she said cheerfully, "you won't be the first man to wear a waist cincher."

Luke sighed, then knocked back the kickstand with his toe and rolled the bike beside her. "I go to the gym four times a week."

Catherine laughed. "You go there to pick up women." Luke's indolence had been a family joke. Yet there'd been nothing soft about the stomach muscles she'd felt when she'd clung to him on the bike, or the hard, tight muscles in his behind pressed between her thighs. There wasn't a flabby muscle on Luke's six-three frame.

"I pay the dues. I can do whatever I want."

He probably bench-pressed two blond gym bunnies. He might give the impression of being lazy, but Luke was no slouch in the flirtation department. Catherine had seen him in action. How many women, despite knowing Luke's views on marriage, wanted him anyway? But she wasn't going to dwell on that today. She was the woman he was with on this beautiful spring day. And she was going to enjoy every moment of it.

On either side of the slightly rolling topography, weeds, shrubs and vines tangled with thick trunks of oak, pine and cypress. There wasn't another house for half a mile. The only sounds were ocean breezes and insects in the long grasses.

"Nick's late," Luke commented as he detoured to angle the monster bike through a patch of sand, parking it against a prefab shed off to one side of the half-finished front porch.

"You work the poor guy like a slave. We barely got here ourselves."

"He's cheap, but he's good." Luke squinted in the wind that ruffled his dark hair. He sent her a grin. "And he's bringing lunch. Now, if I could just get him to give up some of his active social life, I might have this house finished next month as planned."

"It's a long commute," she said casually. A month? My God, there was no way she could pull this off in a month. Could she?

"Well, the office won't be practically across the street as it is now, but an hour's commute these days is nothing. Come on, I want to show off everything before Nick gets here."

Catherine followed Luke slowly as he walked up the wide, shallow redwood steps onto a deep porch. He bounced lightly, testing each tread. His fingers lingered as he trailed them up the simple banister beside the front steps. He took pride in his craftsmanship and it showed. Luke had a hedonistic pleasure in textures. He always had. She was jealous of the attention the wood was getting.

Catherine swallowed hard, remembering the night of her dateless junior prom. Luke had come to spend that weekend with his father. Exuberant as always, he'd burst into her room and found her crying. He hadn't known what to do with a weepy female, and had plucked the hairbrush out of her hand. More, she'd been sure, for something to do with his hands than to console her, he'd ended up brushing her hair for hours as they talked. Luke looking at the back of her head, Catherine watching his face, unobserved, in her vanity mirror across the room. She never did remember what they'd talked about, only that it was the first time she'd experienced sexual awareness. For her, it was the night their relationship had changed forever.

That was the night she'd realized she loved him.

Her ponytail brushed between her shoulder blades and she shivered, remembering the sensual pleasure of Luke's fingers in her hair, against her nape.... *Get a grip here,* she warned herself sternly, as she waited for him to unlock the massive oak door. Before she followed him inside, she bent to pull a weed that had managed to grow through the wood slats.

"Gonna plant that in a pot?" Luke turned, indicating the two-foot weed clutched in her hand, soil trailing from its roots.

His smile tangled up in Catherine's heart. Sunlight stroked his dark hair and magnified his strong, unshaved jaw. His long, lean body looked breathtaking in washed-almost-white jeans and a short leather jacket. He looked handsome, disreputable and too sexy for a small-town girl from Oregon. Yet she wanted him more than her next breath. She held out the droopy weed. "Got a pot?"

"And a window," he said dryly. "Here, give me that. I'll take you on the twenty-dollar tour." He took the plant, tossed it outside, then brushed off his hands.

"Twenty bucks, huh?"

"And worth every penny. Careful where you walk. Not all the nails are countersunk in the subflooring."

The square entry echoed their footsteps as she followed him into a large room filled with sawhorses, paint cans, lumber scraps and other paraphernalia of construction. Sunlight streamed through the plastic-covered windows. The room smelled of fresh wood, mudding compound and dust. She sidestepped boxes of nails and a mountain of Sheetrock to cross the room.

"Wow. This fireplace looks great." Catherine ran her hand lightly over the enormous natural stones, then glanced at him over her shoulder. "Did you carry even one of these monstrous rocks?"

He gave her a horrified look as he removed his jacket, tossing it onto a stepladder. "Are you kidding? What do you think Nick is for? Poor spindly fellow, he needed the exercise."

Catherine shook her head. "You're terrible. What was the bet?"

"Who could eat the most soft pretzels." He puffed out his chest, stretching his black T-shirt over hard muscle. Catherine's mouth went dry. "I ate twenty-three."

"Gross. You must have been sick as a dog."

"Well, yeah. But it was worth it." His grin was infectious and her heart leaped ridiculously as he laid his arm across her shoulders and stood beside her, looking at the wall of stone with pride. "There are over two hundred fieldstones embedded in that thar li'l ol' fireplace."

Reaching to the cathedral ceiling, and about fifteen feet wide, it hardly qualified as little. She shook her head, used to Luke's and Nick's ridiculous but harmless bets.

"When are you two going to stop that nonsense? You've been betting on anything and everything since fifth grade."

"We did a sealed bet when we'd stop."

Catherine shook her head again and slipped casually from under his arm. The back of her neck tingled and her knees felt wobbly as she strolled over to the plastic-covered bay window.

"Oh, Luke, this is absolutely glorious. Look at this view. Are there any deer out there, do you think?"

"Several. I saw a doe and her fawn last weekend."

He walked over and leaned against an exposed stud,

his arms folded as he watched her from hooded eyes. *A stud leaning against a stud. How appropriate.* Uncomfortable under his scrutiny, she shifted without looking at him.

"Are you okay?"

"Of course," she said brightly. "Why wouldn't I be?"

"You just seem…I don't know…different."

"Different? How?" Since when?

"I don't know." He looked as puzzled as he sounded.

Excruciatingly aware of him watching her, she didn't know where to look, what to do with her too-large hands and feet.

"There's Nick! Is that his new car? I'll go out and help him carry whatever he's brought for lunch."

If she took a breath in there, Luke didn't hear it. She dashed out of the room, fiery ponytail bobbing against her shoulders, her sneakers echoing in the vast, empty room. Luke stared at her retreating back, avoiding the view of her tight little butt in retreat.

He shook his head and followed her outside. Just in time to see her fling herself into Nick's open arms.

Scowling, Luke jogged down the stairs, gave a cursory glance at the screaming red BMW parked beside his bike, and dug into his back pocket. When Nick caught his eye over Cat's head, Luke flashed him the twenty in his hand. The top of Cat's head reached Nick's jaw. Luke didn't like the way they had their arms looped about each other's waist as they strolled toward the house together.

He'd seen that look in his partner's eye about seven million times. Luke wanted to gently set Cat aside and pummel his best friend's and business partner's face into the dirt. Twice, for good measure. He settled for a meaningful glare.

Nick grinned. Still holding Cat under one brawny arm, he snagged the money out of Luke's fingers. "Thank you kindly, son." He chuckled, stuffing the bill into his front pocket.

Cat glanced from one to the other and raised one red eyebrow.

"License plate. Has two threes in it," Luke explained, keeping abreast with them on the steps and porch, but unable to squeeze through the front door. He glared at Nick, whose mockingbird-blue eyes held the devil today.

All three of them paused on the threshold.

"We could try it single file," Cat offered seriously, her head doing the tennis match waltz to see who was going to cave first.

"No," Luke and Nick agreed. Nick pulled a quarter out of his pocket. "Call it."

"Tails."

The coin caught the light as it twisted in the air, then landed on Nick's palm. "Step back, pardner. The lady's with me tonight."

Luke scowled as he followed them into the living room. There wasn't that much heavy lifting to do. He could have done without Nick's help today.

CHAPTER THREE

"WELL, HONEY, AREN'T you absolutely, outrageously gorgeous?" Nick released Catherine's waist, only to capture both her hands. He held her in front of him, arms spread wide, their fingers entwined, as he checked her out from head to toe, and all ports in between. She gave him a frank stare back. She'd adored him for almost twenty years. Almost as long as she'd known Luke. It puzzled her why, when Nick was a truly delicious hunk of manhood, she'd never felt any of the sparks that ignited at just the thought of Luke.

"In eight months," she teased, "I had two more calls from you than I did from Luke. I had to come and see for myself if you guys were behaving yourselves."

"I gotta tell you, sweet thing, if I'd known you'd get even more beautiful, I would've called three times a day."

Catherine pulled her hands free and gave him a mild look. "Three times a day, huh? What on earth would we talk about?"

"Your fantastic hair." Nick reached out and fingered a few strands near her face, then lowered his smoky voice. "Your skin, your eyes, your mouth—"

"Hey, Stratton, give it a rest. Cat's immune to your dubious charms."

Although Catherine felt the pulse of Luke's presence

in the room, she managed to ignore him and to encourage Nick. "More. More."

Nick's answering grin revealed two long, sexy dimples in his lean cheeks. His dark hair had a tendency to curl. He kept it cut short, reminding her of the profile on a Greek coin. He was a clotheshorse, and his tall, spare body looked good in whatever he wore. Today he'd dressed in Dockers, his only concession to work a pair of immaculate workboots. His lavender golf shirt made his blue eyes look violet.

He grinned wickedly at Luke. "We're going to have to keep Princess under lock and key while she's visiting, won't we?"

"I'm not visiting." Catherine pushed his hand away from her hair, which he'd been absently fondling. "Dragon over there is letting me stay with him until the house is ready."

Nick stuck his hands in his pockets and gave Luke a level look. "Is that so?"

"I'm not going to be moving in before the turn of the century unless you two get to work," Luke told them shortly, dropping the last torn piece of sandpaper he'd been shredding to join the others at his feet. He cast Nick a mildly belligerent look.

"Please tell me my portfolio is still in your capable hands?" Nick begged with utmost sincerity. Four of Catherine's savvy trades had made his new Beemer possible.

"Safe and sound," she assured him. "Boy, I'd kill for a cup of coffee." She edged past Luke, who didn't like losing and was obviously still smarting over two losses in one morning. "Guys?"

The men followed her into the kitchen. The oak

cabinets had been installed and gleamed in the sun streaming through the plastic over the kitchen window opening. The naked plywood countertops looked ready for tile. A card table shoved into the refrigerator opening held a coffeepot and several sealed jars. A commercial water bottle sat on the floor under the table. Catherine set about making coffee as Luke divvied up the assignments for the day.

"Plan on taking a *short* break," Luke warned his helpers. "Here." He handed her a how-to-install-tile book. "Bone up on this while you finish your coffee."

"You're trusting me to do this after glancing at a book?"

Luke shrugged. "How could a compulsive personality screw up?"

Catherine pulled a face. "Let me count the ways." She tucked the book under her arm. "You're nuts, but I'm game. Gimme my supplies, boss."

"Get your coffee first, and I'll stick what you need in the bathroom down the hall." Luke accepted the brimming paper cup Catherine handed him. "Yo, Nick? Did you say you brought lunch?"

Nick went out to his car to retrieve the cooler while Luke showed Catherine what needed to be done in the guest bathroom.

"You're not going to stay in here and watch, are you?" Catherine sucked in her stomach to make room for him to maneuver around her in the compact bathroom. With a neat knee bend, he set the box of tiles he carried on the floor. Catherine averted her eyes from his crotch. He looked up. Their eyes met and she blushed. She could've sworn she saw an answering heat in his eyes. But then, it was pretty dim in here. Much to her embarrassment, she'd mistaken that look before.

"Nick hasn't gotten involved with anyone in the last couple of weeks, has he?" she asked, hoping to redirect her thoughts.

Luke rose slowly. "Why do you want to know?"

She laughed. "Gee, let me think. He's tall, dark, handsome, owns his own business, is single and has most of his own teeth."

"He owns half a business, and he's the last man you should be looking at." Luke bent to retrieve a large can of mastic from beneath the sink and used a screwdriver from his back pocket to open it. It smelled noxious. "You know Nick'll never commit."

"So? I like him."

"Good." Luke slapped a notched trowel down beside the can. "So do I. Let's keep it that way."

Catherine leaned against the doorjamb with her arms folded. Willpower kept her voice even as a bubble of laughter caught in her throat. "Talk about the pot calling the kettle black!"

"Would you move...thanks." His sleeve brushed her chest as he maneuvered past her to the door. "Think you can handle this, or would you rather paint?"

"I'd rather talk about Nick."

"Yell if you get stuck."

Catherine heard his workboots pound down the hall to the kitchen. She grinned.

"I SEE NO end of problems if she stays with me indefinitely," Luke said morosely over his shoulder as he and Nick installed custom-milled molding in the master suite. "Why couldn't she have stayed in Beaverton where she belongs?"

Nick, standing on the ladder, took a few whacks with a hammer as he drove a nail into the twelve-inch-wide oak. "By herself?"

"She has friends there," Luke said, then hammered a few finishing nails into the baseboard. "And she sold the house."

"It's not like Catherine to burn her bridges. She means to stick around, I guess."

"She asked me to help her find a husband."

Nick's teeth flashed in a devilish grin. "Whose?"

Luke snorted. "That's the problem. Everyone we know is just like us."

"What's wrong with us? We're good-looking, own our own business, have decent cars and can flash the cash." He twisted on the ladder to look down at Luke.

Luke hadn't liked the way Nick's eyes had danced the moment he'd seen Cat this morning. He didn't like the way his best friend had kept his arm wrapped about Cat's slender waist, either. He gave Nick a pointed look.

"She's got great girl parts," Nick said with far too much enthusiasm. "I'd be more than happy to take her out."

"Don't you suddenly start ogling her parts," Luke warned. "Everything from the neck down is strictly off-limits."

"Her lips are fair game?"

"Consider her verboten from head to toe, and all parts in between. Does Cat look desperate for a date? She wants a lifetime commitment. Someone stable. Faithful. A guy who'll see no one but her. You aren't even on the *D* list of candidates."

"Do you have an *A* list?" Nick asked, amused.

"You and I are going to work on it," Luke said with grim determination. "At first I tried to talk her out of it. But you know Cat. Once she's set on something she's like a pit bull."

"More like I know *you*," Nick said. "When Catherine wants something, *you* bend over backward to make sure she gets it."

"She's never asked for much, and she deserves to be happy. I'm hoping it'll be a case of be careful what you wish for. So…how many of our friends fit the 'decent-guy, keeps-his-hands-to-himself, faithful' description?"

"Catherine's a beautiful, intelligent woman. She must've been kidding about finding her a husband," Nick said. "Why would a woman who looks like she does, and makes money hand over fist, want to tie herself down to one guy? She'll have to beat men off with a two-by-four as soon as word gets around she's available."

"I prefer she do it in Oregon." Luke stood, dusting off his jeans. "I'm starving."

The bathroom door was almost closed as they walked by. "Hey, Cat." Luke rapped on the door. "Ready for lunch?" She was on her knees behind the door. He could just see her endearingly large feet poking out.

"Yeah, I'm famished. Almost finished here. Go ahead and start without me. Hey! Make sure you guys leave something edible."

"See, that's the problem," Luke said, picking up their conversation as they entered the kitchen. He dragged the lid off the cooler Nick had left on the counter earlier. "It's gonna be impossible finding someone whose intentions are halfway honorable. Do you want tuna or... what's this? Mystery meat? Here, take it, whatever it is."

Nick removed the wrapping and raised his roast beef sandwich to his mouth. "Tell her you don't want her here."

Luke sent his friend a level look. "I can't do that again, Nick. You know that. I have a history of telling Cat she's not wanted. Prince of a guy that I am, I started the day her mother left..." Luke scrubbed his jaw. "She cried herself sick for four days."

"She was seven years old."

"Yeah. And that was the last time I saw her cry. Think of all the times she *didn't* cry when I embarrassed her by telling my friends I didn't even know her. That was even worse."

"Give yourself a break. You were a teenager. She followed you around school like a sad-eyed puppy. Hey, *I* told her to bug off on more than one occasion."

"She used to scrunch up under that berry bush way in the back of the middle school playground, remember the one? Just scrunch up under all those thorns after I'd told her to get lost. I'd walk by and see her, and feel lower than the scales on a snake's belly. That sad little face, and all that crazy red hair. And she refused to cry. I could see she wanted to, but damn her stubborn pride, she refused. And I'd walk away, laughing with my friends, and leave her there."

Nick bit into his three-inch-thick sandwich, catching the sliced pickle before it hit his boot. He stuffed it back between the slices of bread, then licked mustard off his thumb. "And then there's her seventeenth birthday."

Luke's head shot up. "Don't go there, Stratton."

Oblivious to the danger, Nick continued. "You kissed

her, she puked. End of story. Fine. She's a big girl now, odds are she doesn't still throw up when a man kisses her. But who knows? Why take the risk of her upchucking on a friend? Hey, I'm sure she'll understand if you tell her to get lost. After all, as you say, been there, done that, got the scars to prove it. Besides, just about everyone in Catherine's life has abandoned her. Why should you be any different?"

Luke closed his eyes. He hadn't told Nick more than the basics. The truth was he'd allowed his passions to get away from him that night, and in the process had scared Cat to death. She'd needed her *brother.* Instead he'd turned into Octopus Man with suction lips and a hard-on that wouldn't quit.

No wonder she'd been sick. And embarrassed. And disappointed in him. Luke glared at Nick, grateful in a perverse way for the reminder. "It's taken years for her to learn she can trust me again."

The pain he'd caused her by switching roles midstream still tortured him. They'd never talked about that night, but it lay between them like the monster in a misty bog. He'd sworn not only to be her brother, but her hero, her protector. Her champion. In other words, he'd be what Cat needed.

"I've got a lot to make up for. I'm not going to blow it." Luke tossed his uneaten sandwich into the box they used for trash. He wanted to pace, but that took up too much energy, so he leaned against the counter.

"Got a beer in here?" He dug through the ice and pulled out two cans. "Hey, Cat?" he shouted, handing Nick a beer. "Come and get it."

He waited a beat for her faint answer, then popped the can and took a long swig. "If she wants help finding a husband, then I'll help her find a husband. Between us, we must know a hundred eligible single guys. Hell, it can't be that difficult."

"Wanna bet?" Nick asked, looking up; his pale blue eyes weren't smiling as he issued the age-old refrain. Polishing off his sandwich, he reached for another. "Engagement or wedding?"

Luke narrowed his eyes. Man. He hated this whole situation. "Wedding, I guess."

"Four months."

"Six. Payoff?"

"Milk in my oldest gym shoe?" Nick asked seriously.

"Get real, Stratton! This is Cat we're talking about here."

"Aah! A Major Bet. Mmm," Nick rubbed his chin. "An all-expenses-paid trip to Vegas. For two."

They shook on it.

"I'M ECSTATIC TO announce the toilet in the master bath flushes," Catherine said to the room in general. She stumbled into the kitchen, then her knees folded and she sat down in the middle of the floor with a thump.

"First order of business—" Luke broke off abruptly as he turned from the window. "You look like hell. What's wrong with you?"

"Your bathroom made me sick."

At the speed of light, Luke came down on one knee in front of her. "How sick?" He pushed her hair off her clammy forehead.

Catherine gave him a look. "Barf sick."

He rose, scooping her into his arms. *Very manly,* Catherine thought as he strode through the house, yelling for Nick to open the damn front door. She rested her throbbing head on his nicely muscled shoulder and closed her eyes to stop the world spinning.

"Take a couple of deep breaths," Luke demanded, stomping to the edge of the porch and sitting down on the top step. Right, like she could draw a breath while sitting on Lucas Van Buren's lap.

"Cat? Breathe, dammit."

She took a shuddery breath. His splayed hand on her rib cage moved with her lungs. She tried it again. It felt good. She couldn't figure out now if she was still dizzy from the glue or if it was Luke's touch making her head spin.

Catherine squinted her eyes open as Nick settled himself on the other end of the step and leaned against the post, a beer can in one hand. He gave her a small, one-dimple smile. "Glue?" he asked Luke, swallowing his amusement with a gulp of brew.

Luke's hand slipped a fraction of an inch down her rib cage as his breath fanned the top of her head. He was probably getting a mouthful of her unruly hair. His hand shifted up again. *Up,* Catherine silently ordered. *Move up more.*

"Fool woman, I told her to open the window."

"The one you painted closed last weekend?" Nick asked.

"Why didn't she say so?" Luke's chest huffed under her cheek. His hand was directly under her right breast. If he'd just move his thumb...

"Perhaps because you weren't listening when she *did* tell you." Catherine joined in the conversation. "Nevertheless, she is a big girl, and should have figured out a way to ventilate her workspace." She tilted her head to look up at Luke's very nice chin. "Aren't I squishing you?"

"No."

"The last time I sat on your lap, I was nine." It hadn't felt nearly this good. Or this dangerous. In fact, what she remembered was feeling safe for the first time in living memory.

"You were covered in mud." Luke's voice carried a reminiscent smile.

"You pushed me." They grinned at each other.

Nick rose with a groan. "Oh, bliss, another trip down memory lane. I have molding to finish installing, then I'm outta here."

Luke, as if suddenly realizing the position they were in, slid her unceremoniously off his lap and plopped her on the step next to him. The front door closed behind Nick.

"That was a stupid thing to do," Luke told her. "If you'd passed out in there, I couldn't have opened the door."

"As much as I thrill at being called stupid, I have to admit I should have thrown my shoe through the window for ventilation. Point taken. Lecture over." She rose, staggered and clutched the roof support. "Oh, ick."

Luke shot up as if someone had lit a firecracker in his back pocket. He grabbed her upper arm and pushed her back down. "That's it. You're useless to me now. I'll never get a lick of work out of you if you keep toppling over and I have to stop what I'm doing to hold you up. You're going home."

THERE WERE EXACTLY twenty-six paces from one wall in his condo to the other. Luke knew. He'd counted them off about nine zillion times. He strode across the living room to glare at the clock near the TV. It was after 1:00 a.m. He'd about worn a path in the carpet. Where in the hell were they?

He cursed taking the Harley to the beach house. With Cat asphyxiated by the damn glue, he'd been afraid she'd fall off the bike coming home. But he hadn't wanted her to go in Nick's brand-spanking-new Beemer, either. Luke did the nine paces from the wall unit to the window like a one-minute mile.

The vertical blinds clattered against the wall as he peered down into the dark street. Unless Cat and Nick were the couple blatantly boinking under the streetlamp on the lawn in the park across the street, they still weren't back. And if they were, he'd kill Nick.

He yanked the cell phone out of his back pocket and punched redial. It rang. And rang. If they were hiding down on the nineteenth floor, at Nick's place, his business partner—ex-best friend was dead meat. Luke slammed the phone off and into his pocket midring. He didn't bother with the elevator, he simply jogged the three floors down, then three floors up again.

Irritated that he was so damn irritated, out of breath and out of ideas, Luke threw himself into his favorite chair. The black leather smelled like her and annoyed him even more. He glared at the open front door, willing Cat to walk in before his murder plans were fully hatched.

"ARE YOU SURE we know what you're doing, Nicolas Stratton?" Catherine yawned, barely awake, and rested her head on the padded headrest of Nick's car, her eyes closed. They'd been parked near Fisherman's Wharf, a good two miles from the condo, for an hour and a half.

"You want Luke to see you as a desirable woman, don't you?"

"It's what I've spent the last six hours telling you," she grumbled, rolling her head his way. Catherine opened her eyes. "I want him to see who I am, but I'm scared. What if this doesn't work? God, I couldn't bear losing the relationship we do have."

"Honey, I think you've only thought through part of this plan. Be brave, be daring, be bold. Moving in with him was a smart idea. But what'll really do it is if he has the opportunity to see you through the eyes of someone else. I volunteered. Don't worry, gorgeous, I have the plan well in hand. And my plans always work."

"Yeah," Catherine said, "except when they don't. And Nick? I want you to promise on a stack of Bibles that you'll never tell him how I feel. This has got to be Luke's idea. He has to make the first move."

"This is woman's logic, right? Chase him until he catches you?"

"Basically. Just promise you won't tell. Never. Do you swear?"

"Constantly."

"Nick!"

He crossed his chest in the vicinity of his heart. "I swear I'll never tell Luke how you feel about him."

"Say that so I can believe it. Because I swear to you, Nicolas Stratton, if Luke gets a hint that he's the one I'm trying to catch before I'm ready to tell him, I'll... I'll tell him about you and Babsie."

"That was in twelfth grade."

"Want to bet he won't still be mad?"

"I give you my word," he said with utmost sincerity.

"Good enough." She squinted at the dash clock. "He's probably sleeping, and we're sitting here like idiots in the dead of night, freezing in the car."

"We could've gone for coffee."

"Nick, you're a lunatic, and I adore you. But if I drink one more cup of anything, I'll float away. Please, can I go home now?"

"WHAT ARE YOU DOING?" Catherine cried as Nick picked her up in his arms. The elevator pinged as it stopped on the twenty-second floor. "Nick, you're going to give yourself a hernia carrying me." The doors slid open. He staggered playfully as he strode down the corridor leading to Luke's condo.

"Put your head on my shoulder, your arms around my neck and close your eyes," Nick said softly. "I'm going to give you the opportunity to be a fly on the wall. Hmm, interesting. The front door's wide open."

Catherine looped her arms about his neck and snuggled against Nick's chest. A nice chest. Unfortunately, not Luke's chest.

"Where've you been?"

Ooh. Luke's dragon roar. Catherine kept her eyes closed, her features lax. She imagined flames spewing from his nostrils. This was a good sign. Nick's plan might just work.

"Hey, old son," Nick whispered. "Princess here is sleeping. Lower your tone to a dull bellow, why don'tcha?"

"Why is Cat sleeping?" Luke demanded, with deep suspicion. She could feel the blistering heat of his gaze focused on her.

"You said you wanted to introduce her to some of our...well, let's just say we did a little par-tay-ing."

"I told you to bring her straight home."

"We came straight back."

"Via Hong Kong?"

"We stopped for a bite to eat. Then she wanted a look at my boat."

"For six hours?"

"Gorgeous day for a sail. Look, she's kinda heavy," Nick said over her head. "Mind if I...oh okay, fine, if you want to stand there bitching at me while *you* get the hernia, that's cool."

Luke's arms tightened around her. Bliss. Catherine's head found the natural and perfect hollow beneath his chin. As long as he didn't get that promised hernia, she was content to lie in his arms and enjoy the moment.

"Poor Princess, she needed the break. The last few months have been tough on her."

"She talked to you?" Catherine heard deep suspicion in Luke's voice. His fingers tightened on her upper thigh. "Catherine Harris the clam, the little crab?"

"It's not a state secret, is it?" Nick asked. "Hey, it's great standing here at one-thirty in the morning, in your open doorway shooting the breeze, a comatose woman between us, but how about a drink?"

"I'm only holding her so I don't rearrange that smarmy, pretty-boy face of yours," Luke snarled. "Next time I tell you to bring her right home, you'd better bring her...no, forget it. You keep your grubby paws away from her."

Don't get overexcited, Catherine warned herself as her heart did a little somersault. What she hoped sounded like jealousy might just be Luke in his defensive big-brother mode. But at this point, she'd consider the glass half full.

"Hey, chill. What's your problem? She's over twenty-one and single. You aren't her father."

"No," Luke said grimly over her head. "I'm her brother."

"You aren't that, either," Nick said softly. "Are you, old son?"

CHAPTER FOUR

THIS ENTIRE SITUATION was untenable, Luke swore. How was he going to hide how he felt about Cat?

From her?

From Nick?

From himself?

He'd done it before with some success. But her power was stronger now. He felt himself sailing directly into the Bermuda Triangle at warp speed.

Luke carried her into the dark bedroom, settled her on the bed and heard the front door close behind his ex-best friend.

He pulled off her shoes and tugged the comforter over her, then left the room and stalked back into the kitchen, where he poured a mug of brandy-laced coffee. Morosely, he sat at his small kitchen table and stared at the oil slick on top of the black liquid before reaching for his PalmPilot. The handheld computer was the nineties version of the little black book.

A. Paul Abbott. Brian Andrews.

Luke transferred names into another file labeled PARTY with all the enthusiasm of a man anticipating a train wreck. Robert Kingston. Cy Kronin...Luke paused. The guy had shifty eyes. Really shifty eyes. He deleted Cy's name. Steve Manfield. Good guy. Quiet. A possible. Bob Nelson? Owned his own company. Had a couple of dogs. A full set of parents...

Luke's folks had been divorced about three years, and he had lived with his mother when Cat and Faith had moved in with his father. He'd disliked both females at first sight. Cat had been tall for her age, with enough wild red hair to cover a small horse, and wall-to-wall freckles. She'd looked sweet, and sad, and a whole lot of trouble. And worst of all, his father had adored her, and Nick thought she was a little doll. His for the taking.

Luke took a swig out of his mug, ashamed as the flood of memories spotlighted his own less than sterling behavior.

Okay, face it. I was jealous as hell back then. He'd been secretly thrilled when, a year later, his father had informed him of his impending divorce. *Good,* Luke had thought with satisfaction. He'd never warmed to Cat's mother, Faith. The irony of her name was not lost on anyone.

There was only one little glitch to Luke's joy at her departure. She'd left behind The Kid.

What kind of mother left a seven-year-old girl with her ex-husband? His father had been delighted. He'd doted on Cat, included her in everything he did. Luke hadn't wanted a sister. He sure hadn't wanted *her.* And he'd told her so in no uncertain terms. On numerous occasions. With all the arrogance of youth, and with no consideration for her feelings.

Later, he realized she'd wanted the same things he had—a father, a mother, a family. To be loved. A place to belong.

Luke felt the sting of shame all over again. To be fair, he'd been a kid himself. He'd felt abandoned and shoved aside. He hadn't, at thirteen, thought or cared about how The Kid felt.

Luke got all the way to the end of his address book. Allan Zukker. Even eliminating those he thought unsuitable for one reason or another, there was still a decent selection. But because the criteria for females wasn't nearly as stringent as those for males, Luke ended up with an unbalanced list—more women than men. Which suited him just fine, except the party wasn't for him. It was for Cat.

He pushed the computer away. He'd even out the list later.

Luke buried his head in his hands. He didn't want the party. He didn't want to introduce Cat to a man who might not appreciate her, might not treat her right. She'd been hurt enough in her life. Cat needed to be loved. Cherished.

Luke pushed his chair back and strode into his living room. Nope. There were no two ways about it. He'd made his bed. Now he had to lie in it. No matter how damn uncomfortable it was. He tossed a pillow and blanket on the black leather sofa and turned out the light.

Yep, he thought, flinging himself down on his back, fully clothed. He was going to have to bite the bullet and help Cat find the man of her dreams.

Even if it killed him.

THE PARTY WAS a roaring success. At the moment, E.L.O.'s "Don't Bring Me Down" was competing with raised voices and the din of heels on bare wood floors. Cat had rolled up the area rugs for dancing.

Earlier they'd gone into a cooking frenzy, each trying to outdo the other. The result was a rather eclectic amalgamation of foods and beverages. Luke's Mexican salsa, tamales and Chinese egg rolls. Cat's spaghetti and meatballs and Greek salad. Everyone was having a great old time.

With the exception of the host.

Cat was across the living room putting the finishing touches to the buffet with a huge leafy something in a red ceramic pot. She'd persuaded him to buy half a dozen plants at the store, insisting he lived a sterile existence without living things around him. No matter that Luke knew he'd never remember to water the things.

He remembered the alarming amount of plants scattered around his dad's house, but had given up without too much of a fuss. Cat was a born nurturer. She needed to be needed, even if by just a few houseplants.

He felt as nervous as a mother bird pushing her chick out of the nest for the first time. Luke watched her without seeming to, and tried to see her as his friends would. With his luck they'd have the immediate hots for her.

At the moment Cat was the center of attention of a pack of chest-puffing, lip-smacking, posturing males. Luke monitored the behavior of his friends with a jaundiced eye. They might as well let her inspect their teeth, check their brokerage statements and call old girlfriends for references.

Mike leaned close to whisper in Cat's ear. She laughed. The sound rippled just beneath the music. Luke felt it in his gut.

Her looks were addictive, her compelling, innocent sensuality impossible to ignore. God knows, he was trying. Her sassy mouth and sharp wit were destined to drive some lucky guy to the brink of madness. His friends circled her like sharks in a feeding frenzy. He intercepted a lascivious look from Ted, so busy flexing his muscles and trying to hide his receding hairline he didn't even notice Luke's warning glower from across the room.

"If you keep glaring like that no one will go near her." Nick raised his voice to be heard over the music, and handed him a beer. "All they're doing is talking about the stock market."

Luke pulled the tab, then took a swig. "Allan had his hand on her ass." Cat wore perfectly respectable, not-too-tight, black pants and a teal T-shirt. She wasn't wearing jewelry, and hardly any makeup. And she outshone every woman there.

"And a very sweet ass it is, too," Nick said. "Chill. The whole point of this soirée is for Catherine to meet people. She's doing fine. Leave her alone."

"I need to stick close. She was really nervous about tonight."

"Nervous about what? Meeting our degenerate friends?"

Luke shrugged, covertly studying the dynamics of the group surrounding her. "I guess." The guys were salivating as they watched her eat an egg roll. "She didn't have much of a social life in Beaverton. I told her the city was too fast-paced for her."

"Ho, boy." Nick chuckled. "In other words, you challenged her."

Paul elbowed Mike out. Decent guy, Paul. A good eight inches shorter than Cat. No one held that squint against him.

Luke turned his glare on Nick. "Challenged her? I was trying to protect her."

Nick took a swig of his beer, eyeing his friend over the can. "By telling an intelligent, attractive woman she'd be out of her depth in the city?"

Across the room Cat did a quick sleight of hand, twisting and piling her hair on top of her head as she talked to Paul and the others by the open balcony door. All that hair around her shoulders must be hot. Still, he'd have to warn her how provocative the pose looked. As her T-shirt pulled across her moving breasts, Rob just about swallowed his tongue.

"She's not as self-confident as one might think," Luke muttered, not tasting the beer he chugged. Allan strolled up and formed another wall around Cat. He said something; she smiled, showing pretty white teeth and no desire to drop the hand she held provocatively on top of her head.

Nick smiled. "Doesn't look the least bit nervous to me."

An annoying tick started in Luke's right eyelid. He scowled. "She's biting her bottom lip. See? There," he muttered. "She did it again."

"God, yes," Nick enthused. "Very sexy."

"That's a sign she's nervous, you sex maniac." Luke glared at him, then narrowed his eyes when he saw the way his friend's eyes lit up with devilry. "What?"

"Huh?" Nick asked, all innocence.

"Whatever you're plotting, forget it. I don't want her hurt."

"Got it." Nick saluted. Without missing a beat, he asked mildly, "Sooo…what happened to Karen?"

"Karen?"

"The girlfriend du jour?"

"I know who Karen is. She's around here some-where."

"Where's Catherine?"

"Over by the CD flirting with... You're looking at her, you lamebrain. Why're you asking me?"

"Don't you think it's a little odd that you don't know where your girlfriend is, but you know Catherine's exact location in a crowded room?"

"No," Luke said shortly. "I don't. It's my job to take care of her. Didn't you come with a date?"

"Are you kidding?" Nick grinned. "And have to look and not partake of this delectable smorgasbord of single women? You invite me to a feast, then expect me to bring a bag lunch?"

"I wanted to give Cat a reasonable selection. It would've looked a little obvious if I'd invited just guys. Not to mention boring."

"And I'm eternally grateful. You did good."

"Putting this together was a lot of hard work."

"Especially since Catherine was the one who did all the hard work," Nick said dryly. "A ten spot says Ted will be date number one."

Luke snorted. "He's showing her that stupid scar he got when he fell off my roof last summer. Probably spinning her some far-fetched tale."

"Women go for that stuff."

"Nah," Luke said absently. The tick over his eye was really getting on his nerves now. "It'll be Allan. Twenty, on..." He peered across the room. Ted had his hands on the back of Cat's neck. "What does he think he's doing? Excuse me a sec."

"It's just a casual massage." Nick snagged his arm.

"Uh-uh. Better change that plan, old son. Incoming. Karen at three o'clock." His smile widened.

"Don't you have moves to make?" Luke muttered.

"You betcha. I'm off to give the guys some competition."

Luke swore under his breath as his friend threaded his way across the crowded room to Cat's side. She gave Nick a wide, friendly smile and took his offered hand. He led her to the small area where a few couples were dancing.

Nick was a suave, good-looking guy. Women liked Nick. Luke himself was a decent-looking guy, and just as suave as Nick was. Women liked him, too. Which was why they were going to protect Cat from smooth-talking men like themselves. That's what Nick had meant.

Competition? Luke watched them walk into each other's arms and move to the dreamy music. Slowly. Competition? Nick? What a repugnant thought.

Ridiculous.

Out of the question.

Luke dragged his focus away from Cat snuggled in Nick's arms to watch Karen shimmy closer. His date looked dazzling in a short, tight red dress, black hair streaming down her bare back, long legs showcased to perfection in red high heels. He didn't feel a single solitary spark. Nothing. Nada. Zip.

Obviously he was a sick man.

Karen slid her arm about his waist. Her perfume, recently applied, smelled great. Unfortunately, it didn't do a thing for him. She looked up at him with heavy-lidded, sultry brown eyes. "Hi, sweetie. Miss me?"

Luke bit back the truth. Karen was a nice woman.

He'd invited her to the party. Now he couldn't wait to take her home. And leave her there. Alone.

"Sorry." He cupped her cheek and smiled ruefully. "I've practically ignored you all night, haven't I? It's been so long since I threw one of these things. I forgot how much work it is. Let me change the CD, and I'll give you my undivided attention." As soon as he could manage to unglue his twitching eyes from Cat and Nick, who were like Siamese twins on the postage-size dance floor. Luke took Karen's hand and led her to the state-of-the-art CD player, where he changed the selection of slow ballads to something loud, fast and energetic. His choice was met with a series of catcalls from his party guests. Tough.

He wrapped an arm around Karen's bare shoulders and led her to the middle of the dancers. She moved into his arms smoothly and, despite the pulsing beat of the music, rested her head against his chest and twined her arms about his waist. She moved sensuously against him.

The problem was, Luke thought, enfolding her in his arms, she was just too…short. That was it. She was too short. She didn't fit. Even wearing those heels, the top of her head only came to the middle of his chest. Which was really too bad. Karen was beautiful, smart, sexy. How unfortunate he'd never noticed how vertically challenged she was before tonight.

With fifty-plus bodies in it, the room was hot. Even with the door wide-open to the narrow balcony, the evening air was stifling. Luke wanted to unpeel Karen from his chest and stand under a cold shower. He concentrated on moving his feet.

Two yards away, Cat danced with Nick, laughing and

chatting and having the time of her life. Luke would have to talk to her. He'd invited at least seven guys specifically for her to meet tonight. She already knew Nick.

Luke rubbed his hand down Karen's smooth arm and turned her so that his back was toward Cat and he could give his date the attention she deserved. Karen slid her hands up his chest and around his neck.

"Too many people here." She ran her long nails up and down the back of his neck. "Bet no one would notice if we snuck out."

LUKE SAT IN the back row of the dark, all-night movie theater. He could have had his pick of greasy, red velvet seats. He was the only one there. Not surprising. It was 2:00 a.m. and an artsy foreign film flickered on the screen, the subtitles barely legible. At this very moment he should have been getting hot and sweaty with Karen. Instead he'd dropped her off, walked her to the door and driven back into the city.

He didn't want to go home, because he wanted to go home so badly he could taste it.

Nuts. He was certifiably nuts. He wasn't sure who he was doing this for. Cat or himself.

LUKE DIDN'T COME HOME.

He and his gorgeous, petite brunette with boobs out to there and legs up to here had disappeared over an hour ago. Catherine refused to speculate where they were or what they might be doing. Might? Ha! Did every woman he lusted after have to be so petite? So available? So…cute? She clenched her teeth.

Ducking out on his own party was rude as far as she was concerned. The condo was still jam-packed with Luke's and Nick's upwardly mobile friends, none of whom seemed to have noticed their host had gone AWOL. Everyone was having a blast.

Catherine's head throbbed and the muscles around her mouth ached from smiling. She was tired of making nice. In fact, she'd pretended to hurt her ankle so she didn't have to dance anymore. Which meant she was stuck sitting in Luke's big black leather chair in the corner with her feet propped up. A captive audience for Ted, Allan, two Bobs and an ethereal blonde named Cheryl.

She let Cheryl entertain the four men while she zoned out, thinking unwillingly about what Luke was up to. Karen had beautiful skin. No freckles on her. Catherine glanced down at her own hands, fisted around a half-filled glass of warm soda. Her skin looked as though she'd been peppered. Ugh. She hated her freckles. Hated them.

One of the Bobs said something, and the others laughed. Catherine had enough presence of mind to smile. One thing she'd learned: there was no point in crying over things that couldn't be changed. She was in this particular polka-dotty skin, and she had to resign herself to living with it. Disliking how she looked wasn't going to change reality.

Besides, she thought, working herself up into a real snit, it was Luke's fault. If he hadn't always shown up with some creamy-skinned, pocket Venus, Catherine wouldn't have grown up hating her freckles, her hair and her height.

She wanted Luke to come home and everyone else to disappear.

Eventually, finally, the guests left in dribs and drabs. Now it was after two, and Luke still wasn't back.

The last to leave, Nick leaned over to kiss her forehead on the way out the front door. "Are you sure I can't—"

"Go." Catherine pushed at his wide chest. "Thank you for offering to help with the cleanup. I'll take care of it next week when I wake up."

"You did good, Princess. You were the belle of the ball."

"I'm delighted to hear it." Catherine didn't bother to stifle a yawn. "Too bad Prince Absent wasn't here to see me shine."

"Oh, he saw enough. Trust me."

"You're a sweet man. Delusional, but sweet. Go home, Nick."

As soon as the door closed behind him, Catherine felt the muscles in her shoulders sag. Overtired, that was all. She was just overtired. Overstimulated. Overloaded.

She imagined Luke in bed with Karen. The salsa and meatballs did a sickening dance in her tummy. She gathered several empty platters from the dining room table on her way to the kitchen for a Maalox.

After changing into plaid flannel pajama bottoms, one of Luke's T-shirts and her ratty slippers, she shuffled back into the living room and turned off the CD player. Ah. Silence.

She surveyed the messy room, knowing no matter how tired, she wouldn't be able to sleep. She almost had herself convinced it had nothing to do with Luke's absence and everything to do with not waking up to this mess.

"You owe me, Van Buren. You owe me big." She

loaded dirty glasses onto a tray and wrinkled her nose. A sickening rush of memories assaulted her. She couldn't smell beer without remembering that night nine years ago.

It had started harmlessly enough; her friends, fake IDs in hand, had surprised her with a visit to a strip joint for her seventeenth birthday. Catherine didn't want to remember the rest of it. If she did, she'd be on the next plane back to Beaverton.

One thing was for certain—the next time she managed to get Luke to kiss her she'd make sure she was stone-cold sober. That was then. This was now.

Same objective. Different game plan. She'd chosen this path, and she'd stick to it. No retreating like a spineless crab. Nothing ventured, nothing gained. Rah rah rah.

She looked down at her clothing and grimaced. Not exactly seductive. But if she suddenly appeared in a slinky black negligee and garter belt, Luke would run screaming for the hills. No. She had to take this slowly and methodically. She'd put the idea out there. Luke had to run with it.

She just had to have the courage of her convictions and not run when the going got tough.

It took more than an hour to clean up the party mess. Luke still wasn't home. "Of course he isn't. What did you expect?" she asked herself, drying the last platter and putting it away while the dishwasher hummed with the final load. "You aren't the only woman who wants him. Duh, Catherine!"

She had to play her cards close to her chest. This time Luke had to make the first move. She just had to be patient. One of her better traits, and one not shared by Luke.

She checked the living room and narrow balcony one last time for stray glasses. Finding none, she went to turn off the kitchen light before going to bed. The place was now spotless. Luke called her a neat freak. Okay, so she was a little obsessive. He was just the opposite. For a man meticulous in his work, Luke was a slob at home. He'd happily leave the same pair of dirty socks, breeding and multiplying, under the coffee table until they walked to the laundry on their own.

Her habits had been ingrained before the age of six. She and her mother had moved seven times, sometimes in the dead of night. If everything was in its place, she'd been able to grab her most precious possessions quickly.

She glanced at the clock on the stereo: 3:30 a.m.

They'd be asleep now. Cuddled together. Karen probably had one of those froufrou beds, all lace and pink pillows. Luke would look outrageously masculine and sexy, stretched out naked—

Catherine ruthlessly cut off the thought and groaned out loud. Living with Luke was going to either kill or cure her.

CHAPTER FIVE

LUKE SNEAKED INTO his own apartment like a thief in the night. He'd seen that foreign film so many times he swore he could now speak fluent German. He frowned. All the lights in the spotless living room were on. Unbuttoning his shirt, he pulled it free of his pants and felt a twinge of guilt for leaving Cat to do the cleanup. Then he considered how he'd have felt if he'd stuck around. Hell, he'd done the right thing.

He almost had a seizure when he saw Cat sprawled out on the leather sofa. She wore one of his favorite ratty T-shirts and a disreputable pair of pajama bottoms he swore she'd had since she was a kid. Her cheeks were pink; her eyes glittered.

"Nice of you to drop by, Van Buren. Pleasant evening?"

"Delightful," Luke managed to answer cheerfully. Man, was she ticked. He stuffed his hands into the pockets of his chinos as he walked around the arm of the sofa. "Hey, thanks for doing the cleanup. Did Nick give you a hand?"

"Yes. By leaving."

Cat drew a leopard print pillow, which hadn't been here a week ago, onto her lap, still glaring. Whoops. He did a quick scan through the open door into the darkened bedroom and lowered his voice. "Are we alone?"

Her cheeks lit up like flamingo-pink neon. "Other than the entire 49ers team naked, and exhausted, in the bedroom, you mean?"

Luke took his hands out of his pockets and sat on the opposite arm of the sofa. Out of missile reach. "It's not out of the realm of possibility that you'd have a man here, Cat."

Her fiery eyebrows shot up into her bangs. "Who are you? What alien life force took over Luke Van Buren's body?"

"Huh?"

"Whose condo is this? I hadn't met any of these people here tonight before in my life! Do you really think I'd sleep with a total stranger? In your home? In your bed?"

"Ahh, no."

"Then don't ask such asinine questions, you turkey."

She curled her legs under her and bunched up her hair in her fist. She wasn't wearing a bra. He remembered that brief, tantalizing flash of cinnamon and cream, and almost licked his lips. Yep, Luke thought. A good thing he'd stayed out.

"Shouldn't you be sleeping?" he asked mildly. What was the point in sitting in a movie theater all night only to came home and find her wide-awake, sexy as hell and in his face?

"I just finished shoveling everything into the dishwasher."

The hectic color had left her cheeks. Her eyes looked bruised and kind of sad, Luke thought. They would have been looking a damn sight sadder if he'd hung around much longer at the party.

"I would've cleaned up in the morning, Cat."

She hugged the pillow and snorted. "Yeah, right."

"So what did you think of Ted?"

She shrugged.

"Allan?"

She did the so-so thing with her head.

"Either of the Bobs? Any of them?"

Cat unfolded her legs. She was close enough to touch. The scent of her body, warm, female, Catherine, made him dizzy.

"Come on, Cat."

"Hey, don't rush me. I'll keep you posted. You've given me enough to work with for now." She stood looking down at him. "How'd your evening with Karen go?"

"Great." *The pits.* Karen had not been a happy woman when he'd left her at her door.

"She seems nice enough."

"Pretty, smart. She's a lawyer."

"Lovely," Cat told him coolly. "She can do your prenup if you two get married."

"She knows that'll never happen."

Luke rose. They were no more than a foot apart. Desperate to steal a kiss from those sweet pink lips, he knew she'd deck him with the pillow she clutched to her midriff.

"Ever heard of common law?"

"This is the second time I've dated her. Besides, Nick and I have The Bet, remember?"

Cat shook her head, slapping him in the face with twenty pounds of hair. The honey-scented strands lashed his cheeks before springing back home. He wanted to grab her by that hair, wrestle her back to the sofa…and get a swift kick in the *cojónes* for his trouble.

"That is one of your more ridiculous bets, Luke.

What if one of you falls madly in love and *wants* to get married before you're thirty-five? It could happen, you know."

"Being in love doesn't necessarily mean marriage. Which is why I consider The Bet a sure thing. I have the edge. I'm never getting married, however old I am."

"You mean you still believe that stupid 'all your emotional eggs in one basket' theory you had at fifteen? That, my darling dragon, is what we women call Lack of Commitment. You just haven't met the right woman yet."

"I meet the right women. Several times a year. Which has always been my point." He frowned. "Are you going to bed?"

"Yes." She stepped out of reach and turned to assess him over her shoulder. "Are we going to the house tomorrow?"

"Yeah. Late-ish. Take the bed again."

He watched her walk to the bedroom. Even in the too large T-shirt, she moved like music. Fluid, graceful and too sexy for his peace of mind. Luke closed his eyes. He needed something else to focus on when Cat was around. Something that wasn't soft, smooth and cinnamon flavored. Something like—

"Sweet dreams, Luke."

"Yeah, you too, honey." Something like—construction. Yeah. That was it. Instead of seeing Cat, he'd imagine building the house. From the foundation up.

"Are you okay?"

He glanced up. She was standing at the bedroom door with a little V of worry between her brows, one slippered foot perched on the other. He wanted to stride over, pick her up, carry her into the bedroom, lay her on his nice, wide bed…

"Just tired."

Excavating the foundation. Lots of dirt. Big piles of dark soil—soft pale, freckly mounds tipped with pale apricot nipples… "See you in the morning," he said gruffly, getting up to click off the light and plunge the room into darkness.

He heard the door shush closed.

Yeah, this visualizing concept stuff was going to work well. Yeah, right!

An hour later, still wide-awake, with excavating the furthest thing from his mind, Luke had to go to the bathroom. To get to the bathroom, he had to go through the bedroom. He dreaded walking through the room with Cat sleeping there. Why had he decided to combine two bedrooms into one? Why had he thought a bigger kitchen warranted removing the guest bath?

Because he hadn't expected Cat to be sleeping in his bed. That's why.

She's sleeping, you moron, Luke told himself, tip-toeing into the bedroom. She'd left the light on in the bathroom. A sliver of golden light slashed across her figure on the bed.

"Ah, Cat," he said softly.

She was sprawled facedown across the bedspread, her hair covering her face and half the pillow. Out like a light. Beside her, tucked up to its furry little armpits by the blanket, was the teddy bear he'd given her years ago. That was Cat. She hung on to things. Treasured things. Coddled things.

He noticed she'd changed his satin sheets for plain white cotton. He sighed and bent to take off her slippers.

The smart thing to do, Catherine decided as she felt Luke's hands removing her left fuzzy slipper, was to turn over and say hi. The sensation of his warm hands on her bare foot sent little electrical currents up her leg.

Pretending to be asleep now was almost as bad as when she'd hidden under his bed on one of his weekends at home. She'd been about nine. Even then she'd wanted to be as close to him as she could get. Eventually he'd discovered her, and hadn't cared that she was faking a deep sleep. He'd hauled her out, dragged her screaming into the hallway, then slammed the door in her face.

The housekeeper had reported the incident to his father, who in turn had punished Luke, and in a natural progression, Luke had refused to talk to Catherine for a month.

Bad idea then. Bad idea now.

He drew off the other slipper, then massaged her instep with strong, sure strokes. She'd never felt anything more erotic in her life. Goose bumps broke out on her skin as he cradled her foot before gently settling it back on the bed.

She felt the drag of the covers under her as Luke carefully pulled the spread and blankets down to her feet, trying not to wake her. Her breasts tingled as if he'd touched them directly. She imagined the glide of the blankets were Luke's hands skimming slowly down her body. Eyes squeezed shut, she pictured his hands on her. Large, hard, long fingered. Smoothing, cupping, claiming.

Moisture pooled between her thighs. Her pulse pounded strategically. She gritted her teeth at the thick, syrupy pleasure her imagination created. She felt the brush of fur, and realized he'd settled Hubert back beside her cheek.

"You're a real pain, Catherine Anne Harris, you know that?" Luke murmured. "I wish you'd stayed in Oregon where you belong."

It took a moment for her overactive hormones to assimilate what he'd just said. *A real pain. Stayed where you belong.*

The delicious sensations left her body in a dizzying rush.

Her heart ached in her chest; the back of her nose tingled. She clamped her teeth together so tightly her jaw ached. So much for wanting Luke to make the first move. He didn't want her. Biblically or otherwise.

No matter how Luke presented his invitation for her to stay, the bottom line, as usual, was that she was in the way. All her life she'd been in the wrong place at the wrong time where Luke was concerned.

Catherine wanted to run. She wanted to go home. To her own bed, with her own safe things surrounding her. But she'd burned those bridges by selling the house and putting everything she owned into storage. At the time that had taken more courage than she'd thought she could muster. But selling and closing up the only real home she'd ever known had been child's play compared to this.

Luke tucked the covers around her, brushing aside her hair. For a brief, electrifying second, his hand lingered on her nape.

She couldn't help it. She shivered.

He swore under his breath.

For several seconds he didn't move. She could feel

him standing there beside the bed. Looking at her. Then she heard his footsteps as he went into the bathroom. The lock snicked. The shower turned on.

Catherine stared up into the darkness, eyes dry, chest aching.

LUKE FINALLY EMERGED from a restless sleep. He hadn't bothered with a sheet. The leather sofa had glued itself to his skin all the way down his left side, and he had to peel himself off like a giant Band-Aid. Thoroughly out of sorts, he yanked last night's chinos over his briefs and staggered reluctantly through the bedroom to get to the bathroom.

The bed was neatly made. How nice. One of them had slept well. He glanced at the bathroom door. Open. He shot a look at his watch. Great. He'd had about three hours' sleep. And where was Cat at eight on a Sunday morning?

After a quick, hot shower, he dressed in his favorite denim cutoffs and a faded red tank top, then headed for the kitchen.

Wherever she'd gone, Cat had unloaded the dishwasher and put everything neatly away before she'd left. He hadn't heard a sound. He searched around for a note. She hadn't left one. Vaguely miffed, he started coffee and decided on eggs Benedict for breakfast. He didn't just save his culinary masterpieces for The Morning After. Although he usually cooked this particular dish for two. And served it in bed.

As SOON AS she walked into the kitchen, Catherine knew she should have stayed out longer. There was a twenty-four-hour movie theater two blocks away. She could have spent the morning there, reading subtitles.

"Good morning, sleepyhead," she said cheerfully, setting a bag of doughnuts and the Sunday paper on the counter to avoid looking at a lot of naked Luke. Tanned, taut, terrific body. Not a freckle in sight. He had the naturally long, lean physique of an athlete without having to do the maintenance. It wasn't fair. But then, what in life was? A familiar tightness gripped her chest.

She turned and reached up to find a mug in the overhead cabinet. "Fun party. I like your friends."

"The feeling was mutual." Luke eyed her black biker shorts and white tank top without comment. There were no secrets between fabric and skin, and despite having been outside jogging in the park, Catherine suddenly felt self-conscious in her skimpy attire. Luke's gaze traveled the length of her legs and back up again to her sweat-damp hair scraped back in a ponytail.

"Been running?"

"Yeah. Across the street in the park."

Even at 7:00 a.m. Marina Green had been crowded with bikers, runners, mothers with little kids, people on in-line skates. None of them had looked at her the way Luke was doing right now. None of them could make her shiver with a mere glance. She filled her mug with cool tap water, drank it down, then casually picked up the half-filled carafe of coffee and poured herself a cup.

Golden sunlight bathed Luke as he sat at the table in the alcove. His skin looked like bronze satin, a cliché, but true. Muscles he'd acquired from hard physical labor, not weights, covered his bones in a fascinating display of hills and valleys. There wasn't an ounce of fat on the man anywhere. And Catherine could pretty much see everywhere.

That faded red tank top didn't hide much. She tried not to stare at a flat brown nipple, showing because he'd twisted to watch her, and the wide armhole had shifted.

She found the milk and sugar and doctored her coffee, then grabbed the white paper bag off the counter.

"There's a gym on the ninth floor," he reminded her as she sat down opposite him at the table.

"Ah, yes. Where you go to pick up babes. I prefer being outside in the fresh air. Want a doughnut?"

Luke shook his head. She shivered as his hair brushed his neck. "I just had breakfast. I left yours in the oven." He looked her up and down. "You're in pretty good shape."

"Pretty good shape?" Catherine pushed aside the greasy bag and rose from the table to flex the biceps in her right arm. "I'm in my prime, pal, and don't you forget it."

He snagged her wrist and held it up. "Look at this, your bones are as delicate as a bird's. I could snap this wrist with no trouble at all."

Catherine disengaged her hand. "If you snapped my wrist you'd have trouble, all right. You'd be wearing the coffeepot around your neck." Goose bumps shot up her arm.

"See, that's what I mean. You look fragile enough to break in a man's hands, but you have an amazing resilience—" He broke off and gave her a look she couldn't hope to interpret.

"Mix fragility with all that firehouse red hair, and a man would have to be deaf, dumb and blind not to want the whole package in his be—life. You're a lethal combo, Cat. They're going to kill themselves falling over their feet, and each other, to have you. And I'm here to make sure the right guy gets the prize. I'm going to keep you by my side, and protect you from the predators, until you make your choice."

It was fascinating to hear his assessment of her. He'd rarely commented on her appearance over the years. She knew his preferences from seeing the women he dated. Petite blondes or brunettes. Not gangly, freckly redheads. So it felt odd to have Luke's entire attention focused on her. Especially at such close quarters.

"I don't need you to protect me, Luke. Although I appreciate the offer. The thought of half a dozen guys trying to coerce me into bed is incredibly appealing." She grinned at him. "I'd like the chance to fight off a few of them myself." She forced herself not to rub her wrist, where his touch seemed to have burned her skin like a brand.

Luke gave her a quirky look. "Am I going to have to impose a curfew?"

"You could try." Catherine smiled sweetly. "Although I believe people are capable of having sex at any time of the day or night, aren't they?"

"They, maybe. You, no. You aren't the type to fall into bed with a sweet-talking man."

"I'm not? Then why did you ask me who I was sleeping with after the party?"

He scowled. "I had to ask. Didn't mean I thought… Cat, you've waited twenty-six years to shed your virginity. I know you. You'd have to be madly in love with the guy. That takes time. Years."

"Years?"

"Hell, yes. Years." Luke drained his mug and set it

carefully on the table. He gave her a serious, now-listen-to-me-kid look. "You want more than animal coupling. More than lust. You want love, respect, understanding. Someone who knows you, who'll allow you to fulfill your potential as a woman." He looked so serious she had to smile.

"Can't I go for a little animal coupling first?"

"Catherine."

"Maybe you and Nick have the right idea. Maybe I should be like you guys for a while before I settle down."

"Like…us? You mean be a…player?" His voice rose. "A lifestyle that's risky, shallow, empty? A nowhere existence, just living for the moment?"

"Sure. Why not? It works for you. I'll play the field, be a party girl. That's a great idea, Luke."

He scowled at the implication that it had been his idea. "You're a woman."

"There are women players. You date them."

"And you're about as far from a player as—as Bambi is from Caligula." The light went on. "Aha! You're just trying to muddy the issue."

"I just thought while I look, I might enjoy living on the edge. Wild, uninhibited, unrepentant sex. Variety—"

"Over my dead body."

"Sheesh, that's a little drastic. I might as well wear a chastity belt." Thank God he looked so appalled. She had no idea what she would've said next. She put up her hand. "Just kidding. Can we change the subject now, please?" Catherine rose from the table and yanked open the oven door. "You mentioned real food?"

"You throw something like indiscriminate sex into the conversation and then want to eat?"

"Sure. We changed the subject. Oh, yum. Eggs Benedict."

She took the plate from the oven, feeling his gaze on her backside. That bit of conversation had thrown them both. She repressed a smile as she uncovered the plate he'd saved for her.

Catherine was amazed that the things Luke cooked turned out so well. He never measured anything, adding and subtracting ingredients to suit his taste buds, which just showed how different the two of them were.

She stuck religiously to the recipe, lined up the ingredients and utensils in the order they'd be used, and never varied anything by so much as half a grain of salt. If she had a kitchen it would consist of natural woods and a jungle of green plants. With a place for everything, and everything in its place.

The condo kitchen was a gourmet chef's dream, with brushed-chrome doors, wide black-marble countertops and a ceiling rack laden with gleaming, well-used copper pots. The counters were cluttered with weeks' worth of newspapers, fancy coffeemakers, a Cuisinart, all sorts of high-tech gadgetry, five pairs of sunglasses and a lonely sock.

In the deep windowsill, Luke had his only concession to plants. The window box Catherine had planted for him when he'd first moved in still flourished. She'd crowded it with various herbs he snipped for cooking. An automatic drip system hooked to the faucet guaranteed the plants' lives.

"Delish," Catherine told him, after swallowing. "Oh. I passed Nick in the lobby. He has a present for you."

Luke set down his coffee mug. "Why?"

"Not what?"

"I know Nick. He's a sneaky devil. If I know the why, I can guess the what."

"You won't guess what this is, I promise."

"Hmm." Luke's glassy focus was in the vicinity of her chest. He must have zoned out, thinking about something, but it still felt as though he were looking. Her nipples peaked to full glory. She casually crossed her arms and leaned forward to brace them against the edge of the table, just in case he wasn't as zoned out as she feared. "Luke?"

His head shot up. This wasn't their usual comfortable conversation. It felt a little strained, she thought, but that was her problem. Luke didn't know she'd heard him last night in the bedroom. Remembering his comments sent a chill skittering through her like dead leaves on frozen ground. Was he trying to find a compassionate way to tell her he wanted her to leave? He'd done it before with devastating effect.

"Oh, yeah. Sorry. I was thinking about—about the foundations for the house."

Catherine looked at him blankly. "There's something wrong with the foundation and you only realized this now?"

"Nope. Nothing wrong. Solid. Firm. Perfect." He picked up his empty mug and brought it to his mouth.

"I think you'd better start taking vitamins." She snatched his mug out of his hand and refilled it. "Here. I'm off to grab a shower." She loaded her plate and cutlery into the dishwasher and avoided Luke's eyes, miserable coward that she was.

"And then I'm going to pack." Catherine nudged

the door closed with her knee and resolutely turned to face him.

"Pack?" he asked blankly.

"Pack." She infused as much chirpy good cheer as she could muster into the words. "Let's face it. This wasn't one of my better ideas, Luke. I'm going home." *Before I make a fool of myself and you tell me to go.*

"Running, Cat?"

"That's not fair."

"What about finding a husband?"

"I can do that in Beaverton."

"You should've thought of that before you sold the only home you've ever known. Where will you live, little sister?"

Her chest ached. "I'll buy a condo, big brother."

"Sounds like a giant hassle to me." His knuckles whitened around his mug. "Besides, we decided you'd stay here. Why buy another condo when in a few weeks this one will be available? Consider it a favor, Cat. I can stay with you when I work late."

"I'm sure my husband will be thrilled to have you tromping through our bedroom to use the bathroom," she said dryly.

"You don't have a husband." He gave her a penetrating look. "It's not like you to make impulsive decisions like this, Cat. What's going on?"

"It's my prerogative to change my mind."

"Not when we have a bet going, it isn't."

"Oh, for heaven's sake! You and your dumb bets! Who cares?"

His chair screeched across the glossy, black-vinyl floor as he shoved it back. "*I* care. It's a matter of honor."

Catherine rolled her eyes. "Give me a break, Van

Buren. I admit I made a monumental mistake coming to you. I don't fit in here. I don't blend in with your yuppie friends." She spread her arms. "Look at me—"

Luke squeezed his eyes shut as if he were in pain. "Go take a shower. We'll discuss this when you're dressed."

"SHE WANTS TO go back home," Luke hissed, eyes fixed on the slammed-shut bedroom door. He stuck his bare feet up on the coffee table and glared at his friend. "What happened last night at the party?"

"Other than the host being eighty-sixed?" Nick asked as he reached for another doughnut.

"I had to take Karen home."

"And Catherine got in a snit when you were gone all night from your own party." Nick shook his head. "Women. Go figure."

"So? My entire social and sex life has to come to a screaming halt because Cat's here?"

Nick put up a powdered-sugar-coated hand. "Hey, that's your choice. Personally I wouldn't want to see anyone else. Not with Catherine around. In case you hadn't noticed, old son, that's one hot babe you have sharing your— Oh, excuse me," he drawled as Luke cleared his throat pointedly.

"I'd switch places with you in a heartbeat, and so would half our friends. Didn't you see them salivating around Catherine last night? Or were you too busy getting it on with Karen?"

"She's a beautiful woman."

"Cat? I know. She's gorgeous."

"Not Cat. Karen. And of course those degenerates

were all over Cat like bears over honey. They're idiots, not stupid."

"What idiots aren't stupid?" Cat asked, emerging from the bedroom wearing white shorts, a black crop top and strappy black sandals. She'd even put on makeup. Nothing overt, just enough to make her look…*more.* She'd done something to tame her hair, then swooped it on top of her head in a sexy tumble held up by gravity. A forties pinup. Nick shot up from his seat and crossed the room in three strides.

"Let me take you away from all this, my lovely Princess Catarina." He grabbed Cat around her waist, touching her bare skin as he swirled her in a circle.

Luke watched through narrowed eyes, wondering where he could hide Nick's body after the homicide. His friend brought Cat's hand to his mouth, then theatrically kissed her fingertips before nibbling his way up her arm, reeling her in against his chest and making her laugh. Cat wrapped her arm around his waist and Nick smiled down at her.

"I brought you a present."

"I thought it was for me," Luke said, as a laughing Nick pulled Cat over to the new gate-legged table by the front door.

"Nope. You get yours later, old son. This one's for Catherine."

"Oh, Nick! Thank you." She picked up the old-fashioned, round fishbowl in both hands, then looked at Nick with shining eyes. There was only one ordinary little goldfish in the bowl, not an entire freshwater aquarium, Luke thought sourly as he watched them.

"This is so sweet of you."

"Hey, I'm a sweet guy—"

"You'd better change into jeans," Luke informed her, cutting Nick off. Preferably at the knees. "We're going on the bike."

"I'm not going on the bike. Allan's taking me."

Luke gave her a blank look. "To my house?"

"Is that a problem?" One hip cocked, she leaned into Nick, holding the bowl with the lonely little fish against her chest.

Lucky fish.

"The sooner the house is finished the sooner you move in, right? Allan's a great painter. He told me so last night. Consider him free labor."

The two of them strolled across the living room like frigging Siamese twins. Nick dug in his pocket. Luke absently took the twenty his ex-best friend handed over as he passed.

"Yeah, I guess." He stuffed the money into his front pocket.

Cat didn't sound as if she were packing her bags anytime soon. Something inside him unwound a little.

"I'll make some calls and round up more people," he said. "We can make a day of it."

Cat glanced at her watch. "Well, an afternoon, anyway. You bet on Allan, did you?" she asked, then glanced at Nick. "Who was your call?"

"Ted."

"You should have told me. They both asked me out today."

"That would be cheating," Luke informed her, not amused that she was amused.

"Oh. Excuse me. I didn't realize there were rules."

The doorbell rang and she disengaged from Nick. "That's Allan. Get the lead out, Van Buren."

She handed him the dumb fishbowl and went to the door.

CHAPTER SIX

NICK HAD GIVEN him a two-by-four. To beat back the guys who were going to swarm over Cat. No kidding. At the rate things were going Luke was going to need it. He didn't like the ratio of men to woman: three to one. In Cat's favor.

He liked women, and considered flirting one of life's greatest pleasures. But it was one of his unwritten laws that he never strung them along. Luke made no secret of his opinion of marriage or any long-term commitment.

The second Cat had left on the arm of good old Allan, Luke called a woman he hadn't seen in months. Suzette was an attractive, petite brunette. Intelligent and witty, she made no bones about being available and she liked his rules just fine.

Half the twenty or so people spread throughout the house were working. The others had taken the grill across the street to the beach for an impromptu barbecue. Luke had posted a work schedule, and despite the moaning and groaning from his press-ganged crew, work was actually being accomplished.

Cat and Allan were painting the guest bedroom. They'd been in there for hours with the door closed. Of course, Luke thought, digging in one of the coolers for a liter bottle of soda, there was no furniture in there yet. But how long could it possibly take two people to paint a small room?

"Trying to use telekinesis to open the door?" Nick strolled into the kitchen and caught him glowering down the hall. Nick levered himself up onto the counter. "I thought you came in here for sodas."

"On my way." Luke held up the bottle and a short tower of paper cups. "Ladies getting twitchy?"

"Suzette and Kirsten wonder why everyone else is slaving serflike while you wander from room to room bossing us around."

"Meticulous planning." Luke shot another look toward the closed door down the hallway. "Bad idea leaving the two women unsupervised, Stratton. Who knows what devious plot they'll hatch while we're not paying attention? Back to work."

Nick slid off the plywood-topped counter. "Has Catherine said anything about leaving since we got here?"

"Nope."

"She and Allan look good together. What'ya think?"

It had been Luke's ridiculous reaction to Cat dragging Allan along that had induced him to invite five million people here in the first place. The house was overrun with bodies. Feeling incredibly beleaguered, he had to be in seven places at once to oversee what everyone was doing. "I think Allan's been in there with her long enough to paint the Sistine Chapel."

"Yeah? Go in there and supervise, then."

Luke swore. "Here, take these in to the ladies, I'll be right back." He handed Nick the soda and cups, then stalked out of the kitchen and down the hall.

Sitting cross-legged on the floor, Catherine glanced over her shoulder as the bedroom door flew open. Luke.

She groaned dramatically and rolled her eyes, making Allan smile.

"He's *back!* Quick, look busy before he gives us another project."

"Har-dee-har-har." In one glance, Luke assessed the freshly painted walls and half-painted trim. "Looks good. Nice job," he told Allan, then said to Catherine, "Can we talk a minute?"

She put her paintbrush down on the edge of the paint pan, then flexed her fingers as she rose. "Anything, as long as I can rest my poor abused arm."

Naturally, Luke was immaculately dressed, while she was covered from head to toe in cream-colored paint. Pounding music, the buzz of a Skil saw and manic hammering assaulted them from every direction as they walked through the house.

"What's up?" she yelled, following him out onto the front porch. Luke made a walking motion with his fingers and led her down the steps and across the scraggly front yard, then crossed the narrow street to the beach. The noise from the house dimmed, overshadowed by the whisper of waves curling up the beach. The gorgeous day was made absolutely perfect because she was with Luke.

Catherine removed her sandals and inhaled the salty air deep into her lungs. "Glorious. Beats paint fumes."

Several cheap laborers off to the right pretended to hide behind the sea grasses when they saw Luke coming down to the water. "Isn't lunch over?" he yelled.

"We haven't even lit the barbecue, Captain Bligh!"

Several of the men called out rude comments, which Luke volleyed back with laughing ease. People naturally gravitated to him. It was one of the things Catherine loved about him—that easy, relaxed warmth he exuded without even trying. He was such an extrovert, so charismatic that he made people happy to be near him. People always seemed to want to do their best when Luke was around.

Together they walked down the beach in the opposite direction of the rowdy lunch crew.

"You're lucky to have such great friends."

"Yeah. A good bunch. You fit in nicely. All the guys think you're hot. The women like you, too."

Catherine felt a warm glow. In the years she'd been taking care of their dad, she'd lost contact with many of her friends. She'd almost feared she might have lost some of her social skills. More than the words, the approval she heard in Luke's voice put a lump in her throat. She was glad she'd put off leaving for another day. She'd have one more Luke memory.

"Where are we going?" She skipped to keep up with his long strides. "Not, mind you, that I object to a break from slaving over a dripping paintbrush for a while."

"Let's sit over there in the shade." Luke pointed at a small sandy dune shaded by a wisp of a tree and tall sea grass. He leaned against the frail, gnarled tree trunk and stared out at the flat blue horizon for a few seconds without saying anything. Catherine's stomach clenched.

She concealed the frisson of unease that coursed through her, the sensation familiar and annoying. Old history. She usually managed to control it, but it still blindsided her every now and then. She'd felt it when her mother had left her with Peter Van Buren. She'd felt it every time Luke had tormented her as a child, insisting she was no relative of his. She'd felt it most profoundly the night of her seventeenth birthday, when

Luke had rejected her amateurish advances. And she'd last felt it when the man she considered her father had died, eight months ago.

She didn't need a psychiatrist to tell her she had a fear of abandonment. *Don't be ridiculous,* she told herself, *no one is abandoning anyone.* Luke was everything he'd always been. A typical big brother. It wasn't his fault her feelings had grown and changed. And it would be unfair to blame him because his hadn't. Luke would never hurt her. At least not intentionally. Pulling her shell around herself like a crab and wanting to hide was a knee-jerk reaction. *Get over it,* she told herself firmly. She'd already decided to leave.

"If this is going to be a lecture about something, save your breath." Catherine sat gingerly on the hot sand and circled her bare knees with her arms. Wriggling her toes, she buried them in the dry, hot granules. "I'll be out of your hair tomorrow."

"That's what I wanted to talk to you about. Look, it's not like you have to go, is it? The house is sold. You said yourself you wanted to make a fresh start. The Bay area's great. In a month or so I'll be living out here, then you can finish turning the condo into the Amazon. Why leave now?"

She scratched a flake of cream paint off her shin. "I'm in the way."

"No you're not, Cat." Luke dropped to his knees beside her. He took her chin in his palm and made her look at him. "You're not in the way at all. I like having you with me."

His touch burned like a brand. Catherine shifted enough to dislodge his hand from her face. Her emotions were already on overload. All the old fears and doubts about making him see her differently came rushing to the fore.

The sun turned the short hairs on his arms the color of coffee; his skin shone with vitality. He was close enough for her to feel the brush of his shorts against her bare thigh. Close enough for Catherine to inhale his unique scent.

She loved him so much it hurt.

"It's a one-bedroom, Luke. And I'm in it. You can't even go to the bathroom without tripping over my stuff."

"I don't trip over your stuff. In fact, if I hadn't insisted you unpack, you'd still be living out of your suitcase. You're so neat I hardly notice you're there."

"You can't bring anyone home."

"At the moment I don't want to. And in the unlikely event that changes, I'll handle it. I'm not a sex fiend, Cat. As much as I'd like to tell you I have a smorgasbord of women who sleep over, I don't. Not nowadays."

"What about Suzette. Or Elizabeth the Wretch?"

"Both charming and delightful, but nothing serious."

"Yeah?"

"Yeah. Stay, Cat." He slung a brotherly arm around her shoulders. "Honest to God, I enjoy having someone to cook for. Besides, look how pink my nail beds are." He stuck a broad hand in front of her.

Catherine's lips twitched. "Your nail beds?"

"All that oxygen your rain forest is producing is good for me. And what would I do if I had the use of all my saucers again, or if I couldn't see the carpet because you weren't there to pick up my socks?"

"You could get a maid, Van Buren."

The temptation to lean into him was overwhelming. His skin felt hot, and the sensation of having it touching hers zipped through her like expensive French champagne.

"A maid wouldn't keep me centered, or laugh at my jokes."

"Just promise me something, okay? If it starts getting to you, just come straight out and tell me. No hurt feelings."

"Never happen. You'll always have a home with me. Always."

She rested her head against his shoulder, hoping he couldn't see her moist eyes. "I love you, Luke Van Buren, do you know that?"

"I love you, too, Catwoman. A guy couldn't ask for a better baby sister."

Zing. Direct hit. After a stunned second, Catherine pressed her fingertips into her eye sockets. Hard.

Luke shifted beside her. "Are you okay?"

"Sand," she mumbled into her wrists. "Darn, that stings."

Not her eyes. Her heart.

"Want me to look?"

No, he wouldn't be able to see anything. He didn't have twenty-twenty vision where she was concerned. "I'll be fine in a moment."

Give or take fifty years.

LUKE RETURNED TO the house alone. Cat had decided to go for a run on the beach. He shook his head. The woman was insane. It was hot out there. He found Nick in the kitchen.

"Everything okay?"

"Yeah. Just had a little chat with Cat. She's staying."

"I'd have made book on that."

"Let's get some work done, Stratton." He and Nick crossed the entry hall side by side, their workboots vibrating on the subflooring. The front door stood open to catch the summer breeze, bringing with it the scent of briny air and the mouthwatering aroma of the beach barbecue. A couple of guys were out on the wide porch sanding, and the sweet smell of the sawdust mingled with the scents of tung oil, paintz and wallpaper paste.

Two different radios blared from opposite ends of the house, each on a different station, naturally—salsa from the back, hard rock from the front porch. Luke inhaled deeply as he stepped through the wide double doors into the great room. Home. It was becoming home.

Suzette and Kirsten, Nick's date du jour, a statuesque blonde of awesome proportions, glanced up as they strolled in, but the music was too loud to have a conversation, and they went back to staining the baseboards.

Nick poured more soda for the two women, then leaned back against the hearth to chug down his own drink before hunkering down to do a little hammering on the floor.

The stone fireplace soared to the cathedral ceiling. Dusty sunshine shone through the plastic-covered windows onto the oak plank floor. The plastic billowed with the breeze like an animal breathing.

Luke envisioned the room filled with his furniture. Two black leather sofas framing the fireplace. The steel wall unit over there. The metal sculpture there. His slick, stylized, monochromatic paintings grouped on the far wall.

He frowned.

Suddenly, a jungle of plants materialized next to the

windows and animal print cushions on the sofas. A bowl with a single goldfish appeared on the steel-and-glass coffee table placed between the sofas.

Suzette rose from her position on the floor and sauntered over to give Luke a hug. "I hope that fearsome scowl isn't aimed at me." She raised her voice and ran a finger between his brows. She had straight white teeth and a very pretty smile. She smelled of Obsession. She had a brain.

She bored him to tears.

"Kirsten and I are declaring mutiny for a couple of hours so we can eat, then go for a swim. We'll come back in time to help you finish the floor in here, okay?" Suzette whipped her shirt over her head, exposing nicely tanned breasts and a flat midriff showcased in a minuscule white bikini. Luke's eyelids didn't even flicker. "Are you coming?"

He'd noticed the woman was barely dressed, but didn't care. He pressed his fingertips into his temples and dredged up a smile. "Yeah. In a while."

Coming? It was a dim memory....

"You don't have to skulk. I'm awake."

Luke looked adorably rumpled as he emerged from his cocoon of blankets to sit up the second she opened the front door the next evening. He'd left a lamp on for her, and the dimly shaded bulb cast a golden glow on his bare chest. He lay back against the arm of the sofa and eyed her yellow silk dress with approval. "You look very daffodilish. How'd it go with Ted?"

Catherine shrugged. "He knows a lot about fungus."

"He's a botanist."

She set her purse on the end table and took off her shoes. "I might never eat a mushroom again."

"Limiting, but not impossible. Will you see him again?"

Catherine shook her head, then picked up her shoes. "No sparks. Let me put it this way. You offered me white bread when what I crave is devil's food cake."

LUKE SAT ON Nick's patio, a beer can balanced on his stomach, his bare feet crossed and propped up on the wrought-iron railing. It had been a swelteringly hot day, so they'd ordered pizza and taken a cold one outside. Now soft, damp fog misted around them as they sat in the dark and watched the lights across the Bay twinkle. Appear. Disappear. The fog oddly amplified, then dampened audio and visual details, making the foghorn sound close enough to touch tonight.

"Hey," Nick said lazily. "Guess who called today? Rochelle Lemmon. She wants us to design the addition, after all."

Luke glanced at his partner. "Our way?" The Lemmon's Queen Anne Victorian was a magnificent lady. He and Nick had refused the commission the month before because the couple had insisted on modernizing the extension they wanted on the back of the house. Remodeling Victorians was not only Luke and Nick's specialty as architects, it was their passion.

"Balconies, stained glass, roof finials and all," Nick told him triumphantly, taking a swig of his beer. "I gave it to Christy to schedule."

Luke's mind raced ahead. He wanted their best craftspeople on this important job. There weren't that many artisans capable of doing the detailed and intricate work required. The characteristic excesses of the style—projected bay windows, towers, turrets, porches, wall carvings and acres of decorative trim and elaborate brackets—required a sure hand and a keen eye for detail.

"Willie to craft the chimneys. Mike McGuire for the crestings." Luke glanced casually at his watch. "If those two aren't done on the Simpson job, the Lemmons will just have to wait."

"They'll wait," Nick said with confidence. He and Luke had a sterling reputation, and their clients were prepared to wait. "Got a late date or something?"

"Cat's late. Monday was Ted. Tuesday night she went to a Giants game with one of the Bobs. On Wednesday, Allan took her over to Ghiradelli Square. Tonight she's at the symphony with Kevin. I've stopped asking who's next."

"That's the whole point, right? Meeting guys?" Nick shifted on his cushion. "What's the deal? Are you p.o.'d because she's a big hit and can change her dates twice as often as her underwear?"

"Do me a favor." Luke paused with the rim of the can poised below his mouth. He lowered the cold metal to his bare chest. "Don't mention Cat and underwear in the same breath, okay?"

He looked out at the faint phosphorescent line of the waves breaking on the beach beyond the wide swath of the park across the street. Several people were out walking their dogs despite it being eleven at night. He wondered what Cat and Kev were doing right now. The show would be over. Coffee, he guessed. Hopefully in a crowded place.

"You know, old son, sometimes you sound more like

a jealous lover than a concerned big brother. Why is that, I wonder?"

"You should write fiction, Stratton. I'm merely concerned that Cat makes the right choices."

Luke felt as though he was going to jump right out of his too-tight skin. He wished to hell he could confide in Nick. He and Nick shared damn near everything. Not only did they own a business together, they were closer than most brothers. There was no one on this planet Luke respected and trusted more.

But Nick wasn't the problem. Luke was.

This was one secret he'd take to his grave. The second his feelings for Cat broke free from their tightly sealed box, he'd be in a world of hurt. Once out, he knew he'd never be able to shove those explosive emotions back where they'd been forced to lie dormant for years.

"And have you seen my place lately?" he said, desperate to change the subject. Which seemed to go from Cat to Cat without missing a beat. "It's overrun with foliage. If she buys one more plant I'll need a machete to get in the front door."

"She's nesting." Light glinted off the can as Nick lifted his beer to his lips by radar. "Look at all the antiques she's suddenly acquired. Shoot, in three weeks she's transformed the place. Plants, furniture, all those pillows, candles. Girl things. Hell, old son, if I didn't know better… Nah. Nothing. Neither of us has ever shacked up with a woman. So how would I know what it all means?

"Oh, by the way," Nick added lazily, "in case I didn't mention it before, Catherine's going out with me next week."

"You?" Luke heard a strange noise, then realized it was his teeth grinding. "'By the way?' Since when have you and Cat had that sort of relationship?"

"Hmm. Relationship." Nick's voice came out of the misty darkness like *The Phantom of the Opera.* "I kinda like the sound of that."

"Oh, no, you don't." Luke dropped his feet from the railing to the floor with a thump. "You keep away from Cat. She's not sophisticated like the women we date. She doesn't know how the games are played. She might fall for all your baloney, and you'll break her heart."

"I won't play with Catherine's heart. Trust me."

"I don't. Trust you, that is. And would you stop calling her 'Catherine' like that?"

"Like what? Her name is Catherine."

Luke's jaw hurt. "You'd better treat her as you've always done. Like a sister." His voice sounded like gravel in the thick darkness. He didn't wait for Nick to remind him that neither of them was Cat's brother. "She trusts you. Behave accordingly."

Their silence was punctuated by a mournful toot of the foghorn. A dog barked. A car shifted gears as it turned the corner. Ted and Cat? Impossible to see from this high up.

"How come you haven't taken her out?" Nick asked lazily.

"Me? I take her out all the time."

"I don't mean to your house to slave, you jerk. I mean on a date."

Luke crushed the can he held, then tossed it in the general direction of the pizza box on the floor. "That would be...not a good idea."

OVER THE NEXT couple of days Luke couldn't stop thinking about Nick's question. Why couldn't he ask her out? They lived together. They were friends. Nothing wrong with asking a friend to the movies or a ball game, was there?

Offhand, he could think of several very good reasons why it would be a bad idea.

The promise to his dad.

The promise to Cat.

The promise to himself.

His—thus far contained—all-consuming lust.

On an "official date" he'd feel as though there was a chance of having more. And the reality was that this was Cat's time to shine. To get what she wanted. To get what she deserved.

She'd spent years cloistered in that big old house taking care of his father. Without complaint, without a murmur as life passed her by. She deserved every good thing there was.

A promise was a promise. It wasn't in him to renege, and he'd rather jump off a cliff than hurt her. Yeah, Luke decided, feeling sanctimonious, the least he could do was keep a low profile, and give Cat what she wanted.

VAN BUREN AND Stratton owned an immaculately restored 1860s Italianate Victorian on the Avenues. It not only housed their flourishing business, it was a shining example of their talent as architects and restoration specialists. Every inch had been lovingly restored, then intricately painted.

There were memories for Catherine in every room of this house. There was a photograph of the three of them in Luke's office the day they'd opened their doors for business. She was proud that it was thanks to her skills as a day trader that Nick and Luke had been able to afford the house when they'd gone into business five years ago. She'd just begun day trading, and despite her show of confidence, wasn't sure at all whether she could make it in that volatile roller-coaster world. But she'd flourished. By trading with the trends, she'd made steady profits, never making a huge killing but never getting wiped out, either, like other traders she knew.

She and Nick sat in the beautifully appointed reception area, which had originally been the ladies' parlor. She'd gone with Luke to buy the faded Aubusson area rug. She'd been with Nick when he'd found the camel-back sofa in an out-of-the-way antique store.

"What I want," Catherine told Nick, "is for Luke to give some indication he sees me as more than someone making his socks magically disappear."

"Unless my friend has cataracts, I can't see how he can miss the obvious," Nick assured her, head down as he searched for something in the receptionist's antique cherrywood desk.

Catherine had decided to drop in on Luke to see if he'd take her to lunch before she went shopping. He'd been out. But Nick had assured her he wouldn't be long.

A perfect opportunity for a little strategizing.

Nick dumped a pile of file folders on Christy's desk. Catherine winced. "What are you looking for?"

"The Stockton bids."

"It's in the file room in the blue file cabinet."

Nick glanced up. "It is? How'd you know that?"

"Because all bids go in the file room in the blue file cabinet. Nick? Could you stop scrounging around for a sec?"

Catherine tucked one foot under her and eased back on the stiff horsehair sofa, spread her soft skirt over her knees and picked up the cup and saucer from the table beside her. She'd acquired a slight tan at the beach a couple of days before, and the scoop-necked, butter-colored linen dress showed it off to advantage. The linen jacket hung neatly over a nearby tapestry chair. She cradled the saucer.

"In the last three weeks Luke's interrogated every single guy I've gone out with as if he's Don Corleone," she told Nick, exasperated. "He's still acting like my brother. I want him to see me as a sexy, desirable female, not his kid sister. I don't know how to make him see me as an adult woman."

"You look all-woman to me, Catherine. Trust me," Nick said dryly. "There wasn't a guy at the party who didn't sit up and take notice."

Catherine shot a wary glance at the etched glass panels in the oak front door before turning back to Nick. "I don't care about other men, Nick. I want Luke to love me."

Nick gave her a searching look, then said softly and with regret, "Will that really be enough for you, Catherine? Having him return your love? Luke's a great guy, but we both know he's got some serious hang-ups about commitment. Those fixed ideas he has about tying up his emotions too tightly. Can you accept that he'll never marry you?"

"Having him reciprocate what I feel will be enough."

"For how long?"

She looked him dead in the eye. "For as long as it lasts."

"Really?" Nick asked skeptically. "Then why did you ask him to find you a husband?"

"To throw him off the scent. Don't look at me like that. It's a given that marrying Luke would be a dream come true. But I know that will never happen. I know him, remember? I'm a lot more realistic than you give me credit for."

"Why do you love him, Catherine?" Nick asked. "Because you've known him almost your whole life? Because he represents security to you? Because you're alone now that your dad's gone?"

"No…maybe. Possibly that's part of it. A small part," she added quickly. "I love Luke because he's honest, and strong and ethical. Because he's got a sense of humor I understand. I love him because when I'm with him I'm…a better me. Does that make sense?"

"Yeah," Nick said with a smile. "It makes perfect sense. Okay, gorgeous, you have a master tactician at your disposal." He grinned, looking charmingly rakish. "Between us, he doesn't stand a chance."

"I want him, but not at the risk of destroying what we have now. You understand that, don't you?"

"Luke's right." Nick smiled. "You are a little crab. You've got to keep advancing here, Catherine. No retreating allowed."

"You're sure, positive, no doubt about it, I have a chance?" Catherine hated her own insecurity. She fought it every day, but sometimes that feeling of abandonment would creep up on her unexpectedly and she'd find herself poised for flight. "If you're sure I'm not making a total fool of myself…"

Nick came to sit next to her on the sofa and took both her cold hands between his. "You want Luke to see you as a woman, right? Then you have to make him stop seeing you as The Kid."

Like she hadn't been trying for the last decade. "And how do I go about doing that?"

Nick's blue eyes lit up devilishly as he released one hand to brush her mouth with his finger. "You dare Luke to teach you the art of seduction."

Catherine, in the process of lifting the delicate china cup to her mouth, almost choked. Her eyes went wide. "You're kidding, right?"

"Nope. Luke knows you don't have vast experience. Ask him to teach you."

Catherine carefully set the cup and saucer on the small fern table beside the sofa. "No one is that naive!"

"Luke thinks you are. Pretend, if you have to."

"I'm a lousy actress, Nick. Jeez-Louise, I'm not even a good poker player. How am I supposed to pull this off?"

"You'll figure it out." Nick, still holding her hand, looked up as the door opened and Luke walked in.

"Ah, here's our meal ticket." He rose, tugging Catherine up beside him, then wrapping his arm around her shoulders. "About time you made it back, old son. Catherine and I are starving, and you're buying lunch."

CHAPTER SEVEN

THEY ATE AT a small French restaurant tucked away on a side street. San Francisco was full of small, interesting restaurants off the beaten path. Luke, who loved to eat as much as he loved to cook, knew them all.

It was fascinating to observe how people, men as well as women, were ogling her two escorts. Luke wore bright yellow suspenders over a collarless blue-and-white pinstripe shirt, navy Dockers and boat shoes, no socks. Nick was decked out in a double-breasted charcoal suit. Both looked hunky and gorgeous. Catherine felt like a thorn between two roses.

"Don't look now, Nick." She did an "over there" jerk of her chin. "But there's a sultry blonde at the table near the pillar who's about to fall out of her seat trying to get your attention."

"Actually—" Nick grinned without looking "—she's had my attention. It's Luke's attention she's trying to attract now."

Catherine's heart pinched. "How lovely. You share girlfriends. It must make life so much easier when you can give each other insider tips."

Luke shot a sidelong glance across the room.

"Want an intro, old son?" Nick murmured.

"Maybe later." Luke picked up his water glass, drank

deeply, then turned to Catherine. "What do you have planned for this afternoon?"

To see you in the middle of the day. "Shopping."

"What kind of shopping?" Nick asked. "If it's clothes, I'll go with you."

"Would you? That would be terrific, Nick, I'd lo—"

"You have an appointment at two, remember?" Luke reminded him. Nick looked blank. "You told me you were seeing…can't remember who it was, but someone."

"Huh? Oh. Yeah. Someone. Right."

"If you want company, Cat," Luke offered, "I've got the afternoon free. I can show you some good places to shop."

The fact that Luke, who loathed shopping, wanted to accompany her, and had outmaneuvered Nick, was grounds for celebration.

"I'd love you to come with me, Luke. I want to look for a couple of pairs of sandals."

She took a sip of coffee and caught Nick's eye over the rim of her cup. Those deep blue eyes challenged her.

"And underwear," she added casually.

"Underwear?" Luke repeated.

"Yeah, you know. Lingerie. The slinky stuff."

Nick rose, tossed his napkin on the table and stood behind Catherine's chair, his hand on her shoulder. "I'm devastated to miss this shopping trip. You know I love to shop. Catch you next time, Catherine." He squeezed her shoulder, then said to Luke, "I'm off to see Mrs. Somebody. Take care of my girl."

THANK GOD SHE didn't model any of the stuff she was looking at. Luke would've had a stroke. As it was he was grateful to be sitting. He was as hard as petrified wood just watching Cat slide wispy bits of see-through silks and laces through her fingers before taking them into the dressing room. Surely to God none of those teddies would fit a grown woman? There wasn't more than five inches of fabric in the entire garment.

"You must be bored out of your mind." Cat emerged, a dozen satin hangers in each hand. Luke sat conspicuously on a spindly, peach-satin ladies' chair.

"I'm fine. Take your time." *I'm far too horny to stand or walk.* Luke dredged up a smile. "Really, Cat, I'm kinda enjoying the scenery. Take as long as you like." He'd never thought to frequent lingerie stores to troll for females. Too bad he couldn't care less about his new discovery. Cat glanced around, as if only now noticing the store was filled with women.

"Almost done. What do you think of these?"

"These" consisted of a bra that looked like two smiles of pale purple satin and a stamp-size sliver of supple, lime-green silk. There wasn't much to the top, and the bottom consisted of a short length of matching dental floss. There wasn't a single fluff of lace or frou-frou on either garment.

"Kinda plain, aren't they?" Like wearing nothing at all.

"I like the colors."

"Then buy them." She'd look like a mermaid, with a sexy, slippery wisp of green covering her long sexy, slippery body. The skimpy top would barely cover her breasts. Those delectable, peach tipped— "Buy them all and let's get out of here. You said you wanted shoes? There are a couple of reasonable places in the next block. I've got an appointment in a couple of hours. We'd better make tracks."

"But you said—"

"Hey, a man can only stand so much of a good thing."

Five hundred dollars worth of intimate apparel fit into a tiny shopping bag. The smaller the garment, apparently, the higher the price.

Luke felt much more himself when they walked into the shoe store. There was nothing remotely sexy about feet, in his opinion. His libido had taken a beating in the lingerie boutique. But now he could relax. He sat on one of the uncomfortable chairs lined up in the center of the store as Cat wandered around. That creamy yellow dress was dynamite on her; the color brought out the fire in her hair. Luke watched her through narrowed eyes. The simple style suited her; the square-necked, sleeveless dress had no waistline and gently fell to just above her knees, setting off long limbs lengthened by high heels.

Around her throat and draped between her breasts, Cat wore a heavy, almost barbaric necklace consisting of large cream and bronze beads and hammered copper squares. He'd bought the necklace and matching earrings and bracelet for her in Africa several years ago. At the time he'd imagined Cat wearing just that pagan jewelry. Nothing else. Instead of hand delivering his gift, Luke had mailed it to her in Oregon. Then he'd turned off the phone and got blind drunk for two days.

"Sorry. Are you in a coma?" Cat asked, giving him a sympathetic glance as she sat beside him. "I'd like to try these, please," she told the salesman hovering ingratiatingly nearby. She gave him her size and a handful of left shoes, and he trundled off.

Luke dredged up a smile and shifted slightly so they weren't quite so close. "I told you, I'm fine. Although

I've got to admit I don't have the patience for shopping that Nick does. Man, that guy shops as enthusiastically as a woman. On the other hand, he never told me what a treasure trove lingerie shops are."

"Haven't you ever bought sexy lingerie for one of your girlfriends?"

"Hell, no!"

Cat laughed. "Why not?"

Luke was saved from answering by the salesman's return with several boxes, which he placed on the floor at Cat's feet like an offering. "I'll be back in a jiff," he assured her, then scurried off for more.

Luke didn't buy sexy lingerie for women. One, because he hated to shop, never went to malls, and frankly, it had never occurred to him to casually stroll into a potpourri-scented "pink" store. Two, because by the time he could order anything from a catalog, the woman would have been long gone, only to be replaced by someone who might not be the same size.

He slouched in his chair. His knee brushed Cat's bare legs as he shifted. She smelled so damn good he wanted to forget the promises he'd made and lick her. All over. Then go back for seconds. And thirds...

The salesman knelt before Cat. "May I?" he asked, removing the shoes from the box beside him and stripping out the paper stuffing. Catherine offered her foot.

The man slid on a high-heeled red sandal. "Oh, my. These shoes were made for you. Look how well they show off this glorious high arch of yours."

"Dream on," Luke grumbled under his breath.

The salesman cast him a wary glance as he produced the other damn shoe. Luke's mouth went Sahara dry. His eyes glommed on, riveted to her slender, tanned foot sliding slowly, slowly into that shoe. She had the sexiest feet he'd ever seen. High instep, neat little toes, nails painted a glossy fire-engine red. His erection had merely been lying dormant. It came back to life in a hurry. Oxygen drained out of his brain, leaving him dizzy.

Cat's feet were sexy as hell.

Who would've thunk it? he thought without humor. He wanted to slide those sandals on her himself. Luke closed his eyes. He pictured himself holding her heel in his palm, his other hand slipping the shoe slowly over her toes. Pictured his hand gliding up the smooth, lightly tanned, highly freckled length of her leg. Up. Up. To a wisp of a thong of lime-green silk—

"Well? What do you think?" Cat stood, wriggling her toes and looking down at him. Luke refocused and cleared his throat.

"Buy them in every color they have."

Cat frowned, then turned to the salesman. "Let me try on a few of the others."

While Cat and the man conferred on colors and styles, Luke congratulated himself on his fortitude and self-sacrifice. He was a prince among men to resist her under so much temptation.

His eyes zeroed in on her sexy toes again.

Yeah, a saint.

CATHERINE SANG AT the top of her voice as she walked into the living room fresh from a shower, rubbing her hair with a towel and heading for the kitchen. She screeched to a stop midnote when she saw Luke. He looked up from the book in his lap.

"Hey. You're home early," she said unnecessarily.

Grinning, he demanded, "What did you do with the money?"

"What money?"

"The money for the singing lessons."

"Ha ha. Spent it the same place you did those dancing lessons, Van Buren."

He wore white shorts and a tank top that had seen better days. He'd changed while she'd been in the bathroom, and had tossed the clothes he'd worn to work on the table by the front door. One of his shoes was near the bedroom door, the other under the coffee table. His socks decorated the lamp shade.

"I had the bathroom door closed. You could have come in and changed in the bedroom, you know."

"Yeah, right," Luke said dryly. His eyes skimmed down the now damp cotton jersey of her sundress and back to her face.

They were having a heat wave. The most she could bear having next to her skin was the skimpy, bright yellow tank dress and cotton underwear. "Yeah, right?"

"Yeah. Right. I could have. But I didn't. Hey. Molly Cruz called. She wants you to call her back."

Catherine plucked his clothes off the table and lamp shade and stood with the bundle in her arms. His shirt smelled so terrific she wanted to bury her nose in it. Luke sweat. She really was losing it.

"Thanks. I'll call her back tomorrow." She took his clothes into the bedroom and tossed them into the hamper.

Luke raised his voice through the open door. "Don't you miss your friends back home?"

"I talk to Molly, Susan and some of the others almost every other day, Luke." She came back pushing wet hair behind her shoulders, enjoying the coolness. "Which is pretty much what we've been doing for the last year or so, anyway. The distance hasn't made much difference."

"Yeah, but wasn't there someone special?"

Catherine frowned at him. What was she missing here? "Susan and Molly have been my best friends since second grade, you know that."

"A guy, Cat. A guy."

"No." She sank onto the sofa, curled her legs under her, stuffed one of the new cushions behind the small of her back, picked up *Sports Illustrated* from the coffee table to fan herself. The cool wet strands of her hair felt great slithering down her back. She swung her head, enjoying the sensation.

Luke stared at her, his eyes somewhat glazed. He cleared his throat. "What about a nipple?"

"A what?"

He looked blank for a second. "Nippon. You know. A Japanese car. I was thinking you probably need a vehicle of some sort. Something small to drive around town. Easy to park. Good gas mileage on the freeway."

She could have sworn he'd said... God, she had sex on the brain. "I don't think I'll need a car, do you? If I want to go anywhere, I'll just take the bus or a cab."

"You can always use the Jag." He looked her up and down. "Heavy date tonight?"

"Nope. I'm in. You?"

"In." For a second she thought he'd go back to reading the book he clutched hard enough to whiten his knuckles. He looked up again. "Want to take in a nice air-conditioned movie?"

"You could have stopped at the words *air-conditioned.* I'd go anywhere cool right now. I had no idea

San Francisco could get this hot." She uncurled her legs and rose to go to the kitchen. "I have yesterday's newspaper. Let's see what's on. As long as it's nothing with gushing blood," she added, as she returned with the paper and spread it out on the crowded coffee table.

"And nothing too schmaltzy," he warned as she crouched down to find the movie section. "Why don't you push the fishbowl and twenty-nine of those plants out of the way?"

"Cleo doesn't like to be moved," Catherine said, lifting the paper over the fishbowl and a thriving dieffenbachia, and closer to Luke. She shifted so that she had to practically lean over his knees to see the print. "No vampires." She ran her hand through her wet hair. "Do you think Cleo is lonely?"

"Fish don't get lonely." He didn't move when she rested an elbow on his knee, but he cleared his throat. "No costume dramas."

She wrapped an arm about his knee and leaned a little more of her weight against his leg. Rigor mortis set in as he froze.

Catherine pretended to watch Cleo blow bubbles and swim in circles as she settled comfortably against him. Her unfettered breast brushed against his bare knee.

"She looks lonesome to me. I think I'll buy her a friend tomorrow."

"Then b—" Luke cleared his throat. "Be prepared to be grandparent to a bunch of tadpoles."

Catherine laughed. "Fish have fish. Frogs have tadpoles."

"Same thing—"

"Not to the frogs and the fishies, it isn't."

"Keep the bowl in the bedroom then. I don't think I

can handle fish procreation while I'm trying to watch CNN."

Interesting subject for Luke to bring up.

"And nothing too smoochie, either," he warned, before she could suggest the new romantic comedy at the Roxie.

Catherine pushed damp hair out of her face. "Jim Carrey?"

"What time?"

"Seven-fifteen." She used Luke's leg to lever herself to her feet. His thigh muscles flexed beneath her palm. "I have to dry my hair."

His gray-green eyes darkened. "And get dressed."

"I'm perfectly decent. Why can't I go like this?"

"Put on a bra."

Catherine hid her smile as she went off to dry her hair.

IT WASN'T A DATE.

But it sure felt like one to Luke. The theater was dark, and the movie, at any other time, would've captivated his attention.

Small problem: Catherine Anne Harris sat beside him. Close beside him. In the old theater, the seats were too narrow and far too close together. He'd had to extend his legs into the aisle to accommodate their length. Cat had to sit at an angle to accommodate hers. Which meant she was practically in his lap. She smelled of peach soap and popcorn, a fragrance Luke was rapidly becoming addicted to.

The huge tub of popcorn was on her lap. When he wanted to grab a handful his arm brushed her firm breast. Without looking at what she was doing, Cat fumbled for the giant soda he held on his own lap. Her fingers brushed his chest. He drew in a deep breath and handed her the paper cup.

"Thanks," she whispered against his cheek, eyes fixed on the screen. Her lips closed around the straw. Luke squeezed his eyes shut in self-defense. He imagined those lips closing around him.

"I'm going out," he whispered harshly. "Be right back."

LUKE PULLED OPEN the door to the men's room. He couldn't handle this. Could. Not. Handle. This.

He sat in a stall and stared at the graffiti on the back of the door. He wanted Cat. No. He more than wanted her. He'd desired women before. But what he felt for Cat…what he felt for Cat was deeper, more complex. Just more, dammit! That wasn't going to go away. In fact, if anything, it was getting worse by the minute.

He couldn't concentrate at work. He wasn't getting any sleep. His appetite was shot to hell. Luke felt the familiar tug-of-war he'd been experiencing for years— his own need balanced with honor. Half of him wanted to come right out and show Cat how much he wanted her. The other half remembered what a tender heart she had, how easily she could be hurt.

Been there, done that.

The night of her seventeenth birthday party came to mind. And the sharp sting of his father's disapproval as he'd yelled, "Don't go thinking you can use that girl to scratch an itch! She's not her mother. Catherine is a forever woman."

His father had been more furious than Luke had ever

seen him. "What would you do with a girl like Catherine once you had her?"

The accurate punch of that statement hit him square on the jaw. What he wanted to do and what his own moral code demanded he do were polar opposites.

He was a man who thrived on sampling.

Catherine Anne Harris was a keeper.

The promise to always be her big brother hadn't been made lightly. His depth of sincerity had been in direct proportion to the hurt and anguish he'd inflicted on her. He wouldn't renege on that now. Even if Cat was sharpening her inexperienced claws on his heart right now, he couldn't go back on his word. He went through The Promise about thirty-nine times in his mind. Bottom line? He'd promised himself and his dad that he would take care of Cat.

Taking care of Cat meant putting her best interests ahead of his own. Ahead of his marauding testosterone, his own lust, his own desires. He was a mature adult, not a hormone driven adolescent. He could deny himself; he could control his base urges. No one had ever died of lust, as far as he knew. He resigned himself to being horny for however long it took Cat to find what she was looking for. When she was settled he could take care of his own physical needs.

Luke didn't want to consider why he couldn't take care of those needs while seeing to Cat's happiness. The two seemed somehow entwined in his mind. If he couldn't have Cat, he didn't want anyone else. Frustrated, but determined to stick to the letter of the law, he groaned.

From the next stall, someone pounded on the dividing wall. "Get yourself a girl, mister!"

CHAPTER EIGHT

LUKE WAS IN the kitchen scraping burned cookies into the garbage disposal when Cat returned home from her date with Dan the following night.

"Phew-ee!" Catherine waved her hands. "That is *mucho* stinky! What are you still doing up?"

"Burning cookies. How was your date?"

Catherine sat on a bar stool and swung her foot. "Fun. The play was terrific. We ate at a fabulous little Italian place off the beaten track called Giovanni's. Do you know it?"

"I was the one who told him about it. You and old Daniel hit it off, huh?"

"Umm. He's charming."

"Just remember, he's been married once before."

"No problem, as long as he doesn't bring his ex to dinner with us," Catherine said cheerfully.

"Devil's food cake?"

"Nah. Strawberry swirl."

THIS IS NOT going well, she decided several days later. One of the problems was she was rarely home. The other was…well, she was being too subtle. She needed to turn up the heat. They were anchored out on the Bay on Nick's twenty-seven-foot sailboat. Even at six in the evening, the heat of the day was oppressive. She felt like the Wicked Witch in *The Wizard of Oz. Melt*ing.

There wasn't a breath of wind, the dark blue water reflected mirror smooth, the air shimmered. Dozens of white-sailed boats, manned by scantily clad people hoping for an ocean breeze, cruised the Bay. In the distance the city looked freshly washed and as picture perfect as a postcard. She could even see the twin towers of their condo beyond Marina Green.

Luke lay sprawled facedown on a towel on the varnished deck. Nick slouched on a folding deck chair, a book on his chest, eyes closed. Both wore swimsuits and a light film of perspiration on their tanned skins.

Catherine, wearing a soft lime-green sundress, and sitting in the shade, sighed. She pulled the light T-shirt fabric farther up her bare legs. "Do you think if I sit in the sun my freckles will join together and I'll get a nice even tan?"

"You've been asking me that same question since you turned fifteen," Luke told her. "And the answer is still no." He reached blindly for the soda beside him. Catherine nudged it closer with her toe.

"Thanks. Remember when you went to Hawaii that year? You came back parboiled and peeling."

"How do you know? You weren't there." That was the year he'd gone to the Pratt Institute in New York to study architecture. She'd felt as though a cannonball had gone through her chest and left a gaping, bleeding hole. Worse even than the day her mom had walked out and left her behind.

"Dad told me about it."

Catherine felt her eyes well, and bit her lip. She'd had wonderful years with her stepfather. Good years.

She had to remember those. But, God, how she missed him. Missed the unconditional love he'd always given her. Missed the feel of his arms around her. Missed that safety and the sense of belonging he'd provided. She closed her eyes and said a quick prayer of gratitude for the years they had shared.

"Hey." Luke curled his fingers around her ankle. His hand was cold from holding the soda can as he absently smoothed his thumb up and down her anklebone. "Dad wouldn't have wanted you to be sad on such a beautiful day."

"How did you know I was thinking about him?" Icy hot shivers sheeted her skin at his touch.

"Your mouth always goes soft and sort of pouty when you're sad. Come on, Catwoman. Give me a smile."

Thankful her sunglasses hid her misty eyes, Catherine felt her heart expand as she looked down at him lying there like a giant sun-loving lion. Miles of smooth, tanned, naked skin; sweat-dampened dark hair; heartbreaking smile.

"Good memories," she said around the lump in her throat.

"I know," Luke said softly. Although she couldn't see his eyes behind his glasses, she could feel his gaze skim her face. He let go of her ankle and she felt bereft.

"It was just one of those quick, sneaky whammies. I'm getting better every day."

"Isn't that a song?"

"Yes. But please spare us and don't sing it."

"Hear, hear," Nick agreed, reminding them he was also on board.

The muscles in Luke's back flexed as he pillowed

his head on his hands. "Man, this is the life. I could get used to it."

A seagull squawked as it wheeled lazily overhead. Wavelets lapped the wooden hull; lines creaked. The boat barely moved. The scent of suntan lotion overrode the salty tang of the water.

If she leaned down and stretched out her hand, she could touch Luke's shoulder. Catherine wanted to touch him so badly her fingernails tingled. Her heart sped up and her palms felt slick on her soda can. She imagined sliding her hands up his back, drawing his half naked body against hers. She imagined Luke blocking out the sun as he angled his head to kiss her, imagined his mouth touching hers....

Imagined him wanting her.

Not like the last disastrous time she'd kissed him, nine years ago. She'd almost knocked him to the floor in her exuberance. What a naive fool she'd been. Of course he'd been repulsed. Even inebriated, she'd known how appalled Luke had been. After several Keystone Cops moves, Luke had managed to extricate himself from her rubbery hold with a firm, no-nonsense grip of her shoulders. Then he'd yelled at her. Or had she thrown up and then he'd yelled at her? She shuddered at the memory.

But that was then, this was now. Luke wasn't going anywhere. She wasn't feeling cool linoleum under her bare feet, but the solid wood deck. She wasn't a beer-giddy, euphoric seventeen-year-old. She was stone-cold sober.

No time like the present. Her heart did an antici-patory jig in her chest. The can made a little popping sound as she squeezed it too tightly.

"Okay. Which of you is the best kisser?" she asked into the heat-induced silence.

"I am," both men said in unison. Luke lifted his glasses off his nose, opened one eye and squinted up at her. "Why?"

"Because I think I need kissing lessons."

"Good idea," Nick said, using a water-filled plastic spray bottle to spritz his legs and chest. He gave Catherine a wink of approval. She kept her expression bland.

"Bad idea. Bad, bad idea." Luke scowled at Nick. "She does not need kissing lessons. Don't encourage her."

"Gee, I'm sorry you don't approve." Catherine peered at him over her sunglasses. "But I'm serious here. This is a skill I want to master. I've heard kissing can be taken to a fine art. I've had the sloppy kind, the dry kind, the icky kind and pretty much everything in between. I want to be taught by the best. So I can even the playing field. Who's it going to be?" She avoided looking directly at Luke while she spoke, lest she chicken out.

"We'll both teach you, Catherine," Nick said. "You'll have the advantage of learning from two masters."

"Forget it." Luke sat up. He had the imprint of the towel on his sweat-sheened chest. "Women are born knowing how to seduce. We should be teaching her what to expect and how to resist. Martial arts. That's what we should be teaching her, for heaven's sake! Besides, Cat's not having two men stick their tongues down her throat one after the other. That's gross."

"Oh, thank you for sparing me that. Sticking your tongue down my throat? If that's how you two turkeys exhibit finesse, I'd rather kiss a frog."

"No frogs in salt water." Nick reached for his shorts lying on the deck under his chair. "If you learn from a master, you won't waste your time kissing a bunch of horny toads. Hey, old son, I'll flip you for it." He took a coin out of a pocket.

Luke look horrified. "You can't flip a coin for something as intimate as a kiss."

"Sure we can. Remember Jennifer?"

"That was different."

Knowing the coin Nick held was double-sided, Catherine hid a smile. "Oh, just ignore him and flip it," she instructed Nick. She shot Luke a glance. "If I don't mind, why should you?"

"Call." Nick prepared to flip.

"Forget it." Luke scowled. "Neither of us is teaching Cat anything. When the right man comes along, he'll do all the teaching she wants. Until then, keep your grubby lips to yourself, Stratton."

"Catherine?" Nick asked.

She shrugged. "If Luke doesn't want to help, then I'd welcome any pointers you can give me. Thanks, Nick."

Nick gave her a sexy, dimpled smile and held out his hand. "Stand up, sweetheart, and let's see what I can do."

"Stay right where you are, Cat."

"Don't be such a grouch." Catherine rose, stepped over him and took Nick's hand. "Okay, how should we do this?"

"Put your mouth anywhere near hers and you'll be fish bait." Luke jerked upright. "And take your hand off her butt."

Catherine struggled to keep a straight face. She

couldn't even look at Nick as he carefully lifted his hand from the small of her back.

"One of us is going to help Catherine out, old son." Nick tugged her against his side. "Why don't you go below for an hour or so? I don't want an audience. Do you, Catherine?"

Don't overdo it, Nick. "Not particularly, no."

Luke ignored her to glare at his friend. "An hour? She wants a kissing lesson, not a detailed road map through the *Kama Sutra*."

Nick pulled her closer. "Anything worth doing is worth doing well."

"No."

"Hey, you had a chance to call it. Either of us would do, right, Catherine?"

"Heads," Luke snapped.

"Damn, I was really looking forward to—"

"Flip the damn coin."

Nick grinned, slid Cat a wink and flipped the coin. It caught the sunset as it spun head over head and onto the back of his hand. He slapped his palm down, then lifted it to look. "Heads it is. Should I close my eyes, or would you prefer I go below and take my time finding something cold to drink?"

"How about swimming back to the marina via Alaska?"

"Luke!"

Nick laughed. "Man, you're a sore winner. I'm off to find some compelling reason to stay below." He quirked an eyebrow at Luke. "Unless you want me to stay and coach from the sidelines?"

"I certainly don't need coaching, but there's no need to make yourself scarce. This'll only take a minute."

"A minute?" Nick gave her a sympathetic look. "Poor Catherine, being instructed by someone with such a limited repertoire. Let me—"

"For a man who couldn't even dredge up a date for tonight, you're a fine one to talk," Luke told him sourly.

"I had a date tonight, old son. There she is. About to be mashed by my best friend. Go figure how I ended up being the third wheel."

I'm damned if I do and damned if I don't, Luke thought as Nick went below. Luke dragged on heavy jeans shorts over his thin swimsuit—the closest thing to body armor he could come up with at such short notice. He shifted his stance so he could pull up the zipper.

"What on earth are you doing?" Cat asked as she flopped into a chair. "You're going to roast alive in those hot things."

True. On the other hand, he was already on high boil just looking at her and imagining his lips on her mouth.

"I don't want to get you overexcited. Stand up."

Cat grinned. She rose from the chair and reached up to hold on to the rigging to keep her balance. It was a centerfold stance, with one slender arm curved over her head, the other at her side. The soft fabric of her dress molded nicely to the gentle swell of her breasts and clung to her hips and long legs.

"Overexcited? By a little kiss? Oh, puh-leeze. Get real."

Ahh. Fighting words. A challenge if he ever heard one. Unfortunately, this was one he'd prefer not to accept.

Kiss Cat? Touch his mouth to hers? Feel her breath? Man. This was a bad idea. Bad, bad idea. Look what had happened the last time. He had to refuse.

The words hovered like something bitter on the tip of his tongue. *Just say no,* he told himself. But he saw the tantalizing sparkle in her amber eyes, the joyous lift of her lips. The knowledge he read in her face—that no matter what she asked of him, he'd come through for her—dissolved his resistance.

He was doomed.

"How do you feel?" he asked cautiously.

Her eyes opened wide. "Just fine. Why?"

"Tummy okay?"

Their eyes met as they both remembered that night. Her chin came up; her amber eyes dared him. "I'm feeling in the pink of good health. Smooch away."

Accustomed to the gentle pitch of the boat, he strolled over to stand in front of her, then gave her a reproving look.

"You have to concentrate here, Cat. There are kisses and then there are kisses. I'll show you how it's supposed to be done. But you have to close your eyes and focus on the subtle nuances." Which would be a nice change from the last time he'd mangled her lips in a fit of misplaced passion.

Tiger eyes alight with mirth, Cat looked up at him. "Subtle nuances? You?"

"Remove your hat and glasses, please," he instructed sternly. He could make this a quick tutorial. He didn't have to get involved. It was just a kiss. Two sets of lips touching briefly. Nothing to it.

Cat dutifully pulled off the baseball cap she'd been wearing and tossed it down the companionway. Freed from the confines of the hat, her hair went berserk. An explosion of shiny Titian-red curls demanded to be crushed beneath his fingers. Luke kept his marauding fingers and itchy palms at his sides.

She removed her sunglasses and glanced around for somewhere safe to put them. He plucked them from her, whipped off his own shades and set both on the chair she'd just vacated. He straightened and scrutinized her face. The anticipation was going to kill him. But now, when he suddenly had the opportunity to show her... whatever it was he wanted to show her, he was scared spitless.

He saw in her eyes the memory of another kiss. Another challenge. But the only miserable consolation about that disastrous night had been Cat's claim to have only vague memories about what had happened. Thank God. He didn't want those memories to taint this. Which was just a simple kiss.

He was delusional. This wasn't just a kiss. He knew that. His body knew that. He just didn't want Cat to know it. He felt the thud of his heart deep in his chest. Felt the tightening of his jeans. Felt a rush of desire so strong, so profound he simply stood there, riding the gentle buck of the waves, and looked down at her.

"How long are you going to stand there staring at me?" she demanded, chin out, eyes bright. She narrowed those witchy eyes, and Luke knew he was on a slippery slope wearing wet, leather-soled shoes.

"In a hurry?"

"Well, no..."

He reached up and anchored her fingers on the rigging with his own. His hand covered hers completely. Slowly, he slid his right hand under her hair to cup the back of her damp neck. The filaments clung to his hand and arm like living flame. A pulse throbbed a jungle beat in his ears. The universe around them bled into soft focus, leaving Cat in sharp relief before him. Beautiful Cat. *His* Cat.

He was going to have to make this a lasting memory.

"You have to take a breath," he reminded her, noticing she'd stopped inhaling completely when he touched her. Her breasts brushed his chest as she drew in a shaky breath.

"Right."

Her green dress wasn't particularly low cut. Luke could just see the freckled swell of her breasts above the fabric. But the thought of that soft material hiding her luscious breasts almost had him in cardiac arrest. She took another shuddery breath, and he caught a glimpse of shiny lime-green silk.

That teddy thing she'd bought the other day. Slick green silk over bare skin. That thong riding between her legs... His fingers tightened imperceptibly on her nape. She tilted her face.

He lowered his head and touched his mouth to the pulse at her temple, and felt her slight start of surprise as he feathered his lips on the unsteady flutter he discovered there. He made soothing noises as his lips traveled across her cheek. Discovered the taste of her skin. Gauged her response to the lightest of touches. He ran the tip of his tongue experimentally across the eyelashes on her left eye. She murmured under her breath. He duplicated the action on her other lid. Her breath huffed out against his throat.

Luke shuddered as her hand crept around his waist. He removed it and patted it to her side, then lifted his mouth a fraction. "That's lesson number...later. Hold your horses, woman." He went back to her eyelids.

"Umm."

Oh, yeah, more than umm.

Her skin felt incredibly soft and smooth under his exploring mouth. He imagined the heady taste of cinnamon as his lips skimmed across her hot cheek, the end of her nose, the other cheek. Cat's fingers flexed restlessly under his on the ropes. Her breasts brushed lightly against his bare chest as she started to lean into him again. He shifted out of reach, dry tinder eluding the gasoline-drenched torch.

"Nuh-uh," he teased, already as hard as the mast.

His lips brushed the corner of her mouth. She made a strangled, yearning sound low in her throat. Luke resisted the primitive urge to crush her beneath him and take her right there beneath the sunny sky, out on deck. Cool your jets. He didn't want to scare her away. Not now. Not when he was so close to heaven.

They touched in only three places: their fingers gripping the rigging, his hand on her nape and the butterfly-light touch of his mouth on hers. Yet his entire body seemed sensitized by her close proximity. Her breath smelled of the Dr Pepper she'd been drinking. Sweet, spicy. *Cat. Ahh, Cat.* Just what the doctor ordered. Too bad he was on a restricted diet.

Luke angled his head slightly and nipped her lower lip with his teeth. She nibbled back. He laved the bites with his tongue. She licked his lip like a frustrated, hungry cat. He brushed his mouth back and forth over hers. She hummed and parted her lips. Luke settled his mouth on hers. Her lips responded automatically, melding with his, anticipating the shift and slide of his tongue.

He was inside.

The scented flavor of her mouth tasted achingly familiar. Luke had imagined this for so long, it felt like coming home. He shuddered as desire, hot, strong and pounding, surged through his body like a drug. He felt dizzy with it. High. Ridiculously, disproportionately happy from one tame little kiss.

But it wasn't tame. It was hot. Wild. Surging.

Teeth, tongues, lips, melding together in a mind-blowing kiss hot enough to evaporate the water of the Bay.

Brake. Brake. Brake.

Luke lifted his head and broke contact. "That should do it."

She looked up at him, eyes dazed, lips damp, cheeks pink.

"Hmm, not bad." She seemed to shake herself out of a fog as she stumbled back a step. "I wonder how Nick does it."

IT WAS THE night after The Kiss.

Catherine snuggled back into the squishy cushions on Nick's sofa, ignoring the movie they were watching. She closed her eyes, picturing Luke's face after The Kiss. Annoyance? Shock at her brazenness? His expression had been impossible to read.

Twenty-four hours later, she still felt the jolt that kiss had given her heart. She wished she could bottle the sensation and take it out in the dark of night to hug close. She'd never felt such a weird mixture of peace and agitation in her life.

It was exactly as if she had come home. As if she had stood outside, shivering in the snow, looking into the window at everything she'd ever wanted in her life.

It was all right there at her fingertips. All she had to do was reach out and grab it.

Unfortunately, he'd suddenly remembered he had a date. They'd sped back to the marina, Nick cranky because Luke insisted he use the motor instead of the sail. Luke had rushed into the condo, showered, changed and raced out as if the hounds of hell were nipping at his heels.

Catherine had lied and told him she had a date, too. Then spent several boring hours sitting through a subtitled German movie staring at the back of some Luke-lookalike's head before dragging herself home.

Despite a restless, sleepless night, she hadn't heard his return. But this morning when she'd left to go out for a while he was sound asleep on the sofa.

Catherine touched her lips. How odd that they felt and looked just the same. When Luke had touched his mouth to hers last night, something inside her had shifted and stirred. Changed. She'd literally felt like Sleeping Beauty awakening from a deep sleep. And she realized she hadn't known what love was until now.

She'd been so blinded by the sheer sexy maleness of Lucas Van Buren that she hadn't noticed herself tumbling headlong into a forever kind of love.

She'd made an eyes-wide-open decision to give herself one last chance at seeing if what she felt could possibly be reciprocated. But she was a realist. Luke wasn't ever going to settle down. What if she got what she wanted? Could she walk away when it was over? *Be careful what you wish for. You might get it.*

Yes. Because the alternative was never knowing, always aching, spending the rest of her life empty and unfulfilled. Something with Luke was better than everything with somebody else. And when it was inevitably over, she'd have the memory of Luke's heat to keep her warm.

Catherine hugged a cushion. Insecurity squeezed her chest. Luke had sure been in one big old hurry to get away from her last night. It had been more subtle than nine years ago only because he had more finesse now. Was she doing irreparable damage to what she already had with him? Perhaps she should leave well enough alone. Luke cared for her; she knew he did. Maybe that should be enough. If she got too greedy, she took the chance of losing it all.

"Hey, Nick?"

With a grin, Nick pointed the remote control at the TV and the sound went off. "Wanna analyze The Kiss?"

She squeezed the cushion to her aching middle. "Let's."

"Scared?"

"Spitless," Catherine admitted. "He sped out of there last night like his hair was on fire. How was he at work today?"

"Like his hair was on fire." Nick's dimples showed. Easy for him to be amused. "You were priceless yesterday, honey. Trust me. The fish might be struggling on the hook, but you just have to be strong enough to hang on to that line."

"I'm terrified. I don't want to force him. I just want— I want…"

"Him to love you as much as you love him." He gave her a sympathetic look. "Luke's a hard nut, you know that. He's got this protective instinct a mile wide."

"The last thing I want is for him to feel obligation."

"Catherine, he can't help feeling some obligation to

take care of you. He's pretty much your only family. It's not in Luke's nature to turn his back."

Her frown turned to a scowl, and her heart felt like a heavy rock in her chest. "Are you telling me Luke is humoring me because of some asinine sense of responsibility?"

"No. I'm telling you Luke thinks he's humoring you because he feels responsible for you."

"Huh? Isn't that the same thing?"

"No, it isn't." Nick picked up a cold slice of pizza out of the box beside him. "Luke wants you, Catherine. Trust me on this. I know my pal. He's about to shed his skin, he wants you so bad. He's resisting the pull with every particle of his willpower. And as we both know, Luke has awesome willpower. Remember when he gave up smoking? Cold turkey. And when we bet we wouldn't drink beer for a month? It was on our first college break. I caved in two weeks. Despite winning, Luke stuck it out the exact thirty days."

"If he wants me," Catherine said, completely frustrated, "why doesn't he just…have me? Why resist? What's the point? I'm here, I'm available. I want him. Dammit, Nick. Why?"

"Have you noticed what type of woman our friend dates?"

"Sure," Catherine said miserably. "Petite blondes, miniature brunettes. Boobs out to here. And of course, all of them are sexy and beautiful. Why do men always have to go for a 'type,' anyway?"

"Other than the sexy and beautiful part, which you are, have you ever noticed how much his type doesn't resemble you?"

Catherine sank her chin into the cushion she was clutching. "Oh, great! Thanks for pointing that out."

"He'll date anyone as long as she doesn't resemble you. Interesting, huh?"

"That isn't an answer, and I think this conversation just took a useless U-turn."

"I'm just reminding you of Luke Van Buren's amazing self-control and willpower. Which he has to spare. Not to mention he's as stubborn as a mule. It's taking him longer than I thought to separate the woman from The Kid. Personally, I've always thought he dated The Many to keep him safe from The One." Before he could explain what that meant, he was interrupted by a loud banging at the front door. Nick glanced up and grinned. "Speak of the devil."

CHAPTER NINE

BAM, BAM, BAM.

It sounded like the fire department responding to a five-alarm blaze. If it was Luke out there, he was about to pound down the door. Catherine sat up from her reclining position on the sofa and curled bare legs under her. She and Nick looked at each other and grinned in perfect harmony.

Bam. Bam. Bam.

"Yo, Nick? You home?"

Bam. Bam.

Nick turned off the lamp, quickly lit the three candles on the coffee table, then came up beside her chair and ruffled her hair so it flip-flopped wildly around her head.

"Rub your lips. Hard," he instructed, before yelling, "Hey! I'm coming, cool your jets!"

"Where were you? Peru?" Luke demanded, almost falling inside the room when Nick opened the door. "Is Cat—there you are." He gave a suspicious glance around. "Why's it so cold and dark in here?"

"Nick bought an air conditioner. Great, huh?"

"What'd it do? Suck up all the electricity?" Luke came farther into the room. One glance took in the flickering candles, their wineglasses, the pillows piled up on the end of the sofa. Another glance took in her shorts and tank top. The third bulletlike look zeroed in on her red, swollen lips. He frowned. His glance shot down to her chest, where her nipples were hard from the cold.

"How was your 'business' dinner?" Cat inquired, stretching out her bare legs on Nick's chenille sofa. She tried for an innocent-but-really-guilty look.

"The client was enthusiastic." Obviously Luke wasn't going to notice her facial expression at the moment. He was still glaring at her chest.

"I just bet she was," Cat mumbled, appalled at the apple-green jealousy she was experiencing. "Want a glass of wine?" she asked, reaching for the sweating bottle in the ice bucket.

"Your mother's on the phone."

She shot him a startled look. "My mother?"

"On the phone. Upstairs."

"You put Catherine's mother on hold while you came down here?" Nick sat on the arm of the sofa, then rested his hand on her shoulder. "Where's she calling from?"

"Didn't ask."

Catherine rose and searched for her sandals. "Last time I heard, she was in Portugal." She slipped her feet into them. "She didn't call collect, did she?"

"No." He pinched the bridge of his nose. "Go see what she wants, and then say no, okay?"

She pushed her hair out of her face. "Sure," she said dryly, then turned to her host. "Thanks for a fun evening, Nick."

"Want me to put…the movie on pause till you get back?"

Catherine smiled. She couldn't look at Luke, but she

sensed a scowl. "No. But hold that thought. We'll finish…what we started another time, okay?"

"I'll be here," Nick told her, sounding sincere and extremely disappointed. He briefly touched her cheek with bent knuckles as she walked by him.

"I'll come back upstairs with you," Luke told her firmly, walking between them to sling his arm around her shoulders and herd her toward the door.

"Give me a few minutes first, okay?"

"Sure." At the front door he took her chin in his palm. A shiver traveled through Catherine's body. "Remember, no is a complete sentence. If you use it enough, Faith might get it."

Not likely. "I'll be fine. Thanks, Luke."

HE FOUND HER standing outside on the patio when he came upstairs fifteen minutes later.

"How'd it go?" he asked, stepping through the sliding door and walking up beside her where she stood at the railing. The phone lay on the table behind her, next to the fishbowl, which she must have brought out for company.

His patio used to hold two canvas-cushioned loungers, a low plastic table and several empty beer cans. It now gave every appearance of being the set for an Amazon movie. A veritable jungle of flowering plants and vines vied for space with clay pots filled with flowers and a forest of candles of various heights and sizes. All it needed was a swooping parrot.

She hadn't turned on the overhead light, but the lights from inside were bright enough for him to observe her pale face and the stiff set of her lips. Cat wasn't a crier. Not on the outside, anyway.

"She's getting married again," she told the stars.

"Aw, Cat." Luke casually slung an arm around Cat's shoulders as they stared out at the twinkling lights ringing the Bay. She leaned against him slightly, and he ran his hand down her smooth arm. Down. Up. Down. Mindful of her brittleness, he angled his head toward hers and rested his chin on her crown. Her hair smelled of lemons and fire, and it felt as soft as a kitten's fur where it brushed his chin.

"I kinda figured that when she didn't call collect this time." Faith always called collect when she needed money. Or a place to stay. Or sympathy. The woman was an emotional vampire.

Man, he was in big trouble when the fragrance of Cat's hair turned him on. "When's the wedding?"

"Next week. This one's in Arizona. She wants me to be a bridesmaid again."

"How maternal of her. And how like her to tell you at the eleventh hour, then expect you to hotfoot it to her side."

Cat turned her head to glance up at him. Her frenetic hair brushed the back of his arm, sending a nice little burst of electricity up his nerve endings. "It's only a weekend. No big deal. I'm used to Faith by now."

"No kidding. This is what? Number nine?"

"This is the man she's been looking for all her life." Cat's hands clenched the wrought-iron railing. Luke felt the muscles in her arm bunch under the pressure. He stroked her skin until the muscles relaxed. "She sounded happy, at least," Cat said quietly.

"He must be loaded."

"So she said. His name is Chandler Roberts. He's her plastic surgeon."

"Convenient. She'll keep him busy. Are you going to play bridesmaid again?"

"Sure." Cat's voice was dry. "I firmly believe every woman should have a closet full of froufrou dresses."

"You aren't the froufrou type."

"Really?" She looked up at him. "What type am I?"

Gentle. Loving. Sexy as hell. "Practical. Sensible. Down-to-earth."

"Thanks." The corners of her soft mouth turned down. "In other words, not in the least little bit like my mother."

"Who is...what?" Luke asked cautiously.

"Sexy, vivacious, beautiful."

"Try obvious, loud, surgically enhanced. The woman's a walking cliché."

Cat smiled. "You have a way with words, Van Buren. Will you come to the wedding with me?"

"Don't I always?"

She smiled, her eyes shiny. "I'm going inside for ice water. Want some?"

"No, thanks. Bring the cookies when you come back."

Luke wanted to get Faith Harris-Ford-Van Buren-Davis-Turner-Collingswod-Ashby-Landry-soon-to-be-Roberts in a room alone for about ten minutes for a reality check. Cat, thank God, seemed to be well enough adjusted. Her mother's frequent marriages were met with calm stoicism. However, Luke suspected Cat's nonchalant veneer was only skin-deep. How could it not hurt her to see her mother choose one man after the other, with no thought, no consideration for her only child? It amazed him that Cat would even consider marriage.

He'd known, even as a kid, that marriage wasn't for him. The thought had always left him cold. Nothing lasted as long as both parties wanted. Someone was doomed to be destroyed. And even if, by some chance, the adults withdrew relatively unscathed, the poor kid left in the middle was always devastated.

After the divorce, his mom had held on to him so tightly he'd sometimes wished he'd had Cat's problem. He remembered lying in bed listening to his mother sob for hours. Even though she'd remarried, she'd never gotten over the divorce from his father. Luke couldn't imagine how Faith did it repeatedly.

Cat returned carrying a large glass of ice-clinking water and the plate of chocolate chip cookies he'd baked the night before when she'd been out with some guy she'd met running in the park. Brian something-or-other. An unknown quantity and therefore dangerous.

Luke sprawled out on one of the canvas-covered loungers and held out his hand for the plate. Cat walked around the low table to sit beside him. She set the cool plate down on his stomach, then took a sip of her water.

They both wore shorts, and her bare leg pressed against his, sending a spear of electricity up his thigh directly into his groin. She smelled of some spicy-sweet powder, a fragrance Luke had associated with her for years.

He wanted to interrogate her about the scene he'd just witnessed downstairs. He wanted to discuss, coolly and clinically, the inadvisability of yesterday's kiss. He wanted to politely request she move off his lounger and sit over there, a comfortable three feet away, where he wouldn't be forced to touch her. But her mouth was pouty, her eyes a little sad, her shoulders not quite straight. He couldn't withdraw his emotional support just because he was having a hard time keeping his hands off her.

"Want to talk about it?" he asked gently.

Cat fished in her glass for a large piece of ice. "Same old, same old." She blew out a huff of air, ruffling her bangs. "Doesn't it ever cool off around here? What happened to the San Francisco breezes I'm always hearing about?"

No breeze was going to cool him off. His concentration was shot, intent on erotic, inappropriate thoughts. Like how soft her skin looked. Like how delicious her lips had tasted yesterday. Like how good she smelled.

"They say the heat will stick around for another couple of days before it slacks off. We could always get an air conditioner." And what had been going on downstairs earlier with Nick?

"No. I can stand it for a while." She ran the ice down her throat, leaving a trail of moisture on her skin, then tilted her head and slowly drew the cube down the side of her neck. The muscles in Luke's stomach clenched, and he had to force rational words through a constriction in his throat.

"What's she trying to entangle you with this time?"

"She doesn't really try to involve me in her life. She only calls when…" Cat waved a dismissive hand. "Hey, that's fine with me. I figured out years ago that what Faith does, and how she does it, has nothing to do with me."

Luke dragged his gaze away from the gleam of moisture on her throat. "What else did she have to say for herself?"

"She'd just returned from Paris." Cat smiled. "She

has a French accent this time. She told me it took a month to purchase her trousseau. Just the thought of shopping that long gives me hives."

"Did she by any chance ask how you were doing?"

"Sure. She asked if I was using the face cream she'd had custom blended for me in Germany. I said absolutely." Cat grinned. "I didn't mention I'd used it all on the neighbors' poor little dog when it had eczema a few months ago."

"Good for you. You don't need any fancy lotions and potions on your skin." Luke's gaze followed the shiny trail of water across the smooth skin on Cat's collarbone. He licked his lips.

"I d-don't?"

"No. Did you kiss Nick tonight?" Luke asked, his voice husky.

"Nick?"

"My business partner. The guy you spent the evening with?" Oh, man. He'd lost his freaking mind. He couldn't even concentrate on a simple conversation because he couldn't think of anything other than his hands trailing that ice. His hands on her skin. His touch making her nipples peak like that. What was he doing? Playing with fire. No, worse. Dynamite. He was playing with volatile, incendiary nitroglycerine. Get your mind off sex. Now.

"Hmm? Oh, Nick. Uh-uh." Drops of water trickled down her chest to moisten the edge of her tank top. "Aren't you hot?"

"Hell, yes, I'm hot!" Need clawed at him. "Go sit over there. No more touchy-feely, Cat, you're getting me sweaty."

He swung his legs over the other side of the lounger.

"Look, if none of the guys I've introduced you to so far have rung your chimes, there are a couple more we can tr—"

Cat made a rude noise. "Don't bother. Your selection's been more than ample. I've found my Mr. Right."

Luke put a finger to his throat. Yep. He still had a pulse. "Who," he asked dangerously, "is he?"

"I'd rather not say right now. Just in case—"

"Just in case?" Luke raked his fingers through his hair until it stood up like a cockscomb. "Cat, if this is Mr. Right, you should be absolutely positive. Are you positive?"

"Oh, yes." She picked up the half-filled glass at her feet and took a long slug of tepid water. "Before I do anything, though, I'd like you to give me some pointers." She sent him a guileless look. "Your input will be invaluable, because—because he's very much like you."

"Like me?"

"You know. Suave. Cool. Sophisticated. A ladies' man."

Luke felt as though he'd just bitten into a quince. "A player."

Catherine smiled. "Exactly. If anyone can tell me how to seduce a player, you'd be the one."

Luke shot off the lounger and paced to the patio railing, his back ramrod stiff. After several heart-stopping minutes he turned to face her. "Are you out of your ever-loving mind, Catherine Harris? Which one is he?"

"I told you, I don't want to tell y—"

"Is he someone I know?"

"Jeez, Luke, what difference does it make? I'm certainly old enough to have an affair and intelligent enough to know when I'm ready for one."

He scowled. "I thought this was Mr. Right? You don't have an affair with Mr. Right, Cat. You marry him. *Marry.* Until death do you part."

"I'm sure the people across the Bay are taking notes. You don't have to shout. And he won't marry me. He has noncommittalitis, just like you do."

"You want marriage. You're a Cancer. Cancers nest. Home and hearth and all that stuff."

"Well, I'll be happy just having him. I can live without the trappings."

"No, Catherine. You cannot. Besides, you said you wanted to find a husband."

"It's my prerogative to change my mind. Now I want a lover."

"I know you—"

"Not as well as you thought, obviously. Stop grinding your teeth like that, you'll wear down the enamel. I can't imagine any sophisticated man would be interested in teaching some little hick virgin the finer points of making love, can you? Now, will you give me the help I need or not?"

"Cat…" Luke pressed his hands into his temples. "A man lives to be a woman's first. It's a fantasy few men fulfill."

"Weird, huh?" Catherine crossed her legs and leaned back on the lounger Luke had vacated. "A man wants to be a woman's first. And every woman wants to be a man's last."

He pressed his fingers into his throbbing eye sockets.

"What's the prob?" Cat taunted. "Don't think you can?"

"Can…what?"

"Teach me how to seduce my Mr. Right."

"If I wanted to, which I don't, I could. But I won't."

Cat leaned back and smiled. "Bet you can't."

CHAPTER TEN

THIS REQUIRED SOME serious mental gymnastics, Luke decided, lying on the sofa in the dark. The new wrinkle had been added three days ago. For a while there the temptation she offered was almost more than a man could take. He'd managed to control himself. Barely. Right now he was waiting for Cat to come home from another date.

A date. How delightful for her.

Thanks to her, Luke hadn't had a decent date in weeks. His love life had gone to hell. He was permanently erect and would go into the *Guinness Book of Records* for the man with the hardest permanent erection in history. Probably for taking the most cold showers per day, too.

Mr. Right.

How could she have found this guy so fast? What did this jerk have that was special enough for her to abandon her lifelong dream of marriage?

And could Luke be chivalrous enough to put his own needs and desires aside if Cat truly had found her Mr. Right? Just the thought of Cat belonging to—

Chauvinist. A woman didn't *belong* to a man. Well, whatever the hell the term was, Luke didn't want Cat doing it with anyone. Not ever.

He rolled over, dragging the sheet under him into a

tangled mess. It was hot again. The door to the balcony stood wide open, a fan belligerently moving hot air around. He'd taken another icy shower. No surprise— it didn't help.

He was wearing the bare minimum—cotton briefs, in deference to Cat. Who wasn't even home. He wished he could at least discuss this with Nick. But Nick was unusually quiet these days. Suspiciously quiet, now that Luke came to think of it.

He punched his hot pillow, then jerked upright, only too pleased to be off the sticky leather sofa as he paced, building up a nice head of steam. He strode into the kitchen and turned on the light. He'd bake bread. He loved to cook. The combination of science and creativity, of tossing raw ingredients into a pot and turning out something edible, fascinated him. But bread making got rid of aggression. The pounding, pummeling and squeezing appealed to him, especially tonight.

He found his favorite mixing bowl, added all the ingredients and started kneading the dough by hand. Pounding his fists into the dough was marginally satisfying. Not as satisfying as making love to Cat. But right now, that wasn't an option.

And who had she gone out with tonight, anyway? Pummel. Had she said? Pummel. Was it Ted? Allan? Was it Nick again? Pummel, pummel, pummel. Who was Mr. Right? It was just like Cat to throw him off the scent like this.

She was doing the dating merry-go-round. Ted. Allan, Bob. Nick. Couldn't she see they were all players.

Luke greased the bowl and left the abused dough to rise under a clean cloth. How did she think he could go to work when he had to stay up till all hours of the night waiting for her? The fact that it was only a little after nine and his usual bedtime was around eleven had no bearing on the matter.

An image of seventeen-year-old Cat flashed through his mind. That damned birthday. He'd known she'd gone out with friends. Through the kitchen window he'd watched her return, dancing her way across the lawn in the moonlight, looking like some delicate woodland nymph. The soft, floaty material of her dress had outlined her bare legs and snugly cupped her breasts. He'd been terrified down to his toes at the immediacy of his body's reaction. It had been the entire reason he'd kept his distance in the previous year. He'd been afraid of the magnetic draw she'd always had for him, the pull he'd thus far managed to resist.

He remembered vividly thinking, *Run. Escape before she comes inside.*

Instead he'd stood there in his dad's empty house, heart racing, anticipation churning in his gut. Knowing he had only seconds to make a clean getaway.

Knowing he'd wanted one taste before he died.

And he would die if his father ever caught him with his hands on her. The little sister he'd promised to protect. The defenseless semiorphan he and Dad had vowed would never be hurt again.

The back door had crashed open, and there she'd stood, swaying in the open doorway.

"Luke, you came." She'd sounded so delighted. Her exuberance had been contagious. He'd risen, hard and ready, to the occasion, and had known right then and there that he was damned.

One moment there'd been a safe, respectable ten feet of linoleum between them, the next instant Cat had flung herself into his arms, clinging like a baby monkey.

His embrace had been as far from brotherly as sugar from salt. Giving her no chance to voice a protest, he'd crushed his mouth down on hers. She'd tasted intoxicatingly sweet as her pliant body wrapped around his in the most compelling, amazing way, pressing her firm young breasts against his chest.

In the eleven years he'd known her, Cat had always been reserved, always trying to remain inconspicuous. Her exuberance that night had been totally unlike her.

He hadn't thought. He'd felt. With more passion than finesse, he'd pressed her supple young body against the refrigerator. He'd kissed her until they'd both been breathless, then he'd kissed her some more. He'd touched her breast through the flimsy fabric of her dress and wanted it all. Wanted her naked beneath him. Wanted her strong runner's legs wrapped about his waist. Wanted to sink into her wet heat and have his wicked way with her.

Finally it had penetrated his brainless state that Cat was struggling in his arms.

He felt the deep scalding flush of shame now, nine years later, as violently as he had then. There'd been no excuse for his behavior. Unless being a twenty-four-year-old with a sporadic love life and a suddenly enormously high sex drive counted.

Horrified at his loss of control, he'd let her go immediately. But not immediately enough to prevent her from throwing up on his shoes.

His horror at his own inappropriate conduct had manifested itself in a scathing lecture on *her* behavior.

With one wounded look, after his betrayal, Cat had fled.

He'd gone back the next day to apologize. Cat had been her usual quiet, contained, cheerful, kid sister self. Luke had been so relieved he'd almost kissed her in gratitude. Well, he was a slow learner.

He did the decent, honorable thing. He'd left her alone, and done everything in his power to reinforce their brother-sister relationship. It had worked out just damn well fine. Until now.

He wondered if they needed architects in China.

"Yum, it smells terrific in here. Been baking?" Catherine tossed her purse on the counter and eyed Luke's apparel. She rubbed her itchy elbow and grinned. He wore a navy-and-white-striped bib apron, and from the look of him, little else. "Interesting new fashion statement, even for you."

"It's hot in here."

"No kidding." Even with her hair piled up on top of her head and minimal clothing, she was hot. Looking at an almost naked Luke made her hotter still. She made a rapid inventory of the kitchen instead. Dirty dishes were piled haphazardly in the sink, and the doughy hooks from the Cuisinart lay on the flour-dusted counter.

She frowned. "What's wrong?"

"Nothing. Why?"

"You bake when you're uptight."

"I bake when I want to eat whatever I'm baking."

Right. "Okay. Is that bread ready?"

Luke shoved the dish towel-covered board across the granite center island. "Help yourself." He uncovered the loaf and snagged the butter dish before whacking off a thick, fragrant, yeasty slice. "Nice evening?" He leaned against the counter, arms folded, ankles crossed.

Catherine slathered butter on the hot bread and took a bite. "Mmm. This is fabulous. It was...terrific." Luke had terrific legs. Hairy, tanned, muscular. Runner's legs. Although he never ran when he could walk, or walked when he could be prone. She couldn't wait to get him prone. "What brought on this spurt of domesticity?"

"I have someone else I want you to meet," he said at the same time. "His name is Steve Manfield."

Catherine reached over her shoulder to scratch an itch between her shoulder blades. "Good grief! I told you, I've already found my Mr.—"

"Please tell me Mr. Right isn't Ted?"

"Nope. Not Ted," Catherine said obediently, and resisted rolling her eyes.

"Well, you should meet Steve before you decide. He's a decent guy. Owns his own insurance agency here in the city. Financially solid. Has a terrific house with a pool, which is appreciating in value every day. Loves kids. Has a couple of dogs. I think you and old Steve will have a lot in common."

"With that glowing testimonial, how can a girl refuse?" Catherine said dryly. "I do, however. Refuse, that is."

"One date couldn't hurt, Cat. Just to be sure."

"I'm sure now."

"We'll double-date this weekend, how's that?"

Catherine shook her head in exasperation. She was sorely tempted to whack him over the head with the breadboard.

"Overkill, Luke. And a total waste of time. Besides, we're going to a wedding. Remember?"

Luke groaned. "I was trying to forge… Why are you scratching like that?"

"Don't ask." She considered squeezing between Luke and the opposite counter to get to the refrigerator and a glass of icy-cold milk. She'd hate to pass up any opportunity to touch him. Especially dressed the way he was right now. A nice slow shimmy, Catherine decided.

Luke waited until she was almost through the straits before he snagged her arm. His eyes did a rapid scan of her arms and shoulders, bared by the pumpkin-colored halter dress. "Are you aware you're covered with a red rash?"

"As a matter of fact, yes."

"Shellfish?"

Catherine rubbed her upper chest, where the welts were now on fire. "Would you pour me a glass of milk, please? I think there was some sort of lobster base in the sauce we had at the restaurant." The little container of crab she couldn't resist at Fisherman's Wharf before going into the movie alone had been worth a little itching.

He took down a glass, filled it and handed it to her. "Here. You ate it anyway." He shook his head. "Stay right there, I'll get the calamine."

Luke brushed past her to go to the cabinet where he kept his vast array of first-aid supplies—a five-year-old box of Band-Aids, a two-year-old bottle of aspirin and the calamine lotion. Luke was, as they said, always in rude good health. It warmed her heart to know he had the lotion, which only she used.

Catherine sipped the milk without tasting it. He had

the neatest, tightest little butt she'd ever seen. Luke in underwear and an apron was the sexiest thing she'd ever seen in her life. More than her skin itched. Catherine bit her lip. What did she have to do? Use Nick's two-by-four over his head? Strip naked and lie on the floor at his feet?

Luke grabbed the paper towels from under the sink and came back with the pink bottle in his hand. "Turn 'round."

The first dab was nice and cold. His stiff cotton apron brushed the back of her legs as he stepped closer.

"What are you doing?" he asked, dabbing away at her shoulders with the calamine-soaked paper towel.

"Undoing the halter so you can get to my neck."

"Stop scratching."

"I'm rubbing."

"Don't do that, either." He pushed her hand gently out of his way, then his fingers touched her shoulder as he patted downward. She felt the warmth of his breath against her skin. It made the loose curls at her nape dance and tickle her neck. Moisture prickled between her breasts and she held her hand there to keep the top of the dress up, and her heart from jerking right out of her chest.

What she'd rather do was let go and turn around. She almost clucked, she was so chicken. Her breath jammed in her lungs. She stayed as she was, back turned, and let him dot and dab at the rash.

She felt like she had when she'd been a kid, standing on the highest diving board at the YWCA, her toes clenched around the end of the board, looking down at that pale blue water shimmering a mile beneath her. Wanting to jump, but sick with the adrenaline rush, breathless with excitement, dizzy with terror. One. Two. Three... She removed her hand and let her dress drop to her waist.

"What are you doing?" Luke demanded, voice hoarse. He stood directly behind her. When he breathed in, the fragrance of her skin blotted out all rational thought. When he breathed out, corkscrew tendrils of her upswept hair fluttered against her bare back. With a silent curse, he gritted his teeth and tried to ignore the unconscious invitation of a topless Catherine Harris. And he only had a view of her slender back peppered with cinnamon freckles, nasty pink blotches and smears of lotion. He didn't have to see her breasts to know she was naked from the waist up. Blood rushed from his head to his groin.

"Unless you're going to doctor all of me, I'll do my front while you do the back," Cat murmured, open palm extended over her bare shoulder. "Hand me the lotion, will you?"

For half a heartbeat their eyes met. Her lashes flickered as she gazed at his mouth for a fraction of a second. Her pupils dilated just a little as she looked up, directly into his eyes.

Heat sheeted Luke's body in a lightning-flash rush. God almighty, Cat had no idea what those amber eyes of hers could do to a man. He knew if he inspected himself he'd find the damned apron tented over his erection. He couldn't look anywhere other than into Cat's eyes.

So near and yet so far.

He wanted her so badly. But he knew if he touched her it would just make the wanting, the needing, the ache, worse. Not only would he have betrayed her trust, if he touched her like a lover, even once, he knew he'd never stop. And he'd never get over her.

It would be an irrevocable step.

One he would never take. But it was killing him.

Wordlessly he handed her the bottle of lotion. She half turned to reach for it, and he had a brief glimpse of the narrow span of her rib cage and one pale, perfect plump breast. His eyes shot back to her face. She seemed oblivious, and he dragged in another breath, drenched with the scent of her.

His physical reaction to her was bad enough to deal with. But this was day-and-night different. An odd feeling expanded through him. A feeling that had nothing to do with his rampant sexual desire for her. It felt unbearably sweet. Poignant. Sinfully rich. His heart hitched, and yearning filled his soul....

Then he saw himself in her eyes. And what he saw was security. Safety. Trust. Promises made. Vows kept. The thought worked as effectively as a bucket of ice water.

Almost.

Torture. And bless her sweet naive heart, she had no idea. She believed she was safe with him. He let out a breath and tried to distract himself. Unfortunately, he still had her rash to contend with. He had to stand close, had to touch, had to breathe. He had to get laid. And soon. He was hanging on by the last sliver of his fingernails.

She trusts me. He dabbed all the way down to the slender span of her waist, making sure only the paper towel touched her smooth skin. "Can you do the rest yourself?" he asked, his tongue sticking to the dry roof of his mouth. He'd go directly to heaven for his restraint, and straight to hell for his thoughts. "Or do you need me to—"

She reached back and tugged at the short zipper at the small of her back. The sides flopped back, revealing the sweet curve of her waist, the gentle swell of her bottom and the beginning of cleavage. He went icy hot.

"Jesus. Did you go out tonight buck naked under this dress?" Luke croaked.

"Oh, good." She sounded relieved. "No line. I have on a thong," she told him mildly. "Feels like there's a whole bunch of itchies, right here." She brushed the pale flesh below her waist—well below her waist—with her thumb, while trying to look over her shoulder. "Can you see them?"

Luke prayed for an earthquake. A flood. A famine. A natural disaster. Something. Anything.

"Luke?"

He dabbed.

She moaned as the cold liquid soothed the burning itches.

He silently cursed. "That should do it, right?" His voice was almost nonexistent, and as hopeful as that of a penitent.

With both hands, she started slithering the fabric of her dress up her thighs. "If you'd just do the back of my le—" She broke off and allowed the material to fall down to cover her legs again. "Never mind."

Thank God. He couldn't take any more.

She rubbed the end of her nose with the back of her hand. "I can do the rest, thanks."

"Did something happen tonight with—who was it?" Luke demanded.

Cat sighed, put the bottle down on the counter, then

used both hands to retie the straps of her dress around her neck. She turned to face him. "Nothing happened with tonight's date," she snapped. "He is not the problem."

Luke touched her warm cheek. Longing rushed through him. He yearned to have the freedom to express all the emotions churning in his gut. He felt like an insensitive jerk. Something was wrong. He let his gaze move slowly over her tight features while she glared up at him. He dropped his hand, didn't know what to do with it, and folded his arms across his chest. She was utterly unaware of how she tied him in knots, and he'd better well keep it that way. He leaned back against the fridge, cocked his knee enough to mask the bulge in the apron, and tried his best to look…unhorny.

"Then tell me what the problem is, Catwoman. And I'll fix it for you."

"My Mr. Right doesn't even know I exist." She glared at him as if it were his fault. "What can you do about that, Luke Van Buren?"

Needing something to do with his hands, he pulled a clean mixing bowl out of the cabinet and placed it carefully on the counter between them. He looked at her. "What would you like me to do? Say the word," he said, gathering ingredients from shelves and refrigerator. He dumped everything haphazardly on the counter beside the bowl. "You know I'd do anything for you."

"How about if you stop moving around at the speed of light and listen, then?"

Luke leaned one shoulder against the fridge. He crossed his arms. "You have to say something, Cat. Or do you want me to guess?"

"Right. Tell you. Yeah. Absolutely."

Luke's eyebrows rose. He waited as she hoisted herself up onto the counter. "I have a problem—"

"And you need my deft touch."

"Deft touch?" Catherine hooted, amused. "You're as clueless as he is, you turkey."

"He who?"

"Mr. Right."

Luke groaned.

She crossed her ankles and leaned back. The silky fabric of her dress slithered up her bare thighs.

"Okay, we can talk about me helping you. If you're absolutely posit— What are you doing?"

She gave him an innocent look. "You said not to scratch. I'm rubbing."

"You're stroking," Luke said in a choked voice.

Cat shrugged. "Whatever. It feels great. This itch is driving me nuts."

"Hell's bells, Cat. Your itch is driving *me* nuts. Stop that! Tell me what the problem is, and let's work on it. Cat?"

"I'm thinking here."

He clenched his teeth, pushed away from the fridge and took out his measuring cups and the big wooden spoon he liked to use for mixing. Without measuring, he tossed butter, then brown sugar into the copper bowl.

"Right. What do you think I should do? Just pull out all the stops and seduce him?"

Luke jerked away from his mixing as if he'd been catapulted across the kitchen. Sugar and butter went flying.

"Hell, no!" He raked his fingers through his hair, leaving glimmering speckles of sugar in the dark strands.

She put up her hands. "You don't have to shout. It was a simple question. You refused to help me by educating me on seduction. Now I'm on my own. The question is how do I make him desire me? Share your vast experience and tell me."

Luke stuck the spoon back in the bowl and stirred it to China. "What's wrong with this Mr. Right of yours?" He broke eggs into the mixture as though he were doing intricate brain surgery.

She laughed. "Look, I know he likes me, but I want him to realize that he could love me. Right now he thinks of me as more of a—a friend."

"What's wrong with that?" Luke demanded. "That's a good place to start. Most couples start with less."

"Fine. Great. Terrific. But I'd like it to move a little faster than another twenty years of friendship."

Something in her tone made him stare at her with added intensity. *Nick. She's talking about Nick.* Luke's knuckles went white around the spoon. He stood very still. "How do you feel about this guy, Cat? For real."

Their eyes locked, and Cat said very quietly, "I love him with all my heart."

CHAPTER ELEVEN

"YOU'RE IN LOVE with him?"

"Yes. Very much."

"The real thing?" Very carefully, Luke put the dough-covered spoon down on the edge of the counter and didn't notice when it clattered to the floor. This was Cat. Cautious, crablike Cat. He stared at her as if she were an alien life force. "Are you sure?"

"Without a shadow of a doubt."

For several seconds he searched her face without saying anything, then sighed and said heavily, "I have a sinking feeling I know who it is."

She shot him a glance. "You do?"

"Nick."

"Nick? Who said anythi—"

"Dammit, Cat. That's exactly what I thought." His voice rose to new heights. "He's a player, for God's sake. A *player*." Luke slammed his fist on the counter. Unfortunately, his hand hit the egg carton. The carton crumpled with a crackle as eggs broke.

Cat tilted her head to look at him. "Appearances can be deceiving," she said mildly. "Maybe he just hasn't met the woman right enough to make a commitment."

"My point exactly." Luke wiped his yolk-dripping fist on a paper towel.

"I believe with a little push, he'll realize he's a little in love with me already."

"A push off a high cliff without a safety net is more like it," Luke said grimly. *Not Nick,* he thought, his gut twisting.

This was his worst-case scenario. It was one thing for Luke to think it was Nick. But to have her confirm it…

The earthquake had come. The famine. The plague and the pestilence. She was in love with someone.

"Hey!" Cat socked him on the arm. "Are you in a coma, or what?"

"You deserve to have some sort of commitment. Jeez, Cat. I said I'd help you, and I will." *Even if it kills me.*

"By doing what exactly?"

Yeah. What? "Make him jealous?"

Cat gave him an odd look. "Make him…jealous?"

"You want to at least have some sort of declaration of commitment from Mr. Right, right? You know how competitive we are. One little hint that I'm interested in you, and Nick will charter a flight to Las Vegas before we've finalized the bet. Are you game?"

For several seconds she was apparently too stunned to speak. She closed her eyes and rubbed her hand across her forehead. "Sure." She smiled. "Why not?"

That seemed to have worked, Luke thought, relieved. "It's late. Why don't you go off to bed? I'm going to finish these cookies, and think about how we can execute Operation Mr. Right."

Execute being the operative word here.

LUKE'S THROAT CLOSED up until he couldn't breathe. His chest felt as though an overweight elephant squatted directly on his heart. He realized that every time Cat had mentioned Mr. Right he'd felt physical pain. Agonizing pain. Pound your head on the wall pain. Rip your guts out pain.

He was going to give her a list of Nick's faults. There were a hundred things wrong with Nick. A million things—

Argh! There was nothing wrong with Nick, Luke admitted reluctantly. He and Nick had been best friends for most of their lives. Nick Stratton was honest. Honorable. Decent. And if Cat wanted him, it was Luke's sworn duty to make sure he protected her until Nick declared himself.

Oh, hell. Just the thought of Nick's hands anywhere on Cat's body made Luke's blood pound like a runaway train through his brain. His teeth ground together until his jaw ached. He wondered where he could dispose of the body.

But then he'd have to comfort her.

And if it wasn't Nick, then it would be someone else.

Luke couldn't leave a trail of bodies across the San Francisco Bay Area just because…just because he didn't want her hurt.

He could've helped her with anyone else…. *Liar!* Luke admitted roughly.

THE NEXT MORNING Luke casually strolled into his partner's office in the north turret carrying two cups of latte. Nick, dressed in a lightweight charcoal wool suit, tie in place, shoes polished, sat with his feet on his desk, staring out the window.

Luke, wearing jeans and a T-shirt, because he was going on-site, took a seat in the visitor's chair opposite the wide mahogany desk. "That's my favorite pose, Stratton."

Nick turned his head away from the city view and grinned. "Hey, old son, what's up? Thanks." He took the cup and popped the plastic lid. "To what do I owe the dubious honor of your presence at nine o'clock on a Wednesday morning?"

"A man can't bring his partner a cup of coffee?"

"Depends on what the man's up to." Eyes suspicious, Nick took a sip.

"I wanted to talk to you about Cat. Catherine."

"Catherine?" Nick frowned. "Why? What's wrong?"

"Nothing's wrong." *Damn,* Luke thought, this could prove to be awkward as hell. "How do you feel about her, Nick?"

Nick leaned back comfortably in his big leather chair. "Are you kidding? I'm mad about her."

"Seriously mad about her? Or mad about her for the next five minutes, like the rest of your harem?"

"And the answer to this question is important to you why?"

"Just answer the question."

"She's beautiful. Sexy. Smart… Hell, I'm halfway in love with her. Why?"

"Halfway in love with her?" Luke scoffed. "Get real. Since you obviously can't even commit to how you feel about her, I'm following up on your suggestion and taking her out myself."

Nick frowned and removed his feet from the desktop with a thud. He set his coffee down. "You and Catherine?"

"Yeah. Why not?"

"You mean like a date kinda thing?"

Nick *was* jealous. "Got a problem with that?" Luke demanded, revving up his belligerence for Cat's sake.

"But she's your sister."

"As you've told me so often, Cat's not my sister. All I'm doing is telling you my intentions."

"I see. And what are your intentions toward Catherine?"

"Honorable." Luke watched his friend's face.

Something flickered briefly in Nick's eyes before he expertly masked it. "Yeah?"

"Yeah!"

Nick took another sip of his latte. "I don't think so."

"What?"

"I said, I don't think so," Nick repeated coolly. "You told me weeks ago that you considered Catherine the next best thing to a doorstop. A sexless…sister. Now you're trying to tell me you want her? Give me a break. Wanna bet you want her because you know *I* want her?"

"No. This is not a betting situation."

"Why not? Everything's grounds for a bet."

"Not Catherine," Luke said seriously. The latte tasted like sweat socks. "Tell me, Nick. What do you see when you look at Cat?"

"A beautiful, sexy, desirable woman."

"That's my point. Cat is more than that. Much more. She's funny and wise, vulnerable and incredibly strong. She's…dimensional."

"Are you standing there telling me *you're* in love with her?" Nick asked incredulously.

"I'm taking Cat to Arizona for the weekend," Luke told him tightly, trying to remind himself that this was a strategy to help Cat.

Nick looked startled. "What?"

"Yeah. Wanna make something of it?"

"Are you in love with her?"

Admission ready to spill from his lips, Luke bit his tongue. Once spoken, the words would be out there in the atmosphere forever. Waiting to haunt and torment him for the rest of his miserable life.

God help him. He didn't just *want* Cat. He loved her.

"Are you?" Luke countered.

"Face it," Nick said. "We both have the hots for her. Vastly different emotions, old son. Vastly. Unfortunately, we both feel guilty as hell because we're so protective of her. Which is why I've held back. I've just been biding my time. We've watched her grow up, we've watched her bloom." He waggled his dark eyebrows. "And bloomed very nicely, too. But that's lust, pal. Just lust. Now the question is, which one of us will—"

"Don't say it." Luke stood up and glared at his ex-best friend. "Don't even think it, Stratton. Cat's off-limits to you from now on."

The pseudoanger was a nice touch. Unfortunately, his heart was racing and his eyeballs felt like they were about to pop right out of his head. *This is just an act,* Luke reminded himself, as he tried to unfurl his tightly clenched fists, to no avail.

"Keep away from her unless you're planning a wedding," Luke growled.

Nick almost fell off his chair. "A wedding? A wedding as in here comes the bride? Are you nuts! What about The Bet?"

"So winning The Bet is more important to you than Cat?"

"I didn't say that. Did you?"

"Maybe."

Nick leaned back, cupped the back of his head with his hands and swung his big feet up on top of his desk again. "Well, maybe from me, too."

"Make up your mind, Nick."

"Ditto."

They glared at each other.

THEIR FLIGHT TO Arizona was uneventful, if one discounted their close proximity on the plane. It was late evening by the time they arrived at the resort hotel. Luke had been lucky to get a room on the same floor as hers at such short notice.

Accompanied by the steamy smells of soap and bleach, Cat's room had a view of the back of the laundry room. No scenic overlook of Camelback Mountain, nor the pool, for Faith's only child.

"Mine's not much better. But I can have them move you if you like." Sitting on the foot of her bed, Luke tried to read her expression as she picked up various objects, fiddled with them, then put them down again. The soft fabric of her lavender dress clung to her legs and hips as she paced. Between the X straps on her back, her skin was creamy and lightly freckled in the lamplight. His mouth watered.

She'd been unusually quiet during the flight to Arizona, even more subdued when they'd arrived at the hotel where her mother's wedding was to be held the next evening.

"Nah, I don't need to change rooms. No big. It's only two nights. Besides, I didn't come for the view."

"Just the spectacle?"

Cat picked up the leather-bound room service menu and smiled slightly. "She does her best to outdo herself every time, doesn't she? No doubt this one will beat them all."

She flipped the laminated pages. "If I ever get married I'll combine all of Faith's most outrageous weddings into one huge blowout. Pull out all the stops. Go for broke." The menu plopped back onto the desk with the finality of a divorce decree. "Except for the elephant. That wasn't one of her better ideas."

"Yeah, elephant poop must've been hell on the laundry bill." *When I get married...* The words hit him like a fist in the gut. "You planning on getting married in the near future?" he asked casually.

She gave him an indecipherable look. "Let's get something to eat before I start gnawing on the fruit in that painting. Come on, Van Buren, get the lead out, I'm famished."

Was she missing Nick? Luke already felt like a pulled-taut rubber band, whitened by the excessive stretch. Any second now he was going to go *sproing*. He was sitting on a giant, king-size bed. Sheets turned back. Chocolate on the pillow. Lights turned low. He wouldn't need anything sweeter than Cat beside him.

Ain't gonna happen, pal. "One would think the guy was terminally dense not to fall over his feet getting to you," he offered casually.

Her lips twitched. "One would think. Do you want to hit the restaurants, or should we get room service?"

She'd been only mildly attentive when he'd told her about his conversation with Nick. Women were like that. Not interested until the knights drew blood. It had been damn close.

"Let's go out and eat, then reconnoiter. If you're not too tired, that is?" He felt too vulnerable right now to be anywhere near a horizontal surface with Cat in the same room. Surreptitiously, Luke glanced at the phone on the desk. No red light blinked, indicating Nick had called. Or Faith, for that matter.

It was 9:00 p.m. The wedding was set for six the next evening. Surely Faith could manage to squeeze in a few moments to see Cat? She hadn't seen her daughter in two years. No loss, as far as he was concerned. Cat picked up her purse just as there was a knock at the door. Their eyes met.

"I'll get it." Only too happy for a diversion, Luke opened the door. Faith What'sit-What'sit-What'sit stood out in the hall, wearing a white silk pantsuit with gold buttons and looking as though she'd stepped from the pages of *Vogue*. For a split second, Luke saw what his father had seen. The flawless complexion. The petite, yet curvy body. The incredible honey-red sweep of her hair. But unlike his father, Luke had always had twenty-twenty where Faith was concerned. She was high maintenance, low return.

He stepped back, opening the door wider. "Howdy, Stepmama."

She did a slight double take. "My goodness, Lucas. What a lovely surprise." She reached up to peck the air an inch from his cheek, then handed him the black silk garment bag she carried. "Put this somewhere, darling. Now, where's my baby?"

"Hi, Mother."

Faith came toward her, hands outstretched. "Let me look at you. Oh dear, I always forget what a big girl you are."

Their hands met briefly, her mother's cool and dry, Catherine's damp. She resisted wiping her palms on her dress. As always, in Faith's presence she felt gangly and plain and as though she took up too much space. She despised her own reaction to this beautiful stranger who was her mother. Faith was a softer, paler, more petite version of her offspring.

Smoky eyes skimmed Catherine from head to toe, swiftly and expertly cataloging to the last cent what each item of clothing had cost.

"My goodness, Catherine, are you still shopping at those dreadful discount stores? And those high heels not only make you simply tower over everyone, they make your feet look enormous."

"She doesn't tower over me." Luke came up behind Catherine and slipped his arm around her waist. "I think Cat has the sexiest feet since Cleopatra. And the only people she towers over are people too short to appreciate her height. With her impeccable taste, she could shop at the flea market and still look gorgeous."

His hand felt warm and solid on her middle. So did his defense of her. *Bliss.*

"How sweet," Faith said with a vague smile. "You always were her champion, weren't you, Lucas? Catherine, I only stopped by to drop off your gown for tomorrow. I've made an appointment for your hair at 9:00 a.m. Now that I see it's just as unruly as ever, I'll have Milo straighten it a little after he cuts it."

"She's not cutting one inch off her hair," Luke said flatly. He looked down at her, his arm still around her waist. "Are you, Cat?"

"Nope." Her mother would have given the hairdresser strict instructions, Catherine knew. She'd been caught unprepared only once. Then she'd found herself with an oddly avant-garde asymmetrical do that made her feel like a lopsided Little Orphan Annie until it grew out. There was no use arguing with her mother now. Catherine would cancel the appointment tomorrow.

"How are you, Mother? Where's the lucky groom?"

"You know it's bad luck for him to see the bride before the wedding. Chandler is staying with a friend until tomorrow." Faith craned her neck at her much taller daughter. "And I think that now we're both adults, you should call me Faith, don't you, darling?" She smiled, showing straight, beautifully bleached white teeth. Husband number five had been a dentist. "We can pretend we're sisters. Won't that be fun?"

Great, Catherine thought wryly, *everyone wants me to be their darn sister.*

This was the first time in living memory that her mother's darts completely missed their mark. Startled by the realization, Catherine knew she was seeing Faith through Luke's eyes. It was a revelation.

Like a cartoon character with a lightbulb blinking overhead, she saw her mother as a sad, lonely woman who filled her life with loveless marriages and buying sprees because she couldn't bear to spend a moment alone. The fact that Faith was a petty, selfish woman filled with her own self-importance had nothing to do with who Catherine was. The knowledge came as a shock. For years she'd felt as useless and unattractive as her mother told her she was. Faith's perception was not reality.

"Something to drink, Faith?" Luke asked, still glued to Catherine's side. She was grateful for his strength. Both his arm and the moral support he provided. However she tried to rationalize, she always felt battered around her mother. "Eye of newt, perhaps?" he added.

"No, thank you, darling. I have to run. I'm having a massage in a little while. I just wanted to give Catherine her gown." She glanced around to see where Luke had put it. "Do come and look. I bought it for you in Paris, darling." She eyed her daughter the only way Catherine had ever seen her mother look at her. Critically.

"Although now I look at you it might be just a teeny bit snug around the hips. You have packed on a little weight, haven't you? And my Lord, what have you been doing to your poor skin? Must you persist on going out in the sun and getting all freckled? Darling, I insist you use that cream I sent you."

"Isn't Cat lucky you're marrying a plastic surgeon?" Luke interjected mildly, his hand tightening fractionally on Catherine's hip. "Not that she'd ever need it. But if she does, in thirty or so years when she's your age, she can also have her face extensively excavated and remodeled free. Of course, by then you'll probably be married to a mortician. Easy come, easy go."

Catherine almost choked. She couldn't look at Luke in case she started to laugh.

"Gracious, Luke. You know I was only sixteen when I had Catherine. I was practically a baby myself."

Faith had slipped up and gotten pregnant at twenty-nine, not sixteen. But for as long as she could remember, Catherine had been blamed for the inconvenience. Her beautiful mother couldn't frown anymore, she noticed. Faith must have had those Botox shots to kill the nerves in her face. It was rather odd to see the expression in her mother's eyes but not see the wrinkled brow that should have accompanied it.

Faith pulled the garment bag away and held up the dress. If nothing else, her mother had impeccable taste.

The gown was a slim, floor-length column of flame-ècolored silk. There was no embellishment whatsoever, just flowing fiery silk jersey, expertly cut on the bias.

"Interesting color choice for a wedding," Luke observed blandly. "Wouldn't black have been more appropriate?"

"Black is no longer *très élégant.*" Faith tilted her head as she held the dress up in front of Catherine. She eyed what was certainly a one-of-a-kind designer gown with a small pout. "I thought the color would be quite striking with Catherine's coloring, but now..."

Not in a trillion years, Catherine thought without hostility. There was no way on God's green earth her mother had ever thought this color would flatter her.

"You were absolutely correct," Luke said with mock admiration. "This will look dynamite on Cat. Admittedly, not everyone could pull off wearing this dramatic hue. For instance, it would completely drain all that hectic color right off your face, and make your hair look a little like straw, wouldn't it? It only works because of Cat's youth and beauty. And of course, the stunning deep color of her hair."

Catherine jabbed Luke in the ribs with her elbow. "How many people are coming to the wedding?" she asked quickly, before the giggle in her chest could burst free. To sober up, she imagined all the wedding guests staring at her butt in the skintight dress. She shuddered. Fortunately, she'd never see any of them again. Her mother never invited the same guests to two weddings in a row. Catherine was the unlucky exception.

"Only twelve hundred. Chandler wanted to keep it intimate, bless his heart."

Twelve hundred people staring at my rear. Oh joy.

Catherine's eyes met Luke's. She saw the answering humor, and the question, *Are you all right?* She gave a small nod. A thousand-plus guests had not been invited a week ago, when Faith had called her daughter. Catherine gave a mental shrug. It wasn't important.

Faith recovered and handed the dress to her. "Well, I did my best. Just suck everything in for a couple of hours. It should be just fine. I must bid you au revoir. My masseuse awaits. Walk me to the door, darling."

Catherine wondered if Faith called everyone "darling" simply because she couldn't remember their names. Probably. She handed the dress to Luke and walked her mother to the door.

"'Night, Faith," he called from across the room. "I'm looking forward to meeting old Chandler tomorrow. Hope we get a chance to chat. Dad filled me in on some of your more hilarious antics. I can't wait to share them with your next new…ah, *this* husband. We should have him rolling in the aisle."

Cat gently closed the door behind her speechless mother. She slid the bolt home, then turned to face him.

Cat had the oddest expression on her beautiful face. Oh, man. Was she going to cry?

"I'm sorry, Cat, I hate the way Cruella De Ville talks to you. Let's face it, your mother is a caricature—"

With a war whoop, Cat raced across the room and flung herself exuberantly into his arms. "My hero!"

Her mouth slanted down on his. Perfect synchronicity; his was right there to meet it. He hugged her close. Man, she felt incredible. She laughed against his mouth, and he'd never felt anything as intoxicating in his life.

"My dragon in shining armor." Her tongue curled around his with pure, unadulterated carnal intent.

His arms tightened around her. She kissed him and kissed him and kissed him. As though there was no to-morrow. He did the only thing he could: he kissed her back. Just for a minute. Just to slake his thirst. Just to quench his centuries-old desire for her. She tasted of the tears she hadn't shed while her mother was in the room. She tasted of joy. She tasted of yearning.

She tasted of heaven.

She tasted…off-limits.

He wasn't Mr. Right, and he'd better take a moment here to remind both of them.

As much as he wanted to go on kissing her forever, his hands automatically circled her waist to hold her at bay. There was only so much he could stand. He dragged his willing mouth away from the sweet suc-culence of hers. He hadn't resisted her for ten years to fail now. "Uh, Cat—"

Instead of answering, she gave him a little hip shove. They landed with a small thud on the bed behind him.

CHAPTER TWELVE

CAT PEPPERED PASSIONATE kisses on his mouth, his chin, his throat.

A blinding, dizzy hunger swamped him, so deep, so profound, he shook with it. Wrapping her more tightly in his arms, he feasted on the softness of her lips, on the slick dueling of her agile tongue, on the press of her slender body to his.

He tried to resist. He really did. He sent up a fervent prayer, but it was too late. Her breath feathered against his ear. How could she know there was a direct line from ear to groin? Panicked, he realized his body parts were disengaging from his brain. The brain that knew this was an incredibly dangerous situation.

The narcotic kiss went on and on. The alarm bells in his head became more distant as she arched against him. With unsteady hands, Luke tried to shift her off his body and out of temptation's way. Unfortunately, his hands seemed to be holding more than pushing.

Cat's eyes turned to liquid amber as she looked down, his name on her lips a shape without a sound. Then she dipped her head again.

He attempted to avoid her avid mouth. Her tongue was extremely sneaky. Her hips wriggled to get more comfortable, in the process hiking her dress up, baring more leg.

"What are you—doing?" he gasped, as her hand stroked down his side, evoking an intense shudder of desire. Her fantastic hair made a fragrant cave about their faces as she pulled the tail of his shirt from his jeans and kept him pinned to the bed with her body. Her eyes, so close they glittered like ancient amber, stared into his.

"Know something?" Her whisper, a hairsbreadth from his mouth, tethered him in place. Never in his life had he been so tempted. Found his need so great. Wanted a woman this much. And for so long. He had to battle the heat curling through him. For both of them. Yet the scent of her filled him to the brim. He…had to…think. Right. That was it. He had to think. With his brain.

She nibbled the corner of his mouth. "You talk too much." She clutched at his hair with one hand, the other busy tugging and ripping at his clothes.

A sensual fog clouded his reason. Her kisses were succulent. Rich with need. Delicious with desire. Her breath was warm against his lips, the inside of her mouth hot. Wet. Sweet. Hungry.

Having her like this felt so good it hurt. There wasn't a cell in Luke's body that didn't crave her like an addict. But he had to be sensible. His fingers curled around her upper arms to gently push her away.

Instead he found his hands sliding over the smooth skin of her shoulders in a caress. "You don't know what you're doing," he said desperately, his voice thick with hope and need.

"I'll get better with practice," Cat assured him, missing the point completely. Taking an ear in each hand, she held his head so he had to look at her. Her pupils appeared dark and enormous. "I'm a big girl, Luke. I know what I want."

She was curious, he forced himself to remember. Of course she was curious. His heartbeat kicked into a higher gear at the look of determination in her amber eyes. Luke groaned. She was long past the age where a woman took a lover. And he was the designated candidate. She considered him safe. She knew he'd do anything for her.

"No, wait. Cat—just—hold on a—"

She was a virgin. If he didn't have several really good reasons why he shouldn't proceed with this, that one would do it. He had to let her down gently. He was going to gently disentangle their bodies. Yes, he was. As soon as he came up with a reason that wouldn't hurt her. As soon as he could move, quiet his own raging hormones... As soon as his brain came back online.

"Uh, Cat? Why don't we talk about this?"

"Oh, Luke. You smell so good!"

A low, primal moan escaped him as she laved a warm, wet tongue over his right nipple. He forced himself not to react. But oh, God—he'd ached for this for weeks. Months. Years. Decades. He struggled for control.

And lost.

"Still sure?" he rasped.

"Please make love to me."

Her eyes lost focus as he bent his head and touched his mouth to hers. The kiss zinged through her bloodstream like potent alcohol. While he distracted her with the amazing versatility of his hot tongue in her mouth, Luke pulled the cotton knit dress down to uncover her breasts.

His eyes gleamed when he saw her strapless, lavender satin demi-bra. "Oh, man, touching you feels like a dream." He traced the pale swell above the cups, making her shiver.

"I'm real."

"Thank God. This looks incredible on you." His smile was feral. "It'll look even better on the floor."

His touch became almost reverent as his hand skimmed across her breasts. She arched upward, encouraging a firmer touch. But Luke wanted to explore. Lazily. Methodically. Catherine moaned as his thumbnail brushed her aroused nipple through the thin satin. While she desperately wanted the exquisite torture to last, her body demanded more immediate gratification.

"Luke…" She took his hand and pressed it hard against her. He found the front clasp of her bra. The cups fell away, baring her to his hot, damp breath. Luke palmed one breast at his own speed, his hand hot against her.

"Better than a dream." He dipped his head and, gentle as a butterfly, settled his lips on her nipple. It felt…exquisite. Then he sucked the hard nub deep into the cavern of his mouth, making her body arch with pleasure. A blinding shimmer of lust shot straight to her crotch. Mindless and frantic, Catherine clutched the back of his neck. Her need went beyond his gentle touches. She throbbed. She ached. She had to have…

"Luke…please…"

His lips closed with delicate greed over the other nipple. She didn't want delicate, she wanted desperate.

"Luke, take off m-my dre—" She swallowed. "Naked. I want to be na—ah!" Long moments ticked by before she remembered what she'd been trying to say.

"No rush," he said between nibbles and licks.

"Yes," she told the top of his head breathlessly as the pressure inside her built. "There is."

"No way am I going to rush through the hors d'oeuvres just because you're greedy for the main course. Relax, Catwoman, you're in good hands."

"Great hands," she assured him. "But *slow* hands."

Luke's chuckle vibrated through her chest. He cupped and kneaded the neglected breast while increasing suction on the other nipple. Driving her insane. Her head thrashed from side to side, her hips arched up off the bed as he blew on the wet bead. He bit down, not so gently, his fingers squeezing the twin with the same intensity. Then he skimmed her dress up her thighs. Catherine vaguely felt the air cool her bare legs. Luke's palm burned a path from knee to upper thigh.

"I…" Air spilled from her lungs as, with a low growl, he kissed her mouth, nibbling and teasing as his hand reached its goal.

…love you.

The feel of his fingers brushing the apex of her thighs through the thin fabric of her panties made her body writhe in response.

His finger dipped skillfully into the top elastic of her lavender satin panties. "Easy. Easy." Luke paused to breathe reassurances, then his mouth came down on hers once more.

Catherine felt her face grow warm as he intimately stroked her. She blushed hotter at the moisture his fingers encountered. While his clever mouth worked magic, Catherine shuddered, her entire body sensitized to Luke's touch. It was electrifying. Amazing.

He grazed the corner of her mouth. His lips traveled over her eyelids to close her eyes against the bright light. She felt the tips of his fingers brush satin-crushed curls, and she shivered deliciously. She moved her legs, aroused beyond bearing.

Luke deepened the kiss. His fingers sneaked into the slick wetness between her legs. He made a sound, almost of pain, as he slid a long finger deep inside the swollen folds. A low, hungry noise came from her own throat. Too much. It was too much. She shifted frantically against the scratchy hotel bedspread.

Luke lifted his head, his eyes dark and smoky. "Still with me?"

Catherine swallowed. Every nerve ending in her body screamed for the sweet release his fingers promised. "I think I've gone ahead," she murmured thickly as the scent of her own arousal mixed with the dark erotic fragrance of Luke's skin.

Dimly she heard him chant her name over and over again as he pressed her face against his hard, sweaty chest while aftershocks rippled through her.

God, she loved him. She loved the twist of his mouth as he concentrated on her pleasure. She loved how tender he was with her. How careful. She loved the deep bass of his voice, and the dark sexy taste of his mouth. She loved the smell of his skin and the silken texture of his hair. She loved having his fingers buried deep inside her.

Her choppy breath huffed. Luke's shuddered to a stop. Good. Suddenly shy, Catherine buried her face against the flat plane of his stomach. And inhaled the unique fragrance of an aroused Luke Van Buren. He smelled like her every fantasy. Her heart, already pounding, shifted into a primitive beat. Reflexively, her fingers tightened around him.

He growled low in his throat, then struggled to get something out of his back pocket and at the same time shimmy out of his jeans. She heard the double thud of his shoes hitting the carpet, the whoosh of his pants joining them on the floor.

"Wallet," he grunted, flipping it open to remove a foil packet. He ripped into it with his teeth, then handed her the rolled rubber.

Catherine stared at the tiny coil. What was Luke doing with a rubber in his wallet? He certainly hadn't been planning on sleeping with her on this trip.... Her heart thudded. *Don't go there,* she warned herself. *Don't even think about that.*

She looked from the condom to the bulge beneath his briefs. "You need king-size, not this dinky sample! Oh, Luke—"

"It'll fit. Trust me. Here." He snatched it back. "I'll do it this time. I have only so much control left."

He sheathed himself, then groaned when he glanced up to see her avid attention focused on his hands. "If you stare at it like that I'm going to come before we even get started."

Catherine wished to God she could switch off her brain. *Tell me you love me. That'd help.*

He shot her a quick smile that twisted her heart. Then made quick work of the small satin triangle of her underwear, tossing the scrap of fabric aside. "Ah, Cat, so pretty."

With one knee, he nudged her legs farther apart and slid into the cradle of her thighs. The sensation of his hardness against the vulnerable portal of her body made Catherine tense.

"Relax, sweetheart."

Reflexively, her body stiffened. She bit her lip and tried to relax. *I love you. I love you....*

The fullness of his entry pinched as she opened to accommodate him. Tears sprang to her eyes and she hissed as her body tried to resist the tearing pain. Instinctively, her hips and knees tried to push him out and off.

Luke froze. "Cat?" He reared up to look at her face. "God, sweetheart, want me to stop?"

She tried to counteract her body's natural instinct, and wrapped her arms more tightly around him so he didn't roll away. This was Luke. Luke, the man she'd loved forever. Luke's fingers in her hair. Luke's breath mingling with hers. Luke's body intimately connected with hers. After what seemed like a lifetime of denial, they were on the same page at last. She wasn't going to ruin it now. "I'm—just hurry up and get it over with, okay?" *Hurry up and take my virginity and get back to the good part.*

The tendons in his neck stood out in sharp relief as he cupped her cheek in a tender hand. She felt him move inside her. "You're hating this," he stated. "Aren't you?"

"No!" He saw right through her. "Yes," she admitted reluctantly. White-lipped, he started to withdraw. Catherine squeezed her eyes shut and tightened her limbs around him.

"Finish." She couldn't look at him, she was so embarrassed.

He dropped his head and rested his forehead on hers. "I should have had the strength to tell you no."

Oh, God. Not again.

A sob vibrated deep in her chest. She wished with all her heart that she'd never made him do something he hadn't wanted to do.

"You've always given me what I wanted. Even when it's bad for me. Finish what I started, Luke. Then it'll be done."

Not once had he said he loved her. Not even a whisper of his feelings for her. What was the main event in her life, was, for Luke, a night of sex with an inept but willing partner. Catherine bit her lip. A fumbling, inexperienced, clumsy partner. Weighty sorrow settled like a lead blanket on her chest. *Don't let me cry. Please, don't let me cry.*

It wasn't Luke's fault that he didn't reciprocate her feelings. She couldn't make him love her. The earlier beauty of their lovemaking dissipated, a crying ache too big to ever be filled.

Deep inside, the old insecurity reared its ugly head. She was seventeen, seeing his face twisted with anger and regret just before he walked away from her. Now she felt the exact same bottomless ache of loss. The same bleak understanding that she was on her own. And always would be.

Just because Luke was making love to her didn't mean she had his heart. And without his heart, their lovemaking was a hollow victory. He was sorry she'd seduced him.

She'd taken the biggest gamble of her life.

And lost.

The wonderful feeling of euphoria was gone, but she held on to Luke as tightly as she could, wrapping him close with limbs and will as he pumped into her like a man possessed.

His muscles trembled as he tried to move more slowly within her. "O-kay?" he panted.

No. Her skin and her yearning felt too raw to tolerate his touch.

"Sure." She buried her face against his neck. She needed a dark room and time alone. She wanted to turn back the clocks to before she'd made monumentally wrong choices with the right man.

Catherine's heart ached unbearably, and tears leaked into her hair as she stroked the straining muscles of Luke's back while he had sex with her.

Iloveyouloveyouloveyou.

Stupidstupidstupid. What in God's name had he done? Still buried deep inside her, incapable of moving, Luke breathed in the scent of their lovemaking. A chill that had nothing to do with the air conditioner raced across his skin. She'd hated it. He'd known the second her body had tensed and she'd realized who was making love to her. Mr. Wrong.

He'd not only taken her precious virginity, but he'd taken it like a no-finesse pillaging Mongol.

"Luke, I lo—"

"Want the light off?" he asked at the same time, rolling away from her.

Silence pulsed, a living presence in the room. "Sure."

He carefully extricated himself from her, not touching more than he had to. She flinched and struggled to cover herself. The pale purple material of her dress was twisted around her middle. She tugged and pulled at it, not looking at him.

God. He'd never seen a more abject picture of embarrassment in his life. He pulled the edge of the sheet to cover her pale, perfect, freckled body. "You're not going to be sick, are you?"

"No." Her voice was muffled by the arm she'd flung over her eyes. The only way his little crab could hide.

He reached out and clicked the light off, plunging the room into darkness, then lay down beside her. Inches separated their bodies. Miles separated their needs.

"That was probably the dumbest thing I've ever done in my life," he said with a sigh. "I'm sorry, Cat."

The pause was so long he wondered if she'd fallen asleep. Down the corridor someone broke the thick silence, filling an ice bucket. The room smelled of sex and heat and lost opportunities. Beside him, Cat lay mute.

"Can you forgive me?" An overwhelming sense of dread settled on him.

"Of course."

"That's not how it's supposed to be done." He filled the excruciating silence with confessions. "And it was my fault. I should have realized that, without love, it would be harder for you to take. I just hope to God I haven't spoiled it for you with the next man."

"The next... You th-think—you think if it wasn't right with you it would possibly be right with someone else?" she asked bitterly into the darkness.

He reached out to touch her. She jerked away. God almighty. Luke pressed hard fingertips into his burning eye sockets. He should be shot.

"Trust me, sweetheart. Yes. Loving the person makes all the difference in the world."

"If you say so." A world of doubt colored her words.

"Are you really okay?"

"Couldn't be better."

"If I go get a warm, wet towel will you let me—"

"No!" She cleared her throat and repeated the word with less vehemence. "I'm going to get up in a minute and t-take a shower."

It was evident what she really wanted was to see the south end of his sorry ass heading north. Luke's elbow bumped her ribs as he rolled over. She flinched. He swore under his breath. Oh, Lord. How was he going to fix this? What could he say? What could he do?

Hands stacked under his head, and out of temptation's way, Luke stared up at the ceiling with an aching heart. Beside him, she shifted restlessly, embarrassed and uncomfortable with him now. He'd blown it and blown it bad. He wanted to slide his arm under her shoulders and pull her back into his arms and against his thundering heart. He wanted to be articulate.

Dammit. He wanted to be Mr. Right.

"You know this changes our relationship, Cat." It had to be said. Because he was trying so damn hard not to let any of the pent-up frustration and emotion seep out of his voice, it came out flat and surly.

"I don't want it to change," Cat said fiercely. She shifted; her leg brushed his. "Sorry."

"You don't want it to change?"

"No. I like things just the way they were before."

"You want to forget this ever happened?" His hand bumped her nose as he reached out to touch her.

"Ow. Yes."

"Sorry. Are you okay?"

"Sure. Hey, Van Buren, don't you have your own bed?"

"Are you crying?" he asked softly. *Yes, she's crying, you insensitive, low-life moron.*

"Sinuses."

"Probably the air-conditioning." *Yeah, right.* "You kicking me out, Catwoman?"

"Don't take this personally, Luke, but you're taking up both halves of this bed, and I need to get some sleep before the main event tomorrow."

How much more personal could this get? Luke thought bitterly. He was completely naked. She had half her clothing on. He'd been so wild for her he hadn't even noticed. Of course she wasn't used to a man in her bed. Especially not Mr. Wrong. She'd been a virgin. Just because he'd never been any woman's first was no excuse.

"Can I at least wait until I get my breath back?" *Until I can think of something to say or do that will make this better for you?*

"Hmm? Oh, sure. Gasp away." The mattress shifted. "I'm going to the bathroom. See you in the morning."

See you in the morning?

He heard her pad across the carpet. The bathroom door slammed shut. He watched for a sliver of light. He waited in vain.

Luke's throat closed. He was no Casanova, but he knew he had more finesse than this. What the hell was with him, anyway? He was so discombobulated with the taste, the touch, the smell of Cat that he didn't know up from down or in from out. Now, when he wanted to be smooth and suave and say the words she needed, wanted, deserved to hear, he'd fumbled badly. Even if he was Mr. Wrong, he should have made it good for her.

Not only had Cat lost her virginity to the wrong damn guy, he'd made her first sexual experience awful. He'd been a lousy lover. And if that wasn't enough, he'd betrayed her trust, broken his promises and hurt her in all the ways a man could.

Yeah. He was a real prince of a guy.

He wanted to love her all night. He wanted to love her forever. Instead he'd behaved like a sixteen-year-old with his first girl. Hell. He felt like a sixteen-year-old with his first girl. With startling clarity, Luke realized that the last few weeks with Cat had been foreplay. Blow-your-socks-off, let's-get-ready foreplay. He'd had about as much willpower as a wet rag.

Luke wiped his damp palms on the tangled sheets. He felt as if he were traveling through an emotional storm. They'd taken an irrevocable step.

He wanted to howl like a savage beast. He wanted to burst into the bathroom, grab hold of her and toss her over his shoulder. He wanted to bring her back to this mangled bed and make love to her slowly, tenderly, until they were both too weak to move.

He wanted to grab her by her shoulders and demand she see that *he* was Mr. Right.

But Cat's feelings had to be paramount. Not his own. He knew Cat inside and out.

Luke jerked upright, eyes narrowed on the bathroom door.

He did a mental forehead slap. Damn right, he knew her inside and out.

No way would his Cat make love with a man she didn't love.

What had he been thinking?

As insecure as Cat was, she would never have slept with him if she didn't love him. The fool woman was trying to be noble and save him from himself.

Luke realized something else. He'd been so busy trying not to seduce her, he hadn't noticed that she'd been doing her damnedest to seduce *him* for weeks.

His heart took flight.

CHAPTER THIRTEEN

BLINDED BY TEARS, Catherine leaned her hip against the bathroom counter. The second she'd slammed the door behind her she'd yanked the dress, wound like a shroud around her middle, up and over her head. She was absolutely mortified.

It didn't help matters that she knew she was the one responsible for her own humiliation. *The idea was for Luke to make the first move, remember?* she castigated herself, while choking back a sob.

Didn't she have enough problems without this? One of the buttons on the back of the sundress had caught in her hair. She was stuck with her face covered, her arms pinned overhead by the inside-out dress, and no way to get free.

This would be funny. In about ninety-eight years.

The harder she struggled to free her hair, the tighter the tourniquet became around her upper arms. Furious, frustrated and trying to cry silently, she yanked savagely at the snarl behind her head. The harder she tried to free herself, the more fruitless it became. The harder she tried to be quiet, the more the sobs hurt her chest. The harder she tried not to love Luke, the more her heart ached.

"Damn. Damn. Damn."

The door snicked open. "Need help?"

Catherine shrieked, then said bitingly, "Dammit, Luke. I'm stark naked here!" It was pretty obvious she couldn't reach for a towel, let alone cover herself with her hands. She started to turn around, then quickly changed her mind. Besides, he'd seen every freckly inch of her already. "Get out, Van Buren!"

"Hmm. This looks *very* interesting."

What a particularly weird situation this was—standing here buck naked, arms immobilized over her head, blind, furious and humiliated. "Find me a pair of scissors, then leave."

"Hair caught?" Although he wasn't touching her, Catherine could feel the warmth of Luke's skin all down her left side. "Why don't you let me try to untangle it instead of cutting it?"

"Because," she said through her teeth "I don't want you anywhere near me. Go away."

There was absolutely no point in rehashing what was obviously a no-win situation. She loved him. He cared about her. Close, but no cigar. She'd get over loving him. At about the end of the next millennium, but by God, she could do it. Starting now when she felt the heat of his hand on her hip. She crowded against the cold porcelain sink.

"I don't want you to touch me," Catherine told him with as much dignity as she could muster.

"Darn," Luke said softly, picking her up in his arms like Rhett about to carry Scarlett up the stairs. He was naked. Why hadn't he dressed? "Isn't that too bad."

"Put me down. Dammit, Luke. I'm not joking, put me do—" He dropped her on the bed. Fresh tears sprang to her eyes, tears that had little to do with the fierce pull on her tangled hair.

"Don't suppose you had a chance to wash up yet?" Luke asked conversationally.

Catherine could feel his eyes traveling down her body, and was grateful for the dress covering her face as she blushed. She wiped her hot, wet cheek on her upper arm. "I hate you," she told him feelingly. "Go to your room."

She heard his departing chuckle. What...? Water ran. He was in the bathroom. Like a contortionist, she felt around the bottom of the bed with her toes for the sheet, hoping to cover herself before he came back.

"Amazing." The mattress depressed as he sat next to her. "Maybe you *should* have joined the circus."

"I won't be at your mercy forever, Lucas Van Buren. Don't!" she warned as he touched her thigh.

"Let me at least do this, Cat." His deep voice sounded achingly soft. "Please?"

The man was infuriating. "At least turn the light off."

The warm washcloth touched her intimately. Catherine almost shot off the bed.

"No."

She'd already forgotten the question... Oh, yes. The light. "What's this? The equivalent of a paper bag over my head?"

Luke laughed. "The equivalent of tying you to the bedpost."

"There are no bedposts."

"Exactly."

Catherine quivered like a horse at the starting gate as he stroked her intimately with the rough terry cloth. The heat of her skin dried the tears on her cheeks. She'd never felt more vulnerable and exposed in her life, and it had nothing to do with being naked. Well, not much, anyway. How could he do this to her? Didn't he know what his earlier rejection had done to her?

Luke efficiently finished bathing her with the washcloth, then tossed the cloth aside. She felt him get off the bed.

"See you in the morning," she said briskly. *Not if I see you first.*

"Ah, my little crab. Convenient that you can hide under that pretty dress of yours. How lucky can a guy get?" The mattress between her feet depressed. She shrieked. She'd pictured him dragging on his pants and walking to the door.

He picked up her right foot. "Don't scream so loudly, Cat. It would be extremely embarrassing if hotel security burst in here and saw you like this. We'll start here."

Catherine's toes curled as his warm hand closed around her instep.

"The first time I fell in love with these feet was…oh, I guess you were about sixteen." His thumb caressed the length of her arch with sure, strong strokes. She tried to pull away, but he wouldn't let go. "You were sitting by the pool. You had on a swimsuit the same color as the water, do you remember? And you were painting your toenails Passion Pink. I thought you were the prettiest sight I'd ever seen."

"You're c-crazy. My feet are huge."

"Nah, your feet are just the right size." Moist breath flirted with her toes. She instinctively tried to tuck them out of sight. Luke chuckled. "Remember when we went shopping? Holy hell, Catwoman, I should be nominated for sainthood! I wanted to grab your feet, and…do… this…." He sucked her toes into the wet cavern of his mouth.

Catherine almost came off the bed. Dammit, she wanted to see…no, she didn't. She lay back against the mound of pillows and felt the slickness of his tongue as he ran it along the underside of her toes. The sensation was indescribable.

"Luke…" She had no idea what she wanted to say, so it was a good thing he ignored the interruption. He licked and sucked and nibbled her toes, instep, arch, heel. It was the most intimate of seductions, yet he'd gone no farther than her ankles.

By the time he set the second foot down on the bed, Catherine's heart raced and she felt as limp as an overcooked noodle, yet as wired as if she'd just run a marathon. Blinking open her eyes, she wished she could see Luke's face. But the darn dress was still firmly over her head.

"Luke, could you please—"

"Now I noticed your ankles a lot earlier, I must admit. You were probably fifteen or so. You'd just bought those gold high heels for that dorky Tony's prom, remember?" Luke's thumb caressed her right anklebone, while his lips skimmed over the left. The sensation shot to her very core. "You came down the stairs and the first thing I saw were your ankles. I about swallowed my tongue. World-class ankles, these."

He paid homage to every indentation. How could licking her ankle be erotic?

"You were dating Anna Silk at the time." Catherine shifted on the bed. Wanting to…wanting. "I was spitting jealous of her, and all those other girls you brought home to introduce to Dad. They were always beautiful…. You don't remember Anna at all, do you?"

"No. I remember a young girl who was all wild red

hair and witchy eyes. I remember wishing she'd hurry and grow up."

His tongue felt slippery and rough at the same time as he laved her anklebone.

"I loved you quite desperately when I was fifteen, you know."

His hands stroked up her calves. "Did you?" Luke whispered.

"Oh, yes…" Catherine's body vibrated like a tuning fork. "I'd loved you from the moment we met. But that was the year of my first full-fledged crush. You were so romantically wounded and brooding."

"Was I?"

She struggled anew with her recalcitrant hair and that darn button. "I must have driven you crazy trailing after you. You accused me of stalking you, remember?"

Luke kissed the back of her knee. His lips felt hot, and the touch of his mouth sent a shaft of pleasure skittering up her leg. "I wasn't very kind."

"No, you weren't. But I understood. You didn't sleep over at the house very often, but when you did I'd try to be with you at every opportunity. I was starting to feel very grown-up, and I couldn't understand why you didn't notice me."

"I noticed. As I recall, you came home from a barbecue and you were wearing those funky shorts that came down to here." The edge of his nail skimmed midknee. "Remember?"

Remember? She could barely think now. "You m-mocked me about those long shorts."

"Only to prevent myself from dropping to the ground and licking these knees. Trust me, Cat. I had dreams about these knees…." His tongue laved each knee in turn, while his clever hands stroked and petted. "Serious fantasies about them…"

Catherine ached and throbbed, her nipples painfully hard. Moisture and longing pooled between her thighs. Luke had to be able to smell how hot he was making her.

Again she struggled to remove the darn dress binding her. But after a few seconds, what Luke was doing took over her every thought. She lay back against the pillows, fisted her hands in her hair and just felt.

"And Lord, your legs," he said hoarsely, skimming both large hands up her thighs. Her muscles bunched and jumped under his expert caress. "I could go on for years about these gorgeous legs. Holy hell, woman. I had more wet dreams about these legs than a man has breakfasts. You laugh. I was a big man about town, and I was salivating over this exquisitely shaped pair."

How could he talk? How could she think? Catherine licked dry lips. "I'm c-covered in freckles."

"Thank you, God." Luke shifted up the bed alongside her. She felt the glide of his hair-roughened thigh travel slowly up hers. "I'm going to spend a long, long time joining the dots. Be patient with me. It'll probably take a lifetime."

Lifetime…?

"I remember the night you stopped being tolerant of me," Catherine murmured. "The girls took me to a strip club. My first time seeing naked guys. My first taste of beer. I came stumbling home and you were standing in the dark kitchen. You wore jeans and a black T-shirt. When I saw you, my heart about jumped out of my chest. I wanted so badly to be sophisticated. Of course, I also wanted to be a petite blonde," she added dryly, wriggling as Luke's agile tongue traveled across her hip.

"You had stars in your eyes and wore a pale yellow dress. It floated around your legs as you dashed across the kitchen and into my arms." His hand skimmed up her thigh, making her breath shudder in her throat.

"You picked me up off my feet and swung me around. It made me dizzy. Then you pressed me against the fridge and kissed me."

"I remember."

"My legs turned to jelly and my head spun. My heart started pounding and my skin went hot, then cold. I'd never felt anything like it."

"You upchucked on my new shoes."

"You pushed me away."

"No. I felt guilty as hell at taking advantage of an innocent young woman who was smashed. I didn't want to compound it by taking you on the kitchen floor."

"One minute you were kissing me like something out of one of my fantasies, the next you were yelling and screaming, absolutely furious that I was drunk and behaving like my mother. You said some really awful things. Made worse by the fact that most of it was true. I *was* a pest. I *was* always underfoot."

"I wanted you so badly I was almost willing to risk Dad killing me. But I thought my touch had revolted you. You were so sick, and you looked at me as though I'd killed your best friend. I wanted that look of sisterly adoration back. But I didn't want you to be my sister."

"I didn't want you to be my brother. I was sick because I'd had too much excitement on top of too much to drink.... Are you going to help me get this stupid dress off my face so I can see you while we have this rather important conversation?"

"In a while. Now, where was I? Ahhh, your belly

button." His mouth moved across her middle, then his tongue darted out and licked a sensuous path from navel to hip and back again. Goose bumps rose on her skin and her muscles fluttered. Her hips jerked.

"June 25, your eighteenth birthday party. Fluorescent pink bikini. There were a million nubile young things at that pool party. Nick came with me. I couldn't take my eyes off you. You were practically naked—"

She'd waited with breathless anticipation for Luke to show. He'd arrived late, stayed half an hour. "You left early."

"Pretty hard to hide an erection wearing a swimsuit." He moved up her body, skimming along her sensitized skin and making her shiver and twitch restlessly.

It was with breathless relief that she felt him shift the shroud of fabric covering her head and arms. He found her hand and spread her fingers over his palm. "Now about your hands. Slender, artistic fingers. I love that you never wear polish on your fingernails. I love the way you tap them on the table when you're pissed off. I love when you run your fingers through my hair. Impossible right now, I know. But later…"

He could have at least uncovered her face. Catherine wanted him to kiss her. She wanted to kiss him back. "Are we done with seventeen?"

He flipped the dress back over her tingling hands. "For now. Ah, these shoulders." He stroked what he could reach. "Poets write sonnets about shoulders like these."

"They do support my neck…."

He ignored her. "Slender, yet strong. You carry the weight of the world on these shoulders. You don't need to." He touched two fingers to the base of her throat. "Do you want me, Cat?"

More than my next breath. "What would I do with you if I had you?" she asked lightly, her heart pounding harder, rougher.

"Let me count the ways."

He cupped her left breast in his palm and flicked his thumb over the engorged nipple. The sweet, sharp sensation shot like a flaming arrow to her groin. She moaned. Luke chuckled, but he sounded choked. Catherine felt giddy with desire. High on love. Delirious with hope.

"But first…" his breath whispered across her right breast; his hair tickled her chin "…I need to pay homage to the most incredible pair of breasts it's been my good fortune to meet."

"W-way too small."

"Are you mad, woman? More than a handful is a waste." He proved it. For several minutes the only sound in the room was Luke's mouth against her breasts. The noises alone should be bottled and sold around the world as an aphrodisiac.

His head shifted lower. And lower. Licking, caressing. Touching. Stroking. Until she couldn't tell where Luke ended and she began. He slid down her body until his clever mouth touched her intimately.

"Ah, Cat. The ultimate prize." His tongue opened her slick folds, delving inside. He nuzzled and licked her like an ice-cream cone. She melted when his breath stroked her thighs as he shifted between her legs.

"This—" he licked slowly up her furrow "—was—" down again "—my ultimate fantasy." His tongue darted inside.

Catherine arched off the bed. He held her cold bottom in his hot hands and kissed her again. Hard. Soft. Deep. Shallow.

Catherine forgot to breathe.

"Don't come," Luke told her harshly. "Don't—" he licked her to the edge "—come." He breathed warm air intimately into her, and his fingers tightened on her behind.

Oh, like she could help it? Her body tensed as tight as a bowstring. Every nerve ending quivered for his touch. She was hot enough to melt, so aroused that the next touch would send her over the edge.

Luke shifted across her body. "I'm here. Wait. For. Me." His penis nudged her opening. A sob burst from her lungs as he slid home to the hilt, smooth, hard, impossibly deep. The pleasure took her breath. Tears ran into her hair. She turned her face against her arm as her heart pounded frantically against her ribs. The tribal beat amplified throughout her body. *I love you. I love you. I love you.*

"Wet and wild. But still tight," he murmured, kissing her throat. "Am I hurting you?"

"N-no." She could barely get the word out. Spread wide by his narrow hips, her thighs quivered as he reached between their bodies and rasped his thumb over her sweet spot, circled, pressed.

"Oh my," she managed to pant, as her skin prickled and scalding heat poured through her. Her body arched. "Please."

"Let go, sweetheart. Let go. I have you."

She fell. And Luke was there to catch her.

Like an approaching storm cloud, filled with heat

and energy, she felt her body flex and tighten as the climax thundered closer. And closer. And—

Her body convulsed. Luke held her tightly, controlling his own finale to slowly, skillfully rebuild her desire, until she climbed again. Another impossible peak.

"I lo— Yes, sweetheart— *Yes*—"

They came together in a burst of light.

Finally her spasms eased, and she lay sprawled beneath him, their skin bonded and slick with sweat. Luke's chest heaved against hers as he dragged in great gulps of air. She felt him move inside her, and tightened internal muscles to hold him there.

"Ah, Cat." He sighed with satisfaction and stroked a still-shaking hand down the damp skin of her throat and over her sensitized breast.

"Are you going to help me get this thing off my head, Van Buren?" Catherine murmured.

"Having your head buried is a perfectly crab thing to do."

"That's a *turtle,* not a crab. Come on, Luke. My arms are killing me." Catherine felt as though she were on a high-wire without a net. Either she quickly acknowledged that Luke's ego as a lover had been sorely compromised by their earlier lovemaking, and he'd done that wonderful seduction to prove he still had it, or she could continue this dream....

She loved him so much it was a physical ache in her chest, yet she felt shaky inside, terrified that this would once again blow up in her face.

He lifted his head and she could feel him looking down at her. "Know what I think, my little crab?"

"I tremble to think, my big turkey." She wanted to stay this way forever. Drowsily she nuzzled her fabric-covered nose against his chest. There'd be time later to unveil and have a reality check. But not now. Not when she had him here like this.

"I think you wouldn't recognize Mr. Right if he bit you on the butt."

She yanked the last few remaining strands of hair knotted around the button and freed her face. "You do, do you?"

His eyes danced with little green lights the second they met hers. "Hell, yeah."

She dragged the dress the rest of the way over her head and tossed it on the floor, then looked him in the eye again. They were only a few inches apart. "Maybe he's so blind you wouldn't recognize my butt if it was—was served to y-*him* on a silver platter!" She finished in a rush.

Luke rubbed his chin. Blast his hide, now he was grinning. "Maybe he would."

"Maybe he hasn't."

He bent his head to kiss her lightly on the mouth. "We're getting nowhere fast, aren't we? Boy, I'm going to deserve a medal when this is all over. Cat, Cat. We're going to have to learn to communicate better than this."

She could still feel dried tears on her cheeks. She tried to read his expression, then blinked at what she saw on his face, in his eyes.

He took her face between his hands. "I love you, Cat."

"Love? What about all those emotional eggs in one basket?"

"You are all my emotional eggs, Catwoman. Every last one. You're love, and hope, and promise." His green eyes darkened. "Do you want what's best for me?"

"You know I do."

"You."

"Me what?"

"*You're* what's best for me, Catherine."

"Catherine?"

"I want you to know how serious I am. You're my heart."

"Obligation. Misguided responsibility. A knight in shining *amore* complex."

"*Amore* is exactly what I feel for you. Let me spend the rest of my life showing you how much I love you." He closed his eyes. This was going to kill him if it didn't work.

"Okay," he admitted raggedly before she could interrupt. "I did make you and Dad that promise that I would be your brother and take care of you forever. I made that promise, Cat, with every intention of keeping it. But I haven't felt remotely brotherly for a long time. I fell in love with you, and now I have to break my word."

She smacked him on the arm. "That was when I was a child, you turkey! Why? Why didn't you tell me?"

"Because I thought you needed family more than you needed a temporary lover. I was waiting for you to grow up and make a rational decision about us. But it wasn't you who had to grow up, Cat. It was me."

"Do you love me, Luke? Really love me? Not a morning-after-gee-thanks-that-was-great-sex kinda love. Not, oh my God, I just boinked Cat and now what am I going to do. But the genuine thing?"

"Yeah." He laughed, a joyful, exuberant sound that traveled through her as hot and pure as sunshine. "Love. As in heart and soul. As in crazy about. As in forever."

"You do, huh?" Cat felt a smile blossom from the

depth of her being. "What about Mr. Right biting my butt?"

"He'd be more than happy to."

"Yeah?"

"Oh, yeah."

Thrilled at his grumble of protest, she slipped from beneath him and rolled over onto her stomach. She pointed to her bottom, where the word *LUKE* was tattooed in inch-high red letters.

Luke stared. "Oh, my God. This must've hurt."

She tilted her head to see him better. "Not as much as you not knowing I existed."

"Aw, Cat." His voice sounded gravely soft. He ran a tender finger along the cursive script. "When did you have this done?"

"For my seventeenth birthday. I've always known my Mr. Right. Luke?"

"Yes, my love?" he managed to reply thickly.

"Bite me!"

CHAPTER FOURTEEN

"WE MISSED YOUR mother's wedding. Do you mind?" Luke asked. He leaned across the armrest between their seats and played with a lock of her hair. The back of his hand kept brushing her breast.

"Nah. We'll catch the next one. When you've seen one, you've seen them all." Catherine touched him intimately under the in-flight magazine on his lap. "Tit for tat," she whispered naughtily in his ear. Luke groaned.

He loves me. Catherine wanted to stand on her seat and yell it to everyone on the plane. She wanted to do cartwheels down the aisle. *Lucas Van Buren loves me.*

They'd missed the wedding, the reception and saying goodbye. They'd only managed to drag their exhausted bodies out of bed and off to the airport in time to catch their flight home.

"What's in that bag?" she demanded of the small sack he'd raced out of the hotel with this morning. "A present for me?"

"You bet." His eyes gleamed and she felt him twitch beneath her hand. He wiggled his eyebrows. "I bought out the hotel's supply of condoms."

She smiled. "How many did you buy?"

"Thirty-three."

Cat almost choked. "Condoms? Thirty-three *condoms?*"

"Too few?" Luke asked, straight-faced. "Don't take offense, Cat. If they'd had more, I would've bought them."

Laughing, she swatted his arm and shifted in her seat. "Behave yourself. We can't do anything—oh, no, Luke. No. Absolutely not—" He kissed her silent.

The captain lit the seat belt sign and announced their imminent arrival in Las Vegas for a brief layover. In a couple of hours they'd be back in San Francisco.

Home. Was there ever a sweeter sound? Home to their big bed. Home to share that big bed. Together. Home with thirty-three condoms.

The second the seat belt sign went off, Luke rose and stepped into the aisle. He held out his hand. "Come on."

"Huh? We don't have to get off."

"I have to stretch my legs."

"And you need me to hold your hand while you do it?" She smiled. "Stay here. I'll keep you so entertained you won't worry about being cramped."

"Not that I don't want to jump at that invitation, but I really do need to stretch out for a bit. Come on, Catwoman, you heard the flight attendant. We'll be sitting in this tin can for another twenty-five minutes." He tugged her hand until she rose. She gave him a curious look before straightening and stepping into the aisle beside him.

The flight attendant, brunette, curvy and petite, gave Luke a smile and a wink. Catherine prodded Luke's back with her elbow and snorted.

As they passed the cockpit area, the attendant leaned toward Luke. "Your fr—"

Luke laid a finger across the woman's mouth. He said something under his breath. She made an expansive gesture with her arm, as if they couldn't have found the wide-open door on their own.

Catherine gritted her teeth.

"Jealous?" he asked, smiling happily as they emerged into the concourse. "Don't worry, sweetheart. If I ever look at another woman, you can cut off my balls."

"Thank you for the offer," Cat said dryly, her amber eyes bright with laughter. "But it was unnecessary. That's something you can definitely count on."

Luke didn't let go of her hand as he tugged her in his wake.

"Hey, look. Slot machines. Got some quarters?" The *kirching* of falling coins blended with announcements of arrivals and departures. Weird. Ignoring her request, Luke kept walking, tugging her behind him.

"Aren't we supposed to stay by the gate?"

"I want something over there." He glanced around, then pointed down the concourse to a flower-bedecked white gazebo sitting incongruously in front of one of the departure gates.

Catherine smiled. "Flowers?"

"Something like that. Come on."

They approached the gazebo, festooned with every kind of flower imaginable and threaded with colorful ribbons. It didn't look like a shop.... Catherine suddenly spotted a guy standing nearby who looked just like—

"Nick! Hey, Luke. Look, it's Nick."

"Hey, gorgeous!" Nick braced himself as Cat flung herself into his arms.

Behind her back, Nick gave Luke a thumbs-up. Luke's heart, which hadn't had a normal beat in forty-eight hours, did a somersault. He met the unholy glee in Nick's eyes over her head. Nick grinned and disengaged.

"Thank God," Luke said coolly. "A murder charge would play havoc with business." His best friend's smile widened. And he still had his arm around Cat's shoulders.

"Having a hard time of it, are you, old son?"

"One might say so." Luke scanned the surrounding rows of chairs and the people seated with their backs to them. "Is your assignment complete, good buddy?"

"With a modification, yeah."

"What are you two up to?" Cat demanded, suspicious as hell. She eyed Nick. "Not that it's not delightful to see you, but what are you doing here?"

"Catherine!"

Before he could answer, Cat was swept into the embrace of Molly Cruz, a friend from Beaverton. Behind her stood Sandra Steward, with her husband, Bill, then a dozen old school friends rose from their chairs to converge on her, all talking and laughing at once. Nick had done good.

For several kaleidoscopic moments Cat hugged and exclaimed with her friends. "This is insane! What on earth—"

"Okay, Cat. That's it, time's up." Luke's heart couldn't take much more of this. "Everyone?" He sounded like a movie director, a nervous movie director, as he instructed everyone where to stand. He'd never been so nervous in his life. Luke snatched the bunch of rather wilted daisies from Nick and thrust them into Cat's hands. People parted like the Red Sea to allow Luke to drag her inside the gazebo.

"Luke, what—"

"I want to be your devil's food cake, Cat. We're getting married. Here. Now. Everything else can be ironed out later."

Cat blinked up at him. "Married?"

"Yeah. Got a problem with that?"

Cat smiled. "No."

"Good. Let's do it. Nick, where's the min—"

"Right here." Nick stepped aside to reveal a miniature Elvis Presley. The top of the man's black bouffant do came to Luke's belt buckle. Dressed in a skintight, white sharkskin suit, replete with rhinestones and stand-up collar, the pint-size minister held a black book in his hands and smiled up at them, showing large square teeth.

Cat eased closer to Luke and gripped his hand tightly.

"Dearly beloved…"

"Till death do us part," Luke whispered to a wide-eyed Cat.

"…gathered here…"

Cat pressed her cheek against his shoulder, eyes alight with love and laughter.

"…I want to live in our house together. I want to have children with you. I want us to grow old together. I want commitment, and stability, and knowing we'll have each other for the next sixty or so years. I want it all, Cat."

"…join Catherine and Lucas in holy matrimony…"

"Look at the cake." Luke jerked his chin to a small table supporting a white-frosted wedding cake. "Devil's food."

How Nick had found someone to make this cake at such short notice, Luke had no idea. He owed his friend big-time.

The top of the cake held a small basket filled to the

brim with eggs. On one side was a tiny orange crab. On the other, a plump turkey. As the minister continued, Luke met Cat's tear-drenched eyes. Her smile lit up his world.

"…man and wife. You may kiss your bride."

* * * * *

TAKE ME

PROLOGUE

"Marry me."

"*Excuse* me?" Jessie Adams narrowed her eyes at the stranger sitting in the back booth of the diner. He hadn't finished his first cup of coffee before he'd beckoned her back to his table.

And she thought she'd heard it all. *Marry me? Oh, brother!*

Outside, rain slashed in sheets across the midnight-dark parking lot, empty save for his low-slung silver sports car. Diamond drops of rain peppered his dark hair and the broad shoulders of his black wool coat. The neon café sign in the fogged window sputtered, illuminating his face.

Lord, he's a hunk. And a welcome diversion tonight. It had been a lousy day. Week. *Month.* Jessie sighed. *This too shall pass.* She'd read that somewhere and hoped like hell it was true.

Briefly she fantasized that Prince Charming had come in for the singular purpose of sweeping her off her feet. That his proposal was for real. Unfortunately the way her luck had been running lately he was a mugger after her last twenty bucks and the take in the cash register.

She gave him another surreptitious once-over. In truth, she was like the cartoon dog chasing the car.

What would she do with him if she actually caught him? The thought made her smile.

"Well?" he demanded.

"Well, what?" Jessie tried not to drool. He smelled so good she wanted to snuggle up to him, close her eyes and just inhale.

"Will you marry me?"

Be still my heart. "Is it Thursday?"

"Friday."

"Sorry, I only marry total strangers on Thursdays." She topped up his coffee. "You'll have to wait 'til next week."

"Next week is too late." His pale gaze sharpened on her face, slid lower to her flat chest, skinny legs, then shot upward. "What the hell happened to your hair?"

Jessie's hand rose self-consciously to the overprocessed orange-yellow blotched clump. "I dyed it." In the hope blondes had more fun. Ha!

"Whatever you were aiming for—"

Didn't work. "I like it," Jessie snapped. Her chest felt hard, heavy and tight. He was a stranger. Why did she care what he thought of her hair? "Drink up. We close in twenty minutes." Thoughts of midnight reminded her of more pressing problems. The two-week notice to vacate her studio apartment had four days left. So far, she hadn't found anything else affordable. She'd move to Sacramento or Tahoe. *If* she had more than twenty-seven dollars to her name. *If* her mother's boyfriend hadn't shown up and swiped her car. And *if* she—

"You're perfect." The man's sexy drawl stopped her from turning away. "I have a proposition for you."

I just bet you do. "Listen, pal, my feet hurt, I have to finish my shift, and as much as I'd like to sit and schmooze, I have to clean the kitchen before I go, so if you don't mind..."

"Hear me out—"

Jessie wrote his ticket and slapped it on the table. "If you want more coffee, help yourself."

There wasn't much to do in the spotless kitchen. Other than a couple of truckers at dinner, she'd been alone all night, which meant zilch in tips. Jessie finished loading the dishwasher, then turned to see the guy, hands in the pockets of his coat, standing in the kitchen watching her.

She knew exactly what this sophisticated man saw. She was no beauty. She was too thin, and if she was ever going to get boobs, she hoped it was before she was old enough for them to sag. Her mutilated hair was scraped away from her face and piled untidily on top of her head like orange and yellow straw. All she had going for her were her eyes. Some trucker had once told her they looked like cow eyes. She wasn't so sure it was a compliment, but at least he'd been sincere.

"How old are you?"

"Boy, you're persistent. Has anyone ever told you no?"

"One too many times. How old?"

Jessie tilted her head and eyed him with undisguised curiosity. He appeared rich, spoiled and used to getting his own way. He had beautiful hands. Long, strong, tanned fingers with clean, shiny nails. Jessie always noticed hands.

She automatically hid her bitten nails behind her back. "Twenty...five."

He laughed. It sounded rusty. "Nice try, honey."

"Twenty-one."

"Legal."

Jessie backed up against the refrigerator as he strolled toward her. There wasn't a snowball's chance of anyone coming in at this hour of the night. He could do anything to her, and no one would know. She flinched when he touched her face. She really shouldn't have been sarcastic last week when the car had been stolen and she'd asked God, "What else can happen?" God didn't like sarcasm. It was Jessie's curse. She sighed. She supposed this guy was better than being struck by lightning.

"Perfect." He turned her chin this way and that, his hand warm on her skin. He smelled even better close up. Jessie's mouth actually watered. Instinctively, she understood he had no sexual interest in her, no need to control or dominate. Her heart wasn't pounding because she was afraid of him...not very anyway.

"How about this, pal? I give you ten seconds to take your hands off me, or I call the cops?" His hand dropped, but the ghost of his light, warm touch lingered on her skin. "What do you want from me?" Jessie asked hoarsely.

"I want you to marry me. Now. Tonight. We'll drive into Tahoe, get married and I'll have you back in time for your next shift."

"You're crazy!"

"I'm desperate," he countered, voice grim.

Who isn't, pal? "Why me?" Jessie slid out of his reach and walked back into the brightly lit diner. He was right behind her. He grabbed a mug off the stack behind the counter and followed her back to his table by the window.

What on earth was a guy like this doing here? The

diner wasn't his kind of place. The only reason people stopped here at all was that it was right on the California border into Nevada. The small coffee shop mirrored a million others across the country. Red vinyl seats, worn down by a million butts, beige Formica tables scarred by cigarette burns, tacky Christmas decorations. The invasive smell of grease and food had permeated the plastic plants hanging in dusty profusion from toggle hooks in the yellowed ceiling.

Jessie tried to ignore the décor. Sometimes she physically ached for beauty. For stability. For some damn thing that couldn't be conned, stolen or sweet-talked from her.

She wasn't opposed to working, but it would be nice to get a break for a change. Unfortunately she wasn't delusional enough to believe a total stranger would stroll into the diner two days before Christmas and sweep her off her worn tennies and lay all that at her feet.

"I'll make this short and sweet." The stranger took the carafe out of her hand and motioned her to the opposite seat, then filled both cups and placed the coffeepot in the neutral territory between them. Intrigued in spite of herself, Jessie flopped down on the scarred vinyl seat.

"This is purely a business proposition." He raked his fingers through his dark hair. It fell neatly back in place. *Figures.* "Here's the situation. My father and his brother owned a development company. My father died ten years ago and he left the company to my uncle Simon with the understanding his half would in turn go to me. I've worked my ass off while my cousin Paul gallivants around the world doing God knows what. That company is fifty percent mine. I've earned it, damn it. Now Simon wants to retire, but he insists Paul and I settle down before he gives his company to a couple of 'playboys'—*his* quote. My uncle, in his infinite wisdom, has decided Paul and I should settle down and get married."

Jessie eyed him skeptically. "For real?"

He nodded curtly. "Unfortunately, yes. To top it all off, the first one to marry gets controlling shares. Simon is obsessed with this ludicrous notion."

"So, what's the problem? A good-looking, rich guy like you must have a gazillion women to choose from."

"I asked someone," he said tightly and with obvious reluctance. "She said yes—to my cousin."

Jessie cradled her forgotten mug between her hands. "Ouch. There must be someone else you cou—"

"They're getting married in San Francisco tomorrow at noon. Our meeting up tonight is going to work out to both our advantages. I'm sure you'd like financial freedom. Do whatever you like? Go anywhere? Sure you do. And all *I* want is a contract marriage. I'm not interested in emotional entanglements. I don't want a real wife, I want a wife on paper. Now. Tonight."

He glanced down at her 34A chest and her name tag. "Marry me, Vera. I'll give you a monthly allowance for as long as you live. Hell. I'll buy this damn diner for you if you want it."

Jessie stifled a hysterical laugh. Her name tag had been left over from the last waitress, and she hadn't cared what people called her. "I don't want the diner." Just looking at him made her silly heart do somersaults.

"Listen, having control of this company means *ev-*

erything to me." His eyes glowed pale and determined. "Surely you've wanted something this badly in your life?" He leaned forward. "Do this for me, and when the time comes, if there's something you want more than your next breath, I'll make it happen. You have my word on it."

"Anything, huh?"

"Anything."

Lust at first sight. The attraction she felt for this man was undeniable. But then what was not to attract? He was unbearably handsome, strong, powerful, wealthy and, most dangerous of all, he *needed* her. The attraction was obviously not reciprocated in the least. However, Cinderella hadn't complained when her prince whipped her out of the kitchen.

"How do I know you're on the level?" *Oh, please, be serious.*

He pulled a business card from his wafer-thin leather wallet and a cell phone from his overcoat pocket. "Here's my lawyer's card. Call him, confirm who I am, ask about my uncle's ultimatum."

Jessie took the card. She was nuts, she was crazy, she was out of her mind for even considering his proposition.... What did she have to lose?

She reached for the phone and began punching in the numbers before she thought to ask, "What's your name?"

"Joshua Falcon."

The man on the other end of the phone was not happy to be woken by a lunatic stranger at midnight. Jessie stumbled through enough questions to confirm that Joshua Falcon was who he said he was, and was richer than Croesus.

The lawyer wanted to talk to Mr. Falcon. *Right now.* Jessie handed him the phone and slumped back, openly eavesdropping.

Watching her, he spoke into the phone. "You're damn right I'm serious." He listened for a while. "In a diner on the California-Nevada border." He looked over at her, his pale eyes narrowing. "Why *wouldn't* she? She's probably getting minimum wage and living in a cramped apartment with her cat. I'll fax a copy of the marriage license and bring the original to your office later." There was a short pause. His laugh made Jessie shiver. "No honeymoon. I'll have her call you back to make arrangements for the settlement."

Joshua listened. "No need for sarcasm. She's worth more than her weight in gold. Oh, and Felix? Call Simon as soon as you get my fax." There was a long pause as he listened. "All right," he agreed with some reluctance. "Take the Lear and meet us at the court-house in Reno at nine. You can hand deliver the mar-riage certificate to my uncle."

He folded the compact phone and stuffed it into his pocket.

"I don't have a cat."

"I beg your pardon?"

"I said I don't—"

"That was rhetorical. Get your coat," he said, im-patiently buttoning his own. He tossed a twenty on the table.

"I don't have a coat, either."

"You don't have a coat?"

"Gee, is there an echo in here?"

Scowling, he removed his coat and tossed it to her. "Put this on and let's get this over with."

"Wow, you certainly know how to bowl a girl over with sweet talk." The wool coat smelled of him. It was thick and dark, and held the scent of potent male and fresh citrusy cologne. Jessie's insides turned to mush. She had that standing-on-the-highest-diving-board feeling. Exhilarating, thrilling terror.

"Christ." He watched as she turned off lights. "I must be more tired and desperate than I thought."

Jessie froze with the keys in her hand. "Listen, bub, I didn't come in here on *my* knees begging you, did I? Make up your mind." The keys dug into her soft palm. "Well?" She glared at him. "Do you want to marry me or not?"

He looked down at her. "God help me. Yes."

AT 9:45, JOSHUA slapped the marriage certificate into the hands of his lawyer, Felix Montgomery.

At 9:46, he walked out of the courthouse.

He did not look at Jessie once.

Prince Charming didn't even kiss the bride.

CHAPTER ONE

December
Seven Years Later

PARTY GUESTS, DRESSED in holiday finery, ebbed and flowed through Simon Falcon's home. From a safe distance, Jessie watched her husband scan the festive throng with pale, bored eyes. Born to wear the stark black tux and crisp pleated shirt, every immaculate inch of him screamed wealth and bone-deep self-confidence. With his aristocratic features and go-to-hell eyes, he was like a king surveying his kingdom. And the dangerous edge of his sex appeal was universal enough to make every female head turn.

Seven years hadn't changed him. But *she'd* changed considerably. No way would Joshua recognize the woman he only knew as his absentee waitress-wife, Vera. And only she knew her sophistication was nothing more than a thin patina. Her standards were now extremely, and friends told her, unreasonably, high. So be it. She was perfectly content with her life just the way it was, thank you very much. There was only one thing she wanted from Joshua Falcon.

Their marriage had given him control of Falcon International. Now it was her turn to get something she desperately wanted from their marriage.

More than anything on earth, Jessie wanted a child.

And Joshua was going to make that dream come true.

He'd promised to give her whatever she wanted more than anything else in the world.

Now she was collecting.

A couple of months ago Jessie had instructed her lawyer to inform her husband she was ready to make her request. Joshua had complied immediately. He'd offered to pay for the insemination process at the in vitro fertilization clinic of Vera's choosing.

Jessie wasn't sure what she'd expected him to do. But sending her off to a clinic to accept some stranger's donation wasn't it! The whole point here was that she wanted her *husband's* baby.

The good news was he obviously had no interest in children, nor did he want anything to do with any progeny. Which was fine and dandy with Jessie. What he didn't want, he wouldn't take away.

She squared her shoulders and took a fortifying sip of wine. Exhilaration made her heart pump harder. She resisted the urge to run her hands over her hips to make sure the silk jersey wasn't bunched anywhere, then righted the circlet of holly she'd woven into a wreath for her hair. Feeling like a gunslinger checking his holster, she choked back a laugh.

The smile died on her lips as she caught Joshua's gaze, holding it, although it took every ounce of her newfound sophistication to do so. Her chin lifted a notch and she saw his lips twitch. Their eyes locked as he started across the room toward her. Blood pounded in her ears. Forty feet…thirty feet…*don't talk to him, lady!*…eighteen feet…

Joshua was taller, fitter, better looking than any other man in the room. Her heart pounded so hard she barely felt the individual beats. Everything about him assaulted her senses as he moved inexorably toward her. Adrenaline raced in effervescent bubbles through her bloodstream. The wine was tasteless as she took a gulp then held the cool glass against her hot cheek. Sixteen feet...

Simon almost gave her heart failure as he came up beside her and circled his arms around her waist. She hadn't noticed his approach. He kissed her cheek. "You look like a Christmas angel in that red dress, honey. What are you staring at so intently— Oh, Joshua's here."

"Stay, Simon." Jessie held on to his arm like a lifeline. "Just long enough to introduce us, okay?"

"Are you sure you know what you're doing, Jessie?"

She'd fibbed to Joshua's uncle, only telling him half her plan. Her laugh sounded strained even to her own ears. "No."

For seven years she'd imagined making love with Joshua. She'd dreamed about it. Longed for it. Ached for it. Every time she read about him, either in the business section of the newspaper or a sleazy tabloid, Jessie had wished she were the woman on Joshua's arm. In his bed.

She'd tried unsuccessfully to banish her husband from her mind and heart while putting her nose to the grindstone in the intervening years. She'd finished high school, gone to college, all the while carefully managing to avoid him. Until tonight.

Now there was method to her madness.

The physical attraction she was experiencing was

as powerful, as terrifying now as it had been all those years ago in the diner. Lust made her mission easier. And if the feelings were reciprocated...

It had taken forever, yet, in a second, he was right there within touching distance. His cologne was more subtle, more sophisticated, than she remembered, but the base scent, the essence of the man, remained. She'd never felt more *female* in her life as Joshua's hot gaze burned through the thin silk of her dress to the pulsing skin beneath.

"Simon." Joshua greeted his uncle, his voice low and husky, his eyes on Jessie.

"Joshua." Simon sounded atypically jovial as he clasped his nephew's hand. "How're you doing, son?"

"Introduce me to the lady." Joshua watched the sunrise of a blush paint her cheeks as he allowed the heat of his gaze to travel slowly from her lush mouth to her eyes and back to her mouth. A cloud of dark, Raphaelite curls framed her face and drifted about her shoulders as she looked up at him. Her brows, dark and silky, formed a gentle arch above eyes of sparkling chocolate brown.

Joshua had reluctantly accepted Simon's heavy-handed invitation to the Christmas party. He didn't do Christmas. For a second when he'd spotted the dark-haired beauty beside his uncle, he'd imagined *she* was Simon's surprise. Considering every surprise he'd ever had at this time of year was a bad one, and familiar with his uncle's wily manipulations, he'd almost turned around and driven up to his cabin in Tahoe as he did every year during the holidays.

He felt sufficiently mellow to wait his uncle out. With her supple, slender body, she was enough of an inducement to make him stay. For now. Her subtle fragrance teased him. A holly wreath nestled in her dark hair. Her skin looked smooth and pale against the flame-red floor-length gown. The matte fabric covered her from throat to ankle in a sensuous sweep, without showing so much as a panty line.

He felt a rush of heat as her small breasts shifted with her breathing. She was doing her damnedest to appear unaffected, but the lady was as aware of him as he was of her.

Joshua felt the familiar adrenaline rush for the start of the chase and wondered if she, too, was thinking of tangled sheets and sweat-dampened skin.

"Jessica Adams, my nephew, Joshua Falcon."

Her name was familiar. "You're the interior decorator my uncle's always talking about. You do good work."

A grin tugged at the corner of her mouth. "Thanks. Simon and Patti are always a pleasure to work with."

And she'd be a pleasure to have in his bed. "Go away, Simon," he told his uncle without looking at him. Jessie's mouth curved slightly as she observed him maneuvering his uncle. Joshua couldn't remember reacting so explosively to a woman in his life. The shiny strings of the tiny Christmas balls in her ears tangled in the darkness of her hair. She rubbed her wineglass against the pulse pounding at her throat.

He used every vestige of control to keep from tossing her over his shoulder caveman style and dragging her to his lair.

The very thought startled him. He was not an impulsive man, nor was he given to flights of fancy. He stuffed his hand in his pocket. He was almost tempted to cut his losses and walk away. Sex was one thing, an excess of emotion another.

Hell. Christmas always brought out the worst in him.

He knew he was looking at Jessie with unabashed hunger. His blood pressure shot up another ten points as he heard her stifle a moan. "Are you here alone?" he asked.

She either was or wasn't available. He'd never competed for a woman in his life. Although, Joshua thought, surprised by his reaction, he might be tempted in her case.

She smiled. "Just me and 299 party guests." She had an extraordinary mouth, generous, her lips pouty without being petulant. Joshua needed a taste. Just one. He almost leaned over to take it but managed to remain fixed in place, his libido jumping. She was available, he wanted her and she appeared interested. It was turning out to be a good party, after all.

He smiled. "Can I take you home?"

"Actually, I just got here," she drawled, eyes bright. "But thanks for offering. Simon," she turned to his uncle with a smile that made Joshua's skin tingle, "I'd love another glass of this excellent Chateau Whatever."

Simon gave them both a pointed glance before he snatched her glass and went off to the kitchen.

Jessie tilted her head a little to look up at him. Brown eyes twinkled as bronze lights of laughter danced in the sparkling depths. She was all sass and flirty eyes. And damn well irresistible. Joshua wanted to bury his hands up to his elbows in her hair, assure himself that it was as soft as it looked. He wanted to run his fingers along her slender curves. He wanted to lay her on cool sheets in a candlelit room and make love to her until she melted like warm honey.

But first things first.

"Before we leave," he said flatly, "I need to make something perfectly clear. I'm married."

Obviously taken aback she gave him a startled look. "Goodness, a philanderer with integrity. How refreshing."

He realized he'd tensed for her response. There was something about her that led him to believe she was nothing like his female companions to date. He hadn't paused to wonder why he'd told her the truth when he'd never bothered to tell anyone else before. She'd be just as capable as any other woman to run directly to the tabloids with the news flash.

His marriage wasn't a marriage at all. It was a piece of paper, nothing more. He knew it, the girl knew it. But this woman, with her glowing eyes and ripe mouth, might not understand.

For the first time since he was a boy, Joshua felt a flush ride his cheekbones. "It's purely a business arrangement. She doesn't give a damn what I do. We've been separated for seven years."

"Poor her."

"The arrangement was mutually agreed on," he said flatly.

"Why bother telling me?"

"Because I don't want any misunderstandings. I'm powerfully attracted to you. Hell, flat-out, I *want* you, Jessie Adams. But I'm not interested in a long-term entanglement, and marriage will never be on the table."

"Because you're already married."

"Because I never have, nor will I ever have, any interest in the state of holy matrimony. I married to facilitate a business deal, she married me for money. If this is a problem, tell me now."

"The *problem*," Jessie said sweetly, "is I don't care one way or the other. And I think it's a bit presumptuous of you to think I *would* since we've known each other all of two minutes. Your marital status has no effect on me at all one way or the other."

"Good." Joshua only now realized how damned boring life had been lately. It had been a long time since he'd felt the roar of his blood and the thrill of the chase.

"Let me guess. Your wife's a petite, blue-eyed blonde?"

Joshua stared at her blankly. He vaguely remembered Vera as a tall, skinny...blonde? Redhead? Whatever. Somehow he'd lost control of the conversation. He wasn't sure where or why, but it mildly annoyed him. "What's that got to do with anything?"

Brown eyes gleamed devilishly. "I'm trying to point out that I'm not your type."

"How do you know what my type is?"

Jessie fluttered her long eyelashes at him. "Small, blond and busty. Would you like me to name them for you?"

"I think I can remember," Joshua said dryly, narrowing his eyes in mild annoyance. CEOs had quailed at that look. She—damn her sassy hide—had the nerve to grin.

"And why would you be so interested in my lady friends?" he asked silkily, suddenly finding tall, slender dark-haired women extremely appealing. The air about her seemed to crackle with electricity.

"What?" Little Miss Sass was distracted for a moment watching *his* mouth. "It's hard to miss your exploits when every tabloid and newspaper finds the subject absolutely fascinating."

A point to the lady for her swift recovery.

Joshua glanced down. Her nipples were clearly delineated by the fabric of her dress. As he watched, the small buds peaked. He stifled a groan and shifted his stance.

"Lord," she said, voice thick, "you are direct, aren't you?"

"If I was any more direct, I'd come right out and tell you I want to take you to bed."

She smiled. "I believe you just did."

"I'm hardly the first man who's wanted to sleep with you."

"You're the first man who's said it straight out within moments of meeting me, with about three hundred witnesses." She didn't move away as he rested his hand on the small of her back. He could almost feel her skin vibrate beneath his fingers.

"I want to see you."

"You *are* seeing me."

"Without all these people around."

"If you're staying with Simon for the weekend, we should bump into each other sometime."

"That's a little too vague for me." He scanned her animated face. Her eyes still danced as she crossed her arms over her chest. At the view of her plumped breasts on the shelf of her arms, his mouth went dry.

He wanted her. He planned to have her. Soon.

"Several of us are going parachuting tomorrow, and since it's too far to drive home, then back again so early in the morning, I'm spending the night here. You're welcome to join us, Joshua."

Her husky voice saying his name made him want to yank her into his arms. He craved her mouth under his. He wanted to back her against the wall and have her, right there in Simon's sunken living room, in front of hundreds of guests. Lord. He couldn't remember ever being this hot, this fast.

Jessie glanced at him under her lashes. She took a small step back. "I've heard people should live life as if their personal diary would be published in the newspaper every day." She looked up at him with those big brown eyes. "I've read *your* personal diary in the tabloids for years. Just standing here talking to you is going to give me notoriety I've never had before. I'm not sure I'm ready for prime time."

More than likely their first meeting would be splashed across every tabloid by tomorrow morning. He didn't give a damn—unless she cashed in on his weak moment of honesty concerning his marriage. Then every snoop reporter in the country would be on the hunt for Vera.

Despite the risk, pursuing Jessie held an indefinable, underlying attraction that had nothing to do with her slender body. Something about her made his heart go from zero to a hundred in seconds and he'd be damned if he knew why.

"Do you realize," he asked, his voice thick, "that we're standing right under the mistletoe?"

Her long lashes fluttered as she glanced up, then directly into his eyes. Yes, her eyes told him. Of course she knew where they stood.

"Lord, woman, don't look at me like that." He didn't

recognize the roughness in his own voice. "What do I have to give you for just one kiss?"

"Here?" Jessie scanned the room.

"Yes, damn it."

"Chloroform?"

"Oh," he mocked, "I think I can find something that works just as well and is far more accessible." He hailed a waiter, and handed her two brimming glasses of pale wine. "Here."

Jessie automatically clutched both glasses as she looked up at him. "What am I supposed to d—"

He touched her cheek, just the barest of touches, and she closed her eyes, tilting her face up. He kissed her softly on the mouth. Christ, it was as bad as eating one damn peanut. She tasted of Simon's excellent Chateau Coutet, laughter and something he couldn't quite put a name to.

His fingers tightened briefly in the springy silk of her hair as her tongue shyly touched his. His lips moved with expertise over hers, Jessie's lashes fluttered then drifted closed. He felt her small breasts brand his chest as she leaned into him. He swallowed her ragged moan as he deepened the contact and lost himself in her response.

And then she was gone.

One moment he was standing with an armful of pliant willing woman, the next *he* was holding two dripping glasses and *she* was several feet away.

"Give me a call sometime." Jessie fluttered her fingers and melted into the crowd, disappearing from view before he could recover.

Joshua felt as if he'd been poleaxed.

JESSIE'S PURPLE-AND-PINK PARACHUTE floated over the vineyard toward the eucalyptus tree windbreak on the south side of the clearing near Simon's house. Joshua shaded his eyes against the sharp winter sun and scowled. He'd had precious little sleep the night before. Thinking about her, knowing she slept under the same roof, had caused him to toss and turn. So near and yet so far.

In his imagination she'd appeared larger than life somehow. Vibrant and intoxicatingly *alive*. She had what the French called *je ne sais quoi,* an indescribable *something*.

Joshua didn't consider himself a fanciful man, but he needed to see Jessie Adams again. Needed to assure himself that what he remembered from the night before was as simple as her unmistakable sex appeal.

Joshua enjoyed sex. He considered himself a considerate lover. He wanted Jessie. It seemed simple enough. And yet... He narrowed his eyes trying to put his finger on it. There was more to her. Something complex. Something intriguing. Something, damn it, that called to much more than his libido.

Which was, of course, a ridiculous assumption based on a few minutes of conversation the night before.

He wanted to chat with her once more before he left to drive back to San Francisco. Get rid of this stupid fantasy he'd built up during the night. Frankly, he reminded himself grimly, he didn't have the emotional fortitude to deal with a woman for more than companionship and sex.

They didn't call him The Glacier for nothing.

High above him, a gust took hold of the thin silk, and Jessie's slender arms madly manipulated the controls against the sudden shift in wind direction. She was losing the battle.

"Hell." Joshua started to run as her feet skimmed the treetops. Behind him, the follow vehicle revved, then bit a wheelie into the dirt road running alongside the vines behind Simon's house. Joshua sprinted to the other side of the trees just in time to see the billowing silks covering Jessie's prone body.

Roughly he gathered the fabric, flinging it behind him until he unveiled her. She looked up into his face and grinned.

"God, that was fabulous!" She sat up, brushing twigs and dirt off her arms. A skintight purple and fuchsia spandex bodysuit clung to every sleek, tight inch of her long body.

"You little idiot," Joshua said furiously, his heart still pounding. "You could've been killed."

Jessie's hand stilled and her smile slipped a little as she unbuckled her fuchsia helmet and tugged it off. Something he didn't recognize flared in her eyes.

"Yeah, my landing left a little to be desired." She tossed her braid over her shoulder. "I'll have to work on that." She stuck out a hand. "Pull me up."

He hadn't imagined it. She seemed to inhale life, to eat it with a spoon, relishing each delicious moment at a time. He knew she'd be like that in bed. Eager. Hot. Passionate and wild. He could drown in those hot, brown eyes. "You like living dangerously, don't you?"

"You have no idea," Jessie managed to say breathlessly as he suddenly tugged on her hand, drawing her to her feet and against his chest in one quick move.

"I want to taste it on you." Joshua breathed in her

already familiar scent that even dust and eucalyptus couldn't mask.

"Taste what?" she asked, a hairsbreadth away from his mouth. She looked up at him, her hand in his against his chest. Her fingers flexed under his but her eyes were steady. "Taste what?" she repeated, her husky voice low.

"Danger." He brought his mouth down on hers like a starving man at a banquet. He knew after he'd slept with her a few times the gnawing want would lessen and become manageable enough to ignore.

Jessie's lips held the sheen of his kiss as he stepped away from her. Joshua handed her the helmet. "I'll call you January first," he told her. Ignoring her bemused look, he turned and walked away. It was one of the hardest things he'd done in years.

He walked faster.

CHAPTER TWO

As PROMISED, JOSHUA called Jessie on New Year's Day.

Jessie made sure she wasn't home.

He called again on the second, the third and the fifth. She'd let the answering machine pick up while she sat in her kitchen listening, his tone getting progressively cooler and more impatient with each call.

Joshua had left half a dozen imperious messages in the last two weeks. She had no intention of falling over herself to call him back. Obviously he wasn't used to being ignored.

She knew she was playing a dangerous game. There was a fine balance as she waited for the timing to be right without causing Joshua to lose interest.

Soon. Very soon, Jessie thought as she drove onto the narrow road leading up to the gatehouse. She'd been startled, no, *stunned,* when Joshua had admitted he was a married man. His honesty, not only in acknowledging his marriage, but the *status* of that marriage, had confused her.

If she hadn't been his wife she would've politely walked away. Her mother had had plenty of married lovers. The ending was always sad and messy.

She sighed. His honesty had disarmed her and made her feel a little guilty about what she was about to do. But he was still The Glacier. Cold. Hard. Ruthless. He was still her absentee husband. He was still the man who was going to give her her heart's desire. A baby. Born in wedlock.

It was the second week of the new year and cold for Northern California. The wind cut through her jacket as Jessie got out of the car. It was after three and she'd missed lunch looking for a particular wallpaper sample at the design center in the city. Her stomach growled.

The little cottage welcomed her with warmth as she quickly closed the front door behind her and headed for the kitchen. She loved the carriage house. It was home. Safe, warm, welcoming, and as permanent a home as she'd ever had. Joshua's lawyer, Felix Montgomery, had taken her under his wing and introduced her to his son Conrad that dizzying day seven years ago.

Con had offered her not only the use of the gate-house, but also a job in his architectural company while she went back to school. Conrad and his partner, Archie, had converted the gatehouse cottage into a charming home for her, then later incorporated the studio when she'd gone to work for Conrad full-time as an interior designer.

They'd helped her transform her life and, in the process, the two men had become her dearest friends and the brothers she'd never had.

The phone rang. Jessie turned off the machine. "Hello?"

"Where in the hell have you been?"

She dragged in a breath. "I believe you have the wrong number," and hung up.

The phone rang again. Jessie tossed a tea bag in a mug of water and stuck it in the microwave. The phone continued ringing. The microwave dinged.

She squeezed out the bag and poured in a little milk. "Hello?"

"This is extremely time-consuming," Joshua said with a great deal of annoyance.

"Who is this?"

There was a pause. "Joshua Falcon."

"Oh. Sorry. I've been getting a lot of crank calls," Jessie told him sweetly. She sipped her tea and burned her tongue. She sat down at the small round table in a weak ray of sunshine and unhooked the calendar beside the phone.

"I've been calling you for weeks."

"Darn. And I kept missing you." She didn't bother trying to sound too sincere. "I've been *so* busy."

"So have I," he said coolly. "I just returned from an important business trip, but I made time to call you anyway."

Jessie grinned. "Where did you go?" Her stomach growled.

"Ireland."

"I've always wanted to travel. Tell me about it." She dragged the cord over to the cupboard and scanned her soups.

Talking to him on the phone was easier, safer, than in person. She couldn't see his eyes. Or his mouth. Or smell his cologne. She wanted a baby from this man. She did *not* want to fall in love with him.

Jessie refused to go there. That path was rocky and filled with potholes. Fortunately, she'd outgrown the gigantic crush she'd had on him years ago. She'd seen what love had done to her mother. No, thank you very much. That wasn't for her. Mutual attraction would get the job done. Quick. Painless. Satisfying. No fuss. No muss. It might be cold-blooded, but *she'd* know who her child's father was. No one would get hurt. Everyone would get what they wanted.

It was a good plan.

She prayed she'd get pregnant immediately.

She held the phone between chin and shoulder as she found a bowl, opened a can of tomato soup and added water and milk to her late lunch.

Joshua gave her the *Reader's Digest* travel tour of Ireland while she mumbled "Hmmm" and "Fascinating" at appropriate moments. And it would have been if she wasn't so uptight about seeing him again. At this rate, she'd develop indigestion.

She was sure as soon as she saw him the panicky feeling she'd been experiencing would pass. Between her "schedule" and his business travel, she'd managed to avoid him since Simon's Christmas party. Unfortunately January was a slow month in the interior design business, and she could've used the distraction of being genuinely busy. She'd have to see him soon, even if the timing wasn't right.

"All right. Enough about my trip." He sounded exasperated. "When the hell am I going to see you?"

"How about tomorrow night?" Jessie glanced at the calendar where the next night had been marked with an X. She'd calculated just how long she could keep him dangling. She didn't want to see him one second more than necessary. Her attraction to him was already putting a crimp in her plans. She had to stay focused, no matter what.

"Tonight," he insisted.

"I'm busy tonight." She lied cheerfully, getting up to place her empty bowl and spoon in the sink. "I'm free tomorrow night or next Wednesday. Your choice." Next Wednesday was circled in red. And underlined. She closed her eyes and prayed he'd pick door number two.

"I'll pick you up tomorrow night at seven."

"I'll meet you at Noble's, near Fisherman's Wharf, at seven-thirty," she said, resigned. There was a long pause. Jessie held her breath. Had she pushed him too far?

He laughed sardonically. "God, you're ornery. All right. Noble's. Seven-thirty." The dial tone buzzed in her ear.

She collapsed back in her chair, eyes closed. She'd done it. She picked up the calendar and ran her finger tenderly around the dates she'd marked in red and underlined. The nights for conception. All she had to do was hold him off a week, until her next ovulation. The prize was worth any discomfort she might feel, any small niggling twinge of conscience she might have. All she had to do was stick to her plan without deviating and she'd walk away with the grand prize.

JESSIE WAS COOL, calm and collected when she walked into Noble's restaurant at precisely seven-thirty the next night. She wore a simple royal-purple dress with a jewel neckline and cap sleeves. Sophisticated and sexy enough to hold him off while beckoning him closer.

Joshua rose to greet her. The hem of her dress suddenly felt way too short, the silk far too thin, clinging to her body in a way it hadn't done at home.

"Hello, Jessie. You're more gorgeous than the last time I saw you." His pale eyes gleamed in the candlelight as he took her hand, and drew her onto the banquette seat beside him. A sizzle of electricity arced up her arm.

"The last time you saw me I was covered in dirt." God, but he smelled good. He looked virile and alarmingly masculine. And he was sitting far too close. Jessie tried to scoot up against the window.

"You were covered in skintight Lycra." His breath fanned her mouth. She struggled to draw in air, mesmerized by his silvery gaze as he whispered huskily. "I've dreamed about peeling you out of it for weeks."

Jessie paused a beat for her nerves to steady, then reached for the menu. If she handled this right, she could make the next date for the following week when it would count. One dinner for one night in his bed. Two dates. *I can do this. I can.*

"The seafood here is fabulous." Her pulse throbbed in her ears. She willed herself to relax. She knew the outcome of tonight. He didn't.

The waiter arrived. "Two specials," Joshua said, neither consulting her nor taking his eyes off her for a second.

His broad chest, covered in shirt, tie and jacket, was inches away. She had a lustful vision of it quite naked. Would his chest be sleek and smooth, or sprinkled with hair? It was alarming how badly she wanted to touch him to find out. "Perhaps I'd like something else."

"So would I." Joshua brushed a wisp of hair away from her cheek. His touch was electrifying. "But I'm not going to get it before we eat." She must have looked as blank as she felt. He gave her a wry smile. "I don't give a damn what the specials are, as long as it's served fast."

Jessie controlled a bubble of hysterical laughter. "We could've gone to McDonald's."

"This was your choice."

"I'm starving." God. If they were this hot for each other they'd burn each other to cinders.

He slid from his seat and held out his hand.

"Where are we going?" Jessie took his hand automatically.

"To dance," he said thickly. "I have to hold you." He pulled her up, then maneuvered her to the small, empty dance floor and tugged her into his arms.

It felt good pressed against the length of him like this. *Far* too good. Jessie tried to put a little space between them. Joshua's arms tightened in a firm, inexorable embrace.

The solid width of his chest felt like heaven beneath her hand. She looked up at him. Would her baby have Joshua's nose? His pale-blue eyes? His mouth?

The small band in the corner played something soft and bluesy. Lord, this is dangerous, Jessie thought, as Joshua moved her expertly around the floor. And expertly against *him*. She should have been shocked by the hard length of his erection pressed against her. Instead her heart leaped, and her skin heated. Her nipples puckered and rubbed against the inside of her bra. She moved a little closer, allowing the slide and sway of their bodies to ease the ache a little. He brought his hand up between their bodies, and clasped her hand against his chest. The backs of his fingers brushed against her nipple making her shudder with longing.

It was no accident. Of course it wasn't. He kept up the slight friction, until Jessie wanted to scream.

His hand felt warm through the thin silk at the small

of her back as he pulled her more snugly against him. His thumb moved in a maddeningly light caress. Goose bumps spread from her back to her breasts in a slow, sweet rush that heated her skin another few degrees and made her heart pound.

Oh, boy. Definitely dangerous.

They were practically making love while vertical. Joshua brushed his mouth across her forehead and Jessie felt dizzy with longing. She struggled to find a topic of conversation to keep herself sensible. "Noble's was the first commercial interior design job I ever did on my own. I'd never done any commercial work until Con convinced Charlie to let me do—"

She glanced up while she was speaking. Why did he have to look at her like that? She licked her bottom lip, losing her train of thought.

Joshua's eyes smoldered; he drew her closer. "You did a superb job." He caught her nipple between the backs of two fingers and exerted gentle pressure. Moisture pooled between her thighs and her eyes glazed.

Her skin felt overly sensitive, almost electrified. *Get a grip, Jessie.* "How would you know? You haven't even looked." She managed a smile, and covered his eyes with her hand. She was demonstrative by nature and didn't give the impulsive act a moment's thought. But touching his bare skin, no matter what part of his body, was a mistake. A huge mistake.

"Tell me what you like about it." Her voice sounded strangled. Joshua's hot breath fanned the edge of her palm, his hips moved in a lazy, age-old rhythm that was making her insane, and his tweaking fingers had her libido at fever pitch. Jessie shifted slightly and rested her elbow high on his shoulder, feeling the play of muscles and the tantalizing brush of his hair on her overly sensitized skin as they swayed to the music. When had their feet stopped moving?

"I like the plaid carpet. And the mahogany paneling, the subtle lighting on the seascapes." He was very observant. The thought gave her a chill. *Watch yourself, Jessie.* "And the brass lighting and the dance floor." She felt his eyes move beneath her fingers.

"Lord," he said roughly, nuzzling her temple. "You smell like sin."

She withdrew her tingling palm and vowed to keep her hands to herself from now on. His lips skimmed her cheek.

"Would you make those sweet little moans for me in bed, Jessie? Would you whimper?" His teeth teased the shell of her ear. "You'd be hot and so sweet." He paused, breathing as raggedly as she, and when he spoke again his words were a fragmented whisper against her cheek. "Do you lie in bed at night and wonder how you'd move beneath me? How incredible it would feel to have me deep inside you?"

The picture came to her in vivid Technicolor and her mouth went dry. She gave him a cool look. "Actually…no."

"Liar." His pale eyes looked as hot as lava. "I can see how much you want me. I can see your heart pounding." He used the tips of two fingers to measure the pulse at her throat. "Right here." He dropped his hand, satisfied as her pulse throbbed even harder.

"I don't like the way I behave around you, Jessie Adams. It's completely out of character and I don't like it at all." He said it like a caress. Like a curse.

She smiled, but inside a frightened little voice silently echoed his sentiment. "I thought I made you hot."

"Oh, you do. Make no mistake about that." A muscle jerked in his jaw. "Hell, right now I wouldn't give a damn if half the press corps sat at the next table. That's how much I want you."

His face was just inches away; she could see herself reflected in his eyes. Jessie dug her short nails into her palms until she regained her senses.

"Wow," she said dulcetly. "That much?" She'd observed men play the game of "I want you until I have you" all her life. "Then it's a good thing we're in a public place."

"Which is why I'm not stripping your clothes off." His brows drew together in a frown. "As a rule, I'm a patient man. Congratulations, you've managed to try that patience to the limit." His fingertips ran along her jaw and left a trail of heat in their wake. His thumb glided over her lower lip.

"You and I have different priorities, Joshua." She struggled to control her own libido. "Satisfying your expectations is on the very bottom of my list. I happen to have a life of my own and you're only a very small part of it."

"That's going to change, Jessie. Very soon I'm going to be a major part of it."

His arrogance and self-confidence were bred to the bone. "Don't be too optimistic, Mr. Falcon. This is our first date and I don't like having a man tell me what to do, or when to do it."

His gaze rested on her mouth before he looked her right in the eye. "Are you telling me we *won't* become lovers?"

"I haven't decided one way or the other—yet." She ignored the little thrill of excitement skimming her nerves. She fought the unwelcome, insidious attraction with a reminder it was a physical ailment, like a cold or the flu, and would pass.

"You'll be the second person to know once I make up my mind." She glanced at the table where the wait staff hovered. "Oh, our dinner's arrived." Her hand slid down his arm and caught his as they returned to the table.

Joshua sat down and flicked his napkin onto his lap with controlled irritation. "Are you always this stubborn?"

"Let's say I'm extremely selective. I don't jump into bed at the drop of a hat. And, frankly, the thought of tossing my underwear into your collection is something I have to think about."

"Will I see you tomorrow?" he bit out, his expression savage. Desire dilated his eyes. Clearly part of him loved the challenge; the rest of him wanted her. Now.

Please God, next Wednesday was the next and last time she planned to see him. She'd see how Mr. Impatience liked waiting another week. She groaned inwardly. At the rate she was going, he might become a vapor trail before *tonight* was over.

"Let's see if we manage to complete this evening unscathed first, shall we?"

Amusement flared in his eyes. Jessie was afraid he knew exactly what she was experiencing. He leaned back in the booth, his expression bland as his hot gaze raked her face. "We'll see just which of us raises the white flag first then, shall we?"

Jessie relaxed the tense muscles gripping her spine.

She didn't even *own* a white flag. He had no idea just how stubborn and determined she could be.

Neither of them was getting any sex tonight, she reminded herself. After dinner she would drive herself home. Alone. It made a world of difference to her nerves when she leveled the playing field. The balance of power was in her hands tonight.

He might *wonder*.

But she *knew*.

THE SUN SHONE BRIGHT as a spring day, but there was still a nip in the air as Joshua strolled beside Jessie at the antiques street fair one Sunday afternoon. She wore blue jeans that did marvelous things to her long legs and heart-shaped butt, a short, screaming orange sweater, and a brightly patterned silk scarf. The outfit was so Jessie, as he was finding out. She hadn't worn the bold colors to attract attention, Joshua knew, although several men had turned to look at her. Jessie loved bright colors. *Happy* colors she'd informed him, eyeing his tan slacks, pale-blue shirt and navy windbreaker with disfavor when he'd met her downtown earlier.

The streets were crowded and noisy. Not the kind of place he'd ever have chosen to spend a Sunday afternoon. And certainly not where he would have chosen to be with Jessie. He preferred his surroundings slick, modern and new. And he wanted this woman to himself. Preferably in his big, black lacquered bed.

An unexpected business trip had kept him out of the country and he hadn't seen her in a week. Her face had come to mind at the most inappropriate times. It annoyed the hell out of him.

Jessie paused beside a table laden with junk. She

ran her hands over chipped cups and tarnished silver, all the while chatting comfortably with the vendor, an older woman with improbable red hair and a tired face.

Joshua admired the way the sun tangled in Jessie's dark hair, and the sweet curve of her cheek and mouth as she spoke. She talked with her hands, too. Animated, alive, interested in strangers. He felt a pang he grudgingly admitted was jealousy.

He wanted her to himself. Yet each time he saw her he became more intrigued by her interaction with others. She put people at ease. The things that drew him to her were the same traits that drew other people. Jessie's obvious joy for life, her enthusiasm, her sheer pleasure in everyday things. He glanced at the elderly lady's face as Jessie asked about a particular item on the overcrowded table.

The woman was brought to life by Jessie's animation, by her interest. It wouldn't have surprised him if she gave Jessie anything she wanted from her table of wares.

"She expected you to bargain, you know," Joshua told her as they strolled away with Jessie's purchase, a beaten-up, tarnished teapot for which she'd paid the asking price. A ridiculous amount for a piece of junk.

Jessie cradled her purchase to her chest. "She's raising her two grandchildren. Oh, look at that!" She grabbed his hand, dragging him through the crowd to look at a sideboard on the opposite sidewalk.

Joshua looked at their clasped hands. Her skin looked pale and soft, her hand small. He liked the feel of it in his. He liked the joining. And he wanted her more than his next breath.

Not just the wanting sexually. Although, God only

knew, he urgently wanted her naked beneath him. But he wanted some of her joy, some of her zest for life.

He didn't ever remember having Jessie's...*zing,* for want of a better word. She crackled with energy. Was gloriously, unabashedly *alive.*

"What?" She glanced up to find him staring at her.

The milling crowd faded as Joshua bracketed her face between his hands and brought his mouth down on hers. Her lips felt smooth and soft beneath his. He eased his tongue into the warm wetness of her mouth. She tasted of the caramel corn she'd eaten earlier. He'd never cared for the flavor before, but, on Jessie, the too sweet flavor tasted like ambrosia.

He stroked down her back and held her lithe body against him in an agony of want. The sun shone brightly on Joshua's closed lids, bathing him in gold. *I've lost it. We're in the middle of the street for heaven's sake! Surrounded by hundreds of people—* A magnitude-ten shudder traveled from his face to his groin when Jessie used both hands to hold his head steady, then lightly stroked his cheeks with her thumbs as he kissed her. Her agile tongue played with his, darting and playing tag until Joshua felt weak and stupid with desire.

Once. That's all he'd need. One time in Jessie's bed. One time in Jessie. Surely to God that was all that was required to get her out of his system. Jessie Adams was just too much hard work. He was used to picking up the phone and having his woman available immediately. With Jessie he had to watch the ball.

Her tongue slipped from his mouth, and an ache of disappointment pressed against his chest. No. His arms tightened about her slender waist. But his Jessie wasn't done with the kiss, after all. She brushed her damp lips across his, once, twice, then nipped his lower lips between strong, white teeth, and all the while her soft hands stroked his face.

Joshua had never experienced anything like it. Hell, he'd been horny before. He'd been turned on before. Sex was fine. Gratifying. A stress reliever. But with Jessie he wanted… What? More? Joshua went hazy for a moment as Jessie's body shifted against him.

She was dangerous…lethal. Damn it, he didn't do commitment. He wanted her to be the same as other women he'd dated and slept with. He *needed* her to be just like them. He wouldn't have it any other way.

She finally pulled her mouth away. "We're going to be arrested if we don't stop."

Joshua looked at her through dazed eyes. "What?"

Jessie smiled, her mouth blush-pink, damp and swollen from his kisses. Her unruly hair flew about in the warm spring breeze, strands stuck on the front of his sweater. Bonding them.

Joshua took a step back and stuffed his hands in the front pockets of his Armani slacks. "I don't do public displays of affection."

"Really?" Jessie's brown eyes danced. "I'll have to remember that the next time you grab me for a kiss in public."

ANOTHER DINNER DATE. Joshua vowed he wouldn't see this woman anywhere dangerous. Like a street fair. Or a parking lot. Or standing beside her car outside the theater in broad daylight.

There was something wrong with him, Joshua knew. He was incapable of feeling true emotion. Oh, he could fool most people, and he was quite proud of his ability to project the illusion. But the reality was he didn't experience emotional highs or lows like other people. He had some sort of missing gene.

He could claim it was because unemotional, uncaring parents had raised him. But he was an adult now, capable of seeing their selfishness for what it really was. No, the failing was his and his alone. It just wasn't in him to have any depth of feeling. It wasn't a problem. He'd managed perfectly well without it for thirty-three years.

It was easier to move on and not linger when he had an affair. No one got hurt. He was upfront and always told the woman that he had no intention of getting involved. Hell, fact was, he *couldn't* get involved. It just wasn't in him. It was always her choice if she decided to stay or go. He never admitted he didn't have the emotional fortitude to sustain any kind of relationship.

Take it or leave it. This was who he was. The Glacier.

Joshua had coldly analyzed his obsessive attraction to and fear of being with Jessie. He didn't want her to get close enough to see through him to his empty heart. He didn't want her to know that what she saw was merely the shell of a man going through the motions. Like Pinocchio, he wanted to be a real boy. Unfortunately he had a wooden heart. If he had a heart at all.

Fortunately Jessie would never know just how much he relished basking in her joie de vivre.

"Are you angry because I went to Paris without you?" he asked, reigning in his thoughts. She'd been quiet all evening.

"A." Jessie broke a small loaf of sourdough bread and absently handed him a chunk. "I'm far too busy to

go gallivanting off to Europe at the drop of a hat. *B,* I wouldn't have gone even if you'd asked me."

"Then why are you so annoyed?"

Her brown eyes were so dark they were almost black as she gave him a waspish glare. "You were gone for *ten days.*"

Joshua bit back a satisfied smile. "Not a lifetime, surely?"

There was a pregnant silence when she said, "I hate playing games," and she suddenly looked frustratingly lost. Some of the heat left her eyes.

"You do it remarkably well," he told her.

She stared up at him, her eyes huge. "I won't sleep with you tonight."

"*A.* I haven't asked you to." He smiled coldly. "And *B,* when we're in bed, we won't be sleeping."

Jessie made a low growling sound. "The reason I agreed to meet you tonight was to tell you to go to h—" She paused to look up as a family settled themselves noisily at the table next to them.

"You were saying?" Joshua ground out over the child's shrieks as its mother stuffed its flailing legs into the high chair their waiter had pulled up. "Jessica?"

She turned back, her expression dazed. "What?"

"You came here tonight to tell me to go…?" He knew damn well what the little shrew was going to say. He wanted to inform her he would go to hell *after* he had taken her to bed and made love to her until she couldn't remember her name, let alone give him so much aggravation.

"To tell you…" She looked at him blankly, glanced back at the fussy baby, then in a split second recovered herself. She smiled. Lord, he had never seen anything more captivating than Jessie's smile. "To tell you I missed you," she said huskily.

The waiter must have been trained to wait for the most inconvenient moment. He chose right then to deliver their entrée, then fussed with salad and plates and refilled water glasses. Joshua sent him off with a glare.

Before he went to hell, before he was driven out of his mind, he was going to have to spend at least a week in bed with this infuriating woman. He didn't like this sensation of not being quite in control. She smiled a sweet, gentle smile before picking up her fork.

Joshua had never experienced anything like this in his life. Not when two people's desire for each other was so palpable. Jessie Adams was just as turned on by him as he was with her. And *still* she held him off.

Half of him was annoyed by her reticence. The other half admired her restraint. When they did finally have sex he'd better alert the fire department.

He glided his fingers up her thigh. Jessie shivered, then grabbed his hand and set it back on the table. For a split second, her eyes flashed. The child at the next table broke into a high-pitched babble capturing Jessie's attention again for a moment. When she looked back at him she gave him a dulcet glance and picked up her water glass. Her cheeks were flushed.

She laid her napkin on her lap. A fraction of a second later, her eyes met his, a warm, soft smile touched the corners of her lips. A jolt of pure desire sizzled through him.

His heartbeat sped up as he said gruffly, "I want you very much, darling, so if you don't stop looking at me like that—"

She laughed, that deep, throaty, sexy-as-hell laugh

of hers. A couple of heads turned, people smiling reflexively with her. "Behave," she told him sternly.

Her mouth, pale and free of lipstick, tempted him beyond endurance. Damn her. "Impossible. You wore that red dress expressly to make me crazy. It did its job. Now you have to pay up."

He leaned forward for a brief taste of her smile, slanting his mouth over hers briefly. He felt the quick, unexpected flick of her tongue. Perhaps he'd better place busy restaurants on his dangerous locations list. Electricity shot through him and he jerked away from her potency. After a quick glance his way and a raised eyebrow, Jessie resumed eating.

Joshua enjoyed the delicate greed with which she consumed her meal. A silky strand of hair trailed down her shoulder. He was sorely tempted to pull out the rest of the pins and see how it would look tangled after their lovemaking. He grew harder just at the thought.

"Tell me about Paris," Jessie demanded, leaning forward. "What you like about it. What you hate. What does the city smell like? Did you walk along the Seine in the rain? What's the food like?"

Joshua laughed at her outpouring of questions. So Jessie. Having her focus her entire attention on him was intoxicating. In the flickering candlelight, her skin looked translucent and incredibly soft. Her long, elegant legs were hidden beneath the table, but he could feel the erotic brush of her foot against his calf.

Once the honeymoon part of the relationship ended, he wouldn't have to invest as much time and energy into getting her into bed any time he wanted her. He didn't like wasting the time *thinking* about sleeping with her. He wanted to *do* it, and then go back to concentrating on Falcon International.

He bought failing businesses, put a competent manager in place, and when the business was once again in the black, sold it off. Much like not having the emotional fortitude to bond with a woman, he didn't form emotional attachments to the companies he purchased, either. Everything about his life was controlled, planned and had a finite ending.

An ending of his own choosing.

It had been years since he had taken the time to slowly seduce a woman. It had been even longer since he had wanted a woman as much as he wanted Jessie. In fact, when he thought about it, he couldn't remember ever wanting another woman as much as he wanted Jessie. Nor could he remember one who actually listened without trying to impress him—which might explain his excruciating patience.

And the fact that he was still around. And very aroused.

Over the past several weeks, and mostly during transatlantic phone calls, he'd discovered they had many things in common: old movies, Japanese and Italian food and skiing. Joshua had no interest in skydiving, bungee jumping or spelunking. Jessie's love of dangerous sports appalled him. Not sure why, but wanting to understand this complicated woman better, he brought the topic up again.

"I don't get the fascination," he finally said, after she'd told him about a recent rock-climbing excursion. "What is it about the danger that turns you on?" Her skin looked soft, the bones in her slender hands almost fragile. He refrained from touching her. He wasn't a hand holder. Had never even thought about it before. He frowned. Even the idea of just holding this woman's hand had appeal.

"Everything." Her eyes looked mysteriously dark in the shimmering light. Her gaze skittered to the table next to them and back. The toddler was banging a spoon on the high chair tray.

"I suspect it's the same surge of adrenaline you get when you…when, you know, you're going to attempt a merger. That heady rush that tells you you're alive. That feeling of power can't be duplicated. I feel invincible…." She shrugged one slender shoulder. "It's hard to explain. Why don't you come with me the next time I go?" She gave him that mysteriously limpid look he couldn't fathom.

"Thanks," Joshua said dryly, picking up his wineglass and taking a sip. "I'll stick to mergers and acquisitions. At least I won't have any broken bones."

"Luckily, I haven't had any of those. Believe me, I'm not into physical pain. Just the rush."

"I don't like you doing anything that has the distinct possibility of leaving you dead or paralyzed." He didn't like the thought *a lot,* he thought scowling.

"I'm always careful." She viewed his concern with a strange expression in her dark eyes. "I've never had anyone worry about me before." Her lips curved in a poignant smile for a moment before she looked down at her lasagna, then back to meet his eyes. "I'll probably stop soon anyway." Something flickered behind those fathomless brown eyes again, then was gone.

"Somehow I doubt anyone could make you do something you didn't want to do." His tone was dry.

She picked up her wineglass. "With the right incentive—" she toasted him "—you'd be surprised."

"I LOATHE THAT MAN!" Jessie slammed the kitchen door at the main house and stormed into Conrad and Archie's family room.

Conrad hid a grin. "Another amicable dinner date?" He folded his newspaper on his lap.

"Grrr." Jessie started pacing. "This isn't in the least bit funny, you know. I've missed out a *gazillion* times because he keeps going on these blasted business trips. Damn it. I'm starting to *like* him!" Jessie flopped down in an easy chair cradling a cushion on her lap. "I don't want to like the blasted man. Don't look at me like that, Archie. I don't!" She grimaced. "At this rate I'll be old enough to be my baby's *grandmother* before we do it."

Archie hid his grin behind his book. Conrad managed to look mildly interested by keeping his expression bland. "Good Lord," he said, tongue-in-cheek. "Sounds like you might have to have a relationship before you fall into bed with each other. How novel."

Jessie stuck out her tongue at him. "How droll." She kicked off her shoes and pulled her legs under her. "Neither of us wants a *relationship*." She said it as if it were the plague. "I just want him to be in the right place at the right time, damn it."

CHAPTER THREE

THE LAZY DRIFT of fog gave an otherwordly charm to Pier 39, a picturesque tourist mecca of shops and restaurants down on Fisherman's Wharf. Jessie tucked her hand into the crook of Joshua's elbow and matched her stride to his. Moisture speckled Jessie's dark hair like liquid diamonds. Their footsteps echoed on the wooden boardwalk as they strolled companionably between tubs of brilliant early-flowering spring perennials and the inevitable camera-toting tourists.

Jessie tugged on Joshua's hand. "Come on. I want to go and see the seals."

She leaned over the railing to get a better look as the animals lolled about on custom-made platforms in the water. "Cute, huh?"

Joshua chuckled. "Yeah, really cute." He turned up the collar of her scarlet wool coat, his hands warm on her icy neck. "You're freezing." He tugged off the soft, warm scarf about his own neck and wrapped Jessie in it up to her eyebrows. She giggled. "How about a couple of gallons of hot coffee?"

"And pie?"

"And pie."

They walked quickly, and found a small coffee shop down a little jog in the boardwalk. The restaurant smelled warm and yeasty and was almost empty.

They selected a tiny, rickety round table with a view of the boats ferrying tourists out to Alcatraz Island and ordered their coffee before removing their coats.

"There are only about thirty choices. We could always order a slice of each," Joshua suggested politely as Jessie scanned the menu for the pie selections. She stuck out her tongue at him.

Joshua's eyes darkened. "I can think of more productive things to do with that."

"Wicked man." She turned to smile up at the kid who'd come to deliver their coffee and take their order. The young man almost stumbled into their table. Joshua sighed. Jessie had that effect on men of all ages.

Pie ordered, coats removed and coffee doctored, they lazily discussed the art show they'd seen together the week before, Joshua's recent trip to Japan, and a large commission Jessie had just started, a bed-and-breakfast in Marin.

The waiter delivered their order and faded away. Jessie picked up her fork, and then put it down again. She pressed a hand to her midriff.

"I'm terrified I'm going to let Conrad down." Absentmindedly, she began to tear a paper napkin into shreds. "The people who own the B-and-B also own a small vineyard in Napa. They're influential, and there's a good chance they'll send a lot of business Con's way if I do a good job." She fiddled with the strips of napkin she'd torn.

"I've seen your work, Jessie. You're a fine designer. They're lucky to have you."

Her cheeks pinked. "Really?"

"Really. But if worry is preventing you from sampling the delights of that lemon meringue p—"

"Oh, no you don't." Jessie pulled her plate closer and picked up her fork again.

She glanced up and, smiling, offered him a bite. He closed his lips around the tines of her fork. She was going to be under him tonight. She was going to feel the fires he'd been keeping banked explode into a fury of passion that was going to leave them both too weak to move.

"Thanks for sharing that with me." He was so turned on he felt feverish. He'd been on a slow boil for months. "I can see how much you enjoy your food. You consume enough for a linebacker and look like a nymph. God, where do you put it all?" His eyes traveled down her slender body to rest for a moment on her small breasts.

"Well, obviously not *there!*" Jessie blushed. "Look at the baby seals or something. I can't eat when you're staring at me like a lion about to devour his Bambi du jour."

"Hmm. Soft, succulent and tender pink."

Jessie rolled her eyes. Joshua calculated they'd be out in the cold another hour at the most. He had an excellent bottle of Cristal chilling at home. He regrouped. "Tell me how adorable you were as a child."

"I wasn't an adorable child at all. I was a homely, gangly child." She smiled. "Which made it tough to make friends. My mother and I moved constantly. We'd move from apartment to apartment, town to town, sometimes state to state, so I was always being shoved into a new school."

"Military?"

"Collection agencies," Jessie said dryly.

He frowned. "You were poor."

"I suppose so, although I didn't think about it at the time. Things were how they were."

"When did you start this love affair with food?" He couldn't wait to feel that avid little mouth all over him. Certainly, thinking of her sexually beat thinking of Jessie as being poor and wanting and having no one to care for her. For some reason picturing her that way pissed him off and made him feel…uncomfortable, damn it.

"Oh, way back. I learned to cook when I was six or seven because it was the only way I got to eat. My mom tended to forget little details like that. At one apartment, we had a wonderful Italian neighbor, sometimes she'd let me sit and watch as she prepared the family's evening meals. The stairwells used to smell incredible." She closed her eyes and inhaled deeply. "Garlic. Tomatoes. Yum. Hot, homemade sourdough bread. I used to sit on the bottom step outside their door and salivate. Just the *smell* of garlic is enough to make me remember that apartment on Ninth."

"God, Jessie." He'd never imagined her as a child, just a sensual woman, born to be made love to.

She waved away his sympathy. "Oh, don't feel sorry for me. Trust me, when I was a kid, it was all a wild adventure. I thought being hungry was normal. And I learned to make a mean spaghetti."

"That's child abuse."

"My mom? No. She didn't hurt me. She just—"

"Neglected you." Christ, no wonder she ate as she did; there would never be enough food in the world to a little girl who was starving. It explained her insistence on always getting a doggie bag even in the finest restaurants.

"It was a bit more complicated than that." Jessie

paused and bit her lip. Her eyes met his. "My mom hooked on the side to make ends meet. There. I said it. Phew. As a teenager, I began to hate her for what she was doing. For how we were forced to live. Basically, I was a huge oops. She never knew who my father was.

"She died six years ago. I didn't like or approve of her lifestyle, but I loved her." She looked at him, her eyes unusually bleak. "In an odd way, now that she's gone, I miss her. Family is important, Joshua. No matter what."

"Family," he repeated dispassionately, his eyes flat. "I thought mine was bad, but my life was a cakewalk compared to yours."

"Tell me. You never talk about anyone but Simon and your cousin, Paul the Playboy."

"Want another slice of pie?"

"Does the Pope wear a beanie?" She mouthed "Apple" to the waiter across the room, then turned back to fix Joshua in place with her chocolaty eyes. "Tell me all the Falcon family's dirty little secrets."

"Read the tabloids. They seem to have everything covered."

"Poo, they make up stuff. Thanks," she said as an aside to the waiter, who'd cut at least half the apple pie onto Jessie's plate. She picked up her fork. "Unless the story about you having an alien's love child is true?"

Joshua smiled. "I missed that one."

"They had pictures," Jessie mumbled around a mouthful of pie.

"Yeah?"

"Uh-huh." She swallowed. "No family resemblance. Talk."

I could've used someone in my life just like you,

Jessie Adams. Looking back, it seemed now to Joshua that he'd always been cold, physically and emotionally. "I was pretty much brought up by the servants before I was shipped off to boarding school," he said shortly, less comfortable when he was the one in the hot seat.

"Poor little rich boy."

Joshua stared at her for a moment before shaking his head. "Not at all. I had everything I wanted."

"Not quite. I bet you missed your mother."

"I missed her when I was *home.* She was always off somewhere. No, what I *wanted* was a Lionel train," he said, annoyed by her misinterpretation of his childhood. "What I *got* was a track that ran the perimeter of our thousand-acre estate with a train that required an engine driver and a full-time staff to keep it running. Not quite what I had in mind to take up to my room.

"Naturally I wanted what I perceived the 'normal' kids had. A yo-yo, or a blue Swiss Army knife, or the brown leather bomber jacket owned by one of the servants' kids. Stupid. I could've bought a hundred of each out of my allowance. But perversely it just wasn't the same. I finally figured out that none of that was the least bit important. I was well taken care of, had an exceptional education and learned, *eventually,* to relish hard work and responsibility instead of growing into a dilettante."

"Oh, Joshua…"

"On the other hand, what I'd really like, right now, is for you to come home with me."

Jessie smiled almost sadly. "Sorry, Romeo. Bad timing."

"Damn."

"You can say that again. How about another slice of pie?"

"WHEN'S THE NEXT DATE?" Archie asked her.

"Tonight. Listen, guys. Don't romanticize this. It's sex. Plain and simple." Except it was getting more complex every time she saw him. She shook her head as Archie started refilling her cup. "None for me, thanks." Jessie withdrew her palm from the rim of her cup then rose and rinsed it at the sink. Drying her hands, she said over her shoulder, "We're going to Noble's in the city. He said he has something special to celebrate tonight."

"Valentine's Day," Archie said cheerfully.

"He's going to get you into bed," Conrad said morosely, running his fingers through his blond hair.

"No, he's not," Jessie said grimly, hanging the towel she'd just used on the rack. "He can huff and puff, but he won't blow my house down." Then she smiled. "Not for two weeks, that is. Won't need to dig out the good underwear until then."

"Better run out and buy some *bad* underwear," Archie advised mischievously, giving her a wink.

Conrad walked over to Jessie and tilted her chin up. "Don't for a moment think The Glacier is going to make an honest woman of you. It isn't going to happen. You know it, we know it, and you can bet your sweet patoot the thought hasn't crossed his mind. I doubt the guy has ever eaten meat loaf in his life."

"In this case, I *am* an honest woman. I'm his wife. At least I am until I hand him the divorce papers. I don't want, or need *either* of us to fall in love," Jessie reminded him. "I just want my baby." *And to get out of this with my heart intact.*

"Then I'd suggest, love," Conrad said, softening his tone, "that instead of buying undies, you go back home and reread Falcon's press clippings before you take your temperature."

JOSHUA GAVE HER pink diamonds for Valentine's Day. He watched her reaction as they sat in a dim, candlelit booth at Noble's.

"Thank you so much, Joshua. These are beautiful. But I don't want you buying gifts for me." That unfathomable look came and went in her eyes.

"You don't like earrings?" he asked sardonically, it was clear she was delighted with the way the pendants brushed her neck.

He'd begun to realize that every gift he gave Jessie was a test. She couldn't possibly pass every one. Couldn't possibly be so genuinely pleased every time. No one was that good. He needed to bring what he was starting to feel when he was with her back down to a manageable level.

"I love earrings, the bigger, the better. And these are absolutely gorgeous." She touched a finger to one large pink drop. "What are these stones?"

"Diamonds."

Jessie flushed and he felt a need to taste the heat. He imagined warming his mouth against the fire in her cheeks.

"I mean the big pink stones."

"Diamonds," he repeated.

"Diamonds." Jessie went pale. "Oh, my God. Joshua! They must be…they're huge."

"Five carats." The receipt had been left in the bottom of the box, as he always instructed his secretary to do. He'd probably see them once more before they got "lost."

"Please, I love them, but I can't accept them." She yanked one off her ear with enough force to bruise. "I adore big, flashy *costume* jewelry. I'd be paranoid I'd lose these." She placed the earring on the table between them as if it would shatter.

Joshua picked it up and reinserted the post in her earlobe. After affixing the earring back, he stilled her other hand. "Keep them. They're insured." Conversation closed.

He felt the warmth of her thigh beside him on the banquette seat. She'd swept her hair up off her neck into a sexy chignon that defied gravity. The pink diamonds glinted in the soft lighting, casting rainbow prisms on her smooth cheeks. Candlelight danced in her eyes as she watched several couples moving slowly around the pocket-size dance floor. The pink jacket she wore rustled as she turned inquiring eyes up to his.

"Don't even ask," he murmured huskily, his breath making a curly tendril of hair dance against her cheek. He had no intention of dancing with her again until he had satiated himself with her body in bed. He was a ticking bomb as it was. "Hell, if I held you that close right now, I'd take you on the floor. Hard and fast."

She smiled that annoying as hell little enigmatic smile of hers. The one that turned the neurons in his brain to live wires and prepared his muscles for action.

"I want you," he murmured. "Right now." He restrained her fingers as she tried to pull away. "You've been holding me off far longer than I've ever waited for a woman."

The soft candlelight flickered on her face, bathing it in an apricot glow that made her dark eyes brilliant and drew his gaze to the sheen of wine on her mouth. She ran the tip of her tongue across her bottom lip and Joshua suppressed a groan. She leaned forward, her elbows on the table. The movement made the neckline of her jacket gape just enough to reveal the soft upper curve of her breasts. He dragged his eyes upward with reluctance and she made a small, low sound deep in her throat.

"I think you must put that stuff in my food when I'm with you." Her voice was so low he could barely hear her. "I've never felt like this in my life."

Joshua cleared his throat. "What stuff?"

Jessie's eyes were liquidly slumberous, and she blushed a velvety pink. "Spanish fly."

Joshua thought he would explode. "Spanish fly is actually cantharides made from the skeletons of beetles."

She grimaced.

Joshua held a laugh. "It causes itching all right, but not necessarily for sex." If possible, her blush got deeper, and she gave a small embarrassed groan. His body vibrated with need. "What we both have is an overdose of good old-fashioned lust." Then he lifted his glass. "To new beginnings."

"To new beginnings." Jessie clinked her glass against his, her smile brilliant before she blithely finished her shrimp.

Half her hair had escaped the pins, tangling with the heavy diamond drop earrings. Reaching out, he freed the silky filaments. His fingers lingered on her neck.

"You know we're going to be lovers, Jessie. God knows, I've been patient and waited long enough. I won't wait any longer. I'm not a man who waits very long for anything. I need an answer."

Jessie laid her hand on her purse, something she did often, almost as if it were a talisman. "You haven't asked me a question." She pushed the last bite of lemon meringue pie around her plate.

"I'm asking now."

"I'm not sure what the question is."

He pulled a folded document from his breast pocket, sliding it across the table. "I want you as my mistress, Jessie." Joshua's voice dropped another octave, his eyes kindling as he watched her mouth. He nudged the papers closer to her coffee cup.

Jessie eased her dry throat with a gulp of ice water. "What's this?"

"A contract. A legal, binding agreement." The sharp focus of his eyes reminded her of a bird of prey. "Read it."

"I'd rather you gave me a brief summary." Her hands balled into fists under the tablecloth. A contract! The bastard. And she'd been feeling guilty at how cold-bloodedly *she* was going about this.

"From now until the end of the year as my mistress," he said baldly, "I pay your rent. Buy your clothes. In exchange, you give me exclusive rights for the duration." Cut and dried. No mention of *his* fidelity.

She remembered Frankie, the fifteen-year-old who'd lived next door to them when she was thirteen. She'd had a huge crush on him. When she'd tried to steal a kiss, he'd called her a whore, like her mother. It had taken three other kids to pull her off him. She'd broken his nose and given him a black eye. She wondered how many people would be needed to pull her off Falcon.

"I'll think about your offer." She coolly pushed away her plate and reached for the leftover bread sticks. She filled her doggie bag then snapped two folds in the top to close it.

"You want me just as much as I want you."

Yes. And if I'd slept with you months ago this wouldn't hurt. "I can't tell you how sorry I am about that."

"Don't apologize for wanting me, Jessie. You're a sophisticated woman. You know the score. You want me and I, God knows, want you. You won't be sorry. I can be a generous lover." He tapped an earring with his finger. It grazed her neck and she felt the chill travel across her skin. "You won't want for anything in my care."

She took a calming breath. "You want me to sign a contract." It wasn't a question.

"What did you expect?" he asked, his face impassive. "A handshake and a gentleman's agreement?"

Jessie's laugh sounded brittle, even to her ears. "I can see why that wouldn't work. Neither one of us is a gentleman." She paused. "What happens after my time is up?" Her voice sounded oddly flat. "Do I just disappear, no questions asked, to that great graveyard for all your old mistresses?"

Joshua merely watched her. Suddenly angry—he was too damn cool!—Jessie shoved the papers back across the table. "I hate to be the one to disillusion you, Joshua, but not every woman finds you irresistible. I thought I could do this but, no, thank you."

This was too impersonal, too calculating. She'd

thought she could handle this part of it, but she'd been wrong. Dangerously wrong. *A little late in the day, Jessie,* she taunted herself.

"I want more than this. I deserve more than this."

"Ten thousand a month."

"W-what!"

"Ten thousand a month, tax free. An apartment and your clothes. And a car."

Jessie gritted her teeth. "I wasn't talking about mon—"

"Twelve thousand. And that's my final offer."

Black dots blurred Jessie's vision. "You can take those papers and shove them—"

Grabbing her purse and paper bag, she stood. Joshua gripped her wrist tightly as she tried to sweep past him. With his other hand, he picked up the contract. "Take this. Read it. I'll give you two weeks to decide."

Jessie stared down at him, her breathing erratic. "One of my best qualities," she said frigidly as she tugged her hand away, "is that I make up my mind quickly. You're a self-righteous bastard, and I'm immeasurably grateful that I didn't fall into bed with you. You're a cold, arrogant—" her breath came out in a rush, her heart pounding so fast she thought she might faint "—jerk," she finished.

She had to get out of here. Now. Her cold hands took the papers from him, folding and then refolding them. Then she twisted them into a tight tube. "Here." She shoved them against his chest. "Try this for size!"

The contract slowly unfurled and dropped to his lap. His fingers tightened painfully on her wrist. "Jessie…"

She shook off his hand, removed the earrings, laid

them carefully next to his coffee cup, then walked swiftly out of the restaurant.

BLAST THE MAN. Couldn't he do *anything* right! On each of her fertile days in January he'd been out of town. In February, he'd been gone at the wrong time again. In a couple more weeks all systems would've been go. With any luck, they would've been in the same place at the same time.

Instead he had to go and irritate her so darn much she'd almost punched his arrogant nose. Jessie wanted to throw up her hands in disgust.

She turned into her driveway. This was a case of "be careful what you ask for." And, God, had she asked for this. An icy wind rattled the car. Jessie laid her arms across the top of the steering wheel and stared sightlessly at her cottage. The ache in her chest made her lay her forehead down and squeeze her eyes shut.

She had been so close. So damn close. Tears of frustration and disappointment seeped between her eyelids. She slammed her fist down on the steering wheel. "I want my baby." Her voice broke and she pounded the wheel again. "You promised me my heart's desire. You *owe* me my baby, damn you."

She lifted her head and stared at the dark, swaying treetops beside her cottage. Joshua Falcon approached a personal relationship exactly as he did a business merger. Why had she been surprised? For him, they were one and the same.

She had two more weeks to calm down. She'd go to

him on her first fertile day, she thought grimly, gritting her teeth.

She'd seduce him.

If she didn't kill him first.

CHAPTER FOUR

JESSIE RANG THE ornate bell outside Joshua's downtown San Francisco condo. He'd mentioned he rarely went home during the week, preferring to stay in his penthouse apartment in the Falcon building to driving the forty minutes to his house outside of town.

She'd dressed with care in a short, moss-green ultrasuede skirt suit that did flattering things to what few curves she had, and high heels of the same color. She'd swept her hair away from her face with combs and left it to fall down her back in a tumble of natural curls. On her ears, she had her lucky four-leaf clovers. In her purse, her lucky divorce papers. She was all set.

Her heart thudded as she heard approaching footsteps. The front door opened. Joshua surveyed her without expression, his sexy mouth grim.

Jessie's heart sank to her toes, that is, until she noticed his eyes fixed on *her* mouth. For a moment, their gazes locked. Her temperature immediately spiked.

"You took your sweet time." He pushed the door open. Without seeing if she followed, he turned and strode across the wide marble entry. He disappeared into another room, leaving Jessie to close the door and follow him.

The living room was expansive, with a breathtaking night view of the city and the necklace of lights on the Golden Gate Bridge. During the day, the panorama would be just as spectacular. A black granite fireplace took up space between the wide windows, pewter andirons reflecting a blazing fire.

Papers and file folders were spread across a granite-and-chrome coffee table the size of a small room. A plate with an untouched sandwich had been pushed aside and replaced with a telephone and notepad. Joshua stood at a built-in bar across the room. He turned as she moved across the thick carpet. "White wine?"

"I'd rather have a Coke."

He added ice to a glass and poured her drink. They both seemed fascinated by the building foam.

"Thanks." Jessie took the glass he handed her, pleased by how cool her voice sounded. *How very civilized we are.*

Without invitation, she sat down, the glass pressed between her palms. The leather quickly warmed to her body temperature as the upholstery enveloped her. Too comfortable. She shifted to the edge of the plump cushions as Joshua lounged on the plush sofa opposite, watching her with disconcertingly hooded eyes.

Jessie's experienced eye took in the vast room. Everything was technically correct. The paintings and sculptures were expensive and well showcased beneath discreet spotlights. The wine-colored carpet, bordered with alternating bands of cream and black, stretched across the enormous room to the windows. Stiffly formal tied-back drapes matched the carpet. No one could see into the windows twenty-two stories above the city. Three butter-soft black leather sofas made a U, facing the fireplace and the two windows with an incredible view of the downtown lights.

There was absolutely no life in the room.

"Conrad did a fantastic job, but whoever did your decorating must have been an android." Architecturally, Conrad had had carte blanche, unlimited funds and a client who had no interest in the project until it was finished. In other words, as far as Con was concerned, a perfect client. Unfortunately, Joshua must have given the designer the same blank check.

Jessie, however, preferred her clients' involvement with the project from start to finish. She wanted them to invest more than their money. When Jessie was done with a house, it was a home. *Their* home. Stamped with *their* personality.

Joshua's eyebrow rose at her android comment. "This is a business residence." He didn't glance around. His attention was one hundred percent on Jessie. "It suits me perfectly."

They *were* talking about interior design...weren't they? "I didn't mean to disturb you." She lifted her chin a notch, intending to do just that—disturb this man of ice until he melted. If she didn't do him bodily harm first. She gave him a limpid glance from under her lashes.

At first glance, his gaze could give her frostbite. *This* was why he was called The Glacier. His expression had not changed one iota since she'd walked into the room. With that icy glare, he'd unknowingly just declared war. She smiled inwardly, because Jessie knew that just beneath that hard, frigid exterior lay the real Joshua Falcon. And she was determined to chip away the solid ice to unearth the lava below. Not enough to get burned herself, of course. But enough to keep Joshua hot and bothered until she had what she wanted. Then he could freeze over again.

"You've disturbed me since I met you, Jessie," Joshua admitted dryly. "You better have come to tell me yes. If not, run like hell." His voice was low and rough.

His eyes met hers—*Oh! Not so cool, after all*—pale and hot, as he scanned her body as though she were naked. "I'm not waiting another second for you."

"No?" Her cheeks flushed as she struggled to regulate her breathing, and she covered the rapid pulse beating at the base of her throat with her hand. It was hard to remember that *she* was the one in control when he looked at her like that. The air between them heated another fifty degrees. Her nipples pressed against her bra, and her skin felt sunburned as her temperature rose.

Their gazes locked as he lifted his glass to his mouth. "Why *are* you here?" The muscles moved in his throat as he swallowed, his pale eyes unblinking as he watched her. That stare was as primal as being pinned in place by the hypnotic stare of a large, dark panther. *I'm going to have you,* it said. *I'm going to devour you from heart to toes. I'm going to start right there at that frantic pulse in your throat and work my way down....*

Foolish imagination. Wishful thinking.

Jessie heard the thudding beat of her heart in her ears. *Down, girl.* This was purely business and biological for Joshua. She had to remember that.

Well, so what? It was the same for her, wasn't it?

Then why was her heart beating much too rapidly? And why were her palms damp? And why were her nipples aching with longing? And why, God help her, could she feel moisture gathering between her legs?

"You gave me two weeks, Joshua," she answered mildly, *and the timing is perfect.* She crossed her legs, and noticed Joshua's hand tightened on his glass as his eyes followed the movement.

"Have *you* changed your mind?" She held her breath waiting for his answer. It was slow in coming.

"No. But I am curious as to why you've changed yours."

Jessie shrugged, and her nipples rubbed against the inside of her bra, sending a shudder rippling through her body. She swallowed hard and held his gaze with some difficulty. How had she ever thought his eyes were cold? They smoldered, hot and clear. She swallowed again and managed to say calmly enough, "It's a woman's prerogative."

"I'm still a… What did you so aptly call me the other day? A self-righteous bastard?"

"And a cold, arrogant jerk." Jessie filled in helpfully. "But I'm here anyway."

"Why?"

"I'm *madly* in love with you." *Madly in love with the idea of walking out of here pregnant.*

"Don't be." His voice was ice-cold, in marked contrast to his eyes and the pulse leaping at his strong tanned throat.

Jessie opened her eyes wide. "Okay, I'm not madly in love with you." *And I plan to keep it that way, too.* A woman would have to be insane to allow herself to become that vulnerable around him. And, Jessie knew, if she didn't have this powerful desire to have closure with her husband, if she didn't want to have his baby, if she had any sense at all, quite frankly, she'd be running as far and fast as she could. And she'd mail him the divorce papers from Timbuktu.

But she *needed* closure.

She *wanted* her baby.

Nobody was going to get hurt.

Joshua would have what he wanted.

She'd have what she needed.

And, God only knew, their attraction was undeniable.

"Have you ever been in love?" she asked, curious if anything had ever dented this man's heart.

"I love my business."

"That's not the same thing."

"It's all I need," he said shortly. "Can we get on with this?" He gave her a penetrating look, then rose to cross the room. Opening a drawer in the desk, he returned with a crumpled sheaf of papers. "Is this what you came for, Jessie?" His gaze fastened on her mouth, then slid, tactile as a caress, up to her eyes. "To sign this?"

Jessie kept her gaze steady by changing her focus so he was a blur. It was hot in here. She wished he'd open a window, or put the fire out...or touch her. Why did she have this sudden compunction to touch him? To taste those stern lips? To run her fingers through his neatly combed hair? She curled her fingers against her palms. What had he asked? *Contract.* "Actually, no."

"Then what the hell are you doing here?" Joshua abruptly came back into focus as he tossed the rolled-up contract onto the coffee table. It unfurled slowly.

Jessie drew a deep breath and said calmly, "I won't sign that contract, but I will sleep with you." Now. Immediately. Soon? Oh, please make it *soon.*

"I won't marry you."

Jessie raised her brows. "Who asked you to?" She made a moue of distaste. "I have no desire to get married. We can sleep together until I…" *conceive my baby* "…we tire of each other. A few days or weeks…" She shrugged. The movement rasped her hard nipples against the silky fabric of her bra. She couldn't control the shudder this time.

"A year."

"Too long-term for me."

"Long-term?" A muscle ticked in his jaw. "*Twelve months?*"

"That's *far* too long." Jessie's laugh was sophisticated and light, with just enough mockery. "Besides, we both know that kind of contract wouldn't hold up in a court of law anyway."

He let that ride, watching her with sparkling hot eyes. "Don't you at least want to know the terms?"

Jessie sipped her drink, letting the sweet fizz slide down her throat as she watched him over the rim of her glass. "No." Anticipation sang in her veins, giving her a rush of warmth that made it hard to keep up the casual facade. Now that the hard part was out of the way she should feel more relaxed; instead her nerves were stretched to the snapping point. He wanted her just as much as ever.

Her mouth went dry despite the soda, and she swept her tongue over her lower lip. His gaze fastened on her mouth and his eyes grew heavy lidded. Jessie felt that look in every pulse point of her body.

"Why are you doing this, Jessie?"

"I told you I'm madly in lo—"

Joshua ran his fingers through his hair in utter exasperation. "You're not in love with me, for God's sake!"

Almost drunk with desire, and giddy with triumph, Jessie was starting to enjoy herself. "Oh, yes. I forgot. I'm definitely *not* in love with you." She choked back laughter as his fingers clenched on his knee. Carnal-induced adrenaline raced through her, her skin humming with it. She relished the stroke of fabric across her nipples, and craved Joshua's mouth there. Hot and wet...

"I have a dinner date in an hour," she told him casually. "Is there anything I should know before I go?"

His jaw clenched. *Direct hit.*

"The contract was supposed to be twelve months. January 1 to December 23. It's March. We've wasted time."

Hey, not my fault. Jessie looked at her glass instead of glaring at him. If he hadn't kept going out of town at the most crucial moments, this conversation would've been history. She could be home right now with her feet up, knitting something adorable.

"Darn, we've missed two months. No extension for good behavior?" Jessie asked with a little bite in her voice. She wished he'd stop talking and touch her. She might not be in love with him, but she was definitely in lust. Who knew lust could be this big? This overwhelming?

Her fingers dug into the soft leather and she crossed her legs again, then quickly uncrossed them. God, she'd never experienced anything like this in her life. Surely it wasn't natural. He hadn't even touched her and her body was on fire. She tried to focus. "What if *you* want to extend it?"

"I won't," he answered unequivocally. "The agreement gives us each exclusive rights. No one else. So forget your dinner date tonight," he inserted in a hard voice.

"Fine." She wanted his hands on her bare skin, on her fever-hot breasts, on her aching nipples. She wanted his mouth…everywhere. She felt the flush of heat rise to her cheeks and swallowed a moan. What was he saying…? "As long as you understand that *I* won't share you, either."

A wicked gleam flared in his eyes. "Jealous, Jessie?"

"No," she said firmly and drank the last of her soda before setting the empty glass on the table beside her chair. "Just fastidious. I want to be sure we understand each other clearly. I won't cheat on you, and I expect the same from you. One slip, and I'll consider the arrangement over."

Her gaze was steady, her heartbeat off the chart.

"I'll take care of birth control."

"I've already taken care of it," Jessie said calmly.

"Fine. I have a condo in the Sunset district. I want you to move in there immediately."

"No, thank you. I have a perfectly nice cottage. And my studio is there. I'm not going to disrupt my whole life for just a few months." *Once,* Jessie thought longingly. *Just once should do it.*

The air around them shimmered with sexual arousal. He was leaning forward, his elbows on his knees as he watched her through hooded eyes. He had the sexiest mouth. She pressed two fingers to her lips. A muscle throbbed in his cheek.

"I won't sleep with you there. Not under Archie's and Conrad's overprotective eyes. You'll have to come to wherever I am."

Jessie saluted smartly. "Yes, sir." She held back a scream of frustration. *Hurry up, for heaven's sake, I'm internally combusting here!*

"I don't like actually sleeping with a woman in my bed. When the alarm goes off, Barlow will take you home."

"Wham-bam, thank you, ma'am?" *Yes! Wham me. Bam me. Anytime in the next ten seconds would be fine.*

"Your choice."

Jessie sighed. "What time will I have to get up to go home?"

"Three."

"In the morning?"

"Your choice."

"You said that already. Fine—3:00 a.m."

"I'll concede the point of your staying at your cottage, as long as you're available when I need you."

"I sincerely doubt that you'll ever *need* anyone, Joshua." *And at the rate we're going, I'll have to wait another month before we do anything, in which case I'll go stark raving mad.*

"And don't get any romantic ideas about love," he said crisply. "This is merely a business transaction."

"It certainly looks that way. I've never met anyone who keeps his emotions so tightly under wraps. No wonder they call you The Glacier." Jessie wondered what he'd do if she grabbed him by the collar and pulled him onto the floor.

"You're not required to understand me. All I want is a mutually satisfying sexual arrangement."

Jessie wanted to throw up her hands. It was easy to believe the man was made of solid, mile-deep ice— if one didn't see his eyes, which were as hot as laser beams. His control was absolutely phenomenal. "I'd feel more…comfortable if you showed at least a little emotion about this. I know I'm not the only one whose hormones go into overdrive when we're together. Do you feel nothing emotionally at all?" Her feet were starting to get decidedly cold. Oh, Lord. What had she been thinking?

"I feel damn primitive about you."

"You don't show it." Jessie put a little taunt in the words.

"If I lost control, you wouldn't be able to walk for a week."

Jessie was determined he would not only not be able to walk for a week, she was now bound and determined she was going to push this coldhearted man right over the edge. She almost rubbed her hands in anticipation, but instead she kept her casual demeanor. "So, let me recap this so we both know where we stand. Fidelity for the duration. For both of us. We'll have sex at your place and the chauffeur will take me home at three in the morning. Does that about cover it?" Jessie asked, not giving a damn, because at the outside that would happen twice.

"As long as I don't have to wear corporate colors." She glanced around the burgundy, black and silver room.

"I buy your clothes."

"I'll buy my own clothes."

"Consider the wardrobe I furnish a uniform then."

"I don't suppose this job has a pension plan—401K maybe? How about medical, dental, profit sharing?"

"You're damn cool about this," Joshua snapped, torn between admiration and irritation. When had he lost control of this conversation? Forget all this damn *talking*. The arrangement was a fait accompli. God, he wanted to go over there, grab her and carry her off to the bedroom like a primitive caveman.

The material of her dress looked butter soft, but not as soft as her pale skin. He could clearly see the sharp points of her nipples through the fabric. He controlled the burning need to leap across the space separating them and feast on her breasts through the fabric. He wanted to rip away her clothes and taste her body. He needed to plunge deep inside her, and feel her hot, wet heat close around him.

He felt as hot and horny as he had at fifteen when he'd seen his first naked woman. He could control himself. God help him, he could. But it had never been this difficult. He was scared to move in case he lost it.

"Yes, I am, aren't I?" Jessie folded her hands loosely in her lap and looked at him with dark, steady eyes. She tapped her fingers on her purse. Her control sent his blood pressure soaring. He'd been restless and edgy the moment he'd opened the door and seen her there. So much for his being The Glacier. What the hell was it about this woman that brought out this latent, primitive need to ravish her? He had been sexually attracted to women before. It had taken very little willpower to control his urges around them.

"Are we done talking?" he demanded through clenched teeth.

"I guess…"

With a swift move that took her completely by surprise, Joshua rose, stalked the three steps between his seat and hers, grabbed her by her shoulders and dragged her from her seat. He crushed her little yelp of surprise beneath his mouth.

It started as a kiss of mastery and domination. He wanted her to know that he was the one in control. She was his, damn her. But the moment Jessie realized what he was doing, her body relaxed against his. Her arms came up around his neck, one hand threading through his hair.

Her action softened the kiss. God, her mouth felt so damn good. He forgot just what it was he was trying to prove. She tasted sweet, her lips soft, her tongue aggressive. The suede fabric beckoned his hands. She smelled of fresh air and Joy. Enticing, and so female. She felt so incredibly good in his arms. He buried one hand in the silken mass of her hair, alive beneath his questing fingers. His other hand caressed the slender dip of her waist, the slight curve of her hip, the enticing firmness of her behind, pulling her more tightly against his agonizingly aroused body.

Joshua sighed against her mouth as her tongue came out and, as delicate as a cat, traced his lips. His hands tightened against her back. "The deal is made," he whispered hoarsely against her throat as his fingers found the concealed buttons of her suit jacket and started undoing them with fervent haste.

"There's one more thing," he growled against the fragrant curve of her throat. Her hands were driving him wild as she struggled to rip his shirt from his pants. He gently bit and she made a jerky little moaning sound that drove him wild.

"W-what?" Jessie's voice was a mere thread of sound, then faded completely as her hands encountered the naked skin of his chest. One hand slid up his back, trailing her short nails down the deep groove of his spine. The other hand slipped lower. Down his belly, her nails cool against his hot skin. She managed to unzip his pants. Her pale skin was flushed, her eyes heavy lidded and as dark as chocolate as she held his gaze.

"Don't ever... My God, Jessie," he groaned as her fingers cupped his sex. "Don't ever...ah, woman!... don't ever look at another man. I'd kill him."

"Fine," Jessie replied weakly as she helped him tear the buttons off her jacket.

"Twelve thousand dollars a month."

Her mouth inched over his face back to his lips. "Ten...thousand. You...said...ten..." She used her tongue to open his lips while her jacket fell unheeded to the carpet behind her.

Joshua cupped her bottom, pulling her hard into the cradle of his thighs and firmly against his erection. Unable to stay away from her succulent mouth, he kissed her again. "Twelve," he groaned, and she bit lightly at his lower lip.

Her knees buckled as he stripped off her skirt.

"I...don't...need your..." His fingers slipped beneath her panty hose. "Money." The nylon slithered down her legs and she swayed against him. "I—" she punctuated each word with a nibbling kiss wherever she could reach "—have...my...w-work." The words came out against his navel.

Joshua groaned. "Fine." His fingers tangled in her hair. "Fine," he said again, distracted as her fingers dragged down his shorts, deliberately skimming his rock-hard erection on the way down. Too gentle. Too fleeting. "Oh, God. That's just fine."

They dropped to the floor in a tangled heap of clothes and limbs, him on top of her. Joshua pulled her face up to his for a searing kiss that rocked them both. "You're going to kill me."

Jessie kicked herself free of the skirt and panty hose tangled around her ankles and tugged his shirt over his broad shoulders. Now he was gloriously naked, too. "Can't," she said fiercely, her hands skimming his wide, hair-roughened chest. "I'm…not…finished… with…you…yet!"

His laugh was muffled by the fascinating silky texture of her right breast, small and perfect. He brushed his lips over one tight nipple, then opened his mouth and closed his teeth around the hard point, and sucked it into the hot, wet cavern of his mouth. Jessie's back arched off the floor.

She twisted her head to nip his shoulder. He tasted of soap and salt. The scent of him went to her head like fine wine. The carpet scratched her naked back, but she didn't care. It was far more fascinating to feel Joshua's chest hairs scraping the sensitive nerves of her breasts and belly.

"Is there…any…thing…ah!…else?" Her lips parted, and she inhaled deeply, her eyes almost closed as she felt the damp heat of his mouth laving her breast. Suck. Lick. Suck… A sharp, sweet sensation shot to her groin. She panted for breath. His fingers felt slightly rough, *hot,* on her skin as he caressed her other breast with his hand, while devouring her with his mouth, teeth and tongue.

"Not…that…I…can…think of…at…the moment. God, you taste sweet." He shifted his head to pay tribute to her other breast. His soft, dark hair tickled her

skin as he shifted, and Jessie got goose bumps. She
slid her fingers through his hair, feeling the heat of
his scalp through the cool, silky strands as she held
his head to her breast.

Jessie sighed with pleasure as Joshua licked a path
between her breasts. Hot and slick, his tongue traced
a sensuous path down the center of her body, making
her burn and shiver by turns.

He looked up the length of her body. "Touch your
breasts, Jessie. Close your eyes. Play with those pretty
nipples, and pretend your hands are mine."

Jessie squeezed her eyes shut and cupped her aching breasts in her palms. Her nipples felt exquisitely
hard. She pressed down. God, it felt good. Relieved
a little of the urgency. She felt Joshua's smile against
her tummy, and took her nipples between her fingers,
squeezing and rolling as Joshua's hot mouth slid down
her body. His hands trailed a burning path down her
sides, a beat slower than his lips.

Jessie's body quaked, and she groaned softly as his
mouth brushed the nest of curls at the juncture of her
thighs. She felt a brief moment of panic and clutched
a handful of his hair. But what he was doing was so
incredible that her fingers sifted through the silky
strands, anchoring his head in place instead.

His strong hands cupped her hips, and her body
trembled as his tongue parted her. She shifted, murmuring with intense arousal as he sucked and licked
her clit, his shoulders keeping her legs apart. Her head
thrashed on the floor. She needed more. Less. *More,*
damn it. She grabbed handfuls of his hair as he plunged
his tongue deep.

The pleasure was sharp and riveting and left her

breathless. His fingers would leave bruises on her hips tomorrow, but she didn't care. She couldn't quite catch her breath. Couldn't quite get her mind to work.

A low throbbing began in her belly, then spiraled hot and delicious when he moved his hand around from her bottom to slide to the inside of her thigh. His finger filled her. Her muscles convulsed around it. A second finger joined the first, Jessie moaned low at the sensation of fullness. His damp mouth returned to her clit, and tongue and fingers worked together in a magical, maddening dance that had her breathless and poised on the brink.

His fingers rotated, he sucked harder, and Jessie let out a wild cry as she came in a hard, sharp spasm that lasted an eternity. Her fingers fisted in his hair, and for a moment everything went black.

When she managed to open her eyes, she saw his face above her. She raised a leaden arm and looped it around his neck, drawing him up. His body was heavy, damp with exertion.

The slide of his body against hers made her pulse leap higher and faster. He kissed her, and she tasted herself on his lips. His tongue bladed into her mouth, hot and slick, demanding and insistent. Jessie had never been kissed like this. Never been the focus of anyone's attention to this degree. It was intoxicating. He was intoxicating. She slid her tongue against his, mimicking his movements.

He braced his elbows on the floor on either side of her, but his lower body, and thick pulsing shaft, lay heavy and welcome between her legs.

Snap out of it! Jessie cautioned herself, horrified at her response to him. She hadn't wanted to enjoy his lovemaking quite that much. "More," she demanded, when she was finally capable of speech. She shifted her hips.

"More?"

Terrified by the depth of emotion she'd just experienced, Jessie's heart started pounding for an entirely different reason as she started to panic. She couldn't afford to form any sort of emotional attachment to Joshua Falcon.

She couldn't. Wouldn't. Must not.

She was here for one thing. And one thing only. Oral sex wasn't going to cut it.

Please don't bind me to you. Just have sex with me, and keep it impersonal. Please. Ha, fat chance! As her mother used to say, "Be careful what you wish for. You might get it." Jessie was getting far more than she'd bargained for when she'd taunted the devil into making love to her.

"Finish it," Jessie begged. She had to have sex and get out. She wanted to run far, far away.

"Patience." Joshua smoothed her hair back from her damp brow, his eyes softer than she had ever seen them. "I want to look at you. You're so beautiful. Beautiful and so damned responsive. The perfect mistress."

Yes, Jessie thought, an odd twinge pinching her heart. *That's what I am, a mistress. A business arrangement. Give me what I want, and I'll give you what you want. A fair trade...*

Oh, God. Please don't take more than my body.

Jessie tugged at his shoulders until his heavy, welcoming weight covered hers. She reached down and closed her fingers around the hard length of his penis. It felt thick and long, silky and...alive. "I want you deep inside me," she begged, not at all sure that her body could accommodate him now that she felt the size of him. Oh, God. What if it didn't fit?

"It'll fit just fine. Trust me," Joshua murmured against her throat, and Jessie realized she must've said her thought out loud.

With a hoarse cry, he slid into her slick heat. Jessie gasped as he filled her, stretched her slowly. Oh, so slowly… "Oh, yes…give…me…baby," she panted hoarsely.

He plunged deep.

Jessie hissed out a surprised breath at the sharp sting, froze, then tried to arch away. For a moment the pain was so intense she gave a keening cry, her nails digging into his bare back. He didn't stop, and she was fiercely glad. "More. More. More," she chanted as she adjusted to his width and length. "I want you. I want you. I want you."

His large hands clamped on her hips, and he gave her a feral smile, filled with triumph. "You have me." He began to move again, his thrusts sliding her body on his shaft in a slick, thrilling roller-coaster climb of sensation.

His thrusts grew stronger, deeper, harder. Jessie wrapped her legs around his pistoning hips, and dug her heels into his lean flanks, feeling the bunch and clench of his muscles.

The sensation was too intense to bear. Jessie's head thrashed on the carpet. Her body felt too tight to remain whole. "I can't…"

"You want more?" he demanded, jaw tight with the strain, dark hair sticking to his sweaty forehead. His pale gaze ate her whole.

Jessie tried to focus her eyes. "No. Yes."

He slid in deeper. "Yes?"

She moaned.

He slid out almost all the way. "No?"

She wrapped her arms more tightly around his shoulders and held his hips in place with her legs. "Bastard."

"True. But is that a yes, or a no?" He thrust deep.

"Yes, yes, yes," she panted. Her hips met each plunge, her body straining for release. Her long hair tangled across her damp face and chest. She ran her hands down the slick, hard plane of Joshua's back, feeling the flex and twist of his muscles beneath the satin of his skin. She dug her short nails into his hips. "Now," she begged, hoarse and breathless, body on fire. "Please. I can't take any more."

"No." He kept moving. Changing the rhythm, changing the speed, changing the depth of his thrusts until she was about to come. Then he'd back off slightly until the moment passed, leaving her body screaming for release.

"Now. Now. Now," Jessie gasped, breathless and dizzy.

"Now?"

"Yes, damn it! Now!" she said hitching her hips and clamping her heels down to bring him in harder. One more deep thrust, she thought, just one more...

He slid a hand between their sweat-slick bodies and touched her, rubbing a finger in her moisture.

"Joshua!" Jessie's body immediately convulsed, and she cried out as she climaxed hard and fast.

Joshua continued his deep pounding rhythm until his cry echoed hers.

He collapsed against her, turning their joined bodies so they lay side by side on the plush carpet. Then he cradled her trembling body to his, his hands making broad tender sweeps down her naked back. His breath was harsh in her ear as she melted under his touch.

"Is it always like that?" Jessie was caught unaware by a yawn, and snuggled into the safe harbor of his arms. His laughter vibrated through her. Her eyes were too heavy to open as he brushed a kiss across her hair.

"No, usually it's not quite as hard and fast. Sometimes it's long and slow." Amazingly he felt himself swell inside her again. Joshua moved his hips slowly, enjoying the sleepy warmth of her.

"Give it to me, baby?" he asked, amused, and her eyes narrowed before she shrugged and glanced away.

She closed her expressive eyes and relaxed beneath him. "I watch a lot of movies, what can I say?"

"The dialogue is vast and varied." He assured her dryly, "We'll have time to explore every nuance of postcoital conversation." He glanced down to see the steady rise and fall of her beautiful breasts and realized with amusement that, contract or not, she was his new mistress, and she was fast asleep.

Using a gentle touch, he traced the perfect symmetry of her face, still flushed and damp from their lovemaking. With gentle mockery, he whispered softly, "Nice of you to forewarn me you were a virgin, Jessie."

JESSIE WASN'T USED to answering to anyone. Especially someone who had sent her home at an ungodly hour the morning after with his stony-faced chauffeur, then called her the next day as if nothing earth-shattering had happened. Her car had been delivered back to the cottage by invisible pixies in the middle of the night.

Joshua had called to tell her he would be in New York for two days. He'd left two messages on her answering machine while she'd been out seeing clients. She'd wanted to ask him if sex with her had been so bad he had to flee the state. She hoped to God that their lovemaking had taken. She didn't think she could go through it again. The intensity of climax with him had been almost terrifying. It had left her shattered and shaky and not quite as confident about her own control of the situation.

Jessie pulled her car into the narrow road leading up to the gatehouse. She'd been single-mindedly concentrating on a hot, steamy bath for the last hundred miles.

It was midnight, and she was absolutely exhausted. She'd gone to see a client in Redding, three hours away, leaving early enough to beat the commute traffic in San Francisco and arriving at the client's small ranch just in time for breakfast.

After she and Karen King had talked drapes and case goods, the two women had wandered outside to see the show horses Karen and her husband bred. Their animals had won competitions from Canada to Brazil. Peter's den was filled with trophies and ribbons.

The last time she'd been out here, Karen had put her up on a placid cow pony and she'd laughingly complained. She'd expected a nice, civilized ride this time, too. But Karen, knowing her preference for a challenge, had put her up on Billy. By the time she realized that she and the horse had completely different ideas, it was too late. She had the bruises to prove it.

Jessie was surprised to find Joshua parked outside her cottage—hadn't even noticed his car at first. She'd forgotten to leave the porch light on. The bitter cold hit her as she got out of her car. The wind snapped the bare branches overhead, and moaned around her solid little stone cottage.

The windows of his Jag were steamed and so, apparently, was he.

"Where the hell have you been?" he demanded, slamming out of his car and following her to the front door.

Jessie unlocked the door but didn't push it open. "I *beg* your pardon?" She had a feeling he was going to be the last straw of her day. Joshua stretched over her, pushing the door ajar and following her inside where it was blessedly warm.

"You heard what I said." He started unbuttoning her kelly-green wool coat as soon as the door slammed shut behind them.

"Yes, but I didn't believe my ears," she said crossly, too tired to move. He was awfully quick with those buttons. The back of his fingers brushed her breasts and her nipples stood up to attention. "Did you need me today?"

"What's wrong with…" he started, obviously perplexed by her waspish attitude. Until he saw the condition of her jeans and sweater as he drew off her coat. His pale eyes narrowed. The jeans had been old to start with. They had merely attained an extra patina of real hard work this afternoon. The poor sweater was another matter. Ripped and mangled, it was going to be fed into the trash as soon as she had the energy to do it.

"Who did this to you?" Joshua demanded with deadly calm, carefully drawing the tattered sweater over her head. Jessie couldn't hold back the wince as the sleeve pressed against her arm.

For the last several hours, on the drive home, Jessie had fantasized about a long soak in a hot bath, not an interrogation. She looked up at his hard face, curious to see his reaction. "Billy," she said sadly.

"Billy?" Joshua repeated coldly as he paused in his perusal of her Technicolor ribs.

Jessie sighed. "Bucking Billy. The cad. The *horse,*" she emphasized, only because she was too tired to clobber him. "He has no idea how to show a lady a good—"

"Billy is a horse?"

Jessie gave him a dirty look. It was weak, but still, she hoped, conveyed her feelings on the subject. "Didn't we make a verbal agreement the other night?"

"Yes," Joshua ground out.

"Well then, why would you think I'd be the first to break it?" *You big jerk!*

"Excuse me," he said stiffly. "I forgot your propensity for danger."

The most dangerous thing Jessie could think of right now was their proximity to the kitchen with its myriad sharp instruments. She sighed. Murdering him now would make life so complicated. Besides, she'd need energy for that. She heaved another put-upon sigh.

Joshua gave her an odd look. "Have you seen a doctor?" He did both a visual and tactile search, his hands cool and unbelievably gentle as they skimmed her body. His eyes were hot and hard. "Do you *need* to see a doctor?"

"No and no." She needed more than his impersonal fingers on her skin. Jessie looked up at him. "I don't know the procedure here. What am I supposed to do when I want you to hold me? Do I have to wait for sex?" She saw his lips twitch. "Because, believe me, as much as I loved what we did on Saturday night, I have to tell you I don't think…"

"Oh, I think I can handle a little light touching without resorting to my basic animal instinct to throw you down and have my wicked way with you."

His touch was gentle as he wrapped his arms around her, but Jessie had never felt anything as wonderful in her life. His firm lips brushed hers. Too lightly, too slowly.

Jessie deepened the kiss herself. What she lacked in experience, she made up for with enthusiasm. Her tongue explored his mouth, and he groaned, holding her more tightly. Jessie moaned. In pain. He quickly let her go.

"I heal quickly," she promised.

"I hope so," Joshua said dryly as he carefully swung her up in his arms and headed for the stairs. Jessie gave a muffled squeak as she went from vertical to horizontal.

"Why do you think I stayed away from you for three days?"

Jessie rested her aching head against his chest. *Because you're so darned perverse?* "I thought you'd lost interest," she said so quietly that when he didn't answer right away she thought he hadn't heard her.

"I left town before I was reduced to mauling you on the floor again."

"You didn't maul me." Jessie was indignant. How like a man to take all the credit.

Joshua turned on the landing, heading for the bathroom. "If I'd known what you'd get up to while I was gone I'd have—"

Jessie stiffened. "Yes?"

"I'd have said, be careful." He'd backtracked. Smart man. Jessie relaxed against his broad chest. She'd never been carried anywhere in her life. It felt wonderful.

He leaned over, turning the handles, and water gushed into the claw-footed tub. "Damn. You're black and blue all over. Why can't you have a nice, quiet little hobby like…needlepoint?" He sighed.

"That doesn't say a whole heck of a lot about my charms," Jessie said, imagining what her battered body must look like, yet too exhausted to move as he undressed her as if she were three years old. The bathroom rapidly filled with steam. "The water's going to overflow."

"I'm not making love to a woman who can barely stand." He turned off the taps when the tub filled to the perfect depth. The man could be annoyingly precise.

"I could lie down," Jessie offered. "The bath mat's soft and fluffy."

Joshua shook his head in amusement. "I'll take a rain check. Tell me about Bucking Billy. In."

She stuck a finger into the water. "Too hot." He turned on the cold. Jessie stood there, letting him look at her bruised, battered, goose-bumpy body, thinking perhaps she'd fallen on her head. Because having Joshua look at her like this was more arousing than embarrassing.

"Unfortunately Billy had seen my likes before. He was no gentleman. I managed to stay on for three seconds. It *felt* like three years. *He* couldn't resist a challenge, either."

Joshua frowned. He was very close, and she noted how the steamy bathroom intensified the scent of his cologne. Her pulsed started throbbing. She hoped he'd kiss her. She hoped she had the energy to pucker up when he did. The timing was still right, maybe she could work up the energy...

At some point he'd shut off the water. "Bucking Billy won." Jessie wanted to enjoy the hot, steamy water; unfortunately, she was just too darn tired to move. She gave Joshua a pleading look, and he took her hand and assisted her into the high-sided tub.

"Ow-ow-ow," Jessie wailed as hot water met abraded skin. She didn't feel the least like being brave tonight.

"Needlepoint," he said grimly, picking up the washcloth slung over the spout. Jessie slid inch by inch under the water, and watched him froth the terry with peach-scented bubbles.

"Boooring."

Joshua ran the soapy cloth over her chest. She glanced down. Her hard nipples poked out of the water. She glanced up. Joshua had noticed. Would he do anything about it?

"Close your eyes."

Jessie looked up at him. "Why?"

"I'm going to wash your face. Close, you stubborn woman."

Jessie closed her eyes. The peach-scented cloth drifted across her cheeks, over her nose, climbed her forehead, then brushed down to her throat.

"Wait," he warned before she opened her eyes.

Jessie kept her eyes closed. It felt nice this way. Warm water lapped at her skin as Joshua carefully rinsed her face. She didn't bother opening her eyes again.

She could feel each one of his strong fingers beneath

the soapy terry cloth as he washed her throat, then slid down to sweep across her collarbones.

He swore, obviously coming across more bruises. "I hope they sent this nag to the glue factory."

Jessie's lids weighed a million pounds each. She had throbbing parts and colored parts and scraped parts, and they were all telling her to shut down and sleep. "He's a nice horse."

"Yeah, right." His hand shifted to her nipples. *Ah.* Her nipples perked right up at the attention. Other body parts started coming to life, too. She shifted without opening her eyes, water lapped the edge of the tub. She didn't hear any water splashing the floor, so Joshua must've absorbed the overflow. Her lips twitched. "Are your pants wet?"

"Yes." He sounded amused.

Jessie blinked her eyes open. He was very close. His pupils had dark blue around the edges. "You could get naked, and come in here with me." It sounded a lot more needy than she liked. "Never mind. I'm not up to any fun and games tonight anyway—oh, that feels great." The washcloth was gone and his slick bare hand was doing cleanup duty on her, apparently, *very* dirty nipples.

"Like that, do you?"

"Hmmm," she moaned. Her lax body slid farther down into the hot water. Joshua's steadying hand braced at the back of her head was the only thing preventing her from drowning. The fall from Billy, combined with the long drive back in the dark, had drained all her resources. She felt punch-drunk and silly and overwhelmingly glad Joshua was here with her.

"This is the second time I've been naked," Jessie

mumbled sleepily. Joshua chuckled as his soaping hands smoothed across her breasts and did an intoxicating slip and slide over her nipples. She wanted to purr.

"In your whole life?" He sounded so amused, she opened one eye.

"In *your* whole life." She yawned. "You've only seen me naked once before. Mmm, that feels wonderful." She spat out a soap bubble as he scooped water over her skin. Runnels of hot soapy water tickled her breasts.

"I'm going to be seeing you naked a million more times, Jessie," he promised. "Preferably without these." Underwater, his finger traced a bruise on her ribs. It was a sweet sensation.

"He took me literally, darn it."

"Who?"

"God. When I was a kid I prayed my boobs wouldn't get as big as my mother's. She was *huge*." Jessie yawned as Joshua chuckled. "I should have waited a few more years until I was a little bit bigger before asking."

"You're perfect just the way you are," he said huskily, his breath fanning her damp face. "Any more would be excessive."

There was something she'd wanted to tell him, but the steamy combination of the water and the unbearably gentle touch of Joshua's hands made her forget what it was. She'd wanted to say…

She was asleep.

Joshua watched her face as he finished bathing her. He'd showered with women before. He'd bathed with women before. But they'd always been wide-awake and responsive. Washing Jessie as she slept was a novelty. Her cheeks had pinked up from the steamy heat.

Her ridiculously long, black lashes lay still and spiky on her damp cheeks. Her sweet mouth curved with a faint smile.

Joshua bent his head and brushed his mouth over hers. Her lips were moist and softer than anything he'd ever touched. Sleeping Beauty, he thought fancifully.

Her sweet breasts seemed to float on the water, the nipples soft and as petal pink as her lips. He brushed a finger across one velvety nub. It tightened in response. "Damn it, Jessie—"

Never before had he wanted a woman so much. So why did it feel so good simply to watch her sleep?

SHE LOOKED HER usual bright and perky self the next morning as she walked into the kitchen, haphazardly rolling up the sleeve of a man-style white shirt she'd tucked into her jeans.

Her eyes widened when she saw him sitting at her kitchen table. "Well, good morning," Jessie said cheerfully, clearly surprised to see him. She was no more amazed than he'd been. He couldn't remember the last time he'd spent the night beside a woman, *not* making love. And despite three cups of coffee this morning, he was *still* trying to figure it out.

"Let me," he said standing up and crossing the room, just wanting to touch her. She extended her arm, and he brushed the sleeve down before neatly folding it up to her purple elbow. Jessie's eyes twinkled as she extended the other arm. Her skin felt warm from her shower and she smelled of shampoo.

She'd put her damp hair up in a lopsided ponytail, which had dripped a damp spot on her shoulder. He noted her total lack of makeup. Any other woman would have rushed to the pots to cover the bruises. For just a second he contemplated Jessie's clear skin and candid brown eyes. There was not a shred of artifice about this woman.

"How do you feel?" He traced her cheek with a stroke of his thumb. She smiled.

"Terrific."

"Terrific?" Joshua handed her a cup of coffee. She gingerly sat down, easing her body into the ladder-back chair. The pine table wobbled, despite the matchbook under one leg.

"How can you feel anything but god-awful? You're black and blue and must hurt like hell."

"Oh, this is good." Jessie almost inhaled her coffee. "Of course it hurts. But I still feel terrific. The bruises and stuff are just a blip on the screen. I had so much fun yesterday, it was worth it." She splashed more caffeine into the purple mug with a red ladybug on it, before she got up to hang on the open refrigerator door like a kid after school. "Wanna share cold pizza?"

Joshua glanced at his Rolex. "It's 7:15 a.m."

Jessie grinned over her shoulder. "And that means...?"

"Usually people eat cereal in the mornings."

"I eat cereal at night." Jessie took out a large rather greasy box, sliding it onto the table between them. There was one slice left. She looked up at him, her eyes dancing. "How do you feel about leftover spaghetti?"

CHAPTER FIVE

IT WAS A GOOD THING she wasn't prone to excessive drinking or tantrums. Jessie swallowed two aspirin, more for the Joshua-size headache than for her cramps, and glared at the calendar.

She wasn't pregnant.

Her cycle had always been erratic, but there was no mistake. The disappointment felt like a physical blow to her chest. Her throat had felt tight with unshed tears for hours.

The times with Joshua were becoming more and more like real dates. She didn't want to *date* the blasted man. It seemed Fate conspired against her, as if the gods were challenging her to get to know him before they allowed her a child.

Jessie walked downstairs into her studio. She knew all she wanted to know about Joshua Falcon. He was impatient, arrogant, dictatorial and rude. He was also generous, insightful and an incredible lover. She groaned. She had told the guys the relationship with Joshua wasn't personal, but it was becoming more personal by the day.

She didn't like it. He had one purpose for being in her life, and one purpose only. She couldn't lose sight of the whole point of this exercise. There was no use weeping and wailing and pounding her breast. If she wasn't pregnant, she wasn't pregnant. Yet.

She'd keep doing it until she got it right.

She stepped back from the samples she'd propped on the three-hundred-year-old refectory table she'd bought for a song and refinished herself. Arms folded, she critically eyed the wallpaper and fabric combination, visualizing it all in conjunction with everything else in the client's living room.

Her own home was decorated in the primary and secondary colors she loved. The sunshine-yellow canvas sofa was strewn with plush pillows in blues and reds and parrot green. Various clay pots held grasses or twigs. A large brass spittoon on her drafting table held the mixed bouquet of iris and daffodils Joshua had sent her a few days ago. The cottage was a comfortable blend of antiques coupled with a very modern drafting table and her computer, which she'd used to prop up the enormous wallpaper sample book.

The client, a retired dentist, wanted Victorian and Laura Ashley. Jessie slowly walked backward, her hands framing the still life on her desk, her head tilted. "Perfectomundo!" She stepped back and walked smack into a hard body. "Joshua." She turned into his arms, lifting her face.

His mouth came down hungrily on hers as he angled her head for a perfect fit. Jessie wound her arms around his neck, pulling him closer. She made a soft sound of pleasure as his hands slid under her flannel lumberjack shirt and found bare skin.

She'd given him a key last month, the day after Billy, although this was the first time he'd used it.

She savored the feel of his fingers against her skin

as his large hand skimmed up her back. "What are you doing here?"

"If it's not obvious then my technique is lacking something," Joshua said dryly. "I came to invite you to dinner. How about Japanese tonight?"

"Great." Jessie unwound her arms. It was becoming too easy to be touched by him. Far too enjoyable to have his mouth explore hers. She strolled across the room, then plunked down in her seat and hit the save button on her computer. "I love Japanese." She looked up at him. "I actually thought it would be hard to fit in with your rarefied lifestyle, but it's not all bad."

"You'd put up with the paparazzi and other hoopla for the food alone."

"The travel benefits aren't bad, either." She wanted to touch him but rested her fingers on her keyboard instead.

"Good, because we'll be eating that Japanese meal I was talking about in Tokyo."

She should have realized, with Joshua, nothing was quite that straightforward.

"Not *we,* Joshua." Jessie closed the wallpaper book before turning from her computer, resting her arm along the back of her chair. In a dark business suit, with a teal tie and his hair brushed back, he looked immaculate, efficient and cool. As usual. She knew she must look like hell with her hair haphazardly piled on top of her head and anchored with a couple of pencils. She wore no makeup and was dressed in black leggings and her favorite red-and-black plaid shirt which came to her knees. She hadn't expected him. Usually at this time of the morning he was entrenched in his office in the city.

She'd left him sleeping at 3:00 a.m. and now, seven hours later, he was insisting she pack for a trip to Japan and leave within hours. He hadn't said a word about it last night.

His eyes went cool, aloof. She knew he was ticked off by her refusal to go. His lips tightened. "Part of our agreement, Jessie, was that you would be available to accompany me on my business trips. I'm leaving out of SFO in two hours. Don't bother packing much. You'll have ample time to shop in Tokyo."

"Please don't tell me what to do, Joshua. I said no, and I mean it." Joshua used shopping trips like a carrot at the end of a stick. Shopping had obviously been an inducement to his other mistresses. She supposed she should be grateful he wasn't observant enough to realize she wasn't enticed by the same baubles as his former mistresses.

He hadn't liked it when she'd refused the BMW he'd had delivered a few weeks ago, either. He hadn't understood the charm of her ancient Celica.

"I have plenty of clothes—that's not the point. You'll have to give me more than a couple of hours notice for these trips. I have clients who require my attention and two bosses who depend on me to carry my share of the work."

His face rigid, Joshua dug his hands into the pockets of his coat. In the bright morning sunlight streaming into her downstairs studio, Jessie could see how tired he looked. Not a hair was out of place and no wrinkle marred his impeccable suit or crisp white shirt, but lines of fatigue were clearly visible on his face. The man worked too long and too hard.

She softened her tone. "I enjoy being with you, you

know that. But we only got back from Greece ten days ago—"

"This is strictly business. It won't be a repeat of the yacht."

"It will always be a repeat," Jessie said with sardonic amusement. They'd spent seven days on his yacht in the Aegean. "I only saw you after sundown." While the men talked business in the luxurious stateroom, the women had tanned up on deck. There were plenty of hot-and-cold running waiters, the Greek sun had baked out the last of her Billy bruises, and she'd been amused by the other men's trophy wives or mistresses. But the time was wasted if she wasn't spending it in bed with Joshua. They had gone during peak conception days. Taking advantage of the golden opportunity was the only reason Jessie had hurriedly juggled her schedule.

"As much as I enjoyed it, taking a week off unexpectedly like that threw me off. I have to finish this before my meeting with Dr. Low on Friday."

"Send Conrad."

"Con's an architect, not a decorator. Besides, Jenn is *my* client, Joshua." She rose and put her arms around his neck. Despite his obvious reluctance to be cajoled, he dipped his head and accepted her kiss.

There was one place Joshua Falcon was not one hundred percent in control and that was in the bedroom. She needed him to respond to her without restraint, and he did. Jessie didn't want to analyze why it had become important but with every breath she took, she wanted to know that, in this, she had power over him. That she could make him melt in her arms. She felt the stiffness in his shoulders gradually ease. His lips felt warm, alive. Her body jolted with the erotic touch of his tongue against hers. His arousal was even more potent; she felt his erection through her Lycra leggings.

She moaned into his mouth and, after a minuscule pause, Joshua's arm tightened around her back, drawing her up and onto her toes, one hand buried in her hair. She heard the anchoring pencils fall onto her worktable as Joshua bent her backward like a bow, his teeth nipping ravenously on her lower lip.

Suddenly he gripped her wrists and brought them from around his neck, taking a step back. His fingers imprisoned the delicate bones. "Come with me, Jessie."

"No. I'm sorry you're disappointed, Joshua. But I have a life, too. My business is important, and when I make a commitment to a client, I damn well keep it."

"You *have* a commitment…" he said harshly, his fingers flexing on her wrists. "To me. Which is far more important."

Jessie twisted out of his hold. His grip hadn't hurt and he let her go immediately. She leaned her hip against her desk and gave him a cool look. Still struggling for a breath, her heart pounded. He was as cold as the spring breeze whipping the trees outside.

"I'll be seeing these clients again next year, and probably the next." His mouth tightened. He got the point. Jessie forged on. "My clients are a long-term commitment, Joshua. By next January you won't even remember my name. I'll be mistress number—" she waved a hand "—whatever." She crossed her fingers behind her back for implying she'd still be around then. By next *month* she wanted him out of her life.

"I'll be gone fourteen days." Joshua searched her face. Jessie had no idea what he was looking for. Capitulation?

"Have a safe trip."

There was a long pause. "I'd like you to do the interior design on the resort I'm buying in Tokyo."

Jessie closed her eyes and sighed inwardly. The multibillion dollar resort in Tokyo was a very big carrot to dangle indeed.

"I prefer residential to commercial." She hardened her heart. She had a bad habit of believing she knew what he was thinking and invariably ended up being wrong. There wasn't a needy bone in this man's body. If Joshua wanted her in Tokyo, it was for his convenience.

He'd told her what a good hostess she was, how well she fit in with his business associates and their wives and mistresses. Fine. Well, this time, he could do his entertaining on his own. She had other things to do and people who needed her immediate attention. Besides it was *his* fault she had PMS.

She leaned over her desk and snagged her day planner. "Let's coordinate this trip and I'll make time—"

"By the time you've thought about it," Joshua stated in a voice sharp enough to chip ice, "I'll have contracted Evelyn Van Roosmalen to do the job." He fastened the buttons on his navy-blue cashmere coat and strode to the door. "I beg no woman, Jessie." He reached for the doorknob. "You only had to tell me once. I won't ask you again."

"Joshua—" The door shut quietly behind him. "Damn!" Jessie spun her chair around before sprawling inelegantly in it. "Damn and double damn."

JOSHUA PUSHED AWAY the paperwork he'd been trying to concentrate on for three hours. Damn her. She was his mistress, for Christ's sake. What in the *hell* did she want? He'd never had a mistress who made him feel as if he were jumping through flaming hoops. And she did it seemingly without guile.

She never complained, usually complied and rarely caused even a ripple in his normal workday. He'd become used to her waiting for him at his house in the evening. Used to the novelty of helping her prepare a meal in his kitchen. Damn well complacent about having her in his bed at night.

He felt annoyingly uncomfortable making Jessie get up to go home. Usually *he* left the woman right after sex. But she refused to let him sleep at her place.

Somehow, spending the entire night with a woman had always implied an intimacy he'd never wanted, a level of trust he'd never experienced. This way the sex act was easy—fast, satisfying and impersonal. Intimacy was different. Intimacy required vulnerability, loss of control.

It was probably a good thing the affair with Jessie Adams was over.

Joshua stared at the clouds drifting by the window of his 727. The pressurized cabin was cool, the way he liked it. Except that he could smell the faint scent of Jessie's perfume on the still air. She hadn't been on his plane since the trip to Greece. The aircraft had been cleaned several times since then and yet her fragrance lingered still. That annoyed him. Joshua scrawled a note to himself to inform the flight crew to make sure the plane was scrubbed down after every flight. His pen pressed so hard he gouged the paper.

He'd been forced to be emotionally independent early in life. He'd learned the lesson well. It was damn hard for him to trust anyone. But, damn it, he wanted to trust Jessie. He wanted it badly enough to relax his guard once in a while, like a dog belly-crawling for a pat instead of the stick.

From the hidden speakers came the faint sound of a dreamy Brahms waltz. Something Jessie would love to dance to, her tall, slender body pressed against his chest, her arms stealing up around his neck, her fragrant hair tickling his chin as she hummed along, out of tune, with the music. Joshua laid his head back against the velvety nap of his seat and squeezed his eyes shut against a headache starting to throb in his temples.

How dare she presume that he would come running back when she clicked her fingers. Like a goddamn lapdog. He didn't need her. He didn't need any woman, least of all her. She was too tall, her breasts were too damn small....

Joshua wished to God he hadn't thought of her breasts. Which, of course, like everything else about the woman, fit him to a tee.

He wished he'd never met her. Never tasted her soft, pouty mouth, never held her in his arms or felt her velvety skin beneath his hand. Never had her slick and panting under him, crying his name as her slender body convulsed time and again.

He hadn't become a millionaire by being dictated to by anyone. He called the shots and people obeyed or were eliminated from his equations. He made a thousand competent decisions a day. Had thousands of people working for him who considered his word law. Jessie Adams was dangerous. She reminded him of things he'd never had.

He'd left Jessie five hours ago and already his body ached for her. Joshua gripped the armrests with fingers that turned white. He was getting too involved. It wasn't emotional, of course. But his body craved hers like a drug. He'd never before bedded a woman as sexually compatible. That was all it was.

If any one of a number of other mistresses in the past had done to him what Jessie had done today, that would have been the last time he'd have seen her.

Hell, he hadn't seen his *mother* since she walked away from him when he was a kid. And he was a lot less forgiving now. He'd been shunted between two hedonistic, uncaring people who had the misfortune to be parents. His mother's pregnancy had been cold-bloodedly calculated to snag Joshua's very wealthy and totally unromantic father. Wife number five, the only wife to give him a child. The marriage endured for three years. Joshua had been the pawn in their power-play game of revenge.

Neither wanted him. Both fought over him. He wasn't being volleyed from parent to parent for anything other than power and money. If his father had him, his mother toed the line. If his mother had him, her expenses skyrocketed as she squeezed his father mercilessly. Until his Uncle Simon and the family lawyer had insisted young Joshua be sent to boarding school where he wouldn't expect anyone to care and therefore would never be disappointed.

He'd never seen his mother again. His father had died of a massive coronary when Joshua was seventeen.

Joshua pushed himself upright and drew the papers on his desk closer. To hell with Jessie. She wasn't worth all this introspection. When he said jump to a mistress, she sure as hell better ask how high.

He paused, his eyes on the phone at his left hand.

He could call her and give her one more chance. He'd make sure she understood she'd been given a reprieve. It was damn inconvenient when he was so busy to be looking for another bed partner.

Joshua picked up the phone.

JUGGLING TWO BAGS of groceries Jessie managed to open the back door into her kitchen as the phone started ringing. Rushing, she set the bags down. Her heart gave an illogical leap. *Joshua.* Apples rolled from the bag and her eggs landed, box open, to splatter on the tile floor. The second her hand touched the receiver the ringing stopped.

Jessie picked up the phone anyway. For a moment she stood there in her kitchen, eggs slithering across her clean floor as she clasped the phone and its dial tone to her chest. Her heart was beating much too fast for a short sprint across her kitchen.

Jessie carefully hung up phone.

May

JOSHUA HAD NOT called once in the three weeks he'd been gone. There had been an unusual amount of hang-ups—people not leaving messages. But Jessie knew that Joshua would always have something pithy to say to her machine when she wasn't there. The hang-ups were just coincidences.

Joshua's absence was intolerable. Once again her *C* days had come and gone while he was somewhere else. Damn him, the least he could have done was call. He'd been gone a week longer than he'd said.

The enormous black wrought-iron gates slid open,

the gold Falcon, wings spread, parted in the middle as she drove her five-year-old Toyota up the herringbone brick driveway to the house.

Joshua's home was a two-story English Tudor set on six acres of prime real estate just south of San Francisco. Behind the stone wall surrounding the property, emerald-green lawns and deep flower beds, filled with a brilliant profusion of spring bulbs, lined the long entry to Joshua's very private estate.

The weeks he'd been gone had crept by, no matter how busy she kept herself. He hadn't even bothered to call her himself this morning. One of his secretaries had called and set up an "appointment" for Thursday evening at seven. Typical Joshua. He was still ticked off that she hadn't gone with him. Jessie wasn't going to tell him how close she'd been to hopping a commercial jet and surprising him in Tokyo.

She was starting to get desperate. Perhaps she shouldn't limit their sexual encounters to just her fertile days. Perhaps she should go with what her body was telling her and have sex as often as she could. The law of averages made a compelling argument for increasing her chances of conception.

She parked beside a brilliant bed of pink parrot tulips, right over the drip pan Barlow had discreetly supplied weeks ago. She grinned.

The crisp breeze played with her hem as she hopped out of the car. Perhaps she should have worn something a little more conservative. She looked like a wild gypsy with the brilliantly colored, ankle-length, ruffled skirt and off-the-shoulder blouse. Hardly appropriate clothing for May, but she'd changed so many times before coming, she finally decided she needed the added confidence of the bright colors.

Her hair was its usual wild, curly tangle around her shoulders and the air currents ruffled through it as Jessie sprinted up the shallow brick steps curving up to the massive black front doors. She shivered. The spring air felt crisp on her bare arms and caused the gold charms on her hooped earrings to tinkle softly as they brushed against her cheeks.

The doors were slightly ajar. She rubbed her arms briskly as she stepped into the dim entry hall checkered in black-and-gray Italian marble. She'd been here so many times, she knew her way around the mansion by heart.

She'd love to redecorate the house out of its official, cookie-cutter, corporate mold. Bold colors, she thought, her skin adjusting to warm air as she closed the front door behind her. Teal and sienna, gold and royal purple. She'd strip the tall windows of their fussy layers of draperies. Let the sunlight pour in to warm both house and man.

Jessie's heels clicked across the marble, dulled a little on the polished parquet of the corridor and then became muffled on the thick burgundy carpet of the formal living room. Every one of his homes carried the same corporate colors as his office, planes and yacht.

Joshua stood at the Palladian windows at the far end of the room overlooking the rose garden. Outside, the gardeners had turned on the sprinkler system. Water sparkled in lazy swoops across the freshly mowed lawn. Other than dropping the sheer back across the window, he didn't acknowledge her arrival.

"I'm here," she said unnecessarily, tossing her purse

onto the white brocade sofa and stepping up behind him. Her heart suddenly pounded with anticipation, her mouth dry. Obviously her body had made up her mind for her.

More sex, more often.

He didn't turn around as she slid her arms around his waist. His stomach contracted, his only acknowledgment. Rock hard under her fingertips, his skin felt warm, alive. Jessie rested her cheek against his broad back. "How was your trip?"

"Profitable."

"Did you get any rest?" Jessie felt the exhaustion dragging at his shoulders beneath her cheek.

"I'm not a child. I know my own limitations."

"No, you don't," Jessie scolded as she felt his stomach clench under her hands. "You push yourself to the very edge. One day you should play hooky with me and smell the roses."

"I suggested that, you declined."

"Japan?" Jessie tried to turn his large body. He remained like a blasted rock. "Tokyo wouldn't have been playing hooky, Joshua. You probably worked eighteen-hour days, and I would have been sightseeing and waiting in a hotel room for you to come to me. Come upstairs, and I'll help you relax." Jessie ran her hands up his flat stomach, pressing a series of kisses on his back.

"Is sex all you think about, Jessie?"

Jessie gave a soft, incredulous snort of laughter. "Talk about the pot calling the kettle black." He had no idea how close to the truth he was.

"We've been apart for three weeks, and all you can think about is going upstairs and having sex."

The smile died on Jessie's face. "Good Lord. You're serious." She moved a step away from him. "Joshua, I can tell how exhausted you are. I just wanted to help you relax. That doesn't always mean we have to make love."

"Have sex."

"Make love, damn it. I missed you more than you'll ever know. And that has nothing to do with sex." *Oh, God. Where had that come from?* Jessie thought, panicked.

"I don't want you to love me."

"I know." Jessie squeezed her eyes shut. *I'm trying not to.*

"And I'll never love you. From observation, love isn't all it's cracked up to be. It binds you, strips away your pride and strength with nothing in return."

"You've had more experience. I'll take your word for it," Jessie hedged. "But I did miss you holding me. Turn around. Kiss me. Please, Joshua." Her voice sounded thick. Her heart took up a dull, heavy beat as he remained facing the window before turning around slowly. He looked down into her upturned face, using a finger to trace the curve of her cheek.

The feel of his fingers on her face was unbearably tender. A contradiction to the rock-hard look in his pale eyes.

"*Did* you miss me, Jessie?"

"Yes. Very much." She ached for him to wrap his arms around her, to hold her close to his broad chest. She uselessly yearned to have him welcome her into his arms. Every time they were apart, it seemed to Jessie as if they had to start again from square one. The man had the worst timing of anyone she knew.

He dropped his hand from her face, reaching into his jacket pocket and withdrawing a glossy black paper bag with gold corded handles. "Here."

She looked at the bag. Jewelry wasn't what she wanted from him. "I told you I don't want you to keep buying me things, Joshua." She refused to take it from him. "Don't make me feel…cheap."

He ran his knuckle down her cheek as he stared down at her meditatively. "No, you're not cheap, are you, Jessie?"

"I'll stay for as long as it suits us both, but I won't be bought." Her cheek was immediately cold as he dropped his hand.

"Just open the damn thing. It's no big deal."

Jessie didn't care about the present. Why hadn't he kissed her? Was this his way of punishing her for not joining him on his trip? She absently took the bag from him, and inserted her hand into the iridescent, gossamer-thin paper inside.

She pulled out a delicate rose quartz box the size of her palm. It was crusted with pearls, what looked like pink diamonds and intricately woven gold leaves. It was feminine, delicate and quite unlike anything he'd given her before.

"It's exquisite." Jessie looked up at him. *Please don't just stand there with that hateful cold look on your face.* "Thank—"

"Open it."

Jessie clicked open the lid. Inside, nestled on a bed of blush-pink satin lay two pale green spheres, each about three-quarters of an inch across. Earrings. She lifted one from the box. It moved in her hand. Jessie stared at it. Not an earring. It had no back to it.

"Marbles?" she asked, puzzled. She flattened her palm, and the small ball rolled across her hand.

"Benwa balls," Joshua told her.

Jessie put the thing back into its box, then gave him a puzzled look. "Benwa balls?"

"You insert them into your vagina," Joshua said, watching her face. "You'll have continuous orgasms when we're apart."

Jessie pulled a face. "Sounds exhausting. Think I'll pass."

"These particular benwa balls were hand carved over a thousand years ago." He removed both balls from the box. "Give me your hand. See how they move? That's because they've been carefully weighted so that they'll continually shift inside you. They're made from white jade found in Myanmar, Burma. This particular jade is called moss in snow—see the little flecks of darker green? They're said to have magical powers."

"Well, anything that can give a woman multiple orgasms without human contact, must," Jessie said with a small smile. "But if these things are over a thousand years old I'd hate to think how many women have... used them. Ew. Thank you for the gift, but I'll *definitely* pass."

Joshua took the box from her and inserted the jade balls. He snapped the lid closed then shoved the box in his pocket. "They're nonporous and sterilized. Do you think I'd give you anything that would harm you?"

"No. But I'd still prefer to have something as intimate as that in its original, sanitized, shrink-wrapped packaging, thank you very much."

"Go upstairs and wait for me," he said coldly. "I have to make a few calls."

Jessie gave him a narrow-eyed look before turning on her heel and leaving the room. She left a drift of Joy and disappointment in the room behind her like an invisible ghost.

He should have given her more diamonds. She'd liked the earrings he'd given her for Valentine's Day. The benwa balls had been too intimate, too personal. He'd been thinking of her pleasure. The antiquities had cost enough to support a small nation, and she'd dismissed their value as casually as she would a Cracker Jack box toy. He'd seen the disappointment in her eyes when she'd opened the damned box. She'd expected jewelry. Something she could wear and show off. Damn. He rubbed the ache between his eyes.

Once when he'd been about twelve, he'd given his mother a purple leather coat. It had cost him his month's allowance and humiliating hours trying to choose the one he knew she would like. The memory of her laughter made him cringe to this day. The color, of course, had been all wrong with her skin tones and didn't he know that she had wanted a red fox fur, for God's sake?

His mother had returned the coat and kept the money. The look on Jessie's face had frozen his marrow in exactly the same way as it had frozen all those years ago. Joshua hadn't liked it then, and he sure as hell wouldn't tolerate it now.

He'd watched her bounce in, her bright figure reflected in the small baroque mirror on the wall beside him. He'd squeezed his eyes shut as her fragrance drifted closer and closer. God, when she'd walked in, he hadn't been able to turn around without making an absolute ass of himself.

If he had, he would've grabbed her and held on tightly. He would've inhaled the sweet familiar fragrance of her hair and brushed his mouth across her velvety check. He'd ached so, missing her.

His need for her was alarming. Jesus. What the hell *was* this? It was more than sex. He was addicted to the taste and feel of Jessie. Addicted to the touch of her hands. Hell, he didn't care where she touched him. Didn't care whether it was sexual or not. He wanted her hands on him.

He'd just realized since meeting her that the only time anyone had touched him in his life had been purely by necessity, for sex, or by accident. Who would have thought that touching could become so damn addictive? When he was with Jessie he felt as uncontrolled as the boy he'd once been trying to hug his mother without blubbering like an infant.

It was easy for Joshua to express himself with sex. Sex was physical, immediate, the meaning unmistakable. His insatiable desire for Jessie was a clear indication of his... Joshua grit his teeth. *What?* God only knew, nothing as clear-cut and simple as physical desire described what he felt for the infuriating woman upstairs.

He didn't understand this emotional churning, or the mental upheaval of titanic proportions he'd been experiencing in the months since he'd met her. Instinct warned he was in way over his head and sinking fast.

He glanced at his watch. Eleven minutes had passed. He turned for the stairs, warning himself to slow down and not appear more eager than was financially advisable. The woman turned him inside out, but she didn't have to know it.

Joshua winced when he recalled his crude question to her about just thinking about sex. Christ. *He* was the one who thought of nothing else. He walked slowly up the curving staircase, his footsteps as heavy as that frozen rock in his chest.

Only the light beside the bed broke the darkness. The room was empty. He could hear water running in the bathroom. Joshua shrugged out of his jacket and loosened his tie. He and Jessie had never taken a bath together. Their coupling was always too fast and hard to waste a moment. Joshua felt his arousal despite the bone-weary exhaustion that dragged at his shoulders and made every step seem a mile.

He envisioned Jessie up to her pink nipples in foaming water, holding out her arms to him wearing bubbles and a smile. She'd be slick with water and desire. He moved into the luxuriously appointed bathroom.

She was still fully clothed. The brilliant orange, red and yellow skirt trailed onto the black-carpeted floor as she sat on the top step near the edge of the tub, her fingers testing the water.

"You're not naked," he said more harshly than he intended. Steam had made her hair curl more tightly and filmed her face and neck with a pearlescent glow.

"Not yet." She stood and wiped her hands on a towel she'd draped on the heated rack next to the sunken tub. She moved toward him with that lithe, catlike grace that made his mouth water and his penis stand to attention. Her fingers finished loosening his tie, tossing it behind him where it landed in the doorway.

She stripped off his shirt, tossing it the way of his tie. Her hands felt cool against his stomach as she unbuttoned, unzipped and managed to draw down his shorts with his pants.

"What d—"

Jessie stopped him midword. "Joshua?" She curved her palm against his cheek.

"What!"

"You're behaving like a jerk." She reached up on her tiptoes and gently kissed his mouth. "I know you're tired. Just don't say anything for a while, okay?"

His forehead dropped to rest on hers, and his arms looped around her slender waist. "Jesus, Jessie," he groaned. "What are you doing to me?"

"Tonight, let me be a friend, even if you are behaving like an ass." She methodically removed the rest of his clothing. "The closer we get, the harder you try to push me away. Sometimes you push too hard and it hurts. So, tonight, we'll just be friends."

Joshua bracketed her face with both hands, closed his eyes as if in pain and then opened them to look down at her, a half smile curving his mouth. "What will my 'friend' do when she sees how aroused I am?" he asked on a huff of air.

Jessie grinned. "Oh, I'm friends with that part, too. Don't worry, I can control my baser side."

"Shoes?" he asked, amused by her enthusiasm. "The shoes come off before the pants, darling." Joshua buried his fingers in her hair as she knelt at his feet. Impatient with how methodical she was being, he cupped her face. "Stand up, Jessie."

She rose slowly, hitching up her blouse where it drooped off one slender pale shoulder. Her dark eyes grew heavy lidded as he stroked the warm, damp skin of her neck, then slipped the elastic farther down her arm.

"I know I don't always respond to you appropriately," he said softly as she looked up at him warily. The woman turned him inside out. "But can we be 'friends' later?" he murmured roughly. "As much as slow turns me on, I need you hard and fast right now. It's been too damn long."

As he talked, he stripped her naked. Despite the blustery weather, she hadn't worn much. Her gypsy-girl outfit was more color than substance. She wore no underwear. Joshua groaned, kicking off his shoes as his mouth hungrily sought hers.

Jessie pulled his head closer, kissing him open-mouthed. He swiftly turned the kiss into a prolonged, nonverbal apology.

He felt *very, very* apologetic.

They sank onto the carpeted steps running the length of the deep Jacuzzi tub. Joshua lay back, and Jessie straddled his hips, holding herself over his erection until she was comfortably situated. "You don't get to call the shots tonight. It's my turn. Just lie there and let me do my thing. Now, put your arms out on either side of you where I can see them, and don't touch."

Joshua's mouth watered as he let his gaze travel from her wild hair, down the smooth satin of her skin. She lifted her arms to shake back her hair, baring the slender length of her throat and the gentle slope of her breasts. He reached for her, but she gently pushed his hands away. "Uh-uh. Tell me what you want. I'll give it to you."

He stretched his arms out along the step. "I want to taste your nipples."

She arched her back, leaning forward, hands braced

on the step near his head. Her dark, fragrant hair fell in a silky curtain around their heads. Her nipple was hard and puckered as she brushed his lips with first one and then the other. God, she was responsive. Joshua latched on to one hard point on her next pass and gently closed his teeth around the bud, then laved it with his tongue. She moaned low in her throat, and he felt the shudder run through her body. He nuzzled his face between her sweet breasts, inhaling the heady fragrance of an aroused Jessie.

"Go down on me, Jessie," he begged, his voice almost unrecognizable.

"Kiss me first," Jessie said thickly. "Kiss me as if you're thirsty, and I'm water." Her slightly parted lips brushed his mouth. Eager to taste her, Joshua allowed Jessie to take the initiative. Her tongue slicked along the seam of his lips and he opened his mouth to her. She tasted achingly familiar. For a moment, he couldn't bear to move as she brushed her soft lips over his and tasted him with her tongue.

"I'm dying of thirst here, Jessie. More."

Her husky laugh tickled his lips. She angled her head and tunneled her fingers through his hair, holding him where she needed him, not that he was going anywhere. Joshua dug his fingers into the thick pile of the carpet, resisting the overwhelming need to touch her velvety soft skin.

She kissed him back boldly, aggressively. Her tongue mated and dueled with his until his erection jerked and bobbed against his leg.

They were both breathing hard when she lifted her

head. Their eyes met for a moment, then, keeping eye contact, Jessie slid down his body, supple and eager.

Joshua's head fell back on the thickly padded stair as her hair flowed like summer rain across his chest. Stomach. Groin. *Ah, Jesus...* She knelt between his legs, naked and glorious, her pale body luminous against the matte blackness of the carpet.

Jessie.

Her fingers were cool as she tested the weight of his balls in one hand, while with her other she brought the tip of his penis into contact with the slick, wet heat of her mouth. And, all the while, her big, brown, beautiful eyes watched his face.

As delicate as a cat, she licked the bead of moisture from the tip, then ran her tongue down the length of his erection as though it were a Popsicle. She wrapped her cool fingers around the base, and his nostrils flared and teeth gritted at the exquisite sensation. He bit back a groan and dug his fingers into the carpet to anchor himself.

Jessie.

Her lips worked the swollen head of his shaft as though she'd done this a million times before. Her eyes lost focus as she concentrated on pleasuring him.

She drew her slick tongue down the length, and then took the head into her mouth and sucked hard. Joshua's shoulders came up off the step, and he let out a feral growl of pleasure.

He grabbed Jessie's slender shoulders and pulled her up the length of his body.

"Not good?" she asked, crawling up the rest of the way on her own.

"Too good." His erection demanded relief, it bobbed

and stroked her flat belly with a mind of its own. "Top or bottom?"

"Top," Jessie decided, voice thick. She took his shaft in one hand and guided it home.

CHAPTER SIX

JESSIE GLANCED AT the clock on her nightstand as she finished dressing for the party. For once she might be ready when Joshua arrived. Grabbing the yellow clutch that matched her dress, she dashed downstairs to her studio to put the finishing touches on the presentation she'd been working on for the past week. It was a nice commission, one she wanted to close.

Despite Archie and Conrad being good friends, they were also her bosses. She'd hardly been bringing in enough to cover her paycheck in the past few months, and she was starting to feel guilty.

When Conrad had hired a new designer for the team a month ago, he'd been quick to assure Jessie that she still had her job. The architectural design firm was simply growing.

It was. Jessie knew that, but she felt guilty all the same. Getting out of bed at 3:00 a.m and then getting out of bed to go to work again at 7:00 a.m. was hardly conducive to a good night's sleep. She was starting to feel the strain.

But neither by word nor deed did she intend Joshua to know that. She'd just have to become more organized.

They spent almost every night together, and every morning at three, Jessie drove herself home. It was ridiculous, not to mention inconsiderate, to wake the chauffeur to have him drive her back to the cottage at the crack of dawn. She didn't care how much he was paid.

That time of the morning was the loneliest Jessie ever felt. If sometimes she needed to cry on the drive home, she wanted to do so in private. Almost five months of being Joshua's lover, and she still wasn't pregnant. The spare room was overflowing with baby stuff. A white wicker crib, a high chair, toys, clothes, books.

She'd tossed out the calendar and the basal thermometer. If rabbits could do it then so could she. The fact that she wasn't pregnant wasn't for lack of trying. Joshua couldn't seem to get enough of her and Jessie was afraid to analyze too closely what was going on in her own mind.

She stuck her client's paperwork, which she hadn't even glanced at, back in the file so she could get up and pace. High heel sandals picking up speed from the doorway to the far wall and back again.

"What am I doing?" she asked herself in disgust before flopping inelegantly into the comfortable chair by the window. There was no point anticipating failure. It wasn't over yet. She still had more than half her "contract" time left. She'd just never thought she'd *need* this much time.

TONIGHT THEY WERE attending an engagement party and Jessie was curious to meet his friends.

"How do you know this couple?" She leaned against the brass handrail in the elevator; it felt cool on her bare back. She wore a bias-cut, silk charmeuse dress and huge dull gold earrings that dangled almost to her bare shoulders.

"Guy works for me. I've never met Ginny."

"How long—" Jessie's eyes widened as Joshua took two steps to close the space between them the moment the elevator doors closed on the parking garage.

"There can't be a yard of material in that dress."

She clasped her hand around his wrist in warning, glancing at the flashing numbers above the door. "Behave yourself."

"You look absolutely delectable in yellow, Miss Adams," Joshua said huskily, surveying her from very close up. His hand went to the back of her neck. "What happens if I undo this little button right here?"

Undoing the halter neck would get him a pair of naked breasts against his chest. Which was exactly his intention. Jessie's fingers tightened around his wrist. He grinned wickedly, hesitated, then removed the threat of his hand.

"You're creasing me," she admonished, grateful the party was in the penthouse, seventy-two stories up, and they were alone in the elevator. She wasn't sure she would have stopped him.

"Silk doesn't crease," he assured her, nuzzling her neck. Her short, sassy skirt rustled over net petticoats. Jessie trembled as he pressed her gently against the elevator wall, her breasts flattened against the hard plane of his chest. He'd been in New York for the last three days and arrived home barely in time to change and pick her up tonight.

"We have about forty seconds before this elevator door opens. I'm just making the most of them," he murmured, a breath away from her mouth.

"I wish we'd stayed home." Jessie fluttered her long eyelashes. "Why'd we have to come to this dumb old party anyway?"

Joshua grinned. "For a bright brunette, you certainly do a great dumb blonde."

"Hey," she said indignantly, leaning into him. "I was flirting."

"You were asking for trouble."

She smiled seductively. "Have I come to the right place for it?"

Joshua made a sound deep in his throat as he lowered his head. Jessie tilted her chin, offering her mouth. He brushed his open mouth against hers, then stroked her lips with his tongue.

She had a vague thought that she was playing with fire, but his mouth was so seductively sweet all thought of propriety fled. He exuded pheromones like a musky cologne and her body chemistry always responded.

Jessie slid her hands beneath his jacket to stroke his back. He kissed her harder, tilting her head back so he could slant his mouth and deepen the kiss. She whimpered helplessly.

He lifted his lips from hers a fraction of an inch, his breath warm on her face. "One more taste before the doors open."

"Living dangerously, Mr. Falcon?" She could feel how much he wanted her. His need was in the depth of his kiss, in the press of his body against hers, in the urgency of his hands. The rigid length of his arousal pressed hard against her.

When the elevator jarred to a stop and the doors slid open, Joshua straightened the halter straps, used his thumb to remove her smudged lipstick from her mouth and then his own.

A dozen laughing, talking people got into the elevator on the next floor of the garage. They were clearly going to the same party. The fragrance of expensive cosmetics and perfume filled the small space. Jessie moved closer to Joshua and he pressed her back into the corner, a wicked gleam in his pale eyes.

"Hold the elevator!" a voice yelled.

Joshua slid his hand up Jessie's thigh. Under her skirt. Eyes opened wide she shot him a startled look. He gave her a sexy smile and kept on going.

Jessie grabbed his wrist and tried to pull his hand away.

"Thanks," the guy said, ushering three more people into the already crowded car.

What do you think you're *doing?* Jessie's eyes demanded as Joshua's fingers slid inside the elastic leg of her panties. He gave her an innocent look back. He stroked a finger in the crease between leg and mound. Her knees went weak. "Stop it!" she mouthed.

Everyone in the elevator was laughing and talking and watching the numbers above the door. Joshua was the only one turned her way. Still... His finger slid inside her.

Jessie's knees went weak. His foot came between hers, and gently spread her feet apart.

Jessie licked her lower lip, then squeezed her eyes closed as he inserted a finger deep between her slick folds. Oh. My. God. Her petticoats rustled around his arm.

All it needed was one person to turn around...one person to look...

A second finger joined the first. She bit her tongue to prevent the moan from escaping, and leaned back into the corner. His thumb brushed her clit. Jessie shuddered. *Brush harder.* She felt the coils tighten. His fingers were deep inside her, and her muscles tightened and spasmed around them as he played her clitoris like a master. Her body throbbed, her nipples clearly, visibly aroused behind a thin layer of silk. She was beyond ready to come. How could so many people just be *standing* there, oblivious to what he was doing to her?

His fingers slid in and out. Faster. Faster. Faster.

Jessie came in a dizzying rush. Her back thumped against the wall, and she pressed her hand over her mouth so she didn't shriek with pleasure.

Everyone around them continued chatting and laughing.

Jessie's muscles tightened as Joshua removed his hand. She flashed a glance at the numbers over the door. Seventieth floor.

His hand was back. No way. In a few seconds that door was going to open and everyone would spill out. She was not going to get caught with Joshua's hand up her skirts and down her panties.

Something cool rolled passed her clit…and again something. She felt a weight deep inside and her muscles automatically tightened in response. She met Joshua's eyes. "What…?" she mouthed.

He smiled.

The door dinged, then slid open.

Everyone poured out, leaving Joshua and Jessie behind.

Joshua had his handkerchief in one hand. He offered her his other hand. Jessie took it, and stepped forward. Oh, my God.

The benwa balls shifted and slid inside her. She stumbled, holding on to Joshua's hand for dear life. Her vaginal muscles clamped down hard. She shot him a narrow-eyed look.

"I'm operating these things without a license, and without instructions," she said between her teeth. "I'm going to get you for this, Falcon."

They followed the noise to the open doors of the penthouse. He smiled, tucking his damp hankie back in his pocket. "All you need to know is muscle control. You can do it."

"Easy for you to say," Jessie groused. "You're not the one walking like a duck."

"I am walking with a limp, however. I haven't seen you in seventy-two hours. God, I missed you."

The unexpected flash of a camera captured Jessie and she started to laugh. "Oh, no, the paparazzi are here." She got the giggles. "Oh, Lord. What if these damn things fall out and roll across the floor?"

"They won't." Joshua squeezed her hand against his body. "Everyone's going to see that picture and want to have you."

"I'll have to tell them I'm taken 'til December." Jessie looked around for a familiar face, trying to concentrate on anything but what was happening to her body. Those benwa balls certainly produced an odd sensation. The more she walked, the more they slid around and the hornier she became.

"Rat," she grumbled under her breath as a nice little aftershock traveled up her spine and she pressed their clasped hands against her aching breast.

He smiled. "Thank me later."

The balls did a slow shimmy. Jessie tightened her pc muscles. Oh, brother. Wasn't this going to be an interesting evening?

There were several of her clients and a few other people she recognized. She turned back to him. He had the strangest look on his face. His playful mood of moments ago evaporated. Once again he was The Glacier. Now what?

Raising her voice above the noise, she stepped closer to Joshua as people surged around them. The balls danced around a bit, then settled when she stood still. Good. Stay that way. "Which is the engaged couple?"

"The joyous couple over by the ice sculpture." Joshua indicated with a nod. He slid his arm around her waist, anchoring her to his side.

"The blonde in the blue dress and the tall guy?" Jessie observed the newly engaged pair as they gestured angrily, oblivious to their guests. In the din, it was impossible to hear what they were saying, just observe how they were saying it.

"That's a photograph I'd put in the dictionary under *divorce*."

"They're not married yet," Jessie reminded him. He *was* in a strange mood.

"Yeah, well, it won't last if they already argue in public like that."

"Not all marriages end in divorce."

"Just more than fifty percent."

"That means almost fifty percent are *happy*."

Joshua touched her cheek. "The half-full glass theory?"

"Works for me."

"Let's agree to disagree." Joshua's hand lingered on her cheek. Jessie searched his face for a clue to his mood. "We'll drink some of their, no doubt, excellent champagne then go home. How does that sound?"

Every opportunity sounded promising to Jessie. "I'd rather have you in me than these million-year-old balls."

Joshua chuckled. "Me, too."

She looked wistfully at the elegantly draped tables groaning under elaborate canapés and soaring ice sculptures. "The food looks good." She shot him a mischievous grin. "How about this, we grab something to eat *before* we push our way over there, say congratulations...or offer condolences, whichever is more appropriate, and then go home?"

"Smart as well as beautiful. How unusual—damn."

Jessie followed his gaze and recognized the busty blonde making a beeline toward them. Her photograph had accompanied Joshua's in the press for twelve months the previous year. "Stick by me. I'll protect you," she said dryly.

Joshua looked as suave and debonair as a man could, caught between this year's and last year's models. "Perhaps we should save time. You go and congratulate Guy and Ginny, and I'll tackle Megan."

Jessie shot him a reproving glance just as the other woman stepped closer. "Megan, hi." Jessie gave her a cheerful smile, stepping a little in front of Joshua, which was a mistake because moving made her little friends dance happily inside her. "I'm Jessie Adams."

Joshua placed a hand firmly on her waist and eased her back to his side again. Out of clawing range, Jessie presumed. He kept a proprietorial arm around her.

Megan Howell narrowed her baby blues as she glared up at Jessie. "Do I know you?"

"No," Jessie said gently, seeing the high emotion under the other woman's flush. "I recognized you from that great photo of you in the *Inquirer* last December." Jessie carefully removed her hand from Joshua's. "I'm sure you want to talk privately with Joshua, so I'll go over and—"

"You might as well hear this." Megan's tone was pure hostility. Jessie moved closer to Joshua, her eyes narrowed on the blonde.

The Glacier was back in full force as Joshua bit out icily, "Say what you have to say and leave Megan."

"I'm pregnant," Megan said defiantly in a too loud voice as she crossed her arms over her plastic bosom. A very elegant tent dress effectively hid any hint of a baby.

Jessie felt an immediate surge of anger. How dare this woman be carrying Joshua's child! Jessie wanted to rip her lips off.

She felt sick with jealousy and heartsore with disappointment. *Megan* was pregnant. Damn it, it wasn't fair. A heavy lump in her throat made swallowing impossible. She looked up at Joshua. He had a very nasty smile on his face.

"Congratulations. Who's the father?"

"You are, you bastard!" Flashlights popped. "What are you going to do about it?" the blonde demanded, not missing a beat.

"Ask you to lower your voice, for a start," Jessie cut in, for a moment hating them both, "unless you enjoy having your private life speculated about over breakfast. Guy and Ginny have invited every tabloid in the universe to their party. So smile nicely and behave like a lady."

Joshua looked at her as if she had sprouted another head. He turned back to his ex-mistress, his pale eyes frosty. "It's taken you an inordinate amount of time to come up with this, Megan." Joshua tsked. "You used to be much faster than this at cooking up money-making schemes."

"I've talked to your lawyers," Megan snarled, her cheeks scarlet, eyes flashing him a grim warning.

"Wise idea." Joshua rested his hand on the small of Jessie's back. "They no doubt told you about the mandatory DNA test?"

"I refuse to harm my baby just because you don't believe me," she said caustically, glaring up at him.

"DNA testing can be done at twenty weeks, Megan, without doing any harm to the fetus. I'm sure Felix gave you the facts." Joshua rubbed his thumb on Jessie's bare back.

"This is obviously a private discussion," Jessie inserted. "I'll wait for you over by the bar," she added to Joshua over her shoulder. She turned on her heel and walked away.

As if the world hadn't come crashing down around her.

HER LIGHTLY TANNED BACK was very straight when Joshua found her on the other side of the room minutes later. She was by herself, ostensibly looking at one of Guy's nightmarish paintings. She made a spectacular picture herself in the barely there little number that showcased her gorgeous long legs and the sweet curve of her spine.

"Let's go." Joshua came up behind her, resting his hand on her naked back. Her skin was silky smooth, shimmering with vitality.

"Let's say our goodbyes to our hosts first. I think they're done with round nine."

He glanced down at her set expression. "Can you walk okay?"

She shot him a look. "I took them out," she said under her breath. "I had ninety-nine orgasms without you. I didn't like it."

He didn't talk all the way down in the elevator. The paparazzi had gotten off several dozen shots of the three of them, he knew, in just about every configuration. Jessie was going to have a million questions. Hell, if she wanted to know what he and Megan had discussed she only had to buy one of the tabloids in the morning.

She rested her head on his stiff shoulder as Barlow drove. Of course, she wouldn't pull away, Joshua thought bitterly, leaning back against pliant burgundy leather. She was his mistress. Another woman was threatening her cash cow. What the hell, she only had to put up with him another few months and she'd be free as a bird.

They exited the parking garage, staring straight ahead before he said grimly, "She was lying—"

He felt her exhale before she said calmly, "I know."

Joshua looked down at her. The passing streetlights dappled her face, making her expression hard to read. "Did you hear what I said?"

Jessie yawned. "Mmm. The baby isn't yours."

There was a heavy weight in his chest. "How do you know?" His voice almost cracked in the middle of the question. Far from being concerned, Jessie was almost asleep.

She squeezed his waist, snuggling closer. "You just told me."

"You believe me?"

"Of course," she mumbled matter-of-factly, although her voice sounded thick. "You're a man of your word. If you say the child isn't yours, it isn't."

He stared at her. There was no doubt in her voice, or on her even features. She believed him. No ifs, ands or buts. She just…believed him. Unequivocally. A wave of emotion swept through him. Disbelief. Acceptance. And something else too powerful, too impossible, to believe.

Jessie rubbed her cheek on his upper arm, sweetly drowsy as she settled her arm across his waist, eyes closed. "As a matter of curiosity, what would you do if she was pregnant?" she asked in a soft, casual voice.

"Thank God that can be proven one way or another in this day and age—"

"But what if—"

"She just got greedy."

"She's trying to blackmail you?" Jessie asked indignantly, sitting up straighter. "That little b—"

"Felix will take care of her." Joshua tucked her back against his side.

"If he doesn't, *I* will," she said firmly, then snuggled against him again. Her hand stroked lazily up and down his side under his jacket.

Jessie tucked her thumb under his belt as Barlow made a hard right at the corner. When Joshua looked down, her long lashes were casting shadows on her cheeks. He tightened his arm around her slender shoulders and held her close.

"I wish—"

"What do you wish, Jessie?"

He felt her small shrug as she whispered dreamily, half asleep, "A little girl. I'd dress her in clean, pretty clothes and keep her safe. She'd never ever be hungry or afraid." Jessie covered a yawn. "But most of all, I'd just love her."

Joshua felt the ache in his chest tighten a notch. Jessie seemed unaware of what she'd just revealed. He knew firsthand a mother's neglect, but at least he'd had someone to care for his most basic needs. Housekeepers and nannies may not have provided anything more than necessities, but he had been clothed and fed and had never known cold, fear or hunger.

As a child Jessie had known real hunger and very real fear. She seldom spoke about those years. She'd never known if or when her mother would come home. According to Felix, Jessie's mother had been picked up for solicitation a dozen times or more. Where had Jessie gone when her mother was in jail? How had Jessie, who had never known security or trust as a child, grown into a woman who trusted so easily?

He was basically a solitary man. He had a few men he called friends, but they were really just business associates he trusted. He had never had a woman trust him as much as Jessie did, understand him as Jessie did. It was a novel experience. Joshua savored it as Jessie's body relaxed against his. He brushed a strand of hair off her cheek.

She was asleep in moments, her fragrant hair tickling his face as it blew about in the warm breeze through the open window. Well, hell, Joshua thought, wanting to laugh out loud. She believed him. No fuss. No muss. He leaned his head against the plush leather upholstery, closing his burning eyes. How the hell could such an uncomplicated woman be so damned difficult to understand?

When she'd said earlier, oh, so casually, that she was taken until December, he'd checked a surge of anger. She didn't have to be so damn complacent about the temporariness of their arrangement. Joshua scrubbed his face with his hand. She turned him inside out, then left him swinging. And somehow she made him think he liked it!

As the gates to the estate skimmed open, Joshua recalled a conversation he'd had with his lawyer just before he'd left for New York last week. Apparently his wife wanted more money. The only time Joshua ever heard from her was when she contacted Felix to up the ante. A small price to pay for a trouble-free invisible wife.

"Jesus, Felix," Joshua had griped. "What's she trying to do, squeeze me dry?"

Felix had looked serious as he'd handed the paperwork over for Joshua to sign. "Hardly. You'd give an employee an annual raise. Why not your wife?"

"I'm giving her enough to support a small country now, for God's sake!"

He might not remember anything about the girl, but she *had* served her purpose. He'd made her a promise. "All right, Felix. Give her what the hell she wants."

He was a man of his word, as many people had learned to their regret.

Joshua carried Jessie into the house and upstairs without disturbing her sleep. She would be awake soon enough.

Joshua hadn't mentioned Megan Howell all week. He'd been more intense than usual, more serious. Jessie thought he watched her as if he were trying to read her mind.

He called her in the middle of the day several days after the party and told her to pack a bag. They were going to Tahoe for a long weekend.

Jessie nibbled the cap of her pen, wrapping the telephone cord around her hand. "How many bedrooms does your cabin have?" she asked innocently.

"One." Joshua sounded amused. "How many do we need?"

"That depends on if I have to haul my butt out of bed at 3:00 a.m.," she said carefully. The cord left red marks on her fingers and she unwound herself, listening carefully to his tone.

There was a slight pause, so slight that if she hadn't been listening for something, she wouldn't have heard it. "I'll throw away the alarm for the weekend."

Jessie laughed. "How soon can you pick me up?"

They flew to Tahoe in Joshua's Lear. He didn't want to waste time driving. A shiny black Range Rover waited for them at the airfield when they arrived.

The cabin was far from a log shack in the hills. It was built of cedar with a wall of glass facing the north shore of Lake Tahoe. It was luxurious, with an enormous bedroom cantilevered over a naturally terraced lawn. The living room and kitchen overlooked towering pine trees and the shimmering blue lake.

Despite the corporate colors, the cabin was less decorated than his other residences, more casual and conducive to relaxing. And there was only one phone. Jessie was thrilled.

Joshua carried their suitcases into the bedroom and came into the kitchen for a snack. "You know what the best thing about you is?" He nuzzled her neck.

"What?" Jessie ran short nails through his silky, dark hair as he pressed her lower body against the stainless steel sink behind her. She nibbled at his chin.

"You never ask me for anything."

The one thing I want, you haven't been able to give me, Jessie thought, turning her face up for his kiss while her heart squeezed hard. There was no use dwelling on it. When it happened it happened.

His open-neck blue shirt was the exact color of his eyes and she had ogled him the whole time she fixed the cheese-and-tomato sandwiches. "Actually, there is something I want," she teased, her finger trailing to the top button of his shirt.

"Lord, woman, you're insatiable."

"I can't help myself." Jessie pretended to pout. "I just love it." She fluttered her lashes, trying not to giggle. "I think...yep, I think it might be one of my most favorite things in the world."

"Take me, I'm your..." He started dramatically then narrowed his eyes suspiciously. "Just what *is* it you love, you little tease?"

Jessie laughed. "Gambling." She stood on her tiptoes and twined her arms around his neck. He smelled of pine and clean air, the stiffness had eased from his shoulders while they were in flight, and the lines of strain had left his face by the time they landed. He smiled down at her indulgently, obviously amused and perfectly relaxed. Her eyes sparkled as she lured him closer, still laughing as she avoided his tickling fingers. She danced backward. "Can we go gambling? Can we, huh, huh?"

Joshua laughingly agreed. It was only after they were in the car and halfway around the lake that Jessie said mildly, "I think it's time you bought a pair of jeans. You look as if you're ready to play polo."

"One does not wear summer-weight wool slacks to play polo, Jess. One wears breeches to play polo," he pointed out drolly as he pulled into a frighteningly large shopping mall at Jessie's urging. He couldn't remember when last he'd shopped for clothing for himself. Years. Normally his secretary called a clothier in London or Milan, and they'd send him what he needed.

Clothes shopping with Jessie was a surprisingly pleasant experience. She didn't dawdle about making selections. She knew exactly what she was looking for and didn't linger if the shop they were in didn't have it. Two hours later, Joshua was the recipient of three pairs of jeans and several shirts he wouldn't have looked at twice if he'd been on his own. He'd tried to tell her he only wore blue or white.

Jessie had coerced several mall-walking senior citizens to come into the store to give him *their* opinions. How could he win against Jessie Adams at her best, and several blue-haired little old ladies?

After depositing his new purchases in the hands of the owner of the local laundromat they went to lunch.

"I hate to ask—" Joshua toyed with her fingers on the bare oak table as they waited for their spaghetti to arrive "—but why did we just purchase clothing that needs to be laundered before I wear it?"

"The jeans have to be prewashed a couple of times before they feel slouchy," Jessie said absently as she watched a toddler across the room trying to get into his baby brother's high chair. She smiled at the ensuing drama.

Joshua glanced over his shoulder to see what Jessie was smiling about. He'd never seen quite that look on her face before.

She gave the waiter a soft smile as he set her plate down. The guy almost tripped on his own feet as he became the recipient of the smile Joshua should have gotten. He shot the hovering kid a pointed glare and almost had a plate of pasta and marinara deposited in his lap as the guy gulped and scurried to make himself scarce.

"I love kids, don't you?"

"I don't know. Probably not." Joshua unwrapped his silverware from the paper napkin. "The only ones I've been around seem…disorganized."

He looked up as Jessie burst into peals of laughter. "Disorganized?" She choked. "Of course they're disorganized!" Her eyes were sparkly with mirth. "They're just learning everything. Even *you* were disorganized when you were a little kid."

Joshua thought if he could bottle and sell that laugh he would quadruple his money. "Actually, I wasn't." He pushed the limp spaghetti around his plate. A pool of watery sauce made a moat surrounding the unappetizing lump of his pasta. "I was a well-disciplined, clean, respectful and organized child from as far back as I can remember."

Her eyes got more liquid as that sweet, soft smile quivered then died.

"Good Lord. Don't start crying, for God's sake." He leaned over and wiped away the mascara under her right eye.

Jessie blotted her eyes with her own napkin. "You had a shitty life," she said fiercely. "I wish I could make it all up to you, Joshua."

"My childhood was perfectly acceptable, Jessie. Don't overdramatize it."

"Your mother was a real bitch."

He smiled. "No arguments there. Are you done poking that revolting mess? I'd like to go somewhere and get some real lunch. Then I'll take you to some den of iniquity so you can throw away my money."

Somehow the glow seemed to have gone from Jessie's face. After playing a few hands of blackjack, with the money she had brought for the purpose, thank you very much, she wanted to go home. Joshua liked the sound of that.

"How about going for a walk?" he asked after parking the car in the carport beside the house. He held out his hand for her and she handed him the laundry and an arch look instead.

"Go put on your new jeans and shirt first." She followed him into the house, immediately throwing open all the windows to let in the warm, scented air before she followed him into the bedroom.

"I just love this house." Jessie flopped down on the king-size bed, watching him with hot-chocolate eyes as he changed. "If I ever have a summer house, this is what it would be like. Far enough away from city noises. Nice, clean air." She fell onto her back as he struggled with the unfamiliar closure of the jeans. "That fabulous smell of pine and lake water. Fishing. Boating. *Gambling—*"

"Jessie?"

"Hmmm?

"Do you think you could help me with this?" He walked toward her sprawled legs.

Without moving and not bothering to hide the smile tugging at her lips, Jessie asked seriously, "Which do you need help with, sir? The buttons or the erection?"

She was bonelessly relaxed against the burgundy spread. Her left knee rose to bracket his leg as Joshua leaned down so his braced arms framed her head. "Which do you think?" he asked huskily.

Jessie reached up and gave him a quick peck on the lips before she pushed at his shoulders, her eyes devilish. "I think you need help with those pesky darn buttons so we can go for that walk."

"Touch these buttons and I won't be *able* to walk, woman."

Jessie lectured him on self-control, all the while her nimble fingers enclosing him tighter than a straitjacket behind the row of metal buttons.

"I don't think I like jeans, Jessie," Joshua confessed pitifully as she dragged him outdoors.

Jessie grinned. "They look ma-a-avelous on you, dahling." She hung back then patted his behind. "Great butt." She linked arms with him and gave him a sultry look. "We'll keep them at my house. I don't want you wearing these when I'm not there to beat the women off with a stick."

"That good, huh?" he asked, highly amused. She gave him a sultry look, and he wondered fleetingly what he had ever done to deserve her and how he had managed for thirty-three years without her.

They walked hand in hand on the lakeshore. The smoldering fire of the sun melted into the water, leaving a dancing, shimmering reminder as dusk stole slowly over the lake. Purple and royal-blue faded into black ridges and ranges, spiked with the suggestion of forest. There was an anticipation of things to come as stars started shining more brightly and the velvety sky darkened to reveal a wisp of a moon.

He took her hands, pulling her against him. She'd changed into black leggings and a thick, white cotton sweater with a wide neckline that kept slipping off her shoulder. Her skin felt cool as he caressed the back of her neck, his thumb finding the vulnerable hollow at her nape. He felt her deep shudder through his bones. God, she was responsive. He touched his lips to her temple.

Jessie turned in his arms, rising up on her toes as she gathered handfuls of his hair in her fists. With a little pressure she brought his face down to hers. "Don't play with me, mister," she warned in a tough voice, and she kissed him, her lips insistent and ravenous.

They eventually had to come up for air. Jessie's dark gaze stayed riveted to his face. "I can hear your mind whirring," he said, amused at her intense scrutiny. "What are you thinking about?" Her lips looked soft and slightly swollen from the kiss. The moonlight loved her face, sculpting it with silver.

She opened her mouth as if to say something; Joshua held his breath for a painful heartbeat. Then she shook her head. "Nothing." She touched his face with a small, cool hand as her eyes seemed to memorize his features. "You make me very happy, Joshua."

He couldn't explain his disappointment. Didn't even try. He dipped his head and feathered a kiss on her closed mouth. She tasted of the rich coffee ice cream they'd bought on the way home. Jessie had eaten more than half the carton in the car and then claimed that the bites she had spoon-fed him had been way bigger than the teeny ones she'd had.

A banner of geese flew across the moon. He turned her and braced her back against his chest. Wrapping his arms about her, he rubbed his hands up and down her arms. "I had no idea," he said into the deep pool of silence, "that I could feel this...content." Jessie stroked her head against his chin, resting more fully against him as he leaned against the trunk of a ponderosa pine, looking at the shimmering lake through a veil of her frothy hair. He added softly, "You make me happy, too, Jessie."

Around them the gentle silence of night drifted as soft as a breeze. The air was warm and fragrant with her floral perfume and the scent of woods and water.

There was nowhere on earth he would rather be than right here, with Jessie in his arms. There was no need for conversation. Even his sexual desire seemed tamed and manageable. He felt...calm. For the first time in memory, he felt strangely at peace with himself.

He had learned his lessons of self-preservation as a child, but with Jessie he found his emotions blatantly *out there*. Sometimes he felt so raw and exposed with her, he wanted to flee back into that same protective, rocky shell he was almost ready to cast aside. And other times, like now, she brought him more joy and contentment than he had ever known.

He didn't want her to know just how vulnerable he was to her vibrant spirit, her gentle eyes and soft mouth. He felt raw enough as it was.

THE NEXT MORNING Jessie went swimming in the lake. Her suit was perfectly decent. Red. Plain. Skintight. Joshua watched her from the window in the kitchen as she played in the shallows like a child. She wasn't a child. As the three kids in a speedboat noticed, making ever smaller circles closer to shore.

The waves were lapping at Jessie's calves when he came out to join her. "Hi." Her smile was brilliant, white and directed solely at him. "I thought you had calls to make."

"Made." He dragged his eyes from her sun-kissed face to the three teenagers who were a little less cocky now.

"You look good enough to eat," he told her as the boys took off, the wake making her sway against him. The tight Lycra of her suit flattened her breasts, but he could clearly see her hard nipples.

"Finished swimming?"

Jessie looked at him under her lashes. "Got a better idea?"

"How does grabbing a blanket and taking a walk deep into the woods sound?" He wiped away a droplet of water from her temple with his thumb, her skin was sun-warmed and damp.

"Why do we need a blanket when we're going for a walk?" His lady had very expressive eyebrows.

JESSIE ROLLED HIM OFF the blanket. A pinecone or something jabbed him in the back as she straddled him, her eyes determined, her hands firmly planted on his chest.

"I don't know why we brought the blanket," Joshua said mildly, as he shifted his hips and Jessie's off whatever was under his bare back.

"'Cause you thought I'd be on the bottom." Jessie pointed out reasonably, her knees nudging his sides.

He reached up to gather her loosened hair back into the scrunchie and out of her face. "Why aren't I on top?"

"You were being too darn fussy." She leaned forward to nibble a damp path up his chest as she spoke. "Everybody knows…one…*never*…bothers to fold their…clothes in the woods."

She reached his jaw, while behind her she slapped at the hand he was using to try to get her hips and other body parts aligned where he wanted them. "I don't want you rushing me," she groused against his throat. "In fact," she took a sharp nip and every nerve in his body stood at attention, "don't touch me at…all."

She gave some attention to his lower lip. "At all?" His hands itched to caress her smooth, damp skin.

"At all," Jessie whispered when they were nose to nose.

"You don't like me to touch you?" he asked. In answer Jessie slid her sweet breasts sensuously across his chest. "Because, darling, I sure as hell love to touch you."

"You will lose control."

Joshua huffed. "Are you telling me or hypnotizing me?" It was damn hard to be amusing when he felt like taking off like a rocket.

"I want to see you lose control. Don't touch." When she paused, he could feel the rush of her blood through her veins as she pressed him down. He closed his eyes, letting his arms fall over his head. "You have too much control," she added.

"There's no such thing as too much control, Jessie," he murmured, using every scrap he had. "Although I must admit, with you I seem to have less control than ever before...."

She looked down into his eyes. "Let me see you lose control, Joshua. Don't think. Just close your eyes and feel." Her small white teeth closed in to give a sharp love bite on his neck before she dragged her body up his and took his mouth in a kiss so sensual, so erotic Joshua had to give himself up. He wanted to howl with the pleasure of it.

He sighed, slitting open his eyes. "Have your wicked way with me." Her nimble fingers slid unfairly up his sides. "I'll only touch if you beg me to."

"I won't," Jessie assured him with false confidence as she nibbled his mouth.

The air smelled of the pine needles she was crushing under her knees. Dusty sunlight filtered through the tall trees, dappling her tanned, lithe body as she drove him wild with a deep, wet kiss. He allowed her to believe she was suppressing him with her small hands pressing his above his head into the leaves and needles that made up their bed.

He had never seen her like this. She tormented him with her mouth. Slowly. Maddeningly. Joshua lay where she had pushed him, half on, half off the blanket. Her eyes got so dark there were almost no pupils. She kissed his cheekbones, his nose, his eye sockets and his forehead before she got down to some serious lip action.

He could smell her sensual woman's essence as she broke contact. He thought he would explode without her moist heat surrounding him. Her breasts heaved as she gulped in air, her hands braced on his chest. She must be able to feel his heart thundering beneath her palm.

Her hair, never tamed, slipped from confinement and tumbled into a dark cloud around her shoulders as she kept her hot center inches away from his straining flesh. She slid slowly down his body, kissing a path toward very dangerous territory.

"This is torture, you know," he groaned as her tongue discovered his navel. He sank his fingers in her hair. She tasted lower. "Jessie—"

"I'm busy!"

He laughed on a huff of frustration as she finally did something about his agony. They probably heard his groan as far away as Sacramento when she skimmed that clever little tongue around his erection.

Joshua gritted his teeth and he closed his eyes, fisting his hands against her scalp. Nothing in his life had ever felt this good.

Cool air blew on a hot place. His eyes shot open. Jessie looked up the length of his body. "Uh…what now?" she asked uncertainly, her short nails digging into his flanks as though if she let him go he would disappear.

Oh, God, she had been doing just fine. Joshua closed his eyes on a prayer before pulling her to sit astride him.

"Whatever you want. Just don't stop," he panted, seconds before she sank home to the hilt. No testing the waters for Jessie. His vision blurred as she started to move. Hot, slick, tight. Agonizingly perfect. He held her hips long enough to start the rhythm.

"I can do it, I can do it," she said through clenched teeth and he let go and left her to it. She was doing a damn fine job.

Her breasts were slick, her nipples dark and fully aroused. "Touch me!" she demanded. He slid his hands up her slim hips to her rib cage, feeling her heart fluttering beneath his fingers like a frantic bird. Fascinated by the absolute concentration on her face, Joshua lost track for a moment. Sweat glistened on her skin, sticking her hair to her cheeks, making her skin glow. Eyes narrowed, her concentration complete, she growled ferally as his hands closed over her breasts. He knew exactly how Miss Adams liked those pert little breasts touched, and he did his humble best.

She rode him with a fierce and beautiful savagery, her rhythm perfect. Her primal mating brought them both to the point of no return before easing up just enough to drive him wild—a high-speed chase over a precipice only to slow down to the speed limit at the last second.

"Your…hands aren't…m-moving."

"I'm in ecstasy." Joshua was polite enough not to remind her of her command.

"You're in *me*," Jessie reminded him, his hands on her hips gently showed her he knew exactly where he was and who he was with bare-ass naked, outside, in broad daylight.

Sweat stung his eyes as she leaned down and bit his shoulder, hard. He knew he would leave fingerprints on her bottom. No one had ever made love to him like this. Hell, he'd never considered making love in the wide-open wilderness until he'd met Jessie.

She was his amazon, a Valkyrie. Pagan in her beauty as she loved him ruthlessly. She was as focused and intense as he had ever seen her. Wild and erotic, as sweat glistened on her skin out here in the woods where any hikers could trip over them. He didn't give a damn.

Her back arched as she took him deep into her womb.

The pleasure was agonizing.

Joshua reached down, touching his fingers to where they joined. Her stomach muscles clenched as he unerringly found the small nub.

Eyes tightly closed, Jessie rose and fell, losing momentum as she got closer and closer to climax. Internal muscle pulsing around him gave him fair warning.

Bracing her, his hands enormous on her pistoning hips, Joshua helped her to a faster rhythm. Until she clenched, curved and cried out his name…

Then she threw back her head and screamed.

CHAPTER SEVEN

"COULD YOU EXPLAIN to me, Felix," Joshua asked grimly, looking at his lawyer across the expanse of the other man's desk, "how the hell Vera can run up twenty thousand dollars in bills in one month and I can't even get Jessie to use one credit card?"

"Which one are you angry with?" Felix asked, keeping his eyes off Simon who sat across the room flicking through a magazine.

Joshua had arrived half an hour ago. Accustomed to his uncle's presence in his lawyer's office, Joshua got down to business immediately. That done, he leaned back in Felix's cordovan leather guest chair and stretched out his long legs.

"Neither. Both. Hell, I don't know. I don't give a damn how much Vera spends, you know that. I just wish to hell Jessie would let me do more for *her*."

"Signing over the Tahoe house should do it. Have you told her yet?" Simon asked from across the room.

"No." Joshua rotated his shoulders while squeezing the back of his neck. "I'll wait for the right moment before I give her the deed."

"December?" Felix asked, checking the thick stack of papers Joshua had just signed to make sure his signature was where it was needed.

"It's not a parting gift," Joshua said more harshly

than he intended, then modified his tone. "She loves the house. I wanted to give her something...." He smoothed back his hair. "I want to make sure she's taken care of when I... She should have the house," he finished brusquely, having no intention of telling either his lawyer or his uncle how happy he and Jessie had been in the Tahoe house. It was none of their damn business.

And he sure as hell wasn't thinking about what Jessie would be doing after December 23. Giving Jessie the Tahoe house was a smart move. He would never be able to take another woman there without thinking of her. It was logical to give it to her.

"She *seems* content not to be seeing as many clients as she did before." Joshua cleared his scratchy throat. "But it will take her a while to build up her clientele after...later. The property will be a good investment for her." He paused. "Has she said anything to either of you about being bored?" he asked casually, picking up his briefcase.

"No," both men admitted in unison.

"Fine." His tone indicated he was done with the conversation. "I'm on my way to the airport. When I get back from Russia I'll give her the deed."

"Jess going with you?" Simon asked.

"No. I'm not taking her on this trip. The schedule is too grueling, and I don't think she's getting enough sleep as it is. Keep an eye on her while I'm gone, will you, Simon?"

"If I can convince her to make the time to see me," Simon said dryly from across the room. "Every moment she isn't with you is spent at your house. Gives her more time to fool around with that mausoleum you live in and fiddle around in your garden. Never seen her happier."

"Is that enough for her?" Joshua asked, recapping his pen and sticking it in his pocket.

"She enjoys being an interior designer, but I've never gotten the impression she's a career woman. Despite the way she looks, Jessie is a homebody." Felix slipped the paperwork into Falcon's personal file. "Hate to rush you, Joshua, but Simon and I have a date with a racquetball at three, and you said you had a plane to catch."

Joshua glanced at his watch. He had plenty of time to get to the airport. He rose, shaking hands with Felix and resting his hand on his uncle's back as he passed Simon's chair. Clearing his throat, he said briskly, "Bring Patti for dinner next week so you can both see the house. Jessie will have everything finished by then, no doubt." He smiled. "Anyone else would take a year to do what Jessie does in a week. She really has a damn fine talent. I'll have her call Patti to set it up." He turned to Felix. "Rustle up one of your attractive blondes and come, too." He coughed dryly before opening the door.

"Sounds like you have a cold there, son." Simon rose, slapping the magazine he'd been pretending to read on the coffee table.

"Allergies," Joshua dismissed. "I'll see you both sometime next week. Thanks for taking care of this, Felix." Joshua indicated the desk where he'd signed several dozen business contracts and his wife's bills. "Oh, by the way," Joshua turned and said casually to Felix, "where is Vera living now?"

Felix's gaze shot to Simon, then back to Joshua. "Uh...Phoenix, when last I heard. Why?"

"Get her number, will you, Felix? I'd like a word."

The moment the door closed behind him Felix turned to Joshua's uncle. "Holy hell, Simon. What was that all about?"

"God only knows," Simon said with a frown. "We've told him for years how much Vera loves to travel. He'll buy that she's on another trip. An extended trip."

"For how long?" Felix asked. "I'm a lawyer, Simon. Joshua is my client. I could be jailed for conflict of interest here. Or worse."

"Never happen." Simon waved away the possibility.

Felix's expression was serious as he said to his best friend, "If he ever finds out what the hell you and I are doing, he's going to have our asses in a sling, you know."

"By then he'll be so madly in love with her he won't be able to see straight, let alone care one way or the other." Simon shrugged on his jacket, loosening his tie.

"Then why are we doing this?" Felix demanded.

Simon scowled. "Just in case he doesn't see the treasure stuck under his nose. There're five months left. *If*—and I say *if,* mind you—Joshua is going to give Jessie her walking papers, she'll have a nice little nest egg to tide her over."

"She most certainly will." Felix grabbed his sports bag from the credenza and flicked off his desk light. "I received the copy of her portfolio from the brokerage house last week. Hell, I never expected that Senses stock to split so quickly. So far we've almost doubled her money. We're up to six million dollars for Vera."

"Close, but no cigar," Simon reminded him. "We decided on ten."

"You decided on ten." Felix hefted his bag on his shoulder. "I hope to hell you're working on how we're going to explain to Jessie why we ignored her instructions and continued taking money every month from Joshua, long after she told me to stop."

Simon opened the door for his friend. "And to think she's been slavishly depositing hefty chunks of her pay checks to pay him back. What she's scrimped and saved will be a mere drop in the bucket." He gave a quick nod of the head. "If he does leave her, I have no doubt she'll be dammed grateful to have financial security. She won't give a damn *where* it came from."

"I hope you're right about this, Simon." Felix crossed to the elevator beyond his office and pressed the down button. "The more I know Jessie, the more I realize she doesn't give a damn about material things."

"She sure as hell likes not working," Simon told him. "They *all* like not working, Felix. As soon as Jessie has that money in her hands, she won't feel as bad. You and I have had her best interests in mind ever since that farcical wedding, for God's sake. Joshua wouldn't care or even miss the money. To Jessie, it could be a lifesaver.

"I'm betting on a wedding in the very near future. Hell, he's given her the Tahoe house. You know how much he loves that place. You know I wouldn't do anything to hurt her. I love that girl as if she were my own daughter. And I know women." Simon laughed, slapping Felix on the back as they stepped into the elevator. "Hell, I had my share of lady friends before I married Patti. Trust me on this. I *really* know women."

JESSIE YANKED A navy velour robe off its hanger and pulled it on over her naked body. Its soft folds engulfed her, surrounding her with Joshua's scent. She rolled up the sleeves and tugged the belt around her waist before going downstairs to wait for him.

Too tired to bother eating, Jessie flopped down on the new sofa in the family room. She tried to read. Even the latest terrifying vampire novel couldn't keep her awake. After laying the book on her lap, she channel surfed and found an old movie. She tried to concentrate on Fred and Ginger, pulling down the soft folds of Joshua's robe to cover her bare toes.

He'd gone to Russia this time. As usual, she'd overdone it while he was gone. Sick of the sterility of his house, she'd persuaded Joshua to let her do something about it while he was away.

Conrad and Archie had been so good to give her a job when she had no experience years ago. This commission would balance things out. And the money meant nothing to Joshua, so for once she had no compunction about spending some of it. At least it was for *him*.

She had adamantly refused his offers of money and expensive gifts for months. She'd refused money, the car, a condo and a hundred other perks he'd offered. When he realized she was in deadly earnest, he'd started giving her beautiful costume jewelry. It was obviously expensive, but at least she wasn't having sleepless nights worrying about losing it. She had to admit she loved the clothes he insisted on buying for her. Things she could never have afforded herself. Things she would never have *needed*. He moved in elite circles. To him, the designer gowns and jewelry were part of her uniform. She hadn't been able to refuse, given his logic.

Little did he know that most of the clothing she had was from her college days. College and clothing he had paid for. That was why she'd worked so hard to pay back every cent he'd given her as Vera. She refused to be bought and paid for. No matter how this relationship progressed, she didn't ever want Joshua to think he'd had to pay for her services.

She couldn't stop thinking about their trip to his cabin last month. It had been a magical time. For both of them. But it had made her reluctantly reassess what she was trying to get out of their relationship.

They had been sleeping together for months and she was still not pregnant. Each month the crushing disappointment had warred with a strange feeling of relief. The relief that the gods were giving them a little more time together.

That weekend had nudged a little place in her mind that said perhaps what she felt for him was more than the need to cold-bloodedly procreate. She'd been struggling with the decision for weeks.

She'd originally decided that having the baby alone, raising it alone, would be ideal. However, the better she got to know The Glacier the more certain she was that she would never walk away from him once she was pregnant with his child. She was positive now that Joshua would track her down to the ends of the earth if he ever found out she had stolen something so precious from him. Because, even if he didn't know it himself, Joshua would make a terrific father.

Once he forgot about his image and they were alone, he could be tender and demonstrative. The man had potential. They deserved the opportunity to explore this relationship. He made her happy. She made him laugh. Surely, there was more to what they had than just sex?

Jessie wanted to find out.

She had shed a bucket of tears before going to the drugstore. She had spent a whole day packing all the baby things and putting everything in storage.

Luckily Joshua was on one of his long trips. For days she had been alternately weepy and then optimistic. Finally she had become sick of the inactivity. The decision had been made.

The small pouch wouldn't fit into her little purse because of the divorce papers. In a moment of indecision she looked at the papers, then at the birth control packet. There was room for only one in her purse... and in her heart.

The decision was remarkably easy. She tossed the papers into the back of a drawer. The birth control fit just fine in her purse.

She'd packed a small bag and had been at Joshua's since.

Redecorating his house into a home had been exactly what the doctor ordered. The busier she was, the less time she had to think. In the last ten days she had supervised painters and wallpaper hangers, had furniture and live plants delivered and generally had a wonderful time changing the house into the home she'd always wanted. Except, of course, she'd never, even in her dreams, pictured a home quite so grandiose. And it was the first time she'd approached a job with her teeth gritted for battle and her brain conjuring up untold fairy tales.

She was worn to a nub, she thought with sleepy

satisfaction, letting her head fall back on the plump pillows. The room still smelled faintly of paint. She smiled.

Not a trace of his corporate colors survived. Instead, she had filled his home with light. Beautiful fabrics and textured wall coverings, flowers and wonderful antique accent pieces had brought it all together. She'd rearranged his priceless art collection, consigning the boring pieces to the attic.

The house had been crawling with people for days, sending Joshua's security staff into fits.

Jessie rested her eyes. She wanted him home, sitting beside her, rubbing her feet as he sometimes did. Or making love to her over there on the floor by the fireplace where he'd filled the missing gaps in her education with alacrity. Telling her what a shamelessly slow learner she was, so she had to keep practicing until she got it right.

Making love with Joshua was the best experience she'd had in her life. Dashing to the bathroom first was going to take some of the spontaneity away.

It was those quiet moments with him she cherished most: Listening to music. Watching an old movie. Talking. It was amazing they had so much to talk about, considering they hardly agreed on anything. But, no matter what the subject, they were both fascinated with looking up strange facts in Joshua's extensive library. When she came up with some off-the-wall question, Joshua would laughingly look it up in one of his many books or on the Internet.

He seemed more relaxed. He laughed more. He seemed to like her touching him even when they weren't making love. And Jessie touched him whenever she felt the urge, which was often. She loved the feel of his dark hair between her fingers. She adored the scrape of his rough jaw under her mouth as she snuggled against him on the sofa. He didn't push her away. If he didn't enjoy the cuddling as much as she did, he didn't show it. He seemed perfectly content to let her tumble against him at whim like a pesky kitten.

Most of the time, if she didn't dwell on not conceiving, she was happy.

His control was phenomenal. Jessie had never seen anything like it. Conrad had been right. It was hard to tell if Joshua ever got really ticked off. She'd learned the angrier he was the quieter he got. Thank goodness he'd never been angry with her.

Their lovemaking was spectacular. Jessie could never have imagined two people being more in tune, more compatible than she and Joshua in bed. Or on the floor. Or on a chair. They were both insatiable. He taught her to be uninhibited and inventive. Jessie blushed at some of her choice locations. She would never be able to look at the stairs again without remembering the rug burns she'd had on her butt the next day.

Jessie had practiced the wind sprint required to get to the bathroom, get prepared, and then get back to the bed. She had practiced until she was fast.

She sighed contentedly and slid down into a more comfortable position on the sofa. Even Fred and Ginger waltzing around the ballroom couldn't force her eyes to remain open.

Joshua come *home*.

JOSHUA COULD HEAR the TV as he let himself in and set his garment bag by the foot of the stairs to retrieve later. A strong smell of paint permeated the air. She'd left the front hall light on for him as she always did when he was late. A small thing, but something he always noticed the moment he walked in.

She'd placed an enormous, and rather ugly, vase on the half-circle table against the far wall. The smell of the massed fresh flowers vied with the unmistakable odor of paint and lemon furniture polish. She'd probably worked his staff mercilessly. To them Miss Jessie could do no wrong. They all adored her. A small, satisfied smile tugged at Joshua's mouth.

He loosened his tie and top button, his eyes gritty with exhaustion as he walked down the short hallway to the family room in back of the house.

"Jessie?"

He didn't remember being this tired in his life. Although his business had gone well, he'd missed Jessie more than he'd thought possible.

"Jessie?"

There was no response to his second louder call. For a moment he stood in the doorway. So much for fantasizing about her silky naked skin on satin sheets. He didn't have the energy right now anyway. He glanced at his watch. Well after midnight. She must have left the TV on and gone home.

The configuration of the room was different, the smell of fresh paint much stronger in here. His head throbbing, Joshua moved to turn off the TV before he went to bed.

The flickering test pattern illuminated Jessie asleep on the sofa, her neck at an impossibly uncomfortable angle, her feet tucked up under his robe. Her lashes cast intriguing shadows on her lightly tanned cheeks.

"Jess," he whispered with intense satisfaction. She was here. Crouching down, Joshua ran the back of his fingers across the silky skin of her cheek.

She slept as she did everything else. Totally. Nothing short of an earthquake would wake her. He took the book off her lap and marked her place.

She stirred briefly, capturing his hand under her cheek with a sigh. With a lightening of his spirits, Joshua bent and lifted Jessie to carry her upstairs.

He lay her gently on the bed, then stripped, settling under the crisp sheets beside her. The room was dark and warm, Jessie's scent tantalizing as she unconsciously snuggled against him. Before he could sleep, he wanted to feel her naked skin against him. He skimmed off the velour robe she'd appropriated and for a moment was tempted to turn on the light. She had a magnificent body and he wanted to see it. Was hungry to see it. But he could wait. Even with the brief glance he'd given the house when he walked through it, he could see she hadn't wasted a moment of the time he'd been gone. Jessie must be as exhausted as he was. She stirred restlessly as he slipped her arm out of the second sleeve, her silky hair frothing over his chest as he settled her against him.

Obviously they both needed to... Ah, hell! Jessie's open mouth found his naked shoulder and sharp little teeth took a nip before her lips trailed like liquid fire to the joint of neck and shoulder. Was she awake? Tired muscles electrified back to life as her tongue sent jolts bone deep.

He shifted to his side, his eyes adjusting to the darkness. Desire clenched in his gut. Now that she'd aroused him, she damn well better be awake! His hand made a slow and thorough inspection of one plump breast, finding the nipple pebble hard. As his body came wildly alive, he groaned aloud. He pressed her against the pillows and took her mouth. He could feel the firm curve of her breasts and hard points of her nipples now flattened against his chest. Catching a handful of springy hair in his fist, he nudged her head up so he could just make out the pale oval of her face.

"You'd better be awake, lady."

"Cyril?" Jessie whispered huskily, as her fingers climbed his shoulders.

Joshua fell on his back, taking her with him. He grinned up at her. "Cyril? You little wretch. How long have you been awake?"

"Since you started ripping off my clothes." Jessie ran her fingers through his hair, the tips lingering on his face. He needed a shave. "When did you get back?" She wriggled farther up his chest.

Joshua captured her hand and brought it to his lips, a feeling of profound...*something* pouring through him. He had no name for what Jessie did to him. He didn't even want to think about it. Her entire satiny length was pressed the length of his body. "Half an hour ago." His answer was muffled against the pulse in her throat.

Jessie's mouth blindly searched for his. His arms went around her. They kissed slowly, savoring the moment.

"I missed you." Jessie's voice was low, husky with need.

Joshua's grip tightened as she moved with catlike grace, her smooth skin skimming over his. He heard her sigh. Shifting her, Joshua ran his hand up her side, her skin shimmering under his hand. He found her breast and tended to it with infinite care.

He'd missed her, too. He hadn't wanted to. For days, the memories of this woman had colored his thoughts. It was unprecedented. It was unacceptable. It was. He nudged her knees apart and settled in the cradle of her thighs. "Show me how much you missed me, woman." He slid into the welcoming warmth of her. They made love slowly, savoring the closeness.

Suddenly her body stiffened. "Oh, damn…I forgot to…never mind."

As her body melted into deep sleep, he reached out and turned off the alarm.

HE HADN'T HAD enough sleep. He must be getting old. Traveling had never dragged at him like this. The trips were becoming mundane. He buzzed Angela to put together a list of candidates for future travel.

Hell, he'd been almost too tired last night to love Jessie. Not that she'd been too chirpy herself. He grinned. He had left her this morning with her face buried in the pillow. He'd stroked his hand down the silky curve of her bare back, lingering on her heart-shaped butt and she hadn't moved a muscle. He'd missed too many mornings when she *wouldn't* have been fast asleep. And he wanted them, damn it. He was throwing away that alarm clock ASAP.

He picked up the phone. "Ange, get me Felix, then have Craig from advertising come up. No, I'll hold while you get through. Thanks.

"Felix? Find out where the hell Vera is off to now. I want a divorce."

JESSIE JUMPED UP off her knees as soon as the Rolls pulled up in the circular driveway in front of his house. She fought the black dots in her vision from jumping up too fast, and tugged off her soil-encrusted gardening gloves. Joshua had left before she was awake this morning. Their first morning together at the house and she'd slept right through it.

She tossed the gloves aside as she pulled open the back door of the car. "You're home early," she said happily, as he swung his long legs onto the brick. "Hi, Barlow," she called over the seat. The chauffeur grinned in the rearview mirror and touched his cap, waiting for her to slam the door shut before he took off to the garages behind the house.

Jessie linked her arm in Joshua's as they walked inside. He set his briefcase down and turned to look at her; a small smile tugged at his mouth. "I have seven gardeners," he said dryly, taking out his handkerchief to wipe her dirty cheek. "Why are you digging in the dirt again?"

"I'll run up and take a quick shower," Jessie said quickly.

"I wasn't criticizing, Jess. You can do whatever you like around—" Joshua sneezed twice. "Damn." He walked into the family room and collapsed on the sofa, pushing one of the new pillows Jessie had bought behind his head and swinging his feet up. He held out his hand. "The house looks great. You did a spectacular job, Jessie. When I have more energy you'll have to give me a tour. In the meantime, come and lie here beside me and tell me what you planted today."

"Ugh, I'm all dirty and sweaty." Jessie's nose wrinkled.

Joshua laughed hoarsely. "I love it when you're sweaty. Come here, woman. I'm too damn tired to chase you upstairs."

He did look tired. His face seemed paler than usual to Jessie as she lay down beside him and felt his arms come around her. She rested her head against his chest, listening to the steady beat of his heart.

She was afraid to interpret what it meant for Joshua to turn off the 3:00 a.m alarm and then come home early the next day. She wondered if she should read *anything* into it before deciding not to get too excited. He was more than tired—she could tell by the way his arms held her. He was more interested in holding her than in taking her upstairs to bed. She stroked his face.

His jaw was slightly rough with the stubble he hadn't shaved at his office. Jessie knew he usually shaved twice a day. His skin under her questing fingertips felt warm and dry.

"Do you feel all right?" She lifted her head from his chest to look up into his face.

His eyes were closed, but he rubbed a small circle in the small of her back where his hand held her close. "Tired," he admitted on a sigh. "Just damn tired."

He was more than tired Jessie realized as she scrutinized his pale face, scorched with two angry red patches on his high cheekbones.

Jessie carefully swung her legs off the sofa. "Come upstairs, Joshua. I think you should be in bed."

He opened his eyes, taking a moment to focus on her face. "Don't think I can get it up right now, darling," he mumbled, his lids drifting shut. "M'be later."

She laughed softly. "No sex for you, big boy." Jessie carefully slipped her arm under his back and helped him sit up. "Do you think you can get upstairs on your own or shall I call Barlow?"

"Own." Joshua leaned heavily on Jessie's arm as he stood up, almost tumbling both of them back onto the deep sofa.

Terrified he would fall, and alarmed at his pallor and disorientation, Jessie managed to get him upstairs and onto the bed. After undressing him and rolling him under the covers, she searched his phone book for the number of his doctor.

"Joshua?" Jessie sat on the edge of the bed. He had fallen into a restless doze. "I need the number of your doctor. What's his name?"

"Never get sick."

"There's always a first time," Jessie said dryly. She rested her cool hand on his hot cheek. "What's your doctor's name, Joshua?"

He coughed, turning his head feverishly on the pillow. "Jessie?"

"I'm right here."

"Jessica. Jessie. Jess," he said softly, rolling over to bury his face in the pillow.

"That's me." Jessie went into the dressing room to call her own doctor to see if she would make a house call.

He murmured her name again, shifted restlessly and hugged his pillow.

By the time the doctor arrived his temperature had climbed to 104. Jessie bathed his hot face in cool water, dribbling some of the moisture between his dry lips. He didn't want to drink, didn't want to take his cough suppressant, didn't want to do anything but sleep. He sounded like a fractious child. Her heart squeezed.

Who had taken care of him when he was a child? A nanny? Had the woman loved him? Or had she just done her job?

Jessie nursed him with TLC. She managed to sponge him down without getting yelled at. First he was boiling, and then he was freezing. He hated the cold wet cloths she ran over his sweaty body. She was sweating herself by the time she'd dried him and made him take aspirin. Then she let him sleep.

Until the next time.

The next day his temperature was down and he was just plain bad tempered. Jessie carried on as if he were being his most charming best. She forced him to drink and take his medication. He couldn't resist her when she closed the drapes and lay down beside him. "Sleep," she'd say, stroking his hair, and he'd rest his head against her without a complaint. He'd be asleep in seconds.

She spent every moment with him in the bedroom, coaxing, cajoling, bullying and browbeating him until he got well. It was no hardship for her to take naps with him. He was a harsh taskmaster when he was sick. Worse when he was recovering.

After five days, he thought he was well enough to use the phone. Jessie had taken it downstairs. He was still too wobbly to try the stairs, and he fumed for hours. A short nap took care of that mood, Jessie thought with amusement watching him sleep on the eighth morning.

Whereas she came rushing out of sleep to get on with her day, Joshua woke with a soft sigh. She loved him best like this. When he was soft with sleep, vulnerable and malleable.

She leaned up on her elbow and touched his forehead. Cool, thank goodness. She'd made him stay in bed yesterday even though he could probably have been up. She'd teased him about how much control she had since he was too weak to fight back.

She slipped out of bed, careful not to wake him. Dressed in navy leggings and a thigh-length cable-stitch navy-and-white cotton sweater, she pushed up the sleeves as she made her way to the kitchen. She had the coffee on and was breaking eggs into a glass bowl when Joshua came in.

"Where's Mrs. Godfrey?" he asked, referring to the cook.

"She took her grandkids to the park."

"Hmm." He nuzzled the back of her neck.

Jessie turned to look at him. He had showered and shaved and dressed in the jeans and dark-purple shirt she'd bought him in Tahoe. "Well, don't you look handsome." She moved to arm's length, eyeing him up and down. "Great buns."

Joshua's lips quirked. "You're looking at my front, Jess."

"Trust me, I know." She grinned up at him, automatically checking his forehead with her hand. Satisfied, she turned back to the stove. "Scrambled or omelette?"

"Scrambled." He pulled the wide neckline of her sweater aside to nibble her shoulder.

She poured the egg mixture into the pan. A comb fell out of her hair to the floor. Joshua bent to pick it up. "I don't know why you bother trying to control your hair, darling. It has a mind of its own."

She used one hand to hold her hair up as she tried to force the comb back into the thickly curling mass.

Joshua smiled, his eyes getting crinkly the way she loved. "That doesn't do any good you know. It won't stay up."

"I can't do anything with it. I probably look like a wild woman."

"It looks sexy as hell."

She gave him a speaking glance. "I'm cooking breakfast here."

He looked at her innocently. "I was just making a comment."

She laughed. They hadn't made love since the night he'd come back from Russia. Considering his libido, she was surprised he hadn't taken her on the kitchen floor by now.

He still looked a little pale. She decided she could always persuade him to take a nap with her after breakfast. The meal would never get cooked though if she had to hold up her hair with her hand. Too lazy to run upstairs to look for a scrunchie, she coiled her hair off her neck and anchored it with a pencil she grabbed from the cup by the phone.

He frowned.

"What's the matter?"

Joshua shrugged. "Déjà vu."

Jessie put four slices of bread in the toaster then looked at him. "Are you sure you're feeling all right? Maybe it's too soon for you to be out of bed. Should I call Dr.—"

"Forget the doctor." He wrapped his hand around the back of her neck, his eyes lambent as he pulled her closer. "I want to drag you upstairs and do sexy stuff to your body until you yell."

Upstairs was good.

She would make a quick detour to the bathroom before they hit the bed. She took the pan off the stove, then draped her arms around his neck and wriggled her eyebrows. "How sexy?"

"How much can you take?" He used his thumb to stroke the slick inner surface of her lower lip, his gaze scorching her face.

The toast popped up behind her. "You just got out of a sick bed." She tried to be reasonable.

"Come back to it with me." He swung her up in his arms and strode out of the kitchen, across the wide entry hall and started up the stairs.

"I don't think you should be carrying me, Rhett. You've been flat on your back for a week." She held on tighter as he picked up speed the closer he got to the bedroom.

He kicked the door shut behind him. "Didn't I tell you yesterday I wouldn't always be weak and lying flat on my back?" He settled her carefully on the freshly made bed. "Now, my pretty, what do you have to say about *that!*"

He leaned over her, the purple shirt doing wonderful things to his pale eyes. He was teasing her but his eyes were hot.

"I say, fine." Jessie started unbuttoning the cotton shirt. Her throat felt dry and her pulse had sped up. She wanted to consume him in large bites. "Hurry." She couldn't believe that throaty voice was hers.

She had no idea what happened to their clothing. Or who removed what. The moment her naked skin touched his, he went wild, carrying Jessie along on a tidal wave of sensation so intense she lost all sense of reason.

Her climax was so explosive, so prolonged she almost lost consciousness. After a while she managed to slowly open her eyes. Sunlight streamed through the open window. Blankets and sheets were mounded on the floor. Jessie could feel a pencil under her right hip. She couldn't move a muscle and she struggled to draw an even breath.

She'd forgotten the detour.

Joshua leaned over her. His face had lost its pallor. His hair was sweaty and their skin was sticking together everywhere they touched. In a moment she would be able to speak. For now all she could gather the energy to do was gaze into his eyes. They held some emotion impossible for her to read. She felt the deep breath he took through her breast and down to the juncture of her thighs.

"I'm sorry."

For a moment she was so lost in the sensual haze she didn't comprehend his words. "What?"

"I'm sorry," he said stiffly. "I lost control. Did I hurt you?" A dark frown pinched his eyebrows together.

"No!" She wrapped her arms around his neck, pulling him down. "I love what we did. I love knowing I can make you forget you're The Glacier when you're with me."

Jessie felt the brief suspension of his heartbeat under her hand. It took her a moment to realize that whatever he had felt in that shattering moment, he'd caught himself and brought his emotions back under control. Damn. She'd just have to try harder. She glanced at him under her lashes. A telltale pulse pounded in his temple. So, he wasn't as immune as he liked to appear.

"There's nothing you have ever done to hurt me. In

bed or out. I promise." He lost some of the concern in his eyes. "I'm starving. Can we go down for breakfast soo—"

The phone rang and she groaned. Joshua's business calls had stopped while he'd been ill. No doubt he'd called his secretary this morning and told her he was up and about. He was definitely up—and about to be cut off. Her fingers walked deliberately down his chest.

Joshua stuffed a pillow behind his head. "What the hell do you mean you can't find...?" He glanced briefly at Jessie. "The principal party?"

She loved his crinkly chest hair, but didn't waste too much time there. He had been gone for ten days, then sick for a week. He had a lot of catching up to do. Her fingers closed around him.

She jumped when Joshua said loudly into the phone, "Then damn well hire detectives. I want her found." There was a short pause. "As death and taxes. Keep me informed Felix."

"Bad news?" She crossed her arms on his chest and tried to read the expression on his face.

"Just someone I need to contact to get some papers signed."

She made tantalizing swirls around his left nipple. "Another merger?"

"A contract dissolution. Felix will take care of it." He looked pointedly at her hands folded on his chest. "Wasn't this hand somewhere else?"

CHAPTER EIGHT

JESSIE EMERGED FROM the dressing room in the hotel room, her arms raised as she struggled with a recalcitrant earring. The flame-red Isaac Mizrahi she wore was one of a dozen designer gowns Joshua had surprised her with for this trip to Monaco.

She'd felt like a kid in a candy store when she'd seen the gowns the hotel maid had unpacked earlier. Each gown was a brilliant, vibrant color, each more tempting than the last. The red chiffon had a short, frothy skirt, no back and a deceptively modest front—until movement revealed the throat-to-waist slit and a tantalizing glimpse of small firm, lightly tanned breasts.

"Why aren't you dressed?" she asked, seeing Joshua sprawled on the bed, his arms folded under his head. Half the bedcovers were on the enormous bed, the other half on the floor. He was gloriously naked.

Jessie met his bold look and his eyes darkened. "Don't you have jet lag?" he asked in a seductive drawl. "Perhaps you should come back to bed and take a little nap."

"Oh, no, you don't, Joshua Falcon. That's what you said three hours ago." Jessie's pulse quickened under the heat of his smoldering gaze. "We've been in Monte Carlo for four hours and already made love twice." She dropped her hand when the earring back slipped home. "I thought you brought me here to gamble."

"I did," Joshua said, rising and coming toward her like a panther, all sinewy grace and rippling muscles, arousal blatant and unashamed. "And to see you dressed like you are now. God, you look incredible." He ran the backs of his fingers inside the narrow opening of her bodice to touch bare skin; Jessie couldn't help arching her back as his hand slipped inside the opening. "You turn me on whether you're clothed or naked. I love the way your lush little breasts play hide-and-seek in this dress."

She licked her shiny red lips, watching as Joshua's eyes smoldered. "Don't get me all jazzed up," she warned, fearing it was already too late. She stood her ground as his fingers played against her sensitized skin.

"I want to see the casino," she said with a laugh, her fingers small around the thickness of his wrist, as she halfheartedly tried to restrain him. He could rip these five ounces of chiffon off her and have her on the bed in a heartbeat.

A tremor rippled across her skin. He saw it and smiled. The backs of his fingers slid from the pulse in her throat to her waist and back again. Her nipples were excruciatingly hard and blatantly outlined beneath the soft fabric of the expensive dress.

Jessie closed her eyes, waiting for Joshua to cup her breasts, to taste her nipples as he had done just before she'd called it quits and run into the lavish bathroom for a shower not forty minutes ago. She'd locked the door, hearing his mocking laughter as she shot home the bolt.

"You love being a woman, don't you?" Just the backs of his knuckles rode the edge of fabric over her midriff. Jessie arched an eyebrow, a trick she had learned from him. He seemed impervious to what he was doing to her as he continued in that soft, silky voice. "I love watching you get ready to go out." His touch moved a little higher. Jessie shivered.

"I'm always fascinated by the way you primp and fuss with your hair when you know it won't stay where you put it. And no matter what, it always looks sexy, as though I've just run my fingers through it." With two fingers, he touched the pulse at her throat, and smiled down into her eyes. Her breath hitched.

"And I'm fascinated by your concentration when you apply makeup. Every move you make is graceful, feminine. You love the textures and scents and ceremony that go with being female."

Jessie felt hypnotized by the sensual timbre of his voice and the rhythmic stroking of his fingertips. She took a step back to clear her head. "Goodness. What brought this on?"

Joshua shrugged. "I've never known anyone who enjoys being in their own skin the way you do." He reached over to pick up a toweling robe, then shrugged it on. He looked back at her with a small frown. "Given the way you were brought up, I don't know how you acquired your amazing sense of self-worth."

Embarrassed and flattered Jessie didn't quite know what to say. A lot of her self-confidence was a protective device she'd perfected growing up. "I somehow managed to teach myself. I realized, even as a child, that my mother's life wasn't mine, and I did everything in my power to make sure I knew who and what I was."

Joshua cupped her cheek. "I admire the hell out of who you are, Jessica Adams." He dropped a light, yet somehow intense, kiss on her mouth, and then strolled into the bathroom.

Jessie flopped down on the bed and stared at the closed door.

THE MAIN FLOOR of the casino was an opulent mix of gilt and mahogany, the very old with some modern concessions. It retained the same air of genteel elegance and lavish style it had when it was built in the early 1860s. Jessie was entranced. "It's not fair the locals aren't allowed in the casino." She was afraid to blink—she wanted to see everything. "They're missing a wonderful part of their heritage."

"A small price to pay, considering they don't pay any taxes in Monaco," Joshua said dryly.

"It's their heritage—" Jessie gazed around her "—not the money that matters."

"Tell that to the man trying to feed his family. Hardly anyone leaves a casino with *more* money in his pocket, Jess. They're doing the locals a favor."

"Cynic. I still don't think it's fair," she said without heat, distracted by the sights and sounds of the casino. Elegantly gowned women and handsome men wearing tuxedos strolled through the vast saloons, their voices an exotic blend of accents and pitch. Her eyes lit up as they wandered through a room with dozens of roulette tables.

"It's only the gaming rooms they're forbidden to enter, little Miss Bleeding Heart," Joshua said, amused. He toyed with the loose strands of her hair at her nape. "Everyone can come to the Grand Theater to see the ballet or opera." He lifted her hand to his lips and kissed her fingers. Her lids drifted closed and she whispered for him to stop. He tasted her knuckles and her skin flushed, but she didn't pull away.

Jessie felt the ripple in his thigh muscles as he brushed against her; she carefully moved away a few inches, brushing her palm up the back of her upswept hair feeling for those loose strands as his gaze remained fixed on her face. She had known she was playing with fire when she put on the dress, but now, as his X-ray eyes touched her naked breasts, she realized she hadn't meant to start a forest fire.

She closed her eyes briefly. If she gave in to this insatiable craving, they would be upstairs naked before she could say *strip*.

"Behave," she warned, then drew in a shaky breath.

He smiled, then tucked her arm through his. "You are a hard woman."

"Shh, I'm absorbing." The smell of wealth discreetly perfumed the air. The aroma of power and money mixed with the fragrance of the fresh flowers overflowing the priceless vases in lighted alcoves along the walls.

Jessie's gold heels sank into luxurious royal-blue-and-deep-black Axminster carpet. The murmur of refined voices wove between the dulcet notes of a small orchestra screened behind a fringe of luxurious potted palms nearly reaching the intricate gold plaster ceiling soaring above their heads.

Joshua's hand rested lightly on the small of her back as they strolled across the enormous casino, his caress absentminded. Jessie didn't think he realized how much easier it was for him to touch her in public now. The familiar contact in a crowded room meant more to Jessie than she'd ever thought possible.

"Now, why are you smiling as if you just ate a canary?" Joshua asked, leading her into the next room.

She looked up at him with sparkling eyes. "I'm happy."

He touched her face with his fingertips, as if he couldn't help himself. "This has all been here for more than a hundred years, Jess. We don't have to run."

"Someone might take my lucky seat." She slowed and looked about her as nonchalantly as she could.

"Find a table. I'll get you some chips."

She caught her lower lip in her teeth and looked up at him with a delicious mixture of terrified anticipation and unholy glee. "Not too many," she warned. "I just want to play at playing for an hour or so."

Joshua returned moments later and Jessie dropped the stack of chips into her purse, turning in a little pirouette as she perused the tables before picking the one she wanted.

"I've died and gone to heaven." She grinned, opening her small Chanel clutch and taking out a handful of black and gold chips. "Come and play with me."

Joshua leaned forward, his lips brushing her ear. "I wanted to play with you upstairs." He pulled out one of the elegant brocade chairs for her.

"Patience has its rewards," she whispered, setting her chips in neat piles on the green baize table. She could feel Joshua behind her as she concentrated on placing her bet.

Actually, she had no idea how to play roulette. She only placed bets on red or black and on the double zero. It was the adrenaline rush she relished as her chips were scraped off the table or returned to her.

With several more chips than she had started with,

Jessie'd had enough. Joshua had stood behind her, his hand possessively on her shoulder and without comment for an hour.

"I'm starving." Jessie swung her legs off the high chair. Joshua laughed as he helped her scoop up her chips.

"You're so predictable." He aimed her toward the five-star restaurant with a view of the bay. "Always hungry. Come on. I'll feed you, and then you can bring me some luck."

After being seated, Jessie took a handful of chips, turning them around between her fingers. "You know, these are so pretty I think I'll just take them home and frame them so I can remember this fabulous trip."

Joshua almost choked on his wine. Jessie's eyebrows rose at his expression. "What?"

"Do you have any idea what those chips are worth, Jessie?" Joshua dabbed at the corner of his mouth with his napkin.

She shrugged. "I don't know. Five dollars?"

"Each chip is worth the equivalent of ten thousand dollars."

"What!" Jessie squeaked, her hand at her throat. "You're kidding. There must be…oh, my God, Joshua. There're at least thirty-five chips here. What happened to the dollar table?"

"That's Reno. This is the big time. The sheik sitting on your right was playing with hundred-thousand-dollar chips."

"Lord." Jessie stuffed the chips into her purse and laid it carefully in front of her on the table. "If I'd known that, I would never have played."

"You were enjoying yourself. What difference

does it make how much the chips are worth? It's only money."

"What if I'd lost?" Jessie felt sick to her stomach. She closed her eyes before looking back at him. He was still smiling.

"It's only money, Jess."

"Yours, Joshua. Not mine. It would have taken me forever to pay you back if I'd lost."

"You didn't." His smile disappeared and a strange look came over his features. He handed her the enormous tasseled menu. "Decide what you want to eat and don't think about it."

Jessie hid behind the menu, her appetite gone. She'd had no idea. She felt so stupid. In such opulent surroundings with Joshua's casual wealth, she should have guessed they wouldn't have dollar chips, for heaven's sake!

She felt like a fraud. Sitting here on the patio of one of the most famous casinos in the world, wearing a designer original. Who did she think she was?

Just Jessie Adams, daughter of a prostitute from Bakersfield.

She'd done the unthinkable. She had complacently believed she wouldn't fall in love with him. She'd thought that it was impossible. That she'd been inoculated and would be immune. As if love were something she had control over!

I love him.

She mentally tested the words, tasting them bittersweet on her tongue.

Oh, my God. How could this have happened? It had been so insidious she hadn't even noticed.

It didn't matter how much she now wanted things

to be different. There *was* no happy ending. She was welfare housing: he was penthouse. He might care for her, but he'd never fall in love with a woman like her in a million years. He'd pick someone from his own social circle.

Not only was she never going to have his baby—hell, no—she had neatly compounded her loss. On December 23 she'd leave without Joshua as well.

The sparkle went out of the evening.

She asked Joshua to order for her. The entire menu was in French, and she didn't understand it anyway. He ordered their meal in his impeccable French before leaning forward and taking her hand. "What's the matter?" His voice was husky, his pale eyes intent as he scanned her face. She wondered what he was seeing there. "Jet lag getting to you at last?"

"I don't belong here, Joshua." Jessie's eyes felt scratchy, her mouth trembly. God, she hoped she wouldn't cry. Not now, not here, in front of Joshua and all these fancy people who belonged.

"You are the most beautiful woman here tonight, Jessie. Of course you belong." He picked up her hand, and Jessie realized too late she'd forgotten to put on the red nail polish she'd brought with her. Her nails were short and unpolished. She curled her fingers in his hand. Even her hands didn't belong. Her throat closed up. She was going to cry, damn it.

"Jessie, look at me."

She raised her eyes and looked at him through a shimmering veil of tears.

"What's this all about?" he asked gently, his thumb rubbing circles on her palm. She bit her lip helplessly. "The chips are no big deal—"

"I'm sorry." Her voice was muffled by the napkin she had pressed to her mouth. "I don't know what's wrong with me." She peered at him over the damask. "It must be jet lag." She glanced up just as the waiter brought their first course. "Saved by the food." She injected a cheerful note into her voice.

Determined not to spoil an otherwise marvelous evening, Jessie got a firm grip on her emotions and picked up her fork.

Jess was sure the Boeuf Alexandra she had just eaten must have been delicious. She liked artichokes, and the truffles were interesting, but she could barely taste them. Damn it. She didn't want to be dwelling on the end when she still had weeks and weeks left to enjoy with him.

For a split second she reconsidered her decision to use birth control. It was darn inconvenient and maybe…no. She'd made that decision and wouldn't retract it.

She straightened her spine and tucked her arm through Joshua's as they left the restaurant. "Where are we going now?"

"You sure you don't want to play roulette a little more?"

Jessie gave a mock shiver. "Way too rich for my blood. In fact, here." She handed him her small shell-shaped clutch. "Stick this in your pocket so I don't have to worry about it. I'll watch you play…whatever it was."

"Chemin de fer. See those tables over there set on the raised dais?" Joshua led Jessie across the chande-lier-lit room. He talked to a gentleman standing guard at the entrance. The man gave Joshua a deferential bow and ushered them into the exclusive area. Chemin de fer was a complicated high-stakes card game, Joshua explained quietly to Jessie, much like baccarat. As he took his seat, Jessie refrained from asking what these chips were worth. She didn't want to know.

All the other seats were taken by spectators. This time it was Jessie who stood behind him.

She enjoyed the action. Even if she hadn't a clue what the players were doing or how the betting worked, she was engrossed in watching. At one point she slipped off her high-heel sandals. The carpet felt luxuriously soft under her stockinged feet.

A waiter brought her a drink which she left beside Joshua's on the table. Dinner settled uncomfortably in her stomach. She was thirsty but wanted water, not alcohol. She looked around for a waiter.

A wave of dizziness caused her knees to buckle. Saliva flooded her mouth. She swallowed convulsively as prickles of hot and cold washed over her skin. Her sandals slipped from her lax fingers to drop with a thud to the floor. Blindly she felt for the back of Joshua's velvet-covered seat. "I n-need to sit dow—" The lights dimmed, and then went out completely.

"Jessie?" She heard alarm in Joshua's voice, which came from far, far away... Something cool and damp moved gently over her face. "Open your eyes, sweet love."

Not Joshua. He had never called her love in his life and he'd never sounded that panicky. Jessie drifted.

"Jessie, open your eyes. Now." How typically Joshua to order her conscious.

His lips. Joshua's lips. He kissed her hand. His fingers felt safe and hard around hers. Jessie's eyelashes fluttered as she managed to drag her eyes open. Joshua was kneeling beside her where she lay on a sofa, his eyes narrowed on her face. "What the hell happened?" he demanded as soon as her eyes opened.

His mouth was white bracketed, his hair disheveled as though he'd run his fingers through the dark strands. There was even a pleat of worry between his aristocratic brows. His grip on her hand tightened as she stared up at him blankly. She winced and he relaxed his hold. Just a little.

Her stomach rolled once, twice and then seemed to settle. So much for the five-star dinner that cost as much as the national debt of a small country.

"Jessie?"

"What?"

"What happened, damn it?" He turned to a shadowy form behind him. "She must have a concussion. She doesn't seem to—"

"I just fainted, Joshua." Rolling her head so she could look directly at him, she managed a weak smile. "I don't have brain damage—I'm fine." She struggled to sit up, grateful when Joshua supported her with his arm. They were in an office. Two men stood discreetly across the room.

"I don't think the rich food on top of all the excitement did my stomach any good. I'm sorry if I embarrassed you."

"You didn't," Joshua said shortly, scanning her face. "God, you're as white as a sheet."

"That's 'cause you just wiped my makeup off." Jessie rested her head against his arm. She was feeling much better now and enjoyed Joshua's worried look. "Please tell me my dress stayed in place, and I fell like a lady."

"There were so many men vying to pick you up we almost forgot why you were lying on the floor," Joshua said dryly as he smoothed back her hair from her face. Her skin felt clammy. His hands felt cool and dry.

"Before I embarrass myself anymore, can we go back to our room?"

"I'll have the good doctor come up to check on you."

"I don't need a—"

Joshua gave the doctor instructions in rapid French before picking Jessie up. She felt as light as a feather, and as pale as a sheet. Her brown eyes were enormous in her pale face. He'd picked up the plastic combs she used to hold her hair up and stuffed them in his pocket.

"Make sure my bottom isn't showing." Jessie closed her eyes as he carried her through the casino to the elevator. Joshua hid his smile, making sure the short dress was tucked neatly against her legs with his arm.

"You're quite decent," he said gruffly, maneuvering her into the empty elevator.

"I feel ridiculous." Jessie's voice was muffled against his pleated shirtfront.

"Everyone thought you fainted very elegantly," Joshua teased as he managed to open the door to the suite and get her inside.

"I know you're not telling me the truth—that I fell flat on my nose in front of a million well-dressed gazillionaires and their diamond-studded wives. I bet everyone saw my underwear." Her lower lip trembled. When she looked up at him there were tears in her eyes. "I'm sorry I embarrassed you."

He used his thumb to wipe away the steady stream trickling down her cheeks. "It's only a big deal to you, Jessie. Nobody noticed, I promise. Seconds before you wilted, the prince and his entourage walked in. Everyone was looking at him, not you."

"It's going to get worse," she suddenly said, her face draining of every vestige of color. "Don't slow down until we reach the bathroom."

Joshua set her down just in time before she was violently sick. He held her head as spasms wrenched her slender body. When he was sure she was done, he supported her as she washed her face and brushed her teeth, then he carried her back to bed.

"Don't." She moaned as he wiped her face with a cool damp cloth. He had never been more relieved than when the doctor knocked on the door some minutes later.

When the man had left, advising rest and simple foods for a few days, Joshua helped a very wilted Jessie undress and crawl back under the covers.

She looked up at him with those big brown eyes as he sat on the bed beside her, careful not to jiggle the mattress.

"Can I get you anything?"

"No, thanks. I feel like an idiot. Why don't you go back to the casino? I'll see you later."

"I'm staying right here, with you." Sliding his arm around her shoulders, he gently pulled her close to his side. "Close your eyes and try to sleep."

JESSIE WOKE HIM the next morning, bright-eyed and ready to start the day. She lay across his chest. He groaned. "You're sick. Go back to sleep."

"Nope." She leaned harder, nudging him with warm sleek skin. "I feel fabulous, and you promised we'd go for a cruise today."

"I'll attest to the 'feel fabulous' part." He slid his hand down her back to her bottom.

"Oh, no you don't." Jessie rolled over, then kicked off the blankets. She was like a jack-in-the-box as she shot out of bed.

Naked and glowing, she paused at the bathroom door.

"Come on, Joshua, get dressed, please?" She fluttered her eyelashes, managing to sidestep him as he backed her against the Louis Quatorze credenza. "I'm taking a *quick* shower, then I want to go somewhere lovely for breakfast."

After her "lovely" breakfast, Joshua found the yacht and crew he'd hired the day before.

Dressed in brief white shorts that showed off her gorgeous legs and a cropped top that made his mouth water, Jessie sprawled in a deck chair beside him. Her ponytail, caught up in a hot-pink scarf that matched the stripes in her top was, as usual, quite crooked. She looked tanned, healthy and sexy as hell.

The crew discreetly kept their eyes on their business as they sailed lazily up the coast.

Joshua had stripped down to his black shorts earlier and settled back against the soft cushions with a sigh of pure pleasure. The hot Mediterranean sun baked his skin as the smell of the ocean and Jessie's subtle fragrance lulled him into a light doze. He opened his eyes when he felt soft lips on his cheek sometime later.

"You're sleeping away this beautiful day," Jessie complained, running her warm hands up his bare chest. He saw his own sleepy face reflected in her sunglasses. Gulls glided above them in a painfully blue sky and the white sails snapped in a breeze he couldn't feel.

"There's a nice big stateroom downstairs," he suggested, lazily running his hand around her back under the short top. She wore no bra. Her skin was hot, smooth and slightly sweaty.

She arched her back at his touch. "With a nice big bed, I suppose?"

"Probably."

"How about lunch first?" She wriggled her eyebrows.

Trust Jessie. Laughing, he took her hand and allowed her to lead him belowdeck.

Chilled lobster and a dozen mouthwatering salads vied with fresh fruit and several dessert dishes, the fare spread out artistically on a long, linen-draped buffet table. The crew discreetly returned to their duties after closing the door.

He watched as Jessie helped herself to a bit of everything. Her plate was piled high by the time she brought it to the small table at the large window overlooking the bow.

"You're going to be sick again if you eat all that," he warned as she bit into a chunk of lobster. She had acquired more of a tan and her skin glowed with health and vitality.

It was hard to believe she was the same woman he'd helped into bed last night. He'd never experienced anything like the terror he had felt seeing Jessie on the floor of the casino. While she'd slept the night away in his arms, he had been wide-awake and waiting to see if he'd need to call the doctor.

"No, I won't." Jessie dribbled mayonnaise on the succulent white flesh before picking up another chunk with her fingers.

She was so damned stubborn. Joshua pushed her bangs out of her eyes then settled back to watch her eat.

There was not a morsel of food left on her plate when she finished. After rinsing her fingers in the finger bowl beside her plate she yawned. "I'm not taking a nap," she warned as if she could read his mind. She dried her hands on the napkin he handed her. Hers was probably on the floor.

He looked at her coolly. "Who said anything about a nap?"

"You have that let's-take-a-nap look about you." She wore not a scrap of makeup and she looked so beautiful she took his breath away.

"I didn't get a wink of sleep last night, Jess. Take pity."

"You just want to do nasty things to my body."

"That, too."

IT WAS A darn good thing they'd taken a nap after they had made love after lunch. Joshua figured he had another long night ahead of him. Because by dusk when they got back to the hotel, Jessie was as sick as a dog again.

She came out of the bathroom, her face pasty. "Don't you dare say 'I told you so.'"

"Crawl into bed, Jess. I've called the doctor." God, he hated this. He watched her, worried out of his mind, as she limply climbed under the covers and closed her eyes.

Joshua paced while the doctor examined her.

"It's not fair. I didn't understand a word either of you said," Jessie complained after the doctor had presented his bill and left.

"He still thinks it's some kind of food poisoning." Some of her color had come back, but she still looked washed out and limp.

"Thank you for being so good to me, Joshua," she said with a simplicity that made him certain that very few people in her life had been good to her. The thought infuriated him. He felt overwhelmed by a damned heart-wrenching emotion he'd never experienced before he'd met Jessie.

He traced the dark circles under her eyes. Was the doctor right? Could a touch of food poisoning and jet lag make her this sick? More than likely, she had caught that damn bug from him last month.

"I did this to you," he said, feeling guiltier than he could ever remember feeling. He felt helpless in the face of her illness. There wasn't anything he could do.

"You don't make me sick." She gave him one of her special smiles, one that pierced his heart, as she reached up to touch his face.

"I probably gave you my cold." Joshua smoothed a thumb across one silky eyebrow and her eyes fluttered. "Close your eyes and rest."

"I just want to go home. I'm too embarrassed to throw up in that fancy bathroom again," she said in a woeful voice, which almost made him smile. "I want to be sick in my own toilet and sleep in my own bed."

"Then home it is," he said gruffly, as she looked up at him with the absolute trust of a puppy. "Close your eyes and rest while I make the arrangements."

PERVERSELY, AS SOON as the plane took off she felt fine. "What are you doing?" she asked from the sofa where she had been made to lie down and take a nap.

"Paperwork. Why are you awake?"

"I'm lonely."

"I'm only four feet away from you, Jess." She tried to look pitiful. He smiled and held out his hand. "Want to sit in my lap?" he asked softly. She felt her heart smile.

"I have to go to the bathroom first." She threw off the light blanket and picked up her purse.

"Are you okay?"

"I'll be back before you've noticed I'm gone."

Jessie made quick work of the birth control. She came out, snapped the door closed behind her, tossed her purse in the general direction of the sofa and padded over to his seat while he watched her with those pale eyes of his. His hair was smoothed back neatly, and he was wearing his yellow Tahoe shirt and jeans. She removed the papers from his lap and placed them carefully on the table beside his wide leather chair.

The engines hummed as she straddled his lap. He leaned back and settled her against his chest, her bottom nestled against him. She put one arm around his neck and the other around his waist, resting her head against his chest. She loved the way his arms enfolded her with gentle strength. "Make love to me," she demanded softly, her hand running lightly down his midriff to the snap of his jeans.

"I don't think that's such a goo—"

She smiled up at him, then her lips came down on his, cutting off words and thought. She rubbed erotically against his instant erection as her mouth clung and seduced. He nibbled gently but Jessie was having none of that. She brought both hands up to hold his head in place as she aggressively deepened the kiss.

He widened his mouth, giving her only moments to be the aggressor before he took over.

"What if Joe comes in—?" she asked suddenly.

"He won't. Don't look away, Jessie. You started this. Finish it."

"Is that a dare?" She ran her fingernail lightly down his now open shirt, and he shuddered. He smelled of soap and the brandy he'd been sipping.

Static electricity spun her hair into wild ripples and curls around her shoulders and down her back. She probably looked like a wild woman. "Make love with me. Now."

The top button of his jeans came undone at her touch, and she slipped her hand inside. There, she encountered crisp hair and hard flesh. He dragged his mouth across hers in a brief searing kiss and then held her wrist firmly away from him.

"There's nothing I want more right now than to make love to you, but let's make it last." Joshua drew her hand up his chest and kissed her palm, and she curled her fingers against his cheek. It felt rough—he needed a shave. Her skin tingled as the tip of his sharp teeth skimmed over the pad of her thumb.

He reached over and picked up the phone beside him on the wall. As he instructed the flight crew, he slowly pulled her T-shirt over her head. His breath felt warm on her bare skin. He put the phone gently back in the cradle. Lifting her with both hands on her hips, he set her on her feet. Methodically, he removed her jeans and underwear in one clever move. Jessie kicked them aside, her hands going to his jeans.

"Let me do it, darling." He rose quickly to shuck off his jeans and shirt, then sat and pulled her onto his lap.

"Here?" Jessie looked over her shoulder. The door between cabin and cockpit was only a few dozen yards away.

"They can't hear us." His mouth found the sensitive spot beneath her ear.

Jessie wrapped her arms around his shoulders as he guided her hips down. The leather chair felt cold on the outside of her calves, his thighs hot. Her back arched as he filled her liquid heat. His hands held her still. "Don't move," he whispered against her mouth then nibbled at her lower lip.

"Oh, God." Jessie closed her eyes. The sensation of him filling her was exquisite. She felt the roughness of his hand move up her side, lingering on the indent of her waist before climbing to her breast. He caught her nipple between his fingers, manipulating the hard bud until she moaned. Instinctively, insistently, she wanted to press down.

His left hand held her hips still. "This is torture," she complained, panting now, body on fire. She blindly found his mouth, sliding her tongue inside only to shudder deliciously at the dark, familiar flavor of him.

She used her own hands to tease and torment him. His nipples were just as hard as hers, his skin just as slick, as he drew out the agony for both of them.

Jessie tasted the salty skin on his shoulder, nipping him with her teeth until she felt him leap inside her. She trembled and pressed down, her body desperate to start the rhythm that would bring them both release.

His hand firmly on her hip frustrated and aroused her. She used her hands to drive him wild, feeling his low growl of excitement in her own bones and tissue.

Blood rushed in fiery trails through her body and electrified her skin.

Joshua shifted his hips slightly, lifting her enough to lave her breasts with the hot, dark promise of his mouth. She clung to his shoulders, digging her short nails into his skin, wild with wanting, frantic for release.

I love you. I love you. I love you, Jessie wanted to cry out loud. She bit her lip instead, her mind spinning, her reason going. She pressed down against the punishing grip of his hand on her hips.

He muffled her shout against his chest as he plunged inside her with enough force to convulse her body, the sensation so piercingly exquisite, tears squeezed between her tightly closed lids. Every muscle, every nerve in her body participated. She arched her back, grinding in counterpoint as she felt the sweet waves of release building.

Joshua's face was sheened with sweat, his eyes glazed and unfocused. Jessie could feel her internal muscles pulling him deeper. She watched through her own sweat and tears as his jaw grew rigid and the tendons in his neck stood out in relief.

The climax they shared seemed to go on forever. Their bodies locked in mortal combat until they collapsed, satiated.

Jessie leaned weakly against him, her arms leaden, her body limp. Sweat cooled on her burning skin. Small tremors shook her as sharp aftershocks clenched muscles and nerve endings already pushed beyond endurance.

One moment she was awake. The next she wasn't. Her hand lay curled against his chest, and her breathing was deep and still uneven. Joshua watched her with a bittersweet twist in his gut. He ran a light finger down her bare arm, her skin feeling like satin. She didn't move. He'd still been inside her when she'd fallen asleep as easily as turning off a light switch. She hadn't even twitched as he'd carried her to the bedroom in the back of the plane.

In that fleeting moment, she was more precious to him than his most priceless sculpture, his most exquisite work of art. Her loveliness had increased as he'd known her—not just the animated face she showed to the world, but the soft, intensely private face she wore when no one was looking.

It was becoming almost impossible to keep any emotional distance from her. Jessie could always make him smile. And each time, he felt an unfamiliar softening inside him. He wasn't sure he liked it, but didn't know how to prevent the odd sensation.

He wanted to gather her against his body, hard, and never let her go. She was a priceless treasure, and he'd been complacent in his possession of her, until he'd seen her so pale and weak.

Only then had he instantly and painfully realized that, unlike a painting or sculpture, Jessie *could* be taken from him. By something even he couldn't fight, couldn't negotiate and couldn't buy.

CHAPTER NINE

ALTHOUGH JESSIE HAD lost some of her tan, she glowed with good health tonight. The lighting illuminated her face as she leaned forward in her seat, absorbed by the action onstage. Joshua smiled as her lips moved silently with the music. Alone with her in the small secluded box overlooking the stage, he couldn't resist running his hand lightly up her back, letting his fingers rest under the thick fall of her hair. She wore a tangerine-colored dress with straps that crossed her smooth back. Her long coral-and-jet earrings made a soft tinkling sound against the back of his hand.

Jessie turned, giving him the special smile that touched his heart. His fingers tightened slightly and her smile widened. "*Phantom* is absolutely wonderful," she whispered, her breath soft against his face as she leaned over. In the flickering light Jessie's eyes sparkled. "Thank you so much for bringing me t—"

She was just too damn hard to resist. He kissed her. Not the way he needed to. That would have them thrown out of the theater. Joshua simply ran his tongue back and forth over her lower lip, tasting the liquid sunshine of her smile. The arm of the plush seat dug into his ribs.

The theater and music disappeared. She moaned as

he pushed aside the hem of her dress and slid his hand up her thigh.

The audience applauded and the house lights came up.

Jessie giggled as they abruptly parted. Joshua leaned back in his seat, and pushed his hair back with both hands in a frustrated attempt at control. He felt his own lips twitch in response to her amusement.

"You're going to get us arrested one of these days." Frustration made his voice low.

Jessie's big brown eyes widened mockingly, dancing with naughty highlights. "Who me?" She pulled her skirt down over her knees. "It's not my fault you can't keep your hands to yourself."

"Yes, it is." Joshua untangled an earring from her hair. "What the hell am I going to do with you, Jess? When I'm around you I behave like a randy schoolboy." And when he wasn't around her he thought like one.

Jessie fleetingly traced his mouth with her fingertips, bringing him sharply back into focus. "And I behave like a randy schoolgirl. So what?" She rose out of her seat, her slender body sensuous and graceful as she reached down to take his hand. "It's hot in here. Come on. Let's go downstairs for something cold to drink during intermission."

By the time they traversed the crowds and descended the stairs to the lobby, Jessie looked pale under her makeup. Joshua thought she'd been feeling better since they'd returned from Monte Carlo. She'd refused to see a doctor. He didn't like worrying about her. He wasn't used to worrying about anyone.

"I'm taking you home."

Jessie looked up at him sharply. "Why?"

"You look like you're about to pass out."

"I'm not. It's just warm in here." She licked her lips. "I'm loving the play. I'm fine, truly, Joshua. Let's stand outside for a little bit and get some fresh air. Okay?"

"It's freezing out there. Wait here. I'll get your coat." He glanced over her head. "Damn, this is all I need."

"What? Who?" Jessie glanced around. "Oh, Paul and Stacie."

Joshua watched as his cousin and wife came toward him. Paul was a decent enough guy, if one didn't expect him to work for a living. As tall as Joshua, with equally dark hair, they had often been mistaken for brothers. But while Joshua worked seven days a week, twelve hours a day, Paul seemed to think the world owed him a living. His cousin had never resented Joshua having the controlling interest in Falcon's. He was more than happy to cash his dividend checks and continue his carefree lifestyle. Joshua hadn't seen either of them in almost a year. He could have gone another year without seeing his cousin's wife.

Petite and blond, Stacie hadn't changed her Grace Kelly hairstyle in ten years. She always wore discreetly elegant, understated clothes and maintained a superior aloof air that had, years ago, driven him mad. She looked dull and far too controlled to Joshua now as she smiled up at him with collagen-enhanced lips.

"Paul. Stacie." Joshua's hand tightened at Jessie's waist as she listed against him. He gave her a worried glance before glancing back at the other couple.

He could look at Stacie dispassionately, her cool blond beauty seemed soulless against Jessie's vibrancy. He couldn't believe he'd ever asked this woman to marry him.

Stacie's contact-lens-blue eyes flickered from Joshua to Jessie and then, dismissing the other woman, back to Joshua. He noticed she and Paul stood several feet apart.

"You've met Jessica Adams?" He asked though he didn't give a damn. The room was hot. Out of the corner of his eye, he saw a faint sheen on Jessie's face.

Diamonds sparkled in Stacie's ears as she shot an amused glance up at Jessie. "Oh, yes, darling, we've met your calendar girl." She laughed. He used to think that trilling laughter sexy. Now all he wanted to do was put his hands around her diamond-encircled throat and squeeze. Hard.

Stacie stroked his arm. Her nails were fashionably long and a deep wine color. Joshua shook her off. He felt as though a spider had crawled along his sleeve.

"No need to be angry, darling. It is an indisputable fact you only keep your mistresses for a year."

"We were just on our way outside for a breath of fresh air." He ignored Stacie. "Nice seeing you, Paul. Come to a board meeting sometime." Holding on to Jessie he moved through the crowd to the doors leading to the street.

"Oh, Lord, it *is* hot in here." Stacie fanned her perfectly made-up face with her program as she followed them. Her perfume, while ridiculously expensive, was as repulsive to Joshua now as fly spray. The foyer was packed, body to body. There was no moving quickly, no matter how much he wanted to. Her voice rose as she said over her shoulder, "Get me a drink, Paulie. I'll meet you outside."

As people gave way, Joshua kept a careful arm about

Jessie's waist. Her face was paler now and damp strands of dark hair clung to the moisture at her temples.

"Do you need to sit down again?" He felt her slender body tremble against his arm and saw her swallow convulsively. "Bathroom?" He was already steering her in that direction as Jessie nodded mutely.

It seemed as if she were inside for hours. Joshua held up the wall. Ignoring the few people lingering about the lobby, Joshua finally pushed open the door to the ladies' room.

"Oh, my God, Joshua! You can't come in here!" Jessie looked up from where she leaned against the vanity counter, a damp tissue at her throat. Her color was back, and she had fixed her hair and applied lipstick.

"You've been in here for hours." The carpet felt plush underfoot as he walked toward her, his gaze fixed on her face. The room smelled of woman. Combined perfumes and powders, silks and furs, the lighting flatteringly muted.

Jessie met him halfway, slipping her hand into his. "Thank you for coming to find me." Her eyes danced. "Is the coast clear out there? Can we go and see the last act?"

"You don't want to go home to bed?" Joshua pushed open the door, ignoring the stares as he ushered Jessie across the lobby and upstairs.

"Nah. I feel great. I was just a little wonky for a minute."

Joshua settled in his seat beside her just as the opening bar of music began. He took her hand, placing it against his knee. He inhaled deeply her scent of fresh peach and Joy. "I'm sorry she took those shots at you."

"They didn't bother me," Jessie assured him. "I

feel sorry for her. Anyone that mean must be very unhappy."

Joshua closed his eyes as the music swelled in time with his heart. Only Jessie could feel sorry for a woman like Stacie. Bringing their clasped hands to his chest, Joshua leaned back to enjoy the rest of the play, Jessie's hand against his heart.

His biggest concern right now was Jessie's health. These weak spells were happening with alarming regularity. He didn't like Jessie being sick. Tomorrow he would insist she see a specialist.

On the way home, she dozed contentedly beside him in the car. But when he was about to take his freeway exit, she'd asked sleepily to be taken to her cottage instead. He could tell that, although she was no longer pale, she was distracted.

He insisted on going upstairs with her, because he wanted to make sure she was really fine. They made love with slow, delicious languor and fell asleep in each other's arms.

Joshua was rudely jerked awake by Jessie's alarm clock. She mumbled in her sleep as he dressed and let himself out.

It was icy cold and pitch-dark as he climbed into the car and stuck the key in the ignition. Damn. The engine turned over, loud in the absolute silence. He rested his hands on the top of the steering wheel and stared back at the dark windows of her cottage, imagining Jessie snuggled deep amid her blankets, sleeping securely the whole night through in her own bed.

He felt…cheap.

He glanced at the clock on the dash then started to laugh.

It was 3:00 a.m.

THEY FLEW TO Tahoe for a few days. The weather was cold and sharply crisp. While Jessie cooked a roast, Joshua sat in the kitchen. She smiled as he meticulously folded linen napkins and stuffed them into the little copper napkin rings she'd brought with her.

Jessie opened the oven to baste the meat. The house was already filled with the mouthwatering scents of the meal.

Joshua, finished with the table, poured two glasses of wine. He set hers on the counter where she'd been cutting the lattice for an apple pie. "I'm starving," he complained, tying a towel around her waist. Jessie couldn't see the point: she was already covered practically from head to toe with flour.

"Take the roast out so it can rest, then we can eat." She waited until he'd set the heavy pan on the counter before saying casually, "How do you feel about Thanksgiving?"

His eyebrows rose. "Thanksgiving?"

"Yes. The holiday that comes in November?"

He smiled indulgently. "I don't care, one way or the other. Why?"

"I love Thanksgiving. Can we come up here for it?"

"Sure. I don't see why not."

She'd never cooked a turkey in her life. Jessie mentally started planning. She wanted the holiday to be perfect. There would be turkey, pies…. This Thanksgiving had to be Joshua's best. She wanted to give him good holiday memories to store up.

The roast leg of lamb turned out perfectly, moist and tender, the potatoes fluffy and the carrots glazed to perfection.

Joshua laughed. "You are the only woman I know who sounds as if she's having sex when she's eating."

She loved seeing him so completely relaxed. He was wearing the jeans she'd bought him last time and a fisherman knit sweater that did very nice things to his shoulders. "I love holidays." She felt warm and dreamy and so content she could melt.

After being told to take her wine into the living room, she lounged in front of the fire while Joshua cleaned up the kitchen. He came and sat on the other end of the sofa, pulling her feet into his lap. He massaged her toes through her thick, wool socks.

"When I was a kid," she said, watching the fire spark and leap in the stone fireplace, "I had a scrapbook. I'd look for food pictures and holiday pictures and paste them into my special book. I loved the pictures of families the best. You know the ones? Happy moms and kids eating Campbell's soup in a big country kitchen."

He stopped kneading. "What happened to the book?"

She felt herself blush. "I still have it. Silly, huh?"

"No." His voice sounded rough, and she turned her head to look at him. "It's damn sad. Why have you never married and had the family you so obviously want, Jessie?"

Tell him, she thought. Oh, God, this was the perfect opportunity to tell him. The words gathered and dispersed in her mind. All the food coupled with wine and the warmth of the fire had dulled her brain. The moment passed.

"I fell in love with the wrong knight."

"How old were you?"

"Twenty-one."

"Did he break your heart forever?" he asked roughly, setting her feet aside so he could throw more logs into the already roaring fire. She watched the sweater stretch over his broad shoulders and the way the jeans lovingly cupped his behind.

"At the time I thought so." *I had no idea how much worse it could get.*

"I never thought such a thing as love really existed." He picked up her feet, pulling off her socks. He tossed them on the floor. His hands, big and warm, closed over her bare toes. "It hardly seems worth the risk of a broken heart."

"What you get from love is greater than the risk of never loving at all." She would have this year to remember for the rest of her life.

"If you get to know someone too well, you can see all their faults and failings." He stared into the orange flames, his jaw set. Outside, the darkness pressed against the windows, cocooning them in a suddenly very small world.

"Or you can learn to care?" she said softly.

He shrugged, looking uncomfortable. "I despise anyone weak."

"Perhaps they were just human?" Who was he talking about? Stacie? His mother?

A muscle jumped in his jaw. "My father saw me as weak."

"You *were* weak, Joshua," Jessie said softly. "You were a child."

"The thought of being that weak again terrifies me." He said it like a grim confession. Jessie's heart ached for him.

"Love makes people strong, Joshua. The love of a mother for a child, or a man for a woman. We all need someone to care about us. We all try to attain that special place where we feel loved and safe."

"People are exactly where they want to be." His eyes appeared particularly pale as he turned to her. "The choices we all make lead us to where we are at any given time. If a person doesn't like where they are then they should make different choices, shouldn't they, Jessie?"

"I suppose so," she answered drowsily. She'd certainly made a series of bad choices. His logic seemed rather convoluted, but then she was almost asleep.

A log popped. Joshua's fingers kneaded her instep. Jessie floated in a warm haze.

"Let's have a party when we get back," Joshua said out of the blue.

"Mmm, okay."

"I want a big party, Jessie. We'll invite everyone we know. You can boss around the caterers and staff to your heart's content." Jessie felt a small smile curve her mouth.

"Like parties suddenly?" she asked around a yawn. She thought he hated parties.

"This one will be spectacular."

"Joshua," she said, on the precipice of sleep. "*Why* are you having a party?"

October

"GOOD TIMING. I just woke up from a nap. Oh goodie, chocolate." Jessie reached for a cookie off the Spode plate. Archie and Conrad had arrived unannounced

at the cottage bearing chocolate chip cookies. She'd
led them into her small kitchen overlooking the vegetable garden.

Jessie absently coiled her hair in a knot and secured
it off her neck with a pencil while the two men exchanged a glance over her head.

"What did the doctor say?" Conrad demanded.

"How are arrangements going for the party tomorrow?" Archie asked at the same time. He handed Jessie
a paper towel, shooting Conrad a narrow look.

"Great." She poured them coffee and herself a glass
of water. "I love bossing people around. I've found I
have a real knack for it." She sat down and took another bite of her cookie. "In fact, I'm going over there
in a couple of hours to check on things and have dinner with Joshua. It's so sweet of him to have a party to
show off the house."

"Yeah," Conrad said dryly. "Sweet."

"Well, it *is*."

"He's proud of the job you did," Archie pointed out.
"Your work has been getting better and better, Jess. He
wants to showcase your talent."

"What a nice thing to say." She licked chocolate off
her thumb as the two men lapsed into a rather loud silence. Jessie sighed. "I have good news and I have…
other news."

"What's the good news?" Conrad crossed his feet
before snagging a cookie he didn't really want.

"The good news is…I'm glad you think my talents
are improving 'cause I'll be coming back to work full-
time…soon." It was pretty weak, but, after all, this was
just the dress rehearsal. Right now she felt as if she

were in the hot seat as two sets of eyes bored into the center of her forehead.

"Well?" Archie prodded when she didn't say anything for a few moments.

"The other news is…I'm pregnant." Jessie looked from one to the other. "And don't either of you say I told you so," she warned as they exchanged glances.

"I thought you were using birth control now."

Jessie pulled a wry face. "*Most* of the time in the last few months, yes."

"It's supposed to be used *every* time," Conrad pointed out unnecessarily.

"Sometimes there was no *time.*"

"Oh, please *don't!*" Conrad rolled his eyes.

"Oh, well, another little thing gone awry with life," Archie said drolly, patting her hand. She gave him a smile.

"You don't consider that bad news?" Conrad dropped his feet to the floor, leaned his elbows on the table and scowled.

"Nope." Jessie bit into another cookie.

"Then why have you been biting your nails?"

"Tonight I'm going to tell Joshua everything—"

"Everything?" Archie's eyebrows rose.

"Everything." Jessie rose to stand by the window. The garden looked sad and gloomy in the half-light. Most of the trees were bare and there weren't many flowers. She had to try to remember that after winter, came spring. No matter what. "Oh, God. What a mess. I'm ecstatic about the baby. Thrilled. Over the moon. But I'm terrified of Joshua's reaction."

"Isn't that a little like the thief that's sorry *after* he's caught?" Conrad asked soberly.

"I wasn't *caught*." Jessie chewed her thumbnail. "I really thought I could pull this off, but you guys were right." She leaned back against the windowsill, braced by her arms. She wore her fluffy pink robe but her feet were bare, and cold, on the vinyl floor. She shivered.

"I should have been up front from the beginning. I thought I'd get pregnant faster. I never planned on *this*." She swallowed the lump in her throat with difficulty before she managed to tell them both what they knew already. "All I've done is fall more deeply in love with Joshua." She sighed. "This is going to cut what little time we had left short. Finding out he's about to become a father won't send him dancing through the streets in celebration."

She pushed away from the window, crossed back to sit at the table and pulled her feet up beneath her. She wrapped her arms around her knees.

"The game was fine when it was just the two of us. But I'm not going to play games with our baby. I can't lie by omission anymore. Besides—" she rested her chin on her knees "—how can I expect Joshua to make a rational decision about us when he doesn't know all the facts?"

"He'll be furious," Archie warned.

"I know," Jessie said calmly. "But I still have to tell him."

JOSHUA WALKED INTO the dining room and surveyed it with a critical eye. The table was elegantly draped with a pale-pink damask tablecloth, the delicate cream-and-blush-colored roses had been part of Jessie's order from South America for the party tomorrow night. China and silver gleamed. Stemware sparkled.

He swallowed the dryness in his throat as he checked his pocket for perhaps the twentieth time in the past half hour. God, he was as nervous as a schoolboy. He smiled self-consciously as he walked back down the hall into his den and poured himself a stiff drink.

Jessie was magic. His talisman against the cold loneliness he'd let fill his life. Jessie was warmth and laughter. She made him believe he really mattered to her. She made him believe she knew a part of him no one else had ever seen. She was soft and loving, and so open and honest with her feelings; it was like looking into a crystal-clear mountain pool.

Joshua sank into his favorite chair. In the gathering darkness he could see part of the curving driveway from the mullioned windows in his den. He'd be able to see Jessie's little red car as she approached the house.

Jessie with her sparkling brown eyes and throaty laugh. Jessie with her electric hair. Jessie with her long, slender dancer's body. She had that sensuous way of moving that always made him want her.

If what he had with Jessie was just good sex, it would have been easy to dismiss. He'd had good sex before. But with Jessie even the sex was different. As much as he'd tried to deny it, Jessie was right. It was lovemaking. It was glorious, blow-the-top-of-your-head-off great. But there was more. There was her humor, her intelligence, her honesty and integrity. With Jessie he had learned to relax, smell the flowers. And finally, in a small measure, Joshua had to admit he'd learned to trust.

He suddenly wished he *had* married half a dozen times, because with Jessie he wanted everything to be perfect. If he'd tried a real marriage before, he'd have the bugs worked out by now.

He rolled up the sleeves of his blue-and-white striped dress shirt then rolled them down again. Was he too dressed up? Was he too stuffy? Should he wear the jeans she'd bought him? Christ, this was ridiculous—he'd already changed twice. He laughed out loud, ridiculously happy.

Jessie would be home soon. They would have a drink, go through to dinner, and after the staff served dessert, he would take the little box out of his pocket. Joshua closed his eyes, leaning back in the big leather chair as he imagined the look on Jessie's face when she saw the ring. She'd get that sexy little twinkle in her glorious eyes, probably jump up and fling herself at him…. Joshua lost himself in pleasant daydreams.

He hadn't heard her car but he heard the front door open. Heard Jessie's high heels on the marble, the wood, the carpet.

He opened his eyes. God, she looked glorious in a royal-blue wool dress and high-heeled black suede boots. She tossed the dark coat she carried onto a chair by the door.

Her hair was curled wildly from the wind, her cheeks flushed, her eyes bright. Without a word she crossed the room and settled herself on his lap, curling her arms about his neck, the sweet curve of her butt nestled against him. She smelled of fresh peaches as she raised her mouth to his.

"Is that a gun in your pocket or are you just happy to see me?" she said in a Mae West drawl.

Joshua laughed, burying his hands in her hair. It was still a little damp and smelled of peach shampoo.

He crushed her mouth with a bruising kiss, plumbing the depths as she relaxed against his chest. Her fingers curled around his open collar, holding on for dear life.

"God, Jess," he managed to moan before she lowered her head again.

"We have to talk," Jessie said against his throat. She sounded reluctant. He ran his hand down the soft wool covering her back.

They were going to have a lifetime to talk. "After dinner. How do I get into this thing?" Her skin was warm as he slowly lowered the zipper down her back, detouring to unclasp her bra on the way down.

After Joshua had peeled away the dress, Jessie stood so it could fall unnoticed to the floor. She looked seductive in tiny bikini briefs and black boots. He slid his hands up her thighs to her hips, drawing her close for another kiss.

She yelped when he swung her up in his arms. With one swipe, he cleared his big burl desk, laying her down on the cool leather surface.

"This feels very naughty." Her voice was husky, her eyes alive, the lights in them dancing. The heels of her boots tapped on the face of the desk.

"You're overdressed." He pulled the small damp strip of satin down her smooth legs. Jessie sprawled bonelessly, her breath uneven.

He dropped the fragrant scrap to the carpet, running his hands up the flexing muscles of her long legs. And he laughed hoarsely when she said in a lazy drawl, "Glad you got rid of that. No wonder I was so hot."

She watched him through heavy-lidded eyes as he stripped off the shirt he'd so carefully put on. Her eyes grew lambent, her knees flexed, as he kicked off his shoes and dragged socks and slacks off in two swift jerks.

He'd wanted it to last. He'd wanted to linger over each delectable soft inch. Showing her how much he wanted her. Loving her until she was too weak to refuse him anything. But the moment he plunged into her tight, slick warmth, the moment he felt the rough suede of her boot-clad legs wrap about his flanks, he was lost.

Their climax was immediate and turbulent, leaving him stretched across her body, his face pressed against her damp neck.

"It *was* a gun in your pocket," Jessie said with a faint laugh.

He gently lifted the drift of hair off her face and used the backs of his fingers to explore the texture of her sex-warmed cheek.

With his other hand he tilted her face up before dipping his head toward her. She gave him a drowsy, sexy look at the touch of his lips on her forehead.

He stroked down her side, enjoying the way her skin shimmered under his hand. He continued to pet her and she groaned, rising up to bury her face against his shoulder. Their bodies were slick with sweat.

"I'll give you twenty years to stop that." Jessie looked like a wanton, pagan princess with her hair spread in a dark cloud, her arms curved seductively above her head. Joshua stood between her thighs, his arms braced against the desk.

"You're insatiable."

Eyes that were almost all pupil stared back at him. Sleepy, sensuous and sated. "That's a problem?" she asked lazily as her foot slid up the back of his thigh, and she ran her hands up the muscles flexing in his arms.

"Not to me, it isn't." Her feet met and crossed in the small of his back; he could feel her sharp high heels drawing him closer. He braced his arms firmly for a moment, looking at her with fresh new eyes, his heart playing an unfamiliar beat.

"You drive me wild, Jessie Adams. When I'm with you I want you. When we're apart I think about you constantly. You worry me. You make me laugh. You make me believe in dreams."

Her crossed ankles proved stronger than his will as she drew him against the open heat of her. Joshua lowered his chest, feeling the pillowy softness of her breasts flatten under him. He whispered against her swollen mouth, "I want to wrap you in a cloud and put you on top of the highest mountain to keep you safe." His gaze never wavered as he lifted her hand to his lips. "I'm excited by you, Jessie, and yet strangely calmed by your presence. You're unpredictable and your crazy hobbies give me heart palpitations. You have the strangest, strongest set of principles of anyone I know, and I'm learning to trust you more than I have ever trusted another human being in my life."

Her face drained of color, deathly pale. He felt the flutter of her fingers as she tried to withdraw her hand from his. "What is it, love?" Jessie bit her lip and worry immediately slammed into his chest.

She closed her eyes for the longest moment then licked her lips before she looked up at him. "I went to the doctor today." Her voice shook. She bit her bottom lip and took a deep, shuddering breath, her eyes dark and huge.

A cold chill of dread raced up his spine. He lifted himself away from her, sex the last thing on his mind now. For a moment he felt as though every particle of his body had frozen. A fear he'd never known drew a black ominous cloud over his vision. It made his heart jerk and his hands sweat.

He blinked, too terrified to look at her and yet too terrified not to. He thrust his fingers through his hair in frustration and swore under his breath. "You went to the doctor today.... Oh, Christ, Jessie." Joshua squeezed his eyes shut, a fist squeezing his heart. He forced open his eyes. Her lips were bloodless, her eyes dark with pain. Oh, God, it was bad, really bad, for Jessie to be this upset.

"What the hell did he say? Whatever it is we can deal with it together. Christ, I have more money than God. We'll get the best specialists on the planet. We'll—"

The phone rang just as Jessie said his name in a terrified, tremulous voice and struggled to sit up.

"Tell me, for Christ's sake," he demanded, ignoring the insistent ringing of the phone inches from Jessie's head. It wasn't like Jessie to be reticent in telling him anything he wanted to know. Her wonderfully expressive brown eyes wouldn't meet his. The phone's insistent ringing was annoying the shit out of him.

"Tell me," he ground out, his back teeth grinding painfully.

"I—I—" Jessie's teeth bit into her lower lip. "Answer the phone first."

"The hell with it. What did the doctor s—"

Jessie grabbed the phone off the hook and handed it to him.

"Yes!" Joshua snatched the instrument to his ear, his eyes fixed on Jessie's averted face. What the hell would he do if Jessie died? What the hell would—

"*What* did you say?" he demanded as he registered what Felix had just said on the other end of the phone. "Vera wants five million dollars?"

If possible Jessie went even whiter. Hell, this evening wasn't going exactly as he'd planned. He'd thought to propose first, explain his sham marriage later. The shit would hit the fan now. Jessie had the strangest expression on her face as she slid off his desk.

"Fine. Give it to her!" Joshua snapped at Felix, impatient to get off the phone. Jessie had pulled on her dress. She looked sick as she frantically searched for her underwear. Joshua found the scrap of satin stuffed between the papers on the floor and handed it to her. She crammed it into her purse and grabbed her coat by the door. "Just pay her off. It's worth it." Joshua slammed the phone down. Jessie stood poised, ready for flight out the door.

"Now, what aren't you telling me? What the hell did the doctor say?"

She wore a sunflower-yellow wool dress which covered her from her throat to midcalf. Suede high-heeled boots in a deep cinnamon matched the turtleneck under the dress. In her ears she wore huge painted sunflowers. She looked vibrantly alive and breathtakingly lovely.

And furiously angry.

"And I couldn't have talked right then if my life had depended on it," Jessica told Felix angrily. She stood before his desk, having driven to his San Francisco office to be there at precisely nine the next morning. "I was so darn mad, I ran. God only knows what Joshua thought." She drew an angry breath. "I know you're *his* lawyer, Felix, but I thought you and I had a business arrangement. So would you please explain to me why 'Vera' wants five—" she almost choked on the amount "—five million dollars?"

The intercom buzzed announcing Simon Falcon. Jessie rolled her eyes. "Did you call him in a panic while I cooled my heels in your waiting room? Damn it, Felix. How could you do this to me?"

Simon closed the door behind him, resting his hand on Jessie's shoulder. "Sit down, honey. This is not what you think."

Jessie shook off his hand and flopped furiously into the soft leather chair opposite Felix's desk. She glared first at Joshua's lawyer, then at his uncle. "What are you two up to? I told you years ago to stop taking Joshua's money." Jessie clenched her fist on her knee. "Damn it, I've almost saved enough to repay what I *have* taken for the past seven years. No wonder he's got such a poor opinion of women. And now you two have made it even worse. God. I can't take much more of this," she said thickly, dashing impatiently at the persistent tears.

"Just hang in there, honey." Simon looked at her worriedly, as he leaned over to pat her hand. "Joshua'll never miss the money. He's a generous man. He has plenty to spare. We just wanted to make sure you'd be financially solvent by year's end." He looked helplessly at his accomplice. "If he didn't fall in love with you. And we—"

"Well," Jessie snapped, "he won't *now,* for God's sake! I don't need Joshua to bankroll me, Simon. I have a job. I can support myself," Jessie said through her teeth. "And in the new year I'll go back to it." She jumped up and started to pace, the yellow dress swishing around her legs.

Both men looked alarmed as tears ran unchecked down her face. She continued to dash them away with her fingertips. "Damn it, damn it, damn it. He already thinks every woman he meets is a conniving opportunist. Now he thinks Vera wants five million dollars for a divorce! Are you two nuts? How could you d-do this to him?"

"Honey." Simon glanced from Felix to Jessie, his face creased with worry. "In a month Joshua…" He searched for the right words. Jessie let the tears fall. She was so tired. So tired of being tired. Crying in front of these two men was the least of her problems.

"A lovely women like you should be worshipped, my dear," Simon said uncomfortably. "Joshua's a fool to let you out of his sight. But you knew this was going to happen."

Jessie drew in a deep, shaky breath. She felt raw to the bone. "I don't want to be worshipped. I wanted to be lo-loved." Her breath bubbled. She hated this. Hated it. "In four weeks, Joshua and I would have broken up." Jessie swiped at her cheeks with the hankie Felix handed her. She got makeup all over it. She scrunched it in a damp ball in her fist. "I don't want his money. I *won't* take his money. Let 'Vera' give him his divorce. But if you two try to take one more cent from Joshua, I'll—I'll do something nasty."

Simon and Felix rose. "Honey, we just did it so when it was over you'd have something."

"I'll *have* something, Simon. Trust me. Something far more lasting and important than money."

CHAPTER TEN

IT HAD BEEN a hell of a morning and it was barely ten. Joshua had told Angela to hold all his calls as he tried Jessie's number for the umpteenth time.

He was frantic.

Where the hell was she? He'd tried calling a dozen times last night. He'd sat in his car in her driveway waiting for her to come home until the sky had lightened over the trees. He'd been too agitated to wait inside. Still no sign of Jessie. He'd talked to Archie, to Conrad, to Simon and, finally, to the hospitals. No one knew where the hell she was.

Unease and worry had turned into dread. She'd sped out of the house so fast last night, she hadn't answered his questions. And as much as Joshua loathed admitting it, the unfamiliar ball of lead in the pit of his stomach was fear. He was tormented with it.

He pressed a finger to his temple, warning himself to rationalize this. He had known she wanted to tell him something last night. Something important. Something she'd found hard to share. What the hell could it be? The suppositions were becoming more and more alarming. In the last hours he had come up with every worst-case scenario possible. And every way he could think of to correct it, rectify it, and make it better. Unless it was terminal.

If it was terminal he couldn't do a damn thing. Even *he* couldn't fix that.

He closed his eyes. He ignored the ringing phone. He ignored the faint hum of voices in the outer office. His concentration was complete and total. His focus unwavering. He wanted to pray but for a moment, had no idea *how.* He figured God knew his track record and wouldn't care. Words tumbled frantically through his mind. He begged, bargained and made promises, his eyes squeezed so tightly shut, they watered.

He reached for the phone again. He'd have Felix send out one of his P.I.'s. He drummed a tattoo on the highly polished surface of his desk as he waited, feeling demented, the ice in his soul making him burn. Christ, for all he knew Jessie could be lying dead somewhere—

Hell, he wouldn't think like that. Joshua looked up impatiently as his office door opened. "I told you I didn't want to be disturbed, Angela, unless it's—" The lead ball in the pit of his stomach dissolved like mist. He slammed down the receiver.

Fear dissipated into something he understood even less. Anger then relief, then something else too fragile to name.

"Where the hell have you been?" he demanded, as Jessie crossed to sit in the visitor's seat opposite his desk. The brave red of her wool suit leached every vestige of color from her face. Her hair was pulled back with a cream-colored clip that matched her high-heeled shoes and blouse. She crossed her lovely legs with a whisper of nylon and pulled her skirt down.

Her face seemed finer boned and drawn this morning. Dark shadows haunted her eyes. She looked fragile, as though she'd been crying.

Joshua's throat tightened. "God, I'm sorry." He cleared his throat. "I'm not angry at you. When I couldn't find you I... Jesus, Jessie..."

"I'm sorry you were worried." She sounded as subdued as he felt frantic. His blood pressure rose two more notches. "I..." She licked glossy red lips and swallowed before she looked up at him. "I needed a little more time."

Worry made his voice harsh. "Where were you last night?"

"I stayed at a hotel in San Jose."

"Why, for God's sake?" Joshua resisted scrubbing his face, instead clenching his hands together on the surface of the desk. His palms were damp. "Don't hold it in, Jessie, whatever it is. Just say it." He resisted the need to hold her. He had never been more afraid in his life. If he touched her now, he was terrified he'd inadvertently break her in half when she told him the bad news. The bones in his hands protested the excruciating pressure being exerted.

Wide brown eyes looked at him steadily. She drew a breath. "I'm pregnant, Joshua."

For a split second the relief that Jessie wasn't going to die was so profound he couldn't speak. His fingers felt arthritic as he slowly released their death grip.

Then he stared at her. Actually *heard* what she said. Pregnant.

He had been thinking the best doctors and specialists in a sanitarium in Switzerland. *She* had been thinking child support.

Rage consumed him.

For a moment he went deaf and blind with it. "You're

pregnant." Frigid anger relit the fuse low in his belly. "You're pregnant?"

He stood, his fists braced on the desk. "Whose is it?"

Jessie flinched imperceptibly. "Yours, of course."

"Not in this lifetime, lady." Jessie's eyes went dark. A thundering pulse pounded his temple. Contempt tightened his voice. "I had a vasectomy years ago."

She sucked in her breath. "Impossible."

Joshua delivered the next thrust as the fire in his gut blazed, his voice dangerously even. "Right after the third of my mistresses claimed I was the father of her child. It didn't work for them, and it sure as hell won't work for you. I shoot blanks."

The heat in her cheeks returned full force as she catapulted from the chair to lean over his desk, her eyes blazing. "You son of a— Why didn't you tell me you'd had a vasectomy? How *dare* you keep something like that from—"

"How dare *I?*" he asked lethally and she collapsed back into the chair sputtering with impotent anger. If looks could kill, he'd be in the morgue.

Her sudden flair of fiery temper was no match for his own icy rage. "Nice of you to look me in the eye as you stabbed me in the back, Jessie." He looked at her with utter contempt. "At least the others controlled their greed until their contract was up. That's why you wouldn't commit by signing the contract, you wanted out the second you found some kind of hold on me. You couldn't wait, could you? You should have done your research before coming up with this far-fetched scenario."

He picked a hair off the shoulder of his charcoal Armani suit. He stared at the curling filament for a moment before dropping it to the floor. He had worn this suit to the theater with her. He would burn the damn thing the moment he got home.

"That's not true," Jessie said steadily, a pulse pounding hard at her throat. "I didn't plan this pregnancy." She glanced away, biting her lower lip before glaring at him defiantly. "Well, okay, maybe at first I did. But then I cha—"

For a moment his emotions blackened his vision. "You planned this from the beginning, did you?"

"Yes. No," she floundered, cheeks scarlet, eyes glittering.

"Well, which was it? Yes or no?"

"I changed my mind." Her voice was unnaturally calm. "I knew I couldn't do it without discussing it with you first—"

"Right." He was old enough to know better. "A 'happy' accident?" She flinched. "You were right," he said cruelly, flatly, his eyes unwavering on her face. "You *are* just like your mother." Emotions started ripping through his control. "Wasn't she a money-grabbing whore, too, Jessie?"

"Oh, God. Don't do this, Joshua." Her voice quavered and he saw her swallow dryly before she managed to say raggedly, "Please." Her eyes went dark, as if a careless hand had snuffed out that vibrant bright inner light of hers. His careless hand.

But he wasn't done yet. Not by a long shot.

"Oh, I beg your pardon. You refused to take my money, didn't you?" His voice sharpened, turned to jagged ice as he demanded venomously, "What do you think those earrings you're wearing are worth, Jessie?"

She put an unsteady hand to a diamond-and-ruby hoop. "I don't kn—"

"Try in the neighborhood of fifty thousand."

Her eyes widened and her hand dropped as though burned. "You told me it was *costume* jewelry."

"The 'bigger the better,' isn't that what you told me?"

"Yes, but I mea—"

"Can't tell a diamond from a piece of glass, Jessie?" he asked mockingly. "You'll have to take a quick gemology class before you get your claws into your next victim."

She took off the earrings and laid them carefully on his desk, her eyes blank and dark.

The chair creaked under his weight as he sat down. "Oh, that trembling lip is almost effective. But you forget. I've screwed the best actresses money can buy. Your performance in bed almost makes this fiasco tolerable." He gave her a cold humorless smile. "Almost."

"Giving me your virginity was worth the jewelry. I consider it a fair trade. What you lacked in experience in bed you made up for in enthusiasm." A chill vibrated through him. "That act would have earned you a small bonus." He paused. "If you hadn't let some other man benefit from what I taught you," he finished savagely as she sucked in air and seemed to brace herself for another blow.

An uncomfortably tight band restricted his breathing and perspiration stuck his shirt to his back. "All the protestation about the gifts I gave you was a blind for the big payoff, right, Jessie?"

"No." Her damn lying eyes stayed steadily on his face. "I told you, I only wanted you."

"Well, you *had* me." His anger almost obscured his vision. "Is there anything else?" he demanded when she sat before him motionless.

"Yes, actually, there is." She touched her purse. "But now is obviously n-not the time to—to—" She waved away her words with a shaking hand. She rose, all elegant grace and proud fluid lines. "I haven't slept with anyone but you, Joshua. When you calm down you'll realize that."

"I'm perfectly calm." His back teeth ground together. "I'll give you thirty seconds to explain how you think this could possibly have happened."

She moved to the back of the chair, putting it between herself and his anger. "I don't think this is the right time to discuss this."

"It's the perfect time," he pushed. "What should we put it down to? Immaculate conception?"

"We made love morning, noon and night. You'd better sue your doctor. Your vasectomy didn't work."

"You said you were on the pill."

"No, I said I'd take care of birth control…." She looked at him and paused before saying, "You're right, yes. I admit getting pregnant was initially my objective. My *only* objective. Not because I wanted to trap you, but because—because I wanted a baby. Then I fell in love with you and I *did* use birth control, except that a lot of times I didn't have time and I—oh, damn it." Large brown eyes filled as she admitted lying through her beautifully straight white teeth.

He watched the performance unmoved. A band of pink painted her cheekbones. "I eventually *did* use birth control, but I didn't realize I was already pregnant." Jessie rubbed her forehead. "I hadn't conceived in all those months…I don't know…perhaps this baby is meant to be born."

Joshua laughed.

She sagged, catching herself with a hand to the back of a chair as her knees seemed to give way. He watched her struggle with her tears. Pride tilted her chin. She had appeared so innocent, so absolutely unconcerned and unimpressed by his wealth. He looked at her, really looked at her and his chest hurt with the purity of her face, the absolute resignation in those liquid brown eyes.

A pulse throbbed at the base of her throat. Joshua had to drag his gaze away from her smooth skin. He knew from personal experience that looks could be deceiving. She was out to get him, just as the others had been. Oh, she wanted money, and lots of it apparently, but she'd come closer to getting far more than that.

Goddamn her soul. She had almost had his heart.

He closed his eyes against the sweet curves of her body, against ever feeling the electricity of her hair against his skin, of ever hearing her small breathy moans of passion. He looked at her for the last time and his voice was as cold as his soul. "I'll call Felix. He'll arrange the usual settlement. You can contact him this afternoon."

Her jaw jerked up. "Can't we talk about this rationally?" Her voice was rough and raw. She looked as though she were trying to push the tears back into her eyes as she pressed her fingers to her cheekbones. She never had a damn tissue when she needed one. The tears came faster. "I love you."

"You love my lifestyle."

She squeezed her eyes shut, blocking him out. Tears

leaked between spiky lashes. He hardened his heart as a sob escaped her. "Oh, no," he growled. "Don't go all pale and piteous on me now. I like you much better when you're spitting like a little cat." His gut burned with the betrayal he felt. This was as close as he'd ever been to striking a woman. He didn't want her looking white-faced and soft. He wanted her to come out of her corner fighting. She had already delivered the fatal body blow, but *he* wanted to finish it, put her on the mat and start counting.

It wasn't like Jessie to just stand there. Why the hell wasn't she defending herself more vigorously?

Because she had planned this all along. Everything had been a lie. Every goddamned word. Every action had been to set him up for this. The big payoff. Her agenda hadn't changed one iota from the first moment they'd met.

He cursed her for having wounded brown eyes and skin so soft and sweet the taste of her stayed on his tongue. He cursed her for trying to pull off a paternity suit. He would have given Jessie his last cent and rushed out to earn more if she'd asked. He cursed her for bringing him so low that he had to grind his teeth and lock his knees to prevent himself from falling to the floor and begging her to stay anyway.

Pain and humiliation swamped him in a tidal wave, so deep, so dark, he thought he might never recover.

"Tell Felix not to bother. I didn't sleep with you for your bank balance or the size of your wallet. All I ever wanted was…"

He raised an inquiring brow, daring her.

"I love our baby," she said and looked right at him. "I don't need or want your damn money." She swallowed with difficulty before saying with awful calm, "I didn't mean to fall in love with you. It snuck up on me and caught me by surprise. I hoped you would eventually fall in love with me. I thought…hoped…" She choked back another sob. "I wanted nothing from you—"

Fury ripped through him. "Except that million-dollar baby," he mocked, not caring as her face crumpled, and she started to shake. He didn't give a damn. "Take a damn DNA test. If it's mine, I'll claim it. But I don't think that'll be an issue."

"No."

"No?"

"I won't take a test. I know who the father is." Jessie dashed a hand across her wet cheek. "And no, you damn well will *not* take my baby. I paid for her in blood. She's *mine*."

He didn't realize he'd rounded his desk until he found his hands clamped on Jessie's slender shoulders. He could see his temper had stunned her. Well, hell, he wasn't done yet. As she stoically stared up at him, a comb fell from her hair. Strands were stuck to the tears on her cheeks.

"Tonight was supposed to be our engagement party. I was going to marry you. I was going to care for you and cherish you for the rest of our miserable lives." He laughed harshly, letting her go. She staggered, caught herself and rubbed her upper arms, shivering violently.

"A little more patience and you could have had it all, Jessie."

"Joshua, please…"

He strode to the closed door ready to snap it open and push her through if she stayed a moment longer.

He heard her draw in a long shaky breath behind his back. Damn her. Damn her to hell.

He punched a hole in the wall with his fist. The sound loud and violent in the unnatural quiet of his office. A mirror fell, shattering into a million broken shards on the thick carpet.

"Well, hell," he said sarcastically. "Another seven years' bad luck." A cruel fist tightened around his heart. His hand throbbed and pain radiated up his arm. He jerked open the door. "Get the hell out. I never want to see your face again."

Her eyes went blank before she closed them. "If you ever change your mind—" When she opened them again, they were filled with regrets.

"Don't hold your breath."

She picked up her purse and straightened, looking from the hole in the wall to his hand, then back to his face. Pale, but resolved, she walked to the door and paused.

"Do I have to call security?" he asked coldly.

She didn't turn, but her fingers whitened on the edge of the thick oak door. Her shoulders stiffened and her chin came up. "Goodbye, Joshua."

"AND I SOBBED," Jessie said disgustedly, dry-eyed and furious. She paced Archie and Conrad's family room. "I cried!" She threw up her hands in disgust and kicked off her shoes.

"You're pregnant with his child and the son of a bitch broke your heart," Archie commiserated. "Of course, you cried."

"He lost his temper." Jessie wrapped her arms around her waist and glared at the far wall. "He was so angry." Tears welled. "So hurt." Jessie pressed her fingertips into her eye sockets. "Damn it, my hormones have gone haywire. Why did I have to cry?"

"Because the closed-minded jerk hurt you!" Conrad perched on the arm of the sofa.

Jessie spun around. "He is *not* a jerk." She grabbed the box of tissues Archie held out as she walked by him. "Well, okay, he can be a jerk." She wiped her nose. "My crying only made him feel worse."

"*Him* feel worse?" both men asked in unison.

Jessie blew her nose. "All the poor man wanted was a nice uncomplicated affair. I wasn't supposed to fall in love with the man."

"Excuse me for a moment as I try to instill a touch of reality into the conversation here. Didn't he contribute to your pregnancy?" Conrad asked, eyebrows raised.

"He claims to have had a vasectomy." The tears dried like a puddle in the desert sun. "I could just strangle him for not telling me that." She was furious all over again.

"Shit, Jess. You are Pollyanna." Conrad snatched a handful of tissues from the box in her hand. Dabbing the trail of mascara running down her cheeks, he said firmly, "Call my father. Get every dime that bastard has. Arch and I will be surrogate fathers."

Jessie gave him a distracted smile. "You two will make excellent daddies, but don't blame Joshua for being angry. I shattered his last few remaining illusions. If this had happened in January as planned, we wouldn't be having this conversation. It's not his fault we wanted different things. He never once in all these months pretended to be anything he was not. Or promised me anything he didn't deliver. I was the one telling all the whoppers. He was starting to trust me." She chewed on a fingernail. "He was so hurt, he claimed he had wanted to marry me!"

"You're *already* married," Archie reminded her.

"Oh, for heaven's sake! *He* doesn't know that!" Those darn tears spilled again. Jessie scrubbed at her face. "I'm the one who betrayed that trust. I'm the one who's been living a lie. If the pregnancy made him angry what's he going to do when he finds out the rest of it?"

"You better skip the country," Archie said, half joking.

Jessie tried to smile. It was an impossible task. "How come when you get your heart ripped out you can still feel it breaking inside?"

She wondered at her own naiveté to think that she could spend twelve minutes with Joshua, let alone twelve months, without having her foolish heart broken into little pieces. She should have divorced him years ago. She shouldn't have carried the divorce papers around with her for years. She should have signed and filed them.

Instead, she had only memories and a handful of papers to prove she had ever known and loved him at all. And a tiny baby who would never know her father. Jessie felt the sting of tears again.

Her throat tightened. She had come to know him so well. How could she hope to salvage his pride after what she had done to him?

She should have come right out and told him who she was. She should have done a lot of things, Jessie thought morosely. What she should *not* have done was fall in love with him.

She had listened to him in his office. And although the words had been cruel, she had seen beneath his anger to the hurt tearing him apart.

Or she thought she had. She couldn't forget that she'd misdiagnosed his feelings before.

She'd looked at the strong lines of his face, so dear and so heartbreakingly familiar. Her eyes blurred as she struggled to store up memories like photographs. It took no effort to remember every line beside his pale eyes, nor the way those eyes had cut through her like an icy laser beam.

Now it was over. Irretrievable. Somewhere, in a small rational part of her heart, Jessie had known it would come to this. Movies and romances had happy endings. This was real life. A woman like her could never in a trillion years bring a man like Joshua Falcon to his knees.

She settled her hand over the small roundness of her tummy. He had inadvertently given her something more precious than Tiffany diamonds or real estate, something she'd wanted more than anything else.

"Be careful what you wish for," her mother used to say wistfully, watching the door close behind another man. Jessie's breath wedged in her throat as it tightened.

"What are you going to do, love?" Archie asked.

For a moment she couldn't speak. She was chilled soul deep. The weight of tears pressing down on her chest was almost unbearable.

"As Scarlett said, 'Tomorrow is another day.'" Jessie managed a wobbly smile before grabbing another handful of tissues out of the box. "But first, I need to cry for a while."

It wasn't only what they *had* that she'd miss. It was what they *could* have had.

CHAPTER ELEVEN

IT WAS MID-DECEMBER. A time of year Joshua already loathed. He felt as though he'd spent the past weeks living in a vacuum. Everywhere he looked, Christmas glowed and shimmered. Every store window blazed with red and green.

He closed his eyes and could see her. Those big brown eyes sparkling, that sweet, succulent mouth just waiting... In his mind, he could hear Jessie's throaty laughter. He could smell fresh peaches. Aw, hell.

All he could think of was Jessie. Jessie mischievously wearing a crown of holly. Jessie laughing up at him before welcoming him home. Jessie, Jessie, Jessie.

Jessie loved holidays. Christmas was her favorite. The story about her dream book had almost broken his damn heart when she'd told it. All those carefully cutout pictures from newspapers and magazines. All those unfulfilled dreams and wishes.

If any of that had been true. He'd convinced himself that even *that* had been part and parcel of her lies. She'd wanted that damn baby. She hadn't had a change of heart. She'd planned and executed her attack with the finesse of a general. Her weapons were state-of-the-art, old as Eve, and had almost worked. God, she had been furious when he'd told her he'd had the vasectomy. Furious!

He didn't want to think about Jessie. The fact that this time of year would forever remind him of her pissed him off even more.

He depressed the button to open the gates to the estate, dreading the dark and empty house. He was glad he'd invited Simon over for drinks before they went out to dinner tonight.

He'd hardly seen Simon since he'd met Jessie. He liked his uncle's company, even when he knew the older man was doing something to manipulate him. Well, tonight he'd tell Simon in no uncertain terms that Jessie was definitely a conversation topic that was off-limits. They'd have a few drinks, get a meal and life would get back to normal.

He'd given most of the servants the month off. He was sick of the dark, accusing looks from his staff. They had adored her. To them, *he* was the villain of the piece. He should tell them about the miracle conception.

Since Jessie had left him, he was getting used to coming home to a dark house. He'd become accustomed to Jessie waiting inside for him. She'd have had every light in the place on in welcome. He didn't even want to think about her warm smile or her comforting arms. The house she had briefly made into a home was now a house again, a place he dreaded entering.

Well, he'd been fine without her before, and he'd be fine again. He didn't need her.

His fingers tightened convulsively around the leather steering wheel. Traitorous little witch. He'd narrowly missed making a complete fool of himself. The tabloid press had already made mincemeat of her. A calendar girl who couldn't even cut the full twelve months. Speculation ran rampant. Joshua ignored it as he always did. It was the job of his public relations team to control what was in the press, only bringing to his attention anything needing his immediate input.

In this instance Joshua turned a blind eye, instructing the PR people to do nothing to stop the innuendo and speculation. He didn't give a damn what happened to her. Jessie had made her bed. Now she would have to lie in it. He didn't even care who she lay in it with.

He wanted to believe she had been nothing but a brief interlude. Quickly forgotten. But the reality was she'd sure as hell changed his life. Never again would he have a mistress for a set period. God, he already felt like a hermit. Sex was the last thing on his mind.

She'd even ruined *that* for him.

He planned to spend the holidays in London this year, and had no intention of telling his friends and business associates there that he was even in the country. Part of him regretted giving her the house in Tahoe. She wouldn't even let him dislike the holidays in his usual location.

It started to rain. A fine depressing mist coated the bare branches of the trees, bowing down the shrubs in the long beds as Joshua pulled the Jag up to the front door. He should change his plans and go somewhere sunny instead, he decided, sprinting up the curved front steps and unlocking the door. Somewhere hot and clean.

Somewhere he'd never been with Jessie.

The first thing that struck him as the front door closed behind him was the smell. He closed his eyes, inhaling deeply.

Obviously he'd gone over the edge. The house was

completely empty, yet he smelled a strong scent of pine and cinnamon and the pleasant aroma of apple wood burning.

Joshua tossed his overcoat over the table in the entry hall and strode down the hallway to his den. And came to a dead stop, his eyes narrowing.

The Christmas tree took up the entire corner by the windows. Brilliant with small white lights, glittering with gold and green and shiny red, the smell permeated the room. In the enormous fireplace, a fire blazed, sending up sparks of blue and orange, which reflected off the packages piled haphazardly beneath the tree. A plate of home-made cookies sat beside the crystal decanters on the drinks trolley.

Jessie.

Joshua's heart took up a frantic rhythm. He drew in a breath as if he were dying.

Jessie was home.

He flexed his still sore right hand. Fool. If she were here he'd kick her out in about two seconds. He didn't need her, and he sure as hell didn't want Christmas, this year more than any other. Damn her.

"Jessie!" He spun away from the room, storming like a demented fool through the empty, quiet house, shouting her name. Everywhere he looked were signs that Jessie had come.

And gone.

Crazed, he threw open doors to unused rooms, banging through closets. His bedroom carried a trace of her scent, but no Jessie. Her side of the closet still held her clothes. Every damn dress he had given her. He slammed the door shut to block out the scent of peaches and Joy and loneliness.

He was enraged at her intrusion. Just when he'd gotten over her. Damn her. How dare she just walk into his house and destroy what little peace of mind he'd found?

The image of his Jessie, big with another man's child, pressed against his synapses. Would that picture *ever* go away? Or would it be replayed with one of Jessie holding the other man's child to her breast?

Joshua went back downstairs. His jaw ached and he realized how hard he was gritting his teeth. She had done this to torment him. He wouldn't allow it. Slipping back into his controlled and more manageable persona, Joshua poured a stiff brandy. Trying to show his appreciation for the 1884 Bas Armee, he ignored the tantalizing scent of fresh-baked cookies.

He took the drink with him, staring down at the presents beneath the tree. A green felt cloth, sprinkled with what looked like gold dust, lay like a blanket over something long and curved. Pinned to it was a note.

Joshua crouched down; his fingers trembled slightly as he slipped the note off the fabric.

"Suspend disbelief," she'd written. "Pretend you are seven years old and you've just come downstairs Christmas morning." Joshua closed his burning eyes for a moment. "I can't be part of your future. I've only been a small part of your present. I wanted to give you back something of your past." She hadn't signed the note.

"Damn it, Jessie." He took a deep gulp of Armagnac.

He carefully removed the cloth then sucked in a breath. It was a train. Perfect in every detail. The Lionel engine, black and shiny, was followed by the coal tender. Behind it, freight cars and flatcars carried smaller presents.

The train disappeared behind the sudden mist in his eyes. Joshua sank to his knees, blinking rapidly. Joshua flicked up the on switch. The train started with a whistle and a moment later a puff of smoke rose from the stack. A reluctant smile tugged at his mouth. It hurt, deep inside him.

She had arranged the track around the room, under the desk, around the chairs and tables. Joshua watched it for almost half an hour, clearing his mind. He had no idea why she'd done it. He didn't want to be charmed.

He stood to refill his glass, absently taking the plate of cookies back to his vantage spot on the floor. Biting into a cookie, he closed his eyes, listening to the clack-clack of tiny wheels on small tracks. He would have given his soul to own this train at seven.

Jessie had remembered.

Jessie who had never received a present until she turned twenty-one. Jessie who'd never owned a toy until she was an adult. Jessie who had never asked him for a damned thing.

A small package slipped from a car as it passed his knee. With trepidation Joshua opened it. Inside was a red Duncan yo-yo. The next package was marbles. The next a Swiss Army knife. Blue.

Each gift represented something he'd wanted as a child. He opened a gaily wrapped package from under the tree and found the flannel shirt she had promised him in Tahoe. The next box contained a brown bomber jacket.

He tugged off his suit jacket and slipped his arms into the sleeves, smelling leather and a faint, faint trace of Jessie. He slipped his hand into the pocket to pull out the long white silk scarf. She'd heard every secret his heart had revealed and made them come true. She hadn't forgotten anything.

He sat back as the brandy warmed his insides and the fire caressed his skin. He picked up a throw pillow off the couch. It still carried her scent. "Damn you," he seethed, crushing the pillow to his chest. As always the scent of her aroused him. He groaned deep in his chest. "Damn you to hell," he said. After all, she had sent him there.

He viewed the dozens of precious gifts and mounds of wrapping paper that lay around him, as his train made another circuit of the room. He'd wanted all these things as a child. And *Jessie* had given them to him. Twenty-seven years later.

As the train continued its route about the room Joshua reached for the last gift beneath the tree. It was a narrow, flat box wrapped in gold paper with an iridescent red ribbon. This gift had been buried beneath all the others, almost behind the tree trunk.

Joshua sipped at his drink. He wanted to believe everything that had happened in his office had been a bad dream. That Jessie had never betrayed him. That Jessie was going to walk in any moment, her liquid eyes loving him, laughing that throaty laugh of hers.

The presents were so typical of her, so unexpectedly right. She knew him so damned well—which was why she had been able to sneak under his defenses and render him senseless.

No. Make that *stupid*.

He turned the last package over in his hand. His fingers twitched against the bow. He frowned as he looked down to see his thumb caressing the silky gold paper. He felt ridiculously reluctant to open this last gift of Jessie's. As if by not knowing what it was, he could keep her here in the room with him for just a few more minutes.

Why the hell did almost everything that woman did have to charm him so? His gaze lingered on the piles of shiny paper tossed about the room. Had she meant for him to do more than "suspend disbelief" for the minutes it had taken to open her presents? Had Jessie imagined he was fool enough to believe that bullshit about both the birth control and his vasectomy not working?

The bitterness of gall filled him. He, a man who never vacillated, never had a moment of indecision or ambivalence, was suddenly filled with the most serious of doubts.

More than anything he wanted to believe Jessie's ridiculous story. He shifted from anger to agony in the blink of an eye. It hurt to breathe. He felt as though he were slowly dying without her. Joshua dashed another three fingers of brandy into his glass and tossed it down his throat.

Gasping for air, he waited a moment for the moisture from the alcohol-induced tears to leave his eyes before he glanced at the Rolex on his wrist. The last thing he needed right now was company. Did he have time to call off the evening he'd planned with Simon? Not unless he caught his uncle on the car phone, and what the hell would he use as an excuse?

I came home and Jessie had been here. If I close my eyes I can smell her. She left me every present I'd ever wanted in my life. The box in his right hand cut into his palm. *And she took away something I never knew I wanted...until I met her.*

He shifted in an attempt to ease the uncomfortable

tightness in his chest and leaned against the edge of his desk. He was no romantic fool. The arrangement with Jessie was no different than he'd had with numerous other women. Jessie's premature departure was nothing more than a mild inconvenience.

"Yeah, right!" Joshua said out loud as the engine whistled and emitted small puffs of smoke. He closed his eyes. The box in his hand crumpled along the edge as his fingers tightened.

The wind picked up outside, clicking small branches annoyingly against the windows. While he had been sitting on the floor playing like a child, darkness had touched the sky and darkened the room. He hadn't bothered with lights. From beneath the chair across the room he could see the narrow beam of the headlight on his train. That small beam, the amber glow of the dying fire, and the little white lights twinkling on Jessie's tree provided enough light.

Joshua put the empty snifter on the desk, then went over to the fire to open the last gift before Simon arrived.

The paper crackled before revealing its delicious secret. The thought made him smile. Just as Jessie had intended, no doubt.

He took the Swiss Army knife Jessie had given him out of his pocket, stroked the smooth plastic with his thumb, then opened the blade and cut the tape.

Sitting on his haunches before the fire, Joshua carefully removed a sheet of paper from inside the box. The paper smelled of Jessie and it took him a moment to open the single fold.

"Joshua," she wrote. "Please forgive me for what I

have done to you. Simon and Felix only kept their silence because I begged them not to tell you."

The paper rustled in his hand. What the hell did Felix and Simon have to do with this?

"I never meant to lie to you, but I wanted a baby so badly. I must admit I would have done almost anything in my power to achieve my goal. I erroneously believed I would conceive immediately. I never for a moment thought that I would fall in love. I think even after I changed my mind about getting pregnant, I subconsciously knew I could never make you love me. There were so many times we were in such a hurry I forgot all about protection."

Yeah. Right!

"I wish I could have been there to love and protect you when you were a child, but since I wasn't, I hope the presents will mean something to you.

"I understand, with your deep mistrust of women, why you didn't believe me about our baby. I know you have been lied to about this before. But the fact remains—we did make this baby together."

Sure, Jessie.

"I know you never want to see me again. I am so sorry for causing you pain."

There were wet splotches blurring the writing. Tears of course.

"If you change your mind…we'll be waiting. If not, then I hope eventually you will be able to forgive me and find a love of your own.

"I will love you forever and a day.

"Your Jessie."

He was tempted to toss the box and its contents into the fire. He'd had enough. She had managed to reduce him to idiot status with the gifts as it was. The band tightened around his chest, just where his heart should have been.

Damn it, Jessie.

The box contained several items. Joshua rose and turned on the desk light so he could see everything more clearly. He couldn't take much more. He wanted to dispense with this last gift before his uncle came in.

It was hard for him to breathe as he opened the next folded piece of paper. Joshua frowned, rotating his shoulder. What the hell...? It was a credit slip from Tiffany's in San Francisco. What had Jessie done? Returned all the jewelry he'd given her? It didn't make sense. Stapled to the back of it was a similar receipt, informing him that the rest of the jewelry was at his lawyer's office for safekeeping.

He held on to it for a few moments before setting it on the desk. He was suddenly dying for another drink, but his feet couldn't have moved across the room right then if he'd tried. Intrigued, he flipped open the next document. What the...?

A cashier's check...for over six million dollars? Where on earth had Jessie got this sort of money? And why was she giving it to him?

He removed a trifolded legal document from Jessie's Pandora's box. It looked well-worn, folded many times as if it had been opened and read many times. Light reflected off a shiny square stapled to the top right-hand corner. His eyes scanned down to the signature at the bottom of the page. He stared for a confused moment at the petition for dissolution of marriage.

He frowned, absently tilting the shiny square to the light. It was a Polaroid picture. A picture of a gangly young girl with wiry orange hair and huge brown eyes, filled with anticipation.

The pain came so suddenly it knocked him to his knees. It ballooned in his chest, making Joshua grimace and squeeze his eyes shut as he staggered back against the desk. The red wave washed over him, leaving him shaken and breathless. Sweat slicked his skin.

Jessie had managed to do what she'd planned all along. Not content with *ripping* out his heart, she had managed to induce a heart *attack* instead.

Headlights swung up the drive. Too far away. Too late.

Joshua snagged the phone, cradling his left arm against his chest. He managed to hit speed dial.

"Hi, this is Jessie. I can't come to the phone right now…"

A firebomb exploded in his chest. Like flame it shot down his arm.

The receiver dropped from his nerveless fingers. It clattered onto the moving engine and then fell to the carpet with a dull thud. Dimly he heard the whistle of the train as its wheels spun uselessly. Then his pulse thundered in his ears, blocking out everything else.

The phone. Had to…911…call…pain… Oh, God. This was it…had to…had…

Black snow swirled, his vision dimmed and he felt himself falling into a dark hole.

"J-Jessieee."

"YOU'RE DAMNED LUCKY," Simon said from his seat beside Joshua's hospital bed.

"I'm fine. It was only a severe anxiety attack." Joshua grimaced, feeling ridiculous.

"It *could* have been a heart attack. The doctor said it was a warning to slow down."

"Yeah. It certainly had that effect." Joshua moved restlessly beneath the covers, his long legs uncomfortable in the too short bed. "Thanks for getting there in time to help, Simon."

"You scared the hell out of me when I found you. Thank God, I remembered I had a key. When I saw you lying there you were so still, and your lips were turning blue. Hell, boy, I almost had a heart attack seeing you like that." Simon got up to pace. Joshua envied him his mobility. They had stuck all sorts of monitoring tubes into him.

Simon ran a hand through his white hair. "You do what they tell you, you hear? They said twenty-four hours' observation and you'd better comply. I have every intention of going before you do, so don't screw up my plans. Understand?"

Joshua shifted restlessly under the covers before reaching over and removing something from the bedside drawer.

"Explain this to me while I wait," he demanded, his jaw tensing. The machine beside the bed beeped.

"What's th—? Oh. Jessie's divorce papers."

Joshua closed his eyes, forcing himself to calm down. The monitor beside the bed emitted several high-pitched, nurse-alerting beeps. She bustled into the room, tsk-tsking, and warned him to take it easy. She took his pulse, straightened sheets and generally annoyed Joshua further. Simon gave him a warning look.

The moment the woman left Joshua said coldly, "Simon? An explanation."

"She said she was going to give you the darn thing. Well, there you have it. Jessie's divorcing you."

"Hard to do since we were never married," he said, needing to hear Simon confirm what he suspected.

"Jessie is Vera, son."

The monitor emitted a series of beeps. "It's true then."

Simon nodded slowly.

Joshua sat up against the metal headboard, ignoring the tape tugging painfully at his skin from his movement. "Are you telling me that you knew all along that Jessie was Vera? All these years when you casually mentioned the new decorator Conrad and Archie were training, you knew who she was?" He winced as he pulled the needle from the back of his hand.

"Got her the job, myself." Simon stared, fascinated, as Joshua ripped another tape and needle combo off his skin. "Do you know what you're doing?"

"Obviously not." Joshua grimaced as a bead of blood welled on his hand. He looked up at his uncle. "Jesus, Simon. Whose side were you on?"

"You married that poor child and walked out on her without even taking the time to learn her name. She became part of the family that day—someone had to help her. Felix and I took her under our wing. It was the least we could do."

Joshua swore. He tossed aside the blankets, swung his feet to the cold floor and stood up.

"Where do you think you're going?" Simon asked, alarmed.

"There's something I have to do. Then I'm coming back to finish off you and Felix." Joshua slammed drawers. "But first I have to find my clothes."

"She always was a grasping little bitch," Simon said mildly, watching his nephew with penetrating blue eyes. Another drawer slammed.

"Don't call her a bitch," Joshua warned through clenched teeth. "Aha." He found his shoes, then his socks. Why the hell couldn't they keep everything together?

"Grasping."

"Jessie never asked me for a thing, Simon."

"Selfish, then. All women are."

Joshua opened the wardrobe and removed the rest of his clothing. "Jessie is the most generous, kindhearted woman I've ever met." For a moment his hands were filled with brown leather and the mingling scents of Jessie and unfulfilled needs. He tossed the jacket on the rumpled bed.

"Incapable of loving a man, though."

"Bull." Joshua pulled on underwear and stood to fasten his pants. "Jessie is filled with love."

"All she wanted was expensive presents. That's what they all want."

"Jessie didn't want presents."

"Wanted the notoriety of being with Joshua Falcon in public. Liked the Lear, I bet."

"No." Joshua slipped on his shirt. "She didn't care much for the Lear. She said she preferred the commercial flights because the people were so damn interesting." He buckled his belt and looked on the bed for his socks.

"Well, hell," Simon pushed. "A mistress should know her place. She should have taken pride in the fact she belonged to you, darn her." Simon glanced at Joshua from beneath heavy lids.

"A woman doesn't belong to a man like a dog, Simon."

"No? Well, I don't see why she was humiliated when the gutter press labeled her your 'Calendar Girl.' Hell, she knew it was only for twelve months."

"Ten." Joshua plopped down to pull on socks and shoes.

"Couldn't go the distance, could she? She didn't even have to put in a full year to reap the benefits."

Joshua searched his pockets. "There were no benefits, Simon. Jessie gave it all back. Hell, the only way I could give her jewelry was to tell her it was fake."

Simon hooted. "And you believed that, son? Hell, a woman can spot a cubic zirconium at forty paces. A clever ploy, no doubt. Women can be very conniving. We men have to watch ourselves. God forbid we give them an inch."

"Give it up, Simon. I know what you're trying to do."

Simon sighed before rising. He gave Joshua a hard look. "Jessie's the best thing to happen to you in your life." Simon turned his back to stare out the window. He watched Joshua in the reflection before he turned around again. "Don't let what your father did with his marriages mark *your* life. You could change that pattern, Joshua.

"Jessie is a fine woman. She has spunk and backbone and as much integrity as you do—and more love in her than a man could use up in three lifetimes. How could any man be so damn stupid as to let her slip through his fingers?"

"Well, hell," Joshua said caustically, feeling the sting of his uncle's displeasure added to his own guilt. "Excuse me for being human!"

"We'll discuss your alleged species later, in the meantime what are you going to do about Jessie?"

"What the hell am I supposed to do? She hit me with a one-two punch to the groin."

"Are you sure it wasn't your heart?"

"I doubt she thinks I have one." Joshua slipped the folded piece of paper off the bedside table into the pocket of his jacket. "Didn't I have my wallet when they brought me in?"

"In the nightstand," Simon said absently. "You haven't lost a thing. Jessie gave up everything for you. She gave up a job she'd trained for and loved. She gave up most of her friends. She remained at your beck and call even when you didn't—beck or call, that is." Simon heaved a weary sigh as he rose from his chair. "Tell me, Joshua, have you ever considered what being your mistress does to a woman like Jessie?"

Joshua eyed Simon, who looked as old as he felt at the moment, but said nothing.

"As men, have we ever considered what it must be like when everyone knows the woman we're with is only temporary? Not good enough to have them stick around. Patti pounded into my head how a woman feels. I tell you, son. It stinks. They're forever scorned and pitied. The trash magazines tear their guts out for public consumption. And we turn around and start hunting for the next woman before they even know we're done with them, oblivious to the carnage we leave behind."

"I've never treated Jessie that way."

"Asked yourself why?"

Joshua gave the older man a penetrating look. "I've thought about it." His tone was grim. "In the past weeks, I've thought of little else."

"Well then?"

Joshua stared at his uncle. "You want this for her very badly, don't you?"

"I want this very badly for *both* of you, son. But mostly for you because, I have to tell you, I believe Jessie could limp along with her life without you. But I don't believe you're going to manage much of a life without *her*."

"She's pregnant."

"Congratulations."

"The child isn't mine."

"Don't be absurd. Of course it is."

"I had a vasectomy years ago."

Simon shook his head. "It wouldn't be the first time nature won over a surgeon's knife. If you have doubts, check it out. Hell, you're already here. When you're finished, ask your doctor for a refund."

Joshua sank down on the side of the bed. "Jesus, you crafty bastard, haven't I gone through enough humiliation for one day?"

Simon smiled. "Guess not."

JESSIE SAT IN her car looking at the diner. This is where it had all begun. The beginning of the end. Rain sluiced down her windshield, blurring the lights. The whop-whop-whop of the wipers was starting to get on her nerves.

A sharp white spear of lightning illuminated the sky: thunder rumbled overhead. Perfect, just perfect. The cold desolation squeezed around her heart, and she choked on the lump in her throat.

Her eyes were dry, but still burning from the last bout of tears, as she got out of her car. Bareheaded, she made a mad dash for the door. The familiar smell of grease and pine cleaner assailed her on the way to a back booth. She removed her damp raincoat and glanced around. Half a dozen customers, most of them truckers, occupied the adjacent booths.

A young family sat at the counter. Mother, father and two cute toddlers. Jessie stroked her hand down her tummy and gave the little girl a smile. The child played peekaboo over the back of her chair until her mother reprimanded her, making her turn around to eat.

Jessie enjoyed the momentary distraction. A gum-chewing waitress rounded the counter and asked if she wanted coffee. She ordered food she wasn't hungry for, then stared morosely at the scratched beige Formica tabletop.

For the past few weeks she'd stayed in a hotel in San Jose. She hadn't wanted anyone to know where she was until she'd figured out what she was going to do, and where she was going to go.

Joshua Falcon's reach was long and deadly. The rational part of her mind told her to move to another galaxy far, far away. Unfortunately, she wasn't that smart. She had other plans.

Her heart did a one-two thump. Anger would have been wonderfully cathartic, but she had no right to it. Other than the way it had been delivered, everything Joshua had said in his office had been true. From his point of view.

She didn't have a leg to stand on. Her pain, however, despite knowing she'd asked for it, was very real. She'd always prided herself on taking responsibility for her own actions. She was one-hundred percent responsible for her own broken heart. Joshua had never lied to *her*.

The waitress set down the special. Jessie poured a blob of ketchup on the plate beside the fries. She *had* wanted this baby. She wasn't sorry about any of it. She waved a fry in the red blob before biting it in half.

She'd taken a chance on love. And lost.

Until the next round.

If she was mad at anyone, it was herself. For believing she could change a man so set in his ways. The Glacier. Rock hard and implacable. Slow to melt. So accustomed to a woman's betrayal, Jessie ached for him.

She sipped the industrial-strength coffee as she glanced around. So much had changed in her life since she'd last been here. It was strange to see everything had remained the same at the diner. The same dusty plastic plants hung from the yellowed ceiling. The same rips marred the same vinyl seats. The same cheap tacky Christmas decorations sprouted haphazardly about the place.

Jessie sighed. At least there were some constants in life.

She glanced at her watch then looked out the rain-sprinkled window. She squinted against the bright flash of lightning that illuminated the almost empty lot. She waited for the thunder but the whop-whop-whop outside sounded more like her aged windshield wipers.

She ate two more fries, eyed the greasy battered fish, then picked up the fork and swam the cod through a ketchup sea.

It was very late, well after ten. Jessie wondered what time Joshua had arrived home tonight or if he was even in the country. What had his reaction been to the tree and gifts? God, she hoped it softened him a little, made what she'd done a little easier to take. With Joshua it was impossible to guess how he'd react.

She'd give him twenty-four hours to digest everything, then she'd use whatever it took to make him see he loved her, too.

Wherever he was, he'd better be alone. Jessie straightened. It was early for mistress number...whatever, but Joshua had been angry enough to ignore his own calendar.

Jessie rested her cheek on her hand and closed her eyes as pain swamped her. She couldn't bear thinking of him with another woman. She'd promised herself she would never read another paper or watch tabloid TV ever again. She couldn't stand the thought of Joshua *kissing* another woman.

Beneath her fingers she felt the warmth of her cup as it was refilled. "Thanks." Jessie wondered what the waitress thought of her sitting here mumbling to herself and opened her eyes.

Unless waitress attire had drastically changed since she'd worked here, someone else had poured her coffee. Jessie's heart leaped to her throat. Wishing, and not daring to hope, she kept her eyes on the pair of size twelve Haas shoes beside the table. She heard the creak of leather.

"Jessie."

The familiar voice sent a shock wave through her. She slowly lifted her gaze. He looked exhausted, but gloriously handsome. His dark hair was disheveled. He wore jeans and the brown bomber jacket over his red Tahoe shirt. He handed the coffeepot he'd commandeered back to the waitress and stuffed his hands into his pockets.

"Have you stopped having evening sickness?"

She swallowed hard, gripping her coffee mug with both hands because she wanted to touch him so badly. "Yes. I feel wonderful now."

Joshua sank into the seat opposite, his eyes fixed on her face.

"How did you find me?" She couldn't tell by his somber expression what he was thinking.

"I leaned on Conrad and Archie. They told me you were on your way up to the cabin. Then I hopped the helicopter. I had a feeling you'd stop here."

Jessie looked out at the parking lot. Amazingly, a black, silver and burgundy Falcon helicopter was parked next to her car.

"I wanted to go to the cabin one more time." Jessie's eyes stung. Not now, damn it. "I was going to mail the deed back to you next week."

He took her hand, his eyes grave. "I wanted you to have it." Joshua's fingers tightened around hers. "Damn it, Jessie." His voice was tight. "This isn't what I came up here to discuss." He ran his splayed fingers through his hair. It stood up in shark fins. Jessie stared.

"If you came for more apologies, you have them." She tried to pull her hand away, but he used both hands to hold her in place. She gave him a pointed look. "But I won't apologize into infinity."

"I don't want apologies."

"I can't handle… What do you want, Joshua?"

"I want you to marry me."

Jessie squeezed her eyes shut. When she opened them the look she gave him was cool. "I don't blame you for wanting to hurt me because of the lies I told you. But please," she started to rise and he held her firmly in place, his hands warm around hers, "please, don't taunt me."

Jessie bit the inside of her lip to keep it from trembling. Her eyes filled with the annoying tears that still plagued her. She stared out the window, willing her eyes to dry.

"Mommy? How come that man's kneeling down by the lady?" The sweet piping voice of the child at the counter brought the noise in the diner to an abrupt silence.

"Turn around, honey. It's rude to stare."

Jessie turned as the child was forced to look away by her mother.

"Marry me. For real. Forever, Jessie." Joshua's voice was so low she had to strain to hear him.

Hope leaped in her heart. She opened her eyes slowly. Joshua was on one knee, head bowed, beside her. "Oh, God, Joshua." Jessie's sob caught in her throat. "Please, don't." She couldn't bear to see him so humbled.

He looked straight into her eyes. His were sheened and his jaw clenched. "Be my wife, Jessie." His voice had an almost imperceptible break in it. "Please."

She reached out and touched his face. His skin felt chilled.

His hand covered hers. "Say yes."

"Get up, please."

"Say yes first."

"We have to talk," Jessie said desperately, not allowing hope to bloom. "There are so many things we haven't sai—"

He rose and put two fingers across her mouth. "Shhh. We have a lifetime to say all the things we want to say." He sank into the seat opposite, his eyes fixed on her face.

She tasted blood as she chewed the inside of her lip. Life was hard enough on a child. She would never subject the baby to a father who didn't love it whole-heartedly.

"It's Thursday," he said, his lips twitching slightly as Jessie looked at him blankly. "Remember? You told me once you only married strangers on Thursdays." He picked up her hand, toying with her fingers. Jessie felt the electricity of his touch down to her toes.

"That was a lifetime ago," Jessie whispered, stunned he'd remembered. "So much has happened in be-tween—"

"Yes. I finally grew up." He sounded impatient with himself. "I should have held on to you then, Jessie. We could have had those seven years *together* if I hadn't been such an insensitive ass."

"You were my knight in shining armor," Jessie told him quietly, her fingers gripping his. His gaze was so serious as he scanned her face.

"A pretty damn tarnished knight." His lips twisted. "I allowed what my mother and Stacie had done to me to color my emotions. And, like a fool, I almost lost the best thing to happen in my life." He tilted her chin with his finger. "Can you ever forgive my transgres-sions, Jess?"

"You know I have." A hot wash of tears bathed her cheeks. Her stomach churned as she fought the impulse to throw herself into his arms.

"Ah, Jessie." He leaned forward and dabbed the tears spilling down her cheeks with her napkin. "I went home late yesterday afternoon," he said, turning the napkin to a dry corner. His pale eyes remained fixed on her. "I was dreading going into that damn cold, dark house one more time. Ready, in fact to put it on the market. You were everywhere, Jess. Everywhere and in everything. Everywhere I looked, everything I heard, everything I tasted and smelled.

"And I realized I could sell all my houses, the yachts, the planes, it wouldn't make a damn bit of difference. Because no matter where I was, no matter what I did, you would always be there with me. In my heart."

She stared at him wide-eyed, her heart in some kind of weird time warp. Too terrified to believe what he was saying. And just as terrified not to.

"I opened each of the presents you gave me and I wondered who had taught you to be so loving. Who had shown you how heartachingly wonderful a loving touch could be. Not your mother. Not a man."

He dropped the soggy napkin and reached in his pocket, then withdrew his handkerchief and resumed blotting her tears. "I realized, almost too late, that what you were giving me was what you had always craved for yourself. Tenderness, caring, trust and unconditional love."

She wanted to say something, anything. But her heart seemed to have stopped beating. The world, her world, had paused on its axis.

Again Joshua reached into his jacket pocket. He pulled out an envelope, then laid a small blue box on the table between them.

"I love you, Jessie Adams. I might be a slow learner, but when I've learned the lesson, I assure you, I never forget. I can't imagine my life without you. Please, remarry me and put me out of this misery."

Jessie stared down at the box with blurred vision. He nudged it closer.

"What about the baby?" She took his hankie from him and wiped her cheeks. He gave her that smile she loved, the one that crinkled the corners of his eyes, and pushed an envelope across the table.

"And I love our baby."

"You don't believe she is your baby," she reminded him, forgetting how to breathe.

"It's…a she? She is my baby, Jessie. If she's part of you, then it's part of me." He smiled. "Do you know what a good father does for his children?"

Jessie could think of a thousand things. She shook her head.

"The best thing a father can do for his children is to love their mother."

Jessie's chest ached.

She dabbed her eyes with the hankie again. "I'll be glad when my hormones get back to normal," she said waspishly. "I hate all this crying in front of you."

He smiled. "You can do anything you like in front of me, Jess."

"What's in the envelope?"

"Open it and see." He took a sip of her coffee. "Only you would be more interested in the envelope than the jewelry box."

She gave him a look before she opened the small velvet box. "This is definitely real." The diamond was not ostentatious, just exquisitely beautiful, surrounded by baguettes, in a simple gold setting. She pushed it across the table and stuck out her left hand. "Put it on quickly," she demanded.

Joshua laughed. Coming around to her side of the

table he eased her against the window. She closed her eyes as his fingers threaded through her hair. She tilted her mouth. Then he kissed her. Softly and leisurely and with every fiber of love he could muster. She felt giddy when he let her up for air.

The few patrons of the restaurant applauded and Joshua made a big production of sliding the ring on her finger. His gaze devoured her face before lowering to rest on her tummy.

"God, Jess," he said breathlessly, one hand reverently touching her through her thick sweater. When he finally looked up, his eyes had filled with tears.

"I love you, Joshua Falcon."

"I know you do, Jessie. And I plan to spend the rest of my life cherishing you. There'll never be a day you won't know how much I love you in return."

"Are you sure?"

"Absolutely, unequivocally, and positively." He pushed her bangs out of her eyes. "Are you going to open this?" he asked, his arm around her. He nudged the envelope closer.

"Is it important?"

"No. Just a small test I had."

"What kind of test?"

"Sperm count."

She looked at the sealed opening.

"And you haven't opened it?"

"The results make no difference to me, I told you that."

"And you'll marry me again and love the baby no matter what that piece of paper says?"

"Without a moment's hesitation," he assured her.

Jessie handed the envelope back to him. "You open it."

"It makes no—"

"Open it."

She watched as he slit the envelope open with his Swiss Army knife, unfolded the single sheet and scanned the test results.

"Well?" She raised an eyebrow.

"It says—" Joshua swallowed roughly and looked at Jessie with his heart in his eyes. "It says you are marrying an idiot who adores you, and that we'll live happily ever after, and have at least two more children."

Jessie felt the smile blossoming from her heart. "I love a happy ending, don't you?"

* * * * *

New York Times bestselling author
SUSAN MALLERY

invites readers back to her beloved series set in
Fool's Gold featuring three newcomers who find love
when they are least expecting it...

Available Now.   Available Now.   Coming June 24, 2014!

"Susan Mallery is one of my favorites."
—#1 *New York Times* bestselling author Debbie Macomber

**The women of Bliss County are ready to
meet the men of their dreams!
See how it all begins in this enchanting new series
by #1 *New York Times* bestselling author**

LINDA LAEL MILLER

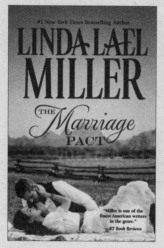

Ten years ago, Hadleigh Stevens
was eighteen and *this* close to
saying "I do," when Tripp Galloway
interrupted her walk down the aisle.
Now that she's recovered from
her youthful mistake *and* Tripp's
interference, Hadleigh and her single
friends form a marriage pact. She
doesn't expect Tripp to meddle with
her new plan to find Mr. Right—or
to discover that she's more attracted
to him than ever!

Divorced and eager to reconnect
with his cowboy roots, Tripp returns
to Bliss County to save his ailing
father's ranch. He's not looking for
another wife—certainly not his best
friend's little sister. But he's never been able to forget Hadleigh. And
this time, if she ends up in his arms, he won't be walking away!

Available now wherever books are sold!

Be sure to connect with us at:

Harlequin.com/Newsletters

Facebook.com/HarlequinBooks

Twitter.com/HarlequinBooks

HARLEQUIN® HQN™
™ www.Harlequin.com

PHLLM870

TERI WILSON

"Charming and
so much fun."
—Sarah Morgan,
USA TODAY
bestselling author

*Unmasking
Juliet*

TERI WILSON

Ever since she was a little girl learning to make decadent truffles in her family's chocolate shop, Juliet Arabella has been aware of the bitter feud between the Arabellas and the Mezzanottes. With their rival chocolate boutiques on the same street in Napa Valley, these families *never* mix. Until one night, when Juliet anonymously attends the annual masquerade ball. In a moonlit vineyard, she finds herself falling for a gorgeous stranger, a man who reminds her what passion is like outside the kitchen. But her bliss is short-lived when she discovers her masked prince is actually Leo Mezzanotte, newly returned from Paris and the heir to her archenemy's confection dynasty.

With her mind in a whirl, Juliet leaves for Italy to represent the Arabellas in a prestigious chocolate competition. The prize money will help her family's struggling business, and Juliet figures it's a perfect opportunity to forget Leo…only to find him already there and gunning for victory. As they compete head-to-head, Leo and Juliet's fervent attraction boils over. But Juliet's not sure whether to trust her adversary, or give up on the sweetest love she's ever tasted….

Available now wherever books are sold!

Be sure to connect with us at:

Harlequin.com/Newsletters
Facebook.com/HarlequinBooks
Twitter.com/HarlequinBooks

H HARLEQUIN® HQN™

™ www.Harlequin.com

PHTW875

REQUEST YOUR FREE BOOKS!

2 FREE NOVELS
FROM THE ROMANCE COLLECTION
PLUS 2 FREE GIFTS!

YES! Please send me 2 FREE novels from the Romance Collection and my 2 FREE gifts (gifts are worth about $10). After receiving them, if I don't wish to receive any more books, I can return the shipping statement marked "cancel." If I don't cancel, I will receive 4 brand-new novels every month and be billed just $6.24 per book in the U.S. or $6.74 per book in Canada. That's a savings of at least 22% off the cover price. It's quite a bargain! Shipping and handling is just 50¢ per book in the U.S. and 75¢ per book in Canada.* I understand that accepting the 2 free books and gifts places me under no obligation to buy anything. I can always return a shipment and cancel at any time. Even if I never buy another book, the two free books and gifts are mine to keep forever.

194/394 MDN F4XY

Name _____ (PLEASE PRINT) _____

Address _____ Apt. # _____

City _____ State/Prov. _____ Zip/Postal Code _____

Signature (if under 18, a parent or guardian must sign)

Mail to the **Harlequin® Reader Service:**
IN U.S.A.: P.O. Box 1867, Buffalo, NY 14240-1867
IN CANADA: P.O. Box 609, Fort Erie, Ontario L2A 5X3

Want to try two free books from another line?
Call 1-800-873-8635 or visit www.ReaderService.com.

* Terms and prices subject to change without notice. Prices do not include applicable taxes. Sales tax applicable in N.Y. Canadian residents will be charged applicable taxes. Offer not valid in Quebec. This offer is limited to one order per household. Not valid for current subscribers to the Romance Collection or the Romance/Suspense Collection. All orders subject to credit approval. Credit or debit balances in a customer's account(s) may be offset by any other outstanding balance owed by or to the customer. Please allow 4 to 6 weeks for delivery. Offer available while quantities last.

Your Privacy—The Harlequin® Reader Service is committed to protecting your privacy. Our Privacy Policy is available online at www.ReaderService.com or upon request from the Harlequin Reader Service.

We make a portion of our mailing list available to reputable third parties that offer products we believe may interest you. If you prefer that we not exchange your name with third parties, or if you wish to clarify or modify your communication preferences, please visit us at www.ReaderService.com/consumerschoice or write to us at Harlequin Reader Service Preference Service, P.O. Box 9062, Buffalo, NY 14269. Include your complete name and address.

ROM13R

CIRCLE OF STARS

"Anna Lee Waldo's exciting story of persecuted Druids sailing west and establishing a colony among the native people of early Florida is a fascinating and dramatic portrayal of an intriguing concept that has tantalized researchers for years—the early contacts between Europe and the Americas. With impressive research and well-drawn, believable characters the distinct nature of the two cultures is clearly portrayed and gives a little-realized global view to the mysterious Druids and the prehistoric Americans. The story is enthralling and the suspense is delicious, one can hardly wait for Madoc and Cougar to meet."
—Jean Auel on *Circle of Stars*

CIRCLE OF STONES

"An engrossing epic that will continue to enthrall fans of sweeping historical fiction."
—*Booklist*

"Readers will appreciate the complex dynamics she portrays within her fact-filled epic."
—*Publishers Weekly*

"A richly drawn medieval saga with complex characters."
—*Library Journal*

More . . .

SACAJAWEA

"A work of uncompromising scholarship and brilliance. It is one of the great books of this or any decade."

—*The Courier Gazette* (Rockland, Maine)

"Magnificently entertaining."   —*Berkeley Gazette*

"A blockbuster historical novel."   —*Fort Worth Star-Telegram*

"Anna Lee Waldo writes her story in a manner . . . akin to the slow, but satisfying knitting of a colorful afghan, filling in the gaping holes in our history."   —*Spectrum Magazine*

"Ms. Waldo's exhaustive research takes the reader on a fascinating, in-depth journey."   —*Daily Herald-News*

"Exceptional."   —*St. Louis Post-Dispatch*

"Engrossing."   —*Detroit News*

ALSO BY ANNA LEE WALDO

Circle of Stones

Sacajawea

Prairie

Circle of Stars

Anna Lee Waldo

St. Martin's Paperbacks

CIRCLE OF STARS

Copyright © 2001 by Anna Lee Waldo.

For a listing of permissions, please see page xi.

Map illustration by Ellisa Mitchell.

ISBN: 0-312-98035-3

Printed in the United States of America

St. Martin's Press hardcover edition / August 2001
St. Martin's Paperbacks edition / November 2002

St. Martin's Paperbacks are published by St. Martin's Press, 175 Fifth Avenue, New York, NY 10010.

10 9 8 7 6 5 4 3 2 1

This book is dedicated with love to Sara, once a Polliwog, who became a beloved Medicine Woman, and to my brother, Eugene (1928–1996), who was Chief Shipmaster of the *Sinopah* and *Rising Wolf*, on Two Medicine Lake in Glacier National Park.

Llan Newydd

ALABAMA
Llan Newydd
GEORGIA

Mobile
Bay
FLORIDA

Dog's Tail

Clearwater
Sandpoint
Charlotte
Harbor

Lake
Okeechobee

Barrier
Islands

Labrador
Sea

Canada

New
Foundland

Nova Scotia

North America

Llan Newydd

Mobile Bay

Gulf Stream

Atlantic Ocean

Bermuda
Islands

Florida

North
Current

Sargasso
Sea

Bahamas

Gulf of Mexico

Cuba

North Equatorial

Caribbean Sea

Central
America

South America

Madoc's First Voyage
To Llan Newydd
in 1170

Epigraphs

I am truly grateful to the copyright holders credited below, who gave me permission to use quotes from their work in my epigraphs. The Welsh spelling of proper names or places may differ with various authors.

Contents

PART THREE

Circle of Stars

Prologue
An Ocean Apart

What is culture? Even anthropologists struggle to define the word. Food, dress, tools, dwellings, laws, manners, art, myths—culture can be described as the manifestations of human existence that are transmitted from one generation to the next, a pool of the collective intellect and memory.

—William Allen, ed.,
map titled "Voices of the World," *National Geographic*

The tan-skinned, old woman was black haired, brown eyed, and not more than five feet, three inches tall. She searched the debris brought ashore by the storm. For three days her heart was in her throat as she looked for her husband. Before the storm hit, he sat with her on their rolled sleeping mats in front of their lodge and watched the rapidly moving black clouds coming across the white-capped sea. The summer lodge was an open square of pitch-laden pine set upright into the earth. It was topped by a thick matting of palmetto leaves laid over a frame of saplings and held firm by evenly placed logs set on either side of the pitched roof. The hard-packed dirt floor was covered with woven mats of beach grass. An outdoor cook fire was laid inside a circle of seven stones.

Now the fire was all gone, blown apart by an angry wind as if it was some flimsy thing children made for an afternoon of play. A ripped floor mat hung in a tree, and the fire's circle of stones lay scattered in the grass. Looking at the seven empty indentations left by the missing stones made the old woman shake with disbelief.

She remembered wrapping a grass blanket around her husband's strong shoulders and muscular legs for protection against the rain, and hunkering against all five feet, ten inches of him. He made comforting clucking noises, like the water hen grubbing for food in the muddy swamp. Then the wind roared and threw a corner of the blanket over her face. She felt her husband brace himself against one of the wall posts as the rain came down on a wide slant and hit the ground with the sound of dropping pebbles. The wind's fingers plucked the blanket from her eyes and threw it sailing into the air with torn pieces from her billowing skirt. Her skirt had been woven the previous day from the curly gray moss swinging from trees near the swamp. She thought the wind was playing tricks and might grab her moccasins, so she leaned over and tucked her moccasined feet underneath the part of her skirt she sat on. The wind was so strong she almost fell backwards. When she sat up, the wind blew against her face so hard she could hardly open her eyes. A little pocket of fright pulled her belly muscles tight. Cautiously she put her hand up to make sure the wind had not taken her hair. She pressed her chin against her chest and told the wind to stop its game; she did not know the rules. The wind took her voice away so she could not hear it and pushed its cold, tumbling breath between her bare back and short leather vest. For an instant she looked up and saw the sand move as if it were a living, crawling thing. She knew the sand's life was a transient thing, borrowed from the wind. Suddenly a spiral of sand rose tall as three or four men standing on each other's shoulders and whirled high in the air. The sun reached through a break in the clouds and shone on the spinning sand, revealing a smoky prism of unbelievable bright colors. She trembled at the beauty of nature and wondered why this beautiful mystery was revealed to her. Maybe it was a sign of something tremendous about to happen. She bowed her head as the dark clouds cut off the sun and the whirling sand danced off toward the breakers. The wind pushed fiercely against her back, and she curled into a ball and prayed it would stop pushing her down and pulling at her clothing. The rain came sidewise in torrents with each hard gust. After a while the rain on her arms became soft and gentle. Night had already swallowed daylight, and land noises were hushed. She thought the wind had heard her prayer and was no longer angry. "I am grateful," she said aloud.

She missed the chirp of the birds as she walked around looking for her husband until the rain suddenly fell hard again. To see better she wiped a hand across her face and thought she would find him in the dry ceremonial lodge, sitting next to the fire, playing the stick game with his friends. She pictured the lodge in her mind's eye with a gabled roof of pine-bark shingles, weighted down with logs, and the four mud-plastered sides held firmly in the ground, buried by five poles on each side, buried as deep as a man's arm. Instead of her husband inside the lodge, she found only dazed people milling around, stepping over dead bodies, and no lodge. Between the bodies were scattered piles of mud and straw and wall posts thrown haphazardly against a row of trees like drift on the beach. She recognized some of the women who ignored the prone, bloodied bodies in the sand and pulled out the wall posts to use as frames for quick lean-tos. They nodded and called her Grandmother. A day after the storm, women were on hands and knees collecting shingle and palm fronds out of the blue-eyed grass to cover lean-tos and keep their children dry. The grass's soft blue flowers were tangled among the tall, thin leaves of sea oats and shiny with rain.

"Let me help," said Grandmother, picking up an armful of wet, slippery fronds. "Have you seen my husband? You know, Beaver Tooth? He was sitting next to me, and—phew—he was gone. Our lodge roof, wall poles, mats, basket of food, and clothing are gone. Where?" She waved her hands in the air and wondered if he went with the dazzling colors of the spinning sand. "Everything carried away by an angry wind gone crazy. In all my life I have never seen anything like it. In a single moment enough sacrifices have been made to propitiate all of the spirits I can name." Her arm made a half-circle to indicate eight or ten inert bodies within view.

"Aye," said Little Mother, holding an infant in her arms. "Same thing happened to me. When the wind became real strong, my sister was hanging on to me—the next moment she was gone, blown away. I heard her calling from a tuft of deer-colored grass then from under a logjam. I looked hard but could not find her. I think it was the wind using her voice." She drew in her breath, sniffed, and pressed her fingers against her eyes for a moment. "I searched the beach for a day. Then I looked down by my feet and saw crowds of dark, shining flies crawling over something on the wet, brown sand. I leaned over for a closer look. I screamed. Blue-green flies rose up and buzzed so loud they scared me. Under that thick cloud of flies I saw Sister's face, pale as button weed. I was terrified, but I dared to touch her cheek, cold as a stone. My belly pinched when I saw her gray mouth half open, smiling. Her eyes were open wide, with a stare like a dead fish. She wore a headband of brownish-yellow sea grapes, like the bride of a sea monster. You know those creatures with the head and body of a man and tail of a fish. I was sick with dry heaves and had to leave. Later I went back, removed the headband, washed her face, and tied her mouth closed. I shook the sand out of her tunic and brushed her hair with a spiny burr. I told her to find happiness wherever she was. I dragged her body to the others laid out, waiting to be buried. I brushed her hair again because it was hard to walk away. I wanted to lie beside her, close my eyes, and sleep forever. Then I thought of my baby, Otter Boy. He and I are a family. We need each other."

"I am so sorry," said Grandmother. "How can we appease an angry wind? I say do nothing. Wind has taken his share of sacrifices from our village. Look at the dead bodies lying around quiet, like it was naptime. This is not a normal fall sacrifice."

Little Mother brushed away her tears on Otter Boy's thinly woven grass blanket that was already wet with rainwater. "It is hard for me to think," she said. "My thoughts are bubbles that break before I can look inside. But I know you are right. Wind has taken more than his share of sacrifices."

"So," said Grandmother, "keep Otter Boy out of the rain. I heard him sneeze. I will fix a little place for him that is dry, then together we shall build a lean-to to shelter the three of us. And so, where is your husband?"

"I never had one," said Little Mother. "I am the girl who followed this boy around for two summers after my mother gave him three racks of deer antlers to perform my Stretching Ceremony. After that I was not satisfied. Something powerful awakened in me. I wanted—no, I longed for the thrill of his stick. Now I believe a girl ten-to-twelve summers need not know the feelings of men and women. Women with daughters ought to put a stop to the Stretching Ceremony. When did it ever start anyway?"

"It has been done ever since I can remember," said Grandmother, dabbing at her eyes. "Some say the first stretching makes it easier for babies to slide out."

"I think it is the other way—easier for a husband to slide in," said Little Mother. "Maybe some ancient male made up this ceremony and women just followed along like baby ducks. We are not always too smart. This boy and I crushed the purple wild flowers underneath us one afternoon in the meadow about twelve, thirteen moons ago.

"The next day he left on a trading mission with his uncle. I have not seen them since. So, I used to sneak out of our lodge at night and find boys here in Sandpiper Point who wanted the thrill as much as I. My mother said it was my punishment when my father, looking for deer, fell out of a tree and died. Then last winter she got the coughing sickness and died. During the storm my sister was pushed or pulled into the water and died. Look what else happened to me, a baby! He came before the storm. I tell you true, the Stretching Ceremony did me no good. The baby, Otter Boy, nearly split my insides coming out. I bled like a deer with its head cut off. I was in terrible pain and frightened out of my head. Someone told me not to complain; this is a woman's life. I told them a woman's life is too short to be filled with hurt and fright!"

"You are not to blame for your father climbing a tree, your mother coughing herself to death, or your sister drowning, unless your hands gave them a push. The hard part of living is to see loved ones die. It happens to everyone. Look, here, Little Mother, can you believe this? A hollow where one of my big firestones sat before the wind went mad," said Grandmother, pointing. She pulled a tattered floor mat from the tree, shook it, and laid it in the hole. "Put Otter Boy there, and I will cover him with a peaked roof of bark and fronds. See, for a few moments he will be fine."

Building a shelter was women's work since time began. Both of these women were adept at putting the logs into the sandy ground and building a lean-to of fronds that would keep the rain off the people inside. When the work was finished, they looked at several other lean-tos. The old woman said, "Ours will do. Stay here and I will find something dry to wrap around Otter Boy. Use your firestones to start a fire and begin drying your own clothing."

By afternoon the rain had stopped, but the sky was still covered with low clouds. "Umm," said Little Mother, feeling in the leather pouch around her waist for her firestones. "Maybe I gave them to Sister. No—I think I lost them during the storm. No matter—all the wood is wet. If there were cook fires, I might beg a red coal. But there are none, so we cannot start a fire."

Grandmother felt around in her waist-pouch and pulled out two firestones and bits of dry bark. She rubbed the stones close to the bark, and when she had a flame, she sent Little Mother for the driest pieces of wood she could find. "Put the bigger log here so it will dry before you put it on the fire," said Grandmother. "You start drying out while I find something more."

Most other cook fires were dead, food was scattered, and what could be found was full of sand and sand fleas. She found some wet flat bread wedged into a basket. She was lucky. The bottom of the basket was sandy, but the bread was fairly clean. Carefully she shook out the sand and fleas by prying open a small hole between the woven strands. The bread would have to be eaten before black mildew and furry blue mold grew on it.

She walked past two lodge poles longer than the height of a man and thought, *Today I have learned that nothing is too heavy for an angry wind to carry.* Then she recognized the poles were roof supports of their summer lodge. Beaver Tooth had carved the supports. He was so proud of them that he had told her he would carry them to the winter camp and use them for lodge supports there. He was noted for his skilled carvings. She had teased him, saying he was not as strong as he used to be and he could never carry those heavy poles unless he had help. "I am not going to be your helper, that is too much work," she had said. He smiled and admitted he was not as strong as he used to be, but he was just as smart and had just bought a beautiful yellow dog, who would do the work, if he made a harness for him.

She found the muddy, yellow dog lying in the grass, with its share of blue-green flies laying eggs in a deep gash on its left shoulder. The grass around the dog was mashed down and broken. The dirt was pawed and bloodied. The dog had a stick in its neck pinning it tight to the ground, but it had struggled to pull itself loose. Grandmother put down the basket of flat bread and pulled the stick out. Blood did not pump out of the hole. The dog was not breathing, and she could not feel a tum-tum, a heartbeat. She knew for certain that the dog was dead and dug a shallow trench with the stick. She lifted the dog into the trench and pushed the bloody dirt and broken wild flowers gently over the carcass. She heard herself moaning as she practiced how to tell Beaver Tooth about his dog. She held her breath a moment to make her voice whisper quiet. Then she said aloud, "And that *was* a dog's life. It *is* a dog's death. A dog's life is short." She thought, *Now what will he do when he hears the yellow dog is dead?* Tears stung her eyes. She told herself tears never brought back anything and scrubbed them away with her fists. "Beaver Tooth! Beaver!" She called and heard only the swish-swash of the sea on the sand. She was near the large pile of driftwood. *Perhaps*, she thought, *he is dry and warm under the drift and playing the hand game with a friend.* She squatted down and poked around. She backed away, stood up, and called again. There was no answer, only the choked private keening coming from others who had found loved ones behind stones, under the drift, and in the dunes.

"With no warning," said someone, speaking loud enough so she could hear, "It was a couple of days ago when that storm arose out of the gray sea. Did you see it?" "I saw whirling water spouts and blasting sand funnels sweep across the land," someone else said. "Not a lodge nor a bird is left on Sandpiper Point. Time to change the name. What do you think?"

"Aye, just call it *Sandpoint*," said Grandmother. No one replied to her sad humor. Since that day, the small village with the overlarge burial mound has been called Sandpoint.

That night Grandmother lay near the drift, away from the wind and tide rise, but she could not sleep. She thought of the colors made by the sun shining through the whirling sand and listened for the deep sound of her husband's voice calling for help. She heard nothing but cries of small children and the hiss of windblown sand mingling with the thunder of the sea. That morning she saw dugout canoes that had been blown ashore and buried under dunes. Some were cracked and twisted around trees that were decorated with shreds of lodge skins, tunics, breechclouts, gray moss skirts, and reed baskets. She pulled a couple of pieces of clothing down and sat under the lean-to next to Little Mother. She peeled the damp blanket from Otter Boy and wrapped him in the dry things. He stopped shivering but continued to whimper softly. She smiled because the fire was still smoldering. She laid on a couple of pieces of wood until the fire was again strong enough to dry out and burn some short, fat logs.

They ate the thin, soggy bread. Little Mother nursed Otter Boy, who stopped whimpering and slept. Then she told Grandmother what a terrible chore it was to take care of such a little thing.

"I have always thought a child was a precious gift," said Grandmother. "I figured it was a privilege and a joy to care for something so small and helpless. I have a recurring dream of being so careful not to break a baby's delicate bones, nor scratch his soft skin. I would bathe him, wrap him in clean, warm clothes, and gaze in wonder as he slept." Suddenly she put her hand over her mouth and looked around.

"It is just a big dream," said the young mother. "You forgot there are things like making diaper cloths to hold cattail fluff or dried moss between a baby's legs. And nursing! A baby sucks harder than a handful of leeches. And then the sharp teeth appear! If Otter Boy bites me, I will choke him."

Grandmother clicked her teeth and whispered, "Little Mother, there is a balance between life and death. Baby's father left. Your mother, father, and sister are dead. But still you are not alone. You have something precious: a tiny, growing life that will renew your spirit."

The rest of the day the sky was clear. The afternoon sun took some of the bite out of the wind. Grandmother missed the gatherings of the sea birds.

The next day the rain fell hard again, making it impossible to look for food. Grandmother could not tell if it was rain or tears or both that ran down her face. Many people were sneezy and sick. Hoping to find her husband, Grandmother helped some men move dead, puffed-up bodies under the protection of a large lean-to that a few women and girls had built during the night when they could not sleep. Two of the bodies carried roofing stakes that the wind had driven through them. Three were pulled from log jambs where they had drowned in the tide surge or suffocated in an avalanche of sand. Most of the others had dark wounds that had not oozed blood for days. The bodies began to puff up and smell rotten.

Chief Brittle Star, the bare-foot man bundled in a leather-hooded tunic and leggings, came out of his lean-to one morning and announced, "Half the village is dead. Burial ceremony is put off until the rain stops."

"Wait," said Grandmother, holding a hand in the air like a flag. "The burial ceremony is important and is past due. Our dead have been too long exposed to the wind and rain. The rats and crows are already fighting over the softening flesh. Let us build a stack of driftwood over the dead and purify our air with a great fire. We can have a burial ceremony and later bury the bones."

"For shame!" said the chief. "You suggest we burn the ghosts of the dead? Their spirits will be cinders?"

"You do not know, because it has never been done," said Grandmother.

"It is an unheard of act. We wait until the rain is gone to bury our dead; we do not, we can not burn them. Old Woman, swallow your words, lest you find yourself over a cook fire, run through on a pole like a wild boar. Troublemakers like you ought to be run out of Sandpoint!"

The men and women moaned in the open, swayed back and forth on their haunches, daubed their faces with black mourning stripes, and scowled at Grandmother. No one dared to bury any of the dead until the chief said the time was right.

The women cut their hair short, painted their faces with charcoal mixed with goose grease, sat inside their lean-tos, and wailed louder than the men did.

Their keening pressed on Grandmother's head. She had slept little since the storm, three days past. She was bone tired, her eyes were red and swollen, and there were deep lines in her leathery, tanned face. Her clothing was damp, tattered, and mud streaked. She had cut her hair with a sharp shell found on the beach. She planned to tear the rest of it out as a mollifying gesture to the wind's angry spirit, whether she found her beloved husband dead or alive. Looking at Little Mother with a blackened face cuddling Otter Boy to her breast made her think of all the times her husband had lain against her breasts while he slept. Now she prayed hard that she would find Beaver Tooth safe. He was the person she loved more than anyone—anything. Suddenly she heard a high scream. It sounded like a hysterical woman, but she was certain it was the voice of the cougar. Her lips twitched making a small smile. The animal had come out of the highlands looking for food. He would make some good meals off that pile of dead bodies. Maybe he would call his family and friends to the feast. In a panic she went back to the big drift pile and grabbed the first person she saw: an old man with rounded shoulders, a long neck, and long, gray hair tied in the back with a palm frond. "The rain has stopped," she said. "Come on! We can bury the dead before sundown. If we wait until tomorrow morning, the stench, beside the hordes of biting blowflies, will be unbearable. Listen, I heard the cougar cry. It is a bad sign. If the cougar calls his friends, they will sniff and urinate on the rotting dead and then go after our sick and wounded like a feast made just for them. Do you have a bow and arrow in safekeeping?"

He looked at her, rubbed his eyes, looked again. In the cloud-gray light his eyes searched her face, and then he nodded his head. "Ahh, Grandmother, is that truly your face underneath mud, mold, and grass stain? Are those your red-rimmed eyes with pouches? Your hair—looks like the back of a sand rat! Ha! Ha! Funny, I have never seen you so unkempt. I recognize only your voice. This storm made a mess of everything. Of course I have a fine bow and plenty of sharp arrows."

"Then use one to teach the cougars what happens when they come around here," she said.

The old man said not to worry. He, Egret, could take care of a cougar. Hey, hey! "Do you know it was I who found your man this morning? He was headfirst in a dune. Brown shit smeared his buttocks. I pulled him out by his bare feet and shook the sand out of his nose and ears, but he had no breath. I truly liked him. I am sorry." Egret lightly touched her arm and walked away before she could see his watery eyes. *Poor woman,* he thought, *once she was the best-looking thing in this village. And today the best thing this village has, even though she looks like an old crone who has lost her enchantment and would as soon quit breathing as wash her face. Poor thing misses her old man. I would like to wash her face and clean her hair to see if she can still look good. I bet my only pair of good moccasins she can. Great Living Spirit! I loved her before Beaver Tooth even saw her. When he did notice her, he let me know she was his by knocking out my front tooth. Oh, he was mean to me and she was sweet and so lovely to me. I guess he was not mean to her. I did like him, once I knew him.*

Grandmother sat on the shore and watched the high swells roll in, curl over in a white crest, and fall into handfuls upon handfuls of bubbles. She heard the breakers mingled with her own sniffling and lingered on wondering at the changing beauty of the water and the earth and the mystery of life. Then she grabbed a handful of her black tangled hair and yanked. She cursed the Spirits for letting her live and leaving her husband dead.

"You fools, you know Beaver was far gentler and more forgiving than I have ever been," she said aloud. "Spirits! Mush Faces, that is what you are! I do not believe you know a thing about us, The People. You are as good as brown slime to let that storm pass here without blinking your yellow, putrid, old eyes. One of you could have told

Wind to go a tiny bit east or a smidgen west and ignore
Sandpoint. You lazy Spirits! Wake up! Look what you let
happen! Why should I honor you? Give me one reason!
Pitooey!" She spit and Wind brought it back to her chest.
She wiped it off with a handful of sand.

People with pinched, anxious faces passed her slowly,
called her name in greeting, but they did not stop. They
understood she was not the only one with problems of survival and an overwhelmingly sad heart. They could see she
wanted to be left alone in her grief.

She got up and went to the large lean-to where the dead
bodies were still laid out, waiting for the chief to announce
the Burial Ceremony. She did not once hold her breath but
breathed the putrid air as if it were the most natural thing
to do. She found her husband on top of the last stack she
herself had made. She put her arms around him and held
him as close as she could and let her tears pour out. "I want
to be with you," she sobbed with her face on his cold, sandy
chest.

In a little while someone handed her a wad of dry moss,
saying, "Like you said, it is time to bury the dead." She
did not see who it was, but she recognized Egret's choked-
up voice. She wiped her tears and scrubbed her face. She
washed and dried her husband's body and tied his breechclout, found in a tree, around his waist. She imagined that
she felt his spirit nearby, so she told him she was not sure
what she would do from now on without him. "First," she
said, "I buried your elegant yellow dog. Next I am helping
a young mother and her baby. This baby is a darling boy
with a round face and big eyes that look at whoever is
talking to him. He reminds me—well, you remember! It
brings back powerful memories to see that baby again. My
arms ached for years to hold him. I must stop thinking this
way. He is a man now, and I do not know what he looks
like. This baby with the big eyes is Otter Boy. He has no
teeth yet, and his little mother is not looking forward to
having them show up. Listen, Little Mother and I might be
bold enough together to tell Chief Brittle Star to forget the
girls' Stretching Ceremony. What do you think of that?
She, like me, believes the ceremony is wrong for young

girls. Can you imagine me speaking my mind to the chief?"
Softly she giggled like a young girl.

Then she heard that high-pitched cry again and knew it
came from somewhere in the big log jamb. She wished
Egret were beside her with a bow and arrow. She began to
grab at her hair again, then suddenly thought, *If I stand
where the cougar can jump at me, the people along the
shore will see me and hear me yell. They will run here with
a club to beat the animal to death. To get rid of a hungry
cougar is to save lives. To get rid of the cougar is worth
letting it claw and gnaw on me to save children. What does
it matter if I die? I will be with Beaver. That is what I
want. Oh, yes,* she thought, *it would be a good thing if I
can save some babies or sick people from being eaten alive
by the cougar. That is exactly what the Spirits intended. So
they are not the fools I thought they were.* "Yu!" she said
aloud. "Good! I apologize for the ugly names I called you,
Spirits. I was wrong. You did not deserve them."

She walked to the jumbled pile of smooth, gray logs
higher than her head. She stepped close to an uprooted tree
that still had its rough bark and whose branches had been
cut for someone's lean-to or a warm fire. She heard several
sharp, quick sounds. *What was that?* She had never heard
a cougar with hiccups before. She heard sobbing. *Someone
is there or that cougar is playing tricks on my ears. What
does it matter?* She bent down and looked inside the tangled drift. As before there was nothing but darkness. She
went closer and heard the scream, but it was softer, like the
animal was luring her closer. She backed out and saw Egret
holding a huge stone. *About time,* she thought. *Good.* She
ducked down and called to the beast, "Come on out here
and fight like a real warrior!"

The next cry was pitifully small. She wedged herself
between two smooth logs and felt around with her hands.
She expected the cougar's teeth to clamp down on her hand,
but she felt only some wet, sticky moss and skittering
hands, or feet, like maybe a sand-crab, no—a mouse in
some kind of a nest. She thought, *The cougar is really
clever at shape changing.* She wiped the pulled hair off of
her hand and reached in as far as she could. There, she felt
the soft moss again. Or was it matted cougar's fur? She

backed out, made the cut-off sign with her hand across her neck, and told Egret to drop the stones. "Hold up that log," she said pointing. "Hold it so that I can get under it. Something is in there, alive."

"Grandmother, you watch out," said Egret with a crooked grin. "It could be a water snake. Something poisonous! Here, you hold up the log and let me drop my stone on it."

"No, no!" said Grandmother, "you hold the log, I will get in there. I am smaller and I can drop the stone. I can do that. Give it to me!" She wiggled herself back in. "Hold the log higher! I see it! Oh, it has big eyes and white teeth. Oh, oh—" her legs were cramped with kneeling. She backed out and let the stone fall from her hands. Egret opened his mouth to cuss at her bungling ways, but she did not give him time to say what she did not want to hear. "Where is your bow and all those fine arrows?" she said.

"I am not sure. I could not find them in all this disorder," he said.

She went back inside the little hollow pushing with her arms. Her legs were stretched out in back of her. "Come here to Grandmother," she whispered, "I am ready for you."

She pulled her body around so she was sitting with her back hunched. She lifted the frightened little thing up and over a skinny log. Then she held it close to her chest. Egret could see her holding something squirmy, dark, and muddy. Around its grimy neck was a band of rainbow-colored beads strung on a strong braided thread. If the beads were clean, she was sure they would be as brilliant as the rainbow colors she saw when the sun shone through the scattered, quartz prisms of sand. When the sun shone through those prisms, she believed it was a good sign. She put a hand over the little thing's mouth to keep it quiet. Suddenly she took a deep breath to control the sharp pain and her beating heart. Instantly she knew what Little Mother was talking about—a baby with sharp teeth. This baby had an extra row of teeth in the top of her mouth. She had only seen such a thing once before and those same kind of double teeth belonged to Egret! She would not tell Egret, or let him think such a little thing had bitten her hand with its sharp, white teeth. *He would knock it out of my arms,* she thought. *No, he will not! This is my day to be strong.* A knot of pressure grew in her stomach. She licked the blood off her hand and waited a few moments for the bleeding to stop, then backed out, careful to keep her head down.

The stench hit Egret. "Is it dead?"

"No!" she cried.

"Hold the stinking beast away from your body," he said, as his brown eyes became wide and his mouth puckered when he turned away to draw in air. "That shitty little beast is sick! Even if it is a cougar kit, it can bite something fierce. No shaman's rattle or herb drink will keep you from dying if you get bit. You are holding it too close. If its breath is yeasty, the wild thing will bite one of your nipples right off, chew it, swallow, and bite the other. You will bleed to death." He picked up another large stone.

Looking at his round, brown eyes, Grandmother thought he looked like he would enjoy such a sight. Actually he was scared to death that something bad was going to happen to her. He wanted to knock the dirty beast out of her protecting arms.

Women can be so stubborn, he thought, *especially this one. She was born with a mind of her own coupled with second sight. She sees things before others see them. Why is she protecting this bedraggled cougar kit? Maybe she knows she will long for something to feed and pet in the days ahead, because she has no man around to fuss over.*

"The village women and shaman are working with the storm wounded," said Egret. "Those wounded will get the healing herbs and songs first before you, if you are bitten. So, drop the beast! Stomp on it! It will bite further than your brown nipples, I tell you."

"Look here!" said Grandmother with a snap in her voice. "I hold a child. A child, born of a human mother. She needs a good wash, warmth of a roaring fire, and loving arms to make her feel secure."

"Poot! No baby is missing," said Egret. "You remember Brittle Star made a village count. I know not where this young thing you have comes from. I believe it is a shape-changed cougar."

"Does it matter?" asked Grandmother. "I found her. I will care for her."

"I told you," said Egret, "each baby in this village is either dead or alive and all are accounted. The chief worked through the bodies, notching the counts on a hide this morning. That baby, my friend, is a wild beast, who shape-changed under those logs. Tonight, he will gnaw on you good. Believe what I tell you."

The baby sniveled into the hollow of Grandmother's shoulder and gripped the backs of her arms with fingers as strong as a liana vine.

"Ah yes," said Egret. "Give me the baby, and I will put him head first in the stream. Then that will be that. He will change back to a real, dead cougar the minute I take him out of the water. I tell you that is the way with these tricky cougars."

"No, do not touch *her!*" said Grandmother, backing away. "I will take my chances. She may have washed ashore after her parents' fishing boat capsized. Who knows who she belongs to or where she came from."

"My Dear One, no bodies have come ashore, neither has an unknown canoe," said Egret, dropping the stone and kicking it. "So, how do you know *she* is not *he*?"

"Same as I know the Spirits—" she wanted to say that the Spirits gave her an unmistakable good sign that matched the baby's neckband. Instead she said, "—left *her* here for me. From now on you will only call me *Grandmother*. I am not your Dear One. And my child is to be called *Cougar,* a fitting name."

Farther than anyone could see, way across the Great Eastern Sea, was an island, east by north from the Calusa village of Sandpoint, called Eire or Ireland. In the year 1151 A.D. neither the Calusas nor the Irish had the slightest knowledge of one another. Even though each group had developed their own, but different, well-established language, customs, mores, religion, and politics, they hungered for the same things: freedom from misunderstanding, security, love, and approval.

Dornoll was a dark-haired, blue-eyed lass, about four-feet six-inches tall, fourteen years old, and wife to an Irish sheepherder. She was washing clothes on a rocky beach alongside a stream when she heard the shrill wail of a banshee, a female spirit, crying a death warning. She pressed her hands against her back to ease the stiffness as she pulled herself upright and peered cautiously up- and downstream. Then she hollered, "Go on with ye! We want no fairy spirit warning about death and such in this family. Get along!" She ran her hand over the black wisps peeping from the edge of her sunbonnet and glanced at the clutches of sheep and goats grazing behind the cottage, their heads high, listening.

The next piercing cry came from the hazel grove and made the hairs on her head stiffen. She moved so fast that she did not concern herself about stepping on sharp stones, or snakes. Her feet slid inside her roomy pampooties. "Seth!" she called. "Seth ap Rees! Come! Get a cudgel and come!"

Seth, five-and-a-half-feet tall, broad shouldered, gnarled and browned by the harsh Irish weather, was outside rubbing his boots with mutton fat to make them waterproof. Startled to hear his wife in a dither, he scrambled to his feet. "What is yer caterwauling about, *colleen,* did yer laundry fall into the creek and ride into the hazels?" He chuckled deep inside his barrel chest. "Keep calm. A light heart lives long," he quoted an old Gaelic proverb.

"Bring a shillelagh! Follow me!" Dornoll breathed so hard she could not say more. She pointed.

Seth took the double-blade ax off the pegs on the front wall of his mud and willow-wattle cottage and followed her to a swarm of midges that hovered over the washing waiting to be spread on gorse bushes.

"Aye, stand in front of the wash heap and listen," she said in a hushed voice. There was no sound but the gurgling of the stream and Seth slapping midges.

He put his arm around his plump wife. "Lass, ye raced yer bones for naught. Ye best get the wash hung before our wee one wakes and cries like a hungry bear cub." He gave her loving pecks on both cheeks and went back to his boots and mutton fat.

She spread the wash, until every bush was covered with all shapes of faded blue and brown linen. She eyed her handiwork and for an instant wished for a fresh, blue tunic for wee Wyn. The cry came again, sounding like the yowling Wyn made when she was cold or hungry. *'Tis a banshee for certes, come back to warn me about something dreadful,* she thought. She tiptoed toward the hazel grove. The crying stopped, and she went through the grove and came out on the mossy bank of the stream where it curved quietly under low branches of red willow. She looked at her reflection in the silent pool. "If ye stay in that water, Dornoll, ye will be as wrinkled as yer dear grandmam," she said, thinking she had heard the squealing of a green woodpecker. She thought, *Ye are a fool,* and laughed. She looked in the hazels for the bird with a crimson crown and yellow rump that was a sign of happiness ahead. The cry came once more, and she twirled around to see a short, wide boat made of waterproofed animal skin stretched over a wicker frame, floating, like an oversized washbasket, between the lower willow branches. It bobbed and dipped each time its cargo made a sound. She moved so the sun was not in her eyes and looked across green water at a babe who had kicked off the wrappings, so bare feet and tiny fists beat the air.

"Oh, mercy me!" she said and slipped off her bonnet, tunic, and pampooties, ducked into the cold water, and peered over the edge of the bowl-like boat. "A Viking-child with fair hair and eyebrows fine as spiderspin." She breathed gingerly. "Ye smell like a scared skunk."

The babe sucked water from her fingers when she stroked his face. She felt the little arms and legs to make certain they were not some ghostly apparitions. She hung on to the coracle and paddled her feet. On the mossy bank she found the foul-smelling coracle so light she could carry it on her head. She placed the coracle beside Seth. "See—something was out there—crying."

He looked at the blue-eyed infant, then at his wife and said, "Is it bath time? Smells like ye need to try again."

"Oh, ye bleedin' daftie! Someone loves this sweet child and rubbed the coracle with skunk-oil to keep wolves away. See how he chews his fist?" She sat cross-legged on the dirt floor of their cottage and took the infant from the coracle. She spread its white blanket on her lap and cradled the babe against her arm to let him nurse. "Slow down, wee thing," she crooned. "Share with yer sister, Wyn."

Seth took the skunky coracle outside to the back of the cottage, while she gave the infant a dry diaper towel padded with clean moss. "The gods have blessed us this day," she said when Seth was inside. "We have a wee *brawd*, brother, for Wyn."

"I suspect his folks were in some trouble and wanted their baby saved. In the old days Norsemen invaded Irish seaports and desperate mothers hid their infants in the sedges, hoping those who remained alive might find them fosterage." He held the baby in his big hands and examined him carefully. "No marks. Some day his folks will want him back."

"A silver clasp held his towel together," said Dornoll.

Seth took the clasp to the open window where there was more light. "On the top are three lions surrounded by an unbroken circle," he said. " 'Tis a life-forever symbol— something druids forge."

"Nay, my husband, druids do not have such fine blankets. This white wool is finer than anything I have ever seen. A long soak in vinegar will cut its musky smell. This lucky *baban* is of royal blood." She kissed the baby's foot and said, "Where do ye come from?"

"The laddie was abandoned and we found him," said Seth. "He is ours."

Dornoll called the laddie Brawd, meaning Brother. His pale hair and eyebrows turned to burnished gold. His eyes changed color with his moods: cobalt blue, like the clear Irish sky, when he was happy; like the blue-gray of the angry Irish Sea, when he was upset; blue-green, like summer grass, when he concentrated on a vexing problem. He pleased Seth and Dornoll as much as Wyn, their true child. The children were told all the stories Seth and Dornoll remembered from their childhood, then Seth began to teach them the way druid teachers taught their foster children. There were stories in the morning and after sup they learned reading and writing and numbers. Brawd was the younger but always asked the more perceptive questions. When he was about five, Seth gave him a paddle with carved swirls on the loom. Brawd set the coracle where the water ran fastest and watched the paddle flash in the sunlight as he made it dip, push, and rise. Later he fixed the craft so that it held a tottery, upright pole on which he strung Seth's cast-off tunic as a sail.

Brawd and Wyn often paddled upstream, looking at the vines that twined through the oaks and the birds that darted ahead from one branch to another. One day he held the coracle steady by wedging the paddle against the rocks in the stream's bottom, and they stared at the wooded embankment of a long ridge or drumlin. He pointed to the standing stones and unknown cowled men who worked silently by lime-washed cottages.

When they were home, Brawd went to Seth and asked, "The men on the drumlin, who are they?"

"Son, they are Taliesin Druids of the Third Order."

"What are Druids of the Third Order?" asked Brawd.

"Ages ago our people called themselves Celts and divided themselves into four orders. Those belonging to three of these orders did not believe in war. They were mystic and realistic at the same time. They believed in the brotherhood of man and called themselves *druids*. Today most everyone who knows of druids has a definition of his own making. There are the bards, singers, poets, harpers, and keepers of history and knowledge of the cosmos and Otherworld gods. There are the lawgivers, judges, and counselors, who are fair and truthful as confidential advisors to lords and kings and have been known to stop wars in the middle of a battle. The Third Order Irish Taliesin are naturalists and healers, concerned with nature, philosophic speculation, and reading omens for lucky and unlucky days."

When Brawd was about seven, he squatted on his haunches beside Seth and asked, "Remember the story you told us about the wise man called Jesus who lived ages ago in a faraway place? Do the druids on the drumlin, who are so wise and know so much, know there was once a man called Jesus?"

Seth had the habit of rubbing his whiskers, as Brawd's questions grew more complicated and harder to answer, to give himself time to think. "Long ago druids had ways to foretell that the Lord God, who is the greatest of the Mysteries because He lives with us and at the same time lives in the Heavens, would have a human son. The Holy Babe, as predicted, was born under the sign of a bright star. Three wise men, who were in fact druids, followed the star to the village of Bethlehem to give precious gifts to the Holy Babe. The three druids were both joyous and sad when they heard the foreshadowing, because they learned the Holy Babe would be the world's greatest Teacher, but He would be crucified long before He was an old man."

"Was His mam's heart broken?" said Brawd.

"I like to think the three druids did not tell her," said Seth. "Sometimes 'tis better not to know what is in the future."

A few days later Brawd said, "Are druids like Christian monks who copy knowledge from one scroll to another for safekeeping?"

"Nay," said Seth. "Druids do not depend on scrolls that can be destroyed by fire, water, or insects, to keep their knowledge. They spend years memorizing it and know more about the Mysteries than anyone."

"One day I would like to ask a druid about sea monsters and the black abyss at the far edge of the sea," said Brawd. His eyes were blue-green like summer grass.

Seth drew in his breath, curled his fingers against his palms to hide the druid, blue-woad half-moon honor marks tattooed into his skin at the bottom of each fingernail. "Some men know of those things better than I," he said, feeling uncomfortable about his ability to continue answering Brawd's growing number of questions.

That evening Seth suggested that the druids, who lived on the drumlin, foster the lad. "The lad's questions should be answered properly," he said.

Dornoll buried her face in her hands and would not look at him. She took the silver clasp from the cupboard and looked at it in the candlelight to see if there were markings he had missed. She found nothing new.

In May, Brawd laid sheared fleece on the floor of the wool-cottage to cool. He noticed a mist, like the bloom on fruit, over the fleeces. He saw them tremble and heard them make soft sounds, like breathing. "Are fleeces living, like a ghost or a flame?" he whispered.

Seth said he had never seen a ghost and was not sure

how they lived. With the logic of observation, Brawd said that a flame ate candles. Dornoll agreed and said she once saw a small flame grow by eating a whole forest and move from one tree to the next as fast as a bear moves toward a honeycomb. Seth said flames move because of gusts of air, but he was not sure if they ate, really ate. He was not sure how flames grew or died or were born. He asked Brawd if a dropped feather was living.

"Nay, I be saying I do not believe so. Although they move in the smallest breath of air," said Brawd with a frown. "Is that the answer to trembly fleeces?"

"Aye, son," said Seth, "Wool is like feathers. The fibers are locked together, and when harvested fleeces cool, they relax, the fibers unlock and seem to stir. See, there is an answer for every knotty point." There was a catch in his breath when he added that neither he nor Dornoll could know the answers to all of his questions. "And you have my habit of saying, *I be*, instead of being proper and saying, *I am*. Good speech tells people you are knowledgeable and studious. I ought to do something about that."

"What will ye do?" asked Brawd.

"Send ye to the druid camp where ye will find the answers and learn proper speech."

"I be proud to speak like my tad," said Brawd. "If 'tis your habit, I would like to keep it and have something of you with me."

Brawd saw the sudden tears that stung Dornoll's eyes. The next morning before he or Wyn were up, he heard his folks talking.

" 'Tis wrong that I, a herder of sheep and goats, and you, a crofter's lass, continue to teach this inquisitive lad, who already knows more about some things than either of us," said Seth. "I be a druid, but I have not been with them for an age. Mayhap I should go with the lad to refresh my knowledge and learn what is new."

"Nay, both of you stay with us. I love you two so much. Brawd is our only son. Wyn will be lost without him. He looks after her, even though she is the older, by mayhap two years," whispered Dornoll.

Their words brought a tingle of excitement to Brawd's spirit, but heaviness to his heart. "I be happy and I be sad," he said.

Part One

Come listen to a tale of times of old . . .
  And ye shall hear how Madoc
  From the shores of Britain
  Spread adventurous sail,
  Explored the ocean paths . . .
  And stood triumphant on another world.
            —Robert Southey, *Madoc, An Epic Poem*,
                        and Pat Winter, *Madoc*

I stood upon the deck and watched till dawn,
  But who can tell what feelings filled my heart,
  When like a cloud, the distant land arose
  Gray from the ocean; . . . when we left the ship,
  And cleft with rapid oars, the shallow wave,
  And stood triumphant on another world.
            —Robert Southey, *Madoc, An Epic Poem*,
                        and Richard Deacon,
            Madoc and the Discovery of America

Part One

I
Cougar

ON THE FLORIDA WEST COAST, 1155 TO 1168 A.D.

> Quite a few of the languages that were once spoken in the
> Southeast [U.S.] are now extinct. For some of these—such
> as the languages spoken by the Avoyels, Taensas, Koroas,
> Grigras, Tious, Yamasees, Ais, Tequestas, Calusas, and
> many, many others—we have no record at all.
> —Charles Hudson, *The Southeastern Indians*

After the big storm, some of the people from Sandpoint
moved to other Calusa villages that were not on a point of
land stretching out into the water, inviting storms to hit.
Egret decided to stay when the chieftain and his three wives
did not leave. Grandmother stayed to be close to the bones
of her husband. Here there was plenty of driftwood to build
a big lodge, everyone knew each other, and fishing was
easy. Little Mother stayed to be close to Grandmother and
raise Otter Boy in a place with fresh water, wild fruit, and
vegetables close by.

Every day for six summers, after gathering wood, Grandmother and Cougar sat and talked, enjoying one another's
company. Grandmother loved Cougar more each day.
Lately, however, some days were more of a trial than previous days because Cougar no longer was a cooing, smiling, and needy baby. She had become a kind-hearted but
independent girl, full of questions. She did not always listen
to what was on her grandmother's mind. Whenever Cougar
ignored her, Grandmother's mind reeled. She felt as if she
was in the middle of a terrible dream.

Today she watched Cougar walk along the beach and

thought of herself as a girl the same age, living south on the shore of Bird Bay, with the small Gull tribe. One morning her parents took their wooden dugout into the swamp to trap alligators for meat and hides and never returned. Gulltown men searched the swamp but found nothing.

After that, the girl seemed older than her years. She lived by herself, learned to cook, built a good lodge, and kept herself neat and clean. She continued to look in all the swampy places she knew and once found a rotting dugout but could not tell if it looked familiar.

Egret, a young man on a trading trip, found her sitting in the sun, singing, weaving reed baskets that she bartered for food and clothing. Each time he came to town she invited him to stay with her. Her life began to change. She had someone to wash her hair, care for her, to make her happy.

She blossomed and became a beautiful young girl. Everyone believed that Egret married her when he was a trader with a large canoe. She never attended the girls' Stretching Ceremony to properly prepare herself for marriage; she became pregnant and never married Egret. She had a baby boy during a time when the winter rains were especially harsh. The weather was so bad that no one went to sea for mullet or snapper. No one dared fish the freshwater stream that had overflowed its banks leaving putrid, dead perch and catfish in the mud. Food and good water became scarce, and the girl's milk became thin. Her baby whined and fussed constantly. Egret, who was truly not married, was in the north trading his fishhooks with the men for their tortoiseshell combs. He was unable to go to Gulltown because of floodwaters hiding and washing out local trails. He stayed in Sandpiper Point and was told that Gulltown had been swallowed by the floodwaters. "No person is left alive," Chief Brittle Star said. Egret was lonely and sad without that beautiful young girl whom he believed had drowned. In the spring he married a widowed woman.

It was a sad year for the young mother in Gulltown. Women made fun of her because she had not gone through the Stretching Ceremony and had a baby by herself. For six-and-a-half moons she prayed to the Spirits to tell her how she could keep her precious baby boy from starving to death. She got no sign from the Spirits, no food and no sweet water. Her breast milk dried up. She had nothing to feed her child, little to eat herself, and could not bear to hear her child cry. So she did what she thought best; she gave away her baby to a married woman who had recently lost her infant and whose breasts were overflowing with milk. After giving her child away, she was so overcome with grief that she wilted. Her skin became pale and flabby. She combed ashes in her hair, which made her look so old that she was given the name Grandmother. She left Gulltown and set out northward to find Egret. It took a long time bartering shell belts, earspools, or gorgets she made for canoe rides from one island to the next to find him. When she did get to Sandpoint, he already had a wife, so she made herself a lodge at the edge of the village and lived alone. A man, called Beaver Tooth, with hair so long he rolled it at the back of his head and held it in place by a thin bone, learned that she cooked well and was courteous, kind, and intelligent. When she showed him she could build a lean-to or summer lodge in half the time it took other women, he said she was his woman. He brought her plenty of meat and fish, and she began to put a little fat under her skin. He washed the ash out of her long black hair and again she blossomed into a beautiful woman.

A few years later, Egret's wife died of coughing sickness. After several weeks of mourning, he plucked out his whiskers, scrubbed his face with sand, bathed in the stream, made his black hair shine with bear grease, and dressed in a breechcloth and a smoky-smelling moss shirt. That shirt smelled wonderful to him. Anything made of the gray, curly moss had to be kept in the smoke from damp wood for one or two days to rid it of the mites that gave the wearer itchy welts. It was time to explain to Grandmother why he had not come back to Gulltown years ago. Grandmother was glad to invite him into her lodge and immediately said she had forgiven him ages ago for taking a wife in Sandpoint. He said he was glad she had not drowned. He said he would like to be her friend again. Beaver Tooth told him she was his woman now and did not need his friendship. It took many moons before Beaver Tooth really liked Egret enough to ask him to go fishing.

Grandmother swallowed her thoughts of days gone by and began to think of recent happy times. Since the Big Storm, Egret supplied her with ducks, geese, fruit, and vegetables. When Cougar was about five summers, she began to help tan hides for their lodge walls. Later she learned to cut and tie all the palm fronds to cover the roof. Grandmother taught her how to use a baited net to get the clams and crabs from the shallow bottom of the sea. She also netted and brought home shrimp and mullet.

Grandmother's nets were made from fibers of the brackish water plant with long leaves shaped like an arrowhead, and they were stronger than those made by the men. So, the village men were happy when Grandmother suggested she trade her nets for deer and alligator hides to make clothing, moccasins, and mend the lodge skins.

Her brown skin became wrinkled like the bark of an ancient possum tree, but her voice was always deep and strong. Sometimes she told Cougar and Otter Boy about her girlhood home in Gulltown. Once she took Cougar south to her home village. Cougar traded her food supply of salted fish to several Gulltown women for corn and squash seeds. She traded the seeds to Sandpoint women for clay bowls for Grandmother. The women found they would rather plant seeds and tend gardens than go out to hunt for wild roots in alligator- and snake-infested swamps. Chief Brittle Star came to see Cougar and told her it was unnatural for The People's women to stay home working in a garden. They had always gone outside the village to harvest wild vegetables and fruit, until Cougar had told them how to plant seeds. Grandmother told him Cougar was a smart girl. He said she was a troublemaker.

When Cougar was eight summers, she made baskets from the pliable stalks of cattail and burr reed from the fresh-water marshes. She went with Grandmother in their dugout canoe to Gulltown to trade for more seeds, then paddled farther south through the marshes to some villages of the Ais tribe. Grandmother could not understand their language and used hand signs and markings in the damp sand to communicate. Cougar said it would be easier to learn the language. Grandmother did not understand how to do that quickly. So Cougar told her how she learned by memorizing the names of things first, especially the name of the trade items. Then she memorized movements, such as run, walk, jump, and swim; then noises, talk, shout, buzz, and honk; then feelings, such as anger, love, sad, and happy. She put words together like beads on a string. There were a few words that sounded like grunts or taking a long breath that she learned to place in the right places along the string by listening to the Ais people talk among themselves. Grandmother practiced new words back and forth with Cougar, but let Cougar translate for her and the Ais women. "That way I listen and make sure the Ais do not cheat," Grandmother said.

"As far as I know, you never accused the Ais of cheating," said Cougar. "Maybe the God of the Tongue created different languages to make it hard for humans to quarrel with one another."

They traded salted fish, nets, and baskets for bean seeds, more hides, and vegetable fibers spun into sewing threads. Trading was good. Everyone enjoyed and trusted a trader who could speak their language.

"Next spring after the rains," said Grandmother, "we will go into the big cypress swamp to some Tequesta villages, and I will see how fast you learn to speak a tongue which is mostly yelps and barks."

The following year Cougar found that the Swamp Tequesta's yelps and barks were used to show the measure of being well pleased with the trade, or the weather, or standing next to a friend; they were not truly words at all. When they spoke words, they were quiet, almost whispers. If one listened closely, the words were still similar to many Calusa words. The trading was as successful as Grandmother could remember. Cougar spoke with the girls her age as much as possible and in three or four days she had mastered the Tequesta way of speaking words for things around them, such as cooking utensils, bedding, clothing, body parts, food, and hunting equipment. Next she learned the words for action. By the end of their seven-day stay she was talking with fewer hand signs and could readily understand what was whispered to her. Grandmother was surprised at how quickly she learned a language and noticed that she put descriptive words in a different category from the names of things. By herself, Cougar had found a way to shorten the memorization process. She had also learned the difference between royal palms and coconut palms and sobal palms. She saw magnolias, hickories, and mahogany trees, and ate water lettuce and duckweed, for the first time.

One evening during supper at home Grandmother said that Cougar had learned to speak the Tequesta language as well and as fast as she had learned to speak Ais last year. "She is a born trader. People love her. She bargains well. She talks with the children, who in turn coax their folks to trade with us. She is fair. Even the men trust her. I think she will be the best trader the Calusa ever had."

Wren was a tall young man already carrying a paunch, who had smooth black hair tied behind each ear with a strip of deer hide. He had taken Little Mother to be his wife, and grunted a kind of displeased bark from his throat, sounding like an aggravated Tequesta.

Cougar felt self-conscious with Little Mother's husband eating with them, so she kept her head down, even though she could feel a few smiles. "I would rather be a tribal storyteller," she whispered.

"You can be a rich woman if you are a trader," said Grandmother.

"I would not let my wife be a trader," said Wren, pressing his thin lips together.

"Is that right?" said Cougar, looking up, forgetting her shyness while right away seeing the inconsistency between his actions and his words. "You gave us some of your wife's salted fish, and we traded them for hanks of woven moss that had lain in smoke over a week. There was not a mite in sight in the whole batch. We traded that clean moss for two feather capes. I guess you would let us trade her fish when we bring valuable things back to you, like the feather cape you are wearing. People say they like your wife's fish."

He scowled. He did not like to be bested, especially by a female. "I will get even with you for making me appear the fool," he said. "I no longer permit you to trade anything my wife makes. If anyone trades her goods, it will be me."

*   *   *

One evening, when Cougar was twelve summers, she sat on floor mats in a circle with everyone in her household after supper. She promised to tell them a good story that she had made up.

After the story, Wren said it was time for Cougar to think about what boy she wanted to perform her Stretching Ceremony. He grinned, letting his upper teeth gleam in the firelight. "If she has no one in mind, I will do it."

Little Mother and Grandmother both gasped and shook their heads. Grandmother said Cougar was not yet old enough.

"Cougar seems old because she learns quickly," said Little Mother. "Believe me, she is too young for the Stretching Ceremony." Her face was red. "We women know the signs to look for. She has none."

"Ha," said Wren. "Men can smell a female ready to bloom, and believe me Cougar is ready to be spliced."

"I cannot smell a thing," said Egret, who came often for supper. He sniffed under Cougar's chin and shrugged his shoulders. "Women always fool me. I can not predict when they are ready for anything."

This very day Cougar had talked to some village girls about the Stretching Ceremony. She believed Wren was getting even for what she had said about trading Little Mother's salted fish several years ago. He carried grudges and never forgot a hurt to his ego. She looked Wren in the eye and said she would never be old enough. "When I find a man I want to marry, which will be years away, I will not need you or a ceremony. The man I choose will be first for me to couple with. I think that is the way it ought to be to establish a trust between couples."

"Tell that to our chief, Brittle Star," said Wren, sucking on his lower lip, "and he will say you think too much for a female. If you do not listen to him, he will ban you from Sandpoint and the Calusa tribes, after he does the stretching for you."

Wren told them about a woman who was sent from her home village because she would not go to the ceremony. Later the woman lived with a man who gave her a newly hollowed-out fishing canoe.

Grandmother scowled at him, reminding him that this was woman's business, so he clamped his bottom lip between his teeth.

Little Mother, sitting with her back against the wall, looked at her husband and was quiet. Suddenly she slumped, so that her arms fell from her lap. She now gazed unseeing into the central cooking fire.

Her going limp frightened Wren, and he blamed Cougar for casting a bad charm by refusing to follow the customs of the Sandpointers. "If you harmed her, I will feed you to the alligators," he said.

That riled Cougar, not because she believed him, but because she too was frightened over Little Mother's behavior. "You will not!" she said. "I have nothing to do with her sleeping there on the floor with her eyes open. Maybe she does it all the time. You should know, she is your wife." The moment the words were out she knew she had said too much. Everyone was quiet and looked at her like she was a spoiled oyster and ought to be thrown on the highest midden heap.

Finally Grandmother said that Little Mother was having a clam-spell. "See there, like a clam, she can not talk or look anyone in the face," she said. "She is unable to hear a word, or to stand and help take the plates from the table, clean them with sand and fresh water before stacking them on the bark shelf Egret made for her."

Cougar got up and began picking up the wooden plates. She dropped one and said, "Oh, poot, clumsy me," and stood looking to see if it awakened Little Mother.

"Sshh, let Little Mother be," said Grandmother. "Her ghost is visiting the ghost of her sister, maybe of her mother and father. Her ghost has a need to be with kin for a time."

"Why does her ghost have a need?" asked Cougar, coming back with a stack of clean plates. She spoke in a low voice and looked sideways at Wren. She did not like him as much as she had a few moments ago. *It is because I have done him wrong, been sassy when it was not necessary,* she thought. *He does not like me either. A person does not like you so much after you have done them a wrong.* She looked squarely at Wren's face and thought, *I am sorry I spoke out of turn. I opened my mouth when I had nothing good to say and I am sorry. I am a loon.* She tried, but could not force the words out so Wren could hear.

Wren's face turned red as though he knew what she was thinking. Cougar turned her face away. For a moment she wondered if she felt bad because she hoped Wren would ask her to be his second wife. *I would like to be close to Little Mother, but not to Wren,* she told herself. *I do not want to marry yet. If Wren asked me I would tell him, No.*

Everyone was quiet until Grandmother answered Cougar's question. "I think my mentioning the Stretching Ceremony frightened Little Mother's ghost. For her that ceremony was a terrible thing and my mentioning it shocked the ghost out of her. She needed to seek her kin for comfort. I did not think before I spoke, and I am sorry. Look at her. You can see how weak a body is without its ghost."

Cougar wished she could say she was sorry as easily as Grandmother. She could see that Little Mother's long black hair had come uncoiled and slipped full length down her back, and her tan face was light as a whistling swan's eggs. "Did she find the ceremony terrible?"

"No, it was afterwards," said Grandmother.

"Did you find it terrible?" asked Cougar.

"No, I never did," said Grandmother quickly. "When it was my turn, I never went."

"The chief should have made you go," said Wren. "It is a female's duty."

"It was a long time ago; people in Gulltown have forgotten," said Grandmother, wishing Cougar would not ask so many questions.

Otter Boy remembered a man who had fallen off the roof of his hut and landed on his head. He never was able to remember anything, nor talk right after that. People said he talked to the Spirits and ghosts in this world. Otter Boy thought how it would be if his mother stayed this way and asked, "Will my mother's ghost come back?"

"You can see her body is waiting for the ghost to fly back inside," said Grandmother. "I think if we put her on a pallet, she will be all right in the morning. If not, we will ask one of the women who knows how to break spells to come over here."

Wren brought in and unrolled Little Mother's straw pallet and with Cougar's help he got Little Mother on it, even though she was not as heavy as the island's tiny doe.

Cougar went back to the supper conversation in a whispery voice and repeated that she was never going to let boy or man put his stick into her until she said he could. She said she was tired of hearing girls and their mothers talk about the ceremony as though it was some special occasion. "Little Mother told me it stings worse than sitting on a pile of ants, and there is blood to prove a man's stick is sharp as cactus spines."

Wren laughed and said, "Little Mother talks too much, and you have a lot to learn. We will all be glad when you grow up and live with someone else."

"Not I," said Grandmother.

Next morning Little Mother was fine, and Grandmother sang an ancient song for her. Otter Boy sat close to Cougar and said, "When I grow up, I can do it for you. No need for you to be bothered with someone you do not want or do not know. I will not hurt you; my stick is not sharp."

"No!" she said and leaned close to Otter Boy and told him he knew too much about her and she knew too much about him. "We are brother and sister! Brother and sister are not supposed to do it. They only marry if one of them is a chief or higher. Hey, I like swaddling you in warm blankets, tickling you until you are giggly. I like seeing you climb over rocks and to the top of the hills. I tingle with happiness when you wrap your arms around me in a tight bear hug. I like to tell you stories and sing you to sleep. You are my darling brother. I look after you so older boys, like Wren, do not take advantage of your kind heart. Remember the time fat, greedy Wren asked you for your soft shirt? You gave it to him, saying that Grandmother had made it from new hides and he was to take care of it. Was Grandmother angry?"

"Oh, yes," said Otter Boy, rolling his eyes toward the ceiling of crossed sticks and woven reeds. "So angry that she said I was a baby and too young to join in the boys' Totem Dream Ceremony. I became angry and said I did not care. Next day she told me she was sorry, loved me, and the soft shirt was a special gift. She wanted me to wear it and to value something she made. At the same time she was pleased that I decided to like greedy Wren well enough to share something of value with him. I told Grandmother I would go to the Dream Ceremony and dream of the otter that would be my totem, so my name would never be changed. Grandmother said she already knew that I would go."

"Of course," said Cougar, "Next summer you will go to the Totem Ceremony and afterwards Otter will be your name. Your mother was wise to give that name to you when you were a baby." Then her voice became very low so that only Otter Boy heard it. "After talking to you, Grandmother said she was going to take that greedy feeling out of Wren, whether he liked it or not. She was not going to watch Little Mother's husband become a give-it-to-me man." Cougar held Otter Boy's hands and told him again that she was never going to attend the girls' ceremony, no matter how old she became. "If your mother and my grandmother send me to the ceremony," she said, "I will run away, or I will be so ill nobody will want to touch me. If your stick touches me, you will break out with red, itchy welts; your skin will feel hot as a boiling soup pot, and in three days you will be cold as a stone."

"You are teasing," Otter Boy said, with his bottom lip quivering, because he was not sure what she could do. "You cannot do such a thing, can you? You are a girl."

"Maybe I can because I *am* a girl." She laughed when his eyes filled with tears. The flush of power over another was irresistible. "Grandmother is right; sometimes you act like a baby," she teased. Then guilt grabbed her. "Listen, actually I have no more power than you. But if you believe I can do what I say, you give me power. I love you best when you are not afraid of me, little brother." She hugged him and told him to go off to the beach to be with the boys who were digging clams.

Otter Boy stood a moment and studied her. She showed signs of maturing this past winter; her breasts had become tiny, pointed tepees. He thought she was the most interesting girl he knew. She could tell a story better than anyone could. His feelings were hurt when she would not take him with her to hunt roots. "This is woman's work," she always said. "Go fishing with the men."

His mother told him girls go through a phase. "While in the phase they give orders to people they care most about. Soon Cougar will be her old self and think more about what it is you want to do. You will see."

Later, looking at Cougar's face, he saw something he had not seen before. He wondered if his mother and Grandmother had seen it. She had a double row of upper teeth. It never showed until she smiled broadly. That look was almost too knowing for an ordinary human. When a shaman conjured up thoughts from the ghost world, you could see he had gained new wisdom by the glow in his eyes. Cougar smiled, and her eyes glowed when she told him things about plants and animals no one else knew, and he could never figure out how she knew. Today it struck him that maybe she too talked with the ghosts, but she was clever and never let herself be pulled into a deep spell, like his mother. And if Cougar said she was not going to partake in the Calusa's traditional customs, she meant what she said. Today he was certain she was one of those women who knew her mind; who was mentally strong, stronger than most men were. She had perseverance. She was a person some would admire and some would fear. He told himself that he should watch her.

That evening, Cougar again asked Grandmother what she thought about the Stretching Ceremony. Grandmother said she thought it best to go along with village custom if one did not want trouble. "Think what you want, but keep it to yourself, is what I think," she said. "We can talk about it, but the words do not go out of this lodge."

"I love you more than anyone," said Cougar, "and next I love Little Mother. But I also love Otter Boy and old Egret. Some of my girlfriends think boys have ticks in their hair. I look at Otter Boy and do not think about ticks in his hair. As good-looking as Wren is, I think I can see ticks in his hair. All I want is for him to be a good husband for Little Mother. I do not want him to look between my legs or show me his third eye sitting on top of his stick. I see Otter Boy's stick most every day, and it is not so much to get excited about. I want a husband who loves me as much as Beaver Tooth loved you." She expected Grandmother to tell her she was thick ribbed and stubborn.

She was surprised when Grandmother smiled and said, "Granddaughter, I am more proud of your wisdom than I can say. It is hard to go against village customs. I know some customs do not make a village great. But I know if you go against the customs, you will have trouble. I want you to be safe and I want you to be happy. I may not be able to satisfy my wants for you, but I will always love you. It is your life. Find a man who is your opposite; one who will not let you take many big risks. Have children of your own, keep them, love them, and you will understand what I mean."

"Do you know who your infant's father was?" asked Cougar.

"Yes," said Grandmother, arching one eyebrow and clamping her lips shut, so Cougar knew she wished to say no more.

The next afternoon when Grandmother and Cougar pulled the heavy net ashore, it was filled with oysters. One by one they picked out oysters and washed the sand off them and dropped them in a basket. Grandmother said that if she went back once more and dragged the shallow seabed, they would have enough to roast for everyone in the village. The Stretching Ceremony was that evening and by the time the morning light appeared everyone would be hungry. They set the net in place with several large stones in the bottom and tied the rope onto a large piece of silver-gray driftwood, then went back to the lodge.

In the evening Cougar went by herself to the open meadow where the ceremony was to take place. She sat behind the drummers figuring no one would look at her or think she was someone's aunt. Half a dozen girls in brightly dyed moss-and-grass skirts stayed in a clutch, nodding and giggling as they kept their eyes on the breechclouted boys or men they had chosen as partners. The males stayed together on the opposite side of the ring of stones, which would be the dance area. In the center of the dance ground was a small fire. Suddenly the drummers began a steady slow beat and from the east side of the meadow came a figure with a bib of white feathers under his chin. A skirt of feathers was tied over his breechclout. Around his elbows, wrists, knees, and ankles were bands of white feathers. On his head and covering his face was a mask depicting a crane. The beak opened and closed by strings that the wearer held in one hand. The faster the beak closed, the louder were its clacking sounds.

Cougar noticed the long black and gray hair hanging out of the bottom of the mask and was sure the wearer was Brittle Star, their chief. He shuffled around the stones and clacked with the drumbeat. He pulled one of the males along with him until all the males shuffled behind him, then the drums became louder, and the girls were brought into the single-file dance by the Crane. When the drumming stopped, someone put more logs on the fire. She saw the couples had oiled their bodies so they shone in the firelight. Sparks flew up toward the sky where the stars were large and bright.

The moon peeped over one of the shell middens where Grandmother and Little Mother were with other women preparing to roast oysters for the Ceremonial Feast early in the morning. So far Cougar was not too impressed with the whole affair. For a short moment she thought she might leave and go help the women at the midden. Then that idea slipped away as she watched the males dance face to face with the females. Slowly the males removed their breechclouts and dropped them inside the ring. They danced so that the muscles of their thighs and shoulders glided up and down. The singers began a soft hum. The Crane became more animated and danced in front of the females. He spun around, and his breechclout moved to the side in a way that made an interesting view. He gently pecked the females on their breasts. This caused some sensual moaning and nervous laughing. The males untied the female's skirts and dropped them near their own breechclouts. The drumming became faster and the humming louder. The flames of the central fire made their oiled bodies shine. Bare breasts bobbed as the dancing became faster. The males thrust their single red eye toward the vee between their partner's legs. This was the purpose of the dance, thought Cougar; to make everyone sexually aroused. Someone, maybe it was Wren, came into the ring carrying a clay vessel incised with tiny squares and poured water on the central fire. Now it was harder to see what the couples were doing. She knew they were lying on reed mats. The humming turned to moaning.

Her eyes adjusted to the darkness, and she saw the couples explore each other's bodies; tongues touched mouths, then nipples; hands caressed lower and then they coupled like animals: the female on hands and knees and the male mounted on her back. The drumming and humming never stopped. Cougar noticed several couples from the audience go past the circle to the far side of the meadow. She squirmed and felt an urge in the pit of her belly that was so strong she too wanted to go out in the meadow. She stayed where she was and tried to shut her ears against the insistent drumming and moaning. When she was certain she was in control of her urges, she looked around and found she was the only one left, except singers and drummers. Close by, Brittle Star had removed his mask and was smiling broadly as he removed his breechclout. Now he was behind her, and she could feel his moist red eye on her bare back. She tried to jump up, but he had his arms around her waist and dropped her skirt to the ground.

The drumming and humming was so loud no one could hear when she cried, "No! No!" She turned and faced him. He laughed and said that was what he wanted. She was on the ground and pinned down by his heavy shoulders. He spread her legs apart and pushed himself inside her. The pain was enormous. She bit his shoulder but uttered no sound. He grunted and moaned in her ear. She felt he would drill himself all the way through to her throat. She bit hard on his other shoulder, and he sucked on her breasts. Then he was up pulling on his breechclout and putting his feathers and mask in place. She put out a foot as he turned to go, and he fell against several circle stones. She kicked sand against the mask, hoping it got into his eyes. He rolled toward the fire and came back with a glowing stick in his crane's beak. She was on her feet and running. Her belly felt like hot coals had seared the inside. She felt something warm run down her leg and was sure she had wet herself, so she ran for the sea, where she lay in the shallows letting the waves wash over her. The salt water stung and the breeze made her cold. Her skirt was at the ceremonial circle. She could not go after it. She could not go to the oyster roast and throw shells on the midden with everybody else. She went home hurting, shivering, and ashamed. She lay on her pallet until the first light dimmed the stars. Then she slept.

II
Brawd

Is beag an rud is buaine na an duine. The smallest of things outlives the human being. This is a reminder of the transience of life. . . . Our ancient ancestors left behind them things that not only outlived them but will also outlive generations to come. . . . The first farming colonists [came to Ireland and Wales] around 3000 B.C. . . . and left us the large stone tombs we now call "court cairns," "portal graves" (dolmens), and "passage graves" (cromlechs).

—Liam Mac Con Iomaire, *Ireland of the Proverb*

On June first, exactly seven years after Brawd was found, the herdsman, his wife, and two children set out on foot for the druid camp above the drumlin. Unseasonably cold air came in sweeping gusts between the hills. The clouds were low and fast moving.

Wyn clung to Brawd's hand and gave him sisterly advice. "Do not sass yer elders. Do yer chores cheerfully. Send me any druid who says a word against ye, and I will pound his tongue out of his head." Then her voice choked.

"I know ye would," said Brawd, "so, I will come back to get ye to learn what ye like best from druids. Fret not, druids teach girls."

Brawd turned and walked backwards noticing that Dornoll kept her head high so the wind dried her tears. He felt a lump in his throat when he ran to her side and said he would always love her more than any other grown woman. She brushed her eyes with the back of one hand, patted his head and smiled. He raced Wyn to the top of the drumlin. His face glowed as he waited for her to catch up. She looked at him sideways, kissed him awkwardly on his cheek. It made him embarrassed. "Walk with Mam. Tad and I will walk together," he said.

Sein, loose-limbed, with deep-set eyes like polished turquoise and hair like a flame around his face, had seen the little family coming up from the stream. He stood on a flat stone to meet them. The wind sent a sheet of rain in their faces. He could not take his eyes off the blue-eyed, blond-headed lad. 'Twas obvious that the child loved the outdoors; he was sun-tanned, his knees were scratched and scabbed, and he held his face up, as though drinking in the wetness. The others huddled inside their bratts and followed Sein to the shelter of the first cottage. Brawd came last, smiling. "I be Brawd ap Seth," he said in a clear voice. He pushed up a yellow lock of dripping hair, pulled up a corner of his bratt, wiped his hand, held it out, and was surprised at his own boldness.

Sein shook his hand. "I be Sein ap Connoll, related to Lug." He watched the lad's broad smile and thought, *So he is called Brawd. He is candid, like his true father, but he has the eyes and mouth, sensitivity and thoughtfulness of his true mother, Brenda. She would be so proud of him.*

"My sister is Wyn, mam is Dornoll and tad is Seth, a herder of goats and sheep," said Brawd. "Was your tad a herder?"

"Aye, he was."

"I like herders and other things."

"Other things?" Sein was puzzled.

"Aye. Answers to wonderment. I wonder why the sky is blue and stars move. Why do ships not fill with water and sink? Is land on the other side of the sea? Are people there? Like us?"

Sein was astonished and pleased with the lad's curiosity. He took the family's wet bratts and hung them over a bench near the center fire.

Seth cleared his throat. "We have come to see if ye would foster our son. We would pay ye twice a year in goats' cheese."

"It would give us opportunity to visit him," said Dornoll, putting her hand against her trembling lips.

"That is reasonable," said Sein. He had blue-woad, honor tattooing around his fingernails, spirals on the back of one hand, and creepers with tendrils on the back of the other.

"Ye have other fosterlings?" asked Seth, looking around.

"We have half a dozen who are memorizing words of Taliesin from *Tuath for Meilyr* and another six who are learning to write."

"I know the story of Cessair and the women who came to Ireland before the flood," said Brawd. "Fintan, Cessair's lover, was the only one not drowned in the flood because he took the shape of a salmon. My sister, Wyn, has also memorized sagas. She plays the small harp and sings stories in poesy. The rhyming helps her remember."

"Smart lass," said Sein. "Do you know that is exactly why the bards recite or sing our peoples' history in poetry? The New Religionists can not take away anything memorized, and the rhyming meter helps the bards remember."

"I did not know," said Brawd.

"You have taught your children well," said Sein.

"Well," said Seth, his eyes dancing, "A herdsman has little to do, but play his harp, tell stories, and sing on winter evenings when the snow is deep and the wind howls."

Sein put two fingers of his right hand on Seth's left elbow, a druid sign, and said, "My brother, your children are fortunate to have an intelligent father who is a believer in the Old Religion."

Seth was suddenly glad that he had talked Dornoll into bringing their son to this camp.

Dornoll handed Sein a linen sack that held Brawd's clothing and an extra pair of brogues. She promised herself that she would never tell that her son was a foundling. She would use the coracle as firewood but leave the blanket and clasp-pin in the cupboard.

Sein praised Dornoll's talent with needle and thread. He said that he had rarely seen wool spun so tight as in Brawd's gray bratt. Dornoll smiled and told him this day was Brawd's seventh birthday.

"May he live as long as he wants, and never want as long as he lives!" said Sein, noticing that Wyn hid behind her mother's skirts. He gently put his hand on her shoulder and took her to meet Eira, one of the druid-healers, whose hair was dark as a crow's wing, same as Wyn's.

Eira led her to the cooking area, reached into a cabinet, and pinched off a piece of bread dough sitting on the rising shelf. She added a little salt and more flour to stiffen it and told Wyn to make it into a cat. Wyn's blue eyes lit up because she knew exactly what to do. She squeezed and kneaded the fistful of dough the way she worked wet, stream-bottom mud. Finally she touched Eira's hand and said the cat was a coney, her favorite. She broke a broom straw into short pieces for the rabbit's whiskers. Eira thought the dough-rabbit with loppy ears was near perfect. Wyn ran to her mother and with hands fluttering whispered that animals could be molded from bread-dough as well as mud.

"Pshaw, honey," said Dornoll, "did ye tell the lady-healer ye have made tiny animals for me from slimy creek-bottom mud since ye were able to toddle?"

Eira told Dornoll that her child had a rare talent, and if she would bring some of Wyn's clay animals, they would sell like barley cakes in Dubh Linn. Eira promised Dornoll two-thirds of the coins from the sales. Dornoll did not know what to say, so Eira told her not to decide until she talked it over with Wyn and her husband. "Whatever you decided the Lord God will know your reason."

From the door of the cottage Brawd squeezed Wyn's hand, careful not to crush the rabbit. He let his mother kiss him on the top of his head, and he clasped his father's hand and said, "Do not worry. I will be all right." He watched his family head for the brow of the hill. They did not look back, which was a relief, because he did not want them to see him wiping tears from his eyes. He went to the edge of the drumlin to wave, but everyone had disappeared. He looked up, saw the low clouds moving to the east, leaving high dark clouds in their wake. He knew it was a sign the rain was not over.

Members of the druid camp sang, made up poems, and found things to do during the wet spell. They mended bedding, clothing, and bridles. They sharpened knives and axes, carded wool, sorted and labeled herbs. On the fourteenth day of rain they all came to the dining hall and sat at the long, plank tables to listen to Liam, who was a white-haired, burly man who sang to the weather gods about the longest rain he could remember. The song was full of energy and exultation. He raised his eyes and implored the gods to listen as he asked that the rain be stopped. "It has passed the point of goodness to trees and grasses. It prepares a path of destruction."

Brawd's eyes were wide and he felt uneasy, as if some evil was about to befall.

Liam, who some thought had a third eye like a seer, closed his eyes, lowered his head, and whispered, "The stream will rise, stew, and fume. Before it becomes calm, it will overflow in a burst of fury." Liam's shoulders slumped. He placed his hands on the table and opened his eyes.

Brawd's face was white with fear.

"Shag it!" said Old Kerry, bald as the day he was born. "I be not superstitious, but I have seen Liam use the secret power of the Mysteries. He can predict certain events if the circumstances are right."

Sein pointed to Old Kerry and said, "In the morning you and Chonroy help the crofter Seth move his family to the hill caves if they are not there already."

Brawd sighed. He believed Sein had good sense, and all would be well.

During the night the animals were restless; the dogs barked. In the morning the rain had stopped. Grasses glittered like fragile glass jewels in the sunlight. The standing stones that stood above the grass shone as though they had been polished with beeswax. Sein sent Brawd and a couple other lads near his age sliding down the muddy drumlin to hunt for two fresh-born lambs and one ewe that had wandered over the edge in the middle of the night. The lads found the footpath half washed-out. They had been cooped up inside for so long that noontime hunger could not appease their wanderlust. By midafternoon, in a little valley, they found the bodies of two lambs wedged between exposed hazel roots. The lads hooted and hollered and dared each other to touch the dead lambs. A swarm of black flies kept them from going too close. A skinny, dark-haired lad, called Conlaf, began to whack a cudgel against a rusty iron kettle half buried in mud and soggy leaves on the bank.

"Let me see that," said Brawd. "It looks like one of the kettles my mam uses over her turf fire."

"Everyone uses a kettle like this," said Conlaf. " 'Tis a discarded thing. Maybe Eira can use it."

"Give it to me!" said Brawd. "See the chip in the lid? For certes, 'tis Mam's!" He grabbed the bail with both hands. He pulled and tugged until it came out of the mud with a sucking sound. Conlaf helped throw off the lid and jerk at the sealskin tied over the top. Brawd said it was probably waterproof protection for apples his mother had stored. The other lads stood in a circle, licking their lips, waiting. Inside was a menagerie of little lifelike clay animals: dogs, cats, horses, goats, sheep, cows, coneys, wolves, foxes, deer, stoats, grouse, frogs, and even crickets. "My sister made them," said Brawd proudly.

"Lassies' trifles!" said Conlaf.

"Worse than a kettle of cow pies!" said blond, blue-eyed Llyn. The boys hoo-hawed and threw mud balls at Brawd, who sat with his arms around the kettle until they left him, muddied and weeping.

He wiped a sleeve across his face and whispered, "Wyn, yer wee animals are safe!" He put the tiny frog in his pocket, covered the kettle, and laid stones over the lid so neither rain nor strangers would find it. He could hear the other lads bleating as they called for the lost ewe. He scrambled after them to say that he was sure they were close to his home-cottage. "It feels right. The hazel grove should be over there." He pointed, struggling through the muck. Then he stopped and squinted. Fear squeezed his throat so it was hard to swallow. In some places the stream flowed into a new bed. Trees were uprooted and lay across one another. His voice was pitched high. "Mam! Tad! Wyn!" There was no answer. His eyes filled with tears. The stream surged, the wind sighed, and the red kite soared in a wide circle, showing its forked, rusty tail and narrow wings. Conlaf called for him to come along back to the druid's home ground. Brawd ran in circles looking for a familiar landmark. He slipped headlong across a rock outcropping and ripped the shoulder of his shirt. He ran into a white thorn, which was a tree of good luck, but he paid it no heed. He was in the sheep meadow. There were no sheep, no hazel grove, no cottage, and no barn. He was bewildered, and his mind tried to hang on to reason. Water could not scour land clean of a stone fence, nor a barn with sheep and goats and a home-cottage. Aye, in the middle of the night the bloody, sneak-thieving stream carried away everything, like ruthless soldiers taking helpless hostages or water taking its own sacrificial gifts.

Alone, he went through brush, crisscrossed trees, leaves, and muck where he remembered the kettle of animals lay hidden. He rested on an uprooted tree that lay across the stream and dangled one foot in the water, while watching a swirling pool periodically boil up white. Suddenly he knew it was not bubbling foam, but something being dragged down by a whirlpool and then spit up on the far edge, only to be dragged down again as it came around near his foot. He inched his way down the tree so he could lean over and pick the white thing out of the water. It was a wool blanket, pulled long and narrow by the water. One end was fastened to the center with a heavy silver clasp. He knew they came from his mother's cupboard. He squeezed water from the blanket, and when he looked down again, he saw Wyn's eyes looking at him from the bottom of the whirlpool. The water had faded her blue eyes until they were pale green fish eyes. Wyn's black hair moved rhythmically, back and forth over her eyes as if to keep the sun out. Her dark brown skin was ghostly white. Caught in underwater branches were the remains of the coracle, a broken frame and shredded hide covering. The oval rim was intact, held together with wooden spikes. *Mayhap Wyn was trying to escape in the round boat when the waters overcame her,* he thought. A cry rose in his throat. "Oh, Lugh! Lord God!"

Grasping the rim in one hand, clutching the tree with the other, he scuttled backwards to the muddy bank. He choked down his fear, pulled off his brogues and breeks, and knew the job had to be done. Afraid or not afraid, he took a deep breath and slid under water. The current was strong. He reached as far as he could to free his sister's body and bring it up the bank. His arms and legs ached with the cold. He came up, filled his lungs with air, but his hands were empty. He pulled in more air and tried again.

This time he pulled her body away from the hazel log, whose branches sawed back and forth with the swirling water. His heart pounded. He lifted the sawyer and pushed hard. The water became muddy as the body rolled. He reached for the body as his lungs felt like they would explode, and the water became black as night. He let himself rise to the top and pushed away from the swirling current. He had blacked out and feared he had breathed in water because he was dizzy. He lay on the bank a while until he decided he was all right. When he looked into the whirlpool, the body was gone. The sun set on top of one of the hills. He looked downstream and saw Wyn's body barefoot in a shallow, with her nightdress billowing around her like a sail unfurled in the wind.

Brawd dragged his sister's body to the center of the flood-cleansed meadow where the home cottage should have been. He piled stones over it to keep the wolves away and thought if he had been home to get her out of the rising floodwater she would be safe. He kicked at the stones and blamed himself for Wyn's death, then he wondered why his parents let her take the coracle. "Aha," he said aloud. "She did it without permission! Aye, she was coming to save me. Oh, my darlingest Wyn!" He wept and when the tears were gone he thought of his heartbroken parents. He pulled on his muddy breeks, carried his brogues, and hummed a death-song meant to accompany her spirit on her journey to the Otherside. The low rays of sun painted the clouds with a pink glow as he slogged back to the druid camp.

Sein worried that Brawd did not come back with the other lads, especially after Conlaf told about the kettle full of clay animals. He sent Old Kerry to the meadow for a look and sat on the brow of the drumlin. His heart quickened as soon as he recognized Brawd faltering up the hillside in the moonlight, dragging a wet shawl, and an egg-shaped wreath. He met the lad halfway, clasped him to his breast, and felt the convulsion in Brawd's shoulders. He sat on the ground and rocked with him in his arms. After a while Old Kerry and Chonroy came up the drumlin to say they had found the bodies of Dornoll and Seth held fast among hazel roots that had washed against a hummock. Brawd's tears soaked Sein's shirt. After a while he stroked the clay frog and told Sein how he found his sister and covered her with stones and sang the sad song until the sun was low and pink. "She was coming for me in the coracle," he said. He held his breath to stop a sudden spasm of hiccups, dropped his brogues, and rubbed a bare bruised foot. Sein asked why he had walked back without putting on his brogues.

"I took them off to go in the stream. They would have pulled me to the bottom and never let me up." He let Sein carry him to his sleeping pallet and rub salve on his bruises and scratches.

Sein went to the kitchen to prepare a draught to help Brawd sleep. When he returned, Brawd was curled into a tight ball with his chin on his chest and his eyes wide and dry. With a quavery voice Brawd said, "I can not remember their faces, does that mean truly all three are on the Otherside?"

"In the morning Old Kerry and I will bring back all three bodies on the cart," Sein said. "Drink this; it will help their faces come to you as you sleep."

Sein could not sleep and berated himself for letting Brawd go down to the swollen stream. His druid training told him it was one of life's Mysteries, which was done and no man could alter. Sometime in the middle of the night Brawd climbed in beside Sein. Man and lad slept until the sun was well up in the sky. Brawd awoke and rubbed a hand over the stubble on Sein's chin.

Sein grinned. "How did I know 'twas you? I be not used to having anyone in my bed."

"How true," wheezed gray-haired Finn from across the room. He sat with a pan of steaming herbs in front of his nose. "You should go to Dubh Linn for a woman once in a while."

Sein picked up a rawhide shoe and threw it toward Finn, the shanahy, and missed. Brawd sucked his thumb and snuggled against Sein, who told him it was time to be up. Sein pulled on his own clothes, dressed Brawd, and took him to the kitchen where Vivian, the blue-eyed herb-woman, had porridge ready. Brawd watched her go in and out of the musty, pear-shaped underground cellar. He watched her auburn braid switch across her back as she sorted good and bad among last winter's fruit and vegetables. Once their eyes met and his mouth trembled because he wanted to say something, but he was not certain if a lad without parents would be heard.

Sein told him to eat. He shook his head and did not open his mouth, thinking that maybe his parents really were not dead, and only sleeping against those hazel roots. He got up and looked out the door. Vivian polished an apple on her apron and held it out to him. He backed away as if it were a griffin, something different, and not seen every day.

"Not poison," she said. "Keep it for later."

He put it in his pocket, followed Sein into the yard, and to the ring of standing stones. At the circle of stones he leaned against one whose sides were carved with combinations of lines, ancient ogham, and lowered himself to the ground that was covered with chips of white quartz. Sein sat beside him and said he often came there to clear his mind and look at life head on. Brawd screwed up his face and said carefully, "If what ye said last night be true, I be an orphan. If ye told me a lie, I swear I will sear yer tongue with a torch." His eyes were blue-gray and his mouth was a straight line. "Did ye hear?"

Sein said he heard and started to put his arm around the lad, but thought better of it. "You were looking for your true mam and tad, but you looked in the wrong place. You are not an orphan."

"Ha, I knew ye lied!" Brawd ran out of the stone circle and threw himself against a wall of stacked torch-poles, whose tops were wrapped with moss soaked in pitch.

Sein went after him and tried to explain that there was a misunderstanding. "Listen to me." He told Brawd that the Prince of Wales, in the province of Gwynedd, was his true father. Brawd got up and held a torch-pole in the smoldering fire-pit.

Sein continued, "Your father, Owain ap Gruffudd ap Cynan ap Iago, was descended from the renowned Rhodri Mawr. Iago studied at the druid school in Glastonbury on the site of the sacred oak grove."

Brawd scraped his heels in the mud, licked his lips, and said that his tad, Seth, told him about the Glastonbury school. " 'Tis long gone, so how can ye know where this bloody Iago studied?"

The logic took Sein by surprise. With a lad bright beyond his years he wondered how he could tell him who he was and still comfort him. Finally he told him that Cynan had fled Wales to come to Ireland to marry Rhagnell, the daughter of Dubh Linn's King Olaf, who was descended from Harold Haarffager, the Norse king first to cross the sea from Denmark to invade Scotland and Ireland. "And your Grandfather, Gruffudd, married Angharad, a black-haired Welsh woman. One of their sons was Owain, your true father. I know because a Welsh bard, Llywarch, a harper and historian from Gwynedd, visits us from time to time. He has all your kin memorized and fitted into a song."

"Nay! I do not want a kin song!" Brawd left the burning torch in the fire-pit and stood in front of Sein. "I be Brawd ap Seth ap Rees, an Irish herder. My mam is Dornoll, daughter to an Irish crofter! I be not related to barbarian northmen who went warring the Scots and my Irish kin! Ye know not what ye speak about." Brawd stood behind a standing stone where he could watch Sein and between hiccups he said he would not live in Gwynedd. " 'Tis all terror and anger there. My tad, Seth, told me that Welshmen fight their own brothers or father when they ought to tend sheep, fish, or sail away. 'Tis a frightful, scary place where New Religionists round up Old Religionists, call them pagans, and cut their heads off!"

Sein agreed and without raising his voice said, "Seven years ago it came to pass in Gwynedd that three lads were born the same night. One died, and one of the two living was also supposed to be dead. But his mother brought him here. You are that laddie."

Brawd's head ached. He could think of nothing to say so with a handful of stones he pelted Sein.

Sein sat on his haunches for a while.

Brawd, whose face was dark, came out from behind the stone, stood in front of Sein and said, "I hate the Welsh prince!" He swung balled fists in front of Sein's face. "If he were here, I, Brawd ap Seth, would flatten his nose!"

"What do you know about the white shawl and coracle rim you brought in yesterday?" said Sein.

Brawd lowered his face to look at his tight fists. Yesterday seemed a long time ago. He did not want to talk about either his baby shawl or the little coracle that he and his sister used to play with. "They are naught but my property, and that is all there is to say about them."

Sein said, soft as butter, "Your true mother and father are as alive as both of us."

Brawd waved his arms and told Sein not to joke any more about such. "Yer words have naught to do with me! Yer tongue will turn black and fall out!"

Sein grabbed him by the back of his tunic and said, "Listen to me, you little whelp. Mistress Brenda, your mam, and you lived in our camp more than a year before Prince Owain sent soldiers to take Brenda back to Wales. She could not let the soldiers know you lived, or they would drown you and smash your head against the nearest tree. The stream carried you to Dornoll, Seth, and Wyn. They called you Brawd and loved you as their own." Sein teetered on his haunches.

Brawd took in gulps of air. "You mean I be not Brawd ap Seth? I be Mistress Brenda's *baban?* I have lived here before? So, in troth what is my name?"

"Madoc is your name. You are for troth the bastard son of the Prince of Gwynedd, conceived under the scrim of especially bright northern lights. You have been given a special destiny by the gods to be leader of the druids."

"No!" said the lad as his face became white as new fallen snow.

"The silver clasp on your baby shawl carried Gwynedd's royal household seal, three lions enclosed in a circle."

"I do not know the seal of Gwynedd," said Brawd, shaking like pudding. "You think I be Madoc ap Owain, son of a bloody Welsh barbarian? Not me!" He sprang up on Sein's back so that Sein lost his balance and fell on his face in the quartz gravel. He pounded Sein's head with tight, hard fists until Sein rolled over and growled, "Leave off! 'Tis luck you do not live in Gwynedd." He grabbed Brawd's flaying arms and held him tight against his chest. "You are here and my *mabmaeth,* foster son. I be your *tadmaeth,* foster father."

"Mistress Brenda—will she—will she come for me?"

Brawd tried to pound Sein's chest. "I do not want to see her! She left me like scum floating on the stream!" He kicked and sunk his teeth into Sein's shoulder. Sein's grip loosened, and the lad wriggled loose and ran like wildfire between the standing stones toward the brow of the drumlin. "I hate ye!" he hollered. "I will not be leader of anybody nor nailed to a cross! Instead I will sail to unknown lands, far, far away!"

With one hand on his aching shoulder, Sein grabbed Brawd's arm. "You are not destined to be crucified, even though right now I want to give it a try. Listen! Your mam will not come here. She lives in the Gwynedd castle bailey in Aberffraw, treated well under the protection of your father. In summer she moves with the court to Dolwyddelan in the mountains."

"Is she his wife?"

Sein said Owain already had a wife, who is ill. "Owain has many friends, some ladies, mistresses."

Brawd stared frog-eyed and croaked, "I have brothers and sisters?"

"You have a full brother, Riryd, who is twice your age and lives with his grandfather, Howyl, Lord of Carno in Clochran, here in Ireland. You have a sister, Goeral, two years older than Riryd. And you have dozens of half brothers with mothers different from yours. For instance there is Howell by Pyfog; Iorwerth by Gladys; Maelgwyn, Cadwallon, and Rhodri by Christiannt. Your same-age, half brother, Dafydd, is known as the son of Gladys. In troth Christiannt is Dafydd's mam and that is a secret you are to keep locked up behind a closed mouth. Do not ask me to name more, my tongue is sorely tired."

All this was terrifying to a seven-year-old. Even with a thumb jammed into his mouth, Brawd could not stop weeping. He would never call himself Madoc. He jerked his arm free, darted fleet as a deer down the drumlin's path toward the swollen stream, scrambled over a boulder, went behind an uprooted oak, and hid himself in a tangle of willow and gorse. He buried his head in his scratched arms, shook like an aspen leaf, and vented giant sobs.

Sein espied him curled safe into a little ball and slowly

walked to the top of the drumlin, turned to the kitchen cottage; inside he poured himself a full beaker of mead.

When the sun sank behind the horizon, Brawd relaxed and his sobs became an involuntary reflex. When he woke, he finished the apple, core and all, and figured that he had no alternative but to accept everything Sein had said. It was his fate. He said his new name nine times so that it rolled off his tongue, then he squeezed through the tangled bramble. He found Sein sitting cross-legged in front of the kitchen cottage with several boys and girls shelling garden peas for supper. He sat, took a handful of pods from the bucket, and shelled them into the pan to prove he was not angry.

That night the women of the camp in white robes took the bodies of Seth, Dornoll, and Wyn to the callow behind the standing stones and placed nine sacred oaks on top of them. Before midnight men in gray robes hummed and moved clockwise in the ritual direction of the sun. Old Kerry sang in old Celtic, "Now, set the pyre on fire!" Eira lay a lighted torch against the logs. By dawn's first light the night's burning was complete and its ashes were cool.

Sein sat on the edge of Brawd's pallet and shook him gently. Brawd's eyes fluttered when he heard Sein say that they had a sacred ritual to perform. "Wear a fresh tunic, your bratt and 'pooties, and comb your hair."

Brawd hopped from one foot to the other.

"Go out behind the sleeping cottage," said Sein, smiling.

When Brawd returned, he slid onto his pallet and hugged his knees close to his chest. "I cannot get dressed," he said. "I do not feel well."

Sein felt Brawd's forehead—no fever. "I understand you feel bad," he said. "But look—if that had been you out there in the water—would Wyn show her respect and say the last farewell?"

"She would," said Brawd and his eyes were bright with held-back tears.

"Then come. This is part of growing up." Sein was gentle as he pushed the pampooties toward him. "Old Kerry cleaned your muddied brogues, but they are not yet dry."

When Brawd was dressed, he picked up the clay frog from the middle of his pallet, put it in his pocket, went to the wash basin outside, splashed his face, and combed his hair with wet fingers. Man and lad walked together. Sein carried two bowls of ashes, one stacked on top of the other. Brawd carried the third bowl of ashes. They passed the women in long white gowns singing as they spread ashes over the fields. The women stopped and bowed to show respect for the man and lad. Brawd nodded back. He could smell the honeysuckle that lined the path along the side of the hill. Yellow blossoms of oxlip and blue harebells bloomed in the grass. The path took them to a stone mound. They walked around the outside kerbstones that were decorated with incised designs of spirals and circles with pocking in the center so they looked like rosettes. Ages ago the cromlech was built for a one-time burial, now it was used as a successive burial.

Brawd asked if the ashes he held were all that was left of his sister. Sein said, "Flesh is bone and water. What happens to a fig when the hot sun dries it?"

"Not much left and 'tis light and crumbly," said Brawd, stopping at the entrance. "Was the spirit carried away by the wind?"

"I do not know," said Sein. "I have never seen a spirit. You have heard of the wee people and ghosts?"

Brawd nodded. His mam, Dornoll, said she saw them. But his tad, Seth, never.

"I have never seen wee ones nor a ghost," said Sein taking Brawd's hand and hunching over as he led the way into the dark, low-ceilinged passage of large stones fitted into sockets and secured by packing with smaller stones. After a moment their eyes adjusted to the darkness. The roof was made of lintels laid across the tops of upright stones, which were marked with spirals and pocking. On one of the uprights was a series of long and short lines. Sein said the combinations of lines represented words. He studied the ogham marks a moment and translated out loud, "When Death comes, it will not go away empty. Good memories are sheltered in this tomb. Smile while you live."

Brawd felt a tingling on the back of his neck as though

ancient eyes watched him. He saw that the passage widened to form a chamber with a deep-set, small, open window. He was silent, hardly breathing as he looked at the little piles of ash on chalky ledges. He spied a small necklace of stone and bone that some unknown child had worn and a double-bladed ax that had belonged to an ancient wood-cutter. Close to his shoulder lay a silver bratt pin, embellished with red enamel and studded with polished amber. His heart fell to the ground and seemed to shatter into a hundred pieces. "I have naught to leave," he said. "My sister loved colorful things."

"Put her ashes in this niche between her mother's and father's," said Sein. "We will go out and gather flowers. Every lass loves flowers."

Brawd's face brightened. Sein was right. Wyn loved blue harebells. He came back with his hand filled with a dozen fragile, bright blue flowers shaped like tiny bells.

Sein filled the parents' bowl not only with harebells but also with daisies and sprigs of fragrant honeysuckle. From under his gown he pulled out the elliptical frame of the broken coracle and placed it around the three bowls of ash and flowers.

"Will they know we did this?" asked Brawd.

"Aye," said Sein.

Brawd smelled the musty air, took a step forward, stretched to touch the frame, and left the little clay frog on top of the harebells. "They will know I think of them," he said.

They walked into the sunlight, where the wild flowers seemed more vivid than before. Brawd said, "Race ye home!" He ran and did not look to see if Sein was in the race.

Sein smiled and thought how pleased Brenda would be with her son. He put his hand on a lone beech tree and moved it upwards, as though feeling the flow of the life-giving fluid in the cambium, and prayed that Brenda one day visit her son before he was grown. His hand moved down, dropped, and he began to run in long pleasurable strides. His arms moved gracefully at his sides. A blackbird sat on a rock outcropping and sang a throaty, glorious song.

III
Stars

ABOUT 1168 — 1169 A.D.

An exception to this rule of exogamy occurred among the Calusas, where chiefs evidently married their full sisters. This custom of sister marriage has occurred elsewhere in the world, though rarely, and usually only among the elite in highly stratified societies. So far as we know, this custom did not occur elsewhere in the Southeast.
—Charles Hudson, *The Southeastern Indians*

Cougar put some green moss from the side of the creek on a flat food board. She found some bluish-gray powder in a little leather bag among Grandmother's things and added a little water to it, until it was thick blue gravy. She painted the inside of one of Grandmother's bowls blue with a frayed end of a fresh willow stick. When the paint was dry, she turned the bowl upside down over the moss. A few days later, the moss was yellow. She thought about that for a while and next hunted a few smooth, transparent, tiny white stones on the beach. She fastened them to the inside of the bowl, with acorn flour mixed with water. In the sunlight the stones glistened like stars. She thought that maybe they would hold the sunlight. Satisfied, she sprinkled water, like rain, over the moss and covered it with the bowl. When she raised the bowl, the moss was spindly and moldy. It was dark underneath the bowl. Her stone stars did not twinkle nor shine like real stars. Disappointed, she ran to Egret to show him what she had done and ask what stars were made of. "If the sky is a bowl covering the earth, why does my miniature earth and sky not work?" she asked. "The stones do not hold the sun's shine nor warmth."

Egret smiled. "You are asking things that even our chief has not asked. You are something special. I have seen only one other girl-child who would dare try to do what you have done."

"Who was that?" asked Cougar.

"Grandmother," he said. "What good did it do her? She never became chief."

"She told me to learn all I can," said Cougar. "The more one knows, the more interesting life becomes."

"Aye, she would say that," said Egret. He showed her that her garden under the bowl had too much water, and no sunshine. "You have to have true sunlight for plants to grow green and healthy."

"How can I put a piece of sunlight under the bowl? What is sunlight anyway?" she asked.

"Throw the bowl away." He sounded exasperated. "Sunlight is warm, like fire, but when I look at it, it blinds me. It is different from fire, but I do not know how, nor how something hot can stay in the sky without falling," he said. "You ask useless questions."

"Grandmother says the moon is cold. Where does it get its light? Do the Spirits hold both sun and moon in the sky?"

"I believe she is right," he said, frowning. "Maybe sunlight reflects off of the moon. I heard that it did. But who really cares?"

"Stars remind me of bits of lightning," she said.

"And so, what is lightning?" he said, scratching his head. "Can you tell me?"

"No. And so, how will we find out?" she said. "Is there a way to capture it and bring it to our lodge?"

"Not that I know about," he said. "Why do you ask so many questions?"

"Grandmother says the Spirits know everything, but they are not talking to me."

"Maybe they will," he said. "When the time is right."

"Right for them or right for me?" she asked.

"Umph," he said, thinking that children these days were far too inquisitive. Serve them right if they had headaches when they were old as he.

It was nearly sundown when Cougar left Egret and started for her home lodge. Half way she saw Little Mother with one hand on her back, the other on her bulging belly, and she was calling, "Please, help—Grandmother is not home."

"I know Grandmother is not home," said Cougar. "A couple of nights ago she said the Dog Star was back, and the air was cooler over the estuary. Next morning she took all the nets she made this summer and went to Gulltown. She said this time of year the water in the bays, channels, and passes is cooler and filled with so many different clans of fish that it would astound your eye, delight the sea birds, and strain the limits of stout nets."

Little Mother lurched to one side and for balance held on to a piece of driftwood. Cougar thought she was having another one of her spells and hurried to support her.

"Grandmother knows this baby is coming any day," said Little Mother. "Why did she leave?"

"I told you," said Cougar. "She went to Gulltown with an armload of fishing nets. Those people know her nets are the stoutest. She will trade them for feathers and quills and show us how to dye them, so we can decorate our clothing. The chief's youngest wife, Frog, and I have been annoying her about the need for quills and feathers. I think she went to keep us quiet," said Cougar. "Nothing to worry about; she will be back before the weather becomes blustery and hard to predict. Tell the baby to wait a couple of days."

"I can not do that," said Little Mother, looking at Cougar with disgust. "How many times have you been with Grandmother delivering babies? You know what to do." She stopped and bent over with the pain. "I do not want to have this baby in front of all these lodges. Oh! Oh! My belly is pinching! My back is killing me!"

"Come on! Hurry, walk fast between the pains," ordered Cougar. "Bend over. That might hold the baby tight, so we can get home." A hummingbird darted around them and followed Little Mother into her lodge. Cougar waved her hands and said, "Shoo, go on! Go home! Not your affair." She talked to Wren, telling him to go outside and find Otter Boy. "It is unlucky for a man to be around a birthing. Egret will feed you, if you take him a fresh rabbit. Otter Boy caught some for you yesterday. I saw them hanging unsalted from the center ridgepole. They will not keep more than a few days."

Wren resented her knowing what went on in his lodge and taking orders from her. Right now there was nothing else he could do but to take a rabbit from his own ridgepole, find Otter Boy, and go to Egret's place.

Cougar built up the center fire and placed a clay pot full of salt-water on a flat stone beside another pot filled with creek-water. She also laid a small reed mat on one of the flat stones. When the mat was warm, she tied it to the middle of Little Mother's back.

Little Mother stood with her legs apart and moaned softly. At the height of a contraction she supported herself by leaning against one of the thick roof-supports. She sucked in air and made a growling sound. When the birth throes were greatest, she gritted her teeth and pulled on a rope attached to the roof-support. All of a sudden she cried out, "Ooohhh," and held her breath.

"Breathe," said Cougar, lying on the floor between her legs the way she had seen Grandmother do. "Water is draining out of you," she said and moved forward, staying away from the bloody wetness on the ground. She pulled Little Mother a step forward by taking hold of her ankles. "This is what Grandmother calls the second half," she said, "after the water sack around the baby drains. The second half is usually faster than the first." She reached up and tried to coax the baby out with her small hands. She felt nothing, only wet warmth. She tried hard to remember what Grandmother would do and say. She looked up and said that she did not want to see baby feet coming out first.

Little Mother took a big breath, held it and pushed, then she relaxed and took small breaths. "You are doing fine," said Cougar. "Grandmother would like the way you use your breath to work the hard pushes."

Little Mother stretched her lips across her teeth, closed her eyes, and grunted.

Cougar remembered the way Grandmother encouraged the mothers. "You have work to do. Another push! Good

work! Come on, one more, one more, you can push!" Again
she slipped her fingers inside and felt it slide around something round and hard as a squash. "The head is down," she
said, wiping her bloody hand on a handful of smoky moss.
"Another push, one more. Aye!" She could see dark, wet
hair. She put up both her hands to catch the baby. She held
the head in her hands and looked into clear, dark-blue eyes,
even the whites were a shadow-blue, then came a tiny nose
and pink lips, quickly followed by the right shoulder, then
the left and a whole baby with its dark, reddish-purple con-
necting cord. The baby's back arched a little; it cried and
Cougar sat up. She held a bloody, but perfect, tiny male
against her own nubile breasts. She gnawed on the tough
cord. When it was bitten through, she pulled out strands of
her own long, dark hair and wrapped them tightly around
the finger-long stub to stop the bleeding.

She cradled the baby in her arms and told Little Mother
to kneel on the floor to expel the afterbirth. She dipped a
wad of moss in the hot sea-water, waved it in the air to
cool, then scrubbed the squirming, crying baby to remove
most of the waxy substance. She laid the tiny new person
on a mat in front of the smoldering center fire and felt a
glow of wonder. She had seen her friend use all the force
she had to push out a real, live, breathing, crying little person.

Little Mother lay on her side with her eyes closed. Cougar buried the afterbirth behind the lodge. She had to be
quick so that a bad spirit would not find the newborn,
shape-change into a worm, and wiggle into the baby's
belly, making it cry day and night with cramps. When she
came back, she wrapped the cord tight with plant fiber,
closer to the baby's belly, and chewed off the excess piece.
She spit the piece into her cupped hand, pulled off the tangled fiber, woke Little Mother, and told her to chew and
swallow the bit of cord. She wiped her own bloody mouth
with crumpled moss dipped into the creek-water. She felt
so good that she laughed when Little Mother said, "You
look like a true cougar cat, who caught a deer, tore open
its hide, and ate the bleeding heart."

"Grandmother says eating a small piece of the cord takes
the pain away and helps a new mother rest. I do not know

if it is true, but do it anyway. It will not hurt." She hummed softly as she again bathed the baby, this time in warm creek-water. She fitted the baby with a moss-packed diaper cloth, wrapped it in a thinly woven grass blanket, and handed it to Little Mother. Then she washed Little Mother clean of blood and fecal matter, fitted a tightly packed moss sling between her legs to absorb the bleeding, and tied it around her waist. "I will check the pack in a while to be sure the bleeding is almost over," she said. "I hope I have not forgotten to do something important." She pulled the fouled mat out from under Little Mother, rolled it to fit between the smoldering logs of the center fire, and watched the flames leap up as it sizzled and burned with a sharp, unpleasant odor. She pushed a clean sleeping mat under Little Mother, who, half-asleep said, "Cougar, you forgot to tell me, girl or boy?"

"You might have looked at his perfect, tiny stick before I wrapped him," said Cougar with a grin. "Look at his dark blue eyes because in two or three days they will be brown, like your own. You are blessed because there was no trouble. I imagined I heard Grandmother saying, 'Do not get excited. This is a normal thing that any mother can do by herself. You are here only to make it easier.' Little Mother, you were kissed by the Spirits because you did not pass into a spell and it was an easy birth."

"That is easy for you to say. My back is stiff and sore."

"You are what Grandmother calls a 'mother-meant-to-be.' "

"Remember the hummingbird that followed me, when I had the big bellyache coming into the lodge?" said Little Mother. "I believe it is a sign the hummingbird wants to be my baby's protector. I am going to call him Hummer." Satisfied and tired, she slept.

Cougar scooped the fouled sand on the floor into a wide-mouthed clay jar, replaced it with clean sand, went home, and slept.

The next day Grandmother came back with a bundle of feathers, quills, and several leather packets of powdered dye. She was not surprised that Cougar alone had helped Little Mother deliver such a fine-looking baby boy. For some time now she had watched Cougar. She studied the carriage of her head and shoulders and her slim body. She saw that Cougar walked with confidence and knew where she was going. She was proud of her, but she sometimes wondered if Cougar ever thought she was headed the wrong way, what would happen. Cougar would not want to admit being wrong.

One day she told Cougar that she wished she was still a tiny kit and she herself was younger. She wished she had found Cougar when she was only two days old instead of nearly two summers. She would have loved to hold a tiny bundled infant, to see the first smile and feel the first tooth and see his first steps.

"Grandmother, you have Little Mother's Hummer to hold and fuss over," she said.

Grandmother said she wished the two of them could climb the hills and wade through the creeks the way they used to. "You used to dance like a water sprite down the middle of the creek while we scooped fingerlings into a palmetto-frond net," she said. "Once we came across a brown bear fishing. You stood quiet and motioned for me to stop splashing. The bear never bothered us, but walked away with a fish in its mouth, then stretched full height against a field pine. He was as tall as we are, if you stand on my shoulders. I was afraid to stand where the bear could smell or see me, but not you. You ran up the bank, stood on a stone, spread your arms in the air, and sang. You said the bear wagged his head in time with your singing. You are different from us ordinary folk. The bears or other animals never bothered you. Eagles and large hawks swooped down to look at you, but never touched you with their wing feathers, beaks, or clawed toes. You were fearless because a scorpion or tarantula never bit you. Mosquitoes and gnats left you alone."

"Maybe it is because I leave them alone," said Cougar.

Grandmother, Wren, and Otter Boy netted oysters, whose flesh had lost the summer, runny consistency and firmed up fat and sweet. They netted oysters for a whole day so that they could have a celebration feast and welcome Hummer to the Calusa tribe.

Soon after the big feast some of the villagers were ill. Grandmother herself ran and ran to the toilet place behind the village. Egret, weak and shaky, came to sing the old songs Grandmother loved, but she hardly listened.

The village Medicine Man was fussy. He kept one hand on his rumbling belly and scratched Grandmother with the teeth of a rattlesnake to stop her runs. He said that he had used the same medicine on Chief Brittle Star and two of his three sister/wives, Frog and Rain, who were also running to the toilet place. "Frog had worms," he said. "She no doubt had them before the feast. Probably picked them up from eating off unwashed wooden bowls. Those women are careless, lazy, and do not scrub with sand. He should have married women outside his own family. It is bad when a man takes his own three sisters to become his wives and not a one of them conceives a child. Besides, I think oysters have turned bad this year. You know the biting insects are still strong. By this time of year they should have all died."

After the Medicine Man left, Grandmother said he was wrong about everything, except the biting insects. The chief's wives had no children because all their lives they had treated the chief like their baby. She did not remember the sisters were careless, but she did remember that they did not cook well. Last fall they had brought undercooked, spiced acorn mush to the Harvest Feast. "It was the spiced acorn mush that Frog and Rain had brought to spread on the oysters," she said. "Acorns have to be boiled long enough to remove all of their bitterness. Frog and Rain know acorns can kill if not boiled most of a day. If one is lazy and stops their boiling too soon and then eats them—it is the end."

Little Mother, weak from throwing-up until there was nothing left but gagging, sat beside Grandmother and wiped her face with a handful of cool, wet leaves. She made fanciful predictions about the life of her new baby. She said in her dreams the little boy would grow up and marry the best-looking young woman in the village. They would be a regular family. He would live long and be as loved as Egret.

Little Mother's belly cramps were gone by afternoon, because she ate a little boiled rattlesnake meat. Earlier she had told Otter Boy that the snake meat would cure nausea and right away he had bagged a fresh rattlesnake for her. She sent some of the meat to the ill chief and his three sister/wives.

The next day the chief's youngest sister, Ibis, told Little Mother that Frog and Rain refused to eat anything, but the boiled rattlesnake settled her and her brother's belly rumblings. Ibis was small and looked younger than she was. She always kept her long dark hair in a single braid that hung down her back, and when she told anyone what they ought to do, the braid moved back and forth like the tail of a horse. She told Little Mother she ought to take her leftover rattler's meat to Grandmother. "Not too much, you hear me," she said, moving her head back and forth. "Too much will make her hot tempered."

So, Cougar fed Grandmother a little of the boiled rattlesnake and prayed that her good health would return.

"Did the rattlesnake help Grandmother's belly pinching?" Ibis asked the next time she saw Cougar.

"Who can tell?" said Cougar. "Grandmother says she is feeling fine and never admits a weakness."

Frog and Rain continued to refuse food for the next couple of days, and one morning Chief Brittle Star found them on their pallets with no breath.

To show his grief, Brittle Star cut his hair short, drew black-and-white stripes across his face, and sat alone on the mossy bank of the river.

Ibis was left to bathe and bundle her dead sisters. She could not face the task alone, so, not realizing Grandmother was still ill, she came to ask if Cougar could help.

"I can," said Cougar, "if Grandmother tells me what to do."

"It is not a hard thing, but if you have never washed a dead person's body, you might become spooked," said Grandmother. "I better go with you."

"I will not be spooked if you tell me what to do," insisted Cougar.

Grandmother shook her head and began to pull her tunic over her head. "I can do it easier and faster. I just need to find my moccasins."

"Do you think you should get up?" said Cougar. "It

might not be good for you. After all, you have not had much to eat. I should be the one to go. Ibis asked me."

"Then go, but come back soon," Grandmother said, pushing her swollen feet back onto the pallet. "Washing a dead person is not much different from washing anyone else, except they are cold and do not talk back."

Ibis was overcome with weeping and could do nothing. Cougar bathed the dead sisters and sprinkled sage inside their wrapping blankets. Finally, she put her arm around Ibis and said it was important to stop crying so that her sisters could rest peacefully in the burial mound. Ibis understood, took a deep breath, and dabbed her swollen red eyes on a wad of moss. She helped Cougar carry the bodies one by one to the burial mound.

Not many attended the burial. The Medicine Man, still feeling weak himself, gave a small performance. He held his head and barely danced, but he did rattle his bone-boxes. Chief Brittle Star was there for the burial, but he was so weak that he had to sit down before the Medicine Man danced. Later, alone with Ibis, Brittle Star said that the deaths of Frog and Rain were the fault of Cougar, because it was she who had made them eat roasted oysters. She was not completely human. Her teeth were sharp as a crocodile's and crowded together so no one could count them. He did not trust her and was not going to speak to her again.

Ibis told Cougar what her husband had said and that it was his grief talking. Grandmother heard and told Cougar that he not only spoke from grief but also from untruth. "Best to ignore untruth."

But it worried Cougar, who was not sure how to ignore a false rumor. She tried to be kind and took prickly pears, sea grapes, and several squirrels to his lodge, hoping that the accusation would stop if she acted kindly toward him. Brittle Star took the food but would not look at Cougar's face, especially her mouth if she uncovered her teeth and smiled. Only later did he look at her and talk to her. Then he asked her why she was blessed by Spirits so that she did not get the oyster sickness. Cougar told him it was because she did not eat oysters. "I was too busy taking care of that fussy baby, Hummer, while Little Mother and

Grandmother were having a good time visiting with all the women," she said, smiling so that he got a good look at her teeth.

After that he always smiled first whenever he saw her. His teeth were larger, and he told himself they negated any spell Cougar's little, packed-together teeth could flash his way.

Once he stopped to say that he was sending Wren to several island villages to find out what they were doing to cure the oyster sickness. He said, "Anything happens to him, I will take care of his wife. I could do the same for you, if anything happens to Grandmother." He reached out to pat her shoulder and smiled. "If you live with me, you have nothing to worry about."

"Why not send your Medicine Man to the island villages to find a better treatment for the oyster sickness here?" she said, feeling queasy in the belly to hear that he wanted her and Little Mother as his wives. She shrugged, trying to convey that whatever Wren found would mean little to her, but more to the Medicine Man. She feared he wanted to talk more and began to move away.

Right on cue, Brittle Star said, "Wren will find the cure. He is one smart person. I will take the cure and be well enough to take another two wives." He looked at her and licked his lips.

She shook her head and mumbled something about his deserving a far better woman than any she knew in the village, and then she went home as fast as was polite.

Wren came back saying he found no sickness in the villages he visited. "No one seems to know exactly what to do to cure the oyster sickness," he said. "Except one chief, who seems to know a lot about healing. He told me that the best cure for any sickness was to wrap up in several fiber blankets and lie in the sun until one's face is shiny with sweat, then toss off the blankets, and run into the cold river water."

When Brittle Star heard that he said the cure was easy, he could do that. By midafternoon he was hot and sweaty. He threw aside his blankets and jumped into the cold water. Moments later the pain in his chest was unbearable. Otter Boy pulled him out of the river, and the chief's legs were so weak that he could not stand. He lay down on the sand, and his heart suddenly stopped. The people in the village could hear Ibis's anguished keening all through the night.

Grandmother was too sick and too tired to weep, but she told Cougar it was terrible to lose a chief, good or bad. She said, "Despite everything, Brittle Star was mostly good to me."

"You think so?" asked Cougar. The chief's death had lifted a terrible guilt from her mind. Now she had no worry that the chief would tell anyone that she had a double row of teeth or that she had waited for him after the Stretching Ceremony, even though she did not.

Grandmother said, "Aye. He made sure that Wren gave me two deer hides, one alligator skin, and a basket of snowy egret feathers when he took Little Mother as his wife. After all, I was like a mother to her while she lived with us."

In the middle of the night Grandmother called to Cougar. "If I meet the ghosts of your true mother and father on the Otherside, what shall I tell them?" she asked.

"Tell them you loved me and gave me the best of care," said Cougar, lying down beside Grandmother. Her thoughts tumbled over one another so that she wanted to cry out with stronger words, telling Grandmother not to go to the Otherside, but her throat closed over the words.

Finally Grandmother turned on her side and said in a slow, low voice, "I am going to tell them about the joy you brought me and that you will be a fine, important woman in the Calusa nation. I will say that you are pleasing to the eye, have a knack for telling the ancient stories, for trading goods. You can deliver healthy babies, think with your own mind—meaning you are interesting, kind, creative, and stubborn as a closed clam shell."

Cougar's throat suddenly opened and she cried, "I forbid you to go to the Otherside! I need you here."

"Shame on you!" said Grandmother. "That is the stubbornness I mentioned. It is not for you to forbid when I will leave for the Otherside. My dear man, Beaver Tooth, is waiting for me." She closed her eyes and rested a moment. When her eyes opened she said, "There is something I have been thinking about. Who will take Brittle Star's place as chief? Secretly, I believe you could do it. Otter Boy is the best male for the job. The council will say you are a woman and Otter is too young. Maybe I can find the ghost of Little Mother's sister and ask her to give Otter Boy the power to be the next chief, before greedy Wren realizes that he was Brittle Star's choice."

"Grandmother, I believe you are teasing," said Cougar. "Tomorrow we will laugh about what you have said. Oh, I do love you with all my heart."

"Look in my sacred pouch," said Grandmother. "The one we sewed red quills on a couple of days ago."

"It is the middle of the night. Can we wait for morning?"

"No, I cannot wait. Inside is a neckband that you wore when I found you. It must have great power, as much power as the wind that makes the sand swirl high in the air and flash the colors of the stones in that neckband. Both have colors like the rainbow. The neckband is yours. It kept you alive until I could find you. It will continue to protect you. Later, maybe you will give it to your daughter, if you ever have one. It proves you are something special, and your life will have a big meaning for The People. I wish that we had looked for my son. He was a handsome baby. The saddest thing I ever did was give him to another mother, because I had no milk to feed him. I always wondered if he had a double row of front teeth like Egret."

"You mean teeth like mine?" asked Cougar. "Egret has teeth like mine?"

"Oh yes. I believe the spirits mark really special people in certain ways, and a double row of teeth is one way," said Grandmother.

Cougar turned her face away. She was not certain that the Spirits could do something like that. She wanted to say that Grandmother was getting old and foolish. But when she looked at the neckband, it was different than she had imagined. It was a delicate necklace of tiny, transparent, colored stones strung on a strong, but almost invisible, cord. She was overcome with its beauty and forgot what she wanted to say.

In the morning she held the necklace up to the sunlight and saw points of shimmering colors reflected on the sand at her feet. Who would put such a precious thing around the neck of a child? It was grand enough for the first wife of a very high chief. She held the neckband of glittering, colored stars for a long time, before putting it in her pocket. It made her think of the star cluster above the western shore that told of winter coming. She fingered the cluster of clear sand bits glued to the inside of her sky-bowl. Her eyes were tearful, but her mouth turned up when she looked at Grandmother.

Grandmother breathed through her mouth and stared at the crossed sticks that held up the ceiling reeds, making a hatched pattern that was pleasing to her eye. She slid to the edge of her pallet and slowly began to pull herself up.

Cougar saw how her hands clamped hard onto the side of the pallet. She put out her hand to help steady her so she could sit up, but Grandmother moved away and said she wanted Cougar to comb her hair. After combing Grandmother's thin gray hair, Cougar kissed her cheeks, saw that her skin looked almost transparent, mottled with thin, brown spots like a single layer of birch bark, and whispered, "Grandmother, how thin you have become. But never mind, I will care for you. And one day I shall find your son and bring him to see you," promised Cougar.

"Oh, if only that could be," sighed Grandmother. "Tell him I have always loved him. It was love that made me give him away. I could not bear to see him starve."

After that, neither one tried to talk. It was an easy stillness inside the lodge between two people, while outdoors there were dozens of people talking and calling to one another, flies buzzing, birds singing, dogs barking, and children laughing. Cougar thought about Grandmother's starving baby. It was the first time she had heard about him. And she never knew Egret had double front teeth. She would have to look hard the next time she went to see him.

Suddenly Cougar heard Grandmother catch her breath with a little cry. Her eyes were closed and she breathed through her mouth. Her breathing sounded shallow.

Cougar laid her on her back and put her face close to Grandmother's mouth; now there was no breath; not a whisper, nothing. She laid her ear on the middle of Grandmother's thin, bony chest. Yes, her heart was beating! "Breathe!" she cried. The beating was faint and irregular, then quiet. "Oh, no!" She told herself to be brave, but she really wished she could cry the way Ibis had done. She looked around the lodge. Grandmother's tunic hung on a wooden peg. Underneath were deerskin boxes that held wild-grain seeds and roots and dried fish. On top of one of the boxes was a handful of small shells Grandmother had kept because they were unusually pretty. Grandmother said pink and tan and white colors were calming. Cougar felt no calmness. Nothing was right. This lodge, this village would never be the same. The something that made this place special was gone. She knew not how long she sat beside Grandmother, letting her thoughts whirl free in her head.

After a while she felt Little Mother's breath on her cheek and a hand cover one of hers that lay in her lap. She pulled her hand away and felt squeezed into a small place, like a pet crow captured in a cage. She nodded to Little Mother, who was weeping, and went to the open doorflap. She could see the people walking by, going about their business. They did not know that Grandmother could no longer walk among them to give advice, guidance, and comfort. She saw a flock of ducks flying low over the sea, looking for food. Underneath the cloud of ducks coming close inshore was the black head of a seal. Suddenly the seal seized one of the unwary ducks from underneath and disappeared with its mouth full. The survivors beat their wings frantically, scattered into the air, and gathered again in perfect formation low over the sea. Now there was no sign of the struggle, and the sea rolled on quiet as before.

Without talking, she and Little Mother bathed Grandmother and dressed her in her deer-hide tunic and gray-moss skirt. They pushed Grandmother's knees up in a fetal position and wrapped her in her own blanket, one she herself had woven. They cut their hair above their ears with the sharpened edge of a shell and slashed their arms with the same shell until they were red with blood. They stood in front of the lodge and keened. That evening Egret dug a deep rectangular hole next to Beaver Tooth's grave and lined it with flat stones. Together they carried Grandmother, whose knees were pushed up against her chest, like a small child sleeping, to the sacred burial ground.

"Has her ghost already begun its journey to the Other-side?" asked Little Mother.

"I believe so," said Cougar, feeling the circle of colored stones around her neck.

The next morning both Otter Boy and Wren went to Egret to say that each of them had decided to be the next chief of Sandpoint. Egret said it was no more than he expected of intelligent young men. Little Mother was so proud of her husband that she puffed out her chest, which was hard to do while carrying a sleeping infant.

Later, when Egret told Cougar, she said, "Grandmother would have been proud. She told me Otter Boy should be next chief—but he is too young, so it will be Wren, because the people will see him as tall and handsome."

There was no time for Cougar, Egret, or Little Mother to go to an isolated place by the river to grieve by them-selves. They were expected to hear what Wren and Otter Boy said about being chief.

Wren told the village people that Brittle Star told him he was to be the next chief. A few nights later he woke up when the stars were their brightest, and one was brighter than all the others. The idea came to him that it was a sure sign that he was the brightest star and he would truly be the next chief. He assured the people that they would keep all of the old customs of the Calusa, and he had some ideas about a few new customs. He did not say what they might be, but said all Calusa customs would be carried out as he, the next chief, saw fit, or there would be proper punishment meted out to those who did not partake.

Ibis interrupted to remind him that he could take more than one new wife; she was certain that Little Mother would not mind. "A new chieftain usually takes the wife of the dead chieftain, like you took me, and if I had a sister, you would be permitted to take her as one of your wives. This gives each wife less work to do and keeps them happy. Little Mother has a sister called Cougar. They have lived together with Grandmother and are almost like sisters. We both like Cougar."

Ibis's words put a smile on Little Mother's face. "I do not mind if my husband takes Ibis and Cougar as new wives," she said. "They are good women. We would be like sisters and best friends."

Cougar clenched her fists and would not look at Ibis or Little Mother, but she whispered to Egret, "I am going to leave Sandpoint for a while. I do not want to be one of Wren's wives."

Egret raised an eyebrow.

Wren sat up, straightened his shoulders, thanked Ibis and Little Mother, and said he would think about another wife, or maybe two. He cleared his throat and said any girl of twelve summers was expected to attend the Stretching Ceremony. "Any girl older who has not been clearly seen to attend will be required to attend the next one." He hesitated a short moment, looked at Cougar, and said. "After I take Ibis for a wife, I will be looking for a third wife, so be patient with me."

There were some giggles and sharp intakes of breath from the crowd.

Cougar thought, *He knows about Brittle Star and me, and he wants everyone to know that I can be a wife—his wife! I do not want to be a part of this!*

"As the new chief, I will participate by giving each of the girls advice on how to keep Calusa men happy," he said, again looking at Cougar. "Other ceremonies will continue as before, and for every ten fish a man catches, he will give one to the chief and one to each family without a man, or where the man is too ill to fish. If a man kills a deer, one of the back thighs shall be given to the chief and the other back thigh is to be cut up and given to families without a man. Also, the chief can ask village men to build him a new lodge and a large meeting hall." Wren waited for his applause to die and then sat down on the ground beside Otter Boy.

Otter Boy got up and stood in front of the crowd. He said that if he became chief, he would not participate in the girls' Stretching Ceremony. A woman would lead the dance, and women would be drummers and hummers. A grandmother or wise-woman would give advice and help the girls understand their role as wife of a Calusa man. Only women could attend.

Otter Boy said that all boys of twelve summers were

expected to attend their Dream Totem Ceremony. Only boys and men would take part in that ceremony. There would be a Summer Trading Fair and weeklong Harvest Celebration, old customs, not kept up since the Big Storm. Then he said he wanted to invite others to live in Sandpoint, so that in his lifetime it would be an important trading center. Everyone stamped their feet and hollered their approval, "Yu! Hey Ha!" He said they would pay more attention to the stars. He suggested a contest to name the star cluster that always comes up over the eastern shore before cold weather and the red star that takes the star cluster's place and shows that storms are imminent. "We will name the box that holds the stars called Three Pearls. When the box is visible, we know the weather will stay cold for a long spell and the biting insects are dead. If you would like, we could name the four stars that form the four corners of the box, especially the top reddish one and the other bluish one at the bottom. We all know when the Dog Star shows up that it is time for the birds to come back to their homes on the ponds and lakes. In the spring we will welcome the geese and ducks back to their nests." The people applauded loudly, shook Otter Boy's hand, and most said he was certain to be one of their best chieftains—when he was older.

Wren was now the chosen chief, and he grinned so that everyone could see he was pleased.

When he was home, Wren told Little Mother that he would fix Otter Boy so that he would never want to become the chief. Little Mother tried to calm him by calling him Chief Wren. She suggested that Otter Boy might arrange hunting parties and lodge-repair parties and build ceremonial fires.

Cougar went back to her lodge and rested with her back against a wall-support and thought of a day several summers ago. Grandmother had told her about the time she and Little Mother were bold enough to go to the round-bellied, smiling Chief Brittle Star and ask him to discontinue the girls' Stretching Ceremony or make it voluntary.

Grandmother had said that Brittle Star looked at them as if they had said something vulgar. Then he said everyone needs a ceremony once in a while. "And he was right,"

Grandmother had said. "It is part of living. To dress up and paint our faces makes us feel good, gives us a chance to get together with our friends, to eat and gossip, to sing and dance. I have changed my mind and now think that the girls' ceremony is a necessary thing, like the Totem Dream for boys who are twelve summers. A girl needs a man to hunt for food, bring in materials to build a fine lodge, and to protect her and her children. The bird or animal a young boy dreams about, after drinking the sacred black soup, is his lifelong totem, his protector and helper. For the rest of his life he depends on the helper to keep his fishing boat afloat, even if it leaks. When a storm hits, his totem will guide him close to shore so he is able to beach safely until the storm passes."

Grandmother said she had reminded Brittle Star of the year of the Big Storm, so he could remember that was the day she changed her name to Grandmother. He had promised the Sandpointers that he would never forget the families who had lost loved ones. But the day Grandmother and Little Mother spoke to him he could not remember that his village had been killed by the wind. Grandmother described it afterwards as sticks and mud, with broken roof poles and uprooted palmettos. She reminded him of cracked and broken canoes, shards of clay pots, and stinking dead bodies. She asked him, where were the totems the men believed in that day? Did the totems help anyone during the storm? He stared at her as if she were a cactus with sharp spines about to jump inside his breechcloth.

Cougar had told Grandmother that she did not believe in special ceremonies. It was unreasonable that a bird or animal from a dream could help in real times of trouble. People had to depend on themselves. She could never tell Grandmother what had happened at the last Stretching Ceremony. She lived in dread that old Brittle Star would brag that he had been first to put his stick inside her. Maybe he told Wren. After all they were friends. Then she had thought of something else.

I often told Grandmother about my totem dream, she thought. *Grandmother did not laugh, but listened to what I had to say about my dreams. In dreamtime I have seen a man with hair the color of the pale, sun-dried grass. He had pale hair on his cheeks and chin. His eyes were the color of lupine and his skin pale as the inside of a clamshell. I thought he was beautiful. I believe I loved him and he loved me. His hands never touched me. He was wise and knew how to use words. He continues to live in my head, but he cannot help in a storm, or in a brush fire, or when the earth shakes and the sea rolls rough with huge swells. But thinking about him helps me think what he might say if he were real. He is my totem.*

She had told Grandmother it was she who had put him in her head when she was a child, young enough to wear nothing on warm days, by saying she should find a husband who was her opposite. So Cougar had smiled and imagined her yellow-haired friend. Grandmother's brown eyes sparkled, and she had smiled kindly.

"You have an imagination," Grandmother had said. "Never mind. That makes you special. Chief Brittle Star has no imagination. His life is duller than mud. His attitude makes my blood hot. He knows nothing about how women think or that they react with trepidation when pushed into an unfamiliar situation. I believe his sisters pushed him around. He was their baby brother. He has left them to their ways and has gone about caring for the village half-asleep. No one has criticized him; he has felt safe."

"He was a bear's ass," Cougar had answered. She suddenly felt bold because she had been so relieved when he had died. *He can no longer hurt girls or spread ugly rumors,* she thought. *The Spirits took care of him just right.* She remembered telling Grandmother that most village women gulp down old ideas that were thought up long ago when the people did not know as much as now. "We are learning new things every day," she had said. "I saw a snake with two heads, one tail. With two heads, Snake can fill his belly fast and never be hungry. No one but you would believe me, even if I took each one to see Snake." She had stood up, looked at the dying fire, and said the fire needed another log. She went out to the woodpile, took a long time because she wanted to feel glad that she was not as blind-headed about the dead chieftain as everyone else, and she asked herself what she was. *Bullheaded* was the first answer that came to her mind!

She remembered when Grandmother first said she was a special gift from the Spirits and began life at two summers. *Grandmother thought I was never born like real people,* she thought. *Am I a wildcat with strange teeth that can shape-change? One day will I change back into a cougar-cat? No, I do not want to do that—not ever! No one around here saw me before Grandmother found me in the big log jamb, or had they? A couple of times I saw Egret look at me in a puzzling way, as if he recognized something. No, I am silly. Egret was just looking at me because I was Grandmother's girl.*

When she finally came inside with a log for the fire, she told Grandmother she was going to talk with Egret to see if he knew what the stars were made of.

Grandmother had said she should hope so and clicked her tongue against her teeth. Egret was older than she and had more learning experience. Cougar had felt Grandmother's eyes on her as she walked along the beach, letting her hair hang loose so it bounced around her waist.

Now, going to see Egret, she missed having Grandmother's eyes on her. Some boys followed her. She laughed and told them to go away. She worried when she saw some older men look at her sideways from the corners of their eyes.

Egret smiled when he saw her walk fast past the men. He came out and invited her inside. He said there were bets on who she would choose to be her man. "Most think it will be me," he said, "because they see you come here so often."

She told him she figured that she had already lived the child-part of her life, and there were things she wanted to look for and think about before she was a woman. Mostly she wanted to leave Sandpoint to look for Grandmother's son. She wanted Grandmother's son to know he had a wonderful, real mother who never knew him, but missed him. "Will you come look for him with me?"

Egret said there was a lot of land and swamps between all the Calusa villages. "We need a log canoe, a dugout, and that will take time. It might be best to look for the woman who raised that boy."

Then she asked if he knew any girl who ignored their

Stretching Ceremony and got into trouble. He said he did not. Then he said that Grandmother did not go to the public ceremony, but had her own that led to the baby she gave away. Egret took her hands and looked at her, and in a soft voice said that he was sorry he never saw Grandmother's baby. "Now I am going to be a nosy old man and look for that boy, my son. It would be wise to go before the spring rains."

Cougar was satisfied with his answer. She had half guessed that he had something to do with Grandmother's baby. Anyone could tell that Egret had loved Grandmother, and Grandmother had a special place in her heart for him. She could ask more questions about that later. Now she asked why the surf flings its spray against sunlight by day to make a rainbow and against moonlight by night to make no rainbow.

"It was always thus," he said. "There is an answer, but I am not smart enough yet to know." Then he told Cougar that he felt a tingle. It grew into happiness because the child Grandmother had found was wonderfully different from the ordinary. "When you were only four summers, you were a real pest, always asking why. You asked me why geese flew north in a wedge every spring. And why did they fly in the same wedge back to the swamps in the fall? Where have they been? Do you know I learned to be a watcher of things so I could answer your silly questions? You made my life interesting. But you are still an awful pest! What are you looking at?"

"Your teeth," she said. "Yours are like mine."

"Oh, Grandmother and I noticed that long ago," he said, as if it was nothing special.

After the spring rains, Cougar took Hummer to see Egret. She said she wished she had asked Grandmother the name of the woman who took her baby boy. "What do you suppose that second mother looks like?" she said, walking back and forth to keep the baby quiet. "Where does she live?"

Egret did not know. He knew only that Grandmother had lived near the village of Gulltown when her baby was born.

"I miss her," said Cougar.

"Me, too," said Egret. "When we were young, we went to the creek, looked at our second selves make funny faces, and washed each other's hair. Afterwards I combed hers and she braided mine. Oh, those were the days!"

"Did you love her?"

"Yes. I still do," he said.

"And you let Beaver Tooth be her husband?"

"Sometimes there are things you cannot have when you want them," he said. "It is something you learn to live with."

"Do you wish you had asked her to be your wife?" asked Cougar.

"Is that what you came to ask me?"

"No. How was fire carried long ago from one camp to another?"

"The people used to put glowing coals in a clay dish of ashes with another dish, with small holes in the bottom, over the top. They put it in a leather basket to carry, because it was too hot to hold. One person was designated the fire-carrier."

"We need to get us a fire-carrier for our trip," said Cougar.

"I hope I am not too old to walk this winter," said Egret. "You want to go places and see things that your home-folks never thought about. Before I am too old to look around, I can help you find the right man. Is that what you want?"

"No," whispered Cougar. "I can take care of myself. I am as old as Grandmother when she lived by herself." She put Hummer in Egret's arms and ran into a hollow in the sand, made by the tide during the night. After a while she looked at crow tracks that showed faint wing markings outside of the wide foot marks and, side by side, the webbed tracks of gulls as they landed. Beyond the webbed gull tracks, the sand was unblemished as the birds flew by free will or fright into the sky. For a long time she looked across the sea to the horizon as if expecting to see something. She thought of something Grandmother had said. "Youth and innocence will not always be your guardians." Suddenly she had one of those prickly feelings that something was going to happen, but she could not hold the thought long enough to examine it. She wondered if she had a real mother, or was she born of a female cougar cat? Or did the Spirits put her with the Calusas when she was already two years old? The hiss of sand mingled with the thunder of the sea did not answer her wonderment.

IV
Blue Woad

1157–1168 A.D.

The British tattooed themselves with woad. The blue dye they
used for this purpose is extracted from the leaves of the first
year growth of this biennial plant. The magnificent designs
of tattooing have been confirmed by the frozen Celtic warriors of the Iron Age excavated in Siberia.

—Peter J. Reynolds,
"The Material Culture of the Pagan Celtic Period"
in Robert O'Driscoll, ed., *The Celtic Consciousness*

One morning Sein asked Brawd why he had not yet memorized *Caesar's Campaigns in Britain*, after he was given
the only Roman scroll the druids had. "You were to bring
the scroll back as soon as you had the work in your head.
Were you not as adept with the Latin as you thought you
were?"

"Well," said Brawd, "I have devoted my time to a discovery that I call 'The Secret of the Sacred Nine.' Nine is
a druid holy number. Come outside and I will show you
with a *ffon*, a stick in the dirt. Take any large number, like
8792, reverse the order to 2978, take the lesser from the
greater and you have 5814," he said drawing the numbers
in the hard-packed dirt. "Add the digits, 5 + 8 + 1 + 4
and you have 18. Then add 1 + 8 and you have 9. It works
with any numbers of two or more digits!" He talked fast to
keep Sein from using the stick on him. He was well aware
that druids believed in free use of the switch if their fosterlings neglected studies. " 'Tis a wonderful discovery!
Check it and see I be right."

"Pythagoras, the Greek, discovered the same trick more

than five hundred years ago," said Sein, taking the stick, and striking Brawd across the back of his bare legs.

Brawd pressed his lips together to will away the stinging hurt. His humiliation was worse than the physical pain. He tried to save face by standing still, with his head up and saying, "By day after tomorrow I will have memorized Caesar. I shall write out the Campaigns this week! I promise."

As calmly as possible Sein said that it was Caesar himself who said the written word causes a loss of diligence in memorizing by heart. He told Brawd to remain on his pallet and memorize.

Several weeks earlier Sein had cajoled three druids, Gorlyn, Conn, and Sigurd, from the Dubh Linn shipyards to take turns coming once a week to instruct Brawd on laws of the sea and shipbuilding. This day Sigurd, Brawd's favorite teacher, would be at the camp.

The thought of missing Sigurd was a rejection that seemed unbearable. Brawd's eyes met Sein's and he said, "Why do you hate me?"

"Lugh's lungs! Laddie, I loved you the moment I first saw you and your mam."

"Then do not slam the door in the face of my learning."

"I could never slam the door on you, nor hate you! You are the finest lad I know. But here is something that you do not know: Your feeling about how I feel has nothing to do with me; it is what you feel and how you feel about yourself."

Brawd brushed the unruly blond curls from his forehead, thought a moment, and then said, "I like the feel of figures in my head. 'Tis measurements of the variations in the water cycle that helped me figure the features of an area in the ocean bottom. Sigurd told me the things shipmasters have to think about. Large waves do not damage ships because they have long wavelengths compared to a ship's length. Breaking waves damage ships. The best ships are designed to produce as small a wake as possible. I like to think about the sea and ships sitting on her face. When I think of men going to a mead feast to bolster their courage, my heart becomes heavy. When I think of war campaigns, I think of dead and crippled men and suffer with sadness. I believe a lord could communicate grievance to another lord through reason and together come to an understanding, so they avoid warring. I can memorize battles, but 'tis not the happiest thing I do."

Sein said he believed hate was easier for men to learn, but love was harder to overcome. "Sometimes you act yeasty, with foamy reasoning, but I give you my word you will have every opportunity to learn all the figuring you can swallow. Sigurd will be here next week. 'Tis time now to memorize. If Pythagoras were alive today, I would send you to Greece to study numbers, astronomy, and the tides."

Brawd's mouth formed an O, and he said he never dreamed Sein would say such a wondrous thing. By this time he thought of Sein as a flesh-and-blood god. "From now on, could ye think of me as Madoc, instead of Brawd?" he said.

The corners of Sein's mouth turned up.

During the next several years Madoc hungered for more knowledge of sailing and distant lands. From Conn, with the fly-away, straggly blond hair, he learned to draw sky-charts. If a ship went north the altitude of the North Star increased and if he went south it decreased. By measuring the altitude variation he could determine how far south or north the ship had gone. He asked Gorlyn, the father of his friend Eira, what ships sailed as far as the icebound land called Thule, where the hunting and fishing was unsurpassed during the summer. Then he made models of the clinker merchant ships and hide-covered curraghs and floated them in the stream below the druid camp. He told Sigurd, whose hands were blackened from tar that covered his woad honor marks, that he preferred the Norse clinker-type craft, which usually had four oarsmen on each side, a square sail, and a deep keel for fast maneuvering in stormy seas.

When Madoc was thirteen, Sein sent him to the Welsh Prydian Druid Camp near Aberffraw on the southwest coast of Anglesey, better known as the Isle of Mon, to be fostered by Archdruid Llieu and to study with the well-known astronomer, a black Welshman named Caradoc. At the same time Sein sent Madoc's best friend to the Prydian Camp. He was black-haired, black-eyed, fun-loving Conlaf, who had the makings of a good healer and was ready to learn from the best, Archdruid Llieu.

Also Llyn, a rangy lad with red-gold hair, who was good with poems and songs, was sent to the Prydians to study with the famous bard Llywarch, who lived near Prince Owain's castle in a courtyard cottage.

The three lads made feeble attempts to learn the differences between the Irish and Welsh languages, but they were too excited to pay close attention to Sein's enunciation. Llyn made up a song:

> "We will see the five peaks of Snow Dun,
>   white and clean.
> Below their slopes lay misty lakes and
>   meadows green."

Madoc hugged the trees and whispered a prayer that Sein would not forget him. He said good-bye to the stream, to fields, to sheep, and promised never to forget Sein. For true remembrance he threw stones and chewed stems of grass.

The day before the lads left Ireland for Wales, Sein said to Madoc, "If perchance you see your dear mother, Brenda, and are permitted to speak, tell her I—tell her I miss her." To hide his broken heart on the day the lads left, Sein used the popular Irish farewell, "Go before the cropped black sow seizes the hindmost!"

The passage from Dubh Linn to Aberffraw was ordinary except for Llyn's singing and Conlaf's treatment of a couple of cases of hives among the messmates to show off his medical knowledge.

The three lads were surprised at the dry look of the Welsh druid camp built on the flat sand, surrounded by a deep ditch with a thin-stick palisade. There were no trees for shelter from storms or the scorching sun. From the front gate, decorated with wild-boar skulls, they could see the sea birds diving for food. Madoc's heart fell at first sight of his new home, and he thought the Welsh druids probably lived like barbarians.

The spring rains came, the grasses turned green, and the

birds trilled mating calls. The smell of warm, wet earth, honeysuckle, and apple blossoms filled the air. Madoc was eager to be on the water with his teacher, Caradoc, whose hair grew like a thick, grizzled, gray mat. One of the things he learned was that there was a tidal bulge on the top side and under side of the earth. He asked if the earth itself was stretched toward the moon like sea-water. Caradoc scratched his head and said that the student asked more questions than he could answer. He told Madoc that for the past two years the Danes had come in the best-built knarrs around Orkney Island and down the Hebrides to the sea-coast of the Isle of Mon to trade and plunder as had their forefathers along the coast of Ireland hundreds of years before. The word *plunder* stayed large in Madoc's mind as he told Conlaf and Llyn about the Danes.

The student-fosterlings from the Prydian camp were instructed to give medical aid to soldiers, farmers, anyone in need. This was a tradition, since Celtic times, that druids tend the ill and wounded without prejudice. Conlaf took to his new medical training like fleas to a dog. He volunteered to treat everything. Madoc was eager to be with his teacher, Caradoc, to test his strength with various coracle paddles. He began to think of himself as a trader seeing different people and lands. Llyn strummed his harp while wandering among the hedge banks and dunes. Often he stayed several days at a time with Llywarch to compose poems about the heroes of Gwynedd. He saw no signs of skulking Danes and felt safe to be alone with only the screech of the sea birds and the whine of the wind, dreaming his own tunes.

One eve when Llyn was late for sup, Madoc and Conlaf were sent to search the dunes in the gray twilight. Madoc said he thought Llyn was probably inside the castle bailey singing to the primroses. The next moment the two lads were filled with sickening horror to find Llyn headless near the shore in a bed of downy stems and soft pink flowers of the marsh mallow. They stared, speechless, at the ragged, red flesh above the brown tunic collar. Llyn's harp lay crushed to splinters. When they looked around, they found no one lurking behind the gorse, nor did they find Llyn's head. The horror of the scene made the lads' stomachs turn inside out. Conlaf went back to the camp for a cart. Madoc continued to look around until his vision blurred and blackness closed over him. Next he heard a roaring and Conlaf calling to him to help load Llyn on the cart. Madoc sucked in a lungful of air. He was not sure he could put his hands on a dead body, especially someone who had been a friend. He put his arms around Llyn's chest without looking down and dragged the stiff, cold body onto the cart. Caradoc and several other druids examined the beach area where Llyn's body was found. They discovered where two keelboats had been pulled ashore on log rollers and a supper fire had been built. They never found Llyn's head. The next morning Llyn's body was dressed in a harper's cloak of feathers and cremated along with his broken harp. Madoc and Conlaf scattered the ashes over the wild flowers on the dunes. Madoc's chest squeezed so tight he could hardly breathe. He stood on a hummock of soft heather under the clear sky and recited Llyn's last poem, praising the deep blue sky. He and Conlaf wept.

To stave off his grief and fear Madoc filled his head with names of the constellations. From Caradoc's charcoal drawing he learned the movement of seasonal winds, the stars, sun, moon, and Venus that went through phases similar to those of the moon. Conlaf studied anatomy from the charts on the walls of Archdruid Llieu's cottage. Llieu always wore druid-gray work gowns and amber jewelry, but he advised the fosterlings never to dress in long, druid gowns. "Wear breeks, shirt, and tunic and never wander the dunes alone."

That winter Conlaf enticed Madoc to indulge in the natural savagery of boys. They caught field mice and dissected them so as to know their anatomy better. Conlaf promised Madoc a magnificent collection of sea shells if he would fetch a dog so he could study the layout of its innards. Madoc got a litter of pups from the camp cook, thinking they would be better for Conlaf's study than being cooked into meat pies. Conlaf wanted to know the cost of such fine specimens.

"A full jug from Llieu's cupboard. Llieu thought it was for you and filled the jug with chickweed tea."

"The cook had a laxative in place of a drink!" said Conlaf, laughing. "The bedamned cook will have a fit!" He held his hands over the nose and mouth of the dogs until their twitching bodies lay still on the sand. He used a bone knife to cut through the belly skins, stretched them open on beechtree bark, and held them in place with thorns. He showed Madoc the positions of the various organs, muscles, and blood vessels. He cracked the heads open and showed Madoc how the brains lay against their skulls.

Madoc had a painful bout of self-reproach and sat on his haunches beside the sea to watch the tide climb the sand to wet the feet of terns and oystercatchers. He wondered why he could see the moon in daylight and never the stars.

Slowly the lads began to love and appreciate the Welsh druids. When Madoc was sixteen, with the help of Llywarch, he made himself known to his true mother, Brenda. Afterwards they became close allies.

Madoc never forgot the evening, several months after coming back from France, when he had gone to the court Bard, Llywarch, with his mother, Brenda. He was so delighted with her intelligence and beauty that he wanted to know the truth about why she left him in Ireland when she went back to the Gwynedd Court. He found her sweeping the dining area in the great hall. She suggested they go to see Llywarch where they could talk freely and admitted that she had something to tell the old bard.

Llywarch was not home, so they went inside the warm cottage quiet as cats. They walked with stealthy steps like hunters stalking deer, careful not to crackle the dry rushes underfoot. They disturbed nothing except to brush away cobwebs in the corner where they sat against the wall. They removed their bratts and waited.

Brenda warned Madoc not to say a word about being her son. "If Owain learns he is your father, he is obligated to kill both of us, including Llywarch and all the druids that kept you alive and hidden."

Madoc drew in his breath and thought of Brenda's words. When their eyes became accustomed to the starlight coming through the single window filled with a waxed linen cloth, Llywarch came inside. He showed no surprise seeing mother and son against the wall, and said he was chilled and bone tired. He rolled out his pallet, pulled off his boots, and climbed between the quilts.

"I came to tell you the advice I gave to Owain about keeping those young village rascals in hand," Brenda said, building up the small center fire to boil water for tea. "And Madoc came with me to ask why I left him in Ireland when I came back to Wales with the soldiers Owain had sent for me. I thought we could tell him."

Seeing Llywarch shivering on his sleeping pallet, Madoc said he could come another time.

"No, no," Llywarch said. "It will warm me to listen to what Brenda has to say and then we will answer your questions. Owain kept me outside most of the evening watching for those wastrels to come back and deface more village gravestones. He never complained about the cold, but I nearly froze waiting for those detestable toads to show up. They were wise to stay at home by the fire. Owain should ask Brenda what to do about their punishment."

"That is what I want to tell you," said Brenda, removing her cap to brush the hair out of her eyes. "A couple of days ago Owain called me to his chamber to discuss the behavior of certain village lads; his son, Dafydd, among them."

"When I was a boy, we were not that irresponsible," said Llywarch. "I cannot believe how today's lads charge around sacred places, the burial barrows, and graveyards. Last week I saw Dafydd and his friends behind the Church-with-the-White-Porch, shouting, tossing a huge ball back and forth, and scuffling in the hallowed, white quartz pebbles. They scattered the pebbles everywhere, never thinking the sacred quartz was meant to stay around the graves and cairns to purify our thoughts of dead friends and relatives. They tipped slate headstones to the ground so the words and carvings were hidden. Some they broke. Nary a parent reprimanded one lad. Instead, a couple of parents came to Prince Owain and asked *him* to put a stop to their lads' wild behavior."

"Owain's soldiers could talk to the lads," said Madoc. "That would chill their spines."

"When the parents left, Owain came to see me," said Brenda. "I asked him why he thought Dafydd was in that crowd. He said Dafydd was the age all lads have a wild streak. Most outgrow it, given time."

"Ho, time has been given those devils, with no luck," said Llywarch.

Brenda stood up, waved her arms, and said, "Exactly what I told Owain. I told him to declare the parents at fault, negligent because they were responsible for their children's behavior. I told him to tie each parent to a tree in the heart of the village and leave them from sunup until sundown for everyone to see. I said, do this whenever their lads or lassies break the Hywel Dda Laws of the province or non-written but well-known laws of the village."

Madoc could not believe his mother was so outspoken. He narrowed his eyes, trying to imagine her advising Prince Owain. "Do you think the prince will carry out your idea?" he said. "Will he let his wife be tied to a tree because of Dafydd's misbehavior?"

"Maybe not, because Gladys is not well, but his cousin, Christiannt, is responsible for the lad," said Brenda.

"This afternoon I was out playing my harp and saw soldiers posting signs and marking large trees to be used as reprimand posts," said Llywarch, pulling the bedclothes as high as his chin. "I wondered what it was all about."

"Christiannt breathes fire and spits out steam!" said Brenda.

" 'Tis troth," Madoc laughed. "My mam tells the prince how to run his province?"

"Your mam is smart," Lywarch said, kicking the bedclothes. "You watch, the prince being a negligent parent will have himself tied to a tree alongside Christiannt and other parents. The people in the village will love him for that. He will give Dafydd a public tongue-lashing, threaten to cut out his birthright, and from now on there will be no wild youths running around the village. I predict the lads will become soldiers hoping to get away from parental goading and more punishment. Soldiers learn to respect discipline. See! Brenda's suggestion is on the mark. She understands behavior."

"Do people in Gwynedd know a woman is telling the prince what to do?" said Madoc.

"Of course not," Brenda said, "and you are to keep your mouth stitched tight."

"Anyway, no one would believe you," said Llywarch. "Now I am feeling warmer. Madoc, what is your question?"

"What directed my mother to come back to Prince Owain and leave me, a helpless babe, in Ireland?" said Madoc in a subdued voice. "I be not whining. I need to know what was in the mind of my true mother."

"Madoc was my precious babe," said Brenda. "I loved him dearly."

"I think it was conscience in her mind that directed her," said Llywarch. His voice was muffled by bedclothes, but his laugh had a hint of a chuckle.

"Conscience?" said Madoc. "You mean like druids believe the eye of God in a person's heart sees everything that is perceptible, in its right form, place, time, cause, and purpose?"

"I do," said Llywarch. "For years, before Owain grew old and forgetful and ignored truth, Brenda loved him and he loved her. He still loves her and will until he dies. Today she thinks of him as a dear, dear friend. While she lived with the Irish druids, caring for you, she was attracted to a man strong in intellect and integrity. He became her mentor."

Brenda's face turned crimson. "Llywarch, be a gentleman. It behooves you not to tell everything you know or think of me."

"Is the mentor Sein, my second foster father?" said Madoc.

"Aye," said Llywarch. "A wise druid knows truth is the sciences of wisdom preserved in memory by conscience. Brenda is like that; strong in will, wisdom, and love."

Brenda signed and Llywarch put a bedcover over his face.

"Mam," said Madoc, "what does that have to do with leaving me, your precious babe? How could you do that? I know next to nothing about you. I know I have an older brother and sister in Ireland. I do not know them; have never seen them. I know Sein, an Irish, druid physician. I loved him. If he loved you, he never told me. He said you are beautiful and would never forget me. But I really never understood why you left me. Before Sein fostered me, I believed I was the true son of a wonderful herder and his wife. I had a sister. I loved all of them. They were my real family until I was seven. Sein said that Prince Owain was my true father and a lady, Brenda, was my true mother. Right away I hated him, you and Prince Owain. I would not believe Sein's words for weeks. After a time I began to like and believe him. When I was fourteen, Sein sent me to Wales to study stars and seamanship. I met my true mam and tad. Now I want to understand. For troth, Mam, why did you not stay in Ireland with me?"

Brenda's heart ached for her son to love her. "Owain believed you drowned in your bath water when you were no more than a few days old. I once made a promise that I would not leave him. I had to go back."

"But I did not drown."

"You are alive because of the quick and wise thinking of your mother," said Llywarch. "To save your life, she kept you away from Owain. With you gone, Christiannt, Owain's cousin, was able to keep her babe." Llywarch sat up and rubbed his gray face. "Surely you have been told that long ago, during the same moon, you and two other babes were born to different mothers in Gwynedd Court. Three wee laddies had the same father, Prince Owain. Male kinfolk tend to quarrel over property and what a father owes them. Owain hated quarreling like he hated stepping into a nest of ground wasps.

"The night of your birth, during sup, I told the story of a man who had been told by a wizard that he would be killed by his own grandson. When his daughter gave birth to triplet sons, the man ordered all three drowned. One babe fell out of the wrappings. The man found him, called him Lug, and raised him. One day Lug was helping the man pare apples and fainted. The man grabbed him, and Lug's paring knife went into his heart, killing him. Lug also died from a wound made by the old man's knife as he was grabbed around the waist.

"I played a soft lullaby on my harp after telling that tragic story and said in a sing-song voice that what anyone said before the hourglass emptied would surely come to pass. Owain jumped up. 'Beshrew you!' he said. 'If I had three sons born under the same moon, I would drown all but one.' He spoke before the hourglass was empty, so he was obligated to do what he had just uttered."

"Aye," said Madoc.

"And so, Owain had made a vow. Later, when he was told of the triple births, he had to see that only one babe lived. Owain's sickly wife, Gladys, had a stillborn babe. Christiannt had a healthy laddie as did Owain's favorite mistress, Brenda. Owain meant to keep only Brenda's babe and give him to Gladys to raise. He was prepared to suffocate Christiannt's babe. But word went out that Brenda's babe had drowned and, grieving, Brenda fled to Dubh Linn. Owain gave Christiannt's babe to Gladys, who named him Dafydd. She was a doting mother and spoiled him putrid. It would have been fair penalty even then, if Gladys had been tied to a tree the moment she could not control her pup."

"So, Mam, you fabricated a drowning story to save two *babi*," said Madoc. "Good for you! I can live with that. An admirable story, a lie with a well-meant reason behind it. I feel better."

Llywarch told him that he made a small grave filled with stones for Brenda's dead *baban* in the courtyard next to the stillborn. At the same time Brenda wrapped her live sleeping babe in a bundle of clothing and held him under her cloak.

Brenda said, "I sat behind Llywarch on his horse and rode out of the royal courtyard and through Aberffraw. Llywarch walked back to his cottage, and I rode on to Degannwy where I found a shipmaster going to Dubh Linn. Christiannt became nursemaid for Dafydd. When I came back to Gwynedd, I became advisor to Prince Owain."

"Madoc, you became the child predicted, hundreds of years ago, to be the druidic savior," said Llywarch. "Your name was a sacred secret at that time, never to be spoken aloud."

"Me?" said Madoc, thinking Llywarch was tickling his funny bone.

"The druids say that your conception took place under unusual, blazing northern lights," said Llywarch. "Outside the whole sky gleamed with sheets of shimmering reds, purples, and yellows. There were sharp snapping sounds when the light undulated rapidly. That aurora meant something to them."

"The bands of color were so close I felt that if I reached I could touch them," said Brenda. "It was a truly spiritual thing."

"I have heard druids say it was a primal thing to see, both frightening and reverential," said Llywarch, "like spirits of the dead announcing a special event to the world. Nine months later, under a full, red autumn moon crossed by triple lines of clouds, a triskele of lads were born at the Gwynedd court. Madoc, your life was signified by the longest cloud line, which fulfilled the ancient prophecy of a strong young man who would lead persecuted druids to an unproved land. There they would find freedom and a long life. The story of your birth has been retold so often that it has become a myth. I suppose the story of your whole life will be a Welsh myth nine generations from now. Druids sometimes have a prescience of things before they happen."

"I always thought that Sein made up that story to make me feel I was not a throwaway lad," said Madoc. "That babe was truly me? I do not feel special."

"Oh yes, he is you!" Llywarch said. "And years later your mother knew you were the wisest choice Owain could make, and so you were appointed Gwynedd's emissary to France."

Madoc had trouble breathing. He nodded and saw his mother and Llywarch smile in the blurred moonlight shining through the waxed linen cloth. "I did not realize Owain chose me because of my mother's suggestion. She hardly knew me then!"

"Brenda, like most mothers, figured her lastborn was more intelligent than most," said Llywarch. "Owain believes any suggestion Brenda makes is the best advice available. We druids believe it was inevitable that you would carry a vellum brief from Prince Owain to King Louis VII of France asking for his military to help the Welsh if the English king, Henry II, ever attacks Wales. Louis, like Owain, dislikes and distrusts Henry."

Madoc looked at Brenda, got to his feet, and put his arms around her. "And I had enough mettle to tell Owain that my friend Conlaf, who was eighteen and a well-trained physician, would be a fine co-emissary. Owain understood that I needed a companion and agreed to send both of us to France if we agreed to wear Augustinian gowns so that our druid affiliation was not recognizable. I can love him for that now."

"And it was your mam who hemmed those gowns and brought them to you," said Llywarch.

"I told you and Conlaf to use the signs of the cross often," said Brenda, "and to wear the prayer beads that I put in the pocket of each gown. I said pray aloud for the people you met. I also said the true value of a human is determined primarily by the measure and the sense in which he has attained liberation from self."

Madoc had repeated her last sentence many times, but had never told anyone that his mother gave it to him. "Owain asked us to keep vellum journals," he said.

"True, and I gave Owain the idea," said Brenda, pointing to herself and smiling. "On the outside the journals were like prayer books that monks carry. Owain told you to keep entries of your voyage until you returned to Aberffraw. I prayed no soldiers, who had been ordered to behead druids, would suspect a couple of lads, dressed as monks and writing 'prayers' in their books, were druids. Most soldiers probably could not read nor write. Owain wanted to read your journals, but his eyesight was poor. I read a few passages to him, but could not keep tears out of my eyes. I kept thinking, These are two lads from Gwynedd and one is my son. Owain teased me for being sentimental over a couple of young fosterlings I did not know. I think he doubted your return."

Madoc kissed Brenda's cheek. "My mother had no doubts."

"Neither did I," said Llywarch. "I said druids have a seventh sense about things like that."

"Your true father wanted to be a druid, and your true mother thinks like one," said Brenda, grinning and giving Madoc a hug.

"Thanks," said Madoc. "I owe both of you my life."

Madoc thought about the fact that druids could read and write, which was a part of their first nine years of training;

they usually spent the next twelve years memorizing whatever was necessary for their chosen field of expertise. At the end of twenty-one years, they were deemed full-fledged druids. They memorized, because written knowledge written on stone, or bark, or vellum could be destroyed. Prince Owain once told him that he remembered when the New Religionists had mutilated important druid writings with fire, water, stone hammers, and insects. Because of memorization, no important new vellum books now existed.

"Until you and Conlaf gave Owain your journals, only a few valuable vellum books were available," said Brenda. "He will make certain those books are preserved so future readers will know what our world was like."

After two years in France and sailing to other places on a trading ship, the lads returned to Aberffraw. Not only had Madoc and Conlaf sailed a trading ship to Bardsey and Lundy Island, they actually had been to the Abbey of St. Denis, then to Paris to see King Louis VII in his castle. King Louis signed a brief stating that he would help the Welsh, if, indeed, the English invaded Wales. Later, due to a misunderstanding, Louis put the lads in a Paris prison. The Moslem, Kabyle, who wore a pink turban, helped them escape to a Danish trading ship. Shipmaster Erlendson was looking for three messmates to replace three who had deserted him in Paris. On the advice of Trader Kabyle, he picked up Madoc, Conlaf, and a prison guard called Troyes. The three lads were fleeing the Paris prison. Erlendson was never sorry he had agreed to take escaped convicts as his messmates. The lads learned quickly and worked hard. Erlendson sailed past Wales to trade in the Hebrides, the Faeroes, and Iceland, which he called Thule. When he finally brought the lads back to Aberffraw, Wales, he paid them generously for working as his messmates. He hoped the gods would bring them together another day.

Prince Owain was pleased to be given the brief signed by King Louis. He was so surprised and delighted with the details in Madoc's prayer-book journal that he gave him all of the old Welsh, dry-beached ships near Landrillo Abbey on the Afon Ganol. "You have studied the stars and seas. Make one or two good ships from the lot and use them for trading," he said. "Years ago I hired traders to use these little Welsh sails for their trade goods. When they left to go elsewhere, we beached the ships. You have studied ship-building with Sigurd and Caradoc, so make one or two good sails from the lot, and use them for your trading. You love the sea as much as I and will be a fine trader."

Madoc could not believe his good fortune, and thanked Prince Owain. He reminded himself how different people were, yet the same in so many ways.

Owain gave Conlaf a handful of coins to study the new disease called *leprosy*. Conlaf was grateful and thought he might ask his friend Troyes, who had studied medicine in Paris, to go back to France with him. Together they could examine twice as many patients and try twice as many cures. However, neither was yet ready to go back to France for fear they would both be jailed. After all, Troyes was the jailer who had helped two Welshmen escape.

Madoc and Conlaf and Troyes wandered through the main street of Aberffraw during the last day of Aberffraw's an-nual Trading Fair. Troyes looked like a Welshman with dark hair and brown eyes until he began to talk with his French accent. Back from their voyage less than a month, Madoc and Conlaf still wore their Augustinian robes. They went to borrow a long grayish robe from old Llywarch for Troyes to wear. Madoc hoped to see Annesta, who lived inside the castle's bailey in the maids' cottage, not far from her grandfather. Often, with other castle maids, she went to visit her grandfather and play a board game like chess. She was the personal handmaiden for Christiannt.

Madoc would never admit he was smitten. However she, with the wavy brown hair and dark eyes, was the girl of his dreams. Often he daydreamed of spending the rest of his life with her and a passel of red-cheeked, laughing chil-dren.

Before the three young men left Llywarch, he told them to find a certain cook, called Clare, at one of the fair's food stands. "He is a friend of mine and a shipbuilder. Greet him and give him these gloves made of raw wool. They will keep his honor marks covered. King Henry's soldiers have been killing more and more druids. Do not talk unnecessarily with anyone."

The air was cold and blustery; the streets were crowded with people bundled against the chill, looking here and there for witches on errands of mischief. The three men watched a vendor selling quills, vials of ink, and rolls of vellum for writing. Another man held out little censers of spiced oil made from the wool of Anglesey sheep. The man swore it was good for incense or rheumatism, which made Conlaf shake his dark head and roar with laughter. They stopped at a booth where roast lamb flavored with herbs was being sold on a stick. The cook's lips were tattooed blue. He looked half frozen. "I came from the Isle of Man, where one day 'twill be known for the cats that have nubs for tails," he said, waving his hands. His fingernails were edged in woad, and blue spirals were tattooed on the back of each hand. He laughed and quickly shoved his hands into his pockets. "I be Clare and come with the tide under the full moon to let you taste my lamb, which will melt in your mouth like butter flavored with mint. If truth were told, I would rather be teaching the trick of cooking metal to shipwrights, but my supply of good iron grows thin, and I turned to my supply of rams and ewes. I learned a cooking trick to make tough mutton soft and delicious as young lamb."

"You understand ships, tides, weather, wadmal, and flax string suitable for mending linen sails?" Madoc asked.

Clare laughed. "Those are less mysterious to me than what herbs to use with what cuts of meat. You three men wear strange gowns, two like the black monks and one like a visiting monk." His voice dropped to a whisper. "Something tells me your gowns are worn for safety, and underneath you wear druid armbands of gold. Are we all friends of Llywarch and followers of the Old Religion?"

Madoc looked around before he spoke. "We do not wear gold armbands, but we protect ourselves from New Religionists, who do not touch monks," he said in a whisper. "If your name is Clare, here are gloves, a gift from old Llywarch. Cover your honor marks." He made his voice louder. "We are half-starved and would be ever so grateful if you would give us several pieces of meat, not fit for selling." Their eyes met for the count of nine breaths.

Clare seized Madoc's right arm, held his fingers in the mystical druid position, and said, *"Quisque sous partimur manes."*

"We make our destinies by our choice of gods," Troyes translated before Madoc could get his tongue moving.

Clare grinned, put on the gloves, and gave each a stick with a generous portion of roast lamb. "I warn thee 'tis hot and will burn thy tongue," he said. Then he mumbled something else.

"Thanks," said Madoc. "If I ever master a trading ship, I choose thee to repair the iron braces."

"If you are ever master of a trading vessel, I, Clare, the Worker of Metals, will go with thee in a minute." He held up his gloved hands. He nodded to several customers to show that he would be with them in a moment. "I long to see and smell more than bleating sheep, sizzling mutton, and pagan purges." With glove tips he touched Madoc's forehead.

"Ever and anon!" said Clare, closing his eyes, and for nine heartbeats staying quiet as a stone. Then his mouth opened and his voice was low and husky. "I know what you do not. You have a trading ship. I have a vision of you with a handful of ships all manned by believers of the Old Religion. Who gives *you* sails? And why?"

Madoc answered the mystical question with his own questions. "Why does water quench fire? Why is one man short and another tall? Why do some men speak of the impossible as truth now and then? Believe this, Clare, Cooker of Mutton, I cannot let you believe an untruth. I be no one, not an owner of a lowly coracle. Excuse me," said Madoc. "I spoke without thought. Truly I have no ship. I be sorry to get your hopes high. I spoke from an inner compulsion, unexplainable. Mayhap 'twas because you have more knowledge than most about ships and metal. I be partial to sailing ships, and we are friends."

"All life connects," said Clare. "Naught happens that is unimportant."

Conlaf pushed in front of the group of men waiting for mutton. He reached across the rough-hewn table, touched

Clare's arm, and said, "*Diolch!* Thanks! Good food. *Hap*, good luck."

" 'Til we meet again!" said Clare. Then he made his voice faint so only Madoc, Conlaf, and Troyes could hear. "Everyone is someone in the scheme of the gods!" Then he looked at Madoc, moved closer, took a deep breath, and said, "I see before me someone of the Old Religion, conceived on a fallen, cold heel-stone, under the shimmering green sky-scrim edged in a rainbow of colors, born in a group of three. You were saved by your own mother to be a druid savior of great merit!"

"Clare has water on his brain," said Conlaf, watching another vendor wave a bunch of dried grass, taken from the churchyard of St. Edern's in Dyfed, saying that tea from the grass was a specific against rabies.

The grass interested Troyes, who stopped to ask the vendor its name, saying that it was more important than where it came from.

Madoc said in a whisper, "There is no way Clare can know of my conception and birth nor about my father's offer of those old sailing hulks that are probably falling apart with dry rot. 'Twas a secret and I should never have told you."

"I be your best friend," whispered Conlaf, watching Troyes. "I would never divulge a secret. You know that!"

"Then Clare's brain is occupied by a water-nixie," agreed Madoc, licking his fingers. "I wonder why Prince Owain wants to please me with rotten ships? He has no idea I be his son, or he would have given me coins also."

"So out of the worthless bunch, why not build one?" said Troyes, who had learned that the grass was actually the curly "pipes" of young fern mixed with wild mint.

"I can scarcely imagine myself with a whole fleet of sails," Madoc answered. "Tell me again why Llywarch suggested we meet this Clare person. To taste good mutton? Or because he is a far-seer?"

"To give him gloves to cover his woad marks," said Conlaf. "Llywarch is kind that way. Say, did you hear the rumor that we are to be given honor marks? 'Tis something we both hoped for in the eventual."

"Honor marks? Soon?" Madoc felt a shiver go up his back as he left Conlaf and Troyes at the druid camp and went to Llywarch's cottage in the castle court to say they had seen Clare and given him the gloves.

As soon as Madoc was inside the cottage his heart began to pound faster. Llywarch's granddaughter, Annesta, petite and dark as her Celtic ancestors, was inside, breathless and red-cheeked, to tell that she had overheard one of Prince Owain's soldiers say that Owain was too ill to rally his troops. "And Dafydd is in the van, the forefront, leading his soldiers to the castle. Lord Dafydd is wearing a boar-crest on his helm and yellow circles around his eyes. His soldiers are painted with bright colors on bare chests and backs and carry axes and maces. They wear fierce war masks and are full of battle ecstasy."

Madoc was tongue-tied.

"Woe is me!" moaned Llywarch, weary of sons fighting their father for power. He thought most of Madoc's half-brothers were scoundrels, with no more notion of peaceably ruling a good-sized Welsh province than codfish. He pointed to Madoc and said, " 'Tis in your favor that your brothers do not know where those old ships, that Owain gave you, are hidden. Go build one as soon as possible. Barter goods around Gwynedd to rebuild others. Believe me, we are going to need ships!"

Madoc cleared his throat.

Annesta spoke up first. "Ships? Trading? Madoc, you are not going away again? You have not been here hardly a week after being Owain's emissary to France."

"I will be gone a month, maybe two," said Madoc, not certain how long it would take him to repair one of those dry-docked ships. Did darling Annesta really care if he went away again?

"Two months! And you have just returned from—only the gods know from where!" she cried.

"Two—three months is not so long," said Madoc, noticing that there was a dimple in each cheek when she smiled.

Annesta was contrite, and there was veiled mischief in her lovely eyes that made him feel off balance. "Of course, but time is different for men," she said. "I wish I could go with you to make my time go faster." Her eyes met his with a look so full of meaning that his legs turned to mush. She put her hand in his, and the longer she left it there the more he thought he might explode. He had to hang on and wait.

Llywarch looked sharply at her.

She smiled at him and pulled her hand away.

"Go with Madoc to the druid camp and have Archdruid Llieu tell you the location of the safe-camp. Come back as soon as possible to tell me."

"Safe-camp?" Fear made her eyes as big as plums.

"A place where Old Religionists are safe from the terrifying circle of Christian soldiers, who falsely believe 'tis their duty to behead anyone who believes in more than one god," Llywarch explained as though she were a child. "We know there is one Supreme God, and 'tis logical that He has lesser gods to help Him. But Christians do not yet know that truth."

Madoc looked at Annesta, slim and pretty as a lark, who sang like one. When she ran her fingers through her long dark hair, it smelled like rose petals. His chest felt too small to hold his thumping heart. He turned to her grandfather and said, "I will take her to the druid camp right away and leave for Afon Ganol in the morning. You will be first to know what I name my ship."

"Clare knows," said Llywarch, smiling, "he is a real wizard. Well, if I believed in wizardry, I would have given you a ring set with a precious crystal that had the property of protecting you against all wounds imposed by sword, arrow, or stone. That is wishful thinking, or else Prince Owain would have had a crystal ring long ago." He put his arm around Annesta and looked wistful. "*Merch*, lass," he said in Welsh. "I feel the event of your marriage. Woe!"

"Grandfather," said Annesta, "I shall choose my own husband, and you shall perform a druid ceremony." She leaned her face against his chin whiskers, but her eyes were on Madoc. She kissed her grandfather's eyelids.

Llywarch kissed his granddaughter's cheek and whispered something that made her blush.

Madoc wanted to hold Annesta's hand, but he dared not with her grandfather so close.

When they were in the bailey, they noticed that every cottage, hut, and shed had an armed retainer beside it. Retainers held scramasaces with broad, thrusting, single blades eighteen-tums long at intervals along the inside of the stave fencing. It was plain that Owain's soldiers were prepared for Dafydd's attack.

Madoc and Annesta hurried through the bailey, out of the heavy gate, and into the village. The cottages were dark and quiet, except for a couple of barking dogs and a crying baby. The two of them sang so that no stray spirits walked with them. Madoc took Annesta's hand, and they walked away from a knot of frightful-looking dragon-soldiers wearing black tunics with slashes of red and yellow paint on their cheeks. The black soldiers carried crimson firebrands and called to a group in blue tunics. Blues answered with savage tremolos. Annesta shivered and whispered that the blacks were Dafydd's soldiers, the blues were Howell's, both Owain's sons.

Horses whinnied and reared frantically. A man in a crested helm slashed a horse from neck to belly and laughed as blood and entrails gushed to the ground. Madoc's heartbeats quickened, and his mouth tasted salty from biting his lip. He pulled Annesta behind brush alongside a cottage. She put her arms around him so tight it was hard for him to breathe. Weapons clashed on hard-leather shields. Several of Dafydd's soldiers were unhorsed, two-barbed pikes went through their leather and pierced their midsections. Extraction of a pike was impossible. Madoc pulled away as his nostrils filled with dust, sand, and ash. He took her hand and kept to the narrow back streets. The smoky, oily stench made him cough. He was charged with alarm, revulsion, and fright at the same time. Annesta held his hand tightly and put the other hand over her face.

"Do spirits of the dead leave instantly?" she asked. "How long is a spirit's path to the Otherside?"

Madoc said he knew little of paths of the living, let alone the path of a spirit. He could understand honor in defending one's land, but never pleasure in the brutal butchery that brought soldiers to their death. Dying for one's land did not seem a great pleasure to him, unless it would end all warring.

"Would soldiers slay helpless people like—like us?" she stammered.

"To slay when another has no weapons is cowardice," said Madoc. "Come! Do I not look like a priest? They dare not touch us." He led her to the north gate of the village where there was glimmering torchlight, and the shivering guard waved them through, saying he did not think there would be much fighting the rest of the day.

At the druid camp, Archdruid Llieu was delighted to see them, and when Annesta asked about the safe-camp, he said it was in the limestone caves near Dubh Linn. "Llywarch knows the place. Listen, it is not safe to go back through the village alone. Not until the soldiers are gone."

Madoc offered to accompany her home in the morning. He hinted that her grandfather worried if she stayed away too long. "I agree the road is dangerous for a lass to travel alone."

"Madoc, do not go from anger over bloodshed to moping over love-sickness," said Llieu, shaking his blond head and squinting his blue eyes. "You will see enough of Annesta when the time is right. Building ships will keep your mind occupied. I will send the lass home with Conlaf." He chuckled. " 'Tis hard to realize, but I was young and had a wife. People said I was not in love with anything but medicine. Actually 'twas half-truth. My Flura also loved medicine, and I thought of her as an ally pledged to heal the ill with me. Our relationship was built on an unbreakable bond between us, more than any emotional love affair." He studied Madoc for a long moment, and his teeth flashed white, then he laughed a big rumble that began deep in his belly.

Madoc felt himself blush.

"When she died, I was devastated."

"I never thought of you with a woman," said Madoc and instantly it flashed across his mind that he talked too much. "I be a sorry fool," he whispered, blushing deep red.

Llieu agreed, but his eyes twinkled. "In one of our weaker moments, Caradoc and I decided we would be pleased if you and Conlaf were druids. We believe you and Conlaf performed well as Welsh emissaries. Before the evening meal, talk with Caradoc. If you agree, he wants to begin your initiation at once."

It was nearly sunset when Madoc went to Caradoc's cottage. Caradoc asked if he had had sup. He said, "No," and Caradoc rubbed a scar on his temple and did not offer him anything to eat, or drink, but suggested that he keep a written log from now on describing his shipbuilding in detail. "Describe your sailing, the location of the stars, and the smell and looks of the land you pass, so that each day can be compared. Written records can be destroyed, but a man also can be destroyed, and what is in his mind lost forever. Later on, shipbuilders and seafarers may bid hard coins for your plans. Using any language, a pilot will be able to find your trade routes if you draw maps."

Madoc said this was the same kind of thinking that French architects used. "They make records that others can repeat at another site. But look at me, I be not an important shipbuilder, or a seafarer."

"Do not sell yourself short," said Caradoc. "What any man does is important. Act cautious, not impetuous. Be fair-dealing as a trader and you will be honored with a mark of distinction, mayhap a ship with a square sail tattooed on the inside of your right wrist." He pulled off his tunic, unfastened the ties of his shirt, and showed Madoc the bluish maps over his back and chest that were full of stars in precise positions. On his right arm was a square-sail ship; on his left arm was a horse. Around all his fingernails were blue curlicues. "Do you agree to be honored this night with your first metamorphosis into the brotherhood of druids? Answer aye or nay."

Madoc remembered the first time he noticed Seth had blue drawings around his fingernails was when he was shearing his sheep. He thought of Sein with similar markings and Owain with a mysterious fish on his right leg from ankle to knee. A tingle ran up his back when he answered, "Aye." Then he said, "I know Conlaf is being so honored this night, but what about Troyes? That man saved Conlaf and me from spending our life in the Paris prison. Now he cannot go back to his own land for fear of being burned as a traitor. He deserves some honor, some recognition. His father was a druid."

"The three of you proved your bravery and intelligence," said Caradoc. "We need more time to study Troyes's abilities and motives. The time for his marks comes later. For you, being a druid will open doors; you will be with others with similar markings. Your honor-price will increase."

Madoc said he had no actual wealth and no status in Gwynedd, therefore how could he have an honor-price?

Caradoc explained that every freeman had an honor-price that could be raised if his fortune or standing was increased, but conversely, it could be reduced if he broke a law or by some other action dishonored his name. "I have seen shamed men fall ill and die." He rubbed Madoc's palm and held his warmed hand on Madoc's cheek. " 'Tis hard to believe, but I am proud to call you my student." He took his hand away and flexed his fingers.

"I be proud to call thee mentor," said Madoc.

"Hush, no more talking from the candidate. I am the seventh son of a seventh son," said Caradoc, drumming his fingers very fast on the table.

Madoc could not watch the drumming; it made him dizzy. He swallowed trying to keep the vibrations out of his chest.

"I have the gift of seventh sight and be calling the god-spirits to speak." Caradoc closed his eyes and thrummed himself into a trance. "In my mind's eye I see you the master of a square-sail—a handful of sails, a circle of nine sails, surrounding the tenth sail, the leader. The nine sails will follow your sail as if you are their kingstone. Your sail goes nowhere I know."

Clare, the man who roasted mutton to a delicious tenderness, once told Madoc that he would be a shipmaster, mayhap a trader.

"I do not see you a long-time trader," said Caradoc as if he could read Madoc's thoughts. "Ten sails leave *Cymru*, filled with mostly pagans, including *myself*. Your name is written in sacred woad on the right thighs of your followers."

"You mean on the inside of their right wrists?" said Madoc.

"Nay, thighs. Hush. What is told to me is beyond my understanding. The gods smile on thee. Thou wert chosen ages ago. Your destiny has been a long-time prophecy of the druids."

Madoc's mother had told him of the midwife's birth prophecy. Brenda's last born would be a leader of men. It was also the prediction of the old Degannwy innkeeper, and Sein said Madoc would be a leader. Even Clare knew what was foretold about his life. Madoc's mind was filled with astonishment. It was beyond belief how the druids from all around knew what he, an ordinary lad in Gwynedd, would do.

Suddenly Caradoc's face paled. "After your Blue Woad Ceremony—you circle the center from which you come and to which you go." He gave a sharp cry. "Your action causes you great joy, but greater sadness." His hands were quiet and his eyes open, but he was unsteady.

Madoc led him to a small pallet and thought that far-seeing had sapped his strength.

"My strength is not sapped," said Caradoc. "I have been in dream-time with no past, present, nor future, only continuum. It leaves me a little bit dizzy."

Continuum puzzled Madoc.

" 'Tis a stream of knowing. An infant cries. He is not hungry; he is clean and dry, yet he waves his arms and legs and cries. He is marking his own special place. 'Tis a place that he sees behind his eyes that will flow with him from time onward. He will find himself in that place when he is grown. I was in your special place and saw you on a ship, wounded. A wound of the heart, that takes a long time to heal. I glimpsed across the sea to unproved land. You must not blame yourself for a broken ship or for lives lost." Caradoc shuddered. "I saw familiar faces, and dark strangers, a young lass with dark-brown eyes looking for you, strange lands and seas, days and nights, happiness and sadness, emotion and logic, life and death, good and evil. I cried for understanding, but 'twas beyond me."

Madoc's knees went weak; he sat beside Caradoc and dared a whisper. "Master, there is no practical or logical reason to believe either of us will be part of such a picture."

"Both thee and me, and many close to us," whispered Caradoc mysteriously. "The faces were there." Then he said it was time for Madoc to see Llieu.

Llieu stripped him to the waist, led him inside a circle of nine standing stones, handed him a beaker, and whispered, " 'Tis a slurry of crushed poppy seeds and mandragora root in red wine to deaden the pain that comes with tattooing. Drink all of it." Other druids stood, in white gowns with arms locked, outside the Prydian circle, singing chants in harmony. He recognized Llorfa and Old Gwalchmai, but he did not see Llywarch and he wondered why. He faced the east, drank, became lightheaded, and swayed with the chants. Llieu pierced the skin around Madoc's thumbnail with a sharp sliver of hollowed bone that contained an inky-blue solution of woad. He punctured around the other four nails. Each puncture was an excruciating pain that made Madoc stiffen and grimace. Llieu spoke so softly that it was hard to hear the words. Then Llieu began piercing around the nails of Madoc's other hand. Madoc tried to anchor himself in some pleasing childhood place. He did not want to faint. A voice asked what he desired most.

He answered, "My true father's love."

"What comes next?"

"The love of a goddess."

"Strange. Are you certes you do not desire to be a leader of men—a leader who loves the sea?"

"Aye, I already love the sea," Madoc said. "My father does not know I be his son and does not love me; I love him. I love the goddess; does she love me? I desire most the . . ."

"Ah, ah, never tell the gods what you desire most. If the gods give it to you, they make you pay. When death claims friends and kin, mourn them, blame no one. Your father loves you. Tell me again, what do you want?"

"I want naught," he heard himself say with no hesitation.

"Aye, make what you want known and you shall have it—for the gods' price. Hide your true desires, like an oyster hides the pearl."

Madoc imagined he was a hungry heron eating up everything in the fen. He saw his body floating away, as a coracle floats on the river. His hands were outstretched like paddles. He heard his name and looked away to avoid the bright torchlight. Llorfa hummed and wiped the sweat from his forehead with a damp cloth. She offered water. He re

fused to unclamp his teeth or open his mouth. The torment
in his fingers burned worse than holding a hot iron. Once
he felt nauseous. Someone pressed on his neck and massaged his back. That was when he heard his name used in
the druids' chant: "The truth is in Madoc's heart; the
strength is in Madoc's arms. The fulfillment is in Madoc's
tongue."

Caradoc put his hands on Madoc's shoulders and raised
his face to the west. The stars were bright, the air was cold,
and the full moon was low in the west. The chanting
stopped and clouds moved over the moon. Caradoc's mat
of grizzled hair moved like a thick mane every time a
breeze whispered. He spoke a triad not heard before:

> "There are three disappearances of famous
>   men from the land of the Welsh.
> The first is Gavran and his men, who went in
>   search of the Green Islands of the floods,
>   and were never heard of after.
> The second is Merddin, the bard of Emrys
>   and his nine attendant bards, who went to
>   sea in a house of glass and
>   the place they went is unknown.
> The third is Madoc, the son of Owain, Prince
>   of North Wales, who goes to sea with
>   three hundred persons in
>   ten ships, but the place to which he goes
>   has no name."

Llieu clasped Madoc's elbows, avoiding his hands that
ached with a devilish sting, and said, "Bless you, my foster
son. We pried, like the devils interested in your soul. You
did not yield. You gave us an image of manly conduct to
hold in our hearts. We praise thee. We praise the Lord God,
and thank the lesser gods who promise to protect thee."

Madoc was filled with wonder and apprehension. He had
become a *druid*.

v
Four Druids

The British Druids were great magicians, and much addicted to divination, by which they pretended to work a kind of miracle, and exhibited astonishing appearances in nature, to penetrate into the counsels of Heaven, to foretell future events, and to discover the success or miscarriage of public or private undertakings. . . . Of the Druidical creed it was an article that it was unlawful to build temples to the gods, or to worship them within walls, or under roof. . . . The Druids, says Pliny, have so high an esteem for the oak, that they do not perform the least religious ceremonies without being adorned with a garland of its leaves.

—John Matthews, ed., *A Celtic Reader*

On a clear day at the beginning of summer, Annesta told Madoc she would bring bread and cheese to the beach if he would teach her to swim. It was easy for her to float, and she learned to move her arms to gain headway and to hold her legs straight when she kicked. They came out blue lipped, shivering, laughing, and hungry. "Follow me to get warm," he said, going over rocks and through the thick brush. When he stopped, she caressed his warm skin. "I worry that you will suddenly disappear," she said.

He looked at her with surprise. "You think I would go away without telling you? Never would I do that."

"I want to go wherever you go. I do not want to be without you, ever."

"I will be a trader; you will be home caring for our flock of wee ones."

"*Our* flock," she said and looked away toward the rocks and sandy banks.

Her hair dried in the breeze and turned up into tight dark curls. Her back was straight as a shipmaker's rule. She was no taller than a hedgerow of wild roses, her shoulders and hips no wider than an ordinary small steppingstone, and she had perfect teeth.

He put his arm around her waist and surprised himself by saying, "You are right—for me." He could tell she was startled. Her body twitched. His heart raced, and a tingle ran down his backbone to his loins. He wanted to hold her close and feel the roundness of her firm breasts tight against his rib cage. He wanted to lay his hands on her back, pull her down on the warm sand, and press his manhood against the vee at the top of her legs.

"There are no trees," she said. "See the beach gulls flying over the rocks and beyond the brush."

To him the beach, sand, rocks, gulls, and water were indistinct; a dull foggy blur. He leaned forward, pressed himself against her, kissed her forehead, opened his eyes and saw she was bewildered, as if she had lost her composure and did not know where to look for it. He bent his knees, put his hand under her chin, and kissed her face all over.

She loved the feel of his whiskers on her chin. She put her face against his and tried to think about the mixture of sensations he had riled up inside her. "I want you," she whispered, breathing deep and hungry, as if she had been running.

He put his arms around her neck, tasted the saltiness of her shoulder, and felt her shiver. Her hair was warm and soft. Her hands moved up and down his back. He thought he might explode. "Aye, me too." He put his trembling hands about her waist and breathed into her ear. "I want you close to me. I really do."

She shivered again.

He looked toward the brush and small sand dunes. " 'Tis not the day for us to be wanting." He ran his fingers through her warm hair and sighed.

"Why not?" she said. "No one is here but us and the sand crabs. Show me how; what to do with my arms." She giggled and rested her arms on his shoulders. He loved her giggles, like a bubbling brook.

"Would you do it?" he whispered and waited a moment for her to answer.

"I would," she said and put her lips against his throat.

Suddenly he felt a special intimacy and pulled her tight against his chest. The crabs scurried in and out of the sand. "Where did you leave the lunch?"

"Hush! Lunch can wait," she said and did not move or pull herself away, but her eyes followed his across the rocks and scrub brush to where the gulls were congregating. "Oh Lugh!" she cried, waving her hands. "Gulls have found our bread!"

"Lugh's liver! 'Tis luck, some kind of luck," he said, taking her hands. He led her back over the rocks and through the brush. The gulls satiated on bread and cheese flew down the shore.

Shaking sand from their clothes, they laughed, dressed, and agreed that they would not have to explain any reckless actions to anyone, especially Brenda and Llywarch. "We lost lunch, but there is something to look forward to," Annesta said, as if talking about the autumnal equinox. "Ya!" said Madoc, blinking. "Next time, the big excitement." His face turned crimson.

It was the morning after the ceremony of tattooing honor marks when Madoc went to Llieu and volunteered to walk Annesta safely back to the maids' cottage. He wanted to protect her from any of the hundreds of soldiers in the streets of Aberffraw and from those milling around the castle gate who would have a closer look at her.

Both had waited days to be alone again. Madoc talked Conlaf into forgetting about taking Annesta home. He said it was his time to do that because he was going to marry her.

"Ya," said Conlaf, "as soon as you build your trading ships and find that your trading business is good. How many years will that take?"

"Just bring her down the trail, and I will take her to her grandfather."

"No skin off my shins," said Conlaf. "I can be with Llorfa. She likes me."

When Madoc met Annesta on the trail to Aberffraw, she

said she could hardly wait until he built one ship, let alone a whole trading business. He said he adored her. They held hands like impetuous children, and he told her again that he would be gone for only a couple of months. "I shall think of you," he said.

"I shall dream of you," she said.

They stopped beside the ancient sacred spring, where sheep grazed all summer long. They ate a little of the dry bread Madoc carried for his trip to the Afon Ganol and had a drink of water. "Do you want to get married the old druid way?" said Madoc. "Just between us. This is the day for it."

"Now? Today?" said Annesta. "I want to have Brenda and my grandfather with us at a church. I thought Brenda could help me make a dress. A wedding dress with rows of tucks on the bodice."

"Brenda likes you a lot," said Madoc. "She will make you a dress any time and go to any church with you. Your Grandfather Llywarch is uncomfortable in churches. He may be unhappy knowing you want to marry someone who is no warrior, no knight, or bard in Prince Owain's court. He told me that he does not hold sailors high on the scale of men with backbone. He believes sailors have a low capacity for intelligent or rational thought. Not many traders come from or go to Gwynedd. I may be the only one he has met."

"I can explain things to Grandfather so he will be pleased," she said. "He likes independent thinkers. And you are certes one of those. Besides," she touched his bandaged hands, "you are a druid now, with honor marks. He will admire you for that. We can have a small druid wedding with kin and best friends. Mayhap Grandfather could marry us. You know he would like that. How would Brenda feel?"

"She would be all right. How about the ancient druid ceremony? It lifts you to the stars and brings you gently back," said Madoc. "Believe me, I can show you."

She looked skeptical, kicked her shoes off, and sat on the mossy embankment. She helped Madoc take off his boots, because his freshly tattooed hands hurt. He lay with his head in her lap and explained the ancient way that druids used to marry themselves. She stroked his blond hair.

" 'Tis a private, glorious, and sacred experience," he said in a hushed voice, as if not to wake the gods nor startle the sheep. "Do not be timid nor worry. Llywarch will understand. I know my mother will. She will be glad for us. First we take time to get to know each other."

Annesta felt there was nothing on earth more important than knowing everything about Madoc.

He had yearned to marry Annesta for a long time. He unfastened her shirt and untied the cord holding up her skirt and underskirt. He was awkward and slow because his tattooed hands hurt under the bandages. She removed his shirt, became shy, and turned her back when he pushed off his trousers. When she turned around, he asked her to lay with him on the cool moss. They kissed fiercely, caressed, and hungrily explored each other's bodies.

He saw her white nakedness surrounded by sunlight, and his arousal made him dizzy with a delirious lightheadedness. He cupped her breasts in his aching fingers, and the desire in his groin grew so strong that he could hardly keep from thrusting deep inside her.

Annesta delighted him by burrowing her face under his chin. She breathed hard, lifted her head, and kissed him on the mouth. Her voice was whispery when she said he was the only man she trusted and loved with all her heart; there would never be another. She was a surprise and delight when she straddled him and pushed her breasts against his chest. She put her tongue against his and he could hardly breathe.

Annesta wanted him, needed him, and was eager to marry him in the old druid way. Madoc felt no hurt in his hands. Both were so aroused they thought of nothing but the overwhelming excitation. They savored the rise and fall of their arousal, letting only rapture weave its enchantment to hold a man and a woman together. Neither could nor wanted to stop the intense emotion.

The passage of time had been meaningless. The length of time it took to make a marriage-chain of clover blossoms had been no longer than an eye-blink. A bubble breaking in the sunlight had been everlasting. Thus, by mutual consent, before they had reached Aberffraw, they had married themselves by the old druid method of coupling by a sacred spring where grazing sheep often drink.

Afterwards Madoc swore he had touched the stars. Annesta had tears in her eyes and said if Brenda and Llywarch had come to watch or if the whole royal court had come, she would not have known or cared. "I was in a cocoon of glorious fire, made by my lover's hands and lips. The finishing sparks did not last long, but the glowing coming down was so peaceful, without a worry." She wiped her eyes and kissed his lips. "I want to do it again. Build your ship and come back tomorrow. I hunger for your kisses. If I do not have them, I will surely die."

Madoc kissed her hard and wondered if he could be without her as long as it took to build a ship or maybe two.

Brenda was not displeased with them, but actually had expected a druid marriage sooner or later. Madoc gave Annesta the last of the coins he had earned coming home from France as a messboy with Shipmaster Erlendson. Llywarch smiled when Madoc said he would become a shipmaster-trader and take the best care of his new wife. Madoc longed to explain his love for Annesta. But there had been no words to describe the most powerful heartfelt emotion in his life.

Two days after leaving Aberffraw to find the old sailing ships Prince Owain had given him, Madoc's hands no longer ached from the tattooing, and he was able to discard the bandages and wear gloves. He carried a blanket and wore his wool bratt wrapped around his blond curls and shoulders. He walked most of the first night and toward the next afternoon he slowed his pace. For a time a dog with furtive brown eyes followed him at a distance. When the dog came close, he saw that there were pink patches of skin showing on its back where the hair had been pulled or fallen out. Madoc waved his hands and told the dog to move off. It slunk off with its head bowed and tail between its legs as if it understood a gruff voice meant a sudden undesirable blow to the head.

After a half-dozen steps he could think of nothing else except his bride. She had charmed him with verses and ballads; made him laugh with her mimics. She could look at him with her eyes so sparkly and direct it was more like being touched than seen.

If Annesta were with him today, he would not be able to keep his hands off her. He imagined her running ahead of him with her long, dark brown hair streaming behind and her long, slim legs cycling. She would turn, smile, and beckon him to hurry. She would couple with him today he knew for certain. Over and over he sang to himself, "I be dizzy for Annesta," until he felt woozy.

A lone wren flitted ahead of him. It was leading him further and further away from his love. Over the top of the next rise he stopped to look at a tiny meadow of rattle flowers, not yet taken by the frost. Each flower had a four-toothed mouth, with two blue lips, one arched over the other, as though puckered, waiting for a lover's kiss. Annesta! How he would like to kiss her warm, salty lips. This kind of thinking made him giddy, so he crawled into an abandoned brush hut. Insects crawled under his shirt and bit at his belly. He was too tired to notice or eat and lay down. He closed his eyes, thought of holding Annesta close, embracing mouth to mouth, shoulder to shoulder. He no longer felt woozy from not eating; instead he had a warm excitement in his midsection, that he imagined was an ever-brightening glow, and he began to dream of the recent past.

When he awoke, he saw the next day wrapped him in heavy mist. He ate a little dry bread and wondered if right now Annesta was bringing clean linen to her grandfather and later would she sweep Christiannt's chamber or perhaps the great hall with his mother, Brenda. Again he tented his bratt over his head and shoulders, this time to keep off the misty droplets. He discarded the limp, pink clover blossoms woven through the braided wedding band Annesta had made. He kept the braided band on his wrist. In the gray rain he lost all sense of time of day. A tiny, pleasant frisson formed in his belly as he thought of Annesta.

The late afternoon sun ate up the mist. He rubbed warmth into his arms and noticed the ring of white skin above his elbow. The ring was made by his student arm-band, which Llieu took for safekeeping, saying that working outdoors on the ships would erase the white ring. He told himself there were two things that he had which were more than enough reason for a New Religionist dragon to separate his head and body: one, the white band of skin on his arm and two, the druid honor tattoos around the base of his fingernails. Thoughts of headhunters made him so uncomfortable that he looked around to see if he was followed. A man could never be certain.

That night he lay down to sleep in a little valley walled off with piles of stones, thinking that becoming a druid and becoming married made a new double beginning for him. He was no longer Owain's emissary to France or a messmate on a trading ship; he was a future shipmaster with the responsibility of a wife. After a short nap, he noticed that the cold mist had washed the air clean of smoke.

In the morning the sun shone pale yellow. He ascended into riparian woodlands thick with stickery furze, and whistled as he walked across terrain broken by rocks and creek beds. He crossed boggy meadowlands and could see trees burnt beyond black, and fragile carbonized cornstalks from previous fires. He thought about his father growing feebler each day.

Prince Owain's words sometimes were unintelligible. He forgot names, places where he was, and what he was doing. He did not walk much anymore, because he could not see well and his bladder was unpredictable. Sometimes the maidservants forgot about him waiting to have his breeks pulled up and fastened, or waiting to have his face washed.

Suddenly his thoughts turned to his New Religionist, half-brother, Dafydd, who claimed to be king even before poor old Owain was dead. Worse, Dafydd's use of the royal nomenclature was with the backing of the English king. Dafydd discarded the old laws of Hywel Dda, which gave Welshmen their powerful sense of personal worth, and superseded them with laws of servitude and subjugation. Suddenly he thought someone was near and looked around. New Religionist soldiers were nowhere in sight, yet he still felt them everywhere. He whistled choruses of lamentations and summoned pictures of Annesta to dance behind his eyes.

At the port of Fair Marsh he hired a curragh to carry

him across the Menai Strait to Bangor. There the yellow grasses, once knee-high food for countless cattle, were now short and brittle under the full pelt of a freezing rain. He kicked against a pile of shattered cattle skeletons. The sharp, mutilated old bones were mixed with newer, roasted beef-nubbed bones. The cattle were gone. Dafydd's dragons, who ate only the choicest, fat-mottled bloody pieces, had butchered them. Madoc slept a few hours in a deserted lean-to and dreamed that Annesta walked the trail with him. Her dark brown curls unfurled like a banner in the breeze. Her face shone, her eyes glowed, and her mouth smiled wide as she sang him a love song.

In the night he heard a scurry in the sod ceiling. He thought it was a mouse coming in out of the cold. When he awoke he said, "Brother Mouse, I leave you this place." Thinking of his own new life, he added, "If you make a change in your life, something interesting is bound to happen."

The salt marshes were frozen. In the light there were iridescent, crystalline sheaths covering every bush and twig. Grass blades glistened in the morning sun that peeked through dark, rolling clouds as though they grew in a fairyland. When he walked against the crystal, it fell in tinkling, icy slivers. He broke through crackling ice in sheltered dingles, walked over slippery ice in rocky hills along the marge of Conwy Bay, and wished Annesta were with him. He hid himself under a thatched roof against a bitter wind and sleet. His eyes filled with tears. It was more than the wind that made him teary-eyed. He would not cry for himself; his life was much better than most. He had the belly-deep feeling that comes to men at rare times when they experience a natural earthly phenomenon as sunlight creating a rainbow interplay on clear, ice crystals when seen from different angles.

He blew inside his gloves to warm his hands. *If Annesta were here*, he thought, *we would look at this unusual beauty until it was too dark to see, then warm each other with pleasures of our lovemaking*. He skirted the village of Degannwy in a flurry of snow and passed rocky outcrops of the Great Ormes Head and the Little Ormes Head.

After seeing candle lights from a group of cottages near

the shore, he spent the night in a shallow rock cave. He believed the village of Abergele was a short distance inland and by the mouth of a small river, the Afon Ganol, that spread out like a fan before its water fell into the briny sea, and he would find a small place called Rhos-on-Sea.

In the clear, cold light of morning, the sparkling, snow-covered mountains to the south seemed less than a league away. Abergele was like a large croft with sheep milling around half a dozen buildings. At the river's mouth he found Rhos with a masonry quay holding a channel of icy riverwater that would be deep enough for small sailing ships, if dredged. He sat against the masonry, out of the wind, and imagined the quay busy with curraghs and other ships during warmer months. Suddenly he spotted part of an old clinker ship on the snow-covered marsh. Walking around it he saw it was more than bare ribs covered with dried slime, as he had first thought. There were oak slabs on the hull caulked with cow's hair spun into a sort of cord. He was sure it was one of his ships because it needed plenty of repairs. He sang, "No man has nothing but misery—somewhere there is joy."

On the clinker's deck he found the planking loose. The crumbly iron nails left wide, dirty brown smudges. *That is the very reason to use nails of deer horn in my ships, instead of iron*, he thought. Midship, like a pregnant mare, the clinker carried a bluff-bowed, broad-beamed coracle. The hull was elliptic; a wicker framework of thin lathes was covered with cowhide. It was small enough to be carried, bottom up, on the shoulders of one man and could be used for fishing close to shore. She seemed in good shape, maybe leaky at the seams, but tar would fix her. And then, he thought, she would ride the sea as lightly as a gull.

The clinker's mast lay on the deck, broken in half, but it once had been secured by two stays on each side and raised or lowered by the rotted halyard still fast in the bow. The leather sail was folded and frozen beneath the coracle. It would be a challenge to get her in shape, but he thought it could be done. His enthusiasm was high, and he clapped his hands. The cold, moist wind made his nose run; he sniffed, wiped a corner of his bratt under his nose, and sat on the deck shielded by the gray, weathered gunwale. The sun shone through the clouds, and he heard the plaintive wails of the herring gulls wheeling in circles about the frozen salt flats and the low, sullen thunder of the breakers that spread white veils of mist across the gray-green waters.

On the sun-warmed side of the clinker, Madoc's brogues broke through the frozen marsh crust. He swore and pulled them out, making loud sucking sounds. He made mental notes on what needed to be repaired. He smelled smoke, looked around, saw nothing, and decided it was only imagination. He looked at the blue sky, grateful there were no dark clouds, but aware that the pale blue this time of year meant cold. He found an icy-wet cowhide rope, frayed, but not rotted, rolled in the bottom of the clinker. He tied it to the prow and used all of his strength trying to pull the old craft through the half-frozen marsh. He thought the snow and ice were a blessing because the ship's keel should run like a runner on a sled after he affixed poles, port and starboard, to hold the ship upright, but the afternoon sun was melting the snow. He worked the whole day pushing and pulling to get the ship out of the swamp and berthed on the bank under the limbs of bare willows. But the work was for naught. He needed help. He rested and looked at the tossing, white wave crests and felt the cold stinging his cheeks. He pulled on his gloves; walked around, looked here and there, and in the small river he spied a fish trap. "Jahoo!" he cried, hoping to see who set the trap.

Past a wide clump of leafless willows he saw a cottage made of logs and creek mud. Smoke rose from the stone chimney and dissipated into the wind. Melting snow dripped from the eaves and clumps of wet snow fell in soft thuds off the roof and off branches of beech trees with bark smooth as greenish skin. The low-slung hide door lifted and four men, dark and short, like true Welshmen, in long, dark gowns, like monks, came out into the sunlight. He ran back to the clinker, unrolled his blanket, and took out his black gown and the wooden cross he had worn when he was Owain's emissary to France. He put them on, tied his yellow curls to the back of his neck, and went to meet the four monks, hoping he could keep his breathing normal and say the right things. The four men said nothing but motioned him to come inside.

The single room was lit by dancing flames of a log fire. The walls had been covered with a layer of manure and thin, dried grasses and painted white with lime. A bunch of dried salted herrings hung from the ceiling by a cord, next to it hung a bunch of dried purple clover used to steep in hot water for tea. At first the sharp odor of urine hit him. In a few moments it was overshadowed by a stronger odor of musty, slippery rushes which covered the earthen floor and the subtle fragrance of a mixture of overcooked vegetables simmering in a kettle hanging beside the flames within the blackened fireplace.

Morgan was first to introduce himself. He had no teeth, but that did not stop him from talking. Glyn had no tongue and could not talk. Rhan was missing his right leg. Efyn, an alchemist, was blind from attenuating ferments of mercury. He could feel air vibrations and the least change in heat patterns so well that most folks did not notice his blindness—right away.

What seemed strange to Madoc was that all four monks knew Prince Owain had gifted him the old clinker and other old, rotting ships. Their prescience reminded Madoc more of druids than monks. He told Morgan he wanted someone to help him move the clinker to higher ground and behind some trees where it had more protection from the weather.

Glyn nodded and drew a map on the stone quay to show that there were other ships further up the mud-bottomed river. He showed by drawing that at certain times the high tide filled the river so that ships could be floated out to the sea. He pulled his gloves off and threw his hands into the air to indicate that for a long time no one had been interested in the old hulks. His hands formed cups, like coracles, which he moved along the map's river to the sea. His hands were tar stained, but Madoc was certain that he saw underneath the stain blue-woad tattoos around the dirty fingernails.

Madoc asked Glyn if he would help move the old ship and rebuild it. "I would be obliged to pay you for your work," he said, holding out a couple of coins to seal the bargain.

Glyn's bony fingers dived into the coins, like a gannet shooting from the sky to snap up a fat fish in its huge bill.

Then he put the coins back into Madoc's hand and led him inside the cottage.

Morgan chuckled and said, "There is no need for coins between us. Some wise men say you can be certes of only what you yourself have seen or lived through. From now on, until something breaks us apart, we are going to live together. If any one of us makes a slight change, something interesting certes will happen."

Madoc thought, *Words come back to cling to me, like iron filings on a black soup pot. One can be certes of only what oneself has seen or lived through.* In the back of a stone fireplace was a black pot hanging on a tripod. Madoc guessed it was a porridge simmering that had been left cold all night. Someone had started it again by adding more ground meal or vegetables, such as peas, and a little water.

Beside the fireplace was a shelf of rough boards on which stood four glass porridge-basins, four glass beakers, and a jar of tarry salve. Leaning upright against the opposite wall were four sleeping pallets rolled in unbleached woolen blankets. Next to them, on the dirt floor, were rolls of musk-ox hide and short pieces of ivory in various stages of carving. Morgan said the four of them once bought a curragh in Dubh Linn and nearly froze to death sailing to the land surrounded by floating crystals, where they traded rolls of wadmal and sailcloth for the hides and ivory.

Madoc wondered if these men already knew that he, too, had been to Iceland.

Rhan sat at a corner table where he had a glass-blowing apparatus. From the bottom of Rhan's long gown a leather pampootie peeked out and next to it was a four-sided wooden peg. It looked like the table leg, except the bottom was covered with a leather pad so that it would not wear or splinter as he walked. Efyn explained that Rhan's leg was lost to a shark, and Glyn had fitted him with the wooden leg. With delicate maneuvering of bellows, Efyn kept a red glow under pale, blue flames in an open charcoal-furnace. By deft twists of Rhan's hand holding a tube, he pierced the bottom of the semiformed beaker. He made quick puffs through the tube that was connected to the hot glass, and like magic there was a drinking beaker Morgan said the beaker was for Madoc's use.

Madoc nodded and rubbed his chest and back. The fleas he had picked up from the straw in various lean-tos and barns were now warm and crawling.

"Lo!" said Morgan. "You do favor the Prince! I guess he has told you that you look the way he did twenty-five years ago."

Madoc did not know if he was irritated or excited to find monks with woad marks who seemed to know a lot about—the things he knew. "Prince Owain does not recognize me as kin," he said. "He is only interested in me making the clinker seaworthy. He believes I will be a trader for Gwynedd."

Morgan said, "We heard from a Moslem trader that Owain is deathly ill, not expected to recover. When the eclipse of the sun takes place, his life will be snuffed out. Have you heard about that?"

"Nay, I have heard naught. Who do you mean, a Moslem trader?" asked Madoc.

"Aye. Kabyle from Al Jazair. You know him?"

Know him! He had arranged for Madoc and Conlaf to get out of the Paris prison. "Ya," said Madoc, cautiously. "I met him in Paris."

It was not an ordinary thing, but no one seemed surprised to hear that Madoc had been to France. *Mayhap Kabyle told you about our blunder of ending up in prison,* thought Madoc.

"Kabyle told us that Owain's son, Cadwallon, was ordained Abbot of Bardsey, then he was blinded by the previous abbot, who was called Robert," said Morgan. "Owain collapsed from anger and the grief of another son suffering because of the bloody English."

"If he is the Robert I know, he is a spy for King Henry, a bloody pretender and impersonator," said Madoc. He thought that the terrible fate of his half-brother, Cadwallon, was another warning to all Welshmen that the king of England could reach out and touch anyone. His knees wobbled. He sat on the floor, grabbed his knees with both arms, and asked, "Where is he—the cleric, Robert?"

"Fled like a dog on the English freebooter's ship," said Morgan.

Madoc thought, *I sailed with that rotten cleric, saw him*

in the prisoner-hole on Lundy, on the streets in Paris, and take money from the English crown. He is the worst kind of New Religionist. His mouth began to dry like plucked apples in the sun. "Cadwallon? Is he still Abbot of Bardsey?"

"Nay, he died from his wounds. Patrick is Acting Abbot. You know him?" asked Morgan.

Of course, thought Madoc, *I have known Patrick since the time I went to Bardsey.* "Aye," he said and asked for a drink of water.

Efyn stretched and said, "Once we worked in the Dubh Linn shipyards, where New Religionists set fire to our curragh and sent us out to sea because we prayed to Lugh, instead of the Lord God. 'Twas luck that Owain was there and told the New Religionists that we were religious men and would eftsoon come back from death to haunt them. Owain rescued us in his fishing craft. If those New Religionists ever find out we live, they will turn as black as the inside of a calcination furnace, and foam with rage, like vinegar on limestone. We made a pact with Owain that when he was ready to rebuild the old trading ships, we would help whomever he chose to be chief shipbuilder and trader."

"Who are the best shipbuilders anywhere?" said Madoc, moving his thick tongue over his teeth.

"Glyn and I," said Efyn. "We are about as good as you will find anywhere around here."

That carked Madoc. "Anywhere!" he said. "Name the best shipbuilders anywhere."

"Aye!" said Rhan. "A triad that comes from Dubh Linn: Sigurd, Conn, and Gorlyn. We worked for them."

"I see," said Madoc, taking a deep breath, "I be right, you are four monkish pretenders—impersonators!"

"Look at yourself," said Morgan, with a twinkle in his eyes. "You dress in an Augustinian gown, wear the braiding of a marriage bracelet on your right wrist. You were fostered with educated men and yet talk like a crofter, using the phrase *I be* in place of *I am.* I hope you learn to laugh."

Glyn made a barking noise in his throat.

"A man needs to see the humor our gods put in front of us," agreed Efyn.

Madoc's mouth fell open and the corners turned up.

Efyn laid his bellows aside and put a hand on Madoc's shoulder. He let his hand slide down Madoc's back to feel the long gown he wore. He reached for Madoc's hand. His thumb ran across Madoc's calloused palm. Then his fingers moved lightly across Madoc's nails and fingertips. Suddenly he yanked back his hand as if stung by a bee. He drew in his breath and let it out slowly. "I feel proud flesh," he said and grinned. "So, 'tis true! You wear a long gown, and there are fresh lines around your fingernails. None of us is a real Augustinian." All four monks were laughing and showing off their honor tattoos. Madoc almost forgot that his half-brother, Cadwallon, was dead.

Efyn banked the coals around the iron porridge pot. He heaped hot ashes over salmon wrapped in beech leaves and said that the local crofters, fishermen, and villagers accepted them as monks. "The people in Abergele and Degannwy buy our glass beakers, basins, and bottles. Some real monks lived in this place before us and called it Llandrillo Abbey. Thus, we are a natural occurrence. 'Tis wiser to be natural, to fit in, than to boast of differences. Tomorrow we shall see what needs to be done on your clinker. You saw our salmon trap. Now we have a salmon supper."

It was the best food Madoc had tasted since leaving Aberffraw. Sometime during supper he felt he had known these men most of his life. He told them that north Wales was like dry tinder, ready for lightning to strike. "Only as long as Owain is alive will Dafydd's dragons not storm the royal court."

Rhan did a little jig on his peg leg and sang a battle song about Owain as he washed the plates and spoons with ashes and then with water.

Glyn laid a fresh fire in the fireplace, and the men, sitting on the floor, asked Madoc questions.

"Is Prince Owain more druid than Christian?" said Efyn.

"Some believe that," said Madoc.

"When he dies, do you think druids will bury him in a place of honor?" asked Morgan.

"Burial in the Bangor Church is the wish of Owain's last wife, and also of his son, Dafydd," said Madoc, eating flakes of salmon hiding in a crease of his gown and licking his fingers. He marveled at the events these men already knew. "Owain believes man discovers truth by reason, not by faith. Owain is used to getting what he wants by reason. When he is told he cannot have something, like a Christian burial—he will have it, not by faith, but by reasonable truths."

"So, you believe Prince Owain is spindle-shanked and gray-whiskered, but not an old fool? His mind still works, slow, but it can reason," said Rhan. "Good for you!"

"To tell the truth, if the New Religionists have their way, they will bury him outside the Church, as an outcast," said Madoc.

"Tell us about your wife," said Rhan.

"Well—a—so—she is a tiny, black Welsh lass, with big shiny, dark eyes. She is intelligent and reliable."

"I like a girl that is smart," lisped Morgan. "So, what is it like to—ah, you know, being fresh married?"

Glyn smiled and moved closer to Madoc.

"Ah, yes," said blind Efyn. "Tell me if I am right. You walked where the ferns gave way to saxifrage and vetch with those soft blue and lavender flowers tangled among the tall grass. There were goldenrod, honeysuckle, pink clover, and the ferns against the mossy bank of a stream that ran along a limestone shelf. She sat on the shelf that was shaded by beech trees and took her clothes off. And it was the first time your eyes saw—"

Madoc blushed and told Efyn his eyes did not see what he thought, and so close his mouth. " 'Tis not your business to know, nor me to tell what I do in private on a mossy bank!"

"Sad for me, you are right," agreed Efyn. "But we are men here and want to know what I imagine, or see in my head. Thou knowest thine aurora is blue and gold? So, let me finish. We know she was the delight of your desiring. Do not deny it—you wanted the pleasure to be everlasting, like a never-ending reflux condenser, but you could hardly breathe and so, for you, the pleasure condensed into a puddle of shivers. So, what about your partner, the tiny woman? I will tell you what I see in my head. She needs a steady flame, not too hot at first to amalgamate her pleasure. Methinks you are inexperienced and know not how to treat a woman with a strong energy field. She wants to be on top of the mountain to capture the rapture every time. So, here is my advice: Take your time, go slow, learn control, hold on, wait for her, reach the top of the mountain together—then let go. She will love you for that." He put a hand on Madoc's cheek. "Though I be blind I see that your blush is as bright as the red stone, the quintessence of mercury. If overheated the quintessence flies out and a puddle of quicksilver is left."

Madoc wondered why he was listening to this alchemist. Perhaps there was nothing else to do, or perhaps he was half enjoying the conversation. He inhaled deeply. "You got it wrong," he said, determined not to play the goat here. "I have had experience. I know exactly what to do. My wife not only loves me for that, but also for what I be."

"And what would that be?" Efyn asked with a chuckle.

"A man who keeps his word," Madoc said without hesitation. "I promised her a druid marriage, and it was the best of that—with ecstasy."

"How do you know?" Efyn insisted.

"You are men with imaginations," said Madoc. "I be finished talking about such a personal thing." The corners of his mouth turned up as he remembered the little squeal, much like a cat's meow, that escaped from Annesta's lips when they climaxed together on top of their mountain-of-rapture.

Next morning the men surveyed the clinker inside and outside. Together the men sang triads and rejoiced that they were not forced to haul the ship to higher ground on a mattress of brushwood. The ice had melted, and it did not take them long to place the old ship where Madoc pointed. Afterwards they took their gloves off to wipe the sweat from their foreheads. Madoc's hands ached from the bite of the wind and burning of the cowhide rope, but the first job was done and he had found four friends. Glyn and Efyn concluded that together they could have it rebuilt before spring ended. The sides and ends would be made higher to prevent heavy sea waves from breaking into her waist. On an old piece of vellum Glyn drew the fore and aft perspectives and said there would be a crew of six, but thirty men could easily ride in her. He drew the ship's interior. At each end of the hold were platforms, under which were pallets and skins for sleeping dry. The hold, thirteen-ells long, would be reached by a ladder and be large enough for a pile of stones for ballast, several dozen barrels or crates of trade goods, as well as a few sheep or cattle with their fodder. She would be like a half-skip equipped with a solid single mast, new square sail, and oak rudder. She would be held together with pins of stag horn. The oar holes would have new shutters to keep out the sea. Madoc wanted her so well built that she could last as long as thirty years and travel from as far away as France and Iceland and somewhere yet unknown.

Madoc studied the drawings. Morgan went up the creek and found a great, round stone to use as the bow-anchor after a hole was bored, through which a twisted, sealskin rope could be pulled.

Rhan knew where there was a tree trunk nearly an ell in diameter that could be rested in sockets on the stern deck. Four sticks could be placed in each end of the trunk. To hoist the sail, the rope would be wrapped around the four sticks; two sailors could haul up so, then the sailspar.

Madoc named his clinker ship *Gwennan Gorn*, meaning *White Horn* because he insisted that white stag horn always be used in place of nails. They worked on the ship using all the daylight available.

Efyn knew how to dope flax fibers in tannin so they would not rot when used as caulking. The five of them braided doped flax ropes and soaked them for weeks in whale oil for waterproofing and pliancy. The one-room abbey smelled so strong of whale oil that even in the coolest evenings the door was left open. They pulled out the clinker's old cow's hair cordage and stuffed in newly doped flax.

One day the wind blew a misty rain in their faces, and Morgan suggested they leave the ship for the afternoon and hike further up the creek to investigate the other sails. As they walked Efyn told a funny story.

"You want to know how I make sapphires?" he said. "I put white quartz pebbles into a red hot furnace for half a day, cool them in water, grind to a powder, mix with salt of tartar, soda, and granulated brass, add a little water and make into little balls. Heat the balls six hours in a reverberation furnace, increasing the heat until they are red hot. When they cool, you have beautiful deep-blue stones, like beads. Ha, ha! To turn a sapphire to diamond, just place it in the midst of melted gold. When heated the color fades. Before I lost my eyesight, I used to make stones that were red on one side and green on the other. I once gave Prince Owain a few sapphires and a rather large diamond to give to his friend Thomas Becket to celebrate his coronation as Archbishop. When Thomas found that the stones were counterfeit, he sent them to King Henry II. Henry was so impressed with the *rich* gifts that he became generous with gifts of money to Thomas. Later Thomas asked Owain for a handful of amethysts to be sent as a gift to the Holy Father in Rome. In my head, right now, I see Thomas stuttering and Owain laughing until tears run down their cheeks. Beautiful counterfeit jewels! What a wonderful, precious prank to play on a paunchy king with bloodshot eyes and an unsuspecting Pope! I imagine whenever those two meet, they enjoy remembering this."

Madoc learned how close Thomas of London and his father had been. He told himself it was up to him to keep his wits sharp while he was in the company of these four counterfeit monks. "Oh Lugh!" he said with a smile. "I want to say something." Everyone stopped laughing. " 'Tis not comfortable if thirty men sleep with their hands on their knees and their chin on their hands. Can we add length and width to my clinker?"

The four pretend monks had already suspected that Madoc wanted his clinker to be the biggest and best. "Certes," said Rhan. "No trouble for us, the most famous shipbuilders here."

Madoc found two more ships that sat in the mud of the tidal flats, both smaller than the clinker. At first he thought none of the ships were seaworthy, nor of any value except for spare parts. He searched each vessel carefully and by the second day found more, and was convinced that four or five of the larger vessels could be overhauled and made into valuable trading ships. One of the small ships was narrow, shallow-draught, and suitable for calm coastal waters.

She would be fast and easily propelled because of her narrow shape. Oars were not her only means of power; there were four large iron rings on each side fastened to the ribs aft of midship that fastened the lines that supported the mast. A single sail would be easy for Glyn to make with his fine, bone needle. He pictured this ship as a slender curragh, to be used for sailing to Ireland, Scotland, through the Hebrides, Orkneys, Shetlands, and Faeroes. If it was fast and well built, there was no telling how far it could sail. People would stand on the wharf waving, eager to see the trade goods she carried. He hummed a ditty and found thirty feet of rusty iron chain fastened to a huge stone anchor, which in turn was fastened to a hawser that was useable. He found a bucket of foul-smelling whale oil on a cog with a broad deck and rubbed it over the chain to save it from further rust. Another ship had a crossbeam placed higher than usual that supported the mast and strengthened the ship's sides. There were no knees fastened to this crossbeam and no extra ribs, instead the upper planking was reinforced inside lengthwise. Madoc was as excited about rebuilding these old, rotting ships as his friend Conlaf had been about healing the stinking lepers on the road to Paris.

Rhan's favorite ship had an open hold around her mast, with decking fore and aft. Her prow had an illusion of overlapping timbers, but in fact, she was carved out of a whole piece of timber. Oar holes were fore and aft, but not amidships. Another had oar-holes the whole length and a wooden dolphin head carved on her prow.

Of course, he thought, *everyone at the Welsh seaports would know Madoc the Trader.* He dreamed that men would line up to be signed on as his seamen.

He had only a few coins left and began to wonder how he might earn more to pay for materials he needed to repair these ships. "If I had one ship, I would barter Rhan's glassware for charcoal, stag horn, brass, iron, linen, leather, lumber, and all the rest needed to make a couple of other ships seaworthy," he said to Morgan.

Right away Rhan found a sandbar of white sand to make the glass that women loved for pendants and ear bobs.

Morgan repaired the slender little curragh with a new layer of skin and a bucket of tar to keep her waterproof.

Madoc used her for shoreline trading and fishing for dabs
for their supper. He went to Llandudno where he heard
rumors that there had been fierce fighting around Aberffraw
between Dafydd and Owain's dragons.

He went to Colwyn Bay to borrow more buckets for tar.
He showed the bucket-man his records kept on a scroll and
told him to put his mark beside the account entry. The man
said he would not lend good buckets against fancy glass
trinkets for collateral. Madoc said Prince Owain was backing his trading operation and that guaranteed the man
would get the coins owed. He was laughed at, jeered, and
hooted off the wharf. He overheard in Colwyn Bay that
Owain had been locked in his chamber because his mind
had gone and left him stark-staring mad.

The last day of December 1169, Madoc sensed something
unusual happening as daylight dimmed with no clouds in the
sky. The daylight became a saffron yellow. No birds chirped,
and Madoc looked up for an instant to see a copper-colored
moon sliding across the face of the sun. He looked away
and sat under a tree to watch the multiple shadows of the
eclipse that came through multiple small openings between
the bare branches. The sun became a mere slice of itself,
then its whole face was hidden. Slowly the moon glided
away and let the sun shine again. Druid training taught
Madoc that if a person watched the eerie fringe of light the
sun left around the moon during an eclipse, he would become blind.

Efyn did not believe the fearful fringe of light came from
the moon's glow. "The moon covers the sun's face, but we
still see the sun's fiery fringe," he said. "If all men knew
such phenomena were predictable, they would be less fearful about natural events."

Madoc sailed alone to Degannwy in the little trading-
curragh, where among the small hills were restless carpets
of chirping gray birds that flew into whirling clouds of
squealing, black-and-white wings when he passed close by.
He learned to listen for wave sounds or echoes off the
rocks. He tuned his senses and estimated his position by
the wind change as it deflected from a seen or an unseen
headland. Between two tall hills, made of solid black out-

croppings, was the sprawling court, surrounded by an earthen berm with a solid wooden gate at either end. Here lived his half brother, Lord Iorwerth, who was affectionately called by his subjects Drwyndwn, or Crooked Nose, because he was born with a misshapen nose.

Iorwerth was blond and blue-eyed like Madoc, but taller and quiet spoken. The two men liked each other. Iorwerth said he would pay coins for as many sacks of Anglesey Island grain as Madoc's ship could carry. His people starved because recent crops and crofts had been burned-out. He had stayed away from the squabbles of his brothers, but said he had runners who told him what was happening in Owain's courts in Gwynedd. It was true that Owain had been isolated. He was feeble and could not fight back.

The two of them decided on the date and place to unload the sacks of grain from the ship to backs of horses provided by Iowerth's crofters. This was a trader's dream. Madoc would supply the grain and Iorwerth would pay. Many people would be fed. Madoc would be able to rebuild a couple more trading ships. Iorwerth's wife, Marared, traded two cowhides with Madoc that he could use for ships' binding and hinges. For payment she took several glass bowls for friends and ear bobs for herself. She said she wanted a milk cow because foster children came to her with bellies empty of nourishment but swollen full of gas. He found a milk cow the last day he was in Degannwy and gave it to Marared for three more cowhides.

While in the town, he met a dark-complexioned, thick-chested lad named Thurs, who had a calm, reasonable voice and druid honor marks on the backs of his hands. Thurs was not more than sixteen years old, and he wanted to build ships. Madoc looked at the lad's sturdy legs and gave him two silver coins to go to Aberffraw with a drawing of the *Gwennan Gorn* on thin vellum for Prince Owain. "Owain will be pleased and give you a box of coins in exchange. When you return to me with the unopened box, you will build ships with me," said Madoc. If honor marks meant Thurs was as honest as he appeared, Madoc's worst troubles were nearly over.

Six weeks later Thurs came back to the Llandrillo Abbey, carrying the vellum, but no box of coins. He brought news: Prince Owain was dead, poisoned by King Dafydd. His body was taken to the Bangor Cathedral. Also, he said, Dafydd's dragons killed one of Gwynedd's best-known court bards, Llywarch, Annesta's grandfather. The old druid camp was empty. "People left Aberffraw under cover of night, like ducks leaving the pond in a storm," Thurs said. "The salty air is so heavy with smoke from burning fields that it seems textured. My Granny Magain worries if I be not where she can see me; so on the way here I stopped in Degannwy to see her. She reads the future in fish innards. One evening while preparing supper she looked at my salmon and said, 'I see you building ships with the trader-priest, who will pay his respects to his dead father in Bangor. The trader is a druid and worth your trust.' In the salmon's innards she saw us sailing, with broken hearts, to an unproved land."

"What does your granny mean by broken hearts and unproved land?" asked Madoc. "She knows you. Does she know me?"

"I can not say for certes. Sometimes she talks strangely; maybe that is why people go to the Inn by the Sea—to hear her extraordinary predictions. For instance, she knew I would break my toe before I stumbled on the threshhold. Ye know those boards that are put at a cottage's doorway to hold the threshed straw on a slate floor from sliding outside? Granny said if I did not stop my running, I would break a toe-bone on the Inn's new threshhold. I was ten summers, too young and hardheaded to heed advice. I ran, tripped, and broke my left big toe. It hurt like fighting furies. She pulled it in place and wrapped it tight. One day, just before I left, she said she would soon be visiting with her dearest Doconn, my grandpa, who has been dead eight years. I have asked myself why she was talking so curious. Did she hear voices? Was it a sign of old age? The day I left, with no warning, while looking at salmon innards, she said, ' 'Tis not safe to trade in Aberffraw.' As if I did not know that after hearing the druid camp was empty. She admitted that somewhere in that mess of fish guts she saw a couple of men looking for something in the Aberffraw druid camp. I knew she was talking about ye, because she said one man wore a long black robe."

"She must be mistaken. I be not thinking of going to Aberffraw," said Madoc. "I be going to Bangor to see where Prince Owain is buried." The more he thought about Thurs's granny the more sure he was that she was Magain, the innkeeper where he, an infant, and his mother had stayed long ago. Thurs's grandmother had given Madoc his name; made up from Ma-gain and her husband, Doc-onn. His tongue burned to ask Thurs about the women from the royal castle.

As if reading Madoc's mind, Thurs said, "After the sun's eclipse, druids from the Aberffraw camp and royal castle, including women and fosterlings, went to a safe-place in Ireland. After Owain died, Lord Howell became Prince. A few months later Howell was slain by his brother, Dafydd, who during the eclipse publicly declared himself King of Gwynedd. Dafydd said he brought the sun back by staring at the moon and willing it to cough up the sun. Even I know that he can not will the moon to cough. He lost his eyesight staring at the sun being eaten by the moon. Granny used to say that if I told a lie my tongue would fall out, not that I would lose my eyesight."

As promised, Madoc found Thurs a room with an old farming couple. It was close enough to the Llandrillo Abbey, so Thurs could walk each day to help rebuild Madoc's ships.

Madoc pondered the changes in Wales for days and worried about Annesta without her Grandfather Llywarch, and about Gwynedd without Prince Owain. His shipbuilding plans went in a swamp without coins! He began to yell at Thurs, who began to leave the shipbuilding early to work for the old farming couple in order to pay for his room and board. He yelled at his four monkish friends. His mind refused to think clearly. One night after sup he told Morgan he was going to sail the newly finished clinker to Bangor then to Dubh Linn to see for himself if his wife, mother, and the Welsh druids were safe.

"Too soon to go to Dubh Linn," said Morgan. He was afraid Madoc might come back by way of the Prydain Druid Camp in Aberffraw. Soldiers and headhunters were rumored to be lurking about the abandoned camp.

"You are telling me what to do?" asked Madoc, in a cranky voice, moving toward the door.

"Do not leave with a flea in your ear!"

That made Madoc angry, and he said, "Nail that flea to a cross!" He tied his belongings together in his gray bratt and slammed the abbey's hide door. The moment he was outside he felt lower than a snail's knees about leaving Thurs and his four friends. The night was cold and dark, with no moon in sight. The silence was like new milk, fresh and heavy. Every step was an effort. He was half-sick with worry about Annesta and where the next silver coins would come from. He stopped to look at the *Gwennan Gorn.* The old, heavy leather sail had been discarded. Thurs had found a torn, unbleached linen sail discarded by Northmen. Glyn mended it good as new and had boiled it clean. Efyn put it in a tannic-acid solution with a tarter emetic, then wrung it out and while it was still damp dipped it in hot woad dye to make it sky blue. Madoc sat in the bottom of the ship, dissatisfied with himself. He thought of the solar eclipse at the end of the year. Of course, the eclipse predicted Owain's death! He should have known Owain was dead! He closed his eyes and imagined taking his tiny, dark-haired wife, Annesta, and his mother on board the *Gwennan Gorn* to the Irish safe-place faster than walking the length of Anglesey. The night sky rolled out of the ocean showing a handful of familiar winter constellations and thousands of bright, twinkling single stars. The air turned cold and he covered himself with his bratt.

He recalled Morgan telling him to work with one commodity before going to the next. "First make all the hulls watertight by replacing rotten boards, planking, and ribs," Morgan had said. "Smear everything with tar. Then work on the masts and crossbeams, sew all linen sails, and make the canvas for forward tents waterproof. All the ships will be finished at the same time."

But, thought Madoc, *if I had my way I would finish one ship at a time, then I could trade for more goods to finish the other ships. My way is better.* He would remind them that the ships were his and insist that they be built in the order he found best. That should be that. The *Gwennan Gorn* had to be more than seaworthy. He thought about getting grain from Ireland and selling it to the lords of the Welsh provinces for distribution to the crofters. The crofters were used to good harvests interspersed with poor. But this year was different because some of their crops were maliciously burned and ransacked by their own king's dragons.

Madoc promised himself that he would sail to Bangor to see if his father was in troth entombed there, after taking a shipload of Anglesey grain to his half brother, Lord Iorwerth. Then he would sail to Dubh Linn to see for certes that Annesta and his mother were safe. He reassured himself that he could count on Sein, Llieu, and his druid friends to keep Annesta and his mother unharmed, but it was his responsibility to see them cared for with food and clothing. He imagined what it would be like to see his wife, to be with her, if only for a day. He tried to convince himself that sailing would be fine training for the crofters' lads. He tossed and turned, went to the masthead, and asked for a sign from the gods to show that his wife was safe. He stood so long that his legs felt numb. No sign came. A man has not only himself, but also good friends to depend on, he told himself again and again. Of course Annesta is fine, otherwise Sein would have sent word. He lay down and slept.

A humming sound awoke him. He opened one eye and squinted in the bright sunlight. He opened the other eye and saw Efyn standing over him.

"I knew you would not run away from your problems," said Efyn. "Instead of blaming us for no material to finish your sorry ships, you are going to help us find materials. Be I right?"

Madoc sat up, grabbed Efyn's hands, pulled him down, and asked if he thought he was a fool to run off in haste. "Be I still welcome here?"

"Of course," said Efyn. "The gods test every man from time to time. How he reacts tells if he grows or withers with wisdom."

Madoc got to his feet and said he needed poles to make a slide to launch the *Gwennan Gorn* into the quay. "I have been thinking of bartering my time as a teacher of young lads in exchange for grain in Dubh Linn or Duglass. Welsh crofters desperately need grain to fend off hunger throughout the winter."

Efyn embraced him and said he had become a real man by changing his anger into good will. "You worry about your wife. Your heart can sing because I know she is all right."

"You know that for sure?" said Madoc.

"Aye, I feel it in my bones," said Efyn. "While you are trading, 'tis a good time to pay your respects to your father."

"A bone-felt thing is hard for me to believe," said Madoc, with a twinkle in his eyes. "Unless you are telling me that your joints ache because of the cold weather. We will finish the clinker and then I will do that trading and sail to Bangor with a crew of crofters and their sons. I hope to find my father's bones honored inside the cathedral."

VI
Llandrillo to Bangor

1170 A.D.

There was an abbey here (12th Century) [Llandrillo-yn-Rhos, near the old village of Rhos] and a plaque recalls the fish trap operated by the monks . . . built over an ancient holy well and of unknown age. The chapel is tiny (11 ft. by 8 ft.) and services are held outside. . . . Traditionally it was from here that Madoc ap Owain Gwynedd (1150–1180) sailed with 10 ships and 300 men into the Atlantic. . . .
  —John Tomes, ed., *Blue Guide: Wales and the Marches*

After much scraping, sawing, nailing, and tarring, the *Gwennan Gorn* sat on log rollers, ready to be launched. Her beautiful bow pointed down a gentle, rush-grown mossy slope. Behind the slope the moors were grizzled with hoarfrost and underfoot the heather roots were crisp. A biting easterly wind frisked through Madoc's blond curls. Thurs and five Welsh crofters, wearing leather gloves, held the ship in place with thick flax ropes. Madoc inspected everything two or three times until he could find no excuse to wait longer. He blew on his red, work-roughened hands, pulled gloves out of the pockets of his black gown, put them on, and called out the signal to let the ropes go.

Going down the slope the ship started slowly then gained speed until she hit the newly dredged river. She made a noise that began low, like the rumble of far-off thunder, increased until it sounded like an avalanche of rock and ice rolling down a mountainside. She plowed through the bulrushes and horsetails, across the mossy mud flats, and slammed into the water that was pushed high up the muddy banks only to splash back into the stream. Nearby crofters watched from the top of the embankment. They shouted blessings, whistled, and applauded. Madoc said later that their cheers made the welkin ring. The gray-haired crofters, who remembered Owain's trading ships years ago, thought the sight of a clinker again floating next to the quay was spectacular. They laughed joyously while wiping the splashed water from their bratts and faces.

An old woman from Rhuddlan stepped to the edge of the embankment, pointed her finger at Madoc, and said that King Dafydd's dragons killed her sheep in the grazing fields, fed themselves, and left the rest to the buzzards. Madoc suggested that she talk to one of the lords of her province. She said that that was dangerous because the dragons used the ancient Celtic punishment of fire in a cage for lords or whoever disagreed with Dafydd. "If King Dafydd's dragons cannot find cages to burn the crofters in, they cut off an arm or leg and let the victim bleed to death," she said. "Dafydd and his retainers slit the bellies of men or women with woad tattooing and pull their entrails out so they hang like ribbons on a woman's dress. He torches cottages and barns, especially when the women and children are inside and the crofter is out of sight. His dragons eat the best parts of slaughtered animals and leave the rest for the wolves and buzzards to have their fill. What are you going to do?"

Madoc hesitated and the woman said, "You are a trader and will see firsthand what is going on. You are a priest and already know what is best for innocent people. I hear that the French king is not going to send his soldiers to help us here in Gwynedd, because our province king is no longer on his side, but on the side of King Henry."

"Yes, I heard the same," said Madoc. The words stung his throat. He was not certain what his role ought to be to stop the slaughter of innocents. He disliked any kind of harsh warring. Mayhap if he could get Dafydd to see the tragedy he was causing to his own countrymen he would stop his killing. But he knew Dafydd was hell-bent on cleaning out the Old Religionists, who were mainly crofters. Killing druids was a passion with him and King Henry. "If Dafydd is gone, there are others to take his place," he said. " 'Tis a dark time in the history of Wales. If any of you have a barn close by where some of my shipbuilders, who are mostly crofters' sons, can sleep, the lads will help you with your crops and give you more security."

"I can take four of your young shipbuilders to sleep in my barn," said the woman, holding up four fingers. "If they bring eats for sup, I promise to cook for them."

Atop the embankment a man, with stooped shoulders and thin gray hairs, looked like Death himself. He pointed his finger at Madoc and shouted so that all could hear. "Dafydd raises levies, stirs up revolt, makes unexpected raids, and takes for himself what should be decided by mutual agreement among the provincial lords and chiefs. I had my arms pulled tight across my back so they came out of their sockets. They left me to die, crying like a baby with pain. My wife pulled my arms in place after she climbed down from a pile of hay in the chicken coop. Then she fell over dead from a spear in her back, which I did not see at first because it was broken off at the spearhead. She had been raped. I went crazy for two, three weeks. My arms are still too sore to bury her. Now I pray for the second-coming of Prince Owain Gwynedd."

Madoc thought the corpselike man probably had little to eat the whole time he was hysterical with grief and pain. "My friend, there will be no second-coming of Prince Owain," he said. "You can work for me as a shipbuilder, if you let three of my shipbuilders bury your wife, and clean the chicken coop so that they have a place to sleep. You will be fed, same as my deal with the lady who spoke before you, but I cannot promise you wages, until I can find a way to get a few coins myself."

"I loved my wife, but smelling a dead person is not devotion," the man said. Then he was so grateful to find a lad who would remove the stink from his place by burying his wormy wife that he gladly offered his chicken coop as shelter to the lad and two others. He proclaimed himself a shipbuilder.

A woman said she had seen the pinched faces and round, gas-filled bellies of hungry children and the hollow-cheeked, famished adults. "Naught like that during the time of Prince Owain. In the fertile valleys there are blackened barns, cottages, and fields as far as the eye can see. Is Gwynedd to be a province of rubble?"

"No!" said Madoc. "There are ways to buy grain and distribute it to those in need, but it takes a wise man with trade goods and coins to do that."

"Praise Lugh!" shouted the woman. "I pray you are the wise man who can buy trade goods."

Madoc gave a silent thanks to Lugh, the god that not only held up all ships on the bosom of the seas but also directed their destiny in storms and fair weather. He held his gloved hands high in the air and blessed the day. "Praise the Lord of all gods, and His lesser gods for this fine day! The *Gwennan Gorn*, launched at the moment of highest tide, is only the first of several seaworthy trade ships to come out of the quay to pursue a favorable business among the traders at various Welsh seaports. Crofters! If your crops are burned out, 'tis not your failure. But if you do not plant your saved seed in the spring and your children go hungry, then 'tis your fault. This trader will give any man credit if he does not have coins for needed goods or grain. I will collect on your credit in a year. 'Tis time enough to grow one or two good crops before then. Is this man fair or what?"

There were shouts of, "Hooray for the Trader!" "He heard us!" "We heard him!" "Aye, he is fair!"

Madoc took measure of the size of the crowd and remembered what Dornoll used to say. "To be hospitable to one's guests is a measure of one's nobility. If ye are stingy, yer guests will mock ye, and ye will seem foolish." He added water and stirred in spices to make a half-barrel of mead a full barrel. He waved the dipper in the air and invited the crowd to have a drink.

The crofters praised Madoc. Their voices buzzed as they planned to purchase grain from the trader-priest and be indebted to him until they had coins from selling next year's crop. It was the only way to keep their families from starving.

Thurs sidled up to a group of crofters. "Did ye know the trader is a pagan, same as us?" He held out his hands. "I saw his tattoos, just like mine. I saved my granny from freezing in the snow the night she stayed overlong looking for a lamb and lost her way in the snow. She gave me my honor marks. You can be sure the shipmaster did something to help someone. He is fearless sailing a fickle sea. He is trustworthy, will sell your goods from one port to another, and give you your fair share of coins. He keeps a list of trades not only in his head, but on vellum, so you can see."

"Aye," agreed a man in the group. "We crofters are like him: fearless of fickle weather. We would like to sail with him."

Another said, "A trader with a ship with pert blue sails is a rare sight, but rarer still is a trader-priest who knows enough to quench a thirst with good mead. I wish I could go with him."

Madoc heard them all say they would like to sail with him. He looked heavenward. "Dornoll, Mam, I hope you can see these folks drink my mead as if it were the best they have ever tasted," he said.

Long planks were laid against the gunwales to load the generous, incoming trade goods: coal, slate, and sacks of salt, a few dried apples, salted lamb and onions, and a large barrel of drinking water. Rhan wrote everything down in an old piece of folded-over vellum. While the men worked, they sang. One man strummed his harp. Druids, especially the Welsh, loved music and believed it helped them work faster and better. They believed that the gods intended men and women to sing more often than cry. Children were meant to laugh. Efyn and Morgan told stories that were bardic poems, more like good, satisfying songs about the ironies of life.

The next day Madoc sailed on a beam of wind and tacked to make short distances. He checked every creak and groan made by the ship. His confidence grew when he found that his ship could roll around sideways and not be swamped like a much larger ship. He began to feel the shape of the sea when he was sailing. Behind his eyes he saw the hole that his ship plowed in the water. He saw the bow, not too blunt or too fine, dive down into a wave. It did not pound on the water or slice it so deep that it came up with a scoop of water to wet the deck. The stern was full enough in the hips to hold enough air to lift her in following seas. When

he could close his eyes and not only feel but see the movement of his ship, it was a glorious thing to Madoc. Whenever possible, the *Gwennan Gorn* was hauled on shore for
the night so that the men had a hot meal and slept where
it was dry. Madoc's first meal, while sailing his own ship,
was oatmeal porridge, butter, and onions. Besides Thurs,
the messmates were three lads from different crofts and
they were seasick at first. After two days they were well
enough to catch cod and mullet, and hang the fillets on
ropes to dry into brittle strips. Some of the strips they
pounded into a powder and stored. Hot water and butter
were added to cod-powder to make delicious, thick soup.

When sailing close to shore, the hairs on the back of
Madoc's neck rose if it was too quiet. Oftentimes he
stopped in the middle of a song and looked for a sign of
one of the dragon bands following him. He never saw any,
but he began to feel unseen eyes and hear footsteps. This
was not the way a man should sail, he told himself. A man
ought to let go of the things on land, not see, feel, or hear
them; he ought to surrender to the water to keep his mind
clear and look about.

In a cloth shop in Duglass on the Isle of Man he saw
Clare, the man who had given him, Conlaf, and Troyes
lamb-on-a-stick at the Harvest Fair in Aberffraw. Clare
spoke softly. "If I be found outside the *keills,* the parish
priest will give my name to King Godred, who is in bed
with King Henry, who will have me beheaded as he did
half a dozen other metal workers last week. The Isle of
Man is naught but a pawn between Scotland and England.
I be ready to go to sea where no one will look for me. I
ask naught but porridge and a place to lay my head when
'tis my turn to sleep."

"Are you asking me to save your neck?" said Madoc.

"Aye. I be saying you need a metalworker."

"I need grain to keep Welshmen alive this winter."

Clare's eyes fastened on Madoc's, and he said, "You
shall have corn, plus a ballast of lead, zinc, copper, and
iron bars before you sail this day, no charge, except take
me with you as you once said. I can make a well-oiled
hinge on a swinging door. 'Tis better than rolling heavy
cowhide up or down."

Madoc's eyes danced.

"All right," Clare said. "I close my eyes, and I see the gods leading you to a box of coins. So, pay me later."

Madoc explained to Clare how much he, as a shipmaster, depended on vellum. "I keep an accurate record of my trades and can recall much more about a storm or unknown shoreline if I stand at the masthead, draw a picture, and write a description. For one who began his education with memorization, it seems strange to be drawing and writing."

Clare excused himself and left the ship. Soon he was back stretching the first of four large pieces of sheep hide taut on a square frame. He scraped the hide thin with a *strickle*, a rounded knife.

"You stole that hide for me?" asked Madoc.

Clare winked and would not let Madoc make an entry of what was owed for the vellum books.

Madoc said, "Do you suggest that I run a pirate ship! Hey, I be no freebooter! I do not steal even if I have a need! I earn what I need or 'tis given to me by free will!"

"Nay, the books have been paid for," Clare said, meaning that Madoc had saved his life and thus the books were a gift. He said he had freely and fairly traded a copper bar, half the size of his fist, for the pieces of sheep hide. Twice he doused the thin skins with hot soda lye to get rid of the fat and grease. He sanded the surfaces with powdered limestone and left them to dry. Then he cut and folded each into eight parts, an octavo. He used thin boards on the outer binding to keep the vellum from cockling, or puckering, and made four books and a leather bag, called a *chemise*, in which a book could be suspended from a cord around Madoc's waist. The messmates used the leftover leather pieces as jar coverings.

"You and I think more alike than you know," said Clare. " 'Tis Lugh's luck that we sail together." He placed two fingers on Madoc's right arm below the elbow. Madoc hesitated until he saw Clare smile, then he was certain Clare could not be a thief and returned the druid sign of brotherhood.

Madoc kept the crew's names along with their duties in the first book. In the second book he kept track of the direction the ship traveled, four times a day. In the others

he wrote and drew what he saw and an inventory of supplies and trade goods and the profits on the goods. He discussed with Clare how best to carry more grain and dried
peas, which were in great demand in North Wales. They
decided the grain and peas could be more easily carried in
the cog-type ship that had a broad-deck and was still under
repairs. A cog was a slow sailing vessel, but did not need
a large crew. She carried no oars, but two long poles. Clare
suggested that oarlocks be installed. "Maybe four on each
side," he said. "I can do that or show your shipbuilders
how." He beached the ship on rollers, made oarlocks, and
mended the hull with hot tar and a concoction of fish oil
and pine gum.

Madoc traded four sacks of grain for a small bag of
sulfur and several sealed jars of white phosphorous powder
to make stink balls, in case they met freebooters who would
try to take their trade goods, especially the metal.

The *Gwennan Gorn* was close to shore when it entered
Traeth Lafan. The fog frightened the messmates because it
was so thick. No one could see the Lafan Sands. They
anchored in the afternoon, and heard the Aber Church bell
toll as it guided the ferry to and from Beau Marais, the
beautiful marsh, through the fog. This lack of visibility
made Madoc remember the last day of December when it
had turned dark because the moon hid the sun's face. Rumor said that was the last day of life for beloved Prince
Owain. Madoc felt an icy shiver creep up his spine as he
thought how delicate and precious life was to people who
admired and loved one another. The ship was anchored off
the coast of Bangor that evening. Madoc woke Clare and
put him in charge of the ship. He said he was going to pay
respects to the memory of Prince Owain and would surely
return before daylight. He paddled a small round coracle to
shore and tied its rope to a handful of bare willow stocks.

The village of Bangor was spread from the seashore up the
side of a steep hill onto the hill's top. Mothers and children
were a sorrowful lot left behind to fend for themselves,
because fathers and sons had gone off to battle. Hearing
babies cry brought on thoughts of Dafydd's heartless drag-

ons as Madoc furiously climbed the twisting dirt path past medlar and blackthorn bushes, past tiny bleak cottages and bumbling sheep until the land began to level off. The hilltop was covered with the thin evening fog and surrounded by a low hedge of plaited twigs, called *bangori*. He followed the path, past the outdoor fires under pots of stew or laundry, where barefoot, unkempt, sleepy children slept in mothers' laps and mangy dogs chased one another, to the wide open village entrance. He found the largest building and had no doubt it was the Bangor Cathedral.

In front was a stone cross, whose arms and shaft were connected by four arcs, giving it a wheel-like appearance. He had heard that sometimes a Relic of the True Cross was enshrined in the hollow head of such a stone. He was not a believer in such rumors because he had looked and found the stones solid. The cathedral's wooden doorway was carved with cherubs, vines, and crosses. He went inside where it was cold and dank. He followed the candle lights and stood, hooded in his monk's gown, to the left of the carved rosewood altar and in front of a marker that stated: *Here lies the remains of Gruffudd ap Cynan.* Gruffudd was Owain's father; Madoc's grandfather. He was a man Madoc never knew and had heard little about. He wondered if Owain looked like Gruffudd. He wondered if Owain, as a child, went to his father with his hurts and as a young man went to him for advice.

The entire cathedral appeared empty of another living person. His brogues groaned with each step until he stood still as stone beside his father's tomb. He could hear his own breathing as loud as waves lapping on the sandy shore. He did not know what he expected, but it was not this cold dampness and deathly quiet that reached straight into his beating heart. He sweated from the long climb and for several moments studied the newly placed gray-and-white marble marked *Owain ap Gruffudd Tywysog Gwynedd*, above the unadorned sarcophagus. He thought his father would have liked the simple arch above the plain white limestone crypt, but not the chill and loneliness of this place.

In truth his father's plans for the coffin had been much more elaborate. For months there had been talk among church hierarchy about moving Owain's coffin outside the church wall. Thus, the sarcophagus had never been sent to the stone cutter, but left blank. Only the lid had been decorated with the name and a few twisting vines around the letters.

The simplicity pleased Madoc. In his mind it reflected the powerful dignity of his father, when he first saw him, better than anything else he could imagine. Again he wished that he could have known Owain as a son usually knows his father. He wished his father could understand his own heartache as he watched the killing of people and farm animals become more and more widespread. He thought, *If Owain had been well, had not fallen apart and left Gwynedd vulnerable to a civil war, mayhap we could have talked as true kin about how to save our beloved country.* Madoc had so many questions to ask his father. *How can I protect my friends—your friends, the druids? How can I even dream of building a trading fleet? Does Gwynedd need a navy if English soldiers come to invade her in ships? With no money and few supplies 'twill take years of bartering for me to finish another ship. If you had known I was your son, what would be different? Would I be dead? I was a coward and afraid to tell you I was your son. Oh Lugh, the last thing I want is to have you disappointed in me.* He reached out and put his hand on the cold, smooth marble. *Must I accept the way things are? Is there something I can do?*

Then the thought of his half-brother, Lord Iorwerth, came into his mind. People respected Iorwerth, thought he should have worn the crown. Iorwerth would distribute grain to the people in need if he could collect it. He kissed the mouth-shaped hollow in the slab, wiped his hand across his face, and smiled a little.

Madoc turned, not expecting to see anyone. There stood a rotund man, handsome, jolly looking, lighting the lamp close to the archway protecting the crypt. He was dressed in layers of clothing. The final layer was an expensive pelisse, lined with white lamb's wool, worn unfastened over his white silk rochet, or surplice, which fastened in a straight band high around his neck. His ankle-length tunic was royal blue trimmed with gold thread. He wore gold-colored shoes that were like the softest kidskin slippers.

His dark brown hair was thin, making his fair-skinned forehead seem wide. His eyes were brown and crinkled with laugh lines at the corners. He wore a red silk cap, the mark of the office of Archbishop, on the back of his head. He carried a highly polished crosier with a gold patriarchal cross on the top. Madoc could tell the man was not used to bathing, because under the sweet scent of perfume there was the subtle sourness of sweat, urine, and soiled under-garments.

The Archbishop's eyes were calm, and his voice was sweet as church bells. "God's b-blessing and forgive me for not extending you welcome right away. I only just no-ticed your p-presence. May your p-prayers be-be answered with p-perfect fruit. I be-be the Arch-b-bishop B-Becket." He spoke with a distinct stammer whenever he put his trem-bling lips together. He saw Madoc's tatty gown and thought, *This unshaven, unkempt, fishy-smelling cleric has come to apply for the appointment of Parish Bishop.*

Madoc thought the Archbishop looked like a giant egg and put his hand to his mouth to suppress his smile, then he remembered his manners and signed the air between them with a cross, bent one knee, and said, "Bless you and may the Lord God give you health. I came to pay my re-spects to—" He wiped his face with the back of his gloved hand.

"B-Brother, I saw you run up the hill from the curragh landing," Thomas's stuttering slowed as he relaxed and spoke in a singsong rhythm. " 'Twould make any man sweat, even in a winter's b-blizzard. My heart leaps, and I be certain you are my new Parish Bishop. I welcome you." He held out his left hand.

Madoc looked at the ring on the third finger. It was gold set with an onyx, carved to look similar to the Archbishop's official seal framed on the wall opposite the sarcophagus. He was expected to kiss the ring. He bent, closed his eyes, and let his lips barely touch it.

Thomas was puzzled and looked at the monk carefully. It crossed his mind that this monk did not speak like a man comfortable with his words and if he removed his black *birrus*, or gown, he would show a strong resemblance to a

Danish heritage, same as his old friend Prince Owain. Thomas's brown eyes danced, and he said, "I get no material gain from letting you kiss my ring, but each visitor who kisses an old, dried ear of Saint Malchus pays the church a measure of grain or a grote of cheese for the privilege. Would you know if I held out the ear of Saint Malchus, or some nobody, or the shriveled half of a dried peach?"

Madoc knew the Archbishop's words were meant to make him smile, and the more he thought about it the funnier it became. "Pfft!" he said, managing not to choke and to keep a straight face. He rested his hand on the smooth marble tomb.

Thomas raised his hand, scratched his neck, and slid the hand under his many layers of clothing and scratched his shoulder. "If ever you wear a hair shirt remember this," he said, "God knows it can itch something fierce. I see you admire Prince Owain Gwynedd's crypt. That dear man was a true friend, a true chief, and a beloved leader. He never hid the fact that he loved the logic of the Old Religion."

Madoc was so surprised to hear an Archbishop talk of the Old Religion with no hint of grudge that he made a choking sound in his throat, as though he had swallowed grit.

" 'Tis no secret that Owain had honor marks," said Thomas. "We both studied Plato, Socrates, and other philosophers in our younger days. We were full of ideals. I admired his shrewdness. He admired my submission to God. He could not submit completely to anyone, even the old gods. Once he said he lived in a crowd, but did not have to live like a crowd. He prized freedom. 'Genuine freedom is intellectual,' he said. I shall always love that half-pagan/half-Christian prince." Thomas smiled warily, not sure what this indigent-looking lad was up to, bishop or not.

"Owain's mind was unsettled toward the end," said Madoc. "He had failed to control his sons. As a consequence, Gwynedd is cut into hundreds of pieces, chewed up, and swallowed by brother at war with brother."

"Aha, you speak part truth. What man has not failed at some things? The same is true with provinces. Gwynedd will rise again. For the love of God, failure is necessary in the succession of events. I see Owain's failure as the result of his forgetfulness of his own importance in the Great Scheme of Things. What say you?"

"I say a chief, a leader of men, should love his people as a father loves his sons," said Madoc, spilling words from his full heart. "A leader must understand people and be ready to celebrate with them in a time of joy. He should plan so that the peaceful times have the more length and breadth."

Thomas studied Madoc another moment. From his manner of speech he believed him to be someone more significant than what he seemed. "Brother, do you believe the Lord sent you to have tea with me in my sitting room?" asked Thomas.

Madoc made the sign of the cross and replied, "I believe in the Great Scheme of Things that some men meet and become friends—or enemies. I be your friend."

"There it is! Sometimes you speak like a well-born lord, and other times you remind me of a well-read, but poorly educated peasant; a miner mayhap or a herder or crofter. Why?"

"I be proud to use the speech of my first foster father, a man not formally educated, but wise from experience and hands-on knowledge. He taught himself to read and write and became a druid. He believed that not only young men should learn the sagas and myths and read and write, but also young women. I loved and respected him. He was my first hero. I owe him so much, but he no longer lives. One way I chose to keep his memory forever alive is to use *be* instead of *am* in my speech, same as he did. 'Tis a habit that would be hard for me to break. I learned from him how to speak Irish, a little Welsh, and the King's English. Do you find my English distasteful?"

"Not d-distasteful, or off-putting. We all have our peculiarities. I stutter." Thomas was certain this young man, who sat under the dark cowl, was not a monk and not his new bishop. It was a pity. Yet there was a familiar sound to the man's voice, an interesting logic to his words. The man was not someone he had met before. Why, then, was he familiar?

The sitting room was richly furnished. The chairs were

covered with purple velveteen. The walls were covered with bright tapestries. On a polished oak table was a silver bowl with fruit. Beside the bowl were silver beakers and a lidded pitcher. Thomas again startled Madoc by saying that he would do his best to see a Welshman appointed Bishop of Bangor. "God knows, we Englishmen are sure to scorn you Welsh as flighty, imaginative, headstrong, and quarrelsome. Might be that the *hiraeth*, a longing for peace, will be nurtured only by a Welsh bishop. In that case, 'twill take a wise man to tame Gwynedd's wild rulers." Then he said he had never met a cleric who sailed his own ship and pointed to Madoc's gown. "You cannot deny it, you are a trader with a clinker. I watched you come ashore in the coracle and thought then that Owain had always wanted to begin trading through the major Welsh seaports."

Madoc drew in his breath.

"Owain had a small trading fleet, when he first became province leader," said Thomas, again surprising Madoc. "English freebooters stole his goods, and the running of a province took all of his time and energy. Say, in this light your eyes are the same shade of blue as Owain's." Thomas did not wait for Madoc's reply. "The last time Owain and I talked was just before Christ's Mass, and he said he had found a shipmaster who would repair his musty, rusty trading ships. A shipmaster who would give Gwynedd honor and importance, he had said, and he predicted the shipmaster would soon have a fleet of ten sails." Thomas stopped and studied Madoc's face.

Madoc was caught off guard and shivered. He pulled his bratt tighter and avoided Thomas's eyes, trying not to tell him anything.

Thomas poured tea into two silver beakers and said, "God gave me a cold stomach susceptible to stress. Tea helps." He added honey, stirred, and took two sips and a bite out of a sweetmeat.

Madoc wondered if Thomas cheered himself with tea and sweetmeats, mayhap other restoratives. He thought he would leave as soon as his tea was finished, although he found the Archbishop fascinating, not at all as he had pictured in his mind.

"So, you are the shipmaster Owain d-discovered and loved," said Thomas.

Loved, thought Madoc. *Loved!*

"I have good eyes and see p-pain when you or I speak of him," said Thomas. "Did anyone ever tell you that you look like him when he was your age? You talk like him. You think like him. There is no denying it, you are one of his sons. I know which one! You are the second son of Brenda! She went to Ireland for a time after the triple birth. One of the babes never sucked air, Brenda reported that her newborn had drowned. Later she went back to Wales, where I met her and liked her immediately. And I suspected that the babe had not drowned, but was cared for in Ireland. Not many women, especially Brenda, would abandon their infant at such a young age. If Brenda had taken him back to Wales, Owain would have killed him. Owain's bard told the old folktale of Lug killed by his grandson. For more excitement the bard said if anyone spoke before the hourglass emptied, the words would be troth. That is foolishness, I know, but before the glass was empty Owain said he would not permit three babes born under the same moon to live in his court; he would kill two of them. And so, according to the old Law of Hywel Dda, he had to comply or else when grown, one of the living babes would surely cause Owain's death. I believe that King Dafydd caused Owain's death. Sometimes when I walk by his crypt I can smell the deadly essence of almonds. There is a story going about that he was poisoned with cyanic acid, something used by alchemists."

Madoc's heart went rat-a-pat-tat, like a drum beating time for a ship's rowers. He could not speak. It was too late to leave. He slid down in his seat. His face burned and his eyes watered.

"Did you know that Owain suspected something amiss with Brenda's story of her babe drowning? He loved women, but Brenda above all of them. He could not hurt her by finding the boy, only to destroy him," said Thomas. "For certes, Owain's spirit is looking down upon us today and knows that you are his son, and is proud to have a son who loves the sea as much as he once did."

Madoc bowed his head so that Thomas could not see

the tears. *Dear gods, mayhap 'tis troth that Owain knew we were father and son.* After a long silence, he rubbed his eyes and looked up. "Do you know Owain's son, Cadwallon, had his eyes pulled out after being made Abbot of Bardsey? The previous abbot, Robert, saw the deed done and returned to England on a freebooter's ship."

"I received a parchment from Brother Cadwallon more than a year ago telling of trouble at Bardsey," said Thomas. "He wrote that Abbot Robert left Bardsey for England somewhere. Then I received another parchment signed by Owain's Welsh emissary to France suggesting I make Cadwallon abbot. Even though Owain was dead, I was certain that Owain had asked this emissary to write the suggestion to me. Therefore I complied."

"I be the Welsh emissary to France," said Madoc. "I wrote on my own inclination. I did not know Owain was dead at the time. I did not know how black Abbot Robert's heart could be."

Thomas stared at Madoc. "Rob-bert?" His lips trembled. "Henry II, recently sent word he is sending me a gift, a cleric, Robert, Canon of Merton, to be my personal chaplain. I was flattered because Henry and I are not friends, surely not gift-giving friends. I learned this Robert was a clerk at Canterbury accused of stealing a silver chalice to sell for wine. Henry sent him to Bardsey Abbey to fortify the island with English troops. That failed, and Robert made his way to Merton Priory. Now Henry has the gall to choose my chaplain. I could choose my own chaplain, thank you. Yet I felt sorry for this Robert. If he is with me, I might change his dark heart." Thomas's long fingers drummed on the table. "You know for troth Cadwallon was blinded by Abbot Robert?"

"I do," said Madoc. "Robert killed Cadwallon. If I were in your shoes, I would defrock your gift-chaplain for a thief and co-conspirator with Henry in the military affairs of Britain. God would bless you." He wanted to warn Thomas thoroughly about Robert, but he stopped, thinking it all sounded somewhat gossipy. He was certain he had already said way too much. Thomas was intelligent; he would soon find out about the man.

"God bless *you*!" said Thomas. " 'Tis no secret how I

feel about that little rooster, Henry, with the gray, bloodshot eyes. He has a dark, reddish complexion, a large, round head and a larger paunch. As God is my witness, he once called me a lowborn clerk and cut off my monetary due. But by God's lips I shall fool him. I shall accept Robert, and in that way I will know what Henry is up to!"

Impulsively Madoc stood and said, "Archbishop, the Robert from Bardsey is like Catilline, the Roman mischief-maker, who in a fit of anger could use poison on his own mother. Please, do not get mixed up with a man like that. I be not carrying gossip, but speak true facts."

Thomas stood and said, "I am used to hearing facts with the sound of spattering mud. You heard me. I can make that sound myself and do. For instance, did I tell you how Henry loves hunting, but after a day on horseback he has supper with his court and never sits down before or after dinner? I read that he thinks standing after a hard day's work riding through woods and crossing ridges will shrink his waistline. Frankly he is no thinner and his legs and feet swell; proof that physical exercise is unhealthy." He squeezed his eyes shut, drew Madoc close, pushed the cowl back, opened his eyes, and smiled as if he had proven something else to himself. "You are the spirit and flesh of blond-headed Owain. When I last saw him, he talked about the monk who kissed his beloved Brenda. His hearing and eyesight had gone poor. He suspected the monk was his emissary to France. He had a suspicion that the monk was Brenda's younger son; the one who is said to have drowned in his bath water as an infant. He truly admired the lad, actually loved him like a favorite son. It was ironic for him not to be able to say anything about his suspicion to anyone, except me. To tell anyone else meant he would have to chop your head off and your mother's! I do not believe he thought of his own death."

"My father knew who I was?" said Madoc. "He knew!" Then he quieted. "You cannot say a word about this, Your Holiness."

Thomas's dark eyes sparkled. He looked amused and kissed Madoc on one cheek then the other and wiped perspiration from his own face. Then his voice was low and mysterious. "Owain told me he promised to pay for repairs on the trade ships, located near the mouth of Afon Ganol, below the old Llandrillo Abbey. Did he tell you?"

Madoc felt the perspiration run down his back. "Aye, he said the same to me."

"The last time we met, he and I talked of many things," said Thomas. "For instance the puzzle of our own deaths predicted to be a year apart. He truly believed he would be killed by a close kin, mayhap one of his own sons. By last year's end it came to pass he was right. Thus, I believe I will be killed near this year's end. Killed not by kin but instead by a trusted friend. Friends talk to me over and over about God and His will. I tell them where there is too much talk about God—there is bloodshed."

Overwhelmed Madoc sat down; sipped his tea. His stomach churned. He wanted to do, to say something that would protect this man who had been his father's good friend. "You cannot trust anyone," he said. "Please, Owain would have told you the same."

"Mayhap you are right, my friend, but I will tell you a secret: Hildegard of Bingen, a mystical prophetess, who calls herself Sibyl of the Rhine, predicts disaster at year's end in Britain when a comet passes the Earth on winter's solstice. Also she says, with tears in her eyes, that is the moment of my death. I am a coward and would prefer to live long enough to die in my sleep an old man. But today I am glad to be visiting with you, Owain's shipmaster-son, who, according to the druids I know, is destined to become a Welsh hero, a savior of druids."

"That is surely flattery and an exaggeration," said Madoc, running his hands through his hair. " 'Tis like a bit of witchcraft, and I dare not indulge in such things. The Romans foretell man's future by studying the influence of the various positions of the moon, sun, and stars on human affairs. The druids study astral phenomena. Ages ago, when druid astrologers determined that Jupiter was ascending to shine within the constellation Aries, they said, ' 'tis the bright, morning star in the east' and when that symbol occurred, they predicted the birth of a great king, a messianic leader, who could deliver people from tyranny.

"You know that I be no messiah, nor kinglike savior. I be not a leader, nor was I born under the mark of an un-

usually bright morning star. I have been told that I was
born when the sky was under a triskele of clouds. However,
I was conceived under an unusually broad band of rainbow
northern lights. The bands of colors danced all around the
night sky making sharp, whipping sounds."

"I have heard about the time the night sky was so bright
one could read words on a roll of papyrus. It must have
been an unusual aurora," said Thomas. "The noises that
accompanied the colored lights, could they have been long-
dead elders speaking with their cold breath about matters
of great anxiety? Prince Owain believed the spirits of those
elders were telling him to rejoice, anxiety would pass."

Madoc smiled and his eyes twinkled. "I be a man of the
Old Religion, not the New, so we are friends and there is
no need to flatter one another. That is the kind of a story
a mother tells her small lad so he gains confidence in himself. It makes him feel important. That story has grown and
may now be called a druid myth."

"I listen to the predictions of today's wise men, and I
have admiration for all druids, Old Religionists," said Thomas. "I believe that my flattery is giving you, my special
friend, a gift, like the sweet smell of herbs. Flattery pleases
both of us, but you, especially, are not going to swallow
it." He chuckled. "Now I seriously ask you to help me keep
my word to your father." He excused himself and returned
with a small silver chest. Its lid was inlaid with wooden
filigree of spiraled tendrils and leaves. He laid the chest on
the table between them. "Take this casket or my conscience
will strangle me," he said. "No need to say anything. I
confess, if you had not come, I was going to take the coins
to Canterbury and buy myself a white velvet scapular with
lace on the strings and a baby baboon for amusement.
Shame on me. My time is short, so what is the point? Put
the coins out of sight, under your robe, my brother." He
blinked to clear his eyes, drew the sign of the cross in the
air over the table, and touched Madoc's hand. "Inside this
casket is your inheritance, your birthright. I thank the good
Lord, Who, in His inimitable way, brought you here today.
The last time I saw Owain he gave me this to give to the
man who was his shipbuilder. Inside are coins that will buy
materials to repair Gwynedd's trade-ships and more. Here

is an even number of small, thin, gold coins. Solidi are
rather rare now, minted thirty years ago in Rome, during
the reign of Pope Eugenius III. Most of the coins are of
silver, which were mined from the rich Welsh deposits of
St. Asaph and sent to the Canterbury mint through Owain's
influence. 'Tis a shame that Owain's profile on the front is
not a good likeness, but in God's honor the reverse has a
cross and my initials, T. B."

Madoc lifted the box. "Well, I—well, I—I—" He stuttered worse than Thomas ever did. He thought, Owain, his
own father, could have had his head lopped off in a wink,
but he had not. His father had truly loved him.

Thomas picked up his beaker and drank the last of his
honeyed tea. "You speak and write with the same keen
vision I admired in my friend Owain," he said, waving his
hand that held what looked like an ordinary prayer book.
"Owain lent this book to me, and I confess that I have read
most of it, especially what you say about Abbot Robert. I
want to give it to you for safekeeping before you sail away.
One day it may be valuable not only to druids but to all
sailing peoples."

Madoc now recognized the parchment cover of his own
prayer-book journal that contained the diary and notes from
his trip to Paris and back to Aberffraw. The parchment
cover was stained from sea-water, sweat, and candle wax.
It was rolled to look like a single scroll so he could carry
it in the bottom of his knapsack on the way home. On the
front page he had written in script:

JOURNAL, PRAYERS and NOTES
by Madoc, Emissary from Gwynedd

"Listen to this." Thomas licked his forefinger and turned
several pages. "Ah, here!"

Madoc braced himself, wondering if he had truly
damned himself by writing too freely of his own thoughts
of the man who called himself Robert.

"12 MARCH 1166 A.D.

"Last night could not sleep. Took a folded parch-
ment to the royal gate guard who could not read.

Told him the note asked the maid, Annesta, to bring hot mead. It was needed for someone in the druid camp. The guard thought it was an emergency. Annesta came out with a pot wrapped in a linen cloth and a mead-beaker tied to her sash. Told her to listen to the old beech tree. "It says, 'Swoosh,' " she said. "It bids me fare-thee-well," I said and told her I was sailing to Paris in the morn. We drank the mead. I said I loved the sea and laid my mother's silk scarf around her neck. The scarf brought me luck, and I wanted it to do the same for her. She stroked it like a pet kitten. At the court gate I kissed her on the lips. She is the prettiest girl I know."

Thomas, breathless from reading without once stuttering, looked up at Madoc's flushed face. "You were a bit of a devil," he said, smiling.

Probably more than you know, thought Madoc, thinking of his adventures with women before he and Annesta were married. He was relieved that Thomas had not read about Abbot Robert but wished that he would not talk about his private feelings toward Annesta. There were other more important things he had written in that journal to talk about. He was thinking about the interactions among disparate peoples that shaped societies. He had written about their conquest with swords, spears, or Greek fire. He had written about epidemics, such as diarrhea or smallpox; and genocide by poison, such as the fatal crushed-almond essence Dafydd had used to kill their father. He knew he had also written about humanitarian things, such as bartering goods for food and shelter.

Thomas's eyes were bright and he said, "I suppose every man goes through the age of romance. Actually I have been in love with Hildegard of Bingen for a long time. The lady hears voices and none of them are mine."

"Well," said Madoc, suddenly thinking that this archbishop was as interested in an ordinary man's love life as much as the four nosy, pretend monks. "Archdruid Llieu saw me come in near dawn and ordered me straightaway to clean out the *buwch ysgubor,* cowbarn, before going aboard the *Morlo.* Thinking back, I later decided 'twas a fair price to pay for the love of a lass to look forward to when I returned."

"You wed the lass when you returned?" said Thomas. "I pray you told her you loved her and that you are brave enough to forgive your brother, who is half-blind, demented, and waiting for the joy of kingship that never comes. I pray that you are honorable and heroic and return love for hatred." There was genuine sadness in his voice.

"I hear your words," said Madoc. "You are wise and speak from your heart. But it was my half brother, Dafydd, who killed my father. Love for that brother is hard to find."

"Life also brings joy, knowledge, and interesting memories." Thomas smiled. "For instance the day you and Conlaf boarded the *Morlo*, sometimes called the *Sea Lion*. The shipmaster, William Hume, a swarthy, heavy-set b-bastard—excuse me—with a black beard and black heart, did not shake your hands but ignored you lads, because you looked no older than fifteen-year-olds carrying brogues over one shoulder. And to prove him right you both unwittingly pulled up your monkish black gowns, which were supposed to hide the truth of your druidry. You revealed tight trousers and faded shirts as you climbed the ladder to the deck." He laughed. "Each of you carried a bundle that held your only tunic, a bratt, your prayer book, sealed briefs, bread and sack of goat cheese, and a metal spoon and knife. No monk carries food. He expects people to share food with him." His eyes twinkled and he continued to laugh.

"Well, it is still the custom for travelers to carry their own eating utensils," said Madoc, not knowing whether Thomas was laughing at him or teaching him a lesson. "Once aboard, I forgot about Master Hume and watched the ship's crew load a couple dozen sacks of grains; balls of wool; bags of indigo, that were dried dye-plants; half a dozen crates of white chickens, and six small Welsh horses. You are right. Being a pretend monk, I was innocent then and did not know the difference between a good blessing and a bad curse. While wearing that long black gown, I blessed every man I met, but it made me feel squirmy. What I loved was the feel of the loaded ship rocking from side to side as she sat low in the water. My curiosity about the ship was overwhelming, and I soon discovered that her oak planking was fastened to bent oak branches, called knees, by wooden nails. The knees were fixed to the cross-beams with iron rivets. The rowlocks were fastened with wooden pegs, called *trenails*. She carried a mast and a sail, which lay in a groove in her deck. The two red sea chests placed next to the last set of rowlocks was where Conlaf and I sat and slept. It was next to squawking chickens. Master Hume said, 'With each squawk the ship fell two inches.' When sup was served, a man with pockmarks sat on a sea chest directly in front of me and asked me to bless the bread and smoked meat. My stomach tightened, and I told myself it would be good to practice being the monk I was supposed to pretend to be for a few weeks. I spoke comforting Latin phrases in a slow, soft cadence as soon as I swallowed the walnut-sized lump in my throat. I even called the man *my son*, bowed my head, put my palms together, and out loud asked the Lord God to bless him and the food we were about to eat. My heart beat in my throat, and I forgot to make the sign of the cross.

"It took less than a day to sail along the coastline of Caernarfon Bay. During that first night there was a gale and we had to do some of the rowing. I wished I had calf-skin gloves to protect my hands from the sting of broken blisters. Master Hume thought ecclesiastics knew naught of sailing and said that an untimely jerk would break an oar or the tholepin. We heard the horses chewing the damp hay and switching their tails at flies and midges. Master Hume said to pray the horses would not switch their tails or we would ship water, and to keep our tongues in the middle of our mouths because he did not want his ship to capsize. The wind blew his beard so that it stood out like a black flag. I prayed out loud for calm and several hours later the wind died. I celebrated by bartering the rest of the goat cheese for a handful of linen rags to bind our raw hands. Both Conlaf and I prayed silently that we would not have to pick up those bloody oars again. The gods ignored us, but not Master Hume, who said we should lead in the singing of hymns that were familiar to everyone. I gave thanks to Brother Cadwallon who had taught us the round, *God in Heaven Watching Babies in Sleep*. This simple religious ditty became ribald when a man in a red cloak sang loud, licked his lips, stamped his feet, and gave us chary glances. We learned later he was the elusive Abbot of Bardsey. We tried to keep monkish faces and not show that we understood their innuendoes as they changed the song to *Dirty Old Men Watching Ladies Bathing*.

"Both Conlaf and I became seasick as our oars beat the sea through the fast and dangerous tiderace between Bardsey and the mainland. Master Hume anchored in the shallows, and the horses moved close to the leeward gunwale. One of the sailors eased into the chilling, chest-deep water and led two horses to shore and picketed them in the meadow of yellow sea-grass above the beach. A wooden ladder was lifted into place as a stairway into the water. To my surprise the wooden framework of a sleeping tent was brought out to cover the shipmaster's carved four-poster bed that was placed above the high-water mark. The abbot stayed with the shipmaster and rarely came to the abbey. The sailors fastened oiled tarps over their sleeping bags and slept two to a skin bag, near the tent. They set up a bronze cauldron on a collapsible iron tripod so that they could have sup before the wind blew sand into their food. Conlaf and I went to the abbey for sup and a bed. I met my half brother, Cadwallon, who looked startlingly similar to Owain. Without seeking the Abbot's permission, he surreptitiously gave Conlaf and me a week's worth of novice Augustinian instruction going to matins and lauds. It was hard getting used to wearing a long skirt. Brother Patrick was walking Death, because Abbot Robert permitted so little food at the abbey. Patrick is now well and Bardsey's abbot."

"Here is something you can add to your journal," said Thomas. "The abbey at Bardsey is the first in Wales, founded during the sixth century by a monk named Cadfan, and later was taken over by Augustinians. 'Tis said that *Myrrddin*, Merlin himself, is buried there, surrounded by twenty thousand other mystics, wizards, and holy persons. The pope promises special indulgences to pilgrims who go there. I told you I have read and reread what you wrote as you began your voyage to Paris, especially where you came to know Abbot Robert." Thomas read aloud again:

"19 MARCH 1166 A.D.

"*Abbot Robert wears a red silk cloak, confides in no one, espies on the monks, and keeps their food sparse. He says fasting gives a man a clearer mind to do God's work. One sack of grain, one crate of chickens, and a pair of horses left to graze in the Bardsey meadow were taken off the* Morlo. *Slate and lumber marked for Bardsey were to be sold on the Channel Islands which are being turned into English military bases, not only to attack north Wales, but also west Normandy. Robert is a keek who works for King Henry II, not the Lord God.*

"Strong language. I had to confirm what you wrote and I did," said Thomas, turning the page. "Next day you wrote:

"20 MARCH 1166 A.D.

"*Abbot Robert said he had been called to St. Peter Port on Guernsey, so came aboard with us. Robert has more power than the pope says Shipmaster Hume. The English plan to build a military fort on Lundy, where the bay can be widened for naval ships. Overheard Robert telling Hume that King Henry would convert the* Morlo *from a trading ship to a naval ship. Hume acted like a wild boar in scalding water.*

"Ha," said Becket, looking up, "and here is more from your own hand:

"22 MARCH 1166 A.D.

"*Worried that we will not reach the French king in time to stave off an English invasion of Welsh territory. Woke out of a dream, looked at black rolling water, nudged Conlaf, and asked about the smell coming out of the Bristol Channel like all of the world's spring flowers put inside a giant funnel and blown this way. Folded my hands in prayer and got up to see what was going on in the prow. Abbot Robert held a tray of fancy lidded-glass thuribles and an ornamented vial in one hand. He wiped his face and neck with a white cloth that was saturated with spicy oils. The smell was so overpowering it made Conlaf seasick. Robert groomed his beard and looked at the stars. I said it was a real blessing, there was no bilge, dried fish, or soured goat's milk smell. At the stern, where the pilot worked the rudder, was the abbot's trunk and boxes with water sloshing half way up their sides. I thought about his silk robes and fine undergarments getting wet and mildewed and the colors running together. I bailed the bilge and some splashed on the abbot's red silk cloak while he talked to us with a perfumed handkerchief in front of his nose. He asked if we would ask King Henry for coins to build a monastery. Conlaf sucked air, and I said we Augustinians were not concerned with money or wealth. Shipmaster Hume stepped in saying he had tarried overlong in Bardsey and would let us off on Lundy where we could catch another sail going into the Western Channel. I told him that the Prince of North Wales had paid him well to take us to the port of St. Valery at the mouth of the Somme. Robert shook bilge from his black boots and said that he dare not leave him on Lundy. 'King Henry will pay you in silver coins to take me to St. Peter Port.' Hume called Robert a thieving abbot and splashed more bilge on Robert's cloak. Robert's lips puckered, and he said, 'You must not judge, lest you be judged.' Finally Hume said he could let us holies off at Harfleur on the Seine.*

"That was an indictment of Abbot Robert, but this whole document is a fascinating memoir," said Thomas. "Most unusual for a druid to put thoughts in writing, but I know why you did. You wanted Owain to know exactly what you did as your country's emissary. 'Tis a story of different cultures. You found the Welsh are not like everybody else and were surprised that others in various nations are far different in all sorts of habits."

"Different not only in language, but in eating habits, agriculture, clothing, thinking, and religion," said Madoc, glad that Thomas had seen the differences. "They will take something from each other whenever they meet. That is what I tried to convey."

Thomas laid the journal gently on the table and then laid his hand over it. "So, this is a bit of history for the Welsh people, written by a man who has become wise, a druid." He pointed to the blue tattoos around Madoc's fingernails. "One day, when you and I are moldering in our graves, this will become something valuable."

"Nay, 'tis a fosterling's thoughts," said Madoc. "I was not yet a druid when 'twas written. But I treasure it. My father, you and I are the only ones who have read it. I thank thee for understanding my words."

"And I thank thee for the warning about Abbot Robert. You need not worry. Life is uncertain. How long we live is up to us and to God. All any man can do is to live well each day. Let us pray together at Owain's vault. Do you know his eyes are covered with rare triangular coins minted more than three decades ago by a man named Halli, in Caernarfon?"

Madoc said he had not heard of Halli. But he had come to Bangor and heard more than he had anticipated. "The gods were good today."

After the prayer Thomas said, "At Clarendon's Assembly Henry approved of an English law to detain Canterbury property. Owain and I protested that law and another law that gave power to twelve men in every village to tell what they thought of men in their village. Your father and I could only see the gross abuse of those laws. Thus, we protested and Henry found it his excuse to exile me. God bless Owain, who gave me permission to stay my exile in Bangor. In my old hunting clothes, I stood with ordinary crofters at his funeral."

"Did he, Owain, look—look good?" said Madoc.

"There is naught good-looking in death," said Thomas, wrinkling his nose.

VII
Hidden Valuables

1170 A.D.

Druids, generally speaking, did not take part in battle. Some appear to have had a personal retinue large enough to be called an army, or at least a bodyguard, but there are very few descriptions or instances of Druids actually fighting. They were, however, supposed to be so articulate that they could destroy a man merely by uttering a satire or curse against him. Whenever Druids appear in tales of battle or warfare, their role is diplomatic. They give judgements, approve or disapprove terms of settlement, and so on.
—John King, *The Celtic Druids' Year*

Back at the old stone pier at Llandrillo-yn-Rhos, Madoc manned the *Gwennan Gorn* with farmers and common laborers hoping to turn them into sailors. Because King Dafydd's men had burned Degannwy's grain fields, many of Iorwerth's people were hungry. Madoc contracted with Lord Iorwerth to sell him a shipload of grain he would buy with some of Owain's coins that Thomas Becket had given him. First his men needed practice before sailing a ship with a cargo of precious grain to Degannwy.

For practice, Madoc had them sail through the deep river called Afon Ganol into the sea. Like all ships, the *Gwennan Gorn* "talked." Each plank, beam and board, horn peg and dowel complained of changing tension. For most of the day the ship had no sail, but was propelled forward by rowers, who leaned over the boards and wished they were dead. These young men had cleared fields, used a scythe, hunted deer, and milked cows all their lives, but they could not keep their gorge down on a rough sea. Madoc remembered how it had been when he first managed something larger than a coracle. Had he been told beforehand, he would not have understood the importance of every small move. "Learn by doing" was one of his mottoes.

The wind pushed the rain into blinding sheets. Madoc struggled with a canvas cloak and hood waterproofed with tar. He stared at the swinging coracles and realized it was not the coracles swinging, but rather the ship itself. For an instant he felt a queasiness in the pit of his stomach. Water sloshed over the deck. His wool stockings, even wet, kept his feet warm. He stayed at the helm and shouted a warning to the crew not to let go of the line of ropes that was tied to the gunwales, or they would be washed overboard. He reassured them that the sea was not angry and was not looking to devour human sacrifices. "Rain and wind are normal when hot air from the south comes in contact with the cold air from the north. All you need is sailing experience. So, stay awake!"

Thurs hung onto the gunwale close to Madoc and coughed up everything in his stomach. His skin was white, and he cried that he was sick to death. The ship caught a gust, and it felt like a boulder fell out of the sky and hit the prow. There was a churning, roaring noise, and the water became harder to slice through. There was little visibility. "Why is the water so black?" said Thurs.

"Everything is black in a storm," said Madoc. "Help me hold the steering oar. Put your hands here. Hold tight. Keep the sea behind you and never allow the ship to put her side to the waves! Where is your rain gear?"

The rain bit Thurs's face. And he could not open his mouth to answer. He closed his eyes. He let up on the steering oar's handle, a bar of hickory wood, to wipe the water off his face. Madoc was gone! The free swinging bar hit him in the stomach, and his breath whooshed out. He opened his mouth to pull in more air, and his hands grabbed at the steering bar to keep himself upright. His hands fastened like steel bracelets onto the bar, and he spread his bare feet wide apart against the deck. He tried to keep the ship ahead of the waves.

Madoc was back with a tarred canvas jacket. He slipped

it on Thurs and pulled the hood up. Thurs did not take his hands off the bar to fasten the front of the jacket. Madoc smiled and fastened the wooden clasps. "I can take her now," he said. "You and the others are not seasick anymore. Therefore, you will be a sailor in no time."

When the rain abated, Madoc ordered the blue canvas sail hoisted. A sail running before the wind was like a giant bird sailing low and steady over the rolling sea. There was an eye-appealing smartness in the full blue sail clewed up to the spar. Looking from the shore it was hard to distinguish the blue sail from the sea. It was a camouflage that Madoc wanted in case there were freebooters looking for his ships or New Religion headhunters looking for him or his Old Religion crew.

Thurs looked at the blisters on the front of his tattooed hands and said he had one huge ache across his shoulders and as far down as the back of his legs. He told Madoc that he dreamed of a dry place to sleep during the night.

"Humpf!" said Madoc. "You are already dreaming. We are going to buy grain for the hungry folks in Degannwy."

When Madoc's ship was filled with grain, he sent Thurs to tell Lord Iorwerth to come with packhorses to the stone pier at Llandrillo-yn-Rhos.

But afterwards, and even years later, he could not remember everything that had happened when that grain was transferred as his ship was anchored at the stone pier. His books were in order, he had the coins for the grain, but things took place that he seemed to have no fore- or afterknowledge about. He could not remember sailing to Dubh Linn after the grain was off his ship.

The druids had seen the *Gwennan Gorn* coming back from Llandrillo-yn-Rhos and lined the shore of Dubh Linn's bay to welcome the shipmaster and his crew. Madoc shook hands with Sein and Llieu who came aboard to look at the ship. Both men said they were sorry. Madoc did not understand why they were sorry. When everyone else left, he stayed behind. He was reluctant to leave the ship. Caradoc, one of Madoc's boyhood teachers, now with gray hair and a long beard, came aboard and asked if he was the guard-of-the-day.

"No, one of my messmates is guard," said Madoc. "Look in the kitchen area."

"Actually I have spoken to Brenda and came to see why you were still aboard," said Caradoc. "Kabyle, the Moslem, who planned your escape from that Paris prison, spent a week at our camp, then he left with a crew of six men to trade along the Welsh coast. I think he wants to sell you his ship for the coins you have in a silver coffer. Why would a man wrap his head in a bedcloth?"

"In his country the cloth keeps the hot sun off his head," said Madoc, putting his hand to his head. "How does he know I have a coffer of silver coins? I have Iorwerth's coins from the sale of a shipload of grain, and I have a few coins left in a coffer from Thomas Becket—no, from Prince Owain. I—I seem to remember some things, then I forget them. I do not remember talking to Kabyle, but I remember talking to Thomas. I do not remember what we talked about, nor when he gave me the coins. After the grain was off my ship, I wondered where the beautiful coffer came from. What did Kabyle say? Did he or Thomas give it to me?"

"I do not believe Kabyle knows, even I do not know that," said Caradoc.

"Aye. It was Thomas who gave me coins aplenty from Prince Owain to buy grain and to pay my crew," said Madoc. "Your sky is covered by a thick veil of brown smoke. Is it from the burning fields in Wales? Or have New Religion soldiers come here and burned Irish crops?"

"Nay, neither," said Caradoc. "A ten-month before Prince Owain's death, on the island of Sicily, in the Middle Sea, not far from Rome, Mount Etna exploded. Blew so much smoke, melted rock, and ash into the air that the earth shook. Without warning, giant waves pushed sea-water inland. The sun has not been seen for weeks and when it was seen, weeks back, 'twas blood red. Summer grass was stunted because of no sunlight. Crops were ruined. Romans starved to death. The few people still alive near the smoking mountain think it is occupied by demons. The mountain is hot in the center and boils up once in a while, like water in a lidded pot."

"I remember seeing the same thing on a barren island not far from Iceland," said Madoc. "I never thought the gods would spread clouds of smoke far out over distant lands and seas."

"Actually, I am here to say how sorry we druids are for your terrible loss," said Caradoc. "Brenda told me." He held Madoc's head and wiped his face with a rag from his pocket. That surprising gesture, as something one might do for a child, brought a sudden, hard ache to Madoc's chest.

Llieu and Sein said they were sorry. "Please, what do you mean, sorry?" asked Madoc. He held his head in his hands trying to remember sailing from the Llandrillo Quay around the island of Anglesey, across the Irish Sea to Dubh Linn. He could feel the rocking of the ship, but he could recall nothing else that took place, even though he thought he had been the pilot. "Is there something wrong with me? I came to see about my wife and mother. When I see them, I will feel better."

Caradoc took Madoc's arm and led him off the ship and away from the people. "You brought Brenda and Conlaf's wife, Llorfa, here from Gwynedd," said Caradoc. "Do you not remember that?"

"Nay!" said Madoc. He hesitated. "The ship fell into a trough, and I thought the wall of water would spill upon—upon—those on deck and swamp the ship. Who was on my ship? I be not certes who was on the ship during or after the grain sale."

"Sit down. I am sorry to be the one to say that Thurs's grandmother, Magain, was killed by Dafydd's men in Degannwy day before yesterday. Archdruid Llieu is speaking to Thurs this very moment."

"I must see the lad. He is only sixteen," said Madoc. "He lived with his granny. She gave him his druid honor marks. Has Brenda talked to him?"

"Wait," said Caradoc. "Remember early this morning at Landrillo-yn-Rhos?"

"Aye, I remember King Dafydd and his troops tried to steal horses with sacks of grain," said Madoc.

"Mona, a handmaiden, was killed in the foray and your wife—"

"Mona, the little handmaiden?" asked Madoc. "No, Nay! What is going on? Please, where is my wife? I want to see Annesta!" He felt sick to his stomach.

"You were going to bring Mona, Annesta, Llorfa, and Brenda on the *Gwennan Gorn*, here to the safe-place after the grain sale. Remember?"

"No!" said Madoc. "I can not! Where was I?" His lips trembled. "I took women on my ship? 'Tis thought to be unlucky to have women on a large sailing ship. They are only to be carried on coracles or fishing curraghs." His heart pounded. "What is happening?"

"There were many headhunters wandering throughout the provinces. The four women, Brenda, Llorfa, Annesta, and Mona had been staying with Iorwerth until they could find a suitable ship to take them to Dubh Linn. When Lord Iorwerth came to pick up his sacks of grain, he told the women to board your ship and sail straight way for Dubh Linn. Climbing aboard ship Annesta was struck and killed by King Dafydd's spear. You held her most of the time while the Degannwy laddie, Thurs, threw stinkballs at King Dafydd and his men, who threw spears and arrows at your ship. Troyes, the lad from Paris, brought your ship here. Some say the spear that hit Annesta was meant for thee. Brenda has your infant daughter."

Madoc tried. He tried hard, but still he could not think straight. Daughter? He had no daughter. He did not believe any of it. He told himself it could not be true. He waited for Caradoc to say it was a terrible joke. Sometimes sailors resorted to such awful jokes. He could not remember his friend Thurs using stinkballs on Dafydd and his men, who shot arrows at his ship. Nor did he know that Troyes could sail a ship. He believed everything would be normal the moment he awakened from this terrible dream. The gods would not permit such dreadful killings to take place. Caradoc led him to a pallet, gave him something to drink, and told him to rest. He drank, but he did not want to rest. He wanted to talk to someone else. His eyes closed, and he snapped them open once or twice. Then it was too much effort to talk. He could not keep his eyes open. So he let them close. He slept for two days.

When he awoke, Brenda put baby Gwenllian in his arms. He felt awkward holding the infant, but he talked with Brenda about the weather and mundane things until the infant howled like a wolfling for food. He stopped mid-sentence, handed the red-faced baby to Brenda, and put his hands around his head.

She wondered if he was ill with some kind of sailor's contagion. She had seen that his mind could not hold thoughts nor string words into a complete sentence.

He could not tolerate being ill, so he had forced himself to carry on a conversation and not complain about a terrific headache. "I have decided to be a seafaring trader, like my friend Kabyle," he said.

Brenda held the baby up so he could see her face and said, "This baby is what you have left of Annesta. She is precious. What are you going to do with her?"

"I do not remember Annesta saying we had a daughter. I do not remember Annesta dying. I have no wife, but I have a daughter! What is that all about? My life is turned backwards. I can not care for an infant. Who will take this baby?"

"I will," said Brenda.

He gave her the coins from the grain sale mixed with those from Owain in the silver coffer. "This will help you with wee Gwenllian's care. I be a poor father. 'Tis the best I can do."

"Thank you," said Brenda. " 'Tis much more than I ask. Listen to your mam, you are not a poor father! You are richer than most with friendship and love from your people, the druids, and your mother. Besides that you have a destiny, larger than most men, to build a colony in an unproved land. Come back to tell us about it. We may return with you, if you permit women on your ship." She kissed his cheek. "Ask the Druid Council for a monetary stipend. They have a cache of valuable things not being used."

During the council meeting he asked for a loan. The druids reminded him that he probably still had coins left from selling grain to Lord Iorwerth and in the coffer his father had given to Thomas of London.

"I gave those coins to my mother," he said. "She is car-
ng for my baby daughter."

The council was mute as they thought about Madoc's words. Madoc rubbed his aching head and thought that was that. He closed his mouth, left the council, and went outside to prepare to go back to Wales to begin trading. He watched the full moon slide under a cloud and in a few minutes come out on the other side. Then he closed his eyes and thought on Gwynedd's beauty, before civil warfare and greed for power ravaged the province. Behind his eyelids he saw the wooded slopes, green valleys, damp moss, rustic stone fencing, white froth of a waterfall slashing through the forest. North Wales was mostly rock and the soil so thin that the stones seemed restless as they forced their way to the sunlight. Then there were the bogs. Because of the rain half of the province appeared waterlogged half of the time. Once on a hill he had heard the churn and gurgle of unseen water beneath his brogues. There were sedgy expanses of ground, half earth and turf, half water, with blossoming bog plants and buzzing insects. He loved Gwynedd and wondered how he could stand to leave and seek another homeland. That was not right, he did not love what was happening to Gwynedd's people by Gwynedd's people. If he thought too much, he could hate Gwynedd, but he would never tell anyone.

He vowed this night to keep Annesta alive by visiting her in his day- and nightdreams. Now 'twas his time to take fellow druids to a place where the air could ring with song. He was the chosen leader and knew not if he deserved the honor. Brenda was certain he did and said the dancing northern sky-lights proved it, as did the words of her midwife and the old innkeeper in Degannwy, who said he was destined for saving the druids. Madoc had seen auroras and talked with the innkeeper. All seemed ordinary, commonplace to him. What had happened in his life just seemed to happen. He was not different from other fosterlings, except that he had more foster fathers, and none mistreated him. He was lucky he loved the sea and his ships; they were now his life. But, by the truth of all the gods, he had loved Annesta most. The sea came second even when she was alive.

No, he thought, *I fool myself, but not the gods. The gods*

*know a man has only one love. I left my wife to build ships.
The gods tested me. I learned that a man gets no more than
he is willing to give. I was not willing to risk myself to
protect her. I depended on someone else to bring her
aboard my ship after I sold grain to Lord Iorwerth. I failed
to protect her, and she was killed by a spear meant for me.
Now my life is changed; I be going to sail to unproved land
and that makes me happy again.*

He did not hear Archdruid Llieu come up beside him.
He hardly recognized him with white hair and a thick grizzled beard, until he saw the tanned, smiling face.

"The council did not dismiss you," said Llieu. "Come
back."

Madoc nodded, but was not certain what more the archdruid expected him to say to the council. He stepped before
the group and said, "My friends, I be not running away. I
be leaving with naught else to do but repair decaying sailing ships. With half a chance I can be the best bloody
shipmaster any bloody druid has seen."

Llieu looked at the lighted candles on the wall, then to
the circle of men staring at Madoc, whose arms dangled at
his sides. "I did not accuse thee of running away." He laced
his hands together. "The council offers you help, but for a
price. Before fleeing the New Religion's headhunters in
Wales, we druids hid our valuables inside my cottage under
my reed rug. If you agree to go to the Prydian Camp near
Aberffraw and return all of the valuables, the council will
give you generous aid for your shipbuilding. When you
have a handful of ships, ten in all, fill them with druids and
farm animals, and sail us to an unproven land where we
can begin again with secure, free lives. You remember the
prediction made by ancient druids about a babe conceived
under a great aurora? The time augurs well for the fulfillment of that omen. We believe you are the prophesied savior, the foretold leader of the druids. What do you say?"

Madoc swallowed and slid his sweaty hands inside the
pockets of his tunic and held his head up. He stood there,
and he did not know what to say. He saw beautiful pictures
of Annesta and the Snowdon Mountains behind his eyes.
He could not say what he saw to the council. He had known

of the prediction since he could remember. It was something he did not think much about. He did not think he was different from other men. He was good at some things, such as mathematics, astronomy, and sailing. He was poor at other things, such as playing the harp and medical surgery. Finally he said in a faltering whisper, "I will do it."

"My foster son," said Llieu, focusing on Madoc's face. "I too lost a wife I loved dearly. You are not all right. Your mind has shut down. 'Tis temporary. Try to remember this: You are no longer a trader. You are a shipmaster and a leader of wise men."

Madoc frowned and drew in his breath.

"English soldiers and their sympathizers are on a rampage to destroy every person with woad tattoos. We have to break or circumvent the circle of terror, before the knowledge that druids have accumulated for centuries is lost. We tried for years, but cannot break the terror, so this is the plan: When you have ten seaworthy ships, each one will take on a six-weeks' supply of food and water, three or four farm animals, and about twenty men. You will lead the sails to an unproved land where men can be free to raise crops, tend animals, study, observe, and live without fear. Now what do you say?"

He thought of the words Becket had said to him about a druid savior. "I understand. I be the one to circumvent the circle of terror," he said. The truth of his own quick answer crept around in his clouded brain. The truth was that his wife had died three days before. He could see that truth on the faces of everyone seated around him. Now he was being asked to fulfill an old druid prophecy. He had never quite believed this day would come. But it was here and he had the responsibility to accept the challenge.

Llieu clasped Madoc's hand and elbow in the druid fashion.

"I thank thee," whispered Madoc. A smile flitted across his face. "Sail with me." Suddenly his throat opened and he called out, "I want you, the whole council, to be on those ten ships! You must suffer no more beheadings!"

Amid the council's loud clapping Llieu said, "Be assured your mind will release your memory a little at a time. A few from the council are ready to sail with you to Aberf-

fraw before the day breaks. There is work for you to do
there." He withdrew his hand from his tunic and opened
his fist to reveal a thong slid through a gold ring with an
onyx stone on which had been carved the house arms of
Gwynedd, three lions, one under the other, on a shield.
"You are kin to the house of Gwynedd and more entitled
to this ring than myself. It belonged to Prince Howell, bless
his soul, who gave it to me years ago for healing his tongue.
You saved his tongue by using the spines of sea anemone to
hold it in place. It was something new, now many physicians
use them to pull skin in place. You never had the dexterity in
your fingers to be a great healer, but you have the mind to be
anything. And there is no question, you are a Chosen One.
My foster son, wear this ring with the same pride you wear
honor marks." He slipped the thong over Madoc's head.
Madoc saw tears in his eyes.

The next day he felt the signet ring around his neck and
thought of the day his ship had been launched into the Afon
Ganol with no special markings on the prow and no flapping banner to arouse suspicion. Suddenly he heard a series
of trills from a harp and looked up to see Conn with a harp
against his chest. His thin hair was flying like wisps of
smoke in the breeze. Next to him a dark-haired lad, with
freckles that stood out as if they were splatter painted on
his pale face and arms, leaned over the gunwale. "A seasick
laddie who has been curled up under planks shielding the
aft deck," said Conn. " 'Tis the fosterling, Brett, whose
folks feared their croft, near Aberffraw, would be ransacked
and burned, so they took him to Archdruid Llieu in the
safe-camp."

Madoc gave Brett a bailing tin. "Work 'til I say stop.
No one gets a free ride," he said. The salt spray lashed
men's faces as the ship dipped and bobbed with the growing breakers. Half of the crofters-turned-sailors groaned and
vomited their insides out as the ship sailed south along
Anglesey's western shoreline as far as Aberffraw. "The
marshes at the coastline now under water were once dry
and occupied by fishing villages," said Madoc, trying to
help the men forget they were seasick. "I believe the sea
rises and lowers in a rhythmic fashion, over hundreds of

years, just as we know the high tides come in twelve-and-a-half-hour intervals, and the moon goes through cycles, taking twenty-nine and a half days to return to the same position. I have wondered if rains and snows are on a rhythmic basis, causing floods during one period and drought during another." He thought it was something they could study when they found their new homeland.

The *Gwennan Gorn* was pulled up on roller logs behind a dune that would protect the trade goods from the wind on Aberffraw beach. Two men set up trading posts on the lee side of the ship. One was Gorlyn, who had an orange-colored mustache that looked like shredded fall leaves, and the other was Conn. They acted like Irish traders and hoped to barter fish oil and dried onions for the latest kind of processed wool that had gone through a fulling mill. They hoped that one of the druid women at the safe-camp would knit them winter stockings from this new kind of wool. The wool was first covered with an opaque clay, tramped on so the absorbent clay removed the grease, and then washed to give it body by shrinking.

Clare and one of the outstanding shipbuilders, Sigurd, with his dark bushy hair hanging to his shoulders, were left in charge of the ship and her crew. Golden-haired Madoc and his friend, tall, dark-haired Conlaf, wore their Augustinian gowns with the cowls up to keep their faces hidden. Each carried a large, folded linen sack under his arm, for holding the valuables they expected to find at the Prydian Camp.

A pain in Conlaf's right side bothered him, so he used a gnarled stick to help him walk over the sandy street outside of Aberffraw. They were surprised to see crofters working outside the village. Some were standing over vats of brightly colored liquids; dyeing fulling-mill woolens. The crofters had long faces and no smiles. Children did not follow the strangers, but dogs ran alongside them barking and nipping at their heels. Looking from the outside, the village seemed to be hiding from itself. Madoc and Conlaf shied away from going inside the village where someone might recognize them. There were a dozen unfamiliar, unkempt cottages near the berm. Conlaf said he had heard that King Dafydd chose who lived where. He also chose what a man was to plant, when to harvest, and what taxes to pay.

Madoc pointed to the unkempt kitchen gardens behind the cottages and said, "Without their ancestral land, people have lost pride and are apathetic. What a waste!" They walked cautiously along the road, past a row of cottages converted to slaughterhouses, where yipping, scavenger dogs sniffed and snatched the smelly offal that was thrown outside. Further on they saw colored banners flying invitingly above open doors and heard laughter and song. These were brothels and taverns, a rare sight in the old days. They heard footsteps, looked around, saw a fleeting shadow, nothing more, and wondered if they were being followed. The thought made Madoc nervous and cautious.

Conlaf climbed the berm and stepped inside an open door. Sheer curtains hung in front of him. Behind the curtains women danced. A naked-bellied, dark-haired beauty did her best to entice him to partake of some obscene frivolity. "Come, Brother, ye shall see sights ye only dreamed. Do not worry, no one asks names or identification. See and experience unforgettable pleasures!" She patted Conlaf's sleeve and said, "Cleric! I will peek under yer gown and give ye a teasing chill! If ye pay, I will let ye peek under my skirts for a heavenly thrill!"

He grinned, scratched his right side, and licked his lips as though they were dry.

Madoc came inside and glared at the naked-bellied beauty that had her arms around Conlaf. "No time," he said. "*Chwaer,* sister, let my brother go before I call a gate-guard to say that your master is not paying his fair share in village taxes. This property on the berm belongs to the village of Aberffraw."

The girl stepped away from Conlaf as if he were a hot barley cake and disappeared. Conlaf had to run to keep up with Madoc, who said that he wanted to go close to the wooden palisade surrounding the castle's courtyard. "I saw a shadow and I think it belongs to the laddie, Brett. It shan't take long to look around and be sure. Then 'tis best to go get the valuables and leave without attracting suspicion."

Conlaf, miffed with Madoc for not letting him sample what the brothel lass had to offer, said, "If I cannot linger a moment with a beautiful, half-naked lady, you cannot linger in front of the royal palisades gawking at the outer bailey, looking for some shadowy figment of your imagination."

The road to the druid camp once had been a wide Roman road built with rectangular stone blocks set on a foundation of crushed limestone. Now the blocks were pulled away, used for fences around sheep pastures, and the crushed limestone was overgrown with weeds. They passed a standing stone with a stinking, headless body of a crofter tied to it. They held their noses and shuddered.

Madoc heard footsteps again, darted into a thicket, and pulled out a wailing, kicking laddie. "Brett, you belong on the ship!" he said between clenched teeth.

Brett trembled at the sight of his shipmaster's ire. Nonetheless he was stubborn. "I know ye are headed for the druids' camp. Tad's croft is not far and I want to see him." His smile was tense.

"How long will it take you to see your father?" asked Madoc. "You have an hour."

Brett nodded. "I will watch the sun."

"If you are not at the druids' camp within an hour, we will go without you," said Madoc, holding Brett by one ear.

Brett stuck out his tongue, twisted away, and ran.

"We have no idea who he will meet or what he will say," said Conlaf. "Lads that age are slippery as loose fish, and they believe everything a stranger says."

"Aw, he is just homesick and scared," said Madoc. "He will be all right once he sees his folks. Remember how you were as a ten- or twelve-year-old, all fire and no heat?"

"Aye," said Conlaf. "I remember the day our friend Llyn took his harp out to the dunes to compose a song and never came back. We found his body without a head. I am terrified of the dunes."

"And remember when we caught field mice so we could study their anatomy?" said Madoc. "One day you asked me to fetch a dog? You thought if you could see where a dog's innards were placed, you would be the smartest student Archdruid Llieu ever had. Instead of one dog, I brought two so I could study and know as much as you."

"That was your untamed time," said Conlaf, making a snorting noise through his nose. "But you could never get your clumsy fingers to separate guts and blood vessels, even when you remembered more names for the innards than I."

"You think you will go barmy having to sail with me, talking to you, giving you orders day after day, no privacy?" asked Madoc.

"Hell, no! You and I understand one another. We sailed south to Paris and north to Reykjavik. We can reread our journals. Llieu said you got yours from Thomas of London. We can talk about those times while we sail to an unproved land. You are the shipmaster, I am the copilot, Brett is a messmate."

The earth mound surrounding the druid camp was covered with runners of bugle plant with spikes of powder-blue flowers. There were uninhibited patches of sandworts here and there. The palisade was unkempt, in some places fallen to the ground, in others burned. The wooden posts with carved faces and bleached boar skulls were gone. The door was off the women's cottage, and the wattle and daub walls were covered with shoots of hazel scrub. Llieu's cottage was burned to the ground. Inside its perimeter some animal had marked its territory. The urine smell was strong. Near the blackened doorsill were clusters of white, starlike flowers on high stalks swaying in the breeze. The bruised leaves smelled like onions. Each man had a lump in his throat and would have gladly beat senseless those who had set fire and pillaged their old homesite. Madoc swallowed and said, "Maybe the local *gwerin,* farmers, did the burning so that Dafydd and his men could not thieve in the druids' cottages." His fists were clenched.

Conlaf cleared his throat and said in a whisper, "I do not believe that. The stones in the ancient circle are scattered and broken into pieces. Gwerin would not do that. The hut with farming tools is gone. Gwerin would save tools."

"You can be sure this was not a Beltane celebration," said Madoc. "No sign of cows or sheep. No carcasses, so none had been slaughtered out of anger. Brett will tell us

what happened. The table and little rug stood about here."
He drew a rectangle in the dirt after kicking more ashes out
of the way. With the toe of his boot, Madoc, tight-lipped,
poked through the ashes looking for something to dig with.
"We can dig with shards from the standing stones." He
scrabbled through the broken stones to find a piece that
would fit his hand and be sharp enough for digging. "I pray
we find the cache."

When they perspired, they took their gowns off and went
to the well for a drink. The well water was full of silt.

"You think people are using ground water for irrigat-
ing?" asked Conlaf.

"No, I think the water was used in fighting the fire," said
Madoc. "And I suspect someone has been digging around
here recently. The dirt is too loose."

"The table was more toward the middle," said Conlaf.
"Move to the right."

After two hours the men had dug three holes, each about
a cubit across and two cubits deep. Madoc stood on the
doorsill, again trying to visualize the location of the rug
and table. He was jumpy and did not like the noises made
by the wind in the trees. He feared someone might be
watching and listening. To keep himself going while digging, he had sung a song in his head that he had heard Lord
Howell sing years ago when battling Vikings had come to
confiscate Welsh seaports, as they had done in Ireland. He
and Conlaf were mere boys, who had hidden in the tall
grass, ready to give first aid to the wounded of either side.
In those days it was the unwritten duty of druid students to
study a smattering of medicine, whether they continued in
that field or not.

> "I love Gwynedd's court, its strong buildings
> And its brave lords who wish to go awarring.
> I love its strand and its snowy mountains,
> Its castle near the woods and its fine lands,
> Its marshy meadows and its green valleys,
> Its white gulls and especially its lovely, lovely
>   women."

Madoc hardly thought about the words belonging to his
deceased brother Howell. Now standing on the doorsill he

daydreamed that he was a druid fosterling, ten or twelve years old, and seeing his half brother Howell for the first time with a tongue nearly cut in half.

Howell had been short and barrel chested. His hairy legs were bare up to his knees and he held a six-foot spear above his head. His nostrils flared and his muscles flexed.

Madoc yelled, "Hold your weapon! We are healers, unarmed!"

"I be Lord Howell, future Prince of Gwynedd!" Howell's spear pointed towards Madoc's heart and glinted in the sunlight.

Conlaf picked up a dead man's two-edged broadsword and choppily cleaved the air backward and forward.

"Pagans!" cried Howell who had seen Conlaf with one hand on the ponderous sword as he tried to cut the tendons in the back of his legs so he would never walk again.

Howell's knees moved, and Conlaf was not able to keep up with them and balance the heavy sword. Madoc moved as close as he dared. He stiffened his legs and hit Howell on the jaw. Howell lurched and stumbled over a half-buried stone. His helm slipped off.

Madoc grabbed Howell's stiff, limed hair and pushed him down on the stone. There was a crack, and Howell fell onto the sand. His mouth opened and bled. Conlaf stood holding the bloody sword like a staff.

Madoc heard the squawks of guillemots flying above the sea looking for fish. He saw the bird's black-and-white wing patches. The sun's glare stung like it was white hot.

He sat in the shade of a clump of dog rose and watched Conlaf let the sword fall. He rummaged in the leather bag of medicines to find a rag to tie around Conlaf's bloody left shoulder, where Conlaf's own sword had hit its mark.

Conlaf laughed and said Howell was shallow-slashed by some dead dragon's sword.

Madoc's head ached. Nausea rose to his throat, and he waited for the dizzy wambling to stop. He trickled water from a goatskin into Howell's bleeding mouth and added a few drops of a yellow, syrupy liquid down Howell's throat so he would not wake up right away.

Conlaf placed a roll of linen under Howell's tongue and

*another in each cheek in front of his teeth to absorb oozing
blood. Then he pinched the flesh and held the tongue in
place so that Madoc was able to fasten it together with
thin, sea-urchin spines. The spines were something Madoc
had wanted to try instead of flax thread because his fingers
were not deft in stitching delicate sutures. The sun had set
and the air was chilly.*

*They buried the dead man under a dog rose. The lads
recited a poem about Anaraed, King of Aberffraw, who
lived more than two hundred years before and died fighting
the Vikings, at the grave of the dead soldier.*

> "This man will not enjoy a victory banquet of
>   boar,
> This man will not taste sweet mead.
> He will fight no more!"

*They laid Howell on the dead man's shield, made a litter
from poles shoved into the sleeves of their tunics, and took
him to Archdruid Llieu, who watched the healing of his
tongue before sending him back to his own army. Over time
the tongue healed so well that Howell saw his big dream
come to pass, and he became Prince of Gwynedd. Unfortunately, Fate gave him a short lifetime.*

"You think Howell ever sang again?" asked Conlaf softly,
sitting at the edge of the hole.

"Yeah, but he liked warring better," said Madoc, letting
his daydream disappear and digging deeper into the earth.
After a while he sat back on his heels and listened to muffled cries. Through his feet he felt the pounding of footsteps. He sat on his haunches ready for anything.

Brett ran between the oaks with his fists dug into his
eyes. He smelled like burned flesh when he threw himself
on the ground and grabbed Madoc's legs. His shoulders
shook as he sobbed. Madoc feared the lad had found his
parents dead. Mayhap burned to death. "An hour has been
here and gone," he said. "What kept you?"

After a few moments Brett said that his family's cottage
was a heap of ash and rubbish. "The barley field was
burned. The well was dry. There was no sign of sheep,

oxen, or people. So I ran to the next croft. It too was burned and the well was dry, but it held a beheaded, mutilated man's body with the hands missing. A small corner of the wheat field had tiny green shoots breaking through the earth. A badger stood on hind legs under an old oak to look me over. Then in a blink was gone into a hole between the gnarly roots." He tapped Madoc's glove that hid fingers tattooed blue around three sides of each nail, pushed his red hair from his swollen eyes, and said, "My tad is pagan. I thought they cut off his hands on account of the woad marks. I wanted to make sure, so I pulled the corpse out and took the left shoe off—five toes! My tad and I have only four toes on the left foot. I could not tell who the man was, so I turned a scorched wooden tub over the body." He tried to hold back the tears and choked when he said, "I swore at the bloody mutilators and prayed my folks moved to another cantref, far out of Gwynedd. They must have. I could not find them."

Madoc shook himself loose to give Brett a drink of silty water.

In a calmer voice Brett said, "There is something unnatural in the oak grove. I want ye to look. Come."

In the center of the grove was an oblong pile of last year's rotting autumn leaves, shoulder high. "Why would anyone do that?" Brett hiccuped. "Leaves are left where they fall. These are heaped up." They scooped the leaves away and found a two-wheeled cart covered over with musty skins. Under the skins were all the things that were supposed to be buried in the floor-dirt of Llieu's cottage.

Madoc gave a little cry when he discovered the bronze box that held Llywarch's folding balance, weights, and his door lock. "Llieu took it out so no one else could see how 'twas made!" said Madoc. There were small harps and lutes, a pouch with flint chips and steel rods for fire making, a leather pouch with precious stones, rubies, emeralds, and sapphires. Another bag contained garnets and amethysts. There was a bag filled only with pearls, which were especially sacred to druids. Brett found a box with moss protecting a dozen exquisite, clear, blue-glass beakers. Conlaf opened a wooden box that was too heavy to lift off the cart. Inside were ten gold torques, each one to be worn around the neck of a druid of high rank. In another were smaller torques, like the ones worn on the upper arm by Madoc and Conlaf when they were initiates. "This stuff comes in small boxes, but only a Titan can lift it," said Conlaf. "You could use it for your ship's ballast."

Neither man suspected that the druids had this much wealth.

"I bet 'twas Tad who hid this stuff!" said Brett.

"Looks to me like someone was going to come back and pick it up," said Conlaf. "Maybe take it to another place."

"When is Tad coming back?" said Brett, looking with expectation at Conlaf.

"Only Lugh knows when," said Conlaf.

Brett kicked at a large clump of leaves covered with black mold edged in gray-and-white threads. "What can I do? I'm useless!" His bottom lip quivered. He bit it and looked in the direction of his parents' burned-out croft. "Mayhap I be an orphan." Tears slipped down his freckled cheeks. He blew his nose on his shirttail.

"Your folks believe you are safe in Ireland," said Madoc. "When they are settled and it is safe, they will find you. Mayhap 'tis troth that your tad saved all this. He did a fine thing."

Brett beamed proudly.

Conlaf tucked the linen sacks they carried under the hides and relashed them as tight as possible over everything on the cart. The binding rope was loose. Madoc ran a stick under the rope and twisted it several times, then wedged the stick's end between the slats in back of the cart to keep the rope tight.

"Nobody, unless they be cracked, would want to buy these musty, mildewed hides or give them a second look," said Brett, pinching his nose.

Madoc heard the hoot of an owl. Owls generally hooted at night. He was uneasy and wanted to leave. He heard something, a dry leaf crackle, a twig snap, but he saw nothing through the trees. He shaded his eyes and stepped into the open to survey the surroundings. He mistrusted every noise, every bush and tree that could hide a dragon or two. "Yeah, that is the plan," he whispered. "Be ready, if anybody asks, these old hides are for sale."

"How can we pull the cart?" asked Brett.

Madoc and Conlaf spent a few moments looking around in the ransacked cottages. Finally Brett said, "How about those linen sacks? Braid 'em."

They made two lengths of braid from the sacks so that two men could pull the cart together. They put on their gloves and gowns and had not gone more than half a dozen ells before Madoc raised his hand. He was sure he heard voices.

At the same moment Brett looked back, saw the despoiled camp, and let out a great keening. It was a burst of grief he could not hold in nor explain, except to sob that he felt abandoned, left utterly alone to fend for himself.

"Crying does no good, so hush now," said Madoc, lifting him up so he could sit on top of the hides. "You want to sail and study with druids?"

Brett sniffed and nodded.

They stayed off the road and walked between the gorse. Madoc still felt that someone watched them. " 'Tis only wind soughing in the oaks," said Conlaf.

A moment later Madoc's feeling was justified. From behind the brush arose half a dozen foot-dragons dressed in heavy-mail vests over yellow tunics; carrying short-handled axes, spears, lances, and shields. The man, who carried a bow with arrows in a carrier strapped to his back, demanded that they stop. Madoc's heart hammered. He made the sign of the cross toward the dragons, who flanked them on both sides. The man with the bow shot an arrow into the air. It came down and pierced the arm of a dragon on the opposite side of the circle. The circle tightened and two other men tried to slash at Madoc's and Conlaf's legs with their lances, but the heavy weapons and mail vests made it nearly impossible to get in a good blow.

Madoc and Conlaf hitched up their gowns, grabbed onto the cart's rope, and ran. They knocked down two men when they broke out of the circle. "You bloody bastards would cut the legs of monks?" yelled Conlaf. They ran faster in an uneven line so that it was hard for the dragons hampered with heavy mail to keep up.

The dragons did not use their shields, believing that monks were not armed. But the one least suspected held a brogue. Brett stood with his bare feet wide apart for balance, whirled his brogue around his head by its leather lacing, and let it fly toward the nearest dragon. The hard sole smashed the man's nose. He screamed worse than a female mountain lion fighting off a wolf that was after her kits. The cart was unwieldy and difficult to pull. "Sit down!" yelled Madoc, who suffered an aching pain in his side that was hard to ignore.

"Keep running!" yelled Conlaf.

The dragons screamed for blood. One of them threw a spear. Conlaf was quick to hold up his walking stick to deflect the spear, so that it clattered to the ground and a wheel rolled over it.

Madoc could feel the sweat run down his face, stinging his eyes. This attack was a race for life or death. He knew which he preferred. He gritted his teeth to endure the pain in his side and told himself he could run through heather pulling a cart faster than a dragon weighted down with armor and weapons. His foot slipped and he swore as his ankle twisted, but he hung on to the rope and ran, as though hungry dogs were on his heels, paying no attention to the pain.

Conlaf let go of the cart's rope, kept running, struck a dragon across the shoulders with his walking stick, and forced him back with the others. One of the dragons yelled to gut the monk. "Lance him between the ribs!"

Madoc bit his bottom lip, ran on, and once was so close to Conlaf that they bumped shoulders. He grabbed Conlaf's walking stick and jabbed it toward the dragon who ran between them. The dragon tried to grab the stick and at the same time jump away from it. He was too slow; Madoc hit him hard under the chin with the end of the stick. It left a bloody hole in the soft tissue to the base of his tongue. The dragon fell to his knees, spit blood, and groaned. Madoc wanted to strike his head. Instead he kept running. He yelled back to Conlaf, "God's guts! I got him!" There were still dragons behind who intended to harry them until they stopped. The cart swerved, and Madoc feared it would topple. Each short breath he took burned his lungs. He was in a panic, thinking his lungs would surely burst. With all his might, he pulled the cart in the opposite direction to keep it from falling over. Glancing backwards he saw Brett swinging his other brogue. It hit the elbow of a dragon. A sharp crack told Madoc that the man's arm broke. Wearing a grin, Brett sat down without being told.

The dragon shook a fist and cursed the audacious monks whose black skirts flapped around their knees as they continued to run like the devil. Running was easier on the hard-packed road in front of the taverns, house of prostitution, the slaughter houses, and one-room cottages. It was nearly dark, and this time they entered Aberffraw. Madoc breathed hard and pressed his hand on his aching side, while watching the gate for pursuing dragons. He hesitated a moment to catch his breath, made the sign of the cross, and blessed the outside guards.

Conlaf told the inside guard that they were bringing in some hides to see what they were worth. The guard pointed to Brett. "My fosterling," said Conlaf. "He is ill." He scratched his nose and took a deep breath. "Say, can you direct us to an astrologer who can tell how long the lad will be laid up?" He remembered to make the sign of the cross.

"All persons, except monks, soldiers, and physicians are forbidden in the streets after dark," said the guard, gazing at the stars. "Anyone else is considered a spy or a pagan and beheaded. In your case I can tell you to try Trevor the Wizard. He is in a hut high on a grassy dune, not far from the wharf. Some say he is a mystic. I can only say he practices magic, like levitation. He has visions, casts spells, and reads the stars, if he is yet alive." He held his nose as the cart slipped past him.

"Bless you," called Madoc, feeling a wave of relief as they headed for the wharf. He looked at Brett's bare feet and pointed to the left one, it had only four toes. He felt giddy, pointing to Brett, and laughed out loud.

" 'Tis myself," said Brett and his face lighted. "I certes found something useful to do! Man, I be hungry!"

"Intuition tells me not to stop anywhere to ask for food," said Madoc. "But reason tells me we have not eaten all day."

"That is not reason talking, that is your stomach. I say

we follow intuition and eat on board ship," said Conlaf. "I want to stay alive."

Madoc put aside his giddiness when he saw two dragons carrying torches come through the gates and talk to the guard. "Hurry!" he said. "More dragons!"

A couple of dogs awoke and jumped to their feet when the cart creaked past them. They sniffed at the mildewed hides, jumped at the strangers, and snapped their jaws. Conlaf kept them away with his walking stick.

"I have never seen the village so dark," puffed Conlaf, trying to take as many short cuts as possible. "No lamplight in the houses. There is moonlight or we would not know where we are going."

A sharp exclamation from Brett made them look in the direction of the Church-with-the-White-Porch. Tied by their hair were human heads, nine of them, on the porch railing. Two had their eyes pulled out. Brett's eyes were wide with fright. He slipped off the cart, choked, and retched. His stomach would not stop its contractions.

Conlaf put his braided rope into Madoc's hands, rubbed the lad's back, and then carried him in his arms back to the cart. "The gods made good my words about you being ill," he said.

Brett moaned that he was too old to be carried like a baby.

Conlaf saw the torches coming closer. "Close your eyes. We best take our chances and go inside."

"You go," said Madoc, watching the torches. "I will stay with the cart and pray the dragons ignore me. Hurry!" Either to be recognized by Father Giff inside the church or to have to talk to the dragons were the last things he wanted. He pulled the cart around to the back and hurriedly wiped out the wheel tracks with his boots. His teeth chattered and his heart thundered. He could hear Conlaf talking to someone and the door slam. Then there was silence. After a while he peeked around the corner and saw two men with torches on the porch. He flattened himself against the back wall, but not before he noticed that several of the heads tied to the porch rail were women. He wondered why Father Giff allowed such a savage thing. A door slammed and in a few moments Conlaf was beside him carrying Brett.

"Father Giff stays at the royal court these days," said Conlaf. "The dragons came to visit the maid. Come on! Out of here!"

"Because I be ill the maid gave me broth," said Brett with bravado as he climbed on top of the cart.

They hurried onto the sandy beach. The cart was hard to pull. Madoc's heart jumped into his throat. The *Gwennan Gorn* was nowhere in sight. "Now I think *I* shall be sick," he said.

They stood close together next to a pile of driftwood for a few moments watching banks of clouds move over the hazy orange moon and heard the roar of the waves that drowned most other noises. Madoc pulled away and crept to the top of a dune. He heard the sound of cordage creaking with the sea-wail. He remembered that there were willows and gorse growing among rocks that made up the beach west of the royal court. He crept back and said, "I think I know where the ship is."

"I be carked!" said Conlaf. "The damned cart will not go through this bloody sand!"

"Go closer to the water where 'tis wet," said Brett, as if the solution should have been obvious.

Madoc put his hand on Conlaf's shoulder. "I swear I saw ships out there on the horizon, but the fog swallowed them," he said. " 'Tis better to sit behind the driftwood until the fog swallows us. Then we can move without being seen. I pray that is the *Gwennan Gorn* creaking behind these willows." The gray mist surrounded them. Brett whimpered, and Conlaf tried to calm him with a Welsh love song.

"I be going to check out the ship and get someone to help us pull the cart," said Madoc. "Do not move—either of you. Stay here."

As soon as Madoc was hidden in the fog, Brett climbed off the cart and wandered on the beach until he slipped on wet kelp and sat on a swarm of fiddler crabs. In a wink he was back beside Conlaf. He crawled onto the cart and went to sleep.

Madoc came back with tall, blond Tróyes, who told

them that there were five ships on the horizon. Clare told
Madoc it was best not to stay beached by the dune if strange
sails came in beside the wharf.

"We moved up the beach to the inlet to be protected by
willows," said Troyes. "One sail came in, blue as the sea.
She came close to the wharf. Shipmaster Kabyle came over
the side. I thought he was going into the brine, but he
jumped to the wharf and tied the ship with a rope. I waited
on the beach for him to come to me. He sat on the end of
the wharf and gazed at the sky. Then he lay down, like he
was sleeping. Finally he stood up. He saw me and waved.
I waved back. He pointed to the east and held up one hand
spreading his fingers, and then he pointed to the ships out
in the bay, there were four, but five counting his at the
wharf. 'Twas called the *Vestri*. He lit a torch, swung it
around his head, and pointed it east. I started to go to the
end of the wharf, but when I looked up he was gone."

"What next?" asked Madoc.

"The *Vestri* turned around and went straight toward the
four others. She went to the head of the line, and the last
I saw they were all headed south. The fog hid them. He
means to take the Menai Strait to Bangor or Beaumaris and
wants us to follow."

"How did he know who you are?" asked Madoc. "Did
he see our ship?"

"I do not know," said Troyes. "He could have asked
while he was in Dubh Linn," said Conlaf. "Mayhap Llieu
and the rest knew you would be coming here."

They backed the cart away from the driftwood, and
Troyes started to pull it across the wet sand toward the inlet.
Suddenly a strong breeze came off the sea lifting the fog
layer so that two torches could be seen coming along the
beach toward them.

"They follow our cart tracks," said Madoc. "Hide the
cart." He helped Troyes push the cart under the driftwood
and rearrange the odd-shaped pieces so it could not be seen.
They kicked sand into the deep wheel marks. When the
torches came closer, they ran into the salt grass, crouched
below an embankment, and smelled the smoky resin from
the torches. Two shadowy figures were clearly visible under
the torchlight. "Climb the dune!" whispered Madoc.

At the top was a disreputable-looking wattle and daub hut, not much larger than a bed-closet. The owner could look out the front door and see every ship that sailed into and out of the bay. Brett looked through a strip of broken daub and whispered, " 'Tis black as a whale's belly."

The torchlight shone on the beach not more than fifty cubits from the hidden cart. Madoc pushed open the door, pulled Brett and Conlaf inside, and closed the door. His hands were sweaty and his mouth dry. With hearts pounding they crouched close together around the fire pit. The intermittent glow of a single coal in the pit was hardly a light. Madoc crouched on a pallet of skins and held Brett in his lap. Above their heads was something dark that looked like clothing hung from the ceiling's crossbeam. Brett sleepily watched a tiny flame jump up and play across a shelf that held quartz crystals and several amphorae.

"We should have gone to the ship," said Conlaf. "This place is so small I can hardly breathe." He raised his hands over his head, hit something, gasped, and looked up. "My eyes can see enough to know 'tis someone swinging with feet cold as ice!" As the flame grew, their skin crawled and the hairs on their arms and napes of their necks stirred from the sight of a headless body hanging above them. The collar of a man's cloak was pulled high and tight around the neck with a rope. On the back of the corpse's white hands were tattooed blue spirals and half-moons.

Madoc smothered the little flame with the hem of his gown, hoping Brett was asleep and did not notice the corpse. He pried dried mud out of a crack and saw the torches moving along the beach as if examining the sand for tracks. "Maybe the gate-guard told them about us coming to see the wizard."

"I believe the guard knew the wizard was dead," said Conlaf.

Brett opened his eyes, looked up, stiffened, and opened his mouth. Madoc clamped a hand over his mouth and whispered, "Lookaway! Do not scream. The men out there maybe did this. They do not think we would stay here with such a thing swinging over our heads." He looked at Brett long enough to count all of his freckles in the light that came through the cracks in the wall. Then he took his hand away and said, "You are a fine lad."

" 'Tis the first corpse I have met that does not stink," said Troyes.

" 'Tis fresh," said Madoc.

Troyes breathed deep and said nothing.

Madoc closed his eyes and listened to the rising wind and the swish of the tall grass. Once he heard voices outside and someone walking through the grass. He held his breath and did not dare to even look out the nearest crack.

They sat in the dark, stale-smelling hut for what seemed hours. They were too frightened to drift over into dream-time, even though they closed their eyes. Before dawn the door opened and a huge man with long, Viking-silver hair came in. He left the door open; saw there was no place to sit, so he stood against the wall. His feet touched Madoc. "Dafydd's dragons are gone," he said in a mysterious whisper. "When fire is applied to the stone it cracks. We all have our breaking point." He stared at Madoc's gloved hands, smiled, took his gloves off, and held his bare hands out for all to see the woad honor-marks. "We can talk. Aberffraw is broken. No one comes out to see ships in the harbor. No harper comes to entertain with songs about Welsh heroes, news, and jokes. No one stands on the street to sell swish-swash mead nor the cheap shiot-drink made from brown flour. When I go out, no small boys come to mimic my walk nor make moustaches from scraps of sheep's wool."

"Why?" said Madoc.

"The head-harvests. People have fled the streets like minnows before the pike. A man who wants to keep fodder in his belly dares not go out. 'Tis a chore to be brave."

"But you are here," said Madoc.

" 'Tis my place. I be Trevor the Wizard," he said and shook his head. "Women are raped by the king's men on open downs so they might beget soldiers for his army. Those who become pregnant conceal it and secretly eat black-blighted rye until they abort. Others have sent their children to border provinces for fosterage. One day I was out gathering greens for sup, my wife and four sons were taken for a head-harvest, public beheadings. Their heads, with mouths and eyes wide open screaming, yet silent, hang for all to see alongside the white church." He drew a gloved finger across his throat and closed his pain-filled eyes for a moment.

Madoc shivered and suddenly saw, in his mind's eyes, his own wife with a gaping hole made by Dafydd's spear in the back of her neck. *Her open mouth is silent, but spills its warm blood on the deck of his ship. Her hair smells of sweet bergamot.*

"Lord Rhodri refused to give his brother taxes and so he is dead," said Trevor. "I heard 'twas King Dafydd himself did the killing. People of Gwynedd are held quiet through fear. Herod, Julius Caesar, Harold Hardruler, and others did the same. It works for a time, but in the end it blows apart. Makes a man like me not want to stand for anything. For days I waited for a ship going to Ireland. For more days I thought about my sorry plight."

"Mayhap this is your lucky day," said Madoc. "But if you do not stand for something, you will fall for anything."

Troyes asked if he saw the turbaned visitor at the wharf the previous evening.

"Ya," said Trevor. "I walked under the wharf. A man, with his head in a winding sheet, was there, looking for the shipmaster-priest. 'Tell him to go home, if ye see him,' he said to me as he lay on the wood slabs of the wharf."

The morning air was cold. Madoc shivered. "Home?"

"A ship can be home to some, but to others a quiet mossy bank suffices," said Trevor, grinning. "No need to shiver. My hanging man is straw. His hands and feet are clay. When the dragons open my door, they think I hanged myself and someone took my head. I always sleep outside in the tall grass with my knife and slingshot. I saw ye come. Ye were brave to stay all night with a corpse hanging over yer heads." He laughed and stepped outside.

Madoc put Brett in Troyes's lap, crawled outside the door, and stretched. "Sail to Ireland with us," he said.

Trevor said it was too late. He had decided he could not abandon his wife or his sons. "There are three more dragons who owe me their lives for the lives of my loved ones. I be greedy for corpses, not patient like old Job. I stand beside Sven Forkbeard. He conquered England in one thousand and fourteen and vowed to give no peace to the New Religionists. Farewell to ye. Sooner, better than later, I be bound for Valhalla."

VIII
Black Drink

1169–1170 A.D.

Black drink, a ritual beverage was a necessary part of all
important council meetings. . . . Black drink purified men of
pollution, served as a symbolic social cement, and it was an
ultimate expression of hospitality. . . . In their own language
the Indians called the brew "white drink" because white sym-
bolized purity, happiness, social harmony, and so on, but the
Europeans called it "black drink" because of its color. It was
made from the leaves of a variety of holly (*Ilex vomitoria*
Ait.), which grows along the Atlantic and Gulf coasts. . . .
—Charles Hudson, *The Southeastern Indians*

During the winter, Egret traded the use of his lodge to a
one-handed man, who had lost his left hand to a hungry
alligator, for his dugout. Nohold had been wise and pinched
the bleeding wrist together as tightly as possible with a long
vine that was twining itself around a sapodilla tree before
he fainted. That had saved his life. It took his nubbed wrist
from one full moon to the next to stop oozing a small dribble of blood, but after he made himself pull the skin tight
over the stump, it healed, even though it puckered like the
top of a closed leather purse with a pull string. Summer
went by and the winter rainy season began when he decided
to use his hunting traps for deer because he could not handle his dugout or an alligator with one hand. The high-sided
dugout was heavy and took two to portage it. The dugout
had been designed for use in estuarial water, with high sides
and a higher prow to keep it from foundering in choppy
water. Around the gulf the waters were only navigable at
night when the wind dropped. Water-skills and navigation

experience and knowledge of the currents were of prime importance if one was to travel prime fishing grounds or from village to village along the keys or the southeast coast of the peninsula. Knowledge of areas of dry land was always precious and could be life-saving in a wind, bad weather, and tides in the bays, sounds, river mouths, and passes. Nohold told Egret where poling his dugout would be safe or dangerous. They took the dugout out together in calm and windy weather so that Egret had some experience.

Most fisher folk among the Calusa tribe used a canoe that was bark- or hide-bound, that was light and could be carried easily by one man. Still Egret was satisfied that the heavier craft would suit him and Cougar just fine. They could carry more gear and travel in most kinds of water in safety.

The first thing that Cougar made that winter was a basket to carry the old blue-sky bowl that was now a firepot holding smoldering punk buried in ash. Next she made a rain-proof leather pack to carry oak-nut flour, another leather pack for salted fish, and one for dried beans. She laid out five bone fishhooks, a stick to dig roots, a stone knife, a shell scraper, three agate spear points, a ball of fiber cord and a bone needle. She had no idea how long they might be gone on their quest for Grandmother's son and reasoned that she and Egret would fish and hunt small animals while they went from one village to another. She decided to make baskets between villages to barter for fruit and flat bread when the oak-nut flour ran out. She told Egret that Little Mother and Otter would be busy with their own lives and would hardly miss them.

Later she thought how much she would miss the first moons of baby Hummer growing and that made her think of all the things Grandmother was missing. She looked around her lodge and saw Grandmother's old gray skirt and gray-feather cape. She wondered if Grandmother would be wearing them if she were alive and pulled both garments off their wooden spikes. She hugged them close to her chest and put her head down so that the sweet-sour smell of Grandmother wafted up to her nose. She closed her eyes and almost believed that Grandmother was standing in front of her ready to embrace her in those strong brown arms. She stepped backwards, the garments still held close to her face. Anguish and loss and anger welled upwards inside her chest and made her eyes sting with a flood of tears. She had touched Grandmother's dead face when it was still warm and held Grandmother's hand as it cooled. The fingers had opened and closed in tiny spasms, then they were still. "Please, do not go," she had whispered, and of course she had gone. Days ago Egret had said it was the way Grandmother would have wanted to go. And so why did Cougar feel so maggoty today? Her tears drowned the cry that formed in her throat. She wanted to berate Grandmother for leaving at the very time she was most needed.

Would Grandmother's ghost come with them to search for her first-born? Why had Grandmother not looked for her son a long time ago? Cougar opened her mouth, nothing emerged, and her face grimaced as she sank to the hard, sandy floor. She cried silently, bewildered and alone. She cried because she had lost the only person who she knew for certain loved her, no matter what she did or said. She could not remember how she got where Grandmother found her when she was near two summers old, wet, dirty, and scared to death. Had she been with a mother and father? Her memory was blotted out cleaner than a newborn's. Living with Grandmother she started fresh as though just pulled out of the breadmaker's oven fully formed on the outside but with spices yet to be added. She never spoke another language, only Calusa, when she finally began to talk. Then, instead of crawling like a baby, she walked, ran, and had no need of diaper cloths. Grandmother gave her security, confidence, and a haven from the large, unknown world. Grandmother taught her equality and reserve. With Grandmother's guidance she discovered she was a fast learner.

Suddenly, her reminiscing disappeared. Someone's eyes were on her and she looked up.

Otter stood in the doorway. "Are you sure you want to search for Grandmother's son?" he said. "Maybe what you will find will not be what you expect. What if you find nothing?"

Still clutching the old skirt and feathered cape, she stood. "I have to do it," she said. "Not searching will gnaw a hole bigger than grief in my heart."

He put an arm around her. "Then dry your eyes. There is plenty to do. Roll that old skirt and cape inside your blanket. They will give you comfort if your own things are rain soaked, or if Egret tips the canoe."

In spite of herself, she smiled. "I will miss you," she said.

The night before they left, Otter reminded Egret that there was an outdoor council meeting at sundown.

Being a council-elder, Egret had thought it would be the perfect time to say he was going to accompany Cougar on her search for Grandmother's son. During the meeting he was careful not to overimbibe in the black drink ritual, a necessary part of council meetings. The strong narcotic drink purified men of pollution and was an expression of hospitality used only by mature men, never by women or very young boys. He vomited once to cleanse his insides so that when he spoke the council members would know his words were not tainted with lies.

Chief Wren drank as though he really liked the taste of the dark-colored, bitter concoction and then vomited until all that was left to come up was the lining of his belly. He staggered around the circle of council men, sat down, wiped his mouth, rubbed his hands on his thighs, grinned crazily, and said he was not so sure it was a good thing to have strangers, old men, come into town to stay. For example, he knew nothing about the old one-handed man staying with Egret. "That old man may be a lookout for the Tequesta who might be planning an ambush to take over Sandpoint," he said, fingering the neck of his tunic and smiling haughtily at the councilmen. "Has anyone besides Egret talked to that man?" He closed his eyes hoping to slow the stars that danced in fast circles above his head.

Egret jumped to his feet and stood next to the center fire so that everyone could see him. "No need to imply that a friend of mine is a party to treachery!" he said. "You all know me and know that I would never dishonor Sandpoint nor the Calusa tribe. You do not see my eyes shift like a fox, nor close to dispel a dizzy feeling; my tongue is not forked, and my face does not sweat and turn red. I do not run my finger around the neck of my tunic making you think it is too tight when it is really too loose. Chief Wren has met my guest and knows Nohold is trustworthy and younger than I am." He wiped a hand across his moist forehead.

"Oho, that is what you say," said Chief Wren, standing straight so that he was taller than Egret, and squinting so that Egret stayed in focus. "Time will tell us about trust and you and your guest." He ran a finger around the neck of his tunic.

Egret was put out by Wren's words. He decided not to say that he and Cougar were going away in the morning. Instead he said, "Chief Wren, you are able to serve Sandpoint well. If the council does not feel you are doing your best, they have the right to select a new chief."

On the way home Wren caught up with Egret and put a hand on his shoulder. "I want you to tell Cougar not to see my wife anymore," he said. "When they are together, they giggle. They wake Hummer and take him to see the wading flamingos, or the orchids, pitcher plants, blooming magnolias, or some foolish piece of wood that looks like a rabbit or a dog. Only the Spirits know what she is teaching my son who giggles with them, but when I show up, he cries. I swear Cougar is a witch and may have thrown a curse on my son. I know for a fact that the old chief, Brittle Star, had pleasures with Cougar. He told me how she fought him at last summer's Stretching Ceremony, like a female wildcat with her sharp claws and teeth—and a row of teeth inside her vagina. Have you ever looked up inside her? A row of sharp teeth! Believe me, if that is not unusual I will eat my crocodile moccasins."

Egret was stunned. He kept his mouth closed and glared at Wren for a long time before saying, "If Brittle Star was not already lying in the ground full of worms, I would put him there!"

"So, I am telling you something you did not know," said Wren. "Brittle Star is dead, and Cougar pretends to be a virgin and will not walk with me among the mangroves, even to gather colorful tree-snails. She says the coral sumac causes welts on her skin. I heard rumors that she is a shape-changer. Ha! I am plenty lucky I kept my stick away from her. Although Brittle Star did not say anything, I believe that a bite from her vaginal teeth is what killed him!"

"What are you saying?" cried Egret. "Cougar, a child who has not bled yet, with vaginal teeth! You have no proof! You cannot pick up on such a crazy rumor! If you were a real man, you would stomp on rumors like that. Kill it right now!"

"If you were a real man, you would put your finger into her vagina and afterwards let the rest of us inspect your finger for bite marks!" He smiled.

"That is not a joking matter," said Egret. His fist shot out from his side and hit Wren in the belly.

Wren gasped, doubled over, and tried to find his breath. He could not draw in air and was so frightened that he dug into the sand with his heels. Egret rubbed Wren's chest hard and told him to breathe. Wren made a funny sound deep in his throat and finally pulled in air. He lay still. Egret told him that he was going to be all right. Wren sat up and said, "Listen, old man, I heard how the old woman, called Grandmother, found Cougar. No one knows where the girl came from, only that after the Big Storm she was here, stinking and soiled as a wildcat's wet kit. I believe a trickster Spirit put her here. As a child she never wore shoes, and the hot sand did not burn her feet; the sticks, stones, and broken shells did not cut them. A man can take the heavy dew at night and the heat of the sun by day, if he is cooled by an occasional sea breeze, but he cannot stand the hordes of black flies. Those flies never bother her. She has a magic oil she rubs on herself to keep flies away."

"It is the same thing your wife makes with rosemary, basil, wormwood, and rue leaves ground to a mush and mixed in rancid fish oil," said Egret. "Nothing magic about it. Calusas have used it since I was a baby."

"Listen, this person—is she a girl or a woman? She can find open spaces no one knew existed, where the wind passes unobstructed and keeps it free of flies as easily as her powerful grease," said Wren. "I tell you, once I tried to trade her a pleasant time in the shallow part of the river, where the duckweed grows, for a handful of that grease.

She laughed and said under the duckweed is where the water moccasin lives. She is a fright. I do not want to see her around my place. I am warning you, she can turn on a friend as fast as an alligator can snap off a man's stick."

Egret's heart was pounding like thunder. He had to sit on the damp sand to think. Never had he heard Wren talk this way. The ideas about Cougar were twisted and not true. He did not want to aggravate Wren or to cause him to hatch his ideas into larger, unfounded stories. "Chief," said Egret, "I do not believe you have to worry about Cougar. She will not be around much longer."

"You put a curse on her?" said Wren, stretching himself to show his height, showing his teeth and hopping around. "Thank you! I owe you something."

"You owe me nothing," said Egret. "I do not put curses on anyone. I have always been a friend to Cougar. I watched Grandmother teach her integrity as well as gaiety, not the pretense of either. Have no fear; your wife hides nothing. Do yourself a favor, join in the walks; hold your son."

"Yu," said Wren, not quite able to control the flap of his tongue. "Before Brittle Star got a bellyache and died, he told me about a dream he had. In this dream Cougar came to his sleeping couch. She was all dressed up with a hornet's nest on her head, decorated with foxes' tails and eagles' feathers. Her tunic was made of a bear's hide with the tail for a trailer in the back. At first he was sure that she came to kill him, and he asked her to take pity, to let him live a full life. She laughed and it sounded like snowmelt falling over a rocky cliff. You know he was not afraid of anything—he could make a wolf howl—but her laugh filled him with fear, and he trembled while waiting for her to say something. Finally she told him she could make an arrow hit a wild goose flying, wade the Big Lake without drowning, outscream a catamount, jump over her own shadow, and cut through the brush like a water jug full of black drink among two handfuls of men. She said she positively knew a skunk from a woodchuck and could dance Brittle Star down any time."

Egret looked at him with his eyes wide, as though it was just a fanciful dream.

Wren looked around suspiciously, to see if anyone had overheard the conversation. "So, you understand my fear of that female?" he said.

"Brittle Star told you this?" asked Egret to be certain he had heard right.

"He did and I am telling you. In his dream the woman told him that she was going to make him suffer for what he did to her if he did not make Otter chief of Sandpoint. She is strong minded and probably meant for things to go hard on him if he did not go along with her. I saw the bite marks she left on Brittle Star's shoulder. Frightful—too many teeth. I never knew a woman like that!"

"Aye, but it was only a dream," said Egret, not opening his mouth any more than necessary.

"Brittle Star was worried because two days before his dream he had promised me the chieftainship. I told him I would slit his throat, as easily as I would slit a fried fish down the back to peel out the bones, if he went back on his word to me. He looked at me with his yellow eyes and said if anything happened to him, it would be my fault, not the female's because he was going to marry her. Now he is dead. I do not know if he ever got around to asking Cougar to live with him and his other wife. I know I had nothing to do with his death. I did not put poison in his food. I did not put a curse on him. I did not tell him to take a sweat bath and then jump into the cold water. His death must have been Cougar's doing. Believe me, she can snuff out a man's life by looking crosswise at him. I shiver every time I look at her. As the new chief, I am obligated to take Brittle Star's wife, Ibis, as my second wife. Am I obligated to make Cougar my wife because Brittle Star, the previous chief, wanted her? Hi-yi, imagine that woman dancing for me. The thought makes me dizzy. Did you ever see that half girl–half woman, Cougar, naked? She will make your blood steam." Wren walked as though his head floated high above his shoulders. His loincloth was stretched in front by his aroused penis.

Egret had all he could do to keep a straight face. *Poor man*, he thought, *he drinks too much, talks too much, and imagines too much*. "Everyone knows you watch the women while they bathe. The men make jokes about it and say you foam at the mouth."

"It is no joke. That one would make any man foam," said Wren. He managed to steady himself when Egret took his arm and led him home. From the doorway of his lodge, he said, "I want that person out of my life. She arouses me with her looks, and I fear the consequences of her kind of pleasures. Yet, if I were alone with her, I would have to have her. She works magic on my stick. I believe that she is a changeling. Did you know she is too knowledgeable for an ordinary female? Maybe she is a spirit changed to ghost who has come to spy on us. I have seen her carry a sharpened deer foreleg that she herself made into a short straight dagger. She can read the clouds and knows when a storm is coming. She can grow medicinal plants. Listen to this: If she cannot find the plant she wants to make a tea to cure your sore throat, she grinds up some black seeds to make your tea, and that same day she puts more black seeds into the ground and sprinkles the earth with spring water. Soon she has the very plants she wanted. No one does this. She frightens me. I want her gone."

"Do not lay a hand on her, unless you want her to put a curse on you. Leave your wants to the gods. Keep your feet steady and your eyes open!" said Egret, thinking Cougar was right. It was time to leave. What could a thick-headed weasel like Wren do for a village? It would be better if Wren were gone.

Before sunup the next morning Egret and Cougar paddled south, keeping close to the islands along the coast. Cougar was glad for the high sides on the canoe. It kept the alligators' noses out of the way. They stopped at Gulltown for two nights, making inquiries about Grandmother's former home. They found no one who had heard of the story of a mother giving her baby to someone else. "We do not know of a man who says he had a second mother," the people said.

Egret thought the people who might know someone like that had moved. Cougar wondered if the man with two mothers had died, and people simply had forgotten about him. Egret said there were more places to go, and they had time for all of them. Their canoe turned east, still following the marshy coast of the Wide River. They followed a piece of swampy land. Inland the water birds and biting black flies lived among the reeds and trees that grew in the marsh. Alligators ate snails and fish in the shallowest water. Cougar used bear fat mixed with herbs to keep the insects at bay. Often, at night, they camped on one of the treeless tiny islands, where there was a breeze, strong enough to blow the flies away. During the day they stopped at all the villages they saw. This marshy land was Tequesta territory. The Tequesta, like the Calusa, were tall and athletic with ruddy complexions. The men twisted their long hair into a bun atop their heads, same as Egret.

The scaly alligator hide was used for high-top moccasins, carrying pouches, and loincloths. The people generally went barefoot around camp; neither men nor women wore clothing on their upper bodies. The women's skirts, similar to the Calusa's, were woven from the curly gray moss after it had been thoroughly smoked to rid it of redbugs, tiny red spiders, ticks, and other biting insects. The people were friendly and wanted to know about the neighboring tribes, whom they rarely saw, except for small raiding parties and one or two traders that came by each year. No one had ever come to inquire about someone who had once lived in their villages. Cougar stared at these folks' fingernails and toenails that were long and filed to sharp points. One woman gave her a shell-bead necklace for a large basket and told Cougar her fingernails were useful weapons against untrustworthy traders. Cougar admired the woman's hairpins of carved bone and fish-teeth bracelets. She traded a small basket for another shell bead necklace.

She learned to use her hands to make the signs most people, especially traders, who traveled from one tribe to the next, understood. At the same time she learned more of the Tequesta words, which were a variant of the Calusa tongue. What had once seemed unintelligible soon made sense as her facility with words took hold. She became more adept with the Tequesta language than Egret.

In the marsh there were lodges reachable only by canoe and a ladder built of mangrove branches tied in place with strips of hide. The lodges were built of small logs covered with tied bunches of long grass and supported by four large logs at each corner, like stilts. Grass-eating bugs lived in the lodge walls, and birds came in to eat the bugs. The people did not try to keep the insects and birds out of their lodges. The gulls and ospreys nested in the dry, insect-littered grass. Tequesta mothers believed that the night cooing of the birds was a comfort, especially to their children. Cougar said the wind brought her energy and the water brought her peace, but it was the familiar sound of ordinary people in a lodge that made her feel at home with the Tequesta.

On the long sandy shore were many lodges with space underneath where high water could roll freely in a storm. The air above was clear of tree branches, but filled with a variety of ducks. Egret said they were near the Big Lake, a good place to stop to rest from the backbreaking work of paddling. Cougar traded her baskets and two shell necklaces for edible roots, water lettuce, and a couple of simple moss skirts. When paddling, Egret had used bunched up leaves against his hands. Cougar had laughed at him then, but now saw how wise he was. Because of the painful blisters on her hands, she went to see the healer and ask the name of this village at the edge of the Big Lake.

Healer was small, about the same size as Cougar, but she looked older than Grandmother; the skin on her face and upper arms was wrinkled and saggy. She said she liked to hold the children that came to her and help birthing mothers, so her fingernails were not long or pointy. Her brown eyes were bright and clear; her teeth were gone; her chin was held up proudly, and she carried a walking stick. She complained with a lisp of the pain in her back and knees and fussed over Cougar as if she were a small child. She bathed Cougar's fiery red palms in a warm, soothing solution, then wrapped them in mittens of woven grass, filled with crushed aloe leaves, and said the village was Duckplace.

The next day the pain in Cougar's hands was gone. She went back to see if she needed a fresh aloe poultice and saw a family of raccoons, a wild pig, and a white-tail deer as she neared Healer's lodge. At the same time she thought Healer was old enough to remember if anything unusual had happened in the village many summers ago. When she saw that Healer had her hands full with two women moaning in the first stage of birthing, she shucked off the day-old, smelly aloe dressing, wiped her hands on a wad of gray moss, and told Healer that she could help. She began to rub fragrant oil on the swollen belly of one of the mothers, who said she already had three daughters and wanted a boy. Cougar spoke softly, nodded, and smiled so that the woman would know that she was asking the spirits to give her a baby boy. Cougar remembered what Grandmother had done for birthing mothers and was careful to watch the woman's progress and encourage her to push when necessary. She began to cut the cord with her teeth. Healer handed her a shell, saying it was better if she cut quickly with the shell; the cut was smoother. Cougar cleaned the crying baby with a handful of curly gray moss and laid him on a grass mat near the glowing embers in the fire pit built of sand and rocks. She cleaned the mother, put moss packing between her legs, and covered her with a fur robe.

She had the mother chew and swallow a finger length of the tough cord to keep her baby well. Then she took the afterbirth behind the lodge to bury quickly before the evil spirits smelled it and harmed the mother. When she came back she handed the mother a tiny violet-colored, sour-grass flower with several stems of three-segment leaves shaped like an inverted heart. "Taste the stem," she said. "It is a sour taste that cleans your mouth and makes you pucker your lips so you may kiss your new baby boy."

The mother was overjoyed to have the delivery easy and end with a perfect baby boy. She named him Jaguar, because that was the translation the Healer gave of Cougar's name. The mother said she wanted Cougar to stay with her, because like the sun, she warmed her spirit, and like a flower, showed her life had beauty.

Healer was impressed and pleased with Cougar's work and asked her and Egret to stay for a meal of clams and water lettuce, then stay the night. Having nowhere else to go to sleep but in their canoe, they agreed.

While eating, the toothless Healer said she did remember a young mother who had given birth alone. It was the time of the Big Flood and no one could go anywhere. "Later the young mother gave her baby to a mother who grieved over a stillborn infant, as her breasts overflowed with milk. That was a bad winter. The give-away mother made one of the greatest heartbreaking sacrifices a mother could make. She saved her child from starving to death by putting him in another woman's arms and walking away." She nudged Cougar. "Funny thing, when that give-away baby was about two summers, he had a double row of top front teeth, same as you. His second mother refused to nurse him and found he could eat most anything."

Cougar swallowed, smiled so that her top front teeth showed plainly and said, "When I was a child, I thought everyone had double teeth in the front. Sometimes Grandmother teased me—in a nice way, saying I was special. Now she is a ghost."

Egret stopped chewing a wad of wild lettuce and looked at Cougar, wondering why he had talked to her about his top double teeth. Was that what puzzled him about Cougar? He had never heard of anyone else but the two of them with teeth like that. When he was young, he kept his mouth half-closed so no one would notice. He was a thinker, a fast learner, and stubborn. *Cougar is like that, smarter than most,* he thought. *She learned the Tequesta language fast enough and figures what people want to hear. It is as if she can read their thoughts.* He remembered hearing Cougar telling one of Grandmother's patients, a complaining woman, that to cure her cramps she should turn her moccasins upside down before going to sleep. Later she told the same woman to rid herself of a sty by running the tip of a brown dog's tail over her eyelid. The woman got better and told Grandmother that Cougar was destined to become a medicine shaman. Egret heard Grandmother say, "Wait and see. Cougar will surprise you."

"Well, I have never seen a ghost," lisped Healer. She wiped the drool from her chin as she ate. "We who help with birthing are often known for slim, agile fingers." She clasped Cougar's small hands and studied them carefully. "I could use a strong young person like you, who herself heals easily and knows how to use her hands and voice to heal others."

"Oh, I do not know if I have the power to be a healer,"

said Cougar. "First I have to find the man who was that give-away baby. If you are still here when I come back, I will stay and learn from you. Did you know that I am a good storyteller?"

"I did not know that," said Healer. "But I know a storyteller and a healer both need a strong, confident voice and plenty of imagination. Hurry back."

"The baby's name? Do you remember?" said Egret.

"He was a regular baby named Owl. He was a young man with beautiful eyes, who married my daughter. People said Hyacinth was wrong to go with him to live with the Tequesta; she should have stayed with me like a good Calusa girl. The jealous women treated her in mean ways, stole her food, and called her names before she left. She would not fight back. She thought grown people should settle differences in a council meeting. There was no meeting and so Owl took my daughter and their baby, Kitten, to live with the Tequesta on one of the islands with little green trees that have red berries the birds like and springs with sweet water. Storms leave the springs bitter tasting and give a person the runs. That island may be in the sea, or it may be in the Big Lake. It was a long time ago when I was there." Healer smiled, sucked air across her toothless gums, and filled one of Cougar's large baskets with comfort-root flour. She took a small basket in trade and told Cougar that she dreamed of seeing Owl and Hyacinth in the summer.

"Ha," said Egret. "If we see them, do you have a message for them?"

"Aye, tell them when it is cold and dark, I am warmed by thoughts I shall see them again."

In the canoe for several days, Egret met the first north wind of the season. The wind brought fog and a warm misty rain. He tried going against the wind in zigzags at first and felt the dreaded nausea overtaking him. He wanted to lie down and close his eyes, but he kept his head up and concentrated on the way the waves were coming at the canoe. When he learned to surf down the fronts of the swells, his nausea disappeared and the rough water did not seem so alarming. The sun was a big silver disk in the mist, almost like a large moon. He turned to Cougar, pointed to the sun, grinned and said, "The space between your top front teeth and your slim, agile hands are like Grandmother's—I wish I had said something about them long ago."

"Why do I have a space between my teeth?"

"Only the spirits know," he said. "When I was younger, I could chew deer hide to a softness that was like a baby's belly. Grandmother said no other man or woman could do better than I. I loved that woman more than life itself. She was so much more than a friend to me." His voice broke and became low. "I cannot believe she is gone. I would do most anything to have her back." He looked past Cougar into the strange, unreal, silver face of the sun.

Cougar turned to look. At first everything was gray all around. She could see islands, then they disappeared, and next they seemed to rest on the fog and float above the water.

Egret dragged the oar through the water and ran his tongue over his dry lips. "I think she did not marry me out of spite. She was provoked because I was not with her when the boy was born. She was stubborn that way, and I was thoughtless and never made it up to her. Much later I told her how the rivers had widened and covered the trails. She thought I had a canoe." His voice was so sad it made Cougar's eyes water and a tightness settle in her chest. "Even after she married she was kind to me. I hoped maybe she still loved me, but we never spoke about it."

He held the oar out of the water, dug a fist into the front pocket of his tunic, and cleared his throat. "Wear these," he said. "I traded Healer my alligator moccasins for mittens made of shark's skin. I have a pair for myself, but yours look better than mine. Ha! Do you believe what Healer said about her daughter not wanting to fight for a safe place in the village? I suppose that the infant boy is now a grown warrior."

"Aye," said Cougar. "That might be. Warriors are men who like to fight, even killing their enemies with stones, arrows, and sticks. Women prefer spreading bad rumors about their enemies. If there is killing, they like quiet things like poison. Why?"

"It is The Way. Men are expected to protect a village or their women. It is a way to add new blood to the tribe.

Warriors steal women from other tribes, and the men are happy they have something new to explore at night. A fight gives the men something to talk about and a way to settle differences. Women give care. They care for the welfare of children and the aged. They tell stories and do the cooking. They are expected to keep things quiet, at peace, not riled up."

"I think fighting and rumor-spreading starts hard feelings," said Cougar. "The stolen women miss their first family and have to bite down hard on a piece of leather to keep from crying out loud, especially at night. I am certain Baby Owl missed Grandmother. Babies have likes and dislikes, fears and insecurity."

"Aye," said Egret. "I think Hyacinth needs to visit her mother. I will bring her to Healer as soon as we find her, if she is really the mother who lost a baby girl during the Big Storm. Think who she and her man are to you!"

"It is what the spirits have done to me!" said Cougar. "If Grandmother was truly my grandmother, then Healer is truly my grandmother, too!"

They checked out several small islands, but found no clues about a man who had had two mothers. Several days later they camped on one of the little islands that was close to the northwest shore of the Big Lake, where the rivers flowed from the north into a treeless, wide-open vista of swampland. They met a man who was so old that he forgot to pluck the whiskers from his red face. He said the story of the mother giving away her infant sounded like something the Ais, living north of the Big Lake, would do. Around the Big Lake Egret was called Grandfather and Cougar was called Granddaughter. The people were generous. The women shared meals of fish stew that they kept in the clay pot for days. When the stew looked low, they added more fish, comfort-root flour, and slices of dried coconut to the pot. After supper they sat outdoors on log benches around the outside walls of rounded grass lodges, where it was cool. Cougar and Egret told about the places they had been. People heard about the storytellers and came to listen. Afterwards they said it was the best time they h~ had in a long time and promised to look for a man ca'

Owl, who had married a woman named Hyacinth.

The chiefs of the villages along the river offered Egret a young woman each night. Cougar noticed that most of them were her age or younger. No one had heard of a baby being given to another mother. These people knew of no couple named Owl and Hyacinth. Some of the younger women liked the name Hyacinth and wanted Cougar and Egret to stay while they had a Name-Change Ceremony. Cougar told them that they needed to add something to the name Hyacinth, or else no one would know one Hyacinth from another. Thus, in one village there was a Red, Yellow, Blue, Pink, and White Hyacinth. Egret said these girls made him feel young, and he was tempted to sleep all day and play with the Hyacinth girls all night. Cougar scowled at him and asked if he had traded his good mind for the pleasures of his body. "It is not a good trade," she said. "Sleep all day and you are going to miss a lot." It was Egret's turn to scowl.

They paddled back to the waterway leading to the sea. Between the marshy shore and little islands they disturbed sandpipers hunting food. They combed their hair, ate mackerel, snapper, grouper, quail, or duck and a lot of flat bread made from Healer's comfort-root flour.

The summer dark clouds rolled in and covered the high sun. "It is going to be a rainy summer and I worry about Otter," said Cougar. "Grandmother had a way of making him feel important. I wish I could do that. I wish Otter were with us."

"Umm," said Egret, exhaling the sound through his nose. "Careful, some wishes come true."

They beached the canoe on a wide gravel bar, took out their gear, turned the canoe over, and put the gear underneath. They wrapped themselves in their blankets and rolled under the canoe alongside the gear, where the air was like sitting next to a pot of steaming water. It was better than being soaked by misty rain all night. Cougar had a hard sleeping. She heard little scraping sounds and wondered was a snake. Egret told her they were small frying out of the rain.

he rain stopped, she got up and saw the breeze d eddies close along the sand. High rolling clouds covered and uncovered a half-moon. The surf was only a wash along the ebb. She took a long time to start a small fire with damp wood and live coals from her fire-bowl. From the water's edge, she pulled a couple of armfuls of new-growth reeds that were good for making tight green baskets. She heard another sound, faint, high, and far away. She wrapped herself in a blanket and sat close to the fire. She passed the reeds over and under each other in interesting patterns to make flat strips. The strips were tied together at their centers; the ends pointed out like rays of sunshine. Suddenly a sound came from the back of a little dune. It sounded like a chorus of bells, soft then loud. It was the sound of a great flight of geese, passing under the bright half-moon, going north for the summer. She imagined the birds like a river of life flowing through the immensity of the night sky. There were short dark rivers, long wide rivers, and then the sky was empty. When the great clamor came back, she thought she could hear the lovely, rustling sound of wings, and once in a while she thought she could see an individual bird, but they were moving fast. Then the sound was gone, the sky over the ocean was quiet, and the clouds were nearly cleared away. She worked more flat reed strips into the rays in increasing circles. Soon the shape of the basket was revealed. Sewing the flat strips in and out over the last woven layer, the rim was made. If a handle was required, it was made last and woven deep into the pattern of the basket and thick enough to hold a load suitable for the size of the basket. *Baskets like this will trade well,* she thought. After a while everything was silent. Cougar's head dropped to her chest and she lay down to sleep.

The weather began to change from cool to warm. The moon of the green budding trees was growing and was soon almost full. It took a warm glow.

They paddled back down the lazy river. It was time to move on before more spring storms came. They called the slow-running river Stillwater. Egret wondered why the alligators left them alone. Was it something more than the wide sides of the canoe? Maybe it was the numinous character of Cougar. He knew she was watching the geese fly north in the middle of the night, but he dared not ask her if she talked with the birds. He wondered if she kept her geese words in the little basket she made while she watched them.

Sometimes she chattered longer than a bunch of squirrels eating pine nuts together. This morning Egret broke into her chatter to say they were going back into Calusa territory. He thought they ought to approach the Calusas carefully, because there was no way to tell what kind of stories Chief Wren was telling. He thought several times that it might be best to stay with the Tequestas, where he could continue to be Cougar's grandfather with no interference.

Cougar found a mossy mound of land where they could spend the night and stay fairly dry even though fog now often hid the waning moon, which had turned the color of newly bleached deerhide. Their canoe lay under a tree with red-brown bark that resembled bad sunburn. Cougar seemed puzzled and said, "Something is coming, not rain nor wind, but I do not know what it is."

Egret laughed and told her she did not have to predict things as Grandmother used to do. "Forget it," he said. "Rain is enough to prepare for."

After supper Cougar again heard a noise. She thought it might be an alligator rummaging around to get the fish left in the bottom of the canoe. She got up to see if she could divert the alligator without getting close to it. First she walked all around the canoe, but saw nothing out of place. She began to believe she heard a snake. Carefully she lifted one of the large mats over the recent baskets she had made for trading. Suddenly she squealed and danced about. Egret looked up and thought she had run into a nest of hornets or, worse, tripped over a stone that was hiding a nest of scorpions.

"Oh, oh!" she cried, grabbing his hand. "Come, look, Otter is here!" She led him running back to the canoe. "Otter, I missed you! How did you get here? You slept in our canoe all night? How did you find us? We went all around the Big Lake."

"Otter?" Egret said. "Really? I see for myself, it is you!"

Otter sat up and rubbed his dark eyes. He said he had forgotten how loud Cougar's and Egret's voices were when he was trying to sleep. "Good thing you did not go back to Sandpoint. Chief Wren says I cannot go back to any Calusa village. Also Cougar is not welcome, especially in Sandpoint. I am a troublemaker, and Cougar is a witch, to be sacrificed to the Rain Spirit when she returns. He might sacrifice Egret, too, but I did not hear him say so. He wants people from the village who agree with him in all things and especially young women who can be trained for pleasuring men. Most of the old people left."

"He sounds crazy," said Egret, sitting in the sand facing Otter.

"I should have kicked him in the belly before I left," said Otter, "except I was concentrating on stealing a canoe and not getting caught." He adjusted his loincloth and sat back on his heels.

"What about Little Mother?" asked Cougar.

"Little Mother is busy with Hummer and is blind to what Wren is doing. His other wife, Ibis, yells at him. One day they will wake up. Their eyes would be open sooner if you were there. Little Mother misses you both. She wept when I left."

In the full morning light Cougar saw the bluish outline where Otter's beard grew on his upper lip and the shadow under his jaw. His face was not as round as she remembered. His long black hair was tied with a thin supple vine and hung down the middle of his back. The muscles in his upper arms and chest rippled when he pulled himself up on his knees. He was tall and intent. He scratched the back of his neck. His eyes watched her, and his mouth turned up in a friendly way that made a tingle run around in Cougar's belly. She had always loved his smile.

He thought, *her hair is longer and her face is clearly oval shaped.* "You are most beautiful," he said quickly, watching her.

She flushed. No one had told her that before, and it embarrassed and pleased her at the same time. She was flustered and did not know what to say. She reached out and put her fingers on a red scar on his left jaw.

He gave a little jerk as if his jaw was still tender. He put his hand over hers and slowly pulled it away. "Nothing gets past your eyes. I told Wren he was full of himself, and he tried to put his fist through my jaw. Luckily I fell down and only have this scar. I am staying with you and Egret from now on."

She pulled her hand away, tucked a strand of hair that fell over her eye behind her ear, and said, "We are not sure where we are going. Maybe Grandmother's son does not want to be found."

Egret saw Cougar's confusion and held his hand up to indicate he had something to say. "I believe the arrangement in Sandpoint is ideal for half-grown men and women; those people who do not want to become adults with responsibility. One day those young men and women will grow old. They will see that a village of old, self-centered folks is a terrible, tired place. They will wish their children would take care of them, and it will be too late. The children will be gone to more reasonable villages to find husbands and wives."

"Listen," said Otter, looking at Cougar. "A week ago my canoe brought me to an island in the sea where a Tequesta couple live. The man has a long neck and a space between his big front teeth, same as you, Egret. No, no, I do not mean he is not fine looking. Only that it is strange how much he looked like you."

"Tell me," said Egret, sitting closer to Otter.

"When the man was a boy, everyone told him that he was twice loved because he once had a Calusa mother, who was unable to feed him. A second mother raised this man. She was a Tequesta with sharp toenails."

Oho, thought Egret. *That is Grandmother's son. My son!*

"This couple lost a baby girl, about two summers old, in the Big Storm," said Otter. "They were fishing, when suddenly a fierce wind hit. Because of the wind, they could not get to land; all they could do was hang on to their canoe. Their baby was asleep, tucked against rolled blankets and fishing gear. Water rose, foamed, and sprayed everywhere. When the storm let up, the baby, along with blankets and gear, was gone. They were away from home, and in the wind-driven rain and water spray they never saw Sandpoint. They were sick with grief, and certain the baby had drowned. They looked along the shore for several days, but did not find her."

Cougar tried to think back to when she was a small girl

and remember a young man, who looked a little like Egret. She wondered if he was the one that made her giggle when she climbed on his lap.

Otter touched Cougar's cheek. "The name of the little girl they lost was Kitten, because she cried like a wild kit. The next day I went back to talk again with the man, Owl. His wife, Hyacinth, said he had gone to find the baby girl who may be their daughter. I told her the girl was no longer a baby. She only nodded her head as if I knew nothing about it."

"Hyacinth and Owl," said Cougar. It was hard for her to believe that this news was true; it sounded made up. She put her head down, waiting for Egret to say something. He was quiet, so she said, "We met an old woman called Healer whose daughter, Hyacinth, married a man named Owl. They live on an island."

"Owl and Hyacinth live on an island, with a row of short trees with red berries," said Otter. "Holly, maybe. I did not ask. Owl almost wet himself when I told him I knew a girl who cried like a cougar kit and that is how Grandmother found you. He said his first mother was called Carries Needles."

Egret gasped, and acted like he wanted to cough, but could not draw in enough air. He stood up, cleared his throat, and motioned for Otter to stop talking. He wiped his eyes and said he was not sure he wanted to hear more. A few seconds later he told Otter to go on.

"Well then," said Otter. "It was Hyacinth who told me that when Owl was a small boy, some older boys told him his first mother adored a trader called Blue Egret."

Egret moved his head up and down, and his eyes watered more. He was not sure he liked people he did not know telling about his youth. It was an invasion and made him feel vulnerable. When he could control his voice, he said, "Carries Needles never married Blue Egret but he always adored her. Carries Needles was the talk of the village because she had a mind of her own and ____ her Stretching Ceremony before she had h___ face was now red as sand cherries; tea___ down his face, and he choked on his wo___ Needles is the Tequesta name for Porc___

Grandmother was called when she was a girl. When I first knew her, she was the most beautiful woman I have ever seen—the most intelligent, most loving, most fun, and most independent." He put his arm around Cougar and whispered. "You are so much like her. I believe you are my true granddaughter."

Cougar wiped her eyes and smiled quietly. She savored the idea that Egret and Grandmother were in love. It was like a dream, and she could not put her feelings in words. She said it would be best to see this Owl and Hyacinth couple and check out their story from the beginning. "We talked with many people from Tequesta villages, but never with a pair like that. We even looked for Hyacinth on the barrier islands. Oh, oh, she could be my mother! That makes Healer—Healer is my—grandmother. Hyacinth needs to visit her mother."

"See, you needed me to straighten things out," said Otter. His smile made his thin, sharp face disarming, and it planted another surprise tickle in Cougar's belly. "What is wrong with this Healer?" asked Otter. "Is she ill?"

"She is as wrinkled as a hickory nut," said Cougar. "But her eyes are clear, and she has not seen her daughter in many seasons."

"I will go with you," said Otter. "People in Sandpoint have to see through Wren by themselves. He is not a chief for those people. He is a chief for himself. His council is made up of men I never heard of, who are also for themselves and talk out of both sides of their mouth. Owl is probably there now talking with them, asking about Cougar and Egret. Think of the stories Wren will tell!"

"What about the man in ___ lodge?" asked Egret, sneezing and rubbing his ev___ ___s knuckles, as if he had walked through a pat___ ___eezing weed. "He is a man of honor. He ___

"Nohold stays ___ ___er. "I rarely talked with him. He k___ ___ ___e I found and came ___ ___ swimming one after-___ ___ould still make it across ___ ___e other side I crashed into ___ ___othing but boots. Crabs were ___. It scared me so much that I wanted to run or be sick. I pulled the body out of the water and turned it over, and between his shoulders I saw two little holes, like a water moccasin or a rattler or maybe a scorpion with a double stinger had bitten him. I thought the little holes were in a strange place for a man who was wearing fisherman's boots. The bite should have been on his thigh or wrist. I dragged the bloated body across the river and to the council house for the elders to look at and identify. The elders you knew are gone, moved away. No one in the village recognized the corpse, but maybe Wren. When he saw it he turned pale, like he was seeing the half-eaten, swollen shell of a man and a ghost at the same time. He knew how the man got in the river. At night I thought about it and knew I had seen those boots. They were No-hold's boots. The man's body was so bloated, discolored, and nipped by crabs that I could not tell what it had looked like in life. It is strange that the alligators had not found him. When I got him to the council house, he smelled worse than a rotting porpoise. I buried him the next day after Wren saw him."

Egret sat with his face in his hands. In his mind he saw a man who was a friend. Was he Nohold or someone else? Wren knew who Nohold was. Why had Wren left him in the river? Egret made his hands into tight fists; he wanted to punch Wren in the face—hard.

Otter continued. "A couple of days later I found a double-pointed dart on a long stick in back of Wren's place. Sometimes he used a dart with pieces of poisonous root attached to get small animals. The day after I saw the dart, Chief Wren said I was no longer welcome. He said he had sent word to other Calusa chiefs to kill me when they saw me. I asked him what I had done to banish me from my home. He said I poked around to see how he ran his village. He said I had no business acting that way. He said it was the same way Nohold acted, and he thought Nohold planned to drive him out of Sandpoint and become chief himself. I told Wren he had too much black drink. He said he believed I was helping Nohold. I asked him how No-hold's boots got on the feet of the dead man. He said the man was a trader of fishhooks and stayed with Nohold for a while. He said Nohold probably drowned him to get his boots back. I said the dead trader had two puncture holes high on his back, and the boots were still on him. Wren's face turned red. He looked away like he was thinking how to correct something that came from his own forked tongue. I think Chief Wren killed the trader, thinking he was Nohold.

"Nohold never said anything against Wren," said Otter. "But I knew he did not trust him, because I saw him look over his shoulder more than once." He rubbed his forehead. "Did you know that Wren sips black drink, a little each day; not enough to purge his insides with retching. He says it helps him think. He claims he has direct contact with the Spirits. He can hear them and they tell him things he has to do. He turned Grandmother's lodge into a house for unmarried men, warriors, and hunters."

"Oh, no!" cried Cougar. "Grandmother would never allow that!"

"The hunters give Wren the hindquarter of every deer they bring in. Little Mother is busy salting and smoking meat. I do not worry that she will be hungry when hunting is bad."

Cougar realized how much she had missed Otter; his level thinking, the flash of his teeth, the music of his voice, and the twinkle of his eyes.

Otter studied Cougar's face and said, "The men who do not have to work, sit around with Wren and sip the black drink. They are fat and lazy. If the Ais or Tequesta attack Sandpoint, it would be the end of Wren. I do and do not want to see that happen. It is like being cut in half, trying to stay logical, when emotions are pulling this way and that. Mother and Hummer are the ones I care about in Sandpoint. The village is unprotected, and I remembered that the Ais like to take women as slaves. Once I made Nohold promise that he would take Mother and Hummer away if there was trouble. I thought if Nohold took them away, he would keep them safe and I would find them."

"How long have you been there, under that mat?" asked Egret, pointing to the canoe.

Otter looked off to the north at the last of the churning gray clouds. Then he grinned and said in a loud voice that carried above the wind gusts, "Since last night. I knew this was your high-sided canoe. I have been watching and trying to follow you. It was hard when all I had was a little bark canoe. It was my lucky night to find a warm mat to sleep under and a high-sided canoe that kept the small creatures out."

"The lucky night was when you found Grandmother's son, a man with a long neck," said Cougar. "I told you we found an old woman healer with a daughter, Hyacinth, whom she has not seen for years. Healer likes us and wants us to stay with her. You, Little Mother, and Hummer could live with her if we do."

Egret was thinking about the man with a long neck. He had seen men with big ears. Ears that stood out so far they seemed to flap in the wind. He had seen men with big noses. But not many had a long neck like his. He heard once that there were animals that had necks so long they could eat the tender leaves high in trees. He wondered about that. It sounded like a story for children. Egret looked at Otter as he would a bird singing a real tune while sitting in the top of a tree. "If the man with the long neck is my son, what will he think of me?"

"He will be grateful you found him," said Otter. "When that long-necked man talked loud, his wife called him Screech."

"Yes!" shouted Egret. "He has to be my son! Grandmother, Porcupine then, named our baby boy Screech Owl." He wiped his eyes with a wad of gray moss. "She told me that our baby was so hungry that he screeched for food. The boy's eyes were brilliant as an owl's. His neck was like a crane's—no, shorter, but like mine!" His chin quivered. "So he was looking for Cougar. Where would he go? If he went to Sandpoint, Wren could do something bad to him. One person poking around means trouble to Wren. That person's life can be wiped out faster than the flash of a firefly."

IX

Ten Sails

Not with a heart unmoved I left thy shores
Dear native isle! Not without pang,
As the fair uplands lessen'd on the view,
Cast back the long involuntary looks!
The morning cheered our outset, gentle airs
Curl'd the blue deep, and bright the summer sun
Played o'er the summer ocean, when our barques
Began their way.

—From Robert Southey's epic poem
Madoc (1805) about the departure from Wales in 1170 A.D.
in Richard Deacon, *Madoc and the Discovery of America*

Outside in the cold predawn, the hungry, tired men pulled the cart away from the driftwood and trudged along the Aberffraw beach to the inlet to find the *Gwennan Gorn* hidden in the willows. On board, Madoc ordered the oars out. Madoc and Conlaf lay on the deck with their heads on coiled rope. Brett lay beside Madoc.

When the three woke, the sky was gray with evening dusk. The ship was anchored in Ireland, in the bowl-shaped mouth of the River Liffey. A cloud of sleek gannets swirled overhead. Each bird had a pale ochre spot on either side of the throat. Thurs and Troyes took the valuables and cart off the ship. Madoc, Conlaf, and Brett trudged behind them to the Irish caves. The druids crowded around to hear how the valuables were rescued. Sein surmised that it was Dafydd's dragons who found the treasure, put it on the cart and hid it, expecting to pick it up later.

Brenda said that she and Sein would like to foster Brett so that he would learn to read and write. Again she lay baby Gwenllian in the crook of Madoc's arm.

This time he held her close to his chest, squatted near the warmth of the cook fire, and rocked back and forth. Gwenllian curled her fingers around his thumb, made gurgling noises, and hiccoughed. It was the first time in days that he had felt really good. This babe of his was easy to hold. He began to tell her a story about clear crystals floating in an ice-blue sea. Finally he told her that he was destined to sail, and Brenda would give her the best of care until he returned. He sang, burst into laughter, and looked up.

"Excuse me," said Sein. "This is important. You are the last and best hope of saving the Welsh and Irish druids. Whatever you do, I know you will give it your best effort. You are well liked, and I am proud to be one of your foster fathers."

Madoc ran a thumb down the side of Gwenllian's face, from her faint yellow hairline to her chin and said, "Do not make too much of me being a shipmaster or a leader of men. I be doing what I want, sailing with people I like, and satisfying a gnawing in my belly to explore pristine land. Look at this baby. She is my daughter, a *prydferthwch*; a beauty she is. One day I will have a hundred stories to tell her."

"That is the troth," said Sein. "I came to tell you that the Prydian council voted to give you a bag of precious stones as reward for rescuing their possessions. You are free to do whatever you like with them. You may repair your ships or buy provisions. However, the council asks that you take all the druids who will risk sailing with you to that unproved land. The council believes that by building a handful of ships and sailing as soon as possible, you will save druids' lives and druids' knowledge. You will become our leader, fulfilling our ancient prophecy."

"That is a great privilege and even greater responsibility. Long ago I learned from you that for every privilege there was a responsibility," said Madoc, fumbling with Gwenllian, who cried as he took Sein's hand.

Brenda put Gwenllian against her shoulder and said, "Not long ago I talked with your brother Riryd. He is a fisherman, who longs to design sailing ships. I told him to tell your sister, Goeral, to come help us with the children here."

"I would like to meet my brother and sister," said Madoc. "Please tell them."

"I taught you that for every reward there is a price," said Sein, holding out a fist-sized leather bag.

Madoc turned toward a torchlight, and his bewhiskered face flushed when he peeked into the bag and saw a rainbow of polished stones. "I never thought to be owner of this many precious stones," he said. " 'Tis more than a reward. I thank the council; my shipbuilders and sailors will thank the council." For a moment his face squinched to hold back an overpowering emotion to put his arms around Sein. "The stones are—are just what is needed to finish all the ships. Our gods have blessed us druids, and I have to thank the council and tell of Brett's bravery. Without the lad we could not have brought your valuables back." He laid out six pale-blue stones and gave them to Brenda, so that she could barter for the things needed to take care of Brett. He looked at Sein and said, "Will you sail with me?"

"I have thought long about it," said Sein, lowering his voice. "I love your mother so much I cannot let her out of my sight for even half a day. 'Tis pure joy to have her beside me. Find your unproved land. Brenda, Gwenllian, Brett, and I shall wait for your return, then we will sail with you. Find a safe place for all of our women and children. In the meantime a few of us men will stay behind to care for the women and educate the children. Recently we have sent someone, a friend, to gather more good men to hasten the rebuilding of your ships. Time is running thin. Go before King Henry and his spies find out what you are up to. Go with the gods' blessings, my son."

For a moment Madoc wondered if he had a right to leave Sein and the others behind. He longed to see his child grow. He had asked the council to permit him to build ships to carry as many druids as possible to a land where they could live free from anguish and fear. Thus, it was not his right to stay—he was obligated to find and save as many druid men as he could. Thus, he thought, *'Tis preposterous to ask mothers and children to sail to a place that I can not name, or say the size, or where it lies on a map.* He clenched his fists and managed to keep his words unemotional. "I will find a place where no women and children have to hide in caves for safety. Then I promise on God's eyren to come back for all of you."

"Son," said Brenda, speaking in a low, tight voice, "we will think of you every day. This is what the gods have chosen for you. It is what the dancing skylights meant at your conception. 'Tis your destiny. Mine is to love and care for Sein, Gwenllian, and the foster children I teach. I feel a great happiness. I pray the gods keep their eyren upon you. So—this is farewell, until next we meet. Oh, there is so much to say. It will be hard to wait for your return." One hand patted the sleeping baby, the other covered her mouth. Her eyes sparkled with tears.

Madoc kissed his mother's cheek and the top of Gwenllian's head, shook Sein's hand, and left. *Oh, sweet Lugh, 'tis hard to leave the people we love,* he thought.

Conlaf would not take one precious stone from the bag, but insisted they were to be used to build ships. After a late meal Madoc and Conlaf boarded the ship in the rain. Madoc anchored the ship north of Dubh Linn, off the shore of Wicklow for the night, hoping by morning the rain would be gone. He pondered the difference between the druid-council rule and the singular rule of his half-brother, King Dafydd. He reflected on Gwynedd's sad plight in the hands of a ruthless leader. He was filled with a longing to be free from fear of his countrymen and some of his kin. He admired Trevor's love of family, understood his fear and anger, but disagreed with his obsession with vengeance. Then he knew, just as his mother and Sein had known, that his days in the province of Gwynedd were numbered.

Sailing was slow the next morning because of wind and summer rain. Madoc took the opportunity to show his crew more tricks to sailing in bad weather. He took them through the Menai Strait, where there was nothing to see through the blowing rain and fog. They met no ship going east on the Strait. The single sail took them easily across Conwy Bay. The wind blew the fog away, and they sailed around the Great Ormes Head and the Little Ormes Head. That is when Brett showed up at the side-rudder, and told Madoc that he told Sein he had decided to sail with the *Gwennan Gorn* instead of letting Brenda teach him to read and write. He said, "In an unproved land no man needs to know that reading and writing stuff."

"You are a barbarian," said Madoc. "Your folks expect more of you. You will learn reading and writing and other stuff as we sail. Now work with the messmates. They already know how to read and write. Welcome aboard!"

Madoc sailed close to shore, always looking for a sail with an Algerian banner, feeling Kabyle was somewhere close. The rain let up. The oarsmen took the ship to the quay of Afon Ganol with the sail lowered. The quay seemed desolate with blackened grass on the hills. Conlaf tied the ship to the stone pier and showed the messmates how to hold a fishline. Madoc climbed down the rope ladder, hiked a league over the burned land to the little river where he believed his four ships, in various stages of repair, were hidden among the willows. The willowy shore was clear. There were no ships! He was numb and ran blindly toward the old abbey. He stood against the abbey's cold, outside walls that were blotched with yellow-green lichens that seemed to glow in the half-light of the cloudy day. Inside, the single room was bare and silent. The floor was hardpacked dirt, undisturbed. On hands and knees he dug frantically with a discarded iron kettle lid, in front of the workbench where Rhan blew glass into intricate designs. He spit on his hands to hold the lid tighter. When it clunked against leather over metal, he sighed with relief. "Aye, here 'tis!" he said, brushing dirt off the leather bag. He shook out the tarnished silver box and looked inside. It was all there, the remainder of the silver and gold coins Thomas Becket had given him. He looked around the bare room trying to figure what kind of fear or rumor made his four friends leave. In his worried concern, his imagination showed him many men in yellow tunics armed with the sharpest of knives, cudgels, and leather slings. He felt as though his heart was squeezed between two cold stones.

Daylight was gone when he returned to his ship. He left his supper of boiled mush untouched. He could not sleep wondering where his ships might be. He woke Conlaf and said that he really wanted him to take a third of the colored gem stones. Conlaf said he would have no use for them in a new land, so his share best be used to buy ships' gear and supplies. He woke Brett and told him he could take a third of the gems and stay in Ireland to study with Brenda. Brett rubbed sleep from his eyes and said, "I have no fancy wishes. Keep yur colored stones to buy ship stuff. Being yur lad is all I want." The words hung between them in the cold night air. Madoc put his oiled canvas-coat over the boy to keep off the fog mist. He put a half dozen of the stones in the deep pocket of his gown and stored the leather bag with the others under his pile of clothing and wondered how much shipgear and food the precious stones would buy for about ten ships for thirty days. Then he went to the steering oar. "Clare," he said, "head east and in morning's first light beach where a ship can be hidden in the willows or tall reeds."

Clare took the ship as far as Abergele, a tiny, fishing village in the province of Denbighshire, where King Dafydd had no authority. He pulled the ship close to shore where she could be beached and partially hidden in the tall reeds.

Madoc did not want to alarm anyone, so he left Conlaf in charge and walked along the swampy shore alone, but he found no sign of his other ships. He sat on the shore and tried to figure how and where Morgan might have taken the ships in case of an emergency. After a while he walked in the opposite direction. His heart was on the ground as he sloshed through reeds. Around a sharp turn he heard singing, looked up and saw, as clear as stones in spring water, four old, battered, partly repaired ships sitting on log rollers far up on the tree-lined limestone shore of a stream he called *Aber Cerrig Gwynion,* White Rock Creek. He walked closer and stared at the ships for a long time.

Hidden on the flats behind the *gele,* men sang as they worked wood laths into bent forms in steaming vats; others stirred hot pots of aromatic pine tar, or bound with thread the edges of newly made sails. Men he did not know shaved and clinchered pine planks, using trenails or wooden pegs that swelled with moisture, onto the frames of the four ships. Other men coiled piles of rope and carried caldrons of coal and quicklime.

Materials were hidden under tarpaulins held down by boulders beside the creek. Beyond the four half-repaired ships were five strange vessels. One of them had the name *Pedr Sant* on her flanks, another the head of a gray wolf carved on her prow, another the horned head of a wooden buck deer, and another with a sand crane with outspread white wings, golden eyes and beak. This last one reminded Madoc of his Danish friend, Erlendson, who had taken him and Conlaf to Iceland on a trading expedition. The sheath of lead that had protected her from shipworms was being torn off, and her hull was covered with a tarred fabric. Erlendson had always said the lead sheath only trapped the worms. He preferred reed caulking and tar as the best way to protect against the worms that burrowed tunnels in the wood. Finally, there in front of his eyes was the *Vestri,* Kabyle's ship, with a citadel being built on her prow. Slots were made in planks of local wood. Then flat pieces, called *tenons* were inserted into the slots. Trenails were hammered into the tenons to lock them in place. Most groups of workers sang or whistled as they worked. Instead of the usual poor fishing village of three or four cottages, Abergele looked spread out beyond the marsh onto the dry flats, like a happily thriving ship-building port. After a while he clenched his fists and roared, "Who dared to move the ships to the *gele?* What is going on!"

His heart pounded as he ran to the nearest cluster of men. A man with a gray wool scarf stopped singing and Madoc said, "What is this? Who are you?"

"My lord, as you can see 'tis a shipyard," said the man with the scarf. "We are shipbuilders, who work for Shipmaster Madoc." He looked down at Madoc's hands covered with gloves. "He will save us druids from being siege-engine fodder."

"He can do that?" asked Madoc, dumbfounded that the man would speak so freely.

"Aye, sire, Madoc can," said the man.

Another lad with a handful of rope and a melodious Irish brogue said, "With ten sails, he will take us where there is no avarice or bloodshed."

Madoc did not know whether to be angry or glad. "Did this Madoc tell you to move his ships from Afon Ganol to Abergele in Denbighshire? It looks like he is running from King Dafydd before he is made a supper for buzzards."

"Aye, if he wants to avoid buzzards and keep his head, he had better run," said the man with the Irish brogue. He touched Madoc's gloved hand. "He is druid, same as you and me. There is an order in Gwynedd, backed by Briton's Henry II, to behead all druids. Look around, *dyn,* man. The men in this shipyard could be without heads by tomorrow if King Dafydd hosts enough troops to discover us, or if we move a bit closer to Gwynedd's border. We are the last of the Old Religionists from Gwynedd, save for the few that hole up in caves and deserted byres in *Iwerddon,* Ireland."

Madoc suddenly thought, *This is what Sein tried to tell me. The druids sent these men, good men, to build these ships as soon as possible. I was stupid not to listen to his words more carefully.* "The chief shipmaster is a true druid and does not believe in force or warring it," said the man with the scarf. "He is our last and best hope."

"How can a druid keep his followers alive and, least of all, himself if he does not fight for his rights?" said Madoc.

"The shipmaster is well known for talking his way out of most anything."

"Really? You give him too much credit. I do not believe he could talk King Dafydd out of a dry biscuit. Who pays for all this shipbuilding?" Madoc's breath came in short puffs.

"We figured this way," said the Irishman, rubbing his hands across his face so it looked like he was trying to brush off the freckles, "if we are dead, our possessions have no value to us, so we pooled them and bartered for shipbuilding goods. We intend to outwit the enemy. Join us? You will not regret it." He took off his gloves and held out his hand. The back was covered with a swarm of freckles and blue half-moons were tattooed around the base of each fingernail. The honor-tattoos looked like lacy, scalloped filigree work.

Madoc looked around in amazement and wondered who, among his druid friends, had gathered so many men in one place. Who had talked these men out of their precious homes and belongings in such a short time? Things were moving faster than he had planned. "Are you offering me a job?" he said.

The man with the scarf gently touched two fingers of his left hand below Madoc's right elbow. "Aye, Shipmaster Madoc will pay for your labor," he said. "He is altogether fair. All you have to do is give up everything you have that can be bartered for building material, and take pride in another honor mark. See," he pushed up the left leg of his breeks, as high as his thigh, to expose the small quarter moon lying like a cradle with a triangle wedged in its trough, " 'tis Madoc's ship. We all carry it."

Madoc was stunned not only by the honor mark, but also by the man's chestnut hair and dark, smiling Irish eyes that reminded him of Brenda. He stared, making the man embarrassed. When he looked away, the excitement ebbed shallow and left him depressed. *I have gone too far*, he told himself. "How do I know you are not all working for King Dafydd?"

"We are followers of the Old Religion! I am Riryd ap Owain and this is my brother-in-law, Willem ap Corwen," said the Irishman, clapping his companion on the shoulder to show they were fast friends.

"Riryd, son of Owain? Owain, the Fearless, the former Prince of Gwynedd?"

"Aye!" Riryd said with pride.

Madoc's heart raced.

"Your luck is good if you join us." Riryd pointed with his thumb, a mannerism that Brenda used. "Watch for a ship called *Gwennan Gorn*. We have orders to attach crossbeams for reinforcement at her mast and to the horizontal knees for holding a forward and aft half-deck. Her forward deck is to be castellated."

Madoc's mouth fell open. It was the first he had heard that his ship was to have accoutrements. He wanted to rejoice and at least say, "Thank you."

"And I am asking your name," said Riryd.

"He be me. I be he—Madoc ap Owain."

"You? Nay!" cried Riryd. "Perfay! Oh, Lugh's liver!"

"Who sez you are he?" said Willem.

"Archdruid Sigurd, the Algerian, Kabyle, the four druids in monks' robes, and Brenda, my mother," said Madoc.

"I have seen those four monks. They look like they have been in the bogs cutting peat," said Willem. "One has no teeth, one cannot speak, one has no right leg, and the other is blind as a mole."

Madoc wanted to shout thanks to the gods for keeping his four friends safe. He grinned foolishly while Riryd walked around him, noting his height, sturdy legs, broad shoulders. His brother's scrutiny made him feel insecure. "What is the matter?" he said. "Do you not like the way I look?"

After a time Riryd said, "Your mother is Brenda, daughter of Lord Howell of Carno?"

"Aye," said Madoc. "Is that important?"

"Important?" said Riryd. "Why, we be full brothers! I thought from what our mother said—I thought you would have dark hair and eyes like a Welshman and be tall like a Viking, but you are short like a Welshman and blond and blue-eyed like a Viking. Is it really you?"

"I should have told you who I was right off. I saw our mother only two days ago."

Riryd put his arm around Madoc and said, "Did you see she is happy as a skylark? She and Sein are like first-marrieds. They can not get enough of each other. Gloryoso! Your daughter, wee Gwenllian, does not look a whit like you."

"She is a throwback to the small-boned, dark-haired, dark-eyed Celts and the darlingest colleen of the Irish camp," said Willem.

Madoc felt another rush of emotion. "You have seen them? Gwenllian is like Annesta, my—my wife. Beautiful just." He closed his eyes so they could not see his pain. When his eyes opened, he was in control and his sorrow hidden. "I be glad and honored to meet you." He fidgeted with his hands. "What about our sister, Goeral? I have never seen her."

"She looks like you. Since *ddoe,* yesterday, she is with our mother, who has always said she looks like Owain Gwynedd. She is married, but no children, yet." He pushed Willem in the side.

Willem started to leave. Riryd called him back. " 'Tis all right, stay." He turned to Madoc. "I said Willem is my brother-in-law. He is married to Goeral and he misses her."

Madoc felt about to burst. He wanted to sing and cry at the same time. "Our mam told me you wanted to build sailing ships, and she wanted Goeral to help her with the fosterlings, but she never said our sister had a husband."

"We came in three ships from Ireland and brought the druids we knew willing to be sailors," said Willem. "I think they decided to come and help with the building after learning how well you and your friend, a physician, outran the yellow dragons, while you had the disadvantage of pulling a loaded cart." He elbowed Riryd. "Archdruid Sein did not come with us, though he insisted we bring Llieu, Finn, Roi, Caradoc, Chonroy, Kerry, and Kei." He counted the people from the Taliesin and Prydian druid camps on his fingers. "Sein and Brenda are with the women and children. They are like a big family on a *tyddyn*, family farm. They plan to have a school for fosterlings. Goeral is staying with them. She will be a good teacher."

" 'Tis odd, but Mam said to tell you that the old bard, Llywarch, died," said Riryd. "You know him? Someone held a red-hot iron to his thigh before he was decapitated. Does that mean anything?"

"Llywarch was my wife's grandfather," said Madoc. "Woe is me! I knew he was dead before Annesta was killed. Mayhap she told me. I do not remember." There was a stricture in Madoc's throat so tight that he could hardly swallow.

"I am sorry, but you are not to worry now," said Willem. "The rest of your people are safe."

Riryd interrupted by taking hold of Madoc's hand. "When I last saw our mother, she talked about naught but you. To me you were a pesky ghost hanging about. I am glad to see you in flesh and blood. I have to tell you that I am an architect, but there is little call for designers of churches, courts, and bridges. They all seem to be built. So, out of desperation I became an Irish fisherman, and hunted krill fields where whales suck. I flensed and rendered oil until I was sick of smelling rancid blubber. When I was in Dubh Linn, my mam, our mam, suggested that I sell my fishing gear and curragh, join you, and create sailing ships. I had already made up my mind to join you before I knew you were kin. I sold my fleet and bought the *Pedr Sant* because she is deep in body with room for sheep, cattle, and fodder. I like her design."

"*Saint Peter* is a funny name for a ship whose owner is a member of the Old Religion!" said Madoc. "But keep in mind, I was called a trader-priest, and suddenly have become a shipmaster who has never seen the unproved lands I intend to find. I would fain like to talk with the *Vestri*'s master, the Algerian, Kabyle."

"The dark-skinned one is everywhere, checking, organizing, checking, organizing," said Riryd. "He asks where you are. He thought you would be here yesterday."

Madoc put his arms on the shoulders of the two men. He began to hum. He could not believe the good fortune of finding his ships with men who were kin, men he could trust, talk to, and enjoy. He promised to meet them again first thing in the morning. "Praise Lugh, I have brothers I like," he said.

His spirits were high when he gazed at the blue-and-white sails that were partially hidden in the reeds and willows on the shore of the calm blue bay. No wonder he had not seen this shipyard last night, or first thing this morning. He was not looking for anything like this. Time had collapsed on him. His dream of taking his friends, the learned ones, the Old Religionists, away from the present danger and giving them peace and freedom to explore natural philosophy was unfolding fast by its own accord.

Yesterday I was a trader, today I be a leader, he thought. *The moment is here and there is no time to prepare. It is time to move into a new role, a point of change, my fate. Is it truly what I was born for? Is it the Epiphany the old druids tell of?* He watched the gulls scatter ahead of him, mixing with another group that was feeding. As he walked a few birds ran ahead to join the larger group. They all stopped, made low chattering sounds, and the whole group turned to face the southwest prepared to fly. They rose as one, tilted their wings as one, and flew in the direction the group had chosen.

A voice behind him said, "The All-Glorious, to whom

we are bound to pray, has finally again brought us together."

Madoc took a deep breath, turned, and let Kabyle kiss him on one cheek then the other. He embraced his old friend, who was wearing the pale pink turban that emphasized his tan skin and brown eyes. He swung his arm around to include the shipbuilding activity and said, "In Allah's name what have you done to Abergele? What is this place? Who is in charge? I heard you were in Aberffraw! To be honest, I do not know where I be going."

"My friend, if you do not know where you are going, any gust of wind will take you there," said Kabyle, laughing so his white teeth shone in the sunlight. "Abergele will be here long after we have gone. For now 'tis *home*. We call it home because it is the last *known* place on this earth that we will work, eat, and sleep. The next place is *unknown* to us or anyone else."

"Home," said Madoc. "So, I be home."

"Since a dozen days ago, I became in charge of preparing ten sails," said Kabyle. "You are in charge of paying for all of them." He waved his hands. He saw Madoc staring at his fingers and thumbs that were bare. Only lighter bands of skin showed where the rings, Madoc once had seen, encircled his fingers. "Sold my gold rings with the various colored stones for ship-fittings," said Kabyle. "May Allah hold your tongue while I look at you and catch my breath. You are no more a gangly lad, but more handsome. Friends in Dubh Linn told me that your trader's life is in danger, same as mine and others who are non-Christian. Our friend Master Erlendson is here with his sail. Look for the crane on its prow. Hey, I heard you married. I want to meet the lass who stole your heart."

"My wife?"

Kabyle nodded, squinted his brown eyes in the sunlight, and smiled.

Madoc sobered and told him what he had begun to remember about losing Annesta. "For a long time I wanted to die, especially in the middle of the night. I have never missed a person so much. I wanted to thrust a sword through my half-brother, King Dafydd. I think of him as a stuck boar roasting on a spit. I be ashamed and sick to death of half-brothers who sacrifice druids in sacred oak groves in the name of the Lord God." Madoc kept his eyes on the ground. "Now I think of venturing to a place where my friends will be safe. Four monks, that are truly druids, and I repaired the *Gwennan Gorn*. I became known as a trader-priest, because I wear this Augustinian gown to save my neck. Now look! I was gone no more than a month, and now you and others are running my play. Sein told me a friend was rounding up more men to hurry the shipbuilding. You are a true friend! I do not know what to say, but to ask the one troublesome question: To sail away from one's homeland—is it irresponsible? Be I naught but a miserable coward?"

"My friend, may the Omniscient, whom I do not question, send you a sign proving 'tis not cowardice to save the lives of more than two hundred learned men. These druids are hard working, intelligent, peaceful, but harassed and threatened by men who think no deeper than an onionskin. You are their solution, their leader, and savior. Even though you are younger than half of the men here, we count on you for advice. Everyone came here because of you. You began the shipbuilding and the fair-trading. We are eager to join. You, then, must be like the spider at the center of the web, always in plain sight, ready to confound the enemy, but not when he expects it. King Dafydd believes he is Gwynedd's great gift and Supreme Lord. He puts his nose in the air and struts, imitating someone who thinks he is cock of the walk. He will keep Gwynedd knee-deep in blood and chaos for years. His English wife, Emma, is sour as rhubarb. She vows to rid Britain of anyone not a baptized Christian! So 'tis prudent to sail away, the sooner, the better. First, however, you shall have a platform in the bow and stern of your ship, someplace to keep your log dry and floating needle from spilling from its container."

"I be overwhelmed with goodwill and would be a fool not to be grateful, even though the plan is developing faster than I can think what to do next," Madoc said.

Kabyle drew in his breath and scratched his turban. " 'Tis true that some Dubh Linn druids spoke about being foolish to sail with you to an unknown land. They held a council and let me talk. I told them 'tis better than hiding in Irish caves or living in Gwynedd. Before the night was over they all agreed with me. Thus, you do not have to think about it. We are all with you. Sein is with you. He stays behind to work with his wife, Brenda, who keeps open the school for fosterlings. He loves your mother more than life itself. So, we sail and you become chief shipmaster, and there begins another story. I am the fool who cast his lot with Old Religionists and used my paltry goods along with theirs to buy shipbuilding materials. Druidlike, I memorized the figures to tell you what was spent, and let them woad-prick a sail on my right thigh. Allah, protect me!"

"So, it was actually you who brought druids from Ireland to work in this shipyard," said Madoc. "I was told the Irish druids were on a retreat! You brought four of my little rotting ships to Abergele for repair, suggested the *Gwennan Gorn* have a fore-and-aft half-deck, and let it be known I would pay for the labor! I thank thee!"

Kabyle tucked his thumbs inside his sash, looked amused, and said, "I wondered how you are faring and heard you visited your father's tomb in Bangor. Allah blesses his memory. You had an audience with Archbishop Becket, and he gave you coins. Do not deny it."

"I cannot," said Madoc and his mouth turned into a lopsided grin. "And what were you doing in Aberffraw?"

"I harrowed hell!" said Kabyle. "I admit I brought over a boatload of Welsh and Irish druids who had been hiding in caves. They said you were on a druid mission. I had some other ships with their shipmasters and crew following me. We took a foolhardy chance that we might find you in Aberffraw and offer help. But you were ready to leave. I talked with the astrologer, Trevor, and admired your boldness running from Dafydd's men while pulling a cart loaded with heavy gold things. I worried like a father worries about his prodigal son when I heard you were rebuilding four measly ships near the old stone quay that is piereed with low arches. So we came to the Abbey of Llandrillo and found four monks, who were really druids, and a handful of young shipbuilders. Half of me wanted to help you, the other half thought I was loopy to be interested in some wild, goder-heal scheme of yours. I preferred to take your ships to Dubh Linn for rebuilding, but they leaked like sieves and this home, out of Gwynedd, was the best we could do."

Madoc's mouth was dry as a hot chimney flue. Once again he was without words. Finally he found his tongue and said, "You have a way of finding things. You are the ideal spy. I would like nothing better than to have you come with us. Help me to fulfill an old druid prophecy." His voice cracked.

"I confess I was about to sell you the *Gray Wolf* and the *Buck Deer*, for an actual druid's ransom, and take my money back to the Mediterranean in the *Vestri*. But it seems my three ships and I must go with you to make an even ten sails to fulfill that druid prophecy."

"Can we come to a bargain for your ships that is satisfactory to both of us?" said Madoc, finding a boulder to sit on and motioning Kabyle to sit on another.

"Truthfully, I want to see that new land more than I want your coins," said Kabyle. "Some of my Algerian sailors heard me say as much and they left me, saying I was throwing away a fortune to sail with a malcontent. They were not learned and still fearful of falling off the edge of the world into the Terrible Black Void where the oceans' waters pour *ad infinitum*. They talked of nothing but sea creatures that spout fire and swallow ships before they fall off the flat world's edge. Now they travel by donkey to seek work around Liverpool. And I be here with a bunch of druids. It was old Archdruid Llieu who promised to find me plenty of men for my ships if I would join your ragtag flotilla. He reminded me of your talent for curiosity, fairness, and getting what you go after. He said a man's willingness to confront the problems of his people in their time of anxiety is the essence of great leadership. That is exactly what you are doing. I thought it out carefully and believe that you will be listed as one of humankind's great leaders."

"That is a lot for one man to swallow. Nevertheless I will work hard at this leadership role. Come with me, I beg you," said Madoc.

"Swith! I am glad you begged; that is more like the ordinary Madoc I know. Thank you very much! I say *ben-*

edicite! Aye, take my ships and I will join your adventure on one condition. Take me to Al Jazair when I am ready to die. We Moslem Algerians have a saying: *The fallen leaves return to the root.*"

"I promise, providing you still want to go to Al Jazair when that time comes." The two men shook hands and Kabyle kissed Madoc on each cheek. Madoc studied one of the ships a few moments and said, "I want to find Master Erlendson of the *White Crane.*"

"Aye, I am acquainted with the Dane with bleached straw for eyebrows. Let us, you and I, make him an offer to buy his ship."

Madoc's eyes lit up like flambeau. "I will bet you a silver penny that he wants to sail with us. We have to welcome him. You do like him?"

"Nowhere is it written that Allah insists I like everyone." Kabyle licked his lips and pointed his nose to the sky. "I wonder why I like you, but I do."

" 'Tis because I depend on you to take charge of outfitting ten sails with stores for at least a month and extra gear for unforeseen mishaps." He reached inside his gown and held his hand open for Kabyle to see two large, blue precious stones.

"Use these, they come from the generosity of our druid friends," said Madoc. "I can use the remaining coins that Archbishop Becket kept for me. From now on keep a chart of the goods you buy and sell, and mark our goods with a drawing of a tiny, single-sailed ship. Tabulate everything and use our trademark. Like you said, I will pay for what we need, including labor if the men insist. I have more stones when you need them. Sell them for denari and smaller sesterces. No need for colored stones in a new land where there are no other people but us."

Kabyle whistled and said, "Ow, you have noticed that I bargain well for goods. I will trade your stones for coins. May Allah send a cuckoo bird to sit on your shoulder and sing sweet songs in your ear. I am going on an adventure that none of my people dreamed of! The Great One forgives me for not bowing to the east five times a day. He knew what He was doing when He put you in my path! I shall be rich!"

Madoc said, "I ask thee, what will coins buy in an unknown land if there is no one there but us? This adventure cannot increase your riches through trading."

Kabyle said, "Wrong. Riches come through many doors."

Erlendson and Madoc greeted each other as if they had been best friends for years and years. Erlendson showed Madoc that the *White Crane*'s prow was newly built. "A year ago I married Meg, the Icelandic woman at her *buiden,* her eating place."

Madoc nodded. He was not really surprised because Erlendson's sailors all knew he had been sweet on that dumpling-faced girl for some time.

"Right away her two sisters and a brother came to live with us," said Erlendson. "I just could not stand having so many in one bed, even though I had made it so big that it filled the room. I told Meg we could move to the Faeroes, if she left the relatives at the *buiden.* I was going to sell my ship and find some lubber's work, but my sea legs could not stand on land. Then I saw all this and learned you were at the center of it. So I talked myself into not selling, but to take the chance of a lifetime and go sailing with you. Meg is happy with her family, and if what I hear is true, and you are a good shipmaster, I am happy with you."

Madoc put an arm around Erlendson. "I cannot promise you sunshine, but I do promise you great welcome in this place called home!" he said. He shook both of Erlendson's hands. The gods had truly blessed him this day.

The day began with a fine, cooling drizzle when Riryd tattooed Madoc and members of his crew on their left thighs with a small sailing ship, Madoc's trademark. Madoc and Riryd sang together as they worked on the steering oar that hung over the starboard side of the *Gwennan Gorn*'s stern. They used a chisel and adz to trim and smooth the wood so the oar was thinner and more maneuverable. A muscular, black-haired, ruddy-nosed man called Einon, who said he was half-brother to Riryd, enclosed the forward deck with overlapping wood planks. His mother was an Irish lady, Semios. Madoc told him they were all kin. Einon thumped

Madoc on the back and told him to be alert because the three of them were also blood-kin to rats, such as Lord Maelgwyn and King Dafydd. The corners of Madoc's lips lifted, and he put an arm around his newfound half-brother. " 'Tis best not to denigrate the king of Gwynedd or his lords," he said. "There are big ears everywhere. I be not a warrior, and I be grateful for the good blood between us."

On the top of the *Gwennan Gorn*'s forward deck were stored half a dozen small coracles. The afterdeck was covered with a sheet of sewn ox hides stretched across wickerwork. The top was not pulled tight but left loose so that rainwater could collect there. By the time the eight pairs of leak-proof oar sockets were redesigned and replaced another week had passed.

Madoc appointed each shipmaster as overseer for his own ship. For example, he was overseer on the *Gwennan Gorn* and Riryd was overseer on the *Pedr Sant*, which needed a windlass. Conlaf sent his men for a three-foot length of tree trunk, which would rest in sockets on his ship's stern deck. Four spokes were stuck in the two ends. The braided, walrus-hide rope of the sailspar used to be hauled up by four men, who struggled and slipped on the wet deck. Now it was no struggle and only two men were necessary.

When a ship was finished, she was given the druid blessing and anchored at Afon Ganol's stone quayside where she could be loaded. The three small ships, the *Dove*, the *Blue Seal*, and the *Ystwyth*, meaning Agile, were already there.

One afternoon Madoc found an old friend from his voyage to France. Shipmaster Gerard, with his tricolored beard, wore a black wool cap over his tousled hair. He told Madoc to avoid the land of ice and snow that the Northmen had found in their unproved land. "We can travel to the Fortunate Isles, take on fresh water, and angle southwest to see what we can find. I will be your mapmaker."

Lord Iorwerth surprised Madoc by coming to Abergele on horseback, leading several packhorses loaded with dried meat, trenails, rope, resin, raw lumber, and other building supplies. He asked Madoc about his baby daughter. Madoc's eyes shone when he told how she smiled and already could turn herself over and hitch up on her knees.

"Quick to learn, like her father," said Iorwerth. Madoc grinned and took him to meet his other brothers, Einon, Riryd, and Willem, who was married to Goeral, their sister. Iorwerth noticed the lad, Brett, helping the men adz the mast for a thirty-footer, named the *Un Ty*, One House. He thought the lad too young to be working so hard. Madoc told him that Brett chose to work; no one forced him. But Iorwerth insisted he take Brett to his wife, Marared, who would give him a proper fostering and education. Madoc introduced Brett to Lord Iorwerth and left them alone. An hour later Brett put his straw pallet under the rearmost part of the bow and told Madoc he was ready to sail. Madoc reassured Iorwerth that he and Conlaf would see to Brett's education.

"I should just grab the lad and ride off with him," said Iorwerth. "Marared would approve."

"He has gone through enough disappointment for one lad's lifetime," said Madoc. "Marared, Lugh bless her, is like my mam, but never worry, she will find another worthy fosterling to fuss over. Leave Brett with us."

The next day Madoc sent Kabyle with Troyes to scout out where Dafydd and Maelgwyn's men were bivouacked. Madoc needed that information before he took all ten sails out of hiding into the wide bay in front of Abergele.

Four days later Iorwerth was home in Degannwy court. Kabyle and Troyes were home in the Abergele shipyard. Troyes could hardly speak his throat was so parched from walking in the hot sun. Madoc brought him a dipper of water. He swallowed all of it in several gulps, then said that Maelgwyn decreed all able-bodied men age fourteen and up, from every Anglesey town and croft, join his army north of Beaumaris on the beach of Llanfaes. "He plans to challenge his brother, Dafydd, for control of Gwynedd," said Troyes. "Lord Maelgwyn will wait until Dafydd's men are frazzled from destroying the very last druid, then he will attack from the south with troops on horseback and from the north with a half dozen of four-man sculls that are colored like the sunrise, red and yellow. Prut and Lord's lungs! A baby can see those ships four, five leagues away! That is my story." He pulled a large wad of wadmall from his trouser pocket and wiped his perspiring face. His eyes glazed with exhaustion and he clung to Madoc, then his knees folded, and he slipped to the ground. Madoc carried him to a sleeping tent and laid him on a straw pallet. "Lad, sleep. You have done the job of two grown men. Afterwards tell me when Dafydd plans to come for us druids."

Kabyle had a beaker of mead while waiting for Madoc. He sat with his back against a pile of lumber and did not stand when Madoc came. The mead made him feel nauseous. He breathed deep and said, "Dafydd has a huge stinking camp near the Conwy River at Llanrwst. I am glad Troyes was not with me. The sentries were jumpy and knife-happy. Dafydd stirs his men into a frenzy. They are ready to explode, to rip the hide off each other! They will rape and murder every woman on the crofts. They will torture the old men before killing them. Dafydd has to put his lads in a battle soon before they cut and slash each other!" Kabyle, pale as a ghost, closed his eyes hoping Madoc's face would stop weaving around and around. He bent his head between his knees, vomited honey-sweet mead, and wiped his mouth on his sleeve. Embarrassed, he pulled himself up and went to the other end of the lumber pile to sit. "I have had no food for two and a half days," he said and looked sheepish.

"There is food and rest here," said Madoc, squatting next to him. "Did you find out when they will battle? Will they come after us in a week, two weeks?"

"Everywhere I walked in that camp there was horse dung, human waste, and garbage. Aarrch! They have waited for weeks for food supplies and horses. When the supplies arrive, five hundred men will come to Aber Cerrig Gwynion 'to wipe the dog-faced, infidel-druids off the land forever.' That conversation I heard two days ago. Between nerves and smell, biting flies and pestering gnats, hunger and howling wolves, I do not see how those troops stand it."

Someone brought Kabyle a plate of warm biscuits. He put the plate on the ground. His stomach growled and he continued. "They know we build ships. They do not know why. They can only think we will start a battle of our own by attacking seaports, Viking fashion." He slumped against the lumber. His head fell to his chest.

Madoc thought, *I have to take charge. I have to give orders to men I myself have taken orders from.* He gritted his teeth, readied himself to tell the venerated men what to do, how, and when to do it. His stomach growled louder than a bear with a sore head. "The sooner we get our ships into the sea the better!" he said. Then he sought out Morgan and told him about the war camps of Maelgwyn and Dafydd. "How much time is needed to complete the building and supplying of our ships?" he asked.

"Another week, maybe." Morgan scratched his head and bent over to pick up a pine chip to clean his fingernails. "We can work under starlight, no torches. We have sailcloth, dressed leather, dressed pine, and oak lumber, brass, stag horn, trenails, corn, water, salted fish, and beef in each ship. We have naphtha, something new for the torches we will use at sea for signaling to one another. We will work out signals when we beach for evening meals."

"We cannot wait," said Madoc. "Hoot! We should have sailed yesterday. Could we leave at the morrow's high tide? We will hug the coast of *Espana*, Spain."

"Aye, you are the Chief Shipmaster," said Morgan, surprised that the time to leave was truly at hand. "Glyn and Shipmaster Gerard are drawing you a map as far as the Fortunates. Then we sail southwest toward the Unknown. Tomorrow's second high tide!"

The dining area was under a blue canvas tent. After sup Madoc gathered the shipmasters and pilots around him. He talked about a communication system from ship to ship by using linen flags by day and flambeaux by night. The flambeaux would be made of wood bound together with a mixture of tow and hemp, soaked in beeswax, or naphtha, and stuck into iron holders. "One flag held high, means to bear to the right; two flags held low, hang back, or stay far apart; two flags held high, bear to the left; three flags held low, stop and form a circle so we can talk; three flags held high, trouble, help, emergency, warning." Madoc struck the pine table with his fist. "We leave on the morrow's second high tide!"

That surprised many of the shipmasters and pilots. Caradoc and Sigurd, seasoned shipbuilders from Dubh Linn nodded, raised their hand in an unexpected salute toward Madoc, and left the dining area to spread the word.

The first high tide came shortly after midnight. Thurs and Erlendson came into camp trailing a long line of horses pulling carts loaded with barrels of mead, salted pork, and mutton, sacks of apples, onions, and grains. Before they could explain that most of the stuff came from abandoned farmsteads, everything, except the carts and horses, was loaded onto ships. Madoc sent them back to gather hay for the horses, which would be loaded into the holds of several ships. "If you find abandoned fish line, hooks, and sinkers, bring them," he said. "And if you wander into the Nant Gwynant woods, bring in more timber—do not bring in any that has been burned or chopped into small pieces."

Erlendson jabbed his fist into Madoc's stomach and said, "You do not have to give me orders for timber, Messmate. I have men looking for dressed rollers for each of the ships. I will store those carts piece by piece in my ship." His eyes sparkled.

Madoc thanked him and walked away, but not so far that he could not overhear Erlendson say to Thurs, "Master Madoc was preparing for this voyage before he was out of wet britches. His wits are quicker than a shark's jaws and his feelings gentler than purple thistledown. But never tell him what I said, or I will show you what is meant by the Viking pink eagle."

By this time the sun was barely under the horizon, shining on the low fog that hung in swirling wisps over the water. The whole shipyard hummed with activity. Apples dried in the bread ovens. They were pressed as they shrank, so when finished they were flat and wrinkled. Milk, strained through rushes, was set in wide-mouthed jars for the cream to rise. The hot pots of pitch sent clouds of vapor to join the fog. Squealing cordage was run up a masthead. There was a rain of hammer blows as workmen replaced deck boards under which they stored waterproof supplies.

Near morning Madoc was seeing the last preparations on his own ship, when he saw Kabyle waving his arms. "What has you so frayed?" asked Madoc, laughing.

" 'Tis not a joking matter!" Kabyle mopped the perspiration from his face with the end of his pink turban. "While purchasing bronze rivets and washers, I learned there are half a dozen sails, with their hulls painted red and yellow, in Traeth Lafan. Also, near Penrhyn, less than a league from Bangor, are three hundred horsebackers. Near Rhul, in the other direction, five hundred men, in yellow tunics, carry axes, wavy-edged daggers, bows, and lighted torches. They march this way on foot. Dafydd thinks we plan a war. He is coming sooner than anyone expected, from two directions, to destroy us. We are caught between the hawk and the buzzard!"

Madoc's skin tingled. "We are not destined to be caught! We move out now! Pass the word!" He was everywhere cautioning the men to be alert and to hurry. There was no turning back. He was aware of only one thing: that his ships would get out before Dafydd's moved in.

Rowers pulled each ship behind the *Gwennan Gorn* where Madoc was formally pronounced Chief Shipmaster. Conlaf was aboard as copilot. The shipyard was deserted, except where the biffins, or apples, had been drying.

Riryd was master of the *Pedr Sant,* which carried six sheep and thirty-two men, including Einon. Master Gerard sailed the *Gray Wolf,* which carried thirty-six men, two swine, and four horses. Sigurd was shipmaster of the *Buck Deer*, which carried thirty-six men, one milk-cow, one dog, and one bull. Erlendson sailed the *White Crane* that carried six sheep and thirty-five men. Kabyle was shipmaster of the *Vestri* that carried three nanny-goats, one billy-goat, and thirty men. Willem sailed the *Dove* with one milk cow, one dog, and twenty men. Troyes was shipmaster of the *Un Ty* carrying two billy-goats and fifteen men. Morgan was shipmaster of the *Blue Seal* carrying two nanny-goats and twelve men. Caradoc, who could not sleep nor wipe the grin off his face, was shipmaster of the *Ystwyth*, which carried ten men and three horses. Madoc was shipmaster of the forty-five foot *Gwennan Gorn*, which carried two milk cows and thirty men. There were two hundred twenty-six men, seven horses, twelve sheep, five nanny-goats, two billies, four milk-cows, two swine, two dogs, and one bull that went asailing for unproven lands. The morning fog and drizzle were burned away by the bright morning sun, and the sky was cloudless the rest of the day.

Without the cover of fog or the knowledge of most of his countrymen, Madoc's ship led nine sails past the Great Ormes head, Puffin Island, around Carmels Point and Holy Head on one of the great adventures of all mankind on the sixth of August 1170.

Before time to bid the sun farewell that day, six small, red-and-yellow sculls, belonging to Lord Maelgwyn, rowed through Conwy Bay. Opposite the Little Ormes Head the sculls were fired upon by flaming torches, stones, and arrows coming from a large contingent of Dafydd's footmen and horsebackers, who had scoured the recently abandoned shipyards looking for a clue to tell them which direction the trader-priest and his ships had gone.

The sailors, the footmen, and horsebackers whispered that the trader-priest's name was on both Welsh and English wanted lists, first for extortion of coins from the Archbishop of Canterbury, second for thievery of money that King Dafydd said was his inheritance, third for impersonating a priest, and fourth for stealing ships and people that Lord Maelgwyn said belonged to him as Lord of the Island of Anglesey. King Dafydd argued that the ships and people belonged to him as king of the province of Gwynedd. Madoc's punishment was set. His tongue and both his hands were to be cut off. There were rumors that he had fled to Ireland, other rumors that he had gone to the coal mines in Powys, and still others that he had freebooted a dozen ships and was sailing for St. Ives in Cornwall. There was no clue to indicate how many ships sailed from the quay into the Bay of Aberglassen, when they sailed, or how many men were aboard.

There was not one tar or pitch barrel, no dressed piece of wood, no torn canvas, no dikers, or stones for anchors, or frayed rope lying about. The firepits, stone milk tubs and bread ovens were gone, filled in with sand and gravel. There was no sign where the wooden benches and long pine table for dining had been. The wood had all been stacked and stored aboard one ship or another. The blue awning, rope, wooden pegs, and pole frame were stored in the hold of another ship. There was neither a sign of leftover food nor refuse in the yard.

The garbage pits were covered with sand and slender stems of bistort and leaves of thrift, so that its location was not discernable beyond the gele. The only indication that any ship might have been recently in the area was in the size of the creek, which appeared to have been dredged and widened. One filled water barrel stood, like a sentinel, on the bank. The cottages around Abergele were silent. The occupants enjoyed a rare spending spree in the village of Rhos after living a couple of weeks in temporary lean-tos. In the village they bought unbleached linen for new shirts and skirts, and undyed wool for trousers and stockings with coins Madoc left them for the temporary use of their cottages and yard.

Part Two

Owen Gwynedd ap Griffith succeeded his father as Prince of North Wales. His death in 1169 plunged his country into civil war. . . . It was due to the civil strife that followed his death and the confusion attending the warring of the princes for the throne that Madoc left his home and discovered the New World, according to many historians. . . .

. . . After Gwynedd's death Howell seized the throne and, according to some Welsh historians, reigned two years. Prince David, gathering friends and some of his kinsmen made war upon Howell, killed him in battle and succeeded him as Prince of North Wales.

David made himself unpopular by his marriage to Emma, half sister of King Henry II of England. Many Welshmen felt that David by this alliance with the ruling family of England, betrayed them into the hands of their ancient enemies. The fears of the nation were justified when soon after the marriage David sent a thousand men to serve under King Henry in Normandy and a little later went to Oxford to enter Parliament and swear allegiance to the King of England. The dissatisfaction among Prince David's people because of the marriage may have been a contributing cause of the ready enlistment of men under Madoc for his expeditions.

. . . The basis for the story of Madoc and his people in Wales and the journeys which resulted in the discovery of America, is found in the histories of Richard Hakluyt, David Powell and Humphrey Lloyd.
—Zella Armstrong, *Who Discovered America?*

X

Pearl Ear Bobs

Two species of penshells (*Pinnidae*) are found in the area:
The stiff penshell (*Atrina rigida*) found in the bays and Gulf
and the saw-toothed penshell (*Atrina serrata*) found in the
Gulf. As a food source, penshells contain a large scallop-like
muscle. It is a very tender delicacy, especially when eaten
raw, but penshells quickly acquire a taste of iodine if not
eaten or processed quickly. Cooking toughens the meat somewhat, but penshells still retain their sweet taste.
  —Robert F. Edic, *Fisherfolk of Charlotte Harbor, Florida*

Egret continued to ask Otter about his trip and why he
could not find the island where there was a woman called
Hyacinth. "How did you get to the island?"

"I talked to a fisherman who was netting what he called
pearl shells," said Otter. "As food they are eaten raw right
away. I liked the taste of the meat. Inside the shells there
were no pearls. It is the luster of the shell that makes them
valuable for ear bobs. If they are filed round, they look like
pearls. A handful of 'pearls' can be made from one small
shell. I traded my mocassins for this pair of ear bobs for
Cougar. There are a couple of colorful beads above and
below each pearl. The beads and pearls match the neckband
she wears. I traded my headband for some shiny thread she
can sew on the yoke of her tunic. See this hairlike cordage?
It looks like rainbows in the light. It is really thin roots or
legs that anchor the pearl shells to the bottom mud. I saw
women sew it into flowers as decoration on the yoke of
their tunics."

"Cougar will like both," said Egret, touching the ear
bobs. "What about landmarks to find Holly Island? Did you

ask the fisherman? I think I could find the place if I knew the markers. You said the island has ancient holly trees that grow in a straight row. The black, purifying drink is usually made from holly leaves. The berries are avoided because they cause terrible stomach aches and purges. Birds like the berries and eat them all day without bad effects. When you were on the island, did you think it looked like the wind blew seeds in a steady line long ago? If those trees with their clusters of red berries are still there, I can not miss them unless the island has moved or is lost. Islands do not become lost."

"I never heard of it," said Otter. "I learned that Holly Island lies behind a larger island."

"I will ask Healer about directions, and you check what she says with what the fisherman told you," said Egret.

They went back to the Tequesta village to ask Healer about the people living on Holly Island where her daughter lived. Healer kept saying that not many people lived there. Cougar told her that the man her daughter married might be called Owl.

"I know that!" said Healer. "My daughter, Hyacinth, married a nice young man who has those funny kind of teeth—same as you and your grandfather. Do all Calusa have that double row of teeth? The Tequesta file their front teeth to sharp points, you know."

"Double teeth in the upper front?" asked Cougar. "I did not know there was anyone, besides Egret and me, like that."

"It could mean Owl is really a Calusa, not Tequesta at all!" said Healer, running her tongue over her top front teeth. "Are you going to leave me and go to see him?"

"I will not leave you," said Cougar. "Grandfather Egret and my friend Otter are going to Holly Island. When they find your daughter, Hyacinth, and her husband, with double teeth in the front, they will bring them here to see you and me. It is hard to wait for that happy day."

In the middle of the night Cougar woke with a dull pain in her back. Maybe it was in her belly, she was not sure, but she knew something was not right. She went outside and behind a tree to relieve herself and discovered she was bleeding. It was no surprise. What even she had hoped never would happen, had. *Oh, Spirits*, she thought, *why do you do this to me now? I am not ready. I would rather have my bleeding begin later—when I feel it is time. Grandmother said it was necessary to bleed to have a baby, but I have learned when a woman is carrying a child this bleeding stops. No woman likes the bleeding. Some wise woman needs to have a talk with you, Spirits, to get the awkward situation straightened out.*

Of course the bleeding marked the beginning of her womanhood, prepared or not. She had not been close to another woman for several moons, since Grandmother's death, and she had forgotten about the changes taking place in her body. She was not certain what to do. Grandmother would have built her a brush shelter twenty or thirty strides from the village. Cougar had heard mothers tell their adolescent daughters they were not permitted to cook or to leave their brush shelter for five days, except at night. For those five days combing her hair would be forbidden. She had heard the mothers ask Grandmother to go outside the shelters at night to sing advice and instructions for a young woman's future behavior. Sometimes Grandmother sang sexual songs for the girls to think about. Because she was a friend with the girls going through this, she had listened to all of Grandmother's songs. When the girls were alone with Cougar, they repeated the songs and giggled, hoping Cougar would impart their meaning. Cougar did not know what everything meant, but she was not hesitant to ask a married friend who might tell. For a moment, under a yellow three-quarter moon, Cougar listened to the dry whisper of sand moving and the rhythmic overspilling of seawater and tried to remember what friends her age had done when they first discovered they were bleeding. She walked around and heard the plaintive, single-note whistle of a bird disturbed by her movement so that it flew in circles over the small breakers before going back to its nest. She went to the canoe where Otter was sleeping.

"Wake up," she whispered. "Remember the breechclout I made for you before Egret and I left? I have not seen you wear it. Now it will do me more good than you. Please, let me have it."

"You want to take my breechclout back? What is wrong with you?" said Otter, half-angry at her for waking him.

"I was hoping you would give it to me without a lot of questions. I know I should have thought of this before, but I hoped it would happen to me later, so I did not think about it."

"What are you talking about?"

"You know, I do not have a woman's belt and I am bleeding."

"I do not know that. What does my breechclout have to do with a woman's belt? Sometimes I can not understand your words, Cougar."

"Well, listen. I need something to hold the moss in place so that I do not bleed all over everything in the Healer's lodge. She is an old woman and does not have a woman's belt. In fact I believe she too forgot that women ever wear such a thing. Otter! Come on, I am desperate. Blood is running down my leg! I hated to ask, but I could think of nothing else. Now I understand why women hide their bodies. Some women say this bleeding is a curse put on them by other women, who do not want men to look at their bodies all the time. Give me your breechclout, and I will let you look at me."

"Why should I do that? I have already seen you. You are skinny with a flat chest like a young boy."

"You have not seen me lately," Cougar said with a smile. "I have two bumps on my chest that grow bigger each day."

Otter got up and rummaged through his small pile of clothing. "I was saving the breechclout for some important day. I really treasured it, because you made it. Now you are going to ruin it. I can never wear it. Do not touch me. These are your unlucky days!"

"That is silly. I might be skinny, but my body is telling me that I am a woman. It is no different than when you start growing facial hairs. Your body is telling you that you are becoming a man. Do you think I, or any other woman, would like to rub faces with you? No! But if I did, I would hope not to be in an unlucky situation. I would get two clamshells and pluck out your facial hairs one by one. Then I would let you rub your face against mine. Hand me your breechclout. I will make you another. I promise—when I have time. If we were in Sandpoint with Grandmother, she would have a celebration for me, because I am now a woman. Here there is no celebration, no feast, no little brush shelter where I can stay for five days without combing my hair. I am a woman with a red leg. A woman's bleeding time is not something to laugh about. It makes me cranky. Remember how your mother used to be at that time? You teased her and made her go to the women's shelter. Are you going to help me or laugh?"

"You look like someone scraped a shell knife on the top of your leg. Wash up!"

"I am going to the deep pool in the creek. It is better than seawater for washing."

"I will go with you and bring the breechclout. That is what brothers are for."

"Thank you. Some men think it is bad luck to look at a bleeding woman. Are you afraid of me?"

"I know you as well as I know myself. Like you said, how could I be afraid of something natural that happens to you? I saw my mother when she was bleeding and bad luck never found me." He made a scurrying sound in the sand with his bare feet. "Race you to the water!" He ran, shedding the breechclout he wore and dropping the one he carried.

Cougar wore her skirt, hoping to wash out the bloody stains and still have a useable skirt when she was finished. She stood waist deep in the cool water. "Aha, cold, but it feels good," she said. She put a little sand on her skirt, then rubbed it between her hands to make sure it was clean, squeezed it several times in the water until the sand was gone, and spread it to dry on a large rock. She swam easily alongside Otter. "Listen to the long hisses, the splashes and whispers of the surf. It seems the sea people are having a grand time talking this night."

The wind had blown most of the day but was calmer now, and there were fewer clouds in the sky. She watched the moon floating in the pool. It looked like the sky-moon's brother, who gave light to the people living in the water. She had never seen sea people but she had heard stories about them. She knew the sky-moon had no brother in the water because Egret had showed her it was only a reflection of the moon. She looked up and, of course, the moon was in the sky. She did not know where the moon's light came from, but she knew it was not a warm light like the sun's. When the moon set behind the dunes, darkness spread across the land.

They stopped frolicking and walked hand in hand back to their clothing. Cougar picked up the breechclout Otter had brought for her. From a pack in the canoe she pulled out a handful of the moss she was going to make into a skirt. She stuffed the moss inside the clout's pouch, then belted the garment above her hips. "This is just right," she said, rubbing warmth into her arms.

Otter stood in front of her and filled his lungs with air. "For a sister, you are even more beautiful than I remember. I—I want . . ."

She looked up and touched his arm. "What?"

"I have not done this before. . . ." he stopped.

"But we have. We have gone swimming so many times. Even when Grandmother thought we were doing something else, we would tumble out of our clothes and swim, then dry in the sun, get back into our clothes, and go after drift for the fire or dig clams. They were good times." She gazed at him and then put her arms around his waist drawing him close. She could feel his stick grow hard against her belly, and it gave her the same frissons she had felt watching the Stretching Ceremony. She sighed and moved even closer. Oh, she did like Otter because they could share everything. She rubbed her belly against him and pushed herself as close as she could. She no longer heard the wind in the trees or the waves slapping against oyster-encrusted rocks.

"I want to give you these ear bobs and this thread that carries its own rainbows," he said. "The ear bobs are made from the shell of the pearl fish. I ate a lot of that fish when I was coming here. It did not have to be cooked."

She was surprised and pleased that he would bring her such beautiful gifts. She slipped the ear bobs into her ears right away, kissed Otter, and danced around him. "Do I look pretty?" she said coquettishly. She felt a little foolish, but she was suddenly anxious to tell him that she wanted to share her life with him. She was elated, but at the same time weepy. The happiness had bubbled over into tears as she danced around him, and finally she rubbed her wet face against his.

"Do not cry," he said gently. "I will not hurt you." He held her face in his hands and said again, "I want—I want you to—"

"You want me to make you something with the rainbow thread? New mocassins?"

"No, I thought about how nice it would look on the yoke of a tunic you make for yourself. I want something you could give me for letting you take back my breechclout," he said softly. "I have loved you forever. You are the only woman I shall ever want. You could think of it as a gift—to me." He gave her a smile and looked away toward the trees. "Come, lie in the warm sand with me." He had known her for twelve years and always thought she was the prettiest girl anywhere. She had the kind of enormous dark eyes that women envied and gave men gooseskin. Her skin was smooth and near perfect, and her dark hair grew longer each year. He had watched her pile her hair on top of her head and hold it there with thorns, or make one braid tied with a thong of leather to ride on her back, or comb it and let it hang loose, like now. When she ran it flew out behind. When the breeze blew it around her face, her laughter and singing came through to make tiny bumps of delight on his skin.

"Otter, I have always loved you. You make me so happy that it spills out like tears. I am not sad, except for one thing. I wish it were you who had done the first stretching of me. I imagined it was you when Brittle Star went inside me. Honest, it was you I wanted."

He let his arms fall and gently pulled her down with him against the back of a warm rock. "This is something I have wanted for so long." He put his lips against her small, rounded breast.

"I, too, have the strong feeling in my belly. But I think this would not be fair to Grandmother. I am thinking I need to wait so I can remember her advice."

"Your grandmother is dead! What does this have to do with her or her advice? This is you and me. This is us." His hand slipped between her thighs to caress the sensitive place. His mouth hugged the flesh on her belly.

She closed her eyes and thought, aye, this was what she too had thought about. She opened her eyes and saw the length of his body. He had grown taller and thinner. Her hand reached out to caress his firm, bare hip. She could hear his breathing above her own.

One of his hands hugged her breast, and the other slid over her flat belly.

This was what had been in her mind just beneath sane thoughts. She breathed deep and smiled. The desperate want was on top of the rational thoughts. The willful want was so hungry it devoured all the other reasonableness. His hands pressed tight against hers, then moved slowly along her arms, up and over her chin. His fingers explored her lips, danced lightly across her nose and eyes, then to her ears, down to her shoulders, and rested on her breasts. He moved his tongue on a hard nipple like a thirsty wildcat lapping water. His breath was warm on her neck. She pushed her hands into his straight black hairs, pressed his face between her breasts, and moved her hips up closer to him. She wanted him, all of him. She was ready. She groaned with desire as he pushed down the breechclout and let her guide him. He plunged once, twice, then gave a powerful shudder. She moved against him, frantic with her unbearable lust. Her fingers dug into his back. He was not surprised at the ferocity of her embrace. He knew her and had dreamed what it would be like to possess her. He whispered shamefaced into her ear that he could no way hold back his need for her. It was something he would have to learn to control—more practice and he would learn. She pushed herself closer to him, and he remembered what Egret had told him about satisfying a woman if he came too soon.

Neither woke until they heard the great flock of gulls shrieking at one another over the small fish that lay on the wet sand atwinkle in the pale starlight. The gentle night breakers dumped handfuls after handfuls of little silvery fish on the sand, all up and down the beach as far as anyone could see.

Cougar pushed herself up, rubbed her back, and saw that the finger-long fish were slim and round with forked tail. She wanted to wake Egret and ask what kind of little fish they were. Some of them danced across her bare feet, making her laugh with joy. She flopped down beside Otter and tickled his bare feet and made him look at the little fish. He did not seem surprised she would be the first to wake, and he smiled. "If we watch, maybe we can get a nice cod for breakfast," he said. "This time of year the cod chase the small fish right up on the shore." He looked down at himself. "What bit me?" His penis and belly were covered with sand and half-dried blood. He looked accusingly at Cougar, who had ducked into the stream and was scrubbing herself as if she had run through something that was hard to wash off. "Wren said you had teeth in your vagina," he said. "Is it true?"

"He does not know anything!" she said. "Wash yourself and you will see that you have no bite marks."

Otter kept staring at himself. "Do not come near me," he said. "There is something wrong here. I do not know what to believe."

Cougar put the breechclout on backwards and adjusted it so that it fit her as well as a woman's belt, then she pulled her skirt on top. "You know I tell you the truth," she said. "It is Wren that would like you to be scared of me, so that you will believe all the false tales he can spew out."

"Am I your husband?"

"No, I did not say that. Did I?"

"Cougar, what is wrong with you? We had the pleasures of husband and wife, and you say that I am not your husband. I say I am."

"I promised Grandmother that I would do the big thing only with the man I take as husband, and I am not ready for the 'taking' part. But you know I wanted you. I wanted you so much that I could not say nay more than once."

Otter groaned and said, "You grew double teeth in the top front, so that when you were a child you could whistle better than any boy. Now you are a woman. You could have grown teeth in your vagina, just to be different than all other women and give men something to fear. Some men like fear with their pleasure."

"Were you afraid?"

"Of course not. Are you going to have our child?"

"No, not yet. I can not have a child if I am bleeding. Every woman knows that!"

"What about me?"

"You should have known. I have to find Grandmother's son before I take a husband. It is my promise to Grandmother. I have to! That is all."

"No man can possibly love you as much as I do. You— you mean everything to me! Come on, lay down with me behind the big rocks where it is warm. If I had bite marks, they are gone. I feel better and will go slow this time. You will see it is better that way."

"I want to! Oh, I do. But not now. You and Egret take the big canoe and find Grandmother's son and Healer's daughter."

He washed himself and pulled on his old breechclout. "I hope you are right about no vagina teeth. I can almost believe you are a shape-changer. Next time we lay together I do not want to find that I have put my stick into a real, live cougar cat."

"Well, what if you did?" she laughed and put her hand over his lips before he could answer.

The moon had become full and then night after night it would shrink back to a mere slice, to a narrow canoe in the sky.

"I have the insatiable hunger for you," Cougar whispered to Otter. "It frightens me. I can not keep my hands off you. I like the feel of your body next to mine. I want to lie with you all the time. When you are gone, I will learn some new stories and the things Healer does to keep people well. Find Grandmother's son. Bring him and his wife here for Healer and me to see. When you come back, I will lie in the warm sand with you and say we are married."

"Promise?" Otter put his arms around Cougar, drawing her close. She promised and put her cheek against his.

Otter found two cod that had followed the fingerlings to the beach before the gulls found them. He woke Egret to show him the cod and tell him the day was right to go to Holly Island to find Grandmother's son. Cougar woke Healer and said the men were ready to go searching for Hyacinth and her man called Owl.

Healer rubbed the sleep from her eyes as she fried the

cod in duck fat and told the men to look for a sink hole in the middle of Holly Island that contained sweet water, except in times of bad storms. "Look for rows of holly. The small trees with scalloped, dark green, thick leaves and red berries," she said. "The island people put the sour juice of wild onions on raw oysters, clams, scallops, and pearl shells that they harvest during cool fall weather. They eat as much sea grape and palm hearts as we do, so you will feel at home. Do not stay long. I am so anxious to see my daughter and her husband that I will count the suns until you return."

She followed them to the beach, still chewing on a piece of the cod. "When you get there, you will see there is only one place to pull in a canoe," she said. "It is on the south side and only a small sand bar. The rest is rock. Not much growing on the rock, until you go inland and see it is like a big meadowland. The drift is used for fuel. Not many people live there; three, four families. During a bad storm, they go to the mainland. Those families are doing something to please the storm spirits, because there has not been a bad storm for years."

When the canoe was out of sight, Healer showed Cougar her supply of herbs and told her how each was to be used. She could tell that Cougar was not interested, so she told her that treating sick people brought new things to learn and think about. "No matter where you live, people will come to you for help. You will be rewarded with food and clothing and family stories. You will always have children around asking to hear a story. They will keep you young."

Cougar did not know if she meant the children or the stories would keep her young. "Have you ever heard the story of a man with pale hair and pale eyes?" she asked.

"Is it a story that frightens young children into good behavior?" said Healer. "My favorite is the story about the giant white panther."

One day she talked to Healer about the loneliness without Egret and Otter. She talked about the injustice of the spirits who permitted people to be gone from sight when they were truly needed by kin or friends they had left behind. "It is not fair," she said. "I do not know what to do any more. I want to talk with Egret and feel Otter's warm hands on my face. I wonder if my real mother and father know that I have lived to be a grown person. I wonder what I will do with my life."

"Everyone asks himself questions that cannot be answered," said Healer. "Listen, I like you. I need you. Any kind of accomplishment in this life requires discipline. Set an objective and work in that direction. You need a man. I will find one for you. You will be a good mother with plenty of children."

"Oh no!" said Cougar. "I do not want you to find a man! What would I do with him? I do not even know what to do with myself."

"You are really bad off if you do not know what to do with a man," said Healer and laughed until tears rolled from her eyes. "A man would know what to do with you!"

Cougar let the tears roll down her cheeks, then she too laughed.

Healer wrapped her arms around Cougar until the laughing stopped and said, "I love you, my dearest granddaughter."

"I may not be your granddaughter," said Cougar sniffling. "It depends on your daughter. If she married Grandmother's son, then I am. I wonder what Egret and Otter are doing. I thought they would be back before the moon grew round again. What can they be doing?"

"Child, wake up," said Healer. "Men! Women will never understand them. Maybe your men are fishing. I have heard that the Calusa men are hungry all the time, so they fish day and night."

XI
First Storm

. . . The mariner became aware of the proximity of land by
listening to the sound of the sea on a strand, . . . and by noting
the flight of birds, like the falcon flying to the south-east. . . .
The principal duties of the crew must have been managing
the large sail, steering, bailing, and standing look-out.
    —G. J. Marcus, *The Conquest of the North Atlantic*

Madoc breathed in the salt air and thanked the gods that
no ship followed their ten sails. For an instant his heart
missed a beat as he imagined his daughter full grown, not
knowing her father. Then reason eased his heart and told
him as long as Brenda and Sein lived, Gwenllian would
know about her father and her mother. Slowly his land-
bound thoughts floated away when his feet were firmly
planted on the deck of his sailing ship. He believed his
feeling was similar to an alchemist's thoughts becoming
more creative when he was in his laboratory.

The sailing men were prepared for an experience that
was completely new and unpredictable. They were tense,
excited, and each one imagined a foretaste of the silver
streams, green unpopulated land, and the freedom to think
and write as individuals. That evening, when the sun was
below the horizon, the air became stuffy. The sea mimicked
the sky, which was a splash of violet, orange, green, and
blue. The colors faded fast to misty gray, and fog closed
around the ships.

Conlaf took his turn with the steering oar.

Madoc was wound too tight to sleep. He thought of
bringing ten ships through the terrible tide race off the tip
of the Llyn Peninsula, and the whirlpools near Bardsey Is-

land's shore that churned the sand and seaweed against the rock buttresses. Caradoc told Madoc that Bardsey Island was once a continuation of the mainland hills. Over the ages the restless sea had cut its way through the land. Madoc had first seen the island when he and Conlaf were Welsh emissaries on their way to Paris.

"I remember 'twas a blue-sky morning four years ago," he said, leaning against the gunwale next to Conlaf, "when we first went through Bardsey's famous tide race. 'Twas the season for planting barley to signify a continuance of life. 'Twas the time of the year when the Old Religionists celebrate the death and resurrection of Attis, the ancient god of vegetation, whose mother was a virgin. Today the Romans celebrate the day as Easter, and say 'tis a time when the son of the Chief God arose from the dead."

Conlaf nodded and quoted words from the well-known druid poet Taliesin, who spoke of three traveling druids, who were wise men going to visit the infant Jesus. "Ah," he said, "other Christian festivals have been placed on certain ancient festival days. The New Religionists hope to transfer druids' devotion to their way of thinking. Four years ago we were young and unsuspecting and ignorant emissaries pretending to be knowledgeable monks."

"We climbed aboard a ship bound for Paris, wearing our black gowns and sitting on red sea chests next to the last set of rowlocks," said Madoc. "I bowed my head, put my palms together, and asked the Lord God to bless our food. I forgot to make the sign of the cross. You bloody goat, you punched me in the side and made me really embarrassed."

Conlaf punched him again and noticed Brett and Brian, a dark Welsh lad, and a couple other messmates wrapped in their blankets, listening to them talk about old times. "Can you believe it?" he said, "We slept next to squawking chickens and a couple of horses going to Lundy."

"I am sleeping next to two cows," said Brett. "I pray for a calm sea."

"Listen," said Madoc. "You can see all ten ships are loaded with supplies, animals, and men. Pray that the cows do not switch their tails, or we could ship water. Keep your tongues in the middle of your mouths. I do not want my ship to capsize."

"Ask for a handful of linen rags to bind your hands before you pick up an oar," said Conlaf. "And during a storm, start singing."

Brian scrambled to the gunwale, leaned his head over, and heaved out his insides. Seagulls mocked him with sharp cries.

"Aye, laddie, get it out of your system," said Conlaf. "The first time I climbed off a ship at Bardsey the messmates came next with the wood framework of a sleeping tent to cover the shipmaster's hand-carved, four-poster bed, which was set above the high-water mark. Good fortune has kissed you because Shipmaster Madoc will sleep under the stars same as the rest of us."

"Has he one of those poster beds?" asked Brett.

"Of course not!" said Madoc. "And you'll never see one on my ships! Here are more facts worth remembering: The first abbey built in Wales was on Bardsey, *Ynys Enlli*, in the sixth century by Brother Cadfan. Later the abbey was taken over by Augustinians and dedicated to Saint Mary. *Myrrddin*, Merlin himself is buried in the sacred ground surrounded by twenty thousand other mystics, wizards, and holy persons."

"If you lads believe twenty thousand, you can believe that the sixth-century Roman pope will keep his promise and give you special indulgences whenever you visit the abbey," said Conlaf with a wink. "Years ago pilgrims fled from the great plague pest and came to the Bardsey Abbey. Shipmasters took huge donations of coins or precious stones from grieving relatives to bring lepers there in winding sheets."

"Shipmaster Madoc, did ye ever bring a leper there?" asked Brett.

"Never," said Madoc. Then he looked at Conlaf who turned his face away and scratched his right hip. It was the same hip on which he had carried a leprous child while on the road to Paris four years ago. Sometimes leprosy seemed to transfer to another as easy as looking at a pretty lass; other times a man could live for years with a wife who had the disease, and he had no sign of it. Conlaf was unlucky because he had caught the disease, but lucky because his leprosy progressed slowly. He had an itchy patch of white scaly scabs on his right hip, but no nodules or deformities, which gave him a modicum of hope even though there was no cure. "I would take no amount of gold or jewels to leave a friend or relative in this god-forsaken abbey, no matter what his measure of wellness or unwellness."

"What is wrong with the abbey? I thought mystics and holy persons went there because it had the best beds and good food," said Brett.

"Henry II is trying to convert Bardsey into a base for launching English ships so that he can attack the Llyn Peninsula," said Conlaf. "From there he plans to have English troops take over North Wales and the west coast of Normandy. France's King Louis cannot be happy about that. Not many people know that Henry wants a military base on Bardsey, on Lundy, and on one of the Channel Islands."

"Four years ago a weasely man, called Robert, was the traitorous Abbot of Bardsey, who expected to become Abbot of St. Peter Port on Guernsey Island in exchange for getting troops on Bardsey and Lundy," said Madoc. "That *drwg*, rotten bloody pirate, was knee deep in English secular affairs. I prayed hard that we could talk the French king into helping Owain's retainers fend off greedy English soldiers, who sailed from Bardsey or Lundy to take over the Welsh mainland.

"At Bardsey we met Brother Patrick, thin as Death, who rubbed his hand over our skulls and said we were two sorry Augustinians. We perplexed him because our souls were clear and our voices true. But we acted like pagans by listening, smelling, and seeing everything. We shunned no knowledge, new or old, good or bad. When he asked, I told him we lived with the world, not apart from it. He said that proved we were kind-hearted, but did not prove we were true Augustinians."

By this time all of the messmates were seated in a semicircle, looking up with wide eyes and open mouths at the two men beside the steering oar and talking about their first big sailing trip four years earlier. At that time Madoc and Conlaf were close to the age of the messmates, who were on their first important sailing trip.

"We found how cold-hearted Abbot Robert could be when he kept food from the Abbey's brethren," said Conlaf. "Brother Patrick never complained, but I could see he was being starved to death. I gave him a rhizome of galangal and showed him how to nibble it to intensify his appetite, keep gas low, and calm his stomach. Madoc found grain for gruel and showed the brethren how to gather fish in a net from a coracle. Listen, when I first met Cadwallon, I knew he was related to Madoc. If either man had worn a bearskin instead of those black gowns, they would have had that same kind of Northman look. They looked like Prince Owain when he went off to do battle in the middle of winter."

Madoc ran his hand through his long blond curls and said, "I looked everywhere and could not find the brief our father had written to Cadwallon. I held up my skirt to look more thoroughly in my trouser pockets. Cadwallon had never seen a monk hold his gown above his waist. He laughed so hard that he had to hold his sides. He said, 'By the Holy Ghost, thou art as irreverent as a goat in a silk shop! 'Twill be a miracle if I can teach the two of you to be monklike in a week.' We memorized a hundred prayers, catechism, litany, and the philosophy of St. Augustine of Hippo. Then he said we could memorize faster than anyone he knew, except his father who, he believed, was half druid. Then we laughed until our sides ached because we knew his father and knew Cadwallon was my half brother."

"I can never forget how that miserly Abbot Robert deviled us all the way to Paris," said Conlaf, giving the steering oar back to Madoc as the tide ebbed and raced down the north coast of the Llyn Peninsula with as much ferocity as it had four years earlier. There were huge black rocks and sawyers caught between underwater crags that made the sea boil, churn, and bubble into white foam. The whirlpools could spin a small boat like a whirligig and smash her against the craggy cliffs or suck her down against rocks, sand, and seaweed.

Huddled together the messmates listened and watched as Madoc manipulated the steering oar. Brian asked if there would be many more treacherous places before coming to the unproven land.

"Only Lugh knows what we will see or run into—tide races, storms, or monsters," said Madoc. "Keep your eyes open and never cry out like an infant. I may have the power of Circe to turn you into swine."

"No sorcerers here," said Brett. "There be only men— brave men who seek a better way to live out their lives than covering up proud honor-marks or hiding in stinking wolf dens to avoid beheadings. You are the shipmaster; we are loyal messmates." He looked around at his fellow messmates as if there was more to say and he had been appointed spokesman. "Ah, umm, some of us wish to continue with our studies. Some of us do not know our history nine generations back, or much about natural philosophy, reading, or writing. Will that kind of knowledge be necessary in a new land?"

"History, natural philosophy, reading, and writing are necessary advantages wherever you might be," said Madoc. "We need scribes to keep track of our planting and harvest time, what crops and how much was harvested and stored. We need historians to mark the date of deaths, to tell about the man's life and the cause of his death. We need someone who knows how to describe the different plants and animals our new place has to offer, how the stars move with the rising and setting of the sun and moon, to compare the new knowledge with what we already know."

The messmates understood and nodded.

"I have extra vellum," said Madoc, "so you who need to practice writing can do so. When that runs out you can draw in the firepan sand."

"We can make marks with charcoal and wash them off the vellum when we wash the sup plates and pots," said Brian.

"And you shall have my journals to practice your reading aloud so we all can hear you. From time to time I will offer suggestions. My journals are all I have to show that I was once a Welsh emissary. Treat them as something precious and rare, or you will wish you were swine, not lads. If you spill porridge on any page, I will beat the bloody tar out of you and cut your ears off. No bloody excuse you can dream up will make me go soft with you."

The next day they sailed into the fearsome stretch of

water south of the Caledonian coast, where Madoc could not talk above the groans and creaks from the planking as it responded to the swells and whirlpools. The ship felt as if it was shaking apart. He kept one eye on the nine ships that sailed close behind and told Brett to fasten a white flag on top of the mast so that the next ship could see it and her men would do the same. He prayed to the water gods that all would come through the *Ynys Enlli* whirlpool without hitting a rock or snag. The planking groaned louder. Wind built huge waves as it roared through rock tunnels, until they sailed past a sheer rock wall with a large proboscidean protrusion that acted as a baffle and broke the waves into millions of water droplets. The cold spray soaked the men quicker than a drizzling rain.

Dewi, bending over an oar yelled, "Lugh! We are going to meet death on the Irishman's Nose!" Another cried, " 'Tis the edge of the earth!" Their teeth chattered and their bones felt brittle as ice. The fierce wind made them colder than if they had gone into the sea.

"Never yell too soon!" called Madoc, arms taut as he held the steering oar. "We will not fall off the edge; there is no edge to a round earth. Know that for troth!"

The messmates drew in their breath, but did not cry out when they noticed Madoc's bloody hands. Watery blisters had broken, and the flesh had become raw as he kept the oar in place. The air was so cold that he was unaware that his hands had blistered. He threw his weight on the oar and drew the ship back towards the center of the channel. Dewi's oar snapped as he cut the water between two jagged rocks. The free end hit the back of Conn in front of him. Conn cried out in pain and doubled over, letting his oar hit the back of the man ahead of him.

Madoc called to the oarsmen to pull. "Hang tight! Heave ho!" He stamped his right foot against the gunwale to mark time. The oars dipped and rose. Skillfully he brought his ship and the nine behind him to face southeast. The steady wind was behind them as they made it safely past the nose of the Llyn. Madoc breathed thanks to the water gods, Manawyddan and Lugh, and congratulated himself on his ability for handling the steering oar. Then his pride turned to humiliation as he remembered something the swordsman, Illtud, said to him long ago, "Purge yourself of the fine achievement that lacks proper talent." If any untrained man had drowned while Madoc was in charge of their rowing, he would have been as guilty as if he had thrust a spear and stopped the man's heart. Madoc wondered if thoughtless men were always repaid at some time for their poor judgments. He had the men push out of the channel on a huge swell and swing around to the south.

Conlaf gave Madoc and the two men, who were battered black and blue by oar handles, a powder mixed in water so they could sleep. He washed the blood off Madoc's sore hands, cut away skin hanging from broken blisters, put on a fishy-smelling salve, and wrapped Madoc's hands in clean rags. He promised the men their pain would lessen by morning. That night the ships beached below Aberdaron and the ships' messmates scrambled off in all directions to search for driftwood to fuel cooking, drying, and warming fires.

After a good night's rest, Madoc saw the blue sky and gave thanks to the gods for fair weather. The crews had little to do this day but let their wounds heal. Some sloshed water on the deck and mopped it dry while others sang.

Dewi's short blond hair spiked in the wind. Suddenly he laid his deck mop aside, pulled off his shirt, and showed off his honor marks that covered both his arms and shoulders. He told anyone listening the history behind each one received for excellence in shipbuilding. The marks were something that made him proud to be a man and proud to be a druid. They signified what he was, what he could do. This was the first time in twenty-five years that he had let more than one or two men see his honor marks. He turned his face so that the wind dried the tears that came unbidden to his eyes. After a noon meal of cornmeal mush with bits of onion, he lifted his harp and played Irish music of great antiquity. The men sang, watched the land, the clouds, and the water. Lundy Island was their first destination to replenish the water tuns.

"Do you keep a journal about us?" Messmate Jorge asked Madoc. He had a large head covered with red hair and spoke in a slow voice.

Madoc seemed surprised by the question. He shook his head and suggested that the messmates take turns reading aloud from his journal. The men stopped singing and came to sit near the messmates to hear them reading. Brett's reading was slow, and Madoc had to help with many of the words. He thought a month or so of reading and there would be a noticeable improvement.

"Let me read some of that," said Jorge, pushing his wide shoulders and flaming head in front of Brett, whose head was black as a carbonized cook pot. Brett slowly handed him Madoc's journal. Dewi strummed his harp softly, making mysterious haunting music. Jorge cleared his throat to make certain each word was pronounced correctly. He spoke slowly as his finger pointed to each word.

The men began to be bored and started to move around. A group formed in the prow and began to sing two-part songs. Madoc hoped that the messmates' writing was better than their reading. But he would not bet on it. He expected some of the men to laugh or make light remarks about what the lads were reading. But no one said anything.

After sup the messmates sat down to work on writing. Brett and Brian copied words from Madoc's journal to ask their meaning later.

Madoc lay on his pallet that night and remembered things. With his eyes closed, he could see the crescent island of Lundy surrounded by slate cliffs and covered with thousands of sea parrots, called puffins, with black feathers above, white below, sharp, triangular orange beaks, and orange-red feet. In the morning he felt out-of-sorts because fog blotted out his line of ships. He went to the boards to relieve himself and took the steering oar from Conlaf, who was glad to get some sleep before the fog burned off and the day became warm and humid. He said, "Sometime on the morrow we sail past Lundy."

Conlaf brushed his damp hair out of his eyes and suggested that they spend the next night on Lundy Island.

"Beautiful Lundy lasses cast their sweet-smelling nets for sailors," piped up old Archdruid Gwalchmai, taking time to tease Madoc, while on his way to relieve himself. "If you let us set foot on Lundy, we may never step off. I am told that Lundy lasses have a powerful effect on men.

I would like to test that effect on a man my age." He chuckled when he saw Madoc turn red.

"I say nay to all of it," Madoc said under his breath, feeling his face burn. The rest of the day men asked more about Lundy and pretended they knew more than they did. Madoc began to half-hope that the fog would stay, and they would sail beyond Lundy before anyone realized.

By noon the following day the sun had dried the fog-wet decks. Madoc's hands were healing, and he wore leather gloves when he took the steering oar. He pointed out Menevis, St. Brides Bay, Bristol Channel, and finally Lundy Island. "Look at the crowd below that has come to see our ships pass by! We must be a glorious sight!" He held his hands on the sides of his mouth and hollered, "Yo! Ho! 'Tis Chief Shipmaster Madoc, Physician Conlaf, and ten manned sails!"

The people on the beach shaded their eyes and chanted, "Madoc! Conlaf! Madoc! Conlaf!"

Madoc's heart skipped a beat when he saw a pretty young woman with a youngster balanced against her hip. "Blackberries!" he called, "Beautiful as ever!" His voice seemed overloud, and he could see she had changed from a lithe girl he remembered to a matronly woman.

Brett said, "Ye know that *merch* with the *baban*? She is puffing up! I bet she has had a poopnoddy or two with her man, and if she has no man, with some sailor who stopped here and dipped his wick."

The blood rushed to Madoc's face. He was galled at the lad's crude observation and no longer heard the crowd chanting. Now he saw the swell of Blackberries' belly and thought, *How could I expect her to—to wait for me? Since her—I married Annesta.* His hands were sweaty and his heart thundered. *A man never forgets his first coupling,* he thought. *I can not deny that I came by Lundy to show her what a big man I have become, but I never intended to stop overnight.* Under his breath he said, "Lugh, I be no better than a whitewashed pig."

The ships did not beach but continued to sail in sight of land through the night.

In the morning after a breakfast of salted fish and hot

water, Madoc told the messmates to complete their chores while Brett read aloud.

"Master Madoc, everyone knows I can read better than that little rat," said Jorge, running his fingers through his unruly hair and pointing to Brett.

"Be still," said Madoc. "Do as I say and I will tell you when 'tis your turn."

"Man," said Jorge, "when I get me a woman, she will do as I say, or I will show her why by beating the stuffing out of her." He winked. "I hear that puffed-up babe on the beach we saw waving yesterday was something special to ye."

"Man," said Madoc, "if I be around, I shall warn your young lady to stay far away from you. You are an old scoundrel, drawn to women as iron is drawn to lodestone. You are no better than a muddy griffin. Did you ever think that words can sting or soothe; educate or destroy?"

"If we had camped there last night, I think I would have had a long look at a naked lady in the bathing pool. I know for troth, I would not come away blind just for having a look. That is a myth mothers tell adolescent sons! I have stirred my stick in a kettle or two." Jorge spit over the gunwale and waddled away with his legs wide apart.

Madoc unclenched his fists and thought Jorge was not what Brenda and Marared had in mind for furthering Brett's education. On second thought maybe it was all right if Brett heard his bragging. It was no more than man's talk. He would hear it sooner than later. He went on with the reading lessons, giving every messmate a turn. Then he let them practice their writing until it was time for another meal. "If my students have not learned, their teacher has not taught," he said, turning to ask Gwalchmai to play some soft lyrical tunes on his harp before mealtime.

Later he overheard Jorge tell Brian that Shipmaster Madoc was a gormless scholar who believed that some of the druid, Welsh, and Roman rituals would be intertwined so that the braid was different from anything anyone had dreamed. "I am not a slow-witted scholar, and my thoughts are not bodged up like our shipmaster's," said Jorge to the other messmates. "Clear as baby tears I heard the him say I was likened to old iron." Jorge had pushed his lips together in a pout, then went on. "The friggin' shipmaster wants us to do reading and writing exercises once every day. If I have to do that, I am not going to wash another pot or pan."

Madoc told Conlaf what he had heard and asked for a suggestion to keep Jorge and the other lads washing the cookware.

"To keep lads that age in the kitchen, you could offer them more rations. They like to eat," said Conlaf. "In fact I believe a couple of them are sneaking food when they think everyone else is asleep."

"I thought it was rats I heard scurrying around the kitchen when I could not sleep," said Madoc. "Thanks, I'll work on your idea." He could not offer more food, because it was not endless. But the lads could add to the supply by fishing.

The next morning he twisted and oiled flax lines for strength. He rolled the lines around blocks of wood, put scraps of dried meat in a basin of sea water to soften for bait, and laid out half a dozen bone hooks. When the lads' practice writing became a torture, he told them to stop. They were going to have a contest to see who could catch the biggest and the most fish. The winners would have a fish supper. His words and the fishing lines sent the lads into a frenzy at the stern's gunwales. They were no better than grown men telling each other about the big fish they had once caught. Actually none of the messmates had caught fish on a line; they were used to nets. The lads tried, but caught nothing.

That night Madoc was worried about his scheme. He realized that they were not close to land where there would be lots of seaweed where tiny fish and shrimp, that the larger fish liked to eat, lived. The next stop, the Fortunate Isles, was a few days away.

The next morning, after breakfast, the messmates read and wrote. Brian used the firepan filled with sand to work on making neat letters. Some of the others used little pads of vellum and quill pens. Jorge spread warm lard over the place the firepan usually stood. When the lard cooled and was solid, he wrote sentences for Madoc to praise. Before noon the study materials were put away and the firepan in place. The messmates boiled water for tea and fried corn-meal cakes in the lard Jorge had scraped off the deck.

While eating, Madoc smelled something burning and found the deck under the firepan blackened. When exposed to air, the hot lard burst into flame and gave off a long tail of black smoke. Quickly the deck was flooded with sea water.

Madoc called Jorge to the steering oar and showed him how to hold it steady. "Messmate Jorge, you will stay with the oar until I come back," he said. "I want to write our direction in the log and yesterday's events in the ship's journal. It will not take long. Think about what you would do if the whole ship caught fire."

Jorge stared at his feet and said, "Aye, Master."

"Call me Shipmaster Madoc."

"Shipmaster Madoc," he said without looking up.

Madoc looked up and saw a front coming in and forgot to tell Jorge to wear gloves to protect his hands. He thought a strong wind could blow them off course. What would they do for fresh water if they missed the Fortunates? A wave hit the ship side-to and flooded the deck. He was alarmed but not panicked. He went to the castellated bow and made a list of things to be done before thick weather. He called orders from the bow. "Clear the deck. Conn, pull down the sail. Tie the lines. Dewi, Conlaf, and Gwalchmai, lower the mast. Messmates, secure all loose cookware. Wrap sleeping gear and clothing in oiled canvas and store in hammocks. Conlaf, watch for seasick men when the wind blows. First check on the animals. Tethers and pens must be secure. Help the bailers."

In his forward half-deck, Madoc put his writing equipment, sand clock, maps, charts, journals and extra vellum, lodestone and floating magic-needle in the cupboard. He noticed one of the smaller messmates coming up to him. It was Brian who grabbed Madoc's arm as the ship lurched. His face was white, his dark hair damp.

"The ship was moving funny," Brian said. "I do not feel good." He bent over and gagged.

Madoc carried him to the deck. He told Brian that sea-sickness would not kill him. The storm would not last long, and there was nothing to worry about. He handed short

lengths of rope to Brett and told him to help the messmates
tie themselves to the gunwale, then to tie himself. "Stay
close to Brian."

Madoc nodded to Jorge, who held tight to the steering
oar, his forehead perspiring. His bare feet were placed
firmly on the deck boards. "Rough out there," Madoc said.
Waves were as high as one man standing on another's
shoulders. The ships seemed to pause in midair then come
crashing down on the opposite side of the wave. There was
no singing as white-knuckled men were at the gunwales
heaving their insides out.

Conlaf was kept busy giving the seasick men watered
vinegar and coaxing them to help shore up a crack in the
hull, where water poured in like a waterfall.

"I held on," said Jorge. He kept a broad smile toward
Madoc. "Did you see me?"

"You did fine," said Madoc, feeling the ship tip to the
left. "Just keep her upright; do not let it put its side to the
waves." The rain hit his cheeks. He took the steering oar
with one hand and gave Jorge an oiled-canvas cloak with
a hood, like the one he was wearing. The water's push on
the oar was so strong that he could not hold it steady with
one hand. His gloved hands were wet and stiff with the
cold. It took all his strength to keep the ship from spinning
as she slid into a deep trough. He saw the coming wall of
water and thought it could swamp the ship and push them
all overboard.

Jorge did not hesitate to put his hands on the oar beside
Madoc's. The ship steadied. The swell crested and pushed
the ship forward. A wave broke over their gunwale and
quickly drained away. Together they pointed the ship at a
forty-five degree angle to take each wave. Jorge pulled his
hood up to cover his wet hair, and Madoc saw the lad's
hands were red.

He said nothing because he was surprised at the strength
the lad had in those skinny hands, arms, shoulders, and
legs. "How would you like to be pilot once in a while?"
he shouted through the wind. " 'Tis a responsibility and you
have to use your head as well as your hands."

Jorge looked at his raw hands and did not speak for a
moment. Lightning rose from the water near the prow,

which pointed downward into another trough. This time Jorge saw Madoc's hands tighten. He did not move, but he pointed to another bolt of lightning that was closer. "If lightning struck the sail or the mast, the whole ship could catch fire."

"Right," said Madoc. He turned the ship so it headed into the wind and the swells. He pushed his hood back, lifted his face to the sky, and let the rain darken and flatten his hair.

Jorge faced him close so that he could hear above the blasts of wind and shouted, "Thank you, Shipmaster Madoc. I would really like that pilot's job. Nobody has asked me what I would like before."

Madoc heard him through the wind's roar, smiled, and yelled back, "Messmate and Sometime Pilot Jorge, tie yourself to the gunwale beside Brian and Brett until the storm blows over."

Jorge saw Madoc's lips moving, but he could not hear as the wind blew against him. "What?"

"Tie yourself to the gunwale!" Madoc shouted and pointed to the stern.

Jorge saw Brian was white as chalk, crying, and hanging his head over the gunwale, heaving his insides out. Hanging on to the wet gunwale with his raw hands, he slid his feet until he was leaning against Brian. He lifted Brian's chin and wiped his face with a wadded rag from his pocket and whispered something in his ear. He tied himself with a rope so that he sheltered Brian from the wind.

Madoc breathed deeply and gave thanks to the storm gods.

XII

Fortunate Isles

> ... The Canaries [Fortunate Isles] were already known to
> early antiquity. In particular, they were frequently visited by
> the Phoenicians, who obtained from them the "dragon's
> blood" [red dye from the *Dracaena draco* tree] and dyer's
> lichen (litmus) used in the production of Tyrian purple. . . .
> The Greeks too knew these islands. . . . The peak of Tenerife
> is visible from a great distance and the smoke billowing from
> its crater can be seen from the West African coast.
>
> —Paul Herrmann, *Conquest by Man*

Madoc warned the other shipmasters about the Scilly Isles'
riptides and strong currents by running three white flags
high on a rope attached to the upper yard. When the last
sail had threaded its way between huge boulders, Madoc
flew one flag low, meaning go on. They sailed passed
Land's End, the granite cliffs of Cornwall, and the rocks at
Liz-Ard Point. At twilight the expedition sailed across the
English Channel toward Brittany. Madoc looked for
friendly, mild, southern currents, instead of the strong
northward stream to the west that Kabyle had warned him
about. Summer was ending. They had not had the luxury
of waiting through winter and leaving in the spring when
most storms were over. If they got past Cape Finisterre,
they would easily make the Fortunates.

The ships strung out through the choppy waters at the
mouth of the Bay of Biscay. To lose sight of one another
could lead to permanent separation with unknown consequences. Madoc raised one flag and flew another low. The
signal meant to close up, keep together.

They sailed past Finisterre and into a sheltered bay,
where Madoc was afraid beaching would gouge out keels

on boulders and piles of driftwood. Then he found a large sandy shore clear of debris and brought the *Gwennan Gorn* ashore amid hosannas. The ship was rolled on logs high out of reach of high-tide breakers.

The barefoot crew wore hoods and flapping cloaks of tarred canvas and divided into two groups. One group searched for dry wood and the other built a smoking fire. Madoc made three torches of raw wool soaked in naphtha and stood them low on a sand dune. A few twinkling stars became visible. Madoc addressed them as the royal sky guards, who kept vigil day and night, clouds or not. He asked the sky guards if they knew where the other ships were. They were silent, keeping their secret.

A second squall line moved overhead and dumped buckets of rain while Kabyle's *Vestri* came in. His men brought out a large blue canvas and tried to make a kind of lean-to against the back side of a sand dune to keep the water off everyone as they ate supper. Stones were laid on the bottom of the flapping canvas. Torches glowed and sparked. Men hollered over the wind to tell how each thought their ship was a goner when mountainous waves struck broadside. The wind died, the fire and torches burned bright, and the men talked easier, even though soaked to the skin, despite tarred cloaks. The air turned bitter cold, and the men crowded around the central fire. Toward midnight they saw seven bright lights moving up and down on the sea. They were sure it was seven torches. They counted again and were certain it was seven ships headed for the beach. Madoc helped the men tie their ships to large boulders on shore. There was handshaking, hugging, recounting narrow escapes, and wolfing down of hot mush. The *Un Ty* was not in sight.

Gorlyn, the shipbuilder, had tamed his straggly gray hair so that it hung in wet, snakelike strands. His narrow face was haggard, making him look older than his forty-five years. He hammered, scraped, and belted out orders on how to repair the storm-damaged ships, especially his loose rudder. Many men keyed up from the storm worked with Gorlyn to ship the rudder so that it hung secure. Afterwards the men found a place to sleep in the damp sand against driftwood.

Conn had a group around him that watched the blue-black bay for the little *Un Ty*. Madoc's supper lay in his belly like a stone as he shouted orders to replace the two lost hull strakes, or two lines of planking along the hull on the *Gwennan Gorn*. When he heard the men sing as the eastern sky blazed with streaks of pink and orange and the dazzling sun rose from its night ride under the earth, he raised his arms in gratitude. He searched the calm golden sea and checked the beaches for the *Un Ty*. He refused to think the worst and avoided Conlaf, whom he knew would say, "It is to be expected we would lose a ship in that storm. Erik the Red lost half his fleet when he sailed less than a week from Iceland to Green Land. We sailed less than a week and lost one ship in a terrible storm. That is something to be thankful for."

Kabyle told Madoc they were near a tribal fishing village, called Vigo, in the kingdom of Leon. Madoc gave him a handful of coins to buy a barrel of wine and more tar. Kabyle explained that the Leonese were not fond of dark-skinned men who wore turbans, so he would take a couple of druid sailors with him. Madoc did not argue, but bent his head, looked at glinting, pearl-like bits of shell on the sand and then looked up at the white clouds. He promised the powerful water-god, Lugh, that if he brought the *Un Ty*'s crew to safety, he would be more thoughtful toward the men by giving each a full cup of wine this very eve. In the afternoon Kabyle and two men came back with a barrel of tar, two barrels of olive oil, four huge stoppered jars of olives, and several sacks of plums to dry in the sun. Madoc asked how three men had carried these things.

Kabyle told him to look in the tall grass growing above the high-tide line. Squatted there were fifty or sixty men, women, and children. They came to see more ships in one place than they believed existed. The chief of the group was middle-aged, a corpulent man, dressed in a brown wool tunic that hung below his knees. He had curly brown hair and a hypnotic presence. He used his eyes like a teacher by directing his gaze not at the eyes of the man he spoke to, but at the bridge of his nose, producing a stare that the student could not return. He stretched out his hand and presented Madoc with three high-smelling, beautifully dressed bearskins. Madoc took the skins, bowed low, and said he appreciated the gifts. The chief looked puzzled and spoke words in a resonant voice that Madoc did not understand. Neither man knew what the other said and looked around for help. Kabyle was beside Madoc to translate. "The chief says he knew right away that you were chief of all these men and ships because you walk alone with majesty. There is worry in your eyes. He sees you search the sea. Shall I tell him you look for a ship?" Kayble kissed the tips of his fingers and flicked them in the chief's direction. "His name is Pico."

"Thank him for his generous gifts and say we are missing one sail since the storm," said Madoc, holding his nose and lifting his eyes to scan the sea.

Chief Pico turned his back on Kabyle who, to him, was an infidel because of his dark skin and turban, then spoke for a moment. Kabyle ignored the turned back and said that Pico was a believer in ancient numens, guardian deities. "He reads auguries in the liver of a slaughtered ram, and yesterday he saw two hands' worth of unusual liver spots in a dead ram. Each hand represented five ships from afar going to a trade fair. He believes that a chief owning ten ships has wonderful things to give away."

"There are nine ships." Madoc counted aloud, pointing to each ship and pausing for Kabyle to translate. "Ask him where we can find the missing ship." Madoc patted the elegant skins. "If he finds it, there is a reward." Madoc lowered his voice. "Do not ask or say what the reward is because I have no idea."

The chief was all smiles at the mention of a reward. Still, he would not look at Kabyle, translator for both men. "At this moment I see your bright red, living aura," said Chief Pico to Madoc. "The aura of a very rich man." He hefted a barrel of wine from the shoulder of one of his men to the ground directly in front of Madoc. "I honor you with three bearskins and a gift of wine!"

Kabyle cleared his throat. "The wine is not a gift. I paid for it like you said. He has the Roman denarii in his pocket."

Madoc tried to keep his face without emotion. He stepped close to Chief Pico and said, "You augured ten ships in your omen. Well done! Find the tenth ship." He nodded to Kabyle to translate.

The chief picked up a pink spiraled shell and said, "I see you at the center! You, a rich man, share the lost ship and her cargo with us. You reward me many silver coins. I treat you well. Tomorrow your lost men will be happy working for our fishermen."

"Oh, no!" said Madoc.

"May an eagle pluck his tongue out by its fat roots," said Kabyle. "He expects a ransom for the *Un Ty,* or he proposes to keep us as slaves, a sign of wealth, valuable property. In my country there is a saying. 'A king without slaves is like cider in a leaky tun.' "

Madoc looked at the seashell in Chief Pico's hand. He followed the winding channel of the shell from the center, like an island, with ever-widening circles of waves. He waited for his anger to subside, then said, "I care naught if the chief is like cider dribbling away. None of my men will become slaves. I give no reward until we find where the missing men are. Tell him I pay fairly for what I receive, but I do not pay for goods not delivered. Tell him I also read auguries and that the stars are in their conjunction, which means he is the one to bring us good news of the tenth ship and her men, who are not, in this lifetime, destined to be slaves."

Chief Pico moved in front of Madoc and looked at the bridge of his nose, seeming to look through him.

Madoc met his scrutiny without a blink. "You are so close, my shadow dims your pale yellow aura," said Madoc calmly, knowing that Kabyle would not translate his words exactly.

The chief put his hand across his eyes to avoid Madoc's look. He wrapped his fingers around the delicate pink shell. It broke. "On the other side of the stone point is a ghost ship with no sail," translated Kabyle.

"And the men?" Madoc's voice was loud.

"Gone," said Chief Pico, "Gone like boiling water."

Madoc sent Conlaf and two others to the other side of the point. If the ship was there, he could not afford a reward of food, nor ships' gear, nor lumber. His men needed all that for survival. He looked at Llieu, who shrugged his shoulders and said, "What you seek is under your nose."

Madoc looked down and saw only the three bearskins. "I cannot return a gift, even if it does smell of dead bear, smoke, and putrid grease. Chief Pico would have my head for such discourtesy."

"For troth," said Llieu. "But you can make something with the skins that will please everyone."

Madoc's lips parted. He wanted to ask Llieu what he had in mind. But it was up to himself to think of something. He was half-sick with worry. The missing men were more important than any ship. He stared at the skins and had not the slightest idea what he could make. Mayhap a couple of capes, collars, or caps? He walked the beach to bring himself into focus. He closed his eyes and cleared his mind. He saw Chief Pico paddling a coracle that spun around and around and got nowhere, like his thoughts. He breathed deeper and raised his face to the scudding clouds. The sun warmed him. He brought his arm up to shield his eyes, and the bearskins slid and settled on his shoulder. He looked at the gray-green sea dotted with an occasional whitecap. His cheek rubbed against the smooth fur. His bare feet dug into the wet, warm sand, and he felt close with the earth, close to his followers. Then a tingle, a whisper, something indescribable caught him by surprise. *The men of the* Un Ty *are nearby*, he thought.

Llieu startled him by taking his arm as if he were an aged man needing support. He led Madoc toward the shallow water and pretended to poke around in the water, with a stick, looking for something. While they were alone he said, "I heard something and hope I have translated correctly. I listened and watched people's hands and faces. They can do the same with us, so I will be quick. Kabyle told me what two old women were saying as they sat over there by the sticker-bush. Last night a couple of Pico's fishermen towed ashore an empty ship swamped with water. Then they spied men bobbing about the sea in a round, basketlike craft. The fishermen were so amused they held their sides and laughed. They pulled the men ashore to examine the little boats. When they looked for the men, they were gone!" Llieu snapped his fingers. "Poof! Gone like smoke!"

Madoc shouted, "I knew it! Master Troyes and his crew are here somewhere. Find them!" He danced around Llieu.

"Sshh!" Llieu looked around to see if anyone noticed Madoc's outburst. He saw no one paying attention and said, "A Cymru shipmaster does not yell and prance like a mountain lion. He remembers his druid training. Wisdom comes to those who are calm and tranquil in spirit. We will find our brothers, who probably rest under some bushes."

Madoc stood quiet a few moments after Llieu left. When he saw old Sigurd wandering back and forth on the shingled beach, he walked beside him and asked if he could cut enough long willow branches to make a coracle frame that would fit the bearskins. Sigurd smiled, patted his gray beard, and said he certes could. "I can also strip the branches and weave them into a neat coracle frame."

It was not long before villagers gathered to watch what this agile old man was doing with the snow white branches. Sigurd measured the bearskins that lay on the yellowed grass, went back to the willow sticks, and began to weave and sing, "They think I am making the world's biggest basket. A big basket, hi ho. A basket to hold a man, hi ho!"

As he headed for the stony point, Madoc found Riryd and asked him to carve a paddle out of a piece of drift, with a fancy claw at the top. He walked through tall beach grass and suddenly saw some suspicious bumps. His heart leaped. The bumps were coracles pulled up on the shingle, flipped over, hull up, and partly hidden in the sand and grasses. Madoc kicked and lifted one of the coracles. There was Troyes curled naked like a sleeping baby. Troyes rubbed his eyes and shivered. Madoc saw the heap of wet clothes and told him to dry them quickly. Troyes's mind, dulled by cold and fatigue, brushed sand off his muscular, hairy legs and said, "Master Madoc, I be sorry, 'tis *Dda*, the goat. I tried to hold him on the ship, but he jumped. We never saw him again. But we saw the three torches you set in a row on the beach. Did you see ours?"

"We never saw yours," said Madoc. "Death and misfortune come to everyone. I say, better the goat than any of the men! Hey, do not jump around like that! Wrap something around your waist. There are women here to eat with us. Bring the rest of your clothes and dry them near the cook fires. Come on, sailor."

Troyes barely comprehended what Madoc said. He did his best to explain that he and his men were half-afraid of the strangers who pulled them from the water in the howling wind the previous night. Bundled in thick black cloaks, the strangers resembled grampuses in the churning sea, and their words were beyond understanding. He and his men ran up the beach and hid in the tall grass. Later they turned their coracles upside down and climbed inside, out of the storm and out of sight.

Madoc helped the others spread their wet garments before a roaring fire. He set them getting their blood moving and warming by opening the *Un Ty*'s sacks of grain: hard wheat, millet, corn, and barley, and set them on huge stones to dry before they had a chance to sprout. Supply barrels were not opened; they were supposed to be waterproof. The *Un Ty*'s crew spent the afternoon dovetailing her broken mast and lashing it with wet leather strips that pulled tight as they dried. A gash in the gunwale, made when the mast fell, was repaired, and the ship was washed clean as the day she first set sail. When the grain was dry and the sacks sewn shut, the *Un Ty* was ready to sail.

Brett found the drowned goat, Dda, rocking in the water against the rocks. He asked Madoc if he could bury the goat. Madoc looked it over and decided it could be skinned and gutted. He told Troyes that his goat would pay the grampuses for fishing him and his men out of the sea. "Your clothes are dry. Get dressed. Come and watch."

Sigurd sewed the brown-and-white goat's skin on the rim of the coracle that was to be Chief Pico's gift. The skinned and gutted goat was given to Troyes to roast over a trench of hot coals. "We will feast with the villagers, then get away from here before Chief Pico has time to think of any of us as slaves for his fishermen," said Madoc, hoping that some of the women would bring things to eat, because one goat would not feed many during a feast.

The curious villagers stood around and talked in little groups. Then one of the women brought a mix of rye flour, water, and animal fat to make flat bread on the hot stones.

Others brought cheese, clay jars of milk, a basket of figs, and hazelnuts. Madoc poured the wine in a tun and topped it with water so there would be plenty to go around.

After the feast the villagers courteously smacked their lips, wiped the grease on their arms and legs to make them shine, and smiled when Sigurd held up the finished coracle. With handsigns and Kabyle's help, Madoc told them the tub shaped like a big furry eggshell was a reward for fishing the men out of the stormy sea the night before. Riryd gave the paddle he had made to the stocky man who brought the cheese. He waded chest-deep into the bay and held the coracle so that the man could get in and pull his legs up under his chin. The man took the paddle as Riryd gave the round tub a twirl before the paddle dipped into the water. The villagers clapped, jumped, and hooted to see a grown man swirling around in a small round boat in shallow water. The man finally poled ashore, put his arms around Madoc, lifted him off the ground four times, and slapped him on the back to show that the gift was something grand. Chief Pico smacked his lips and waved his arms to indicate that he wanted everyone to stand back and watch because he was going to show them how to ride the coracle. The crowd cheered.

Madoc spread the word that the ships were ready to leave one by one. Chief Pico spun round and round as the *Un Ty* and *Pedr Sant* were pushed off the beach. Then the *Gray Wolf* and *White Crane* were floating. A few villagers helped push ships into the bay and load the log rollers onto the decks. The *Gwennan Gorn* was last to store her log rollers and be pushed away. Madoc waved as the rowers took the ship past the twirling, bouncing Chief Pico, who clung, for dear life, to the sides of the coracle bobbing across swells made by the departing ships.

The druids in each of the ten ships gave a silent blessing for a safe day and night. Behind each ship was a phosphorescent wake that faded, disappeared, and reappeared among the gentle evening waves. Kabyle, feeling the need to do something more than keep the rudder straight on his ship, moved beads back and forth on his abacus. He figured they had gone as far as two hundred and forty leagues, as the crow flies, from Abergele.

The next day the ships sailed along the Portuguese coast where they could see small deltas and deep river valleys. They pulled into a secluded bay for the night and beached in a large basin surrounded by steep mountains on two sides. The grasses were soft, sweet smelling, and most comfortable under sleeping blankets. In the morning the men gathered armloads of the fragrant grass, tied them into bundles, and stored them aboard each ship for animal feed. They replenished their water from the river. Around noon there was hardly a breeze as they rowed past a shoreline of jagged rocks. The sails hung like limp clothes on a line. They were in the doldrums and travel was slow. That gave the men time to wonder if each ship had enough dried fruits, onions, and nuts to avoid the bleeding-gum disease. Some wondered what would happen to them if there was no land in the southwest. On Erlendson's ship someone said, "Maybe we will sail west forever and perish from thirst and starvation!" On Caradoc's ship someone said, "Mayhap we ride in a great circle!"

The druids were thinkers and used logic when talking among themselves. However, like all men, sometimes they questioned each other's knowledge and intuition. They sometimes even questioned Madoc's wisdom. Dewi scratched his head of reddish brown hair, looked at the backs of his strong hands, cracked his knuckles that were large as unshelled hazelnuts, and said, "The Fortunate Isles might be a figment of the chief shipmaster's imagination. Of course I have heard the Algerian Kabyle talk as if one could actually spend time on one or two of those islands. But I never heard of them from anyone else. So, what if they do not exist, and the Algerian is puffed up with wind to make himself look big in front of Master Madoc? He talks about Plato's Lost Continent, yet no one has found that land, not even the mysterious rock."

Tipper, short like the old Celts, with dark hair and eyes, said, "Dewi, all of yer life ye have been a drystone mason, clearing the Welsh landscape for pastureland. Ye kept yer head down close to yer stone-shifting and thought of naught but fitting stones, not even of looking up to see the graceful slopes of *Moel Siabod* while resting yer back. Yer goal was to weave the strongest, levelest stone wall in Gwynedd. Ye never bothered to imagine land beyond the Irish Sea."

"And why should I?" said Dewi. "Years before I bent to my work I loved the stately, sharp, blue-black Snowdon Mountains. I remembered the names of the mountain peaks like the names of a royal family. I thought of Moel Siabod as king, with the craggy tip of Yr Wyddfa, the queen, peeking out from behind. To me the ridge of Tryfan was the prince arching a shoulder on the right. Then when I began to work, I hunched over and imagined those stones were put in my path by the little people. With my head down, my ears heard the faraway calling of curlews, bleating of sheep, and singing of larks. Gwynedd in midsummer has a pleasing, sweet, musky fragrance. There is no reason to take an interest in foreign places. No reason, until recently when my land was taxed so heavily I could never hope to pay. My land and animals were confiscated by rogues, who knew neither drystone walling, nor sheepraising. The royal court had a secret head-harvest list with my name. My enchanted land became my fire and brimstone. I became a recluse and shook like a leaf in the afternoon breeze when anyone spoke to me."

" 'Tis no wonder ye have not heard of these foreign places," said Tipper. "The day before we left Wales I had the opportunity to see a map drawn by the false monk with no tongue, Glyn, who travels on the *Blue Seal*. I saw the Fortunates placed off the coast of Africa. The Algerian told the mute that the islands are sometimes called Isles of the Blessed and some believe them to have a fountain that gives eternal youth to any who drink there. The mute hooted and the Algerian agreed, saying, ' 'Tis an ordinary waterfall fed from snowmelt off mountain peaks.' He sounded like he had been there. Ye know how there are waterfalls gushing down the sides of Snowdon in summer?"

Dewi nodded and his mouth gaped open.

"Master Madoc is wise, a man we can rely on."

Dewi nodded again.

"So, Madoc shan't tell us anything foolish to make hisself look big. He is a man who values integrity. I say trust him."

"Who says I do not?" said Dewi. " 'Tis the Algerian I be not certes of." And he closed his mouth.

Madoc turned his ship eastward in the morning to give his men one last glimpse of a world they were familiar with. They sailed along the coast of Portugal and by evening everyone could see the range of small hills above Tagus Estuary, which marked another eighty-three leagues from Cape Finisterre. Madoc led the ships up the River Tagus so that they could see that Lisbon was a jumble of age-old, earth-drab cottages surrounding the Se, and a cathedral newly built twenty-three years earlier of gray stone so highly polished that it appeared wet. He showed his crew an ancient Moorish wall surrounding a multicolor-tiled castle. Nearby were cottages with a fresh revetment of charred peat mixed with water matted over the outside as a caulking.

Dewi pointed to the dry-walled pastures with sheep, swine, and cattle. The old and new was enclosed by a gravel girt except where the city spread itself to the harbor. The ships beached among the willows were hidden from the bustling Lisbon seaport. On shore the evening meal was black olives mixed with mush and fresh cod that a dozen men had caught by using nets strung between several coracles at the river's mouth where salt and fresh water mixed.

Kabyle felt completely at home in these waters and told Madoc that there could not be much more than three hundred leagues before they would see the volcanic cones of the Fortunate Isles. After supper Madoc laid out the vellum map. Kabyle was surprised at Gerard's and Glyn's accuracy in drawing the area around Cadiz and Tangier and the Strait into the Mediterranean. He said that the Madeira Islands were also of volcanic origin. "When the Madeira are sighted, we will know to go directly south to the Fortunates. Allah, the Generous, is being easy on us with fair weather."

Glyn nudged Kabyle and smoothed out the ground so he could write. "The sea gods will challenge us. They like for us to accept the challenge and thereby expand our knowledge and skills."

"Your sea gods and Allah may be brothers!" said Kabyle with a mischievous grin.

Madoc pointed his finger at Kabyle and said, "My friend, if I would let you, would you back out, take your ship, and go home to Algiers?"

"What? You think I am a lubber?" He drew a small, wicked-looking knife from inside his sash and moved it in circles over his head to show that he severed whatever threads of duty bound him to his country. "As the sun's rays go forth, so do I go with friends that I deserve, friends who have as much wisdom as I." He looked at Glyn, who became tense like a cat watching a bird, and replaced his knife. Glyn relaxed. Kabyle roared, "I am with you wise and foolish, but glorious, druids all the way! Your sea gods may reduce all of us to insignificance, but Allah possesses inscrutable sovereignty!"

In the next couple of days the men suffered various degrees of sunburn and salt-water blisters that became boils and then festering sores that burned like fury. Nothing seemed to keep the blisters from forming on bare feet as they sloshed through the salty water on board the ships. Only if they stayed out of the water did Conlaf's milky ointment dry the blisters. They traveled one hundred and ninety leagues in three days of gentle winds and made up new songs. They passed several small, barren, rocky islands. Mussels crusted the rocks where kelp and surf grass grew. They passed the main Island of Madeira with its lofty peaks and the rocky coast with red-and-yellow blooms of prickly pear cactus. Several of the rocks had wave-eroded tunnels where water and mist ran through. There were no inhabitants. They sailed due south in a good stiff breeze for two days and were in sight of the Fortunates and the Grand Canary Island with its mountain peak, the Tenerife, rising from the deep ocean floor. The shore was lined with rich green grasses and dark-green broom with pink flowers. The sky filled with clouds of greenish-brown wild canaries and black oyster catchers. There was the sweet smell of wood smoke and manure.

The ten ships were met by groups of smiling, kinky-haired black men and women, who wore short skirts made of loosely draped black fur, like a dog's short hair. The people were of medium height, with good physiques and health. When they were ashore, Kabyle told Madoc that these people had come from mainland Africa in dugout canoes. Their huts were sticks tied with strings of brown, rootless seaweed. The air bladders, that once kept the plants afloat, hung like pale tan grapes. Packs of black dogs ran here and there barking, causing flocks of oystercatchers to fly away. The people spread apart and called to the dogs. In a moment all dogs, but for two or three, were out of sight in palisaded pens.

Kabyle held up a bucket to the nearest man and asked with strange words if they might fill their water casks. The people moved closer as the man grinned and pointed toward the mountain, whose top was covered by a cloud. After the man spoke, Kabyle explained that the snowmelt was coming down the mountain so there was plenty of water in the pool below the falls. The messmates stumbled forward on wobbly legs that felt uncomfortable without the pitch and roll of the deck. They brought back buckets of water to top the barrels and fill the pots and pans and buckets that would not be used for anything else. This was the last stop before they found the ideal place in the unproved land they were looking for. Some of the men looked around the island. Flocks of sand grouse strutted up and down the black, porous volcanic sand. Knots of smiling people untangled, spread apart, sang, and danced with children and dogs at their heels. Several sailors ran to pet the loose dogs, whose dripping tongues licked the salt from their whiskered faces. The sailors laughed and put their arms around the dogs' necks. They felt like boys letting a cold nose sniff and touch their skin.

The natives put their hands over their mouths and stopped singing. A low moan came from their chests like the rush of water sluicing down a mountainside.

Kabyle told the men that the natives were asking them to keep their hands off the dogs. "They are afraid you are hungry!"

"Lugh's whiskers!" said Brett. "I saw a bone pile near the waterfall and wondered what kind of animals they hunt. They do not hunt! They raise dogs—to eat!"

The sailors let go of the dogs and fell on the black sand to catch their breath. The dogs barked and the natives started up their singing.

Madoc could not call out orders because his words were drowned in the noise of singing and barking. He felt the good weather would not hold, and they were better off sailing than sleeping the night there. The village smells irritated him, especially the unclean dog pens. The women showed off in capes made of short, red-and-purple dog's hair, and he suspected that these people raised the dogs not only for their meat but also for the hides, which surely they had dyed with something unusual. To him it was undignified to change the color of the dog's hair. He motioned for his men to go to their respective ships.

Whenever Madoc was on land, he could not wait to get back on board ship, the same as Master Erlendson. Even though he felt easier on board ship than on land, he knew there would be a time when he would feel he must put his feet on land. Then, on solid ground, the salt air would beckon and again he would not be able to stay away from his love, the sea, and her changing moods. It was a spiral and he was caught in it.

On the fifth day from the Fortunates, Madoc checked the food supply on his ship. There was enough hay and water for the two cows for about three weeks. They were getting six beakers of milk each evening from each of the two cows. The cream was agitated in a goatskin to make butter. Whey was used in cooking. Cheese curds were mixed with mush that was made from pounded grains. He figured there was enough food and water for twenty days.

Suddenly Madoc saw smoke coming from the *Dove* that sailed directly behind the *Gwennan Gorn*. The *Dove*'s sailors ran here and there sloshing buckets of water. He yelled, "Fire!" and ordered three torches lighted and held high for the trouble sign and waved for the *Dove* to come alongside so he could find out the trouble.

Willem hollered, " 'Tis naught! Messmates wanted a hot sup! Timbers in the decking blackened along with sup. Doused with bilge water. We sup on ash."

Madoc's mouth turned up and he hollered, "Heads up! Wind ahead, then rain! Collect rain in your oiled tarpaulin to help digest the ash! Stay in sight!" He waved and had his torches doubled so the ships behind could see them in the lashing rain.

Heavy wind came out of the northeast. The sea spun great frothy curtains. The lines were hauled down and the sail reefed before the ships were blown farther south than

Madoc had planned. Everyone thought that the high swells
and wind would go down when the rain came. By midnight
the overcast and rain thickened. Everyone's clothing was
soaked. Madoc shivered and his arms ached as he maneuvered the ship between towering swells. He put his hand
on a taut rigging line that vibrated with tremendous energy
and charged through him as hard as lust. The shocking
charge reinforced his idea that a shipmaster was bound to
his ship, same as a baby was bound to his mother.

Oiled tarpaulins had been spread over the waist of the
ships, creating a tentlike crawl space where a man could
look after the animals and bail the rising water. The crew
in ships with leeboards took in the boards so they would
not dip like a plough and lift water over the gunwale. A
couple of the ships had fastened leather war shields at an
angle to the gunwales. The overlapped shields deflected the
water as it broke against a ship. Madoc grinned and was
proud of these creative men. His bailers worked in hour
shifts. Bilge swirled under the decking. Water was thrown
out as fast as it splashed in. Not only bailing buckets were
used, but also the messmates' pots and pans.

Gwennan Gorn creaked and groaned, rose on the high,
gray-green waves and sank into the wide, nearly white, spu-
mescent troughs. The cows mooed, switched their tails, and
batted their heads on the inside wall of their pens and added
to the confusion and panic of the crew. Madoc found it
difficult to hold the steering oar. He prayed the nine other
shipmasters were holding tight. Wind gusts made it impossible for the ships to stay in a straight line. There was
naught to do but sing and bail, or sink into a watery grave
and be silent forever. He twisted the steering oar slowly
back and forth to keep from shipping the full brunt of the
wave crest onto his deck. A three-man-tall wave was all he
ever wanted to see. He tried to keep an eye on the bobbing,
dipping ships behind him and notice how each man reacted
when jobs were changed to give them a rest. Wind blew
the tarpaulin away from a corner lashing, and it flapped and
snapped like some crazed flat monster. It jangled Madoc's
nerves. The tarpaulin collected rainwater, but it was mixed
with salt water so not worth saving, even for the cows. He
saw Conlaf scratching his right thigh where the white, scaly

leprosy patch was growing little by little. *Damn the bratling near Paris that infected him*, he thought, and pictured the stooped, disfigured mother. Conlaf had carried her child on his hip to ease her painful walking. A good deed rewarded with a dreadful, incurable disease.

He gave Jorge the steering oar and went to the castellated prow to bring the logbook up-to-date. The ship trembled and swayed and made it difficult to make notations. He wrote about the men's good morale and health, the ships condition, and its food supply. From the bow he dropped a wood shaving into the sea and using a sandglass figured the time it took the shaving to reach the stern. He knew the length of the ship and was able to figure that they were moving about ten-to-twelve leagues a day in the storm. He wrote the numbers in the logbook. He checked their direction according to the needle on a floating cork in a basin of shallow, swaying water. On the basin's edges the four directions were written. The letters blurred. Madoc's chin rested on his chest, and he was aware of his fatigue.

He lay down on the aft deck under a sheet of ox hides for a moment and thought of the time he was a boy watching rolling waves. He noticed the water that was stirred up rotated in an ellipse that was lifted and carried forward, then down and back to where it started. When he was twelve, he figured out that a wave broke when the ratio of wave height to water depth was about four. In a coracle close to the Irish shore, he figured that a six-foot wave broke in eight feet of water. He learned that when rising tides coincide with storms, they are frightful. He closed his eyes and thought of his wife. He knew this was no place to go. It always left him depressed. When she had died, his heart had shriveled and shattered into a thousand slivers. Now a healing was taking place so that he could think of her without his throat closing up, even though his heart remained hollow. Suddenly his thoughts came back to the present. He could not shirk the duties at hand. He must keep his mind and himself alive. A man's conquest at sea was over himself. He shook his fist at the pelting rain. "Lugh, what I think does not count for a wet cow's pie!" he said aloud. "I be taking all these good men to some place without a name! I can hardly fix my ship's position. 'Tis a

steady and sent ⌐⌐⌐⌐ OF STA
in the ship's bow. Then he ⌐⌐ps
golden mats of hair on the back of his
barrel of olive oil close to the gunwale. "⌐⌐⌐⌐ ⌐round
it, punch holes in the sides, and toss it overb⌐⌐

Dewi did not ask why, but made half a dozen openings in the barrel with his knife. The oil seeped out and made the deck slippery and dangerous. Madoc tied a rope around Dewi's waist, lashed the free end to the masthead, and Dewi heaved the barrel over the stern. The oil left a streak in the wake and partly calmed the highest crests. Madoc prayed it would be useful to the nine ships coming behind them. Lightning streaked across the gray morning sky and thunder reverberated in every plank. Biting salt spray lashed the faces of the men. The pelting rain did not stop until the next morning.

Then the men attended neglected chores in a glorious blaze of sun. Tiny wave crests glittered like thousands of stars. Grain sacks were opened and left on the deck to dry beside sodden blankets and clothing. The barrel of drinking water became so warm the men called it tea. The cows stopped giving milk. They pushed moldy hay around with noses that were covered with putrid sores, but they did not eat. The fermenting hay was spread out to dry around the sides of the stalls.

Madoc threw out fungus-ridden onions but kept the wormy grain and rancid butter. One water barrel was bitter with salt and was dumped. He suggested rationing water and eating every second day. The men complained, but went along with it.

There was not another ship in sight. Madoc was not certain of his location, except what he could read from the floating needle. He whittled three small sticks, not any larger around than his index finger and about twice as long. He tied them together to make a triangle. That night he looked at a circle of stars and could not remember seeing

... stick of his
... He estimated the
... ween horizon and pole star.
... drift, he might find a way to
angle and ... ds and make a map of his route in
If he ke... ortunate Islands. He looked back at the
pinpoi...rcle of stars and worried over the possibility that
relat...
...was lost.

The next morning the sun seemed to be a little higher
in the sky. Madoc drew a thin line on his map to show the
direction he figured his ship was sailing. He prayed they
had not been blown in a great circle. He scanned the horizon and thought he saw a line of ships against the gray
in the northwest. When he blinked, they disappeared. Conlaf looked and could see no strong line of demarcation
where the gray sky met the gray sea.

"Your eyesight is poor," said Madoc. "Have you been
drinking your ration of water?"

" 'Tis only half a beaker, what does it matter?"

Madoc said during the storm he had tasted water that
blew in over the gunwales, and it was surprisingly sweet.
He wondered if there were places in the ocean fed by underground springs, same as in a lake. "We could look for
fresh-water upwellings."

Conlaf looked at him with haughty impatience. "Are you
greedy for corpses?" he said. "No man can drink the sea.
What you tasted was surely rainwater. If you have naught
to do, collect fog that condenses on everything at night. I
can use it on cracked lips and bleeding tongues."

Before sunup the messmates scooped the water droplets
hanging from the gunwales with spoons and tin cups. They
wiped the moisture from the deck with bits of wool and
squeezed them into a cooking pot. The soothing, moist
wool was saved to rub over parched bodies when the sun
beat down on the open ship. By midafternoon the men wet
their shirts and caps in the sea to keep cool.

Conlaf continued to see none of the ships that were visible to Madoc. He watched the men's depression from
water-and-food deprivation grow deeper. They were listless
with round, bloated bellies full of rumbling gas. He

squeezed his lips together to keep...
lanced boils on the *Juans'* feet or thei...
...pened pieces of bone. The ankle an...
and there was spots on their bodies. ...
...llen, and they had chronic sores o...
his own body with his ou...y
pink skin was puckery and...ng white skin had...sa...red,
hard as dried leather in the sun. ...e tried to keep his de-
...ng of his right side. The
hydration a secret until he found ...er...ne else was also
...ed every day, it became
having debilitating night sweats and explos...e diarrhea.

One afternoon Madoc asked if his eyesight could be truly going sour the same as his memory. He admitted that he had to think two or three times about everything he did before remembering to act on it. "Something is happening to all of us," he said. "At night I hear men blubbering like babies in their blankets. I bite my tongue and take a deep breath to hold back tears. Look at us. We have become so thin that our skin tingles and our bones feel hollow. The cows are skin and bones. Strings of saliva hang from their mouths. There are scabby sores on their udders and they stopped bawling. The constant wind dehydrates us."

"We could drink the cows' blood," said Conlaf. "I can butcher them one after the other, save the hides, let the messmates roast the rest. Think of the pleasure of sucking on the bones!"

XIII

Puffer

Cougar and Healer found herbs in the green hills and swampy meadows. At home they hung them by their stems to dry. Cougar found that the quiet in Healer's hut was soothing, and she could let her imagination create a story to tell the children later in the day. She helped Healer treat patients, who waited outside the hut each morning, with herb teas, a soothing salve rub, a wet compress, or a vinegar shampoo to rid a child of head lice. She advised some to come back in two or three days to have a painful carbuncle drained. She treated fractures by wrapping them tight to make sure the bone healed properly. Often she rewrapped a broken arm or leg with flat chips of wood beneath the wrapping above the bone to keep the limb straight. She told Healer to give all broken or cracked bones to her because she could put them in place faster and wrap them tighter.

"See, I told you I needed a strong granddaughter," said Healer. "The spirits saw my weakness and sent you."

Late one afternoon, days later, the sky was darkened by heavy, gray clouds streaked with yellow. The plants looked deeper green, and the ground seemed to be a brighter brown. A great gust of air swished through the open huts and a sharp crack of lightning, like a jagged streak of pink, pity so few people will ever know if two hundred and twenty-six courageous men in ten ships sailed westward for new land and drowned! Some may say we fell off the edge of the sea!" He came out of the enclosed prow and called the dark haired crofter, Tipper, to hold the steering oar steady and sent Jorge to rest in the dry, castellated platform in the ship's bow. Then he called Dewi, the man with golden mats of hair on the back of his big hands, to roll a barrel of olive oil close to the gunwale. "Tie a rope around it, punch holes in the sides, and toss it overboard."

Dewi did not ask why, but made half a dozen openings in the barrel with his knife. The oil seeped out and made the deck slippery and dangerous. Madoc tied a rope around Dewi's waist, lashed the free end to the masthead, and Dewi heaved the barrel over the stern. The oil left a streak in the wake and partly calmed the highest crests. Madoc prayed it would be useful to the nine ships coming behind them. Lightning streaked across the gray morning sky and thunder reverberated in every plank. Biting salt spray lashed the faces of the men. The pelting rain did not stop until the next morning.

Then the men attended neglected chores in a glorious blaze of sun. Tiny wave crests glittered like thousands of stars. Grain sacks were opened and left on the deck to dry beside sodden blankets and clothing. The barrel of drinking water became so warm the men called it tea. The cows stopped giving milk. They pushed moldy hay around with noses that were covered with putrid sores, but they did not eat. The fermenting hay was spread out to dry around the sides of the stalls.

Madoc threw out fungus-ridden onions but kept the wormy grain and rancid butter. One water barrel was bitter with salt and was dumped. He suggested rationing water and eating every second day. The men complained, but went along with it.

There was not another ship in sight. Madoc was not certain of his location, except what he could read from the floating needle. He whittled three small sticks, not any larger around than his index finger and about twice as long. He tied them together to make a triangle. That night he looked at a circle of stars and could not remember seeing it before. He looked at the pole star along one stick of his triangle and the horizon along another. He estimated the angle to be eighteen degrees between horizon and pole star. If he kept track of speed and drift, he might find a way to pinpoint where he was and make a map of his route in relation to the Fortunate Islands. He looked back at the unknown circle of stars and worried over the possibility that he was lost.

The next morning the sun seemed to be a little higher in the sky. Madoc drew a thin line on his map to show the direction he figured his ship was sailing. He prayed they had not been blown in a great circle. He scanned the horizon and thought he saw a line of ships against the gray in the northwest. When he blinked, they disappeared. Conlaf looked and could see no strong line of demarcation where the gray sky met the gray sea.

"Your eyesight is poor," said Madoc. "Have you been drinking your ration of water?"

" 'Tis only half a beaker, what does it matter?"

Madoc said during the storm he had tasted water that blew in over the gunwales, and it was surprisingly sweet. He wondered if there were places in the ocean fed by underground springs, same as in a lake. "We could look for fresh-water upwellings."

Conlaf looked at him with haughty impatience. "Are you greedy for corpses?" he said. "No man can drink the sea. What you tasted was surely rainwater. If you have naught to do, collect fog that condenses on everything at night. I can use it on cracked lips and bleeding tongues."

Before sunup the messmates scooped the water droplets hanging from the gunwales with spoons and tin cups. They wiped the moisture from the deck with bits of wool and squeezed them into a cooking pot. The soothing, moist wool was saved to rub over parched bodies when the sun beat down on the open ship. By midafternoon the men wet their shirts and caps in the sea to keep cool.

Conlaf continued to see none of the ships that were visible to Madoc. He watched the men's depression from water-and-food deprivation grow deeper. They were listless with round, bloated bellies full of rumbling gas. He squeezed his lips together to keep from screaming when he lanced boils on the mens' feet or their bleeding gums with sharpened pieces of bone. The ankles and feet of most men were swollen, and they had chronic sores on their arms and legs and bluish spots on their bodies. Conlaf began to believe that by rubbing his own body with fish oil his leprosy would heal. Already the flaking white skin had disappeared, and there was new pink skin forming on his right side. The pink skin was puckery and, if not oiled every day, it became hard as dried leather in the sun. He tried to keep his dehydration a secret until he found everyone else was also having debilitating night sweats and explosive diarrhea.

One afternoon Madoc asked if his eyesight could be truly going sour the same as his memory. He admitted that he had to think two or three times about everything he did before remembering to act on it. "Something is happening to all of us," he said. "At night I hear men blubbering like babies in their blankets. I bite my tongue and take a deep breath to hold back tears. Look at us. We have become so thin that our skin tingles and our bones feel hollow. The cows are skin and bones. Strings of saliva hang from their mouths. There are scabby sores on their udders and they stopped bawling. The constant wind dehydrates us."

"We could drink the cows' blood," said Conlaf. "I can butcher them one after the other, save the hides, let the messmates roast the rest. Think of the pleasure of sucking on the bones!"

XIII
Puffer Fish

For the Calusa, fishing was not just an economic endeavor—it was the mainstay of their lives. . . . Their religion, art, and social institutions depended on successful harvesting of the marine environment. . . . The legacy of their maritime heritage is obvious from the marine refuse that comprises the mounds—the foundations of their major villages.
—Robert F. Edic, *Fisherfolk of Charlotte Harbor, Florida*

Cougar and Healer found herbs in the green hills and swampy meadows. At home they hung them by their stems to dry. Cougar found that the quiet in Healer's hut was soothing, and she could let her imagination create a story to tell the children later in the day. She helped Healer treat patients, who waited outside the hut each morning, with herb teas, a soothing salve rub, a wet compress, or a vinegar shampoo to rid a child of head lice. She advised some to come back in two or three days to have a painful carbuncle drained. She treated fractures by wrapping them tight to make sure the bone healed properly. Often she rewrapped a broken arm or leg with flat chips of wood beneath the wrapping above the bone to keep the limb straight. She told Healer to give all broken or cracked bones to her because she could put them in place faster and wrap them tighter.

"See, I told you I needed a strong granddaughter," said Healer. "The spirits saw my weakness and sent you."

Late one afternoon, days later, the sky was darkened by heavy, gray clouds streaked with yellow. The plants looked deeper green, and the ground seemed to be a brighter brown. A great gust of air swished through the open huts and a sharp crack of lightning, like a jagged streak of pink, flashed above the northwest horizon. The sky became darker and the yellow clouds turned a sickly green. After another flash and a loud crack, the sickly green clouds broke open and spilled cold, round, white seeds. The seeds bounced and rolled off the huts and across the ground and deposited themselves in crevices and small gullies. Without the warning of another wind gust, the hail stopped, but the wind and rain continued all night.

Two days after the storm, when the patients were gone, Cougar sat outside and waited for children to come to hear her stories. First she asked if the children had a story they wanted to tell. Turtle, a shy skinny girl two summers younger than Cougar, said she had a true story her brother had told her. Her black hair was finer than most but uncombed and tangled like wild vines, and she wore nothing on her feet.

"This is a true story because Brother was there to see with his own eyes and hear with his own ears," she said. "Brother would not be here if it were not for an old man and a young man in a high-sided canoe in the *pa-ma-okee,* grassy water. Brother was looking for the fish with a small mouth and feeble teeth that he could catch in his net. He caught nothing but puffers, and he met these two men looking for Holly Island. Brother shared a meal of spiky puffer fish with the two strangers."

Cougar could think of no one but Egret and Otter. "Puffers are not good eating," she said, making her face wrinkled.

"The old man was smart. He was a Calusa and knew how to prepare them. He scaled and cut them into thin strips while they were alive, and they ate the puffers raw. Brother learned that the uncooked poison in the puffer does not make a man sick, instead it gives him a clear vision. In Brother's clear vision he saw the large canoe belonging to the two men, but he could not see the two men. They laughed when Brother told the men that they would be out of sight by tomorrow. The old man said he was looking for Healer's grown daughter. Brother was so surprised that he stood up in his canoe and said he knew Healer. The canoe lurched and Brother, with heavy black stones for spear points in a bag at his waist, fell into the water. He sank, could not get the bag untied, and thought he was going to drown. The two men pulled him up, took him to the shore, and pushed on his chest so water gushed from his mouth. The next day Brother led them to Holly Island. When he waved good-bye, they were safe in the big canoe. Brother thought the vision had meant he was the one who would be out of sight. He said he was so full of happiness because the two strangers had broken the curse of his vision."

Cougar's breath caught in her throat, and her eyes widened. "And so, what next?" she said.

"Brother said that Healer's daughter and her man used to live here. One day, a long time ago, they went out fishing and a bad storm caught up with them. Wind dropped their baby girl into the sea. The baby grew up in the deep part of the sea, and her hair grew down to her waist, like mine. It is now greenish-brown, like sea weeds."

Cougar ran her fingers through her hair and asked Turtle if anyone had seen the girl with greenish hair.

"No, I have never heard anyone say that."

"And so, I do not believe a real girl can live in the sea," said Cougar. "She could not breathe water, you know. Did your brother see the two men after he left them on Holly Island?"

"Yes, I think so," said Turtle. "And he believes an air-breathing girl can live in the sea."

Cougar was hardly able to hold back her excitement to hear more words about Egret and Otter.

"Tomorrow I will take you to Brother. I will tell him you want to hear more of the story about the two strangers."

Cougar ran into the hut and found the vinegar jug and a strong shell with points on the edge that was used as a comb. She washed Turtle's hair with wild apple vinegar and combed out tangles and lice.

With a fist-sized stone Cougar pounded her comb until it broke into two pieces. She gave half to Turtle. The full moon rose above the treetops before Turtle went home.

That evening Cougar asked Healer if the puffer fish was good to eat.

"I would not eat it," Healer said. "But the Tocobaga and Tacachale and Calusa eat them during special rituals, such as a Solstice Ceremony. They believe the puffers give them an insight of what is to come next. I never paid much attention, because I was not inclined to keep those nasty fish around. I am a healer and I do not believe they do much healing. I do not know about the future, but believe we best let it come to us without foreknowledge."

"Oh, I would like to know the future. I might be able to do something about an unpleasant event. Something like avoid it," said Cougar. "And one day I might try a puffer fish, scaled, filleted alive, and sliced really thin. Puffer might just tell me something I need to know."

"Humpf! What you need to know is more about healing and less about storytelling," said Healer. "One day I will not be here to tell you what I know, and you will be expected to mend broken bones, abscesses, coughing, stuffy noses, abdominal pains, weak eyes, and the bleeding flesh of mothers birthing babies."

"Maybe a bite of raw puffer will tell me what I am going to do," said Cougar.

Healer looked Cougar in the face. "These days young people talk back to their grandmother? I do not want you to go away. Stay with me. You will always have something to eat, a place to sleep, and me to talk to in case you have a sad, joyous, or frightful event."

The following afternoon Turtle came again to hear Cougar's stories. Her hair was combed and her face shiny as a newly fired clay bowl. Afterwards she asked Cougar to come with her to meet Brother.

Cougar told Healer she would be back before the sun set.

"Look out! Here comes an event," Healer said. "Look the young man over. Bring him here so I can put a love spell inside his head. He will believe you are most desirable, and he will know exactly what to do."

Cougar shrugged indifferently and followed Turtle to a small hut where Brother sat behind a smoldering fire. He had bronzed cheekbones and an aquiline nose. Weather had hardened his thin body. He held his head high and his arms folded across his chest. He wore no more than necessary: soft moccasins, a breechclout, and a faded red-fiber band across his forehead. He motioned for Turtle to leave and for Cougar to sit across the fire from him, and his eyes studied her. "The old man said Healer's granddaughter was staying in this village. The young man said you told stories to the children. And so, you are Story Teller?"

"I am Cougar," she said, sitting cross-legged. "I came to hear what you know about my grandfather, Egret, and my friend Otter who have not returned from Holly Island."

"They went to Holly Island all right. They asked about Owl, a secondary ceremonial priest, whose wife is the daughter of Healer. These men, your relatives, wanted Owl and his wife to come here to see you and visit with Healer."

Cougar could feel his eyes searching her face for some clue about her true identity.

"Aye," she said. "Are they coming?"

"Owl and his wife listened to their story. They could not believe their baby was not drowned but lived all these years in a Calusa village. When the strangers said their daughter was now living with Healer, her own grandmother, Owl became angry and swore that he was there when the wind toppled their canoe and spilled their baby into the sea. He said their baby was living like a fish in the sea with other drowned babies who had green, waving hair. I have heard fishermen say they have seen soft, green baby hair near shallow beds of fish. Owl's woman cried when he told the strangers that he believed they were tricksters looking for an undeserved reward."

"And so, Owl convinced Hyacinth that if they went with the strangers to see their daughter, they were in for some kind of trick?" said Cougar. "They could not believe their daughter was breathing air today and sent the men away? Did Owl know that the old man was his true father? They both have a short, double row of teeth in the front of their upper jaw."

"What happened? What made their mouths like that?" said Brother.

"I think maybe the first teeth never came out when the second teeth came in, and they grew together."

"I heard something like that about Owl," said Brother. "His teeth are why he was chosen as a Tequesta priest. It is said that a double row of teeth filed to points are a frightening sight. I never saw them, never knew this Owl. Actually, I liked the two strangers a lot and I believed them. I caught up with them again as they poled their canoe away from Holly Island and into the Grassy Water. We were close to the trees, where the alligators sleep, when lightning flashed and the wind blew a black cloud open so it spilled its cold, white seeds. Their high-sided canoe lurched and leaned. The two men were unable to angle the heavy canoe into the waves so it would stay upright. It turned over and spilled them out. I tried to get close to their splashing and yelling. The white seeds pounded my head, the back of my neck, and hands. I waited for the men to pop their heads up into the air, turn their canoe upright, and climb inside. Hungry alligators awoke, splashed until the water turned red, and went back to sleep."

"Oh, no," whispered Cougar. "You looked for them. You found them!"

"I tied their clumsy overturned craft to my canoe, even though it was filled with water and heavy. Those two men were fair and honest and now I wonder if they went into the sea to find the girl with the long greenish hair. They told me that they had told the Holly Island couple that they would bring their daughter back to them. I think the girl still lives in the sea. I think she made the storm that gave us those white, watery seeds. She did not want to come out of the sea, even to be with her own people. She has fallen in love with a fish her size, and they have minnow children to care for."

"I told you that girl—their daughter, is me," choked Cougar. She was stunned and angry. "You can see I am not a fish with minnow children. I do not believe that Egret and Otter have gone into the sea looking for a baby girl with green hair. It is not possible. They swim. They float. And so where are they?" She felt her chest would burst open. She could not believe Egret and Otter were drowned. "You should have gone after them! You could have waited longer for them!"

Brother said there was not a thing he could have done differently in the storm. He sat quietly until Cougar was calm then he asked her about the white seeds. "Can they be planted?"

"Of course," she said, rubbing her eyes, "but they will

not grow. The storm spirit sent the seeds. He turned them to water. Water turns the brown grass green. Everything but fire needs water to live. What is the matter with you? A *person* can not live *in* water." She thought maybe Egret and Otter had grabbed onto a piece of downfall and floated unnoticed to land, and she began to feel better. She asked Brother for directions to Holly Island and told him she was taking Egret's canoe for a couple of days.

She went back to Healer's place. Healer was gone, so she began to pick the fish bones, discarded stems, and seeds out of the sandy floor. She swept the floor smooth, tidied the bowls and baskets, and hung discarded clothing on twigs sticking out of the wall. She did not look for anything to eat because the thought of food made her nauseous. Just before dark, she went to the place where the tall cattail grew and found the high-sided canoe tied to a crooked mangrove.

She found three paddles in the bottom of another canoe and closed her eyes to wait for a sign from the spirit of Otter or Egret to tell her what to do. No spirit spoke. She opened her eyes and decided that if she took one paddle the loss would not be too great. Her mind was crowded with the image of an overturned canoe in a thrashing sea. She went to Healer's spring for a jug of water. She stirred the water with a small stick, chewed on the end of the stick, and turned around three times before dabbing water on her eyelids. Healer once said spring water on her eyelids would give her wisdom sufficient for getting through the day. She washed and filled a discarded jug with water, put it in the bottom of the high-sided canoe, found two dried chili peppers still clinging to their vine among the weeds, and put them in her pocket. She plucked the last of the dried blackberries on the bushes near the hut and left half of them inside for Healer.

Cougar was poling the canoe long before sunup. The new day was about over when she ate the blackberries and looked for three pines that pointed west. She poled past the pines then beached for the night. She was so angry with the spirits on the Otherside for taking Egret and Otter that it was hard for her to sleep. Next morning she looked for the palmetto palm that Brother had told her to look for. It had a raft of twigs and leaves at its foot, where four small river mink lived. The sun came through the trees and showed Cougar that the mink were yellowish-brown with white chins. As she paddled past and headed into the mangrove forest, the mink scurried into the water and swam around her canoe. Then they ran up the palm tree and watched her paddle away. She thought their little ears and muzzles pointed in the direction she was to go, a good sign. Carefully she made her way through the palmettos and bald cypress trying to avoid their knees and crisscrossed roots. Poling blistered her hands, and she pulled off leaves from the cypress to make pads to put inside the mittens Egret had given her. That eased the pain. She watched gulls fly off a garbage heap of decaying fish, bones, shells, and mildewed hides on an island's west side. *I am getting close to Holly Island*, she thought and rubbed some of the crushed leaves around her eyes so that she would stay awake. As the day grew warmer, she wanted to stop and sleep. She saw a big island in the south where there were several small deer standing in the shallows, eating water plants, and flicking flies with their short white tails. As soon as she was around the island she saw another good-sized island in the northwest. *That should be it*, she thought and was certain she could see a row of holly trees. As she rode closer, it was a row of black rock. Against the rock she saw the moving, glowing light of the water fireflies, phosphorescent creatures. She thought of Otter and Egret seeing the same things a few days before. Tears spilled down her cheeks. *They were my family*, she thought. Her throat pinched. She wiped the tears, not wishing to have red-rimmed eyes *if* she found them alive.

"Accept fate with enthusiasm," Grandmother used to say. She also had come to see Owl and his wife, Hyacinth, Healer's daughter. *Healer is nice enough*, she thought, *but not like my first grandmother*. When nothing in the sea of trees and grass was familiar, she felt utterly alone and wondered if, in this place, the stars in the night sky would be the same as they had been at the Healer's place. If these were Tequesta or Tocobaga people, would they understand her words or she understand theirs? She shrugged her shoulders thinking she would listen carefully and pick out the words she did know and piece together the rest as best she could. She would listen to the names of familiar things, like river, sky, hut, man, woman, food, and sleep. She loved Otter and Egret and was sorry she ever lost patience with them. Her paddling was not steady, but the uneven strokes ate up the distance so that it was not long before she could smell smoke and see more mounds of discarded fish bones, shells, rotten vegetation, and excrement.

Suddenly she saw many fishing canoes and smaller craft in the bay. It looked like a celebration. *Maybe it has something to do with harvesting,* she thought when she saw a small dugout filled with coconuts and another filled with small ears of corn. She found that there were wooden docks built above the water surface that ran parallel to raised shell banks. This island held more people than Healer had thought. She pushed past the tethered canoes and found a place to tie her canoe near the front of a dock that met a footpath leading to a group of huts with their thatched roofs extending over outside stone flooring. They were the first porches she had seen and wondered why more people did not build such a pleasing thing onto their huts.

Without thinking she said, "I will ask Egret about that." Hearing her own voice she looked about. The people along the docks and in the boats seemed to be occupied with their own business and paid no attention to her. She saw a young woman wearing yellow streaks on her cheeks, a feather cape on her shoulders, and leather sandals on her feet. She knew that the huts with porches were for royalty or the shamans. The woman wearing feathers was probably a priestess.

The woman came down the dock reciting prayers against evil and bad luck and held her hand out to Cougar. Cougar thought she meant to help her out of the canoe and reached out, clasped her hand, and stepped stiffly onto the dock. When she let go, the woman thrust out her hand and asked for a token for the privilege of tying the canoe to the dock. Cougar pulled out the two chili peppers and laid them side by side on the woman's hand. The woman smiled and motioned for her to follow.

The woman had been cutting live puffer fish into slices. The fish flopped around on the cutting board. This was interesting to Cougar, especially when she was offered a thin slice. Cougar was hungry and popped it into her mouth. When she chewed, the fish tasted sweet and bitter, and she thought it would have been good with a small piece of chili pepper. The woman must have read her mind because she used her bone knife to cut the peppers into tiny squares. Each square was placed onto a slice of fish. She handed another fish slice to Cougar, who said that she had poled and paddled before sunup to get here, and she was hungry for more than a few slices of puffer fish, although she was glad to have tasted it. The woman clearly spoke Calusa words and said, "I have chosen you as a Dreamer. Eat more tiny slices and have a short sleep. Afterwards you will tell me what you saw in your dreams. I will tell the Chief Priest, and he will tell the crowd in the city's main street what the future will bring to the ordinary people."

"Why not have the priest eat the puffer slices himself?" said Cougar. "You cannot tell the future from my dreams."

"Silly child!" said the woman, looking from under dark brows. "Dreamers test the raw puffers to see if they are poisonous this time of year."

"Oh," said Cougar. "Good for me."

"Thank you for bringing chili peppers." Dark Brows wiped her face in a way that did not smear her paint.

"When I left, I did not know that I would give the peppers away," said Cougar, telling herself to watch out for this woman. "I did not know about your celebration. I came looking for a man called Owl and his woman."

"Owl is a priest. He makes predictions about the sun and moon eclipses and when the rains will begin and stop. He tells us when to have special feast days to praise our spirits. His wife takes care of children who are left without a mother and father. She has done this ever since she lost her only child in a storm."

"Only child?"

"Aye." Dark Brows pointed to the huts with porches. "Their place has a blue-and-red door. Hyacinth is in the City Square. Sleep and I will take you to her." She pointed to a stone bench with a hide pallet filled with straw.

"What is this day?" asked Cougar, feeling sleepy.

"The First Day of the New Year. Last night we heard

the cry of the cranes coming back where the water is warm. That is the sign to finish the harvest, before cold weather. We honor the harvest spirits and the returning cranes. What does your family call you?"

My family, Cougar thought. *I am going to meet my family. I do not know what they call me. I have to tell them what I am called.* Colors seemed brighter and her head felt funny. She thought she was going to be sick. The dazzling sunlight put sparkling red outlines around everything, making her dizzy.

"I am Cougar," she said and lay down, closed her eyes, and soon thought she was on the beach at Sandpoint, where the sand was hot but did not burn her feet. Her mind told her this was something she imagined. She shaded her eyes and looked out across the sea where something was floating against the incoming fog bank. She saw a line of elongated, upside-down huts each with a single bluish wing, which was so close to the color of the pale sky, the fog, and the water, that each one was almost hidden. She chased a couple who turned back, pointed their fingers at her, and called her vile names. She did not know what to say to them and became tired of running. She sat on the beach to watch as the huts floated toward her, and their wings swelled in the wind.

Soon the huts were close enough so that she could see people moving around inside. They came closer, and she could see a couple of ghostly pale faces, like spirits of the dead. She wondered if they were Egret and Otter coming to see if she was all right. She waded into the shallow water and called to them. She waded and the people in the first hut waved back as their hut came up to beach on the sand. Their hair was long. Some had hair on their pale faces!

Then she saw him! His hair was almost white. It was light as dried summer grass. His eyes were a pale blue color, the same as the huge jaybird wing hanging from a pole in the center of his upsidedown hut. He was waving but something was wrong with his arm. He did not hold it out straight. His hand was too large. *It is swollen,* she thought. *Did something bite him, a red-bellied spider, or an alligator? Was he in a fight or an accident?* He said something she could not understand. She heard her name,

"Cougar! Cougar!" How did he know her name? Her heart raced. She ran through the water toward the floating huts, but they faded and were barely visible against the blue sea. She called them back, but they disappeared into the fog. Disappointed, she put her hands over her face and when she took them away Dark Brows was looking at her.

"You saw something? Something unusual?"

"Aye!" Cougar said. "I ran after the people; I do not know them. They called my name. I thought they were—I do not know who they were. I rested and I saw the pale-faced, light-haired man on a floating hut with a blue wing. His arm is hurt and he is coming here."

"Who is coming?" asked Dark Brows with suspicion. "There is no one but the very old with pale hair. Is he an old man or the white panther that is said to bring us good fortune?"

"Not a panther, a young man I have seen in my dreams. He does not seem to mean much to anyone but me, and maybe it means something will happen to me, and it has no real meaning for the priest and all these people on Holly Island."

"Did the pale one give you a message?"

"I could not understand his tongue. It was not Calusan, Tocobagan, or Ais."

"Maybe he used the hand-signs which are known by everyone from the southern mainland along all the east and west barrier islands, across the southern waters to the Big Islands."

"He used his hands only to wave. That is why I know the right arm was hurt."

"Tell me about the floating hut."

"It was a big canoe shaped like a hut with one wing," said Cougar. "It was not a hollow log, not made with straw and grasses, but with logs cut along their length, fastened so they lay over one another. I do not know what the wing was, but it was not feathers. It was woven tighter than the gray moss we weave into skirts. It was more like hide scraped thin. From a distance it was almost hidden against the blue sky and water. It moved with the wind like something soft and did not become tattered. These people look like they are from the spirit world. The pale ones might be ghosts of men who lived here long ago."

"Women? Where were their women?"

"I saw no women with the pale ones," said Cougar.

"Do you think the spirit men are looking for women?" Dark Brows creased her forehead into a frown. "Were you frightened?"

"I never thought of them not having women. In my dreams I am never afraid. I feel safe seeing the man with pale hair."

"Well, we all know that after a person dies his skin color turns pale, a ghostly white," said Dark Brows. "I do not know about the hair nor do I know what the blue wing is. Those are puzzles. Have you ever seen a hut rise off the water and fly like a big bird?"

"No—but maybe in powerful, strong winds a hut can be blown so the pieces fly all around, even into the tallest palm tree. After a big storm Grandmother found me, not in the top of a tree but in the sand under gray driftwood."

"Where do you come from?"

"No one knows," said Cougar. "That is what I am trying to find out. You can see I am not a ghost." She held her brown arms out and her face close to Dark Brow's face to show that she told the truth.

"You are a scout that was sent ahead of the floating huts to point out the best-looking women to go with ghost-men to their spirit world?"

"Oh, I do not believe that!" said Cougar sliding off the pallet.

"Follow me. We shall see what the Chief Priest has to say," said Dark Brows.

Cougar looked out into the bay, which now seemed to be a logjam of canoes and people trying to come ashore to join the festivities in the town's courtyard. It was more congested, more confused than Cougar imagined. Behind the royal court was a wide circular street in front of a string of one-family huts built close together. Behind those huts was a smaller circle of larger huts built farther apart and in the center was an open market and a game field. The center was filled with milling people. A row of holly gave shade to one side where there was a round, stone-edged spring where people stood in line to drink the salt-free water. This time of year the spring was low, and the stone steps that led down to the water were dry. She guessed that the spring had been much higher when there were only a few families living on the island. She wished Healer were here to see how this place had grown.

"I said I would take you to Owl's wife," said Dark Brows. "She stands over there by the Solstice markers."

"Where are her children?" asked Cougar. "The children with no mothers or fathers?"

"Each year, for a handful of days before the Solstice, the children are kept in the sacred temple that is on our highest flat mound. You can see the sun's light touching the side of the Children's Temple. Its beauty is a compliment to our chief who said how it was to be built to last forever as a memorial to him. The children are fed our best food, bathed, dressed in new clothes, and then they are thought of as precious gifts to be given to the rain god. After that, the rain god thanks us by giving us plenty of good water for drinking and cooking, even in the cold season when there is no rain. We have underground cisterns built on top of the highest mounds that hold the rain. It is up to us to pray that sea-water does not creep into the cistern."

"I do not believe sea-water goes that high," said Cougar. "But I never thought of saving rain-water. That is clever and a memorial to your chief. What do you mean, the children are 'gifts given to the rain god'?"

"We put one small, beating heart on top of every cistern," said Dark Brows. "Maybe two if the water is low and there are enough children. Then the rain comes and those little hearts are eaten up."

"Eaten up? By rain?" Cougar was astonished.

"Aye, eaten."

"I did not know rain could eat. Some animals look for food in the night. Have you seen animal footprints? Animals can find those hearts. I shiver to think about it. Are you making a bad joke?"

"Nay, it is done every year and every year we have water."

"Maybe next year you ought not sacrifice little children

and see if you have water," said Cougar. "If I were Chief of Holly Island I would do that before taking any more hearts from anyone, especially your children."

Dark Brows looked shocked that Cougar would be so bold to even suggest such a thing. She could not get over this young woman's impudence. "Who do you live with?" The young woman's words were insinuating, defaming, scandalous, and far too outrageous for her age. Wherever did she learn to think in such a disconcerting way?

"Healer, my grandmother." *Of course it was old Grandmother who taught me to think for myself and to question ideas that do not seem right*, she thought. *It is fortunate that Grandmother never knew Dark Brows.*

There was a large circle of skull-sized stones with a straight line of fist-sized stones passing through the center of the circle, cutting it in half. The feathered alignment-sticks were planted at each end of the diameter line. Cougar studied the Chief Priest. He was short enough to walk under the hollies without ducking his head. He stood, letting his shoulders droop, while he waited for the time when the sun would almost set into the horizon in the west. Before setting, the sun aligned its last rays with the top of the far stick and then moved right up to the near stick without a waver.

Cougar knew when the light became too bright to watch it would fall off both sticks. At sunrise the light had moved in the same way but in the opposite direction over the tops of the markers. Egret had told her that the sun turned north when the weather became cool and in the spring it turned south. Egret was never a priest and did not believe that men had the power to tilt the sun either north or south. He said the sun moved by its own force one way or the other and was dependable; it never failed even if the day was full of clouds or rain.

Dark Brows pointed to a woman standing apart from the crowd. She wore a shawl of colorful feathers over her head to keep off the sun. "That is Hyacinth," she said. "Stay with her while I talk to the Chief Priest, who is about to read the position of the sun as it sets. He will tell us if it coincides with the sunrise position. When he announces that the sun rides the right path, I will come for you. Then you can talk with him." She disappeared inside the crowd, and Cougar wondered what to say to the woman wearing bird feathers.

Are you my true mother? she thought. *I like your looks, but do you have a kind heart? You care for children, but let the priest use their little hearts for gifts to an unseen rain god. What does the rain god do with those gifts of little baby hearts? Does anyone here really know?*

Cougar wished that both Egret and Otter were with her. She stared at the woman and wondered how to say, "Are you my mother?" Clouds covered the sun, the air cooled quickly, she shivered and could not say anything.

The woman pushed the multicolored, feathered shawl from her head to her shoulders. Her hair was twisted, drawn to the back of her head and fastened with green twigs that still had their little green leaves. Her complexion was clear, and her eyes were dark with a black ring drawn around them so they looked large. She wore a gray moss skirt that went down past her knees and matched the color of her sandals. Her ankle bracelets were made from dried red berries strung on coconut fiber. She laughed and said, "It is a hot day for this time of year."

Her laughing made Cougar think of the cool breeze that was coming through the big, round sea grape leaves, and she wished that her feet had sandals and that one of her ankles had a bracelet. She was glad she was wearing the circlet of small, transparent, colored stones that she had been wearing when Grandmother had found her and the pearl ear bobs Otter had given her.

The woman looked closely at her ear bobs and her neckband. "What pretty things. The neckband reminds me of something I have seen before. I am sure it was something precious like a marker for a special child. The ear bobs are expensive looking, like something a lover gives his favorite wife. They look good on you. Exquisite. I suppose it cost your father a full season of hard work."

"That is why I am here. I want to ask my father if he made the neckband when I was a baby," said Cougar. She let her cool hand rest on the warm neckband and thought, *Why would a mother not recognize the neckband she fastened around the neck of her own baby girl?*

"Your father was a man who shook stones in a box of sand and water to make them smooth? Where did he find such beautiful colors? Did he drill holes to push the thread through?"

"I do not know my father."

"My husband was a stone polisher, before he became a priest. Now he must learn to perform magic to impress the people. He is good with his hands. I always said he should have been a healer. My mother is a healer. You have the same kind of hands. But you are too young to be a healer."

The woman reached under her feathered shawl and brought out a handful of coconut pieces. She offered Cougar a hunk of clean white meat and pointed. "Look there, Chief Priest is moving to the eastern stick to see the sun set. Will the sunlight line up with the head and heel sticks?"

"It always has," said Cougar, eating slowly. "I have come a long way to see you and your husband."

"You mean you have come to see the priest push the sun from the south to its northern path?" said the woman.

"Do you think your priest is strong enough to do that?" Cougar asked, pointing to the small, gray-bearded man whose tanned face had paths of white scar lines on translucent skin over jutting cheekbones. His eyes were like beady black seeds darting here and there. He had colored feathers on the yoke of his long tunic.

"Oh, yes. He does this twice a year, and he is always strong enough," said the woman.

"What if the priest was not here?" asked Cougar, with a mouth full of coconut.

"Another would take his place," said the woman, "Owl, my husband, could do that. You are too young to be so full of questions. You must have a cute little name. I cannot be wrong. Let me guess. You are called Fingerling."

"No. I told you, I am Cougar, named by my first Grandmother. And you are Hyacinth?"

"Aye," said Hyacinth. "Who told you? You still look like a tiny Fingerling."

"Your mother, the Healer told me. So, do you know you have a living daughter?"

"No," said Hyacinth, "I do not."

"Do you want one?"

"No."

XIV
Starvation

Scurvy took many forms, its characteristic signs were putrid, bleeding gums and blue-black spots on the body. Generally, the first signs of the disease were pale and bloated complexion, listlessness, and fatigue. Eventually, internal hemorrhages caused weakness, lethargy, stiffness and feebleness of the knees, swelling of the ankles and legs, chronic sores, putrid ulcers, and breathlessness following any exertion. Advanced cases were marked by coughing and pains in the bones, joints, and chest. Profuse hemorrhages and violent dysenteries reduced the patients to extreme weakness. During the last stage of the disease, . . . [there is a] breakdown of previously healed ulcers, chest pains, difficult respiration, and sudden death.

—Lois N. Magner, *A History of Medicine*

Near sunset Dewi saw grampuses circle the ship and laughed at them. Madoc watched the half a dozen small whalelike animals bump against the ship then leave. The first time Tipper saw them he said that they could line up side by side and swim against the ship and turn her over. That made everyone more watchful. The pod of grampuses, black on their backs and white on their bellies, returned the next day at sunset and showed great agility as they played around the ship. The largest one, about a tall man's height in length, acted like the leader and moved his nose up and down as he passed Madoc at the steering oar. Madoc noticed that these animals had tails that were horizontal with the surface water; fish tails were perpendicular. The grampuses communicated in high, sharp squeaks. Madoc wondered if they knew he was lost or knew where the other ships were. Then he wondered if the gods tested him by putting crazy thoughts in his head. When he closed his eyes, he could see eight sails traveling in a straight line behind the blue-sailed *Vestri*. He opened his eyes and there were no sails, but he saw fish swimming among smiling grampuses that were about a foot long with big rolling eyes.

Dewi and Tipper caught the fish on their own plaited horsehair line with hooks made of bent brass nails and pieces of leather shaved into thin, wormlike strips. As fast as Tipper swung a fish from the water into the ship's waist, Dewi unhooked it and replaced the leather worms. After an hour they had several high-sided willow baskets filled with tough-skinned fish. The leader of the grampus pod spouted from his crescentic blowhole, as if to say "farewell," and they disappeared. Tipper and Dewi believed that the grampuses had brought the fish close to the ship to be caught.

Because of the thick bone that protruded from the fishes' back, they were too hard to clean. Their white meat was bitter as gall. Everything about them was unpleasant, except the sweet, juicy, tiny heart and liver. Messmates filleted the stringy meat into strips and tied it on a line to dry. They threw the bones overboard but saved the skins for bait. During sup the men agreed that sucking out the innards of the fish was one of their most satisfying meals in days. The ship seemed to stand perfectly still.

Before the sun went down Dewi and Tipper were fishing again, hoping the grampuses would bring back more of the tough-skinned fish. Suddenly Dewi said, "Take in the lines!" He pointed to a dark mass, longer and wider than the ship, floating near the water's surface. " 'Tis *kraken*! I have heard the Northmen say it has arms that can wrap around a ship and crush her to bits!"

The dark, shadowy creature had more arms than anything Madoc had seen. "Oars out!" he said. "Row! Fast!"

Everyone stood against the starboard gunwale and watched the *kraken*, which seemed to have two huge eyes in the center of its big round body and ten, long, waving arms. Two of the arms appeared longer and more flexible than the other arms. The water turned inky black, and the buzz began as Tipper told what he had heard of sea monsters that could change to gruesome creatures or swallow ships whole. No one actually believed his stories, but no one had ever seen such a sight as a huge ten-armed sea monster that could spit out enough ink to hide itself. The rowers sang, "dip, lift, in, out," in a fast cadence that kept time with the oars.

When the water was clear, Madoc went to his forward, enclosed deck and wrote all he could remember about the sea beast and drew a picture showing that its arms stretched far past the bow and stern of the ship. He looked up and saw six ships sailing in a straight line off to the right. A blue sail, like Kabyle's, was in the lead. He hollered, but of course they were too far away to hear. He waved two flambeaux and thought a couple of the ships waved flambeaux in response.

Conlaf could not be sure he saw the ships and said he believed Madoc was hallucinating.

The *Gwennan Gorn* was unable to reach the six sails that Madoc saw floating in and out against the horizon because of the strong local current and the wind.

Tallesin, a corpulent young crofter, who had seen his wife and child murdered by Dafydd's retainers, said the ships were a mirage, and Madoc was taking the *Gwennan Gorn* into oblivion.

Madoc assured him that land was just over the horizon and said that he had found another place where the seawater was cold and hardly salty. He wanted to try the semi-sweet water on the cows. "Bloody hell!" Tallesin laughed uncontrollably. He dumped the water bucket across Madoc's feet and accused him of trying to kill the cows. "I will have no part of this. You are mad! A stark, raving-mad shipmaster!"

Next morning Tallesin and his friend, Garth, a towering bulk, had orders to scrape the sea-salt encrusted deck. Tallesin became irascible and said he could hardly breathe in the humid air and thought they should scrape in a shaded area. "I feel limp as dead seaweed, my head aches, and my eyesight is so blurred that I want to keep my eyes shut."

Garth called him a complainer and told him to keep busy and the time would pass faster. "Mayhap ye miss the lovely Welsh songs ye used to sing with the pipes. While ye scrape, sing along with me.

"The churl did blow a grating shriek,
The bag did swell, and harshly squeak,
As does a goose from nightmare crying,
Or dog crushed by a chest when dying."

"My chest is tight and will not open up to sing," complained Tallesin. "My head throbs, my belly rumbles, making me nauseous."

An argument broke out, and the two men wrestled on the briny boards. The dried salt cut and burned their flesh. Afterwards they huddled under the tarpaulin and cursed each other.

Conlaf cleaned their cuts and asked how they felt.

"I feel if Shipmaster Madoc knew where he was going, we would be there!" said Tallesin. "He is taking us over the Edge. He told us the rain would calm the sea. Did it? I remember, when the rain came, the wind blew hard, the sea was mighty ruffled. If he can tell one lie, why not another? Look, now the rain has stopped, the winds have dropped, and the wet clouds are dragging themselves away so the sun can break through. The air is cooler than the sea, and the air tastes like water from the mountain streams on the Snowden slopes. But there is something out of place. Now the sea is too warm, too salty, and too clear. Brown weeds drift with a strong current just under the surface. 'Tis unnatural. Something is wrong. We are headed for the Black Abyss! If the shipmaster does not get us away from this cursed place and find a real breeze to open the sail, I shall punch him in the nose harder than ye did when ye kicked me in the balls!" He pulled his fist back ready to attack.

"You mangy dog!" Garth snapped, suppressing a surge of anger. Have ye naught better to do than to make malicious remarks about the shipmaster? He is doing his best. I promise ye if ever ye get into strife he will not let ye down. Ye ought to thank him for keeping this leaky tub afloat!"

"You think right," said Conlaf, carrying a clay jar under his arm. He daubed stale lard mixed with dried jimson blossom on the men's salt-water blisters. "This will kill the pain and heal the blisters. You men ever been so spent your eyelids will not stay open?"

"Ya, weary to death and all out of patience." Garth stopped scraping and stood up. "Yesterday, in a fit of annoyance, I kicked Tallesin between the legs and changed his baby-maker to a damn gob of tar. Could ye give him extra lard for the pain I caused?"

"Tar?" whispered Conlaf, closing his eyes.

Tallesin blinked to push away his own blurriness, pulled his balloonlike trousers down, and said, "Look where his damn foot landed like a hammer. Did ye ever see one so black?"

Conlaf wanted to turn away and lay on his blanket. "Looks like blood pudding," he said.

" 'Tis pure fire to make water, which is darker than year-old mead," said Tallesin, shaking his head like a bear with a sore nose.

The sight of the black thing made Conlaf's skin crawl. "A compress of water-lily root will take away the swelling," he said and scratched his right hip that had begun to tingle.

"Leave it swelled," said Garth. "His women friends will bless ye for it."

"Ye are the worst kind of fool." Tallesin's honor-marked hands balled.

Conlaf wanted to knock their heads together, but he had no strength. He put each man on opposite sides of the narrow pen holding the scruffy cows and reminded himself that ordinarily a druid could easily control his emotions. Self-control was one of the first things he was taught. Now control was a thought-out effort. Old habits seemed to have nothing to do with the violent moods the men were having. He wished he were in a feather bed with cool linen covers and a pitcher of water on the table. He scratched under his right arm.

Tallesin put his hands in his trouser pockets so that no one would notice their trembling. He hung onto the cows' pen to steady himself. He had not felt so rotten in his entire life. His legs were too weak to carry him. He scowled at the scrawny cows munching dried seaweed as if he had not noticed them before.

That evening the clouds came back to form a high dome under the sky. By midnight the dome lowered and a misty rain fell. When the rain let up, Madoc stared over the steering oar to the horizon and counted seven ships instead of six. He called to Conlaf, "Count the sails ahead."

"Aye. Seven flambeaux winking at us," said Conlaf. "Actually I think they are stars. I see no sails."

"Two ships missing!" said Madoc, wiping the mist from his face and giving the steering oar to Conlaf until morning.

"Sshh! I hear something," said Conlaf. "Do you hear it?"

"Peevish voices?"

It was Garth and Tallesin arguing over something. Then the voices stilled and the ship rolled, pitched, and plunged as the wind moaned through the rigging. The sea lifted, pushed, and smothered the ship in salty spray. With the first hint of dawn, Madoc said the rain was over. The sea reflected the waning moon. The air was warm and oppressive. The slosh and scrape of the bailing shovels halted. There was rainwater in the loose tarpaulins and hides over the wickerwork of the afterdeck. Madoc drank a handful of the water. It was sweet, like moldy cowhide. He asked Tallesin and Garth, who sat huddled together, to fill several buckets with the good rainwater from the tarpaulins.

Garth said, "Master Madoc, this cheeky Tallesin crawled to my bailiwick in the night and passed out. I am holding him."

Madoc stepped over the two men snuggled between damp blankets. Garth groaned and muttered under his breath. Madoc put his fingers around Tallesin's neck searching for a pulse and ran a hand inside the stinking tunic to feel a heartbeat. With the other hand he lifted the eyelids. He wiped his hand across the wet deck and held it close to Tallesin's face to feel his breath. He looked up and said, "Dead."

"Sir?" said Garth. His eyes were wide with sadness and fear. "I did not kill him. I would never kill a friend. I did not. Did I?"

"Nay," said Madoc. He woke Conlaf and told him Tallesin was dead. "You and Garth do what needs to be done."

"Now?" said Conlaf, barely able to keep his eyes open.

"Before sunrise."

Huffing and puffing, Conlaf and Garth shoved Tallesin's heavy body over the gunwale. By then the crew was awake, and Madoc told them that Sailor Tallesin had passed to the Otherside. Garth began singing a haunting dirge about a soul traveling the high airy trail to tranquility.

Tallesin's body stayed beside the ship buoyed up by the air in his wide trousers and full-sleeved shirt. The eyes seemed to stare accusingly at Garth, who pushed the body of his friend beneath the water with an oar. It disappeared for a few minutes, but reappeared. Garth swore and poked at the corpse again, trying to turn it facedown. It turned faceup each time. Tears ran down Garth's cheeks.

Madoc grieved the loss of one of his men but because he suffered from thirst and semistarvation, he confused his sad feeling with weakness. He stiffened and sounded vexed. "Stop your driveling so you can clear your mind and connect with your friend's free soul."

"He stares at me, like I killed him." Garth sounded like he was carked.

"Take your oar and sit with the rowers," said Madoc.

The rowers pulled the ship due west at sunrise. Tallesin's body was not seen again.

A few days later Conlaf stood near Madoc waiting to take his turn at the steering oar. He asked if Madoc had seen the lump on the back of Tallesin's head. Madoc said he had not. "I saw it when I heaved the body overboard. Garth said it was caused when Tallesin fainted on the rim of the water barrel." Conlaf believed the blow broke something in Tallesin's head that made him blind and dizzy as a drunken trader. Then Conlaf blamed himself for the death, saying he should have trepanned to relieve the skull's pressure. "I should have looked at him when we heard them talking. I thought I was too wrung out to go, but I could have done it."

Madoc said Tallesin might have died anyway; besides he was the one who ordered the men to scrub the deck. During the scrubbing is when they argued, and Tallesin was kicked and complained he did not feel well. "I was bone-tired and did not think straight, so maybe the death is on my hands." He drew in his breath, put a hand on Conlaf's shoulder, and said, "Put this behind us and look after the living. Garth refuses to eat and speaks to no one. His eyes dart here and there like some caged animal. At night he rocks back and forth muttering to himself."

"The trouble is in his head," said Conlaf. "Like us, he believes 'tis his fault." Suddenly he realized that probably no one was to blame; it was out of their hands days ago. Of more importance was the belief of some of the men that death on a ship opened the veil for spirits on the Otherside to play mischief. With the veil open, the spirits would coax more of the living to join them on the Otherside. "I am a physician and have an obligation to say something to the crew," said Conlaf. "What can I say?" He stared at his bare feet.

"Tell them that you have never seen a spirit while sailing a ship or standing on land," said Madoc.

For the next few days the sun shimmered on the water and parched everything dry on the ship. The sea was quiet, warm, and strewn with floating brown seaweed with bladder-shaped berries. Madoc left the limp sail up, even though there was no breeze. Each morning and afternoon he had the rowers unlash the oars and row a few leagues. Then one day some of the men said that the oars frightened the fish.

That same day Garth stood by the masthead and held his oar close to his breast like he would hold a lover. His matted hair was rakish. His eyes rolled and his face shone with perspiration. He held his trembling hands out as if making a benediction. His voice was raspy. "I will send fish to ye," he said. "No one need be hungry. I know where the fish are because they call to me to rest in the still waters." He perched himself atop the port gunwale, clung with bare feet, and hunkered on his haunches. Quiet as a cat pouncing on a bird, he was gone. Everyone heard the splash and the sound of water slapping the ship. Dewi and Tipper flung ends of loose ropes into the water. Madoc shouted, "Garth, you bloody fool! Grab a line! No joking around!"

The ropes fell short. Garth seemed not to see them.

Madoc whirled another knotted rope above his head and let it go. The knotted end hit the sea ahead of Garth. When the rope reached him, he pushed it away, let it sink. Madoc ordered the oars brought out. The rowers kept the ship alongside Garth. Everyone coaxed him to grab an oar. He smiled, raised an arm and called, "The fishes beckon me!"

"I be coming after you!" yelled Madoc. "We could sight land on the morrow!"

"*Avaunt*! Begone!" yelled Garth and disappeared under a mat of yellow-green seaweed.

Madoc tied a rope to the gunwale and around his waist and went out looking for him. He found nothing. Conlaf and Tipper came into the water and also found nothing, only hundreds of small eels wiggling near the underside of the weed mat. Most had bodies that were glassy-clear, scaleless, and covered with mucus, making them nearly impossible to grasp.

No land was sighted the next day, and the crew moped and sang death songs, wondering who would be next to leave the ship. Dewi began to talk about spirits coaxing others to depart to the Otherside. Before evening the men looked suspiciously from one to another. Madoc tried to be cheerful, but his light-hearted banter faded when his cracked lips bled and his bony hands on the steering oar became shaky.

Several days later the water churned like a tornado had struck off the stern. The men saw dark forms thrashing among the large-headed fish. Brett said, "Sea monsters!" and would not go near the gunwale. He believed the creatures could leap out of the water and pull a man overboard. The monsters swam continuously around the ship, often rocking it by slapping their tails against its sides. Brett said it made him dizzy-sick to see them swim without a rest.

Madoc tried to calm him by repeating what he had learned years ago from Shipmaster Erlendson. "These monsters are naught but sea sharks, and they have no air bladders like regular fish. When they stop swimming, they sink like a stone."

Dewi did not help by saying, "I heard if the stomach fluid of a yellow-belly sea shark touches human skin, the skin dissolves!" Some of the crew nodded to show they too had heard the same thing.

Not to be outdone, Tipper said, "I be told that a sea

shark has to roll over on its side in order to bite at all."

"That cannot be true," said Conlaf. "I have seen them bite head-on at a fish. Blooded water brings hordes of them. They charge straight at a steering oar that is moving, but if it is still, they leave it be. So, I be telling you—do not rock the ship until the sharks leave!"

"Is Garth giving them orders to frighten us and gobble our sweet-tasting flesh?" said Brett, clutching the top of the water barrel.

"The other way around, I think," said Madoc. "Knowing the onions were gone, and the little bit of corn meal left was filled with worms, and our bellies growled for food; he sent us the sweet, big-headed fish."

Barri, an agile, black Welsh crofter from Abergele, suggested eating one of the cows.

Without taking a vote or asking permission, Conlaf unfastened the stall rope from one of the scraggy cows. He prodded her to stand up. Both he and the cow moaned and groaned with the exertion. The other cow bellowed pitifully. Conlaf unsheathed his dagger and tipped over the cows' water bucket, spilled the precious, slimy drinking water. He had decided to butcher both of the miserable animals and catch every drop of sweet blood in their water bucket. He reasoned that it was a crime for men to die of thirst while these sorry beasts looked on with large, stupid eyes. He licked his lips and could almost taste the delicious, warm, thick red soup trickling down his parched throat. Both cows swung their heads from side to side. He imagined the nearer cow smiled and turned her head so that he could have a clean swipe at her jugular vein. His hand clutching the dagger raised. With no warning, his arm was jerked down and pulled behind his back.

The dagger clattered to the deck. Madoc's eyes blazed and he picked it up. "Bloody fool! I did not think you could be so stupid. Obviously I was mistaken. I gave no orders to butcher a cow!" He shook with anger and outrage. "Give each cow a chance and it will serve us well in a peaceful land." He felt betrayed. Conlaf had disregarded ships' rules that the only one who gives orders is the shipmaster.

"Friend," yelled Conlaf, " 'tis better both cows die to

feed us than have all of us starve! You can see we are on a death ship!"

The confused, hungry crew heard the words *death ship* and gathered to see what it meant. Madoc jabbed the air with Conlaf's dagger and said that he was in command, and no one, not even the ship's physician, could act without his order. That was mutiny, he thought, and from now on he would need to keep close watch on both beasts if he wanted them to thrive in the unproved land. He told the men to go back where they were and ordered Conlaf to put the dagger away before he took his turn at the steering oar. The men went back to their work. There was nothing to see, even the sharks had gone.

The next morning Conlaf stood alone in the bow with his eyes glazed and his face uplifted to the sky. His whiskers had grown to a scraggly black beard, and his hands were clasped together in front of his chest. His lips moved as though he were a schoolboy reciting the raids over Offa's Dyke. He was using an ancient druidic technique of clearing the mind of all thought except for an important matter that was to be discussed with another person not present.

Madoc watched him from the steering oar, then closed his eyes and let his own mind clear. Suddenly, in his mind's eye, he saw that the men in the missing ships were safe. He opened his eyes and saw Conlaf still facing the cloudless sky. He called to him. "My friend, did you tell Llieu to throw out a flare of Greek fire when he spots land?"

Conlaf's eyes were red rimmed and crazed. With his dagger in his hand, he came toward Madoc shaking from head to foot. "You are killing us by keeping the bloody cows alive!" The sailors had heard their angry words and circled around them to find what the hullabaloo was about. Conlaf held his breath until he had to inhale. Then he held his breath again.

Madoc's heart pounded loud as a drum. His hands perspired. He saw how easy it would be to lose control of a ship. With a lunge, he grabbed Conlaf's hand and wrenched the dagger free, but not before it laid open a deep gash from his right shoulder to his elbow.

Conlaf went berserk. He grabbed Madoc and shook him as if he was shaking fruit from an apple tree. Madoc could not swallow. He heaved his shoulders to throw Conlaf off. Blood spurted from his upper right arm. He put his foot out and tripped Conlaf, who fell on the bloodied deck.

"You are trying to kill me!" said Conlaf in an alarmed voice.

"No," said Madoc, giving the dagger to Dewi. He held his bleeding arm and ordered Conlaf taken to the bow. He bound him with chains to the large wood anchor that Clare, the metal man from the Isle of Man, had braced with iron. Each man had felt his dry mouth become moist and secretly wished Conlaf had killed the cows. The men kept their heads bowed so Madoc could not see their eyes. Madoc tried to tie a cord around his bleeding, upper-right arm to stop the flow, but he failed. His men were unmoving as statues, even when he lowered his head between his knees to keep from fainting from loss of blood. Finally Tipper told him to lean against the gunwale and asked Conlaf how to dress the shipmaster's wound. Conlaf, in a daze, said nothing. Tipper asked Conlaf if he was in possession of his reason. Conlaf blinked as though he only now saw that Madoc was wounded. He tried to free his hands. "Unbind me!" he yelled.

Tipper told him he could not. "You are being punished for trying to kill the chief shipmaster."

Madoc's arm throbbed as though it were on fire. He clamped his teeth together to keep from passing out.

Conlaf said the wound needed soaking.

"Soaking?" asked Tipper, puzzled.

"Tincture of witchhazel in my leather case," said Conlaf. "Lugh on a ladder, let me do it!"

"Nay," said Madoc, trying to hide his ever-growing weakness. "You spent your foolishness like a mutineer, so I shackled you for insubordination." His heart was heavy as a sack of lead, but he told himself it had to be done or he would lose control. He flinched when the witchhazel hit the gash. Conlaf turned so that he could touch Madoc's hand. Madoc asked himself if Conlaf realized what had happened.

Madoc gritted his teeth, glared at Conlaf, who was sick with starvation, as were the rest of the men. He was a sorry sight with cracked, scaly, purple lips and dull eyes—a bag of bones, pale as moonlight with a red spot in the middle of each hollow cheek. His skin felt hot and dry, and his breath was short and fetid. His eyes filled with tears when he looked at Madoc. He said he was tired as a hunting pup and did not have the strength to open and shut his eyes. He was at the end of his frayed rope and not able to heal himself. He said he could not recall going after the cows, defying the shipmaster, losing his temper, and slashing Madoc. He looked around and said, "My dagger is gone. Who took it? Lugh, I just want to sleep. My legs—weak as watered mead. Believe me, I could never hurt Shipmaster Madoc, my best friend." Finally he told Tipper how to push the flesh together so as to leave no ridge of proud flesh, nor barely a scar. He told him not to wrap the bandage tight or 'twould cut off the flow of blood, causing Madoc's hand to rot. In that case Tipper would have to ask him how to amputate. "Lugh's lungs!" he said. " 'Tis a nasty wound. Fie on the lout who did it!"

Brett confessed to Madoc that Conlaf had given his rations to him once in a while.

Madoc made sure Conlaf was fed each day's ration and kept clean as possible, when all he had to be washed with was sea-water that could make a man's skin blister if used overmuch. He believed, as long as he acted rationally, the men would continue with their sea duties, keeping the ship clean, checking the ropes for wear, and plugging leaks with tar and wadmal. He was realistic and knew it was not himself, but the sight of the other ships on the horizon that would keep hope in the hearts of his crew.

Again it was the sharp eyes of Brett that saw the seven ships against the horizon near sunset. They were like seven black silhouettes. After that the men ate their single meal of half-cooked fish, sat on the deck, and counted the ships on the horizon. When the fog rolled across the horizon so they could not see, they swore at the gods. Brett and two of the messmates continued to read aloud from Madoc's journal about Paris each day. When the men began to mutter among themselves and share the darker details of their lives, the messmates listened. Then they challenged the men to make up elaborate menus to see who could outdo the other by imagining things they would like to eat when they next stepped on land. The time taken for reminiscing and daydreaming grew. The men urinated more than usual. Madoc asked Conlaf if the urine might be drunk to conserve every bit of water. Conlaf shook his head. Drinking urine would be as bad as drinking sea-water. He suggested they squeeze raw fish between two boards, throw away the pulpy flesh, and save the juice. He thought the flesh of the fish took water from their bodies, and it was worth trying to drink only fish juice for a couple of days.

"With only juice we will have naught to chew!" said the ex-fisherman, Barri, who wore a peaked cap of gray wool. "Men want meat!" He had not only woad markings around his fingernails, but also a turtle tattooed on his left cheek. His shoulders twitched, and his teeth scraped over his parched lips.

Three days later the men were feeling a little better. Conlaf was permitted to eat with the others, but not permitted to give away food or water rations to anyone. Dewi and Conn took his place at the steering oar, and he slept through the night.

"When the fish are gone, we shall slaughter the cows," said Madoc several afternoons later. He exchanged quick glances with Conlaf. He had thought about what was best for the starving men for a long time. " 'Tis better to save the men than the cows if we do not find fruitful land soon."

"I agree with that," said Conlaf. "Just the sight of the tragic cows chills my blood. Nevertheless, I did wrong if I charged you with my dagger. I was out of my mind. Knowingly, I would never hurt you. Never! I am more sorry than I can say." His eyes watered.

Madoc never regretted putting Conlaf in chains; yet it broke his heart to see his best friend fettered. "Your attitude has improved as has your sanity," he said. "I believe you."

Conlaf fully expected to stay shackled two or three more days, but smiled with relief when Madoc ordered him unshackled and told him to look after the sick men. The rest of the day Madoc kept an eye on Conlaf as he gave out bits of powdered herbs and put salve on the worst saltwater sores. For the next few days every eye and ear was alert for another threat from Conlaf. None came.

"How are we going to join the ten sails into one line?"

said Conlaf one evening when he took the steering oar.

"Make use of the sail, the northeasterly winds, and sea currents," said Madoc.

"What if we cannot join the other ships?" asked Conlaf.

"We will join them on land," said Madoc. "I watch the two ships behind us and the other seven against the horizon every moment I be awake. If there be land, the seven sails will tell us!"

"Will we see elephants on that new land?" said Brett.

Barri hooted and said, "There is no such beast. Are you going giddy?"

Brett laughed to show that his mind was healthy. "One night it was hard to sleep, so I read by moonlight what Madoc and Conlaf had seen in Paris," he said. "You can learn a lot at night when the moon is full with no rain or fog."

On the next fog-free night the men watched the falling stars and wondered where they went when their lights went out. They slept and dreamed about a rain that would fill the empty water barrels. At the steering oar that night Madoc saw seven flares, indicating that the seven ships against the horizon were bearing starboard. That puzzled him, but he kept his line of three ships going in a southwesterly direction. He ordered the rowers to take their positions, saying that with some powerful rowing they might be close enough to communicate with the seven sails in the morning. After a few hours of hard pulling, he ordered the second rowers to take the oars. He could not sleep and before morning noticed more brown sea grass and a new long slim fish swimming in the grass. He squinted and tried to make out who was the lead sail of the seven. He let Conlaf take the oar and went to the afterdeck and wrote about the previous day's flaming sunset that slowly faded to gray, then black, revealing a hundred shooting stars on the underside of the night-sky's bowl. Near dawn he rolled into his blankets, closed his eyes, and the next thing he knew he was awakened by shouting.

"*Ynys*! Island! *Traeth*! Beach! Starboard!"

Far ahead on the starboard side was a wide strip of land. His ears rang, and a tingling feeling of joy ran through him. He could not wipe the huge grin from his face when he looked at Conlaf and ordered the rowers to make every effort to move the three ships closer to the line of seven before noon. " 'Tis fitting that we give thanks," said Madoc.

"Why?" said Conlaf. "Why thank the gods? If we do our duty, they will do theirs."

Nevertheless, in the manner of a druid thanksgiving, the men, including Conlaf, joined hands to form a ring and swung their clenched fists high in the air four times. On the final swing they shouted, "*En!*" which meant, "We who live!" These men, who were as near to being skeletons and still alive, sang four-part songs and Welsh cants for pure joy.

The rowers worked rhythmically. Madoc leaned over the gunwale and saw that the seaweed was frequent now. Some of the leaves were coated with ribbons of sea-slug eggs. The slugs surprised him by flying like birds among the waterweeds. With a hook on a line, he pulled seaweed onto the deck and picked out a beakerful of small white crabs. Each crab was no larger than his thumbnail. He pinched a tiny crab and popped it into his mouth. The taste was not bitter, more like a dilute medicinal—iodine. The soft shells crunched pleasantly.

Dewi's mouth watered and he said, "Look there, our shipmaster has plenty for himself to eat. The well-fed does not understand the lean."

Tipper glared at him and said, "Do not speak ill of the shipmaster. He is as lean and hollow eyed as ye and me."

Dewi glared back until Tipper dropped his eyes. "Be I not here? I was anxious as ye to leave a land that had been in my family for nine generations. King Dafydd, for his own power and glory, gave my land to the English king. Under his influence my land was scorched, its edibles wasted, its animals butchered, my wife and babies brained against my sacred oaks."

Thinking about Gwynedd's terrible deterioration, Tipper said, "Ye be entitled to grumble once in a while. But I remember my homeland as a paradise with green meadow, blue, snow-fed lakes circled by distant purple peaks."

Madoc glanced at them and gave Dewi the beaker of tiny crabs saying, "More can be had by any man just for the taking." Dewi's neck turned red. He gave the beaker to

Tipper, saying the gods share with a person who is generous. He got his fish line and pulled in more seaweed. Tipper helped him pluck the tiny crabs. Soon the messmates were working with them and in no time they filled two large cooking pots with tiny crabs.

Each change in marine life indicated a change in the sea's currents. Madoc noticed the subtle changes much earlier and knew they were approaching land. He looked up and saw two sea swallows fluttering overhead. Birds were a certain sign land was not far off. The land appeared gray and shaped like a pyramid. Madoc wondered if it was clouds that made a peak over the land. He had seen clouds that stayed in the same position for so long that they looked like solid ground in the form of cliffs or low sandbars. The land did not move, but near midday it seemed to become clear and grow into an island. Madoc let the oarsmen rest during the warmest part of the day. In late afternoon the island's pyramid melted and lost itself in a white haze near the water. The wind began to blow, and Madoc had to keep changing the steering paddle so they were not blown in a northerly direction. In the twilight, he watched the towflares of the seven sails and saw they too kept their ships aligned alongside the land. He grinned and thumped Conlaf on the back. "See that pinpoint of bluish light? 'Tis Greek fire!" His eyes squinted. "The ships anchor! Their flares bob in unison. They wait for us. *Avaunt*, go toward the land!"

A great cloud of golden-headed gannets wheeled and swirled overhead, cutting off most of the sky's light on the beach. As the ships came nearer, the birds flew off, like thick, black, flapping clouds, into the gray fogbank that hovered over the sea. It was night when the *Gwennan Gorn* was anchored in shallow water beside the other nine ships.

Men from the ten ships dropped over their sides, clambered down the rope, and waded to shore, not waiting for coracles to be lowered. The reunion was noisy and bursting with emotion. Everybody talked at the same time. There was laughter, hugs, and sadness. Five other men besides two horses and a goat had died.

Archdruid Gwalchmai said in a loud voice, "Look at it this way! We are here, where no other men have been, and we are alive." The men stood quiet, thinking about being alive. They watched Gwalchmai pick up his harp, thinking how they all looked the same as old Gwalchmai with stringy hair and ragged beards that touched their chests. Their clothing was tattered and encrusted with salt and fish oil. Their bare feet were bloody with open sores. They were scruffier and smellier than any person any man had ever seen. With eyes that shone with wetness, Gwalchmai led them into a song of thanksgiving.

Madoc thanked Gwalchmai and gave a heartfelt hosanna for Shipmaster Kabyle, who had kept seven ships together after the big storm. Kabyle embarrassed Madoc by asking what happened to his arm. "Did you tangle in a fog bank and could not see where you were going?"

Madoc sat on a drift log and heard Conlaf draw in his breath before he said a word. "Well, yes, my reason went behind a cloud and I fell onto a blade," he said, with no intention of saying he had a disagreement with his ship's physician. " 'Twas a stupid accident. During the storm I had to hang on to the steering paddle for dear life; my ship, bull-bowed and round-bottomed, skated sideways, right and left with the beam wind."

Conlaf relaxed and told about sighting sea sharks after the storm and admitted that he, same as some of the other men, became weak as watery gruel and despondent as any man could be. "We could have lost our ship more than once, but our shipmaster would never let us give up."

Madoc kept his eyes down so no one could see his shame. "For troth, I have to tell you that I do not remember the three or four days after two of my good, decent men died—one drowned; the other died on my ship's deck. I believe a man can go stark mad from lack of food and water and the constant sea spray. Our measure has been taken. I be not worth so much."

Caradoc asked, "Well now, how many of us would be alive today if we had stayed in Gwynedd?"

"Fewer than are here, I be certes," said Conlaf.

"So, was Madoc correct when he said there was land west of the Fortunates?" said Caradoc. "Of course, you know he was right. That is worth something."

"We will spend the night on this island and in the morning explore for water and game," said Madoc.

Half a dozen driftwood fires were built. One by one stories were told of food stores depleted, spume rolling across the decks, and men calling to the sea gods for mercy. Sigurd told how his men hacked holes in the sides of the large-headed fish and drained the liquid into beakers for drinking. Erlendson, whose tongue was swollen, said in a lisp that a couple of his men cut the same species into sections and twisted them in a cloth to free the juice, which was caught in cooking pots and rationed as drinking water. "It tasted worse than bilge."

While listening, Madoc lay back in the sand and let his eyes drop shut. He never knew that Llieu examined the red healing line on his arm and shoulder and rubbed it with a sheep-oil paste of mashed poplar buds. Llieu told Conlaf that the scar would fade to a pale line no wider than that made by a manure fork on a clean barn floor.

Conlaf glanced at Madoc sleeping, rose to his feet, ran the tip of his tongue over his chapped lips, and said, "There are many ways of measuring a shipmaster's worth. Is he fat and his men lean? Is he at ease and they weary? Is he receiving praises and his men feeling humiliation? Does he bribe his men to obey orders? Is he afraid to punish wrongdoers, lest he create a mutiny? Shipmaster Madoc meets every one of those measures on the right side and more! He treated us as equals." He cleared his throat. "One time I was a bloody fool, and he tied me hand and foot for a whole fortnight for going against orders. I do not remember having ahold of my dagger. But if I did, I could have killed two cows and my best friend. I deserved my punishment. Tipper, a crofter and fine seaman, repaired the damage I did to Madoc's arm. For troth, I was crazy—as were others from time to time. Shipmaster Madoc never acted irrationally, even though he says he had lapses of memory. None of us saw that in him."

The crew from the *Gwennan Gorn* clapped. "*Iawn!* Right!" they said.

Other men from other ships retold their grim stories. The men's and animals' deaths were not only tragic but, at the same time, elevated to the plane of heroic. Finally, to help the men relax and sleep, Gwalchmai told riddles as he softly played his harp. "What is sharper than the sword?"

The druids sang out, "Understanding!"
"What is swifter than the wind?"
"Thought!"
"What is whiter than snow?"
"Truth!"
"What is blacker than the raven?"
"Death!"
"What is lighter than a spark?"
"The mind of a woman between two men."
"What is sweeter than mead?"
"Intimate conversation."

Two-hundred-plus men lay in the sand in a circle around six, tiny driftwood fires and slept as the fog hovered quietly over them.

Early the next morning Riryd and Willem and Brett walked in the same manner as they walked on board ship, with a slow gait, their feet spread wide so they had maximum weight distribution and could not be thrown off balance. They found large tufts of yellow grass with dry roots abrasive with grit. The grass would give the emaciated animals something to munch on. Sigurd complained there was no fresh water on the island, only tough grasses, sand, broken shells, and lizards. Gerard said Madoc did not know where they were, except on an unproved island. "We may all be fools," he said.

Shipmaster Gerard, of the *Gray Wolf*, said, "Chief Shipmaster Madoc and physician Conlaf were only lads when they sailed with me from Lundy to France. And not ordinary lads, they were Welsh emissaries, pretending to be black-robed Augustinians, going to see the King of France. Now I am here of my own free will, following these men because in my homeland I could have had my throat cut for being what I am, a druid. We may be on a barren island today, but Madoc will get us on something better tomorrow or the next day. Have ye noticed how life can suddenly turn around and hit ye between the eyes?" He turned around and pointed to the cloud of terns in the sky and a smaller cloud of brown birds with a long feather in their tails. "The birds are no fools. They are finding food, seeds or insects."

When Madoc woke, he rubbed his sunbrowned, sunken, bewhiskered face and longed for sweet, cool water. He picked up a fistful of wool that had soaked up fog droplets during the night and gave it to Brett to suck on for carrying an armload of brittle grass to the emaciated cows aboard the *Gwennan Gorn*. He did not want to spend another night on that barren island.

Kabyle came to tell him that five days earlier some of his men and himself had seen a star with a tail of fire fall into the sea. "It looked to be no more than a few leagues from the ship. My men said it was a sign that food would fall from heaven. They want to wait here another night to see if 'tis true. They hope the food is dark bread made from rye wheat. They are tired of fish. We are all tired. One more night here will not matter. Why hurry? Who are we going to meet?"

Madoc searched the sky. He saw only the high blue dome with a slow-moving, relentless sun and the thick circling clouds of birds, sometimes blotting out the sun, sometimes covering the sand close to the water, searching enthusiastically for small sea creatures to fill their bellies. Among the men there was not enough enthusiasm to fill a thimble. "I remember watching the falling stars," said Madoc. " 'Twas a lot more than five days ago. And I believe it meant naught for us. Tell me, can your messmates show other messmates how to catch birds for sup?"

"Aye," said Kabyle. "Birds will taste good for a change."

Madoc coughed and announced that the men could rest here one more night and be ready to leave at dawn. He was exasperated with himself for feeling so tired and achy. His throat hurt, and he wanted the messmates to run out and grab handfuls of birds without being told. He was hungry, but he did not want to do anything. He felt hot and dry. He was confused, inefficient, and easily provoked. He imagined the men secretly scorned him. He was irked because they were druids and should have forbearance. He asked Conlaf about the crankiness.

"Each man lapses into his own private dream of home, loving relatives, or hungry sea monsters. Some talk to imagined friends or foes. Others cry dry tears and try to keep their deterioration secret from the others. They miss a taste of their own kind of food and their homeland more than they ever dreamed. They miss the women," Conlaf said truthfully. "The men eye one another and their own thoughts make them nervous."

Madoc should have known, but his wits were muddied and in the next moment he forgot Conlaf stood next to him and lapsed into his own dream of hunting with a high-rumped, crinkle-haired, white hound, that looked more like a beast in a French royal tapestry. In his daydream, light came between the leaves of the beech trees. The breeze carried the smell of fresh clover, and a slim young woman with shining dark hair that hung to her waist and shining brown eyes walked at his side carrying a bow. She placed an arrow butt end against the taut bowstring, pulled back, smiled, and let the arrow fly. A doe fell in front of them. The dream was so real that Madoc cried out, "You killed a living thing! A thing with a heart and soul that loves life the same as we!"

Tears streamed down the woman's face, and she said, "Why are you cranky with me? I killed the doe to save your life. It was an exchange, her life for yours. I want you to live."

Madoc blinked and the woman was gone and so was the doe. His knees were mush and his arms quivered. He scanned the earth's rim and jammed his fists into his eyes to clear away the dream. Conlaf's steady arms encircled Madoc's twitching shoulders. He rebuked Conlaf for not minding his own business. He was ashamed of Conlaf's pity and his own lack of control.

The sky brightened in the east. Nothing resembling bread had fallen, and it was time to look for more suitable land. "The Western Sea has to have more than sandy islands and thousands of birds," said Madoc. "We will tire of eating birds and gritty beach grass just as we did fish and kelp without good water to wash it down."

Three days from *Ynys Tywod*, Sand Island, Madoc, still achy, found himself in a strong northern cross current moving in a wide gyre. The wide path of sea had become aquamarine. He wondered if the color change meant there was land ahead. He could smell the damp, rich, salubrious smell of marshlands. The idea of land with lush grass, game, and fresh water made him lightheaded. He heard the rhythmic

pounding of the surf and imagined he heard a voice. He
told himself it was another dizzy spell, but the phantom
voice insisted that he raise his eyes to the horizon. He was
stubborn, refused, and closed his eyes. A gull screeched.
He opened one eye and saw a dazzling white wall, like
great chalk cliffs against the horizon. "Land! Land ho!" he
shouted. The gull disappeared and a patch of green crept
away from the white cliffs. Then the cliffs disappeared.
Whirring clouds of tiny tan birds flew from the north across
to the southwest as though they were leading the ships to
the tiny patch of green. He spied a bay and from it rose
thousands of bigger birds with long wings, thin tails, and
hooked beaks. He now knew that the chalky cliffs were
actually layers of fluffy clouds shining in the light from the
sunset. He adjusted the steering oar so that he could go
west across the fast cross current. The clouds moved east,
and it was twilight when he led the ships into the sheltered
bay. Not only was there a wide sand beach, but also an
aber, the wide mouth of a dry creek that once flowed over
huge rocks and gravel out into the sea. Before they
beached, a cloud appeared overhead and rain poured out of
it. Messmates laid out pots, plates, and beakers, and the
sailors let their blankets soak up precious water that later
could be squeezed out. The men raised their faces to the
sky, their mouths wide open. The animals licked the wet
deck inside their pens. It was a marvelous time that lasted
less than six dozen heartbeats. Afterwards the air felt
steamy.

It did not take long to discover that there was little green
grass and no source of fresh water. This was another island.
The messmates collected drift for their cook fires, then they
plucked, gutted, and roasted the big birds with the long
wings for sup. The birds were caught by throwing oiled
tarps over them and stepping on their necks until they suffocated. After sup, Madoc reminded the messmates from
all the ships to gather as much fresh grass as possible for
the animals on their particular ship. He coughed and swore
under his breath about his hoarseness and the sore throat
that hurt every time he spoke. Then he gathered the shipmasters around him and asked if they had noticed the strong
northern current before coming into the bay.

"I had trouble with my steering oar," said Willem.

"I did not quite believe what I had run into," said Kabyle. "It was a current, strong enough to carry a ship northward. I had a frightful time keeping my ship on a southwesterly course."

"I was a fool to get into a different current's set," said Erlendson. "That is where the color of the water changed to a bright blue-green."

"I got into it, too, thus I do not believe you were a fool," said Madoc. "I want to talk about those strong currents. If there had been winds blowing in the same direction as the current, only Lugh knows where we would be now. Water in that fast current is warm and truly salty. There seemed to be low hanging clouds that rained on the beach wherever the water was warmest. Did anyone else notice that?"

"The current tore up the floor of the sea, constantly changing its depth is what I noticed," said Caradoc.

There were gasps, whisperings, and head noddings before anyone else admitted that he had noticed the same phenomenon. Riryd said he, too, had found the fast water more salty than he would have expected, and every shade of blue moving in a wide band northward as far as he could see. "There are more mysteries in the sea than I had ever thought."

"I be wondering if a ship is caught tight in that warm, northbound current, would she sail straight for Iceland?" said Madoc.

"Goder-heal!" said Conn. "Exactly what I am thinking. The current will take us north, back where we came from, if we need such a thing!"

The shipmasters were now as excited as children who had sifted through the sand to find agates and instead found sharks' teeth. They nodded vigorously to one another and spoke of the amazement in finding that each had experienced the same, strong, northbound current. However, none, but Madoc, had thought to ask about it, to discuss its possibilities.

"What trouble would we have going across the current in an easterly direction?" said Llieu.

"Depends on the strength of the wind," said Madoc. "We have already experienced that coming southwest. If we follow the current, we would go north, then east, then south and west in a huge circle. 'Tis something to ponder while we are at sea."

"Does this mean we are close to being carried right over into Black Doom?" said Troyes.

"Nay, no one has ever seen Doom, as far as I know," said Madoc.

"Mayhap seen it, but not come back to tell about it," said Caradoc.

Kabyle told the men stories of Eric the Red, who took twenty-five ships to Greenland. During the first storm, six ships were lost. Five turned back at the first sight of crystalline ice-mountains in the sea. Fourteen landed. "Three hundred and fifty men and women, with livestock and gear, settled in Greenland. Ten years later the colony expanded to a thousand," said Kabyle. "I believe we are certain to do better under the leadership of Madoc."

"We have not lost one ship," said Caradoc.

"But we have no women," said Conlaf.

"And no one is going to turn back until we have built a decent village, even though we have discovered a fast-moving northbound current to sail on," said Sigurd.

Two mornings later Brett spotted more green islands and one of them had trees. The trees caused pandemonium on the *Gwennan Gorn*. Brett pulled off his shirt and waved it. The men shouted. Madoc beached his ship on rollers on the shore of the Island with Trees. A light wind billowed the sails on the other ships and brought them to the shore. Songs of happiness flowed through the air. Madoc thought that the kelp beds swayed with the water currents as if keeping time to the singing. Joy flooded through him so fast that he could not speak. He was like a lost child who had suddenly spied his family. He was first off his ship, and he ran to the other shipmasters who were directing the placement of the poles so their ships could be pulled on shore past the tide line.

A colony of herons were routed out of the heavy-leafed trees. They circled overhead and landed along the edge of the water, leaving trigonal prints that were quickly deleted.

Madoc told his messmates to catch enough birds for sup.

Then he talked with Erlendson and Caradoc, who said they, too, were low on provisions and had lived off a few small fish that were so tough that they could not be gutted and filleted or split up the back to save them for smoking. "We kept the heads and frames to make fish soup, but in the end had to salt and dry them," he said. "We were hungry so we ate them."

Madoc told them that like a miracle, before the sun set for the last few days, schools of three- to four-foot-long fish with large heads that tapered to slender and deeply forked tails swam around his ship. The fish fought hard not to be caught. Everyone was awed by their change of color in the air, from shimmering gold to green, then blue to pure silver as they died. He thought it sad and humbling to see so close up and graphically the ebbing of life. He told them it made him think of Tallesin dying of starvation and Garth drowning in the green forest of kelp. He asked if it was possible that Garth had traded his life for the fish, so that those on the *Gwennan Gorn* might live. He closed his eyes and rubbed his temples. His throat hurt and no matter how much sleep he had, he was exhausted. Both Erlendson and Caradoc thought it possible because they had caught many of the same kind of fish. "The fish's meat was sweet but tough, and my crew took turns fishing most of three nights to bring in a few of the bloody, luminescent fighters," said Erlendson.

"Same thing on my ship," said Caradoc. "The fish tugged hard on a line, changed direction, tore the hook loose, and swam away with it dangling from its mouth or gills. My men were so hungry that they laughed and cried and swore at the same time."

As soon as each ship was pulled ashore, the rest of the men scrambled over the gunwales and ran pell-mell to the tall grass, panting and still buzzing about the northern current that made it hard to keep their ships on a western course. Each ship had to reset its sail often, because the wind seemed to change with the current. The men were dehydrated from wind and sun. The long, cool grass was a comfort for some men to lie in. Then Brett, who could not stay still, found the tree-shaded rocks that held precious rainwater in every indentation. The men went crazy. Conlaf tried to stop them, to tell them not to drink too much, too fast. Thirst was so strong that all ears were deaf to his words of warning.

Madoc gulped water that lay in a stone indented into several basins. He threw away his salt-encrusted bandage and washed his scarred arm in one of the basins. He let the warm, sweet rainwater run through his hair, over his face, and down his shoulders. He drank again. Never in his life had he tasted anything so enjoyable, so satisfying. He lay beside his rock and watched the men scramble for pockets of warm, sweet-tasting water. They knelt or lay on their bellies and drank from cupped hands. Three men sat in a huge concave rock, like a cauldron, with water up to their chin to drink, sing, and thank Lugh. Most paid no attention to Conlaf, the physician, and gorged themselves until their bellies distended, rock hard. They were the ones who suffered severe cramps, became violently ill, and could not look at a supper of roast heron. That night Conlaf had no time for sleep, but continually reassured the men that they would recover. The men rolled back and forth on the beach in agony until they vomited and felt better. Only then did they understand why Conlaf had warned them.

In the morning Madoc discovered several dozen large sea turtles basking in the sunshine. He and a couple of men, who felt better, dug pits in which to roast the turtles. Grass and twigs were twisted together as fuel. It was the best, most tender meat they had had in weeks. The messmates from all the ships sliced the meat, spread it over poles held by Y-shaped branches in the sand, and let it dry over a slow, smoky fire, which kept the hordes of flies away.

Next, the messmates shoved dehydrated cows, sheep, goats, and horses from the ship, down wooden planks, to the juicy green grass. They were tied to trees so that they could crop the grass but not wander to the rocks to gorge themselves on water. No one told the messmates, until it was too late, that the animals would suffer bloat from filling up on the rich grass after they had had only brittle, dried grass for several weeks.

Before sailing, the ships' hulls were scraped of barnacles and retarred. Erlendson sang Norse verse honoring the old gods, legendary heroes, and trolls as he checked the beechwood blades of the steering oars, the oar locks, and inspected the rigging and wooden crossyard on all the ships. If the old flax rope looked frayed, he had one of the men from that particular ship reeve up a new rope alongside the sail. Someone took down the old one and mended it.

From a hill, the sailors could see a string of the sandy islands, like a chain. The shallow sea around each islet was bright green in the sunshine and became olive green where the bottom fell away to great depths.

Brett found figs as large as a man's hand hanging from inland trees. He and Troyes, who limped on his stiff right leg, gathered all the good figs they found on the ground into a large tarpaulin. When others came for figs to dry and store on their ship, Brett climbed the trees to pull them loose. The men found it easy to pick them off the ground. Erlendson found a strange yellow fruit hanging from large-leafed trees. When the skin was peeled, the soft fruit lying against big seeds was orange colored and had a fine, sweet taste. He gathered as much as he could to replace his depleted store of mushy, moldy onions. Madoc suggested to Brett that he and Brian bring in as much as he could find room for on the *Gwennan Gorn* and then help other messmates gather some for their ships. In his mind's eye he saw all the men, skinny as skeletons with sunken eyes and cracked lips, healing themselves on this Island of Trees. Caradoc had his messmates pull in large conch shells from the sandy, shallow sea bottoms and crack them, remove the hand-sized piece of meat, and put it on rocks to dry. After a few days, the men began to feel better from water, fruit, and plenty of meat.

Troyes asked Brett if it was true that he was like a bagpipe, never making a noise 'til his belly was full. Brett laughed and said that was not really true, and Troyes ought to come around after sup to hear him read. "I am reading Chief Shipmaster's journal and what he did after he left Paris."

"I will come around and see if he wrote true," said Troyes. "I was with him by then. Matey, it better be right, or I will have to take over your story and finish its telling."

Brett thought for an instant that Troyes's sea-green eyes held the cold glint and cunning of a falcon. Then he thought, *I am reading him falsely, because I know he has a big heart and is as kind as a dolphin.* "Hold on," said Brett. "There is something I have learned, beside reading words while studying from Master Madoc's journals. Druids actually use that dirty rye smut to heal their wounds."

"I know that," said Troyes. "Any good physician knows about that. What else did ya learn?"

"Storytelling is at the heart of human experience. When stories are told, the teller, or in this case, the writer, Shipmaster Madoc, uses all of his knowledge of life, philosophy, and history. He shapes the familiar for his audience into something he has seen or experienced in a way that is concrete, vivid, persuasive, and thus, easily remembered. More and more wonderful stories are made every day from our adventures in these unproved islands, and they reveal information not told in the old, druid, formal council meetings."

"That is good," said Troyes. "Believe me, if what I hear you read or tell after sup is as good as you make it sound, together we shall encourage all the storytellers to spread the lore. There has to be a storyteller on each ship."

xv
Around the Dog's Tail

There are ... hundreds of barrier islands [along the coast of the Carolinas, Georgia, and Florida], ... some scarcely more than [sand or] a spume of cedar and palmetto. They are all remnants of an Eocene ocean floor. The islands themselves are encircled (except on the ocean side of the barrier group) by passementeries of rich marshlands. ... Millions of years ago, the supercontinent was ripped apart by drifting tectonic plates, creating Gondwanaland and Laurentia—Africa and North America, respectively. Fossils of plants and animals deemed indigenous to Africa have been found embedded in the ... [islands'] limestone.

—Roy Attaway, *A Home in the Tall Marsh Grass*

Madoc drew the shipmasters around him and told them he was heartened to see how fast all the men had recovered. He told them that there was no fresh water on the island so they would leave at the evening's high tide. "Pack the dried conch and fruit. Fill the water barrels with the rainwater."

Willem held up his hand and asked about the lake that Master Kabyle had found.

" 'Tis a lake made by a bank of conch shells damming a salty spring. I do not know how to explain a pile of conch shells that dams a spring to form a salty lake. Can the sea run up under this island?"

"There is more to say!" said Kabyle. "This morning I stood on the shell midden and gazed into the lake that was like liquid mercury. I saw my reflection as easily as if I looked into a piece of polished silver." He paused and leaned forward. "I looked at the reflection of trees and standing before them I saw four brown men." There was a gasp and a whispering like the rustling of dry autumn leaves. "These men wore nothing but short aprons in front. Their hair was long and black as coal. They had sticks in their mouths. Once in a while each man would take the stick out, pucker his mouth, and blow out smoke. At first I thought they had a fire in their throats. But that can not be true. So I kept my head down and watched in the water. They touched the end of the sticks to the fire that burned beside them. They sucked on the sticks. And blew the smoke out of their mouth. I have never seen such a thing!"

There was more buzzing among the shipmasters. "What kind of stick?" asked Sigurd scratching his head and rubbing his red-rimmed eyes.

"I could not tell," said Kabyle. "After a while I began to wonder if I was seeing these strange men under the clear water, so I threw in a handful of shells. When the water's surface was smooth there was nothing. I went to the shore in front of the trees. There was nothing except a thin line of smoke from a little fire. And a few leaves, brown and dry, as big as my hand. Some were rolled into sticks. I was tempted to bring them to you, but praise Allah, I heard a twig snap. My heart stuttered and I ran."

Everyone was silent thinking about the strangers who sucked in smoke. Finally, Riryd said, "There are no other men here. We are the first. You made that up."

A few of the men snickered. Kabyle held his head high. He knew what he had seen and said he would take anyone to see the place.

Brett ran across the beach carrying something over his head. "Master Madoc! Look! Look, what I found—a beaker! A funny beaker. Look at its handle. Avast! There are men, strange men, here." His face was red, either from running or from looking at the beaker with its long handle.

The beaker was small, one piece of red stone, with a carved figure of a kneeling man. The beaker's handle was his long phallus. The beaker's inside was blackened from burned matter that was still in the bottom.

"Well-a-way!" said Madoc. "Where did you find this?"

"On a crib, a ridge, behind a wall of rocks," said Brett. "Can a man be so long? We look like god-awful babies beside this. Whoever are these men? 'Tis something!"

"Something, but what?" asked Madoc. "This cannot be ordinary treacle left to dry in the beaker's bottom." He passed it around. "Maybe 'tis a fire carrier. Someone made it. Who? One of the men Kabyle saw?"

This was something unexpected, something bold, not at all like their own plain beakers, bowls, or stone carvings. The men could hardly wait to hold the beaker. When they held it, they chuckled nervously, guffawed, and scratched their whiskered faces at the thought of meeting someone with such a large organ.

Kabyle rolled his eyes skyward, slapped his knee, and said, "May Allah praise those men and let us be lucky enough to see their women!"

Troyes held up a foot-long, finger-wide roll of crumbling brown leaves. "I found this on the same crib," he said. "The end of the dried roll was charred. Someone said they were dulse, the edible sea algae with wedgelike fronds. Someone else said they were tinder that smolders and is used to start a cooking fire. It was a puzzle."

"By Allah's good will," said Kabyle. "This is it. They rolled the leaf into a stick, held it to a coal, and put it in their mouth and sucked in the smoke. That is what I saw!"

"This dusty, crumbly leaf?" said Erlendson. He held one end to the cook fire. It did not burn with a flame but smouldered like peat. He put the stick in his mouth, sucked, coughed out smoke, and gave it to Kabyle.

Kabyle rolled the stick over his tongue, inhaled, and the stick's end glowed. He blew smoke from his mouth and coughed.

The men passed the stick around. Each one smelled it and gingerly sucked a little smoke. The smell reminded Brett of bergamot, horsemint, and for a moment he was acutely homesick for the Samhain fires. He dug his fists into his eyes, breathed deep, and said, "On the crib is a burly tree carved into a wooden seat with legs, a head, and a tail. It looks like no animal I have ever seen."

"I would like to see it," said Madoc. He left Kabyle in charge of the men and followed Brett across a green meadow to a forest of fig trees that grew on a hillside, where the earth was lashed together by sinuous roots. They brushed away silken webs. Hundreds of yellow-headed, green-bodied, raucous birds sat in the lower branches of the trees. When Brett walked under the trees, the birds flew and swirled about, crying to one another, looking like hanks of brightly colored yarn.

"Little parrots!" said Madoc. He remembered seeing parrots at the royal court in Paris.

Brett walked backwards to watch the green-and-yellow movement in the trees. "The parrots eat the fruit," he said. On top of the hill they looked on the other side of the island. "I kind of hope we will see the men Kabyle saw. Then I hope we will not," he shivered. "Where did they come from? I thought no men lived on this side of the Western Sea."

One side of the little hill fell away to the seashore. On that side was a worn, woven ladder built into the sandbank, leading downwards about five ells. Brett ignored the ladder and showed Madoc the seat that looked like some kind of well-fed beast with a man's head, a bird's tail, and four legs.

Madoc sat and leaned his back against the weathered wood to catch his breath. The back and front of the chair towered over him. He felt an indescribable power as he looked out toward the sea to a chain of greenish islands as far as he could see. When he sat the opposite way, he could see a landscape of surreal beauty: fruit trees, a meadow, and a tiny, swampy lake with a well-defined path all around the perimeter. The path was like a run eroded by ages of use. His heart thumped. So, mayhap men did chip and smooth out the rock into bowls to catch the rain. "From here one can rule this whole island and the sea around it," he said.

"The seat is faded and covered with dust. It has been here a long time," said Brett. "Who put it here?"

"I cannot say," said Madoc. "But it will be here long after you and I are gone." He hunched forward and wiped fine, wind-blown sand away with his hand. The wood was so finely polished at one time that on the underside it felt like it was coated with oil. Not far in front of his feet, close to a wall of first-sized stones, was a fire pit. Brett said that that was where he found the god-awful cup.

Madoc was quiet for several moments. "I think this is some kind of ceremonial place, like our stone circles. I think that the headman sits here." He kicked at a stack of drying leaves and took several to examine later. "You want to sit a few minutes to see how it feels to be head man?"

Brett sat with his chin in his hands. "This does not make me feel like a king." He moved on the seat so that he could lay his head on the head of the magical beast and his feet on the tail. "How do I look?"

"Like you need a cape of rabbit skins or parrot's feathers and a gold circlet on your forehead," said Madoc. He walked around the wall examining the stones that formed little ledges and nooks. There was a fine grit on everything. No footprints, only his and Brett's. No meat bones were discarded near the firepit. He concluded that there was no eating on this little rise of hardpacked earth. He wondered how the man was chosen to be left here with the smoking sticks, isolated from his other tribesmen. He wondered if the inhaled smoke made a man feel dizzy, giddy, wide awake, or sleepy. He looked into the wall crevices for some hint of other leaves or grasses, but he found nothing but a rotting withie ladder fastened against the embankment that led to a narrow stream of water. "The ladder takes the men down to the beach," he said. The near shoreline was a damp, purple-brown mud lot, as though the water rose and descended with the tide. On the far shore were high outcroppings of black rocks with wide cracks in which bristles of yellowed swamp grass grew. The air was pungent with the smell of decaying vegetation and marsh gas that was trapped under the surface of the mud. Warmed by the sun the gas expanded and burst through the surface in loud pops. It left little holes in the mud that quickly filled up with water.

Brett put his arms around the wooden figurehead, pulled himself over on his stomach, and his hand slipped into the beast's mouth. "Here 'tis! I found it!" he squealed. From the jaws of the beast he pulled out a twisted mat of dried mushroom stems with flat heads. "More weed? Smells like dry cow dung. Mayhap Master Kabyle can tell us what this stuff is for! Do we dare take it back?"

"Pull out a little for a gift for Master Kabyle and stuff

the rest back," said Madoc. "If eyes watch us, we do not want to appear greedy and offend them. Mayhap the mushrooms are infused, soaked in water for a drink, or rolled up in the leaves. 'Tis a mystery. Mayhap the spirit of a dead king who once sat here is close by. I have a prickly feeling."

"I like Shipmaster Kabyle," said Brett. "He is like you when he explains things so that I understand. He never makes fun of me."

"Aye, you cannot go wrong liking him," said Madoc. "He may look different because he wraps his head in a scarf. But he uses his head for good thinking. He is wise like our archdruids." Madoc put a hand on the warm tousled hair of the boy.

A lizard that had been sleeping unnoticed on the warm ground was disturbed and scuttled up to the wooden seat. Its tongue flicked in and out. Brett made a choking noise in his throat and through gritted teeth said, "Let us get out of here. I see the king's spirit and 'tis ugly!"

Madoc took Brett's hand, looked at the lizard in the center of the seat, and chuckled. He wished he knew the significance of the mysterious seat. For a second, he wished the lizard could speak and tell him the secrets of a special ceremony, the chants, songs, and mystical words.

In the morning Troyes and Kabyle watched Brett scratch his head until the scalp was red. Together they examined his head and saw tiny, pale eggs attached to the hairs and the moving, tiny, flattened bodies of lice. Laughing, the two men carried the lad to the large caldronlike rocks holding sun-warmed rainwater. The three of them first emptied their pockets, washed their fishy-smelling clothes, lay them in the sun, and then they sat in the rainwater. They scrubbed Brett's tangled hair with a handful of sand and rinsed his head underwater. When Brett kicked his feet and sputtered, they believed his lice were drowned. The three sat in tree shade waiting for their clothes to dry.

Kabyle twirled his metal firesticks, lighted one of the rolled leaves Brett had given him, and took a couple puffs to make sure the end was glowing. Brett showed him the handful of crumbly mushrooms he had taken from his pocket. Kabyle mashed the mushroom crumbs between his thumb and forefinger, sprinkled some on the end of the smoking leaves, then he folded the rest inside the wrappings of his turban. He sucked on the leaves, first taking the smoke in his mouth, then boldly breathing the smoke into his lungs. He exhaled little gray puffs, and his eyes shone. He saw Troyes as a gargoyle with a huge head, huge hands, two hairy legs, one that would not bend at the knee, and feet edged in a golden yellow. He passed the leaves to Troyes, put on his dry clothes, and moseyed back to the ships. Neither Troyes nor Brett hurried to follow him.

Brett lay back on the moss and dangled his feet in a quiet pool, hoping that the black tadpoles might nudge at his toes.

Troyes's head seemed to expand with each puff, so that he felt sure he could understand more than ever before. He loved the clear sing-song sound of Brett's voice. He heard the wind grind the grains of sand against one another. At the same time he could hear the thunderous crash of the waves long before he could see the foaming water began to curl along their tops on the rocks. Colors were brighter. Water in the stones shone with a luster actually seen only on polished metals. The black, mucky humus at the foot of the tree was velvety soft. Brett's face glowed against the brilliant green fern beside some black rock. His body was surrounded by a shining rainbow aura, beautiful like the ceiling of a French abbey. The sight of Brett's white body lying on the brilliant green moss aroused him; made him think of slim, young girls he had known. A surprising rush of throbbing tension rose in his loins. He passed the glowing leaves to Brett. "Kabyle did it, so you can! It makes my heart beat fast and gives great pleasure. Come on! Suck a little. See, like this." He puckered his mouth and kissed Brett at the same time he handed him the smouldering, tightly rolled up leaf.

Brett inhaled, made a face, coughed, and laid the rolled leaf on a stone. "It gives me no pleasure. How can ye stand it? The taste is worse than sour cabbage!"

Brett kicked at a fern clump, where a brown-and-yellow snake lolled and slithered out of sight. The two of them walked single file back to the line of ships.

* * *

Conlaf, as always, was curious and wanted to experiment with anything new and different. Late in the afternoon, when the ships were ready to sail, he took a long pull, and another, and another on the rolled leaves that had been sprinkled with the crushed mushrooms. He sat on the sand and stared at some sandpipers wading in the sea snapping at tiny shrimp. The birds glowed. The long bills looked sharp as needles. Conlaf put his hands over his head thinking that the birds meant to drill holes in his head. He heard someone scream and realized it was himself feeling the birds tapping on his skull. He ran down the beach.

Madoc ran after him. Morgan, Llieu, and Kabyle were right behind. When they caught him, he was lying faceup in the sand, his eyes glazed and his breathing a series of gasps. His heart beat so hard that Llieu saw the throbs move his tunic up and down.

"Looks like he sucked too much on the smoking leaves," said Kabyle. "Should we make him vomit?"

"Nay, do not move him!" said Llieu. "Stand so the sun does not shine on him. He needs something to calm his heart. 'Tis racing like a mad dog." He knew of no faster way to make an infusion of fox-glove than to chew some of the herb himself. He reached inside his tunic and brought out one of the small packets he always carried because he was a physician. He put a pinch of the grayish powder on his tongue, soaked it a few moments in his mouth, pushed up the sides of Conlaf's mouth, and let the saliva mix drip in.

Conlaf arched his back. His face was red and his dark hair matted with perspiration. Madoc held Conlaf's mouth closed until he saw his throat move and knew he had swallowed.

Llieu kept his hand over Conlaf's chest so that he could feel the heart thumping. "This smoking stuff influences men's behaviour," he said. "Some men laugh and cavort, others cry in a rage and tear at their hair and clothing." He frowned at Kabyle, who hovered over the patient and shoved him out of the way.

"Avast!" said Kabyle, "the smoking-stick does not belong to us. 'Twill punish us." He stamped a foot and made random gestures with his hands to attract attention. "Listen! Mushroom smoke catalyzes Physician Conlaf's life forces to react faster and faster. His lungs and heart are working to a trilling cadence of pipes and drums. He is living so rapidly that he could be an old man by nightfall!"

The men on the beach listened and believed, even though Kabyle was not a physician and none had heard of such a malady. They stood like trees in a calm while the words soaked in, then there was a mad scramble to put out the smoking sticks. The other men, who had recently sucked up smoke of the mushroom powder, were wandering away, holding on to one another. Someone shouted that the sea was blood red. Their uncontrollable laughter floated on the sea. Some men splashed in the sea-water and swore their arms were red. Someone else cried that the breeze scalded his skin right off his bones. He lay down and covered himself with sand.

Roi, a young man who had been a druid fosterling in Dubh Linn with Madoc years earlier, climbed a tree that held red, fist-sized fruit. When he was half way up, he stood swaying on a branch, screamed, and flapped his arms like a seagull.

Brett watched with wide eyes and held his breath as Roi fell like boulder, with a thud. One arm twisted under him, and he spewed vomit over himself. "Sweet, leaping Lugh," said Brett.

Kabyle helped Roi to his feet and cleaned him as Archdruid Llieu pulled the broken arm straight. Roi screamed and tears rolled down his face. Llieu tied the arm firm between two pieces of driftwood. Roi wiped his eyes and told the crowd around him that he could have flown if only he had climbed higher. "Or the magic smoke changed my shape into only a half gull."

" 'So, 'twas the half not changed that made ye fall," said Brett, who held his nose against Roi's sour smell.

By evening-meal time everyone appeared normal. Those who had inhaled the magic smoke swore they had seen land, sea, and sky through a new set of senses. Conlaf believed that small doses of the mushroom smoke could alleviate symptoms of great pain. "I have bruises on my arms and legs and never felt a thing. I do not recall when the bruises were made." He asked Kabyle for the remaining dried, orange mushrooms to use for medication and asked Madoc to show him the ancient seat.

Madoc was angry with Conlaf for overimbibing himself on the smoking stick and said 'twas time for sup. On the beach the messmates were preparing the evening meal of fruit. "There is no time for tramping about," said Madoc.

"Why not stay one more day?" asked Conlaf.

"Place is too small," said Madoc. "Not many wild animals here for meat if our animals die without producing young. The rainwater will dry. The lake is briney. There are indications that strange barbarians live around here. We need a larger place, with a wider stream or river, more trees for lumber to mend ships and build cottages." He looked around, alert for any sign of hostility among the sailors, found none, and he finished quickly. "I promised you a true homeland. And that is what you shall have! We set sail at high tide."

The rising winter moon was full and bright. The oarsmen sat shivering at the benches ready to work up a rhythm with their oars and sing words about where they were and where they slept. They would tug at the water for as long as the shipmaster said. On more than one ship, skinny cattle, horses, sheep or goats stared unblinking at the fresh water and grass in their pens. Soon the thin horses munched noisily at their grass. The scraggy sheep pushed at one another as they slurped at the fresh water. The scrawny mooing cows were noisier than the emaciated barking dogs. There was a babble of voices disagreeing or laughing, waiting for Madoc to give the order to sail. There was music of flutes and harps, and foot tapping as someone demonstrated the steps of a dance or how he could juggle four fist-sized stones at one time. Above all, there was the clear song of the chief shipmaster, who sang out instructions for the night sailing.

Madoc lifted a single torch, the signal to head out to deeper water. He watched the flicker of the single torch from each ship circled around him, and then they were out in the open sea with bright twinkling stars and bright bursts of phosphorescence in the water every time the oars dipped or moved. He sang, in a soft voice, a lullaby he remembered from his childhood, to assure his men that they were leaving an undesirable place and going to a desirable place. They had nothing to fear. He licked at the salt on his cracked lips and heard the scurry of soft feet close by. He looked around for rats and saw Brett's face, pale as the full moon. Brett was biting his bottom lip and holding a pair of raw-wool stockings that were still greasy, stinky, and overlarge for the lad. "Why are you not asleep?"

"I do not feel well." Brett's bottom lip trembled. "I feel the hot breath of strange spirits strangle me. I cannot breathe. I see filmy haunts drift through tree trunks. My thoughts are muddled. My head spins. There is a flame in the pit of my stomach, and I cannot shoot a stream any higher than—yer knees. Can it all be caused by spirits of the strange chair or the barbarians Kabyle saw?"

" 'Tis the warm day's moist air; the cool night's fog of this place. You are out of breath because you have been too long without decent food. Water and fruit run through us like going through a sieve," said Madoc. "You have the old blue-devil feeling. Everybody gets it now and again."

"The chair spirits are angry with me!" insisted Brett. "Mayhap the spirits are hidden in the moon! It seems overlarge this night."

"Without the moonlight, 'twould be darker than inside a stone."

"Something terrible is going to happen."

"Not to me," laughed Madoc, dropping one hand for a rest from pulling hard on the steering oar.

"To me," sobbed Brett, putting his hand inside Madoc's. "I do not want to be a grown-up."

Madoc snorted. "Sure you do. Be proud of being a man! Men do not cry. Men roar and stamp their feet so the gods can find them to bestow good fortune on their heads. Come on, I will show you!" He kicked up his heels and stamped his feet in a little dance. He waved his arms and bellowed like a bull in heat, then raised his head and cawed like a hawk that had found an unprotected warren of baby conies.

Brett tried to imitate the stamping and kicking dance, but he could not make his voice loud enough for a good roar or caw.

Madoc wondered what he could do to bring the lad out of his melancholy.

Brett felt like a coward. He had left his beautiful homeland, a place he might never see again. He did not know if his folks were dead or alive. "I be naught but a square-headed scut."

"I told you," said Madoc. " 'Tis naught but the blue-devil feeling. I will let you read more of my journal to me. Tell me what I saw when I was in Paris. Guess first." He let Brett hold tight to the steering oar while he went after the vellum journal.

Brett heard the familiar rustle of the dry vellum pages and thought it sounded like a cat with a rough tongue grooming her whiskers. "I think ye saw a mermaid with the softest tail that can wind around a man like a long leg."

"No," said Madoc. "But I did see a man hanged. Not a sight I enjoyed. It gave me the blue-devil feeling. Maybe you would rather read stars with me tonight." He felt like kicking himself for being insensitive.

Brett wrapped himself in his blanket and tied his thin pallet to the gunwale before he lay down close to Madoc's feet. They talked about mermaids, sea monsters, whales, and porpoises for a while. Then they turned to unicorns, wolves, mountain lions, barbarians, and hermits that might be in the new land. Madoc was not convinced there would be barbarians or hermits where they were going. Then he let his head roll back, and he talked softly about the changing position of the stars.

Suddenly Brett asked if Madoc was cold.

"Bleeding cold," said Madoc. "Damp and cold." He pulled his blanket up around his ears.

"I think ye are the best storyteller," said Brett. "Are ye doing what ye dreamed of doing when ye were my age?"

"Aye. I love sailing. I like the thought of helping these men find a safe place to live in unproved land. Whatever sacrifice they face, I face. We follow our conscience and decide on the best course together. I will get you and these good men to a land where all can live in a manner you dream of, peace and freedom and hope."

"Ye are my hope," said Brett. "I hope I be like ye. I will be glad to see the day I find silk on my upper lip."

"Thinking of the future is good," said Madoc. "A wise man once said, 'You must think of the future, to have one.' "

"Maybe I can not see that far," said Brett. "My mind is always dark. I wonder about it. Is wondering an unhealthy sign? How do ye feel? Are ye happy?"

" 'Tis healthy; you are fine," said Madoc, closing his eyes. "Be I happy? Lugh, I be frightened to death most of the time. I never thought there would be living men on unproved land."

A flying fish came out of the water at dawn and hit the ship's deck with a thud, knocking the air out of itself for a couple of moments. Brett picked it up, and Jorge said it would make a good breakfast. "Ya, for the shipmaster," said Brett.

A little later in the morning the ships were letting their sails carry them between small islands that were no larger than a good-sized barnyard. The sky was covered with dark clouds. A silver bolt of lightning crackled from one mast to another leaving a thin trail of blue smoke. The sails were lowered.

On the ships struck by lightning there were men who whispered that the goddess of death, Hela, had sent a warning, but no one could decide exactly what she warned them about. The anchors were lowered so that the hooks might catch on to something to stop them from being pushed off course, way out to sea, by the wind. The anchors found nothing to hang on to in the deep water. The wind came from everywhere, tossing the ships from side to side so they groaned and creaked. Some of the newly tarred seams split, letting seawater seep in, soaking blankets, pallets, dried meat, and fruit. The sailors did not cry out, but did what they could to stop the sea from taking over. More jagged lightning came down among the ships. A tip, like an eye, of blue light sat on the mast of the *Un Ty*.

"Listen," said Madoc. "The bright blue eye is crackling and fizzing as it looks down on the men on the *Un Ty*. And her men stand like soldiers looking up at the top of the mast."

"Hela is sending a warning to us," said Brett. "Her eye watches us. Do ye think she is wondering if any of our men, maybe Troyes, would kiss her—on the lips?"

"You have an imagination that beats all," said Madoc.

"Is it right for a grown man to kiss a lad on the lips and put his tongue inside a lad's mouth?"

"I do not know any man who would do such a thing. Of course it is not right! The man is not right! Did you know someone like that?"

Brett sighed like a tired old man.

The thundering subsided, and the ten sails drifted out of their straight line. Sailors on each of the ships caught the drizzly rain in open water barrels and every available bucket and kettle. Soon the water barrels were brim full, and the men and animals had plenty to drink for a week. The air became so warm that the men did not wear their oiled-canvas coats. Brett kept his clothes on, day or night, rain or shine. The men took off tunics and shirts, pushed their hair back from their eyes, and let the rain wash them. During the rain Brett was seasick, chucking his guts over the gunwale. Afterwards he scrubbed his hair, the knees of his trousers, and the front of his tunic hoping to restore them to some measure of cleanliness.

The rain stopped, and the refreshing breeze billowed and dried the sails. Madoc kept the *Gwennan Gorn* in the lead, sailing due south along the coast from island to island. In the evening they beached on the marshy bank of a small island. The messmates ignored the tiny pink crabs, barnacles, and shrimp floating with the beds of kelp. In the muddy shallows they found fiddler crabs and large blue crabs which they roasted in charred holes already dug in the high clay banks. The men talked about who might have dug these round holes in the greasy clay and what those unseen barbarians might be like. Their imaginings went from fire pits for cooking and warmth to sadistic rites of human sacrifice by brown barbarians living in the marsh.

Each day now brought more birds. The men gave names to them, Yellowbeak, Redlegs, Brighteyes, and Fisheater. Brett was particularly fascinated by a species that deliberately flew at and pecked smaller birds on their heads, making them regurgitate. The bigger birds ate the partly digested food and the messmates called them Bullies.

The humid breeze from the shore brought more oppressive rain. Clothing never dried, even if hung between spits of rain. The men frowned, whispered, and complained in little groups about how the moisture-laden air caused their friends to be cranky. The motionless, nighttime air smelled rotten, like marsh gas, and made the men more moody. Finally someone said it was the change of wind direction that worried the men.

"The wind change makes them find fault with things like damp blankets and cold food," said Madoc one evening as he gave the steering oar to Conlaf. "They accuse each other of stealing mislaid shirts or caps. Little things."

"Are you telling me that they are working up to a rebellion? Are the men tired of obeying ship's rules?" asked Conlaf. He scowled and his face was dark.

"Nay, nay!" said Madoc. " 'Tis not rules. 'Tis the indignity of aimless living. They are painfully aware of every little change. When the wind blows in the wrong direction, they worry that it will not blow back toward *Cymru*. They lose heart."

"They would go back to Wales?" Conlaf's forehead wrinkled. "Mother of Lugh! Do they remember why they left? Do you have to tell these men over and over that there is peaceful land with no fighting, no treachery, no tax on croft animals, grain, or flax waiting for them with water, fruit, and game? To lose heart is to lose confidence and meaning in life. Where is their patience, forbearance toward the small hardships? We all have problems!"

"In the last few weeks they have had more experience than most have in a lifetime," said Madoc next morning when he came back to take over the steering oar. They watched the morning red sky pale to pink before becoming daylight blue. "Their hearts are worn out. Mayhap knowledge of some new, unfound land will restore their hearts." He counted the small stones tied at fathom intervals as he let the depth rope slide through his hands. "Can not find the bottom."

The daytime breezes blew away the humidity, and Madoc's sailors sang songs about their ancestors and recited verses about their home country. By afternoon the ships had moved closer to a string of small barrier islands. Now the only sound was the dip of the oars as the men watched the coral reefs and the unusual fishes. Some were bright yellow; others were red and blue with bold black band and eye marks on wide dorsal fins. There were fish that were green as grass with wide bodies and large scales. The jaws were fused above and below to form a hard, pointed beak. The sailors called them seaparrots. Madoc did not beach the ships on any of the islets and watched carefully as they passed the mainland, or perhaps it was only a larger island. It was dense with vegetation, snakes, and the sounds of singing insects. No one thought this kind of land was desirable for their new homeland, but Madoc became excited when he saw that it stretched as far as he could see. He brought the ships close to the shore and was disappointed to see that it was only another string of islets close together. The sailors hardly looked when he pointed to the canes in the bogs and the trees draped with a lace that rippled like smoke. The trees seemed to be breathing when the gray-green lace rose and fell with the breeze, needing nothing but damp air to grow. The gauzy leaves of the trees were soft needles that fanned out toward the sun like delicate green feathers in a peacock's tail, and they filtered the sunlight to a soft glow on the dark, mucky floor that bubbled like thick soup and gave off noxious odors. Pointy stumps grew around the wide, flaring tree trunks.

Madoc drew pictures of the trees, birds, and fishes. He wrote descriptions of the pink-and-white coral reefs and said these were sights he wanted to hold true for all time, and he had to put them down as he saw them.

Caradoc wrote on thin sheets of bark tied together with thongs. He said every known reason for memorizing everything had vanished. There was no one in this strange land who would destroy writings. "What we see cannot become altered by a bard's fanciful, embroidered memory, nor be destroyed by a frustrated priest who can not believe what we have seen. We can read to our children, and they will believe."

"There will be no children if we have no women, and no more lambskin or even calfskin for vellum if our sheep and cows drown," said Tipper. "No one, but us, will know what we find. But I do agree it is good to write or draw what we see. I can cut pens from the quills of feathers and make ink from oak galls, or green-skinned holly or black-berries, or lampblack mixed with lichen. Acting as scribes will give us something to do, to study, to talk about, and fill the place of women."

"You have been too long at sea," said Dewi, "if you believe tree bark takes the place of a woman. I bet your stick lays limp as a sea slug. If we cut it off, you would never miss it."

"Hey!" said Tipper, "speak for yourself."

One day the ships sailed through a flock of white birds with long necks, and the men thanked Lugh for their evening meal. The messmates peeled off the little clothing they wore and swam beside their meandering ships, grabbed the birds' feet, wrung their necks, plucked their feathers, and gutted them and called them long-necked chickens.

The naked swimmers made Madoc think of Garth and Tallesin: skin bleached white, bloated, probably torn to shreds as sharks and other fish ate clean the bones. He imagined the bones scattered on the shifting sands at the bottom of the sea. *Death, however peaceful it appeared, is a work of violence,* he thought. There was no such thing as a natural death. There was no premature death, no such thing as an accident. Deaths were preordained, caused by existent and recognizable destinies. For two nights running, before Garth and Tallesin left, there were no green sparks of light, no phosphorescence, in the water. He wondered if that was a forewarning that the two men would drown. How could he know for certain? He should have said something out loud to someone. To anyone! Oh woe! He doubted that a man's spirit lived in the sea with the fish. On the other hand he had seen things he could not explain, such as fish changing color. He was glad when Jorge called to the swimmers, and they were safe aboard their ships.

The day after that the ships zigzagged between spongy islands that were no more than floating debris with moss and fern holding them together. Madoc watched for game, but saw nothing except lizards, snakes, large hairy spiders, turtles, and birds. He heard the whirring of countless sting-ing insects that invaded eyes, ears, nose, mouth and drove his men crazy. They covered themselves with clothing or blankets and nearly suffocated from the heat. In the evening they saw fireflies dart among the trees and fought hellish mosquitoes that choked the air and caused the cows to moo in a high pitch. They heard horses on other ships neighing with irritation. Madoc thought this part of the earth was made up of hot ooze where an aimless cycle of small animals, not fit to eat, and vegetation, not fit for consumption, lived and died. Mayhap this was how the earth looked in the beginning or maybe how the earth would look in the end.

December 2, 1170, was a cool morning and more memorable than Madoc, climbing the masthead to tighten the lines, ever dreamed. For a moment he watched a few men scrub the *Gwennan Gorn*'s deck and thought how well the men had learned. Each crew on the ten ships knew what to do now without being told. They were a team and he was proud of everyone. He looked around the horizon before coming down. "Look!" he called. "There—an inlet starboard!" He blinked his eyes and looked again. A small stream flowed into the bay. Then, seeming to come from nowhere, hundreds of little green parrots concealed the sun. They wheeled and flew towards the inlet as if pointing the way. "A good sign!" hollered Madoc. "We shall sup on land this day!"

More than two hundred men singing rounds and happy ditties climbed down from beached ships and began to run up and down the shore. Shipmaster Girard and his crew from the *Gray Wolf* pointed out driftwood for cooking fires. Madoc and the messmates waded into the warm water with bailing buckets to scoop up crabs with bluish-green appendages. They heard a pinging sound like a handful of pebbles thrown into water and found large shrimp flickering across a shallow feeder creek, the bottom of which was rocky and clustered with barnacles.

High on the bank, Llieu found a large, bare circle where the soil had been packed hard. The outer perimeter of the ring was mounded with a midden of oyster, snail, and clamshells. He poked into the mound and found bones of small animals. "This is a place where people gathered to eat," he said. "Maybe they gathered to celebrate seasonal rituals or trade. Twice the number of men we have could be sitting side by side in that gathering place."

"It has not been used for a while," said Kabyle. "See all the saltgrass growing over the shellmounds." He bent and picked a round-leaved creeping plant, an asterlike flower, and a jointed, cylindrical, leafless green stem that was turning red on one side. He found alkaline-loving small trees similar to hickories growing in the gathering place. "I do not know these plants," he said. "They will be something for me to draw and describe."

Madoc could not take the grin off his face. This place was exactly what they had been looking for. A place, already cleared, with sweet, fresh water and plenty to eat. He was sure there were animals around the stream and told a couple of the men to be prepared with slingshots and arrows.

Excitedly, nine-year-old Brett pulled on Madoc's sleeve and took him away from the hubbub of supper preparation. They walked a way along the bank until they could no longer hear the men.

"There is game!" Brett whispered and pointed to a small buck deer.

Madoc's heart leaped with joy. Here was the place for the druids' new land. He hunkered down and cautioned Brett to be still. The deer waded leisurely across the stream to the other side where it chewed green shoots. Then it heard or saw something that made it raise its head and perk up its ears. Madoc heard a low rumbling, almost like a dog growl, looked up, and drew in his breath. He had never seen a cat so large. Brett's eyes were wide as hazel nuts. He sat on a flat stone downwind from the cat, whose tail was black, matching the tips of its ears and either side of its upper lip. She lay, wide awake, in shoulder-high grass overlooking the creek.

The deer ran.

With a sinuous grace the huge cat pulled herself up on slender hind legs, then on short front legs. The bed grass was slippery, but her paws were equipped with claws.

Madoc felt Brett cling to his scarred right arm.

The cat leapt over the grassy bank and pounced on the small deer. Her claws dug into the withers and pulled the head down. Her pointed teeth ripped into the deer's throat.

Madoc bit his tongue to keep from crying out. Brett hung on to his arm.

The deer struggled to back away. The cat's hind feet raked and rived the deer's abdomen into red ribbons. Blood flowed to the ground, absorbed, and left a tacky, dark surface.

Madoc shuddered. Brett's eyes closed, and Madoc put his arms around the lad's shoulders.

The cat dragged the dying deer up the embankment to the grass under a long-needle pine and gnawed the head and a front leg. She ate everything on the leg down to the bone. When her hunger was sated, she covered the carcass with scratched up pine needles, licked her bloody paws clean, wiped her face, and went back to the bed of packed grass. Her tail switched once then curled around her hind legs. She slept.

Madoc was half-shocked, but totally fascinated by such a vicious act to satisfy hunger. He thought about the cat most of the day. That night Brett said he did not want to sleep by himself and snuggled against Madoc's chest.

Brett dreamed of the big cat eating the deer and woke thrashing around, trying to get warm. He woke Madoc, who asked what the problem was.

"Men are strong, big, like the cat," said Brett. "I am weak, little, like the deer. If there is another death, it might be mine."

Madoc felt the lad shudder and said, "Hush, 'tis naught. So, the big cat ate the deer. You have seen big fish eat little fish. 'Tis a law of nature. No use crying and waking us both up."

"If we leave this place to the cats, I will not have to sleep with ye," said Brett.

Madoc saw no reason to stay beside the little creek if it upset Brett. Surely there were other places they could find that were better. He called the shipmasters and archdruids together and told them what he and Brett had seen. They agreed that if there were more wild cats than deer, this place could be dangerous. Archdruid Gwalchmai said if there were cats that large, they could and would certainly run off with the sheep and goats.

That evening Madoc lay on the warm sand with Llieu and Sigurd. The water was calm and small fish, like mullet, were jumping. The men heard them leave the water and flick their tails in the air. They watched the stars for a while and Madoc said he was sure that the guards had moved. "Here they are closer to the western horizon than they were in Wales." Sigurd reminded him that the North Star underwent regular variations in brightness every four days, and he had noticed that this variation was still taking place. After that Madoc said how pleased he was with Brett. "The lad has improved beyond all expectations. He no longer clings to me or to Conlaf. He takes orders from Shipmaster Troyes without talking back or looking like a pot of boiling water was thrown in his face. I believe all the men like him and feel obligated to look after him. He has more teachers and father figures than most lads his age. His folks, wherever they are, would be proud of him."

Then Llieu talked about the grain seeds they had brought with them. He was not certain they would grow well in the sandy soil they had seen on these islands. He talked about the blackberry thickets he and Clare had found earlier. "Clare was disappointed the berries were gone. But we found aspen and pine next to a fresh-water stream. And we saw coney, foxes, mice, and a deer. Mayhap there is nothing but islands in this part of the earth. Nevertheless I am certain we were on one of the larger ones." His curiosity prompted him to wonder if the island was as large as Anglesey. The men went to sleep talking about how they would divide the men to examine the next large island. They slept in the smoke-path from the night-fires, without the nagging whine of clouds of mosquitoes.

They followed the sandy shore southward for three days of rain. On the fourth day Brett scrunched his face like a blowfish when he pointed to two dolphins leaping together high and clean out of the water inside a little bay. "Garth and Tallesin sent us a sign to stay here," he said, watching, but he did not see the dolphins arch up for air again. "So, what kind of shelters are we going to build, or will we make the ships steady on logs and live aboard for years and years?"

The further south they sailed, the muckier the beaches

became. It was hard to distinguish between water and the coast of the small islands. One night the ships wove between the islands, careful not to run too close to the shores because of the enormous masses of coral just under the water that was clear as air. Caradoc stood forward with the lead line which was fashioned with a lead weight tied on the end of a cord with knots every two ells. Caradoc tossed the weight ahead of the ship and just as Madoc sailed the ship over the spot, he hauled the line tight as it hit bottom. Caradoc counted the knots and called back the depth. The *Gwennan Gorn* needed at least three ells of water to give her at least half an ell clearance when it was calm. The ship slid sideways into steep waves. Madoc's heart pounded because there was no way to tell if there was a rocky ledge underneath as Caradoc called, "Sixteen—twelve—twenty-four!" His heart missed a beat as they passed over the shoal. A wave broke over the deck.

Before dawn there were few bird cries, once in a while an unexplained rustling of leaves and unseen splashes were heard. The ships disturbed the water's smooth surface. The oarlocks creaked and the water whispered as the oars sliced through it. When on the seaside of the islands, the tide slapped against the hull of the ships. Looking into the water it was easy to see minnow-sized fish riding on the back of fish with wings and thin tail. That was the morning the *Vestri*'s oarsmen rowed beside the *Gwennan Gorn*. "We have changed direction!" yelled Kabyle. "West. Not south! This seems to be a large island. I watch for a bay suitable for landing."

"Fine, if 'tis unoccupied," called Madoc.

The ships remained as close to shore as was safe. After a couple of days traveling west, weaving in and out among endless small islands, but always keeping the large land in sight, the ships turned north. There was no definite current in the quiet shallow sea. One whole day they were becalmed and depended on the oarsmen. Gulls and oyster-catchers stood in the white sand at the water's edge, all facing the same direction. Raucous, gray-blue herons followed the ships. Huge worms, snails, and snakes slithered and twined through fern and horsetail grass. Shrill, red-winged blackbirds flitted from tree to tree. Olive-brown squirrels flew out of treetops with all four legs stretched so they looked like tiny fur blankets in flight. The vegetation was thick with pink flowers at the edge of a pine-woods. Madoc saw badgers, wildcats, and a small, high-antlered deer. There was some talk of the best way to hunt small deer, but no one volunteered.

That night there was no wind. Everyone worked naked, hoping for a breeze to cool them. The messmates swam, glowing with the phosphorescent creatures that Brett called wet-fireflies. Later there were short squalls making it hard for the men to sleep. The sky was dark, and flashes of lightning left ghostly shadows among the men and between the ten ships sailing one behind the other. By morning the seas were steep and the motion of the ships was violent. Word passed down the line of ships that most of the mess-mates were seasick. On Madoc's ship Caradoc and Conlaf were sitting with the messmates, holding their hands over their bellies and moaning. Everyone knew that time healed seasickness, and once it left it never returned until after they set out from land once again.

Conlaf said the world was all angles. When the ship heeled over, getting anything from his physician's bag was a chore. "I hate this," he said.

Madoc said one moment was calm and the next, when it took all his energy to hang on to the steering oar, was a damnable surprise each time. "The weather has become the god we love and fear."

"Hate," corrected Conlaf, heaving from as far down as his toenails over the gunwale.

Brett and Brian said they were too ill to get Madoc's journal and read. "This is exactly the time I would like my mind to take me to another place through reading, but I can not go," said Brett.

"My eyes and my belly are connected in one dizzy, gaggy, run-to-the-boards place," said Brian.

Jorge made them both drink the dregs of the cider vinegar. The looks of the murky brown, slimy liquid only added to the lads' nausea.

Madoc was thinking about moving out to sea, where there would be a good breeze at their backs to refresh the lads who were feeling so nauseous. Suddenly Caradoc called out that there was only half an ell between the keel and the top of a bed of coral. They sailed between sand islands and into a bay formed by the freshwater mouth of a river. The wind was dead astern with the surf on either side. There was a terrified feeling in the pit of Madoc's stomach; he had no choice, the ship was moving too fast. He had little time to figure out which way to go; he had to start turning, a sharp right, a left, and then the feel of sand grinding under the keel. Swishing sounds. He was on a sandbar with the current whirling around. Madoc turned as white and sweaty as the men who hung on to the gunwales with sweaty hands. He had just made the unforgivable mistake of running aground.

"Do not worry, the tide is coming, and we will be able to get off soon," said Conlaf, suddenly feeling fine and laughing as he pointed to nine other ships aground along the shore because they had followed the *Gwennan Gorn* like the game of Follow the Leader. The ships dropped their anchors. A few men from each ship were allowed to go ashore immediately. Those men clambered down the rope ladders and waded, not thinking of getting into the coracles. These men wanted to shuck off their seasickness as soon as possible. The men still aboard wanted to lie down and sleep in a ship that rocked as gently as a cradle. Madoc, their wonderful leader, had given them this welcome opportunity. He sent word to the men on the ships to arm themselves with sticks and stones and those on shore to do the same. "We have no idea who we might find," he said.

There was no sign of human habitation, no huts, no shell middens. There were only tracks made by birds and small animals that had drunk from the shallow pools along the river.

Madoc, Troyes, and Kabyle carried long, pointed sticks to stab small edible animals, like rabbits or turtles, as they explored inland. Madoc headed for the pine-woods and suddenly put a finger to his lips. "Listen, do you hear drumming?"

"By the hair on Allah's sacred chin I do!" said Kabyle. "What manner of animal can that be? Keep behind the trees."

In the muddy area Troyes found a clay pot with a skin

stretched over the top. He pulled hard to remove the skin and found the pot partly filled with water.

Kabyle whispered that he had seen drums filled to various levels with water to create the different sounds on the islet of Al Jazair.

Troyes pushed the skin back over the top and thumped on it with his strong fingers. The drumming vibrated inside Madoc's chest. Shivers ran down his spine. He put his hand on his chest to keep the vibrations out. It reminded him of demons that crofters often said could live inside inanimate objects, such as strange-shaped stones. He did not believe in demons—but he had never felt this kind of deep pulsating. He wondered whose spirit was hanging about. "Troyes, stop that! There are barbarians around. Leave the pot," he said.

Troyes's face turned ashen as he imagined strangers' eyes following him as he ran alongside Madoc. When he reached the beach, he stopped to catch his breath. "Do you think barbarians watch us? Where are they? In the tree-tops?"

"If some strange people came unexpected onto your land, would you watch them?" panted Madoc.

"If you were a barbarian, would you make sacrifices to your gods to make the incomers go away?" asked Kabyle.

Madoc's thoughts were clear. He would not let his men stay on shore for any longer than necessary. He would rather get them all safely back on the ships and the ships off the sandbars. He was more fearful of an incipient tempest on land than any squall sweeping the water. Those that had brought in game were ordered to clean and dress it aboard ship. Some big nuts with milk and white flesh were carried to the ships. Finally, using the coracles to carry the water barrels to the river, they filled them and then grass was cut for the animals. Before dark every ship was loaded and remained anchored in the green sea for the night. Next day the sun came over the horizon in a blaze of orange. The gulls squawked and circled low. The *Gwennan Gorn, Buck Deer,* and *Ystwyth* rowed upstream to explore the wide river.

The sun turned the riverbank's black muck into a steaming morass resembling blood pudding. At noon, Sigurd ran up three swatches of blue linen on the back of the *Buck*

Deer, to indicate trouble. There were brown men, in aprons and wide headbands of woven fibers and colored feathers, poling four dugouts around the river bend. The dugouts stopped in front of the ten sails. They dropped large, perforated shells and stones tied to fiber rope as anchors.

From the gunwales the druids watched them dip poles with hoops of withie nets into the water. Each time a pole was dipped, it brought up one or two pan-sized fish. They had green cane spears tipped with spikes taken from crabs and bony tails of fish. Madoc was glad he had thought to tell those left behind to arm themselves. In one of the dugouts a man speared a large fish and let it go, spear and all. The cane kept the fish afloat and when the fish was played out, the man swam to pick it up along with his spear.

"We might learn something from them," said Madoc.

The brown men appeared to ignore the strange sails after the initial surprise, and when their dugouts were filled with fish, they poled out of sight chanting some unintelligible word.

The druids stayed on their anchored ships the whole afternoon to fish. At nightfall they were again alerted by three blue flags on the mast of the *Buck Deer*. Three more dugouts were seen in the riverbend. One man tended fires that burned in clay basins elevated a little above the top of the dugouts, while the others speared fish. Everything was quiet until the men on Sigurd's *Buck Deer* began a ruckus with iron pots and metal spoons.

The fishermen poled closer to the ships. When close enough to see the color of the druids' clothing, the fishermen rattled off strange words and held up their spears. The druids held up empty hands to show that they were not warriors. The fishermen grinned, aimed, and threw the spears so they arched high and landed on the ships' decks. One hit and stayed in the wood siding of the *Ystwyth*. One struck Madoc's right arm, leaving a jagged flesh cut from a fish's tailbone. The natives said, "*Kaw-lu-zaw!*"

"These folks are telling us 'Hello!' or 'Farewell!' " said Madoc, wrapping his shirt around his arm.

"I think they asked us something," said Dewi. "We held out empty hands. Maybe they thought we did not have fishing gear. So, to them we were poor ninnies, and they threw their gear up to us so we could fish the way they did. They did not mean to hurt you."

"Mayhap," said Madoc, rubbing his aching right shoulder.

Madoc had his ship turned and led the other two sails out of the river, that spread like a brown fan into the brackish bay, to the open sea. The ten sails headed north along the coast, still staying in sight of land. Madoc was puzzled by the change of direction and wondered if everything went in a sunwise direction in this unproved land. How large was the island?

Occasionally they stopped for fresh water and fruit. They saw a few scattered villages, so they never stayed long in one place. Once during strong southwesterly winds they beached until the sea calmed. The men said they felt eyes watching them, but no hostile appearance was made. Madoc worried about readings from the astrolabes, the sunstone, and his floating needle. All three devices said the ships were no longer going south or west, but north. That was hard to understand. They sailed in and out of more small sandy islands. "What does this mean?" Madoc waved and called over his gunwale to Morgan. "Does naught work in this new land?"

"Possibly, this is no island," lisped Morgan. "We sailed around a dog-tail or tonguelike projection attached to a large land."

"A peninsula," said Madoc.

XVI
Holly Island

The solstice defines either of the two points at which the sun reaches its greatest declination north or south. Each solstice, winter or summer, is upon the ecliptic midway between the equinoxes, and therefore 90 degrees from each. The term is also applied to the time at which the sun reaches its highest point, when it is farthest north or farthest south of the equator, about June 21 and December 21.

—Robert Jastrow and Malcolm H. Thompson,
Astronomy: Fundamentals and Frontiers

"Who are you? Where do you come from? What do you want?" asked Hyacinth, with suspicion.

"I am your daughter," said Cougar, biting her lower lip. "I come from Sandpoint, a Calusa village, now I stay in Duckplace and help Healer, your mother. She wants to see you."

"Oh no, no!" said Hyacinth. "You cannot be our daughter. She is a baby on the Otherside. My mother does not know what she is talking about. She gets yesterday mixed with today."

"Imagine how hard this is for me," said Cougar.

"I have to sit down," said Hyacinth. They sat together on a log where lizards were sunning. The log was alongside the court where the High Priest paced back and forth waiting for the sun to move lower in the sky.

"Did an old man and a young man come to see you?"

"Yes. Are you saying my mother had something to do with them?"

"No, coming to see you was my idea. That fine old man was my grandfather, Egret. He was your husband's father.

The young man was Otter. He was—my friend, almost like a brother. I was told—their canoe capsized in a storm after leaving your island." The words were hard for Cougar to say while watching Hyacinth's stern face. She took a couple of deep breaths before saying, "So, I came to see you, my true mother. I invite you to come with me to see Healer, your true mother." She tried hard to keep her eyes wide open so the tears would not run down her cheeks, but she could not hold back a blink, or keep the quiver away from her lips. Hyacinth's forehead was sloped like most of the islanders. She wanted to tell Hyacinth that her husband's head was never pushed down in the cradleboard by Grandmother, who did not believe in such mutilation.

Hyacinth stepped close and put her hand under Cougar's chin so she could tip her face up and look it over. Cougar wanted to ask if she was happy to see that Grandmother never put her in a cradleboard. Hyacinth drew in her breath and cried, "Oh, Great Spirits! You have double front teeth like Owl! Is it a trick?"

"I have had these teeth a long time. I have been called *Biter*," said Cougar, trying to make a joke.

Hyacinth kissed her on the forehead. "Aye, Owl was teased like that until he was grown. He never wanted to open his mouth nor hold his head up. I thought he was, and is, quite handsome. Those strangers, those two men that came to us, we did not trust them and Owl sent them away. Now—I am not sure. I want to believe you are—our beautiful daughter, but she was so little. You are nearly grown. You do have teeth like my husband, but you speak so well. Our baby can say only a few words!" She twisted one end of her shawl. "I do not know what to do. I kept telling Owl that the older man looked like him. Both have graceful, long necks. What was his name?"

"Egret was his name," said Cougar. "Did you see he had double front teeth like mine? He was a trader. Long ago he loved a woman called Porcupine, who was Owl's mother."

"We did not give him a chance to say much. I did not see his teeth. I was afraid of him because he looked like Owl. I thought he was one of those persons who can change looks. Maybe he was actually a water bird who had the power to change into a man. Owl thought he was trying to make us believe he had our baby girl, so we would give him something valuable in exchange."

"Listen to me, Egret was not like that! Porcupine, my true grandmother, was Tequesta. She did not believe in crushing a baby's head or filing his teeth. She was caught in a winter flood and did not have enough food for her firstborn. She gave her baby boy to a woman whose baby was dead and whose breasts leaked with milk. That baby boy grew up and married you. I have not long known that Porcupine and Egret were my grandparents. Recently I have learned from Healer that Owl can blow a song like the mocking bird between his double front teeth. I would like to hear him. I believe Healer is my other grandmother. So, I helped her, a kind-hearted old woman, and sent Egret and Otter to find you. They did not return."

For a long moment Hyacinth put her hands over her mouth, then she took them away and said, "Does my mother know who you are?"

"She knows. She knows a lot, but it is hard for her to believe. I want you to tell her when you are with her. Your mother said, each person has his own marks; some are visible, others not. She showed me the round, dark spot on her right ankle, and she said it was the mark of a special healer. She said you healed broken hearts. I guess she meant the children you care for. But I ask you what good do you do, if, in the end, those children lose their hearts?" Right away Cougar wanted to bite her tongue. The words had slipped out, spoken by themselves. Embarrassed, she looked down at her dusty feet and thought, *Hyacinth's hands are small like Healer's and mine. This woman is my real mother.*

Hyacinth was surprised by the way Cougar spoke her mind. *This young woman is too bold*, she thought. *She thinks deep and deep thinking means trouble.* "Maybe you are a shape-changer and do not understand that life is a circle, a path around a living area. One lives around the circle from beginning to end. People must travel the circle to be inside the living area. For some the path is smooth; others find it rough or slippery. For some it is long, for others it is short. Every life that gives up its ghost helps those who are still traveling the circle to be happy. To be

happy means we have kept the spirits happy. The rain spirit
is happy with the precious gift of a child's beating heart.
The village is happy with fewer mouths to feed. The chief
is happy with fewer boys growing to an age when they can
challenge his leadership. I am happy that I can do what the
chief says is my obligation. I am sad to lose any child in
my care, but I will have more children after the season of
rain and sickness. Then I am happy again. That is Life,
even for a shape-changer like you."

"Happiness is only half of life," said Cougar with con-
viction. "The other half of a real life is conflicts, uncertain-
ties, and disappointments. If a child is killed for his heart
to be left on top of a cistern, he no longer has the life that
the spirits gave to him. He did not give you permission to
kill him. A man, full grown as a warrior, knows what could
happen to him and may permit himself to be killed for the
good of his village. A child does not understand that kind
of good. A child wants to live. He wants to trust those who
care for him. Put yourself not in an adult world of ease,
but in a child's place and be prepared for most anything.
Then you will change your thinking and see what I mean."

Hyacinth was again shocked by Cougar's words. She
was uncertain who this beautiful girl was: a ghost, a shape-
changer, a priestess—but certainly not her daughter. Whoever she was, she could have her tongue cut out for her
words or thoughts. She wished her husband were here to
deal with this strong-minded young woman.

Cougar circled mysteriously behind Hyacinth and looked
down at her right ankle, thinking, *What if Hyacinth is not
certain who I am and sends me away? If she is my mother,
she must believe that I am her daughter! I am on the verge
of making her see how alike we are.* She spied a round
stone and sucked in her bottom lip anticipating the hurt the
stone would cause when she stepped on it. She told herself
that she had no choice. The stone rolled under her foot and
her ankle twisted as she fell. She groaned, sank to the
ground, and grabbed Hyacinth's right ankle. She pushed the
ankle bracelet up, and there on the back of her ankle was
the round, dark spot, no bigger than a thumbnail. It was a
replica of the spot that Cougar and Healer had! Cougar
stood precariously on her left foot and said she was sorry

she was so clumsy, then blurted out that she had a similar spot on the back of her own right ankle, the one she had sprained. "It is another sign that we are related. Your mother, Healer, has the same kind of a spot."

Hyacinth put her hand over her mouth again and squeezed her eyes shut. When she opened her eyes and took her hand away, she said, "Dear child, I have dreams about my baby girl every night. She is two summers old. Let me see your birthmark. Aye! That is it, the only blemish our baby had when she was born! It matches mine and my mother's so perfectly that long ago I knew she was special. We wondered if there would be a double row of teeth in the upper front. We promised not to file them like the Tequesta, because my husband's had never been filed—he was Calusa, so I became Calusa. We named her Cry, Crying Kitten. She had a me-yeow, like a baby panther."

People were clapping and whistling all around them because the Chief Priest had announced that this was the beginning of the Winter Solstice and New Year festivities. The sound of singing and drums came from one of the mounds on the outskirts of the city. The sky put on one of its best shows; bright pink and orange streaks flared out on the clouds along the eastern horizon and changed to pale pink and yellow before fading before the moon rose.

"Look," said Hyacinth, "the moon rises full at the beginning of the New Year."

"Yes," said Cougar. "This is the time of the least sun and longest night, and the moon will be fat and full. Egret told me that this time of the year the moon is closer to the earth than it has been all year."

Her words startled Hyacinth because they sounded so much like her husband, who knew such interesting things about the wonders of the sky. She was certain that she would like to know this strange and wonderful woman much better. Yet she hesitated and wondered why someone would teach a young woman so much. What made her speak up against established tradition so freely? Did she understand that she could be severely punished for her unguarded remarks?

"The moon spirit watches us," said Cougar, thinking she could be no happier. She hoped that the ghosts of Grandmother, Egret, and Otter could see that things were going just fine for her. Maybe the fat moon was a big eye in the sky that spirits looked through. She hopped along because walking intensified the pain in her twisted right ankle.

Suddenly Dark Brows was back and talking into Hyacinth's left ear. It was so noisy Cougar could not hear what was being said. Hyacinth repeated, "No" several times. "The Chief Priest wants to see her," said Dark Brows in a louder voice, pointing to Cougar. "He believes she is an advanced spy for a malevolent band of ghosts who have no women and so want to steal ours. Chief Priest wants to make certain that none of the village women take ill or disappear. He will keep the woman where she can talk to no one." She pointed to Cougar and said, "Come."

"But—I am not a ghost from the Otherside," cried Cougar. "You have it wrong! I do not want to see your Chief Priest! This is my mother. I have not seen her—in a long time!"

Hyacinth grew pale and stood back, saying not a word, but letting Dark Brows take Cougar, who was crying and kicking.

The old, hook-nosed Chief Priest grinned when he saw that Cougar was slim and barely a woman. He ran his scarred, rough hands over her breasts and licked his lips. His hut was next to a larger hut where the loud music came from. He hummed along with the singers and did not ask Cougar to explain anything to him, but tied her to a tree next to his hut. She thought how quickly her joy had turned to despair and heard someone snuffling softly. It sounded like laughing or crying. "I am Owl's and Hyacinth's daughter," she said in a loud voice, realizing that the snuffling came from her. "I should not be tied like a thief or an enemy that has come to steal your valuables. Please! This is unfair!" When nothing happened, she asked for water, and the Priest shook his head, causing the thin gray hair to move back and forth across his narrow shoulders.

"No comforts," he said. "If you slip out of these binders, I will know you are a ghost." He held a stick across one shoulder that could hurt if he decided to use it. Cougar had no way to move away from him.

She closed her eyes but would not let tears run down

her cheeks. She thought how lonely she would be until Hyacinth could talk the Chief Priest into letting her go. The binding hurt her neck, wrists, and ankles. After a while she let herself go limp to see if she could sleep. She thought of her true parents coming to get her. Was not Owl a Lesser Priest? He could do something. When would he come back and talk with Dark Brows and the Chief Priest? She wondered what the Chief Priest really wanted. He had not asked her anything. He had hardly looked at her after she was tied to the tree. Hyacinth could offer him something for her, maybe a feather cape, or a bone scraper, or a stone knife with a bone handle? Maybe if she gave him Egret's canoe he would let her go. In her head she asked Egret what he thought, but all she heard were the brown insects hitting the leaves and bark of the tree and skittering around. The insects were scary, big, finger-long, beetlelike roaches. There was no place to hide. The sunshine had been warm, but the cold emptiness of the moon and stars were close to unbearable. A rat or rabbit passed close enough to brush against her legs, but she did not see what was chasing the little animal. Maybe a ground rattler. She shivered and thought, *No matter, they can chew my eyebrows off, but they will not bite my flesh.* She must have dozed because the loud drumming and singing had stopped the next time she opened her eyes. She wiggled her toes against the sandy dirt and thought she smelled rain.

Dark Brows, who no longer had her face painted, brought a jug of water and bowl of something that smelled of fish. She bathed Cougar's face and wiped it dry with her shawl, which was woven from the gray skirt moss. Cougar said she needed to relieve herself. Dark Brows frowned, clicked her tongue against her teeth, patted Cougar's face, and brought in a wide-mouthed jug from behind the tree and unfastened Cougar's bindings. "Poor, unlucky child," she whispered. "Maybe the Chief Priest will make you his slave, or give you as a gift to a man he owes a favor, or give you to a woman he especially admires. I cannot guess. The woman, Hyacinth, likes children and said she would take you. He said it was not her turn for a gift. And I am not supposed to talk to you."

Cougar felt her heart fall to the ground. She rubbed her

neck and arms, then her hands and legs. To be able to move about was glorious. While she sat on the jug, she tried to see if there was a way she could get away, but it was too dark. She thought, *In the morning when there is light I will find a way to leave.* "I did nothing wrong. I should not be here," she said when Dark Brows, who was strong as an alligator, tied her to the tree.

Dark Brows leaned close to Cougar's ear and again whispered, "There are things worse than beetles. Nothing is as deadly as a knife pushed under your ribs as the priest's fingers grab your beating heart. Swallow your words, before they suffocate you. Eat to keep alive." She fed the cold stew to Cougar with a bone spoon.

The stew was thick and hard to swallow. The taste was spoiled fish. Cougar thought it was something the Chief Priest had last night and should have thrown out, instead of keeping it for another day. There was no need to be stingy about food. This time of year there was plenty for everyone, including the sea birds. She longed to say, "Help me out of here," before she gagged. Dark Brows held her fingers across Cougar's mouth so that she could not push out the food or talk. Her fingers were cool and gentle. Cougar swallowed without chewing. She curled and uncurled her toes on the sandy floor. Dark Brows shook her head and placed a sandaled foot across Cougar's toes. "Do you hear me? Be still. You do not want to attract attention. Some insects are curious. They creep up to take a peek and snap! Black, shiny scorpions hide in cracks and under a stone and are quick, but their sting is not so dangerous. You will feel it, hotter than fire, but it is not as bad as a rat gnawing your toes, fingers, or ears."

"Insects and rats?" blurted Cougar.

The woman pressed down on Cougar's toes. Cougar bit her tongue and reluctantly opened her mouth for the next spoonful, swallowed and opened her mouth, and swallowed again. The woman patted Cougar's face and pushed the jugs behind the tree.

"You tried to help me, and I was full of myself, only thinking of a way to get past you to get out of here," whispered Cougar, trying to put on a good face. "Will the Chief

Priest come back? What is Hyacinth doing? Whose side is she on?"

Dark Brows shook her head and was gone.

Cougar slouched against the neck binding and knew she had only herself to count on. She tried to think of a story to tell little children when she was away from this nightmare. In her mind she retold some of Grandmother's stories, until she heard scrapings against leaves. In the moonlight she saw rats climbing the low, crooked vegetation. The rats had come to eat the overripe, purple sea grapes that lay on large, round, red-veined leaves. Then she saw several scorpions hide in a rock crevice. None was longer than her index finger and each had a narrow tail that curled over its back. She realized that Dark Brows had taken a chance, not to be heard by someone who might be listening. Dark Brows had warned her about things she should have thought about by herself. *Be still and the scorpions may not sting and the rats may not bite*, Cougar told herself. *If only one stings or bites, I could get over it. If more come at me, I will yell like an angry panther! Let someone hear me!* She kept her eyes on the crevice. When the full moon moved behind a tree, it was hard to see the crevice. The night became scary. She thought of the story Grandmother had told her about scorpions killing each other by stinging themselves when circled by a ring of fire. She wondered how long they would stay in the crevice. Maybe a long time, if they found water or other insects down there. Then she remembered that Grandmother had told her that scorpions could go a whole year without food or water. Her eyes grew heavy, and she wondered how many days she could stand upright without sleep. She wished she could scratch the itch on her nose. She wondered if it would actually rain.

A burning, hot sting came to the inside of her left foot. The sting was worse than stepping on a hot coal or putting a foot in a wasp's nest. She had not seen the scorpion leave the crack in the rock. When she looked down, she could not see her feet! She tried lifting her foot, but that made the ankle hurt like hot pitch. She was certain a scorpion was stuck to her foot by its stinger, and she had no way of pulling or shaking it off. Her left foot became numb and then her ankle and leg. She held her foot up and was certain she saw the dark body of something pressed against the sole. She tried to remember what Dark Brows had said. Maybe if she tried to clear her mind and not panic the numbness would disappear before morning. Her foot was swollen and her toes felt fat and close together. She could not wiggle them. A tear slid down her cheek. She looked at her thigh to see if it was turning black, but she could not tell. Being numb was better than the awful sharp hurting. She was nauseated and imagined the scorpions had a spirit and wondered if their ghosts were pale when they died. She hoped her scorpion would die when its stinger was pulled out. She was ill. The thought of the stinking stew coming up was enough to make anyone ill. How long was it since she had eaten? She vomited and hoped she had missed her toes. She turned her head to the other side so the stench of her vomit was less. She was not really bothered by the smell; she was used to whatever the human body gave since working with birthing mothers. She had always burned their fouled grass or straw and replaced it with fresh. What she did not like was leaving the mess so it could be stepped in and spread around. The moonlight was gone. She thought it must be morning soon. She would be happy to see Dark Brows again and maybe clean the mess herself, if Dark Brows would let her. Surely if the Chief Priest wanted her to stay awake someone should check on her, but no one came. The night became colder. There were more scorpions, but she did not worry about them. She told herself that if she was going to die, so be it. There were people who cared about her. She thought of the time after an evening meal that Healer had said, "I think you have my hair, not your mother's. Her hair was fine and thin, not thick and heavy like yours. Let it grow. I never cut mine. When it is hot, I twist it up on my head. When it is cold, I let it down to keep my ears warm. Long hair gives a person strength." Little Mother also cared about her, and she did not know that Egret and Otter were gone. *Oh, no, not gone! They cannot leave me alone! Where is Owl? Did he go to Duck-place to see his mother or Sandpoint looking for me? Oh, Spirit-of-Travel, do not let him go to Sandpoint!*

Cougar thought, *My mother and father do not really*

know who I am. They do not want to know. And so, it is
all right to leave Holly Island as soon as I can. I am old
enough to live by myself. For Spirits' sake! I am old enough
to be married to Otter. I can take the canoe to Sandpoint
and bring Little Mother and Hummer to Duckplace. Healer
would love both of them!

The torchlight was so bright she had to close her eyes.
She turned her head a little, opened her eyes, and saw Dark
Brows and Chief Priest. The old priest laid something beside the rock's crevice and scorpions came out to look it
over. He scooped them onto a piece of bark, gently tapped
them into a clay jar, and put a wooden stopper on the top.
He mumbled, scraped his sandal in the sand, and sand over
the vomit. He looked at Cougar's left foot, pulled the clinging scorpion away, and hit it with his sandal. *And look*
there! That scorpion did not turn white when it died, and
my leg is no longer numb!

Dark Brows pulled the wide-mouthed jar to the front of
the tree and nodded to Cougar. The Priest undid the bindings. She walked carefully on her sore foot and sat on the
jar. There was a wickerwork cage beside her with some
small animals inside. One of them was gnawing the wickerwork trying to reach the seagrape on the ground. She
could see yellow eyes and long rat-tails in the torchlight.
She imagined how it would feel with teeth gnawing at her
ears, nose, arms, hands, belly, and feet. If they were hungry,
it would not matter to rats where they chewed. She breathed
a thank you to the seagrape because its berries were ripe
and most attractive to the rats. When she finished relieving
herself, she wondered if she could get away if she ran fast.
She hunkered over the cage to look at the rats, which were
full of seagrape. She pulled out the wooden latch, tipped
the cage on its side, and the door opened. She stood up
and ran for the nearest tree. She felt faint and crouched
behind the coral sumac, with smooth red-brown bark, and
round orange-red leaves and berries, to catch her breath.
The sumac would give her an itching rash if she touched
or rubbed against the leaves. Her belly growled, her head
spun, and she was sick again. She quietly retched over and
over, not only the fish stew but the green bile made from
food she had eaten yesterday. She tried to clean out her

mouth with saliva and spit it out without moaning or groaning.

Dark Brows screamed as if she had seen a coral snake. Chief Priest told her to shut up, waved his stick in the air, and said, "Do not be like that. You are safe. See here, I closed the rats' cage." Dark Brows held the torch out to him; he used the stick to knock it from her hands, and the grass caught fire. Dark Brows was tottery and grabbed on to him. *No,* thought Cougar, *maybe it is not her who is tottery.* Old Chief Priest was disoriented and trampled the burning grass. He looked out into the brush for Cougar as she climbed into a tree. Neither he nor Dark Brows seemed physically able to run through the brush looking for her. They clung to each other. Cougar thought she saw Dark Brows wave in her direction. *I think she is telling me to hurry on. She is holding the chief back, pretending to keep him out of the fire! If I get away, he will think I am a ghost! Good, that ought to frighten him.*

She climbed down from the tree, kept herself hunched over, and ran up a small mound and down the other side. Her legs felt like they would fold under her any moment. She was angry because the chief intended for both the scorpion and rats to bite her. She was weak and still half-sick. She smelled the damp decay of the swamp, and it was sweet compared to the vomit she had left behind. She wondered if the stew had been poisoned. She saw a mangrove forest ahead, felt the marsh suck at her feet, slid against tangled, arching roots, pulled away from the tidewater, huddled against spreading branches, and looked around. She wanted to find her canoe. Nothing was familiar, not even the mangrove's fruit with hanging roots. The roots grew so long that they became fixed in the mud before the fruit separated from the tree. She pulled off a fruit that had not yet sprouted roots and began to suck on its cool, sweet flesh. She ate another, believing that it settled her stomach. She listened to the comforting sound of the wind in the top of the trees and the waves slapping against shell-encrusted rocks, but heard no one running through the scrub. Orange flames flickered among the tops of several trees. The morning sky was gray with heavy rain clouds. Cougar walked back through the village without stirring suspicion and found the small dock and the high-sided canoe. She wanted to go to the house of her mother but was certain that act would bring trouble, and she could not do that to the mother she hardly knew. *I must leave my mother, forget I have seen her, and leave the father I have not yet seen,* she said over and over to herself. She unfastened the rope holding her canoe to the dock and poled away. She saw flames rushing up a tall palm and bare-backed men sloshing water from clay jugs around the tree's base and others pushing hard to fell the tree. She thought that the brown roaches and big hairy spiders living in the duff would have to run for their lives.

After a while she was certain no one followed her and she rested. There was something sweet and safe about being part of the water, close to every wrinkle in its skin, like a small turtle riding a chip of wood. For half of the day she went back over the same route she had come. Then she turned, headed away from the Big Lake, and followed the river back to the Big Bay and to Sandpoint in the rain. She thought only of Little Mother and Hummer, and ignored the fact she had not brought food for this trip. She planned how to tell them that Egret and Otter no longer lived and then ask them to live with her and Healer. They would be a family again. It was something good to think about. She never once thought that Little Mother might not want to leave Wren.

The evening sky stayed gray, the air was heavy with a fine mist, and she tied the canoe to a low cypress branch loaded with lacy moss moving slowly in the short whiffs of air. She slept with her body pulled up into a loose curl in the bottom of the canoe. The mist made her clothing damp and sour smelling. She dreamed of playing with Hummer, who was two summers old now. The child hung back, not wanting to go near her. She felt a kind of desperation take hold, because of the child's rebuff. She thought of her true mother's indifference—or was it a rebuff? Her heart dropped and would not come up where it belonged even the next morning after she awoke, relieved herself, and scrubbed her face in the river. She looked about and saw a vinelike flower growing around the low branches of the cypress. She pulled up several of the vine's tubers and placed all but one over the edge of the canoe to dry. She had never eaten the tubers of this large pink flower without first drying them. They were usually pounded into flour, then animal fat and water were added, and the mix heated on hot rocks until is was brown and crisp. She had no firestones to build a fire, neither did she have any kind of fat or grease. Whatever the food she wanted to eat, it had to be eaten soon after picking. If she was hungry, she could not wait days and days for drying. She rinsed her mouth and let the water dribble over the edge of the canoe. The vine's flowers had no smell, but the tuber tasted both sweet and bitter. Cougar thought it was fine and ate two of them. Then she swallowed great gulps of water and poled along the Stillwater toward the west.

Two days later she came to the familiar point of land that lay in the long fingerlike mouth of the river. She expected to see the usual piles of driftwood along the shore of Sandpoint and people pulling clams out of the sand during the afternoon's low tide. She saw neither and wondered if this was really her old home. She beached the canoe up-island and walked back, uncertain what she would find. Egret's hut, now Nohold's, was by itself in a stand of tall beach grass. She stood outside the open door and called softly, "Nohold, this is me, Cougar, who has come to see you."

More mist smelling of salt and decayed fish came in from the sea. Feeling weak from not having much in her stomach made things seem different. She looked around. She was glad she had not gone to see Little Mother. A good rest would do wonders to make her feel better. She went inside where there was less light. "Nohold, are you home?" she asked again and heard a moan from the back of the place. She followed the sound, and the smell of refuse and excrement became strong. "You need to clean your place," she said, looking at a skeletal man lying on a filthy straw pallet. "Remember me? I am Cougar. I have come to care for you."

His lips turned upwards into a thin, grotesque smile. "Thank you. I have waited for you people to come back."

She thought, *you people* meant Egret and Otter.

"Did Little Mother come to see you?"

"Nay, because of Chief Wren," he said, drawing in shallow breaths. "Wren says when and where she can go. I am off limits, because I talk against his scarring. I do not want tracks made from gar teeth on my flesh. He says the more scarring lines denote the most bravery. I do not believe any marks of bravery are honest from him. Wren is the man who killed my brother, thinking he was me." He became quiet, resting.

She wondered if that was the story of the man who was found dead in the water with nothing on but Nohold's boots. She began to look around for food and found comfort-root flour and a little rancid goose grease. She filled a clay jug at the spring and pulled up several tufts of cress. She found his firestones and some dry drift.

She helped Nohold hold his head up to drink a little warm water with tiny bits of cress, a little grease and bits of the crisp bread. He did not drink much. He needed a wash. His whiskers were stuck together from vomit or some kind of food he had spilled on himself. His body smelled like the toilet place. He needed the straw replaced in his pallet. *I can do that tomorrow*, she thought and asked Nohold if he was all right.

He groaned and coughed. He leaned over the side of the pallet, helpless in a fit of coughing. Cougar put an arm around him. He gripped her arm with both his sweaty hands. She could feel the heat of his thin body. She pounded his back hard until he coughed up a gob of mucus onto the dirt floor. It was a trick that she learned from Healer to help wheezing patients breathe. She rubbed his back for a few moments then laid him back on the pallet. She remembered that Healer always looked for flecks of blood in the mucus. She went out and found a flat stone, came in, scooped up the mucus, and took it back outside where she could see. There was nothing red or pinkish in the gob, and she flung it far to the back of the hut and smiled. When she went back inside, he was asleep and his face felt cooler than before.

She ate nothing but lay with her blanket near the open door where the air was fresh. She slept through the night.

In the morning she threw her moccasins at the two rats

that scurried in the straw around Nohold's pallet. She bathed him and put her blanket around him. She let him rest while she threw the old pallet outside and replaced it with a pile of fresh beach grasses. In the middle of the pounded dirt-and-sand floor he had laid out large flat stones for baking bread or setting a clay jug of water to heat at the edge of his fire pit. She built up the fire and soon had warm flat bread ready for him to eat. He turned his face away from the food.

"It is your turn," she said. "I have already eaten. You have to get well to come to live with me near the Big Lake. We will take Little Mother and her baby, if they will come with us."

He tried to please her and sucked in three or four mouthfuls of soggy bread that she had dunked into water to make swallowing easy. Then he looked at her with sunken eyes. His mouth was closed as he thought over her words. She let him lie back and began to straighten and clean his hut.

The silver driftwood walls were mortised with dried rushes. The thick thatched roof was rounded and pointed at the middle so that rain could run off no matter which direction it came from. At the point there was a hole to let the smoke out, but it could be covered with a large piece of hard leather. The leather was held in place with a large stone. The stone and leather piece lay on the roof waiting to be used.

"No baby," said Nohold, startling Cougar as she was gathering his soiled clothing for a wash.

"Aye, Little Mother has a baby boy called Hummer," she said.

"No," he said. "Hummer is gone."

"Gone where?"

"Wren," he said. After a long wait he added, "At first boy babies were found dead and only girl babies survived. Now it is just accepted that boy babies hardly ever survive birth. A puzzle to me, so I figured it out. Boys grow up, become warriors, and could challenge Wren for chieftainship. Wren says, 'Look at me. I am your chief forever.' He has said the same words for a long time and now believes he will live forever. There is only one lad as young as ten summers in our village. He belongs to Wren's best warrior, a man called Rabbit. The child will probably be a gift to the warrior spirits, the rain spirit, or some unknown spirit. It will be a way to get rid of him before he becomes old enough to think for himself and is smart enough to see what Wren truly is."

"Impossible!" she said. "The men in the village can figure things out by themselves."

"No. They have plenty of food, women, and good shelters. They show their bravery by letting Wren and his subchiefs scratch deep scars in their flesh. When people are living well, they let their leader think for them. Now, forget the things I said. I am delirious with fever!"

Nohold went back to sleep. She sat in the doorway of the hut and plaited her hair so it hung down her back. Cougar washed the sick man's clothing in the water that filled a hole she dug in the damp soil below the spring where she had found cress. She climbed the driftwood ladder in the back of the hut and spread the clothing on the roof to dry. Now she was ready to see Little Mother.

She walked across the beach to examine the place where all the drift had once been. She could not believe that the little village of Sandpoint had used all that driftwood for building or burning. There did not seem to be any new huts. What had Wren asked them to do with the drift? Did they really do what he said? Little Mother would tell her. She looked out at the water and saw something so unusual that she stared and did not believe what her eyes told her. Far away on the sea, toward the horizon, there were floating huts with pale blue wings. If they were canoes, she would not have been surprised, because it could be a fishing party or a tiny village that was looking for another place to live that had better water or better hunting. She closed her eyes thinking that maybe when she looked again the horizon would be clear. When she opened her eyes, nothing had changed. There were the huts, each with a huge billowing wing gliding across the water. Maybe they are some kind of waterbird, she told herself. They are too big to ever come here. I had better find Little Mother. She hurried down the path to Grandmother's old house, not sure where Little Mother lived. The door was open and she looked inside. It smelled like men. Pallets were left unrolled on the floor, which was made up of blocks of grassy turf. The grass was worn short and yellowed, but the roots held the sand together so that it made a good floor covering. No one seemed to be about. She went to the next hut and asked a young woman where Little Mother was. The woman looked at her and cried, "Cougar!"

It was Wren's number-two wife, Ibis. The women stared at each other until Cougar said, "Is Little Mother here?"

Ibis nodded and asked where Cougar came from. Cougar pointed back toward the trader's hut.

Ibis made a gagging sound and touched Cougar's arm. "He is ill."

"Aye. Why?"

"He tried to save the babies," she whispered.

"I would do the same," whispered Cougar.

"You do not understand. Wren says the trader will die, because he does not follow our custom. Young boys will be jealous of Chief Wren's greatness, and it follows that they will be tempted to band together and take away his chieftainship. We can not have that. It would be wrong. We are a peaceful village."

"What a waste. All those babies dead."

"It is not a waste. Our chief makes a gift of the babies' hearts to the spirit of the rain and their bodies to the spirits in the sun. Rain Spirit eats the little hearts in the middle of the night. Sun Spirits are so thirsty they suck the bodies dry. The trader must leave or die. You ought to leave him be. Stay away from him."

Cougar remembered Holly Island. She found it hard to believe the same thing had happened to the people in Sandpoint just since she had left. Did they not remember what Wren was before he became chief? "The trader is not going to die," she said, "and Chief Wren is wrong."

"Are you interfering?"

"Does Wren do that often? Make people ill?"

"Only those that break our customs or cross him. It sounds bad, but he is good to us. He sees we are fed, and if we are ill, he finds us a healer. He is generous and wants us to have a permanent marker for our village on the point. It will have his face chipped in stone for all to see."

"I can imagine it. A monument to himself," said Cougar.

"You watch him put more than his face on the stone. He will have the stone chippers draw his boasts on the other three sides. A picture of a great hunt, a circle of women seeing to his every need and pleasure, a house of scar-faced men ready to do battle for him."

"If he would go to all that trouble, the people in Sandpoint would celebrate. This will be a famous trading point real soon. Come with me. We will find Little Mother, who is gathering greens by the spring," Ibis said, rubbing her brow. "When you see her, do not criticize Wren. She is still angry at him for Hummer's death."

"I do not blame her. I think you, too, are angry with him. Maybe you are afraid to have a child, because if you had a boy he would drown him or bash his head against a tree trunk. Some leaders have sight only for themselves. That kind of sight is not for the Calusa people, neither is the strong desire for a man to be well remembered not only in his time, but in all the time that is beyond him. He wants to be known forever as someone great, even if during his own time he was not so great. He does not think of his people. He thinks only of himself. There must be lots of great people in Sandpoint, both men and women. Their names and deeds ought to be on the monument. Killing babies, men, and women in his own village, is that something to be proud of, to be remembered as something good?"

"He is away now with his men looking for a big stone for the marker."

That reminded Cougar about the floating huts coming toward their shore, and she told Ibis about them. Ibis smiled but was not sure what Cougar was talking about. The floating huts were still too far away to see clearly. Ibis thought they might be the end of a rainbow or the beginning of a storm. She could not see the pale blue wings against the sky, but she enjoyed talking with Cougar, who was so different from the women she was used to.

Cougar could see that Ibis had straight, white teeth, and if her hair were washed, she would be quite pretty.

"If the men are gone looking for stones, where are all the women and children?" asked Cougar, thinking the quiet village was deserted.

"Women stay inside with their babies."

"They never used to do that," said Cougar.

"Well, when it is a day to go after water, the chief sends out a crier, so we all go at the same time. Remember that?"

"No, we used to go out for water or roots or drift whenever we needed them."

"The crier lets us know what to expect, sun or rain, hot or cold," said Ibis. "He is good that way. We never forget what to do; he reminds us. There are no children except the little girls, and if they are old enough, they learn to cook, to sew skirts and tunics, so they stay inside. If they have started bleeding, they are taken to the women's hut and taught the specialties that pleasure men. The chief has made this a real nice place for men and women to live. What do you think?"

"I think it is nice if you want someone to do your thinking for you and if you do not have a boy baby," said Cougar. "Do you ever want to get out to smell the rain, or look at the grass moving in the breeze, or see the clouds? Do you ever wonder what color the ocean is on a certain day?"

"You do not live here anymore," said Ibis. "You seem to have an answer for everything. When we find Little Mother, we can be friends. We could sit on the beach and look at the ocean together. Did you know that she is growing a new child and prays it will be a girl?"

"Would that be good news to your beloved chief?"

"I do not think he cares if she has another child or not. He has much to take up his time."

"I mean if we are friends and look at the ocean together."

"We do not have to tell him we are friends or what we talk about." Her eyes shone with the anticipation of doing something she had wanted to do for a long time. "Little Mother should be coming back about now. She had better be home when the men come back."

"Now you are thinking," said Cougar. "Tell me how long either of us would last if Chief Wren found out we looked at the ocean without him saying we could."

"You are impossible," laughed Ibis. "Go on over there. See Little Mother sitting on the grass? Her basket is full of greens."

Little Mother was so delighted to see Cougar that she cried and laughed at the same time. She confessed she thought Cougar had drowned. When they got home, she put water in a jug to make tea and squealed when she found she had no more dried clover heads. Ibis, feeling brave with Cougar around, went out to pick some.

Then Cougar told Little Mother that Otter and Egret had drowned during a storm. Little Mother told her Hummer had drowned. Wren, his own father, had held the little boy's face in the spring until his body went limp. The two women cried together. For comfort, Cougar combed Little Mother's graying hair. Cougar saw the swell in the front of Little Mother that made her look like a gray fox with the bloats.

"I am staying with Nohold," Cougar whispered. "When he gets better, we will go to a place near the Big Lake. Come with us. No one will hurt your baby there."

"Do not say words like that. Wren says Nohold will be dead when he gets back. I am forbidden to see him and know I will not be able to see you when Wren is here."

"We can leave before he comes back." Cougar told Little Mother about going to Holly Island to find her true mother and father.

It seemed like a grand, made-up story to Little Mother. But the longer Cougar talked, the more she believed. "I can paddle the canoe while you look after Nohold," said Little Mother. "I do not know much about caring for the sick."

"You had children; you know something. I will tell you what to do," said Cougar. "Can you give me a little dried fish or any kind of meat? Nohold needs it for strength."

"I can give you dried fish, coconut, and some hickory nuts, and show you the duckweed in Big Spring," said Little Mother. "You will never starve if you stay here."

"Aye," said Cougar. "But Nohold will if no one brings him food. He is out of everything, except comfort root."

Little Mother asked how long Cougar had been in Sandpoint and pouted for a few moments because she had talked with Ibis first. She got over her pique when Cougar made her laugh by telling about the fire that was started from a torch on Holly Island.

"Those people deserve some calamity for being rude to

you," said Little Mother. "Imagine sending scorpions to bite you."

"Well, think what your chief and husband might have done, if he had thought of scorpions. He might have used them on Hummer or Nohold or someone else."

"Please do not say those words—not out loud," cautioned Little Mother. Her lips quivered. She looked ready to cry again.

"What about Ibis?" asked Cougar.

"She's all right. Come on. I will help you carry this stuff to Nohold's place. We can get her and have clover tea at Nohold's place."

Nohold was pleased to have three women visiting him and filling his place with laughter. "When are the men coming back?" he asked.

"No one knows exactly, but we will be warned," said Ibis. "I have a cousin who lives near the Big Spring. The men always stop at Big Spring to rest and refresh themselves before coming into the village. She will come the back way to tell us."

"I knew you did not stick to Wren's crazy rules," teased Cougar. "Now is the time to plan how we are going to leave even before that cousin comes to give warning."

For the next couple of days Little Mother and Ibis took turns helping Cougar care for Nohold.

Every day Cougar looked for a glimpse of the string of huts with blue wings far against the horizon. For three days she did not see them again and thought it was because of the fog. Or if they were birds, they had flown away. She wondered where they had come from and where they were going. She wanted Little Mother and Nohold to see them. She wondered if they were the same huts she saw in her dream on Holly Island. Or was it all a false picture, like seeing puddles of water, on a hot day, far ahead on the trail?

One day after coming back from Big Spring with a basketful of duckweed, Cougar lay on the warm sand to sleep for a while because she had stayed up most of the night talking with Nohold. They had talked while they walked on the beach in the moonlight. She hoped that if someone saw them, they would think they were two women out at night to relieve themselves. The more they talked the more Cougar thought it best to tell every woman in the village to come to the beach to see the floating huts. Then when the men came home, they would hear the same story from all the women, and the men would ignore Nohold, who was getting better every day.

The following day was clear with no clouds. Ibis and Little Mother could see the floating huts clearly this day. They ran inside to tell Nohold and Cougar. He wanted to see them right away, but Cougar made him sit still while she and Little Mother pulled more whiskers out of his chin and put a gray skirt and thin, hide tunic on him and made him swear he would not talk to anyone on the beach. He smiled, said Cougar was more bossy than Chief Wren, but sat quietly beside her and shaded his eyes to see the spectacle on the sea. Cougar told Ibis and Little Mother to bring the other women to the water's edge as they had planned.

There were enough women and girl babies to fill the rounded area where the big pile of drift had once been. They talked and screeched until someone suggested they get canoes and go out to see better who lived in floating huts that were coming closer and closer.

"Nay! Nay!" cautioned Ibis. "We do not know what this strangeness is made of. Wait until the huts are closer. They could be big birds, with big appetites, you know."

The women were used to being told what to do, so no one questioned her idea to wait.

The first hut was being pulled onto the shore by several men wearing trousers and shirts. That was a lot of clothing for a warm day. The hut had a little covered porch at both ends, like the hut with a porch Cougar had seen on Holly Island. Her heart beat faster as she moved closer to see if these men had come from Holly Island. Who had sent them? Her mother and father? The vile, insect-carrying Chief Priest? When she studied them again, she was so awestruck she could not move. She stood in front of all the women as if she was going to talk to them. *I can not say a word*, she thought. *Zot! I must look like a log planted end-up in the sand.*

The other huts were also towed to shore and pulled up

on peeled logs. One hut scraped its bottom on a gravel bar. The bottoms were covered with shellfish, barnacles, and seaweed.

She saw the man with the pale hair, and his right arm was scarred with a long pink line and held tight against his chest. He was singing. Others sang with him. He waved his good arm. She brought her arm up and waved back, but it was an awkward gesture. *If this is not a dream, it is something unusual.* An opportunity, Grandmother had said, is something unusual.

The man with the pale hair had surprising sky-blue eyes. Her first thought was that he belonged to the sea. He walked toward her with his head up, no eyes on the ground. The muscles in his arms and legs flexed in a rhythm that made her feel awkward. He was broad shouldered and one arm swung easily at his side. His feet were bare and pink skinned, like a newborn baby. The skin on his face, arms, and torso was as tan as her own skin. She looked at his baby-pink feet again and giggled.

Ibis tugged on her arm. "We must leave. Our men are coming. They have already seen the floating huts and the strange men. Wren is preparing his men to invite the strangers to a feast. He said the pale strangers are like ghosts and suck on air. The dark-haired ones eat worms and grubs. If you go to the feast, eat nothing. Some food we women will be told to prepare will kill the strangers! We should not be seen here."

"Why not?" said Cougar. "I bet you that the men will come to look around. Of course, they will come to invite the strangers to their feast." Ibis turned and disappeared into the crowd of women, shooing them towards their homes. All of a sudden Cougar looked around, saw the pale-haired one coming closer, and something else in the tall grass caught her eye. She put one hand in the air as a warning, stepped back, and pushed Nohold against Little Mother so they fell in the sand. Her hand stayed suspended in the air for several seconds.

"What is wrong?" asked Nohold.

"I am losing light. Is it late?" she said, looking dazed, and fell in a heap.

"Get up!" whispered Nohold, seeing women's bare feet

scuttling around them. She did not answer. He saw the stone knife in her back and sniffed the smell of redcap mushroom and May-apple juice. It was stuff used to kill bears. Some of Cougar's moss shirt was puckered up into the wound with the knife.

"She is breathing!" Little Mother said, getting to her feet.

"Do not touch her!"

"Get out of here!" whispered Ibis.

"Ibis and Little Mother, go home! I will take care of her!" whispered Nohold.

Part Three

In the history of the Madoc legend, the decisive moment was the shift to the North American mainland. As with many such migrations, this effected a profound qualitative change. A tradition of a "Discovery of America" became a tradition of "Welsh Indians." The Welsh Indian myth in turn became perhaps the most powerful and influential, certainly the most persistent, myth of American westward expansion. Its entry into history was explosive; in the last years of the eighteenth century, something like a Madoc fever broke out in America. In its essentials, however, the myth had been created in the seventeenth century.

William Herbert, Earl of Pembroke wrote in 1634: "Madoc ap Owen Gwyneth discovered America about three hundred yeeres before Columbus. . . . From an innate desire to travell and to avoid domestique broiles, he put that in action which some old prophetique sayings gave him light and encouraged him. . . ." Herbert remembered a prophecy penned long since by the noble Bard Taliesin . . . "he put to Sea without bidding his kindred farewell, least too much love or hate might have withdrawne him." Herbert had Madoc sailing from Abergwili (probably a corruption of Abergele in north Wales, an area rich in *Gwennan Gorn* stories). He reached land, and then ranged the coast to find settlement. Here Madoc planted and . . . raised fortifications and left 120 men behind him on his return.

—Gwyn A. Williams, *Madoc, The Making of a Myth*

XVII
The Man with Ghostly Pale Hair

Warrant number one, (October 3, 1580 executed by Dr. John Dee) runs: "The Lord Madoc, sonne to Owen Gwynedd, Prince of northwales, led a Colonie and inhabited in Terra Florida or there abowts;" the claim therefore was to *Terra Florida*. In the summation this claim, which was based on a colonization venture attributed to the son of an authentic prince of Gwynedd (who died in 1169), was used to establish British title to "all the Coasts and islands beginning at or abowt Terra Florida . . . unto Atlantis going Northerly," and then to all the northern islands extending as far as Russia.

This abrupt, bare and startling statement is the first direct, authentic and public reference we have to Madoc as a discoverer and colonizer of America.

. . . Madoc's *Terra Florida* obviously ran into head-on collision not only with Columbus but with the papal Bull of 1493 and the Treaty of Tordesillas of 1494 which had divided the New World between Spain and Portugal.
        —Gwyn A. Williams, *Madoc, The Making of a Myth*

In the morning Madoc had the ships beach on the rain-damp sand in a little bay. He divided the men, according to the ships they sailed on, into three groups to explore inland. He sent one group to the north and another south. His group, including Troyes's, and Riryd's men stayed behind to scrape barnacles off the bottoms of ships and to tighten loose caulking with heated resin peeled from the long-needled pines. Lost caulking was replaced with the lacelike air plant.

Madoc's messmates found fibrous leaves of a low-growing tree that would replace the straws in their worn brooms. Then they harvested the large, wild oat heads to grind into flour with the stone pestle in the iron mortar on board their ship.

Lugging the last sack of oats up the ladder to the ship's deck, Brett became aware of a low buzzing sound, like bees swarming. He realized that he had been hearing the noise in the background for some time. It was louder now, hissing like steam escaping from a lidded kettle. He had no idea what it was, and he looked around several times before he saw dark-haired, near-naked tan bodies, wearing small aprons tied around their waists, crawling stealthily through the grass in the direction of the ships.

At the same time there were three huge stones being pulled on skids, which were barkless logs held together by vine-creepers. Whenever the vines wore through enough to break apart, the four men wearing breech clouts stopped pulling and rewrapped the logs with fresh creepers. Quickly they tunneled holes in the sandy soil under the logs to wrap on fresh creepers to keep the logs together. The large, unwieldy stones were left on their skids on a point of land that seemed to collect driftwood coming into the harbor. The men who had pulled the skids stacked the drift high on the shore to dry. Afterwards they shaded their eyes and looked over the ten ships as if they were a bunch of beached whales. The men were puzzled and pounded their foreheads.

Brett was certain the natives wondered what the ships were and what to do about them. He saw that the druids, standing gaped-mouthed beside heaps of barnacles they had scraped from the ships' keels, were more naked than the barbarians. It was not unusual to see men on board ship naked when the day was warm or rainy. They kept their clothing dry under oiled tarps.

And then he saw the women walking toward Madoc. He could not move nor call out a warning, because he was so startled seeing these unexpected, strange people. After a while he put a sack of oats he was holding on his shoulder under a tarp, hung his damp blanket over the gunwale, and stood there with Brian and Jorge to see what was going to take place between the chief shipmaster and the strange women.

Brett wondered how he could bring trousers to the druids, then thought it was not necessary, because the barbarian women paid no attention to the pale-skinned men. It was only the chief shipmaster they had their eyes on.

Madoc had been inspecting the caulking when he heard the hissing. More startling than men hissing as they crawled in the grass were the women walking toward him. The lead woman was small with long black hair. She wore a filmy skirt and a sleeveless tunic made of the gray air plant that the men had pulled from the trees to use for caulking. Her tunic's yoke was trimmed with colored bird feathers. There were two women; one was pregnant, close behind the leader, and the others followed in a big, whispering huddle. Their faces were serious. The leader approached Madoc with her hands extended, the palms upward, to show she had nothing to hide.

The hissing became a buzzing sound and then a strident gobble. The men half-hidden, crawling through the grass, were not as dark as the Fortunate Islanders. Bone daggers were tucked inside their waistbands. A few of the barbarians wore short, feather capes. All of them were barefoot. Their straight, dark, long hair was held on top of their heads by mud. Dried frogs', lizards', or snakes' skin was added for personal decoration. Bangs hung stiff on their foreheads like thatch on a roof. Their foreheads sloped backwards, and the backs of their heads were flat. This made them look like they had been rolled over and flattened by a huge stone. In fact, when they were infants, their heads had been bound by boards. Their faces, chests, arms, and legs were scarred.

This unusual sight made Brett shiver with distaste. He looked around at the familiar bunch of naked, bewhiskered, tattooed sailors and spied a couple of them in tattered trousers and tunics. *We must look equally strange to these barbarians*, he thought.

Madoc was face to face with the young woman, whose face had not been deformed into a flat forehead when she was a baby. She extended her hand and touched his face. He drew in his breath. She was quite beautiful. Her clear, brown eyes studied him. Her skin was flawless, no scars.

She smiled and he blinked because a small cloud of fine sand sailed on the breeze past his face. In that single eye blink she cried out, grabbed the pregnant woman and the other one behind her, pushed them to the ground, and then fell on her knees. Looking at him, she pushed her hands away from her chest two or three times as if telling him to leave quickly. Or was she pushing something unseen? He could not tell which. He put one hand out to help her up. *No, no,* he thought, *she is not just kneeling; she is holding herself from falling.* She slumped to the ground. *How odd. What is she doing?* He walked closer, expecting to see more women coming to help. He was startled. The women were gone. Where did they go? He bent over the lass, and his heart jumped into his throat. A short bone knife, like a dagger, was embedded, along with a scrap of her tunic, between her shoulder blades. He put his hand on her neck. She was warm and there was a pulse. Her eyes were closed, her breathing was strong, and another sound, like wheezing, became louder. He looked up. Dozens of men, all a head taller than he, rushed out from the bushes. None of these men paid any attention to the wounded woman. Instead they walked around and over her as if she were dead; nothing to worry about, nothing to care about.

Madoc held his hands out to them and said, "Peace!" Then he spoke the same word in Welsh, *heddwch*, and in French, *paix.* The barbarians shook their heads, became quiet, and stared at him.

Conlaf said, "That lass is scared and playing dead. I saw it happen. The dagger came from a man in the brush. He stood to throw the dagger, and I saw a red handprint on his left cheek. When the dagger hit, he went down on all fours and became one of the crowd. In a couple of moments he stood again, ran, and climbed onto that fancy seat." He pointed to a litter carried by four men. "Do not touch her! Leave her for her people. Lord God, there are hundreds of them with sloped heads and taller than any one of us!"

Madoc held both of his hands over his head and turned around so the barbarians could see that he carried nothing, no weapons.

The litter came through the tall sea grass that swirled in the wind. A man, not much older than Madoc, rode the litter. He had a red handprint on each sweaty cheek. His mouth was open, and he was sucking in air as if he had been running.

"That is the man who threw the knife," repeated Conlaf. "Looks like he is their prince, king—their leader."

Conlaf is right. The chief lord, their king, is coming for the lass, thought Madoc. The barbarians faced the chief, and Madoc thought they looked no different than dirt-grubbing crofters with broken fingernails and scarred faces. He guessed a farming village lay behind the dunes. The litter was lowered, and the chief stepped out from multi-colored, feathered cushions and mats. He turned around four times. Each time he was closer to Madoc. On the right side of his head was a large red scar where his ear had been. On his arms were star- and crescent-shaped scars. He pulled off his feathered cape, stepped out of his breech-clout, and dropped them inside the litter. His chest and back were scarred with slash-and-puncture wounds. Behind his knees were ugly purple scars that caused him to walk with a stiff limp. A fresh wound on the right thigh was healing into contracted fibrous tissue. Conlaf called it a *cicatrix.*

Amazed by these deformities, Conlaf moved closer for a better look. "That man is a warrior, a special fighter in addition to being chief," he said.

"He is courteous," said Madoc.

"How so?"

"He made himself naked, showing he has no weapons, before he stood beside me."

"I am impressed! He is king of scars." Conlaf smiled and the chief smiled.

The chief hobbled forward, made a growling noise in his chest, poked at the wounded girl, and when she did not move, he kicked sand in her face. She lay still as death with her eyes and mouth squeezed tightly shut to keep out the swarm of sand fleas. Madoc cleared his throat as loud as he could and pushed two of the barbarians aside so that he could enter the circle of men around the chief, who held out a crosier with three fluttery little pieces of dried skin with brownish hair on a circular frame attached to the top.

Madoc looked at the locks of hair waving on the crosier and realized they were not hair but rather the soft neck feathers of birds. "Peace," he repeated, staring at the man's scarred chest on which a shell gorget lay with a carved, fan-tailed bird surrounded by circles and lozenges, or diamond shapes. Both men looked at each other, studying what they saw.

Madoc looked into the chief's steady dark eyes. He rolled his fists into tight balls and set his jaw. This man had the same kind of arrogant, crazed, power-hungry look that he had seen in the eyes of his half-brother, King Dafydd. Madoc's top lip twitched, and he wanted to hold it firm between his teeth. He barely breathed. He heard the breathing of the barbarians surrounding him. He reminded himself that the chief was unarmed, yet he feared that if he moved the wrong way or made a rude sound, the chief would trip him with the crosier and then stab it through the soft flesh of his abdomen. His stomach cramped, and his mouth dried up faster than a muddy creek in the hot sun. A cricket chirped as Madoc again held out both hands, palms up, hoping he was not expected to strip naked to show he was unarmed.

The chief said something, which was no more than a cackle. He stepped close and began to finger Madoc's beard.

Madoc lowered his hands to his sides and willed himself to stand still. Perspiration slid down his back. He heard Conlaf's fast breathing and knew he watched the lass on the ground.

The chief felt Madoc's yellow curls. Suddenly he pulled up one of Madoc's legs, pushed up the trousers, patted Madoc's knee, and pinched his thigh; then he chortled, pulled up the other leg, looked at the knee, pinched, and hooted.

Madoc supposed his legs looked as white and hairy as moldy cream to a barbarian. He smiled, but he did not laugh with him.

The unintelligible, throaty hum started again. Barbarians, as scarred as their chief, swarmed around the druids, who had stopped all work on their ships to come and look at the strange men.

The muscles in Madoc's neck and chest were tight. The barbarians were not the way he had imagined at all. Before leaving Wales, he had thought there were no people in the new land, not even Skraelings, whom the Vikings had found in their new lands.

The grotesque-looking chief stepped back and again held out his crosier. His eyes flicked here and there across Madoc's unblemished skin. Then he spied the woad honor marks. He touched Madoc's hands and smiled. Madoc showed him the half-moon with a triangle, his ship-symbol, on his right thigh, and the chief said, "Ah ha! Yu!" Madoc stepped back as if he were following a leader's steps in a Welsh jig.

"He approves of your tattoos and wants you to take his scepter." Conlaf's voice was so close that it startled Madoc, and he jumped forward at the same time the chief came forward. Madoc reached out, and his thumbnail bit into the smooth shaft. The scepter was made in two parts, a shank and a horn head carved in the form of a bird with an open beak. Fluttery pieces of feathered skin were tied to the head with leather strips.

"Stay here," Brett said to Brian and Jorge. "I have to give something to Shipmaster Madoc."

The chief held one hand, palm up, towards Madoc. His head did not move, but his dark eyes swept across the ten ships, back to the nearly fifty bearded men and red-haired Brett, who had come off the ship and now stood beside Conlaf. Everyone held his breath waiting for something to happen.

For an instant, Madoc saw his own men through the chief's eyes. They were bewhiskered, dirty, and sullen. Those that had clothing looked like the worst kind of villains and made his skin crawl.

The chief fingered Madoc's trousers.

Conlaf said, "The King of Scars wants a real gift from you."

Madoc figured his only trousers were a gift too precious. So he smiled, trying to think of something else to give the man.

The chief's mouth opened, and he sucked in air and blew it out. His nostrils flared, and his gaze was trancelike. When he held up his left arm, everyone saw the ridged scar across the bend in his elbow. The arm had a permanent bend. The silence became tangible.

Out of the corner of one eye Madoc saw Conlaf put his arm around Brett and whisper. Brett flashed him a smile and said out loud that he had figured the crippled king would like the beaker with the long stem.

The chief smiled with his eyes on Brett.

Madoc said, "Good lad," and heaved a sigh of relief as he took the beaker. Just then his inner voice whispered a warning.

The chief's hand shot out for the beaker. He waved it above his head for all to see as though it was some long-lost family heirloom just come to light. He smiled and made a halo in the air with his hands around Brett's red hair. Against his dark face, his teeth, chiseled to points, shone white and sharp. He crouched awkwardly and with a heavily scarred hand, caressed Brett's left foot. He whooped as if it was the best thing he had seen in days.

A birth defect, or scar, seemed to be of enormous importance. The chief touched Brett's face gently then touched his own to show that both were whiskerless. For a brief moment his eyes became clouded, rested on the lass curled in the sand, and he seemed sad. He pointed to her and said words Madoc did not understand. The woman's flimsy moss skirt had torn, and Conlaf had covered her with his frayed shirt. The chief pulled off the shirt, put it on and pointed to Conlaf, indicating that he could have the girl, a generous gift. He held his nose, making it clear that he was not fond of dead women.

Conlaf shrugged his shoulders, sat beside the lass, tucked the torn skirt around her like a burial shroud, and gently put his hand over her closed eyes.

The chief made a chuckling sound in his throat and lifted Brett for his barbarians to see the foot with four toes. He patted Brett's flame-colored hair and squeezed his left foot approvingly.

Madoc said red hair and four toes were naught, just some whim of nature. He reached for Brett saying, "Please, put the laddie down, Your Majesty."

The chief did not understand and smiled a kind of silly smirk. He stepped backwards, looked puzzled at the drawstring around the neck of Conlaf's shirt, and signaled his men with his eyes. They unsheathed their short daggers and held them ready to slash anyone who moved.

Madoc remembered that the chief had left his dagger in the litter after he removed his breechclout. His inner voice screamed its warning anew.

Brett began to kick so hard that the chief set him down. Before anyone took a deep breath, Brett scooted into the crowd of druids. He was next seen in the arms of Troyes, who limped slowly toward the *Un Ty*.

The chief laid the cool beaker against Madoc's hot cheek.

Madoc wondered if barbarian protocol indicated that he lay the end of the feathered stick against the chief's cheek. But he did not have time for that, because the chief ran past him, pushed Troyes aside, picked up Brett, and laid the beaker four times on his head. The barbarians surged forward around Brett.

Madoc elbowed his way through the swarm of barbarians.

A man, with a huge scar of crisscrossed lines on his breast, smeared greasy stuff between his hands that had missing the index fingers. He laid his hands on Brett's cheeks and left red, mutilated handprints. By hand signs the king indicated that Brett should sit opposite him on the litter.

"Nay!" said Madoc. "You can not have our lad!" He shook the scepter in anger so that its feathers quivered. The carved bird's beak was open so wide that it reminded Madoc of a Welsh cleek, a stick used to grab a sheep's leg. He lowered the scepter and grabbed the chief's leg in the bird's beak so the chief could not move without falling.

The wrinkles between Troyes's brows deepened as he picked up Brett and hobbled across the beach as fast as his lame leg would go. His wavy dark hair flew out behind, like a miniature dark sea.

The chief raised one hand, and his men answered with a clucking sound, slashing the air with bone daggers. Some pulled slingshots from their breech clouts, loaded them with stones, and pulled them taut in front of their cheeks, all pointing at Troyes.

Madoc jerked the scepter so that the chief had one fewer leg to stand on; he fell.

Barbarians with daggers and slingshots had the upper hand against druids without weapons. They twittered like birds, ran along the beach, and surrounded Troyes and Brett. The chief scrambled to his feet, and Madoc held him so that he could not limp backwards to the safety of his slingshooters. Madoc looked for anyone to help hold the chief, but his men had left to help Brett and Troyes. The chief jabbed his fist into Madoc's scrotum. Madoc doubled over in pain, wishing he had thought to do that.

Conlaf rolled the lass on her side, pulled the dagger from between her shoulders, and was satisfied that if the blade was dipped in something poisonous, not much had gotten into the wound because of the wad of mossy tunic that had gone in around the blade. Madoc gave the knife to Clare, telling him to wrap it with leaves and not touch it because it might have been doctored with something. Clare said that he wanted to hold the wound together with his fingers. Conlaf told him to let it bleed to wash out the wound, then it would be safe to pinch it tight. The lass's mouth was pinched tight, and she did not make a sound until she was lifted on Conlaf's shoulder. Her breathing became uneven as she held her breath and ground her teeth to bear the pain.

The chief, using something sharp, scratched Madoc's left arm, making it sting like fire. He hit Madoc on the chest with his fist, causing him to fall onto the hot sand. His eyes shone like onyx firestones as he went back to his fancy litter. Two barbarians carried Troyes, who was bound hand and foot, to the litter. The chief held Brett as if he were a cornhusk doll and bowed four times to the corners of the earth. He lifted Brett into the litter beside Troyes.

Madoc's men threw sticks and stones toward the litter but without other weapons, there was nothing he could do with two thirds of his men away from camp. He hoped those men had not found trouble. He yelled and slashed through the crowd with the scepter. Barbarians shoved him aside as though he was nothing more than a scrawny barking dog.

At least a couple dozen armed, near-naked, facial-hairs-plucked men glared at the gaping, fifty or so unarmed, be-whiskered druids. No one seemed to notice that Conlaf and

Clare were walking toward the *Gwennan Gorn* with the wounded barbarian woman.

Madoc hollered in an angry voice that no one could take his men or shove him around. The wind carried his voice far down the shore. His fists balled and a stone from a slingshot hit his bruised chest. The pain made him feel sick, and he swallowed hard to keep from vomiting in front of the barbarians.

Brett screamed and Troyes was purple with outrage because he was tied to the litter. The chief sat between them with a hand on each. The druids swarmed toward the litter but were easily pushed back. Stones from the slingshooters peppered them. Old Gwalchmai was hit on the back of his head and fell to his knees.

The chief paid no attention to the commotion. He nodded and four men raised the litter, trotted into a grove of pines, and disappeared.

Madoc breathed hard. He tried to speak. His chest hurt. He hoped to see the men, who had left early in the morning, returning. He saw Clare and Conlaf carrying the barbarian lass up the rope ladder into his ship. *So, we have a hostage,* he thought.

Clare laid the lass on a blanket in the bow. Conlaf opened his medicine bag, smeared the wound with smelly black salve, and wrapped an old shirt around her like a wide bandage. She coughed and drank the water Clare handed to her. Conlaf shook his head and made her understand it was not good to cough. He closed his eyes so she would know he was telling her to sleep, instead she tried to tell him something about a pointed roof or a shelter in the grass. He brought her a stick of charcoal and told her to draw. He made a picture of a leaf-covered lean-to on the deck. She smiled and rubbed it out and drew a picture of Nohold's hut. She tried to tell him that inside was a person who was not well, and she wanted that person brought to her before his life was taken away. When she was asleep, Clare told Conn that when it was dark they would find the person she talked about. He was sure it was the pregnant woman.

*   *   *

Madoc helped Gwalchmai to a place where he could sit with his back against a gray piece of drift. He dug damp sand and laid it on the swelling.

Everything had happened so fast that Madoc said he did not know whether he was standing on his head or his heels. He rubbed the swollen knot on his chest with cool sand. Some of his men were beating the ground with bare feet, howling, and shaking their fists. He told them to stop; it would do no good. The barbarians were out of sight running somewhere along a path among the pines.

Madoc sat with Gwalchmai and thought for a while, then together they went back to the *Gwennan Gorn*. Madoc put on a shirt and boots and stood where he could talk to his men. He told Clare to take care of the girl, who would sleep until the next morning. "This is naught what we expected. Go about your business of scraping barnacles and caulking the ships. Conlaf, Caradoc, Thurs, Riryd, Dewi, and I are going after Brett and Troyes. Be ready for anything by arming yourselves with sticks and stones. When the two exploring parties come in this evening, keep them informed. Tell them 'tis best to reason with the barbarians, if possible. Pray we do not have to fight our way out of this! We do not understand barbarians, and they do not understand us, but I think we could, in time. We have one of their women. She will help us know what they are like. Kabyle is in charge of the camp and the ships."

Riryd said, "Brother, I will never understand them. They ignore their own wounded." He flexed his hands. "I suggest we leave this place as soon as we collect all the men."

Madoc waved the scepter. "I hope it is that easy," he said. "I will negotiate with plenty of hand waving, like butterflies. If that does not work, I will think of a bee and use a stinger, something unusual."

"Stinkballs!" hollered Gwalchmai.

"Healing salves," said Conlaf. "You saw their scars and cuts."

"If you are not back by nightfall?" asked Sigurd.

"Feed yourselves, and the lass only if she awakens," said Madoc. "Lugh, I hope everyone is back by nightfall. Oh, did anyone see their horses?"

"No! Barbarians do not have horses," said Llieu with a snort.

"But they have sacred numbers such as four," said Madoc. "If we are not back by the time the moon is halfway across the sky, bring us four horses. Follow the path to their village. We will be there."

Caradoc pushed his hair from his face and said, "I wonder if these barbarians are happy and cheerful, or sad and pitiful. I will learn a few of their words so I can communicate with that bloody chief. I keep wondering where the women went. Why are the men scarred and crippled? Why was one young woman to be killed? What sort of people are the barbarians who live here?"

"We shall find out," said Madoc. He motioned that it was time to go.

The six men followed the barbarians' trail about a league from the shore. When they lost the trail, they clawed through a pine grove to wild, broken terrain. Walking was hampered by many downed trees. Beyond lay a swampy muck with seedy brambles of sumpweed and sawgrass. They picked up the trail on high ground lined with stones. It reminded them of an old Roman road. Madoc used the scepter, the feathers fluttering at the top, as a walking stick and as a lever to push debris from the trail. When they came to a narrow canyon with a stream flowing below, the druids were surprised to find a fiber-rope bridge held at both ends by guy ropes tied to windfall. They crossed one at a time with mincing steps, as the bridge swayed and bucked with each step. Madoc bounded across last and pressed them to hurry.

"Chickens speak plainer than these barbarians," said Riryd.

"Are these scarred, slant-eyes, long-heads real people?" said Dewi. "I never saw uglier *cwmni,* company."

"They scare the stuffing out of me!" said Thurs.

"I was wrong when I believed we left irrational behavior and killing behind us," said Caradoc.

Madoc did not want to be pestered with chit-chat. In his mind's eye he could see Brett and Troyes sitting with their hands tied, their mouths drawn in a straight line too scared to speak, and their bodies swaying with the litter's motion. "Only they and the Lord God understand their tongue," said Madoc. "Look at the suspension bridge! That shows they are real, thinking people. My concern is to find Brett and Troyes." Out of nowhere an outrageous thought popped into his head. *Maybe the barbarians never saw a redhead or a light-skinned, black-haired man. Maybe the two hostages are something to show off to their dark, swarthy people.* "Brett is our fosterling, not theirs." His voice rose with anger. "Troyes is a free man. They have to let both of them go!"

The men followed the trail further inland. On either side were strange, tall green spears, covered with sharp needles. The green spears gave way to pines half-strangled by vines and swags of gray-green moss. Next they were in yellow grassland. Overhead the sky was cloudy. There was an oppressive feeling in the air, like an approaching thunderstorm.

At the foot of a particularly steep hill, the men were met by slobbering, mangy, wolflike, yellow-haired dogs who yipped and growled with bared fangs. Madoc held up his hand, a signal to stop. For a moment they looked at the unusual mounds that were arranged in a circle, like a wheel, at the bottom of the hill. The seven "spokes" were shallow burials with the heads meeting in the center and the bodies extending outward with legs splayed apart. Most of the bones had been exposed, possibly dug up by the dogs.

Madoc wanted to look the burial over and talk about it, but he knew that the quicker they found Brett and Troyes, the better it would be to negotiate their release. At the same time he could not help but feel a peculiar kind of curiosity to understand this land and its people. He felt an unexpected delight that there were people here. That meant there was water and game for food. There was an unexpected feeling of energy because the old, familiar rules of patience, forbearance, and tolerance were in force, but in a different way. New rules had to be invented in order to endure this new place. These people knew how to live here. Madoc's people were not certain they wanted to stay.

On top of the hill were dozens of thatched oval huts,

whose roofs were covered with cane mats and decorated with conch shells.

As if waiting for something to take place, many barbarians milled around an open space, like a courtyard or ball field, behind the village.

The sights seemed unreal, like a dream, to Madoc. He had no idea such a place existed and estimated that the village was larger than Aberffraw. He nodded and smiled at moist brown-eyed women with sloping foreheads and flawless faces. Some of them screamed, pointed their fingers menacingly, and ran away. Scar-faced men chipping spear points over a pile of reddish chert turned serious, spiteful, and threatened the druids with jagged hunks of stone. Naked, slope-headed, sun-browned children, all female, waggled their tongues and threw clods of dirt.

Madoc could not figure why these people had no male children and why they were antagonistic. Had they never met strangers? Neither he nor his men would hurt them. He wanted only to talk to them, understand them, and then take back Brett and Troyes.

He spied the empty litter in front of a large withie hut. Dirt steps led down to the front opening. He was heartened when the door flap was pushed aside and the smiling chief, with pointy front teeth, beckoned to him. He followed as the chief limped down stairs cut into the dirt to the hard-packed dirt floor of the single room, half-buried into the earth. Opposite the steps was a row of leather boxes. Each was large enough to hold the cut-up carcass of a good-sized deer.

Daylight, coming through a wide opening in the ceiling, shone on a milling crowd of a couple of dozen barbarians. He guessed that the room was forty-ells long and fifteen-ells wide. Log benches were topped with pairs of carved stone statues of scarred warriors. They were as tall as the distance from a man's elbow to his fingertips. The air within the room was tense, and sour with the smell of unwashed bodies.

He was so relieved to see Brett and Troyes sitting next to the statues that he whistled through his teeth, charged past the barbarians, and cut the cord binding their hands. "Follow me up the stairs and out the door," he said.

Without warning, the most agonizing pain he had ever experienced hit his shoulders. He turned to see the grinning face of the man with the huge scar on his breast. The man held something pointy in his right hand that was without its index finger. He threatened to scratch Madoc's face if he interfered with the men rebinding Brett and Troyes.

Brett was silent.

Troyes swore.

Madoc's blood rushed for action inside his veins. He wanted to fight. Fighting was not a druid's way. He was beside himself with anger and frustration. He breathed deep and centered himself in the druidic fashion, so that he would better be able to cope with what came next.

The barbarians growled, and the deep sound vibrated in Madoc's chest like thunder. His five men were separated, and then each man was surrounded by several scarred barbarians. He leaned on the scepter and thought, *Barbarians are smart. They know the Roman trick of divide and conquer.* Showing he was intimidated by a man with a round scar on his chest would be a sign of weakness, so Madoc sat on top of a leather box where he could easily see Brett and Troyes.

Pulling him to his feet before he could blink an eye, a man with sunlike scars on the backs of his hands, with big ears and a pursed mouth, gave Madoc a fright. The man threw open the box. Inside was a child's skeleton, curled up.

"I sat on top of the remains of someone's highly revered relative," Madoc said out loud. The man with big ears pointed to the chief, who was taller than Madoc and spoke in chicken-like squawks. Madoc froze, but his eyes and ears were alert. Big Ears did his best to tell him that the dead child had belonged to the chief. With words and hand gestures he said the dead child had the name of a bird, so did the chief, but they were different birds. The child was named after a small bird with fast, whirring wings. "A hummingbird," said Madoc, moving his arms as fast as he could. Big Ears grinned and shook his head up and down. "So the chief is called something small—like wren?" asked Madoc, with hand signs. It seemed possible that Wren was the chief's name. It was hard to be sure, but between words, facial expressions, and hand signs it seemed that Chief Wren wanted Brett to take the dead child's place. Wren had killed his own male child to show his strength, his power. He had also killed many male children. Troyes would take the place of all those other unfortunate male children. Today Wren had become angry and killed his pregnant wife's friend, the good-looking female. He was sorry he had not killed his pregnant wife. Madoc was not sure that was the real story.

Big Ears rubbed his belly in wide circles, smiled, turned his mouth down, closed his eyes, and circled his head with one hand as he spoke in strange, deep-throated gobbles. He managed to make the gobbles sound frosty when he explained by hand signs that when Conlaf tired of the dead woman, he would put her bones into a wheel-like burial. The chief's pregnant wife and other woman were gone. He made it seem like they had disappeared, flown away.

"What is he saying?" asked Caradoc. "You younger men can understand his words better than I. The sounds are all scrambled together to me. Are those the bones of his child or that limping chief's?"

"The chief's name is Wren, and Wren's hands are covered with blood," said Madoc. "They think the chief killed the pretty young woman who appeared to be a leader. So, do not say what you know about her. He wishes he had also killed his wife, the pregnant one. He is going to put the pretty leader in one of those burials that look like wheel spokes. The bones in the box I sat on are what is left of the chief's little son, named Humming Bird, and Brett is to take his place. Troyes is to take the place of others who are dead. This story is too much! I must have it all wrong."

"*Non!* I am not replacing any barbarians!" said Troyes.

"Ye would not give me to a barbarian, would ye?" said Brett, trying to keep his lips from moving.

"As long as I am here, that limping lizard of a chief will not have ye," said Troyes. "I promised to look after ye."

Madoc thought what to do next, as he nervously fingered the edges of a hole broken in the bottom of the clay jar beside the child's skeleton. *First thing*, he thought, *is not to tell the barbarians that the leader of the women is still alive. And no woman can fly away, even if she is pregnant.*

With a disgusted facial expression, the man with the big ears made it clear that Madoc was discourteous to touch the clay jar that was precious grave goods.

Madoc forced a grin and said, "I figure the jar was killed, so its soul could escape and be with that of the deceased." Something sharp raked across his right arm, leaving four rows of scratches that oozed blood. "Hey! Why did you do that! That arm has had enough scarring!" His mouth went lopsided from the pain.

The man with the big ears answered, and Madoc could not understand his caterwauling, but he did see the set of gar-fish teeth held in one hand.

"Why?" said Madoc, holding out his aching arm that oozed blood.

The man held his head high to show four gashes on his cheeks and then his scarred arms and chest. He drew his lips back and made another slash at Madoc's other arm. The barbarian's front teeth were filed to points the same as the chief's, and there was a double row of white scars from the corners of his eyes to his mouth.

Madoc did not think the scratchings were anything to be proud of nor to grin about. He wanted to lash out, forget courtesy, and punch Big Ears in the face. How would he like that? He balled his fists and held one under the man's nose.

"Do not do whatever ye be thinking!" yelled Troyes. "Do not use physical force when it can be avoided."

Madoc pushed aside his desire to strike out and stammered, "I—I know that! How was I to know—'twas a—a *beddrod*?"

"Beth-rot?" imitated Big Ears moving his tongue in and out.

"Aye, grave enclosure, a bone box!" snapped Madoc, meeting Big Ears's gaze eye to eye. Neither man blinked for several moments. Madoc's intuition told him that the man could easily match him in a battle of wits if they spoke the same tongue. He imagined the man's eyes drained like canals through the deep scratches at the corners. Impulsively he pointed to himself and said, "Madoc." He pointed to Big Ears and waited for him to answer with a name. Big Ears furrowed his brows a moment, then convulsed with laughter as he tried to imitate Madoc's word. "Maa-tuck!" There was a glint in his eyes. He flexed his upper right arm where there was a scar resembling a rabbit. The rabbit's fur seemed to move, to fluff outwards.

Madoc sang the words, *Thank you, Troyes,* inside his head. Troyes's intuition was true. The man was communicating. "Rabbit!" Madoc said aloud. "You are Big-Eared Rabbit!" He hopped like a rabbit and pointed to the tattoo on the barbarian's upper arm then to his chest.

"Raa-bite!" Rabbit laughed heartily at the funny way of saying his name. He stepped close. The gar teeth were still in his hand. They made Madoc step back. Rabbit made strange sounds pointing to the various paraphernalia in the room. Madoc knew the sounds represented each item and pointed to a huge bow standing upright beside several arrows. Rabbit uttered a string of words. Madoc repeated them then tried again.

Madoc, who was noted for his good memory, could not twice repeat the unusual sounds. He realized that communication was going to take some time.

Rabbit showed him a pile of leather-and-cane shields; some were decorated with seed pearls, others were painted with lozenges and circles. There were helms, or headpieces, made of leather and rolled bundles of furs and hides. A raw slab bench held leather boxes of weapons, slingshots, and daggers and stones on a tether. Rabbit pointed to war drums and bird wing-bone whistles, and to bone clubs with wooden handles embedded with pearls or bits of polished copper. *War material. These people are fighters. Who are their enemies? Where are their enemies?*

Madoc thought about the irony of traveling more than a month across a vicious ocean. His men had survived starvation on part of that long voyage in their eagerness to escape war and the evils of men's violence against one another. And now they were in the middle of an unknown clan of warriors. The thought appalled him, and he was ready to vent his horror with a tongue-lashing for anyone who looked at him cross-eyed. He could see neither Brett nor Troyes. He bolted from Rabbit and pushed his way back to the stone statues where they sat with their hands tied, the same as before. He felt foolish and the back of his neck turned red. He sat quietly and avoided looking toward Rabbit.

Troyes leaned over and nudged Madoc so he would notice the young woman with a high, flat forehead. She carried stacks of grass mats on top of her head that was peaked on top like a Welsh thatched roof.

"I think I saw her before," said Madoc.

Brett wiggled, trying to pull his hands free. "I have a scary feeling."

"Scary," said Madoc. "This has been a scary day."

"Like—something is about to happen."

"Stay still," said Madoc. "We will be on the ships in no time."

Brett trusted Madoc and knew he was obligated to do what the chief shipmaster said. The nine-year-old already knew that to obey his superior was a responsibility he had taken on when he chose the privilege of sailing with the druids. He said with no joy in his voice, "For ye I stay still a while longer."

The chief, always staying close by, put his big hand around Brett's neck and opened his mouth so that Brett could see his front, pointy teeth.

Thinking he was being strangled and eaten alive, Brett screamed. The chief threw him over his shoulder, shuffled to the wall opposite the stairs, and stood there with the lad in his arms. Troyes was carried there by two men and placed on a floor mat. The crowd moved to form semicircles in front of the chief, who glared and waved his free hand for the eight newcomers to sit on the mats next to him where he could watch them.

Madoc's teeth ground together. He did not sit. Instead he grabbed the chief's hand away from Brett's windpipe and squeezed hard. "Let the lad be, or else I shall lay curses on you more painful than the curses of the Norse giant, Loki. I wish I could tell you about him. Then I would tell you that in our thinking you are not supposed to be here, but in a fiery-hot, underground cave!"

Chief Wren's hand hurt. He understood the anger in Madoc's voice and let go. He stood Brett on his feet and untied his bindings.

Madoc grabbed Brett's arm and wasted no time dashing

for the door. Instantly, the barbarians swarmed, pushed them back, and Brett fell in front of the chief.

Madoc waved his fist in front of the chief's face. "You, you have no right to make any of us stay."

Wren's lips formed a thin, down-turned arc, and he loosened Troyes's wrist binding.

"Pourrie merde d'oie!" said Troyes, lowering his eyes. "Do not be afraid, Little Brother Brett. The barbarians do not know what we say or what we can do."

Rabbit thumped Madoc on the back, patted the red scratches on his arms, and turned his mouth down as if asking forgiveness.

Madoc gave him a tart look, and his heart pounded so hard he could barely think. "How do we get out of here?" he whispered to Conlaf.

"Turn ourselves into small crickets."

"I know naught of magic," sighed Madoc. "But there are Brett and Troyes without bindings."

Wren gave Brett the phallic beaker to hold, bowed four times in front of Troyes, and all eyes were on the chief. He harangued with passion in a torrent of whoops, clacks, grunts, and gobbles. His flow of words emitted a strange splendor, and Madoc knew he had worked hard on his speaking skills and why he was kept as this village's supreme leader. When he finished his tirade, he flexed his lame legs as far as possible and pointed to Troyes's lame leg and to Brett's foot with four toes. He looked haughtily at Madoc, suggesting that he had no special marks, except the tattoos. The barbarians hissed. There was no doubt what that meant. Madoc, with good legs and feet, was out of favor.

"King Wren is in pain from tight scar tissue," said Conlaf. "Salves or something more might give us some respect. He would still have scars, but not as much pain." He patted the medicine bag tied to his waist.

"Aye," agreed Caradoc.

"He likes my lame leg," said Troyes. "Here it gives me status. Maybe he thinks I am a lord."

"Give you a smile a tum long and you take an ell," groused Madoc.

"We need to understand them," said Riryd. "Learn their language."

"Trust them, mayhap they will trust us," said Dewi.

Madoc perspired and his thoughts went this way and that way. He did not want to start a confrontation that he could not finish without bloodshed. He wondered if he could work through Rabbit to convince Wren to release Brett and Troyes.

Chief Wren gave the druids a stern look and held Brett close to one side and Troyes close to the other side. Rabbit sat behind them on a pile of skins with an arm across Troyes's shoulder.

A one-eyed barbarian with copper ear plugs motioned with his head and hands to make it clear that he wanted to trade for the wool cap Troyes wore. He fingered Troyes's long, soft, black hair.

Troyes said he had no desire to wear plugs that would turn his ears green. The one-eyed man knew he had been rebuffed and shuffled away in a huff.

Wren's brown eyes sparkled. He snatched the cap and tossed it after the man.

"That cap is not yers to give," said Brett shaking his finger at Wren. "Where are yer manners?"

The one-eyed man picked up the coveted cap, bowed toward Wren, looked at Troyes, and grinned.

Troyes drew back his lips making a grimace that was no smile.

Rabbit left Troyes and came to sit beside Madoc. He playfully pulled the back of Madoc's yellow hair and side-whiskers. Madoc half-turned and pushed Rabbit's fingers aside. Rabbit was amused, smiled, and patted his own scarred cheeks. He twisted Madoc about so that he could see the women with flat trays of steaming food come down the steps. He mimicked Madoc's facial expressions, his Welsh and English words, and patted his stomach. He growled low in his chest, like a dog growling over a caught coney, and smacked his lips.

Madoc wondered if that was his way of saying he was hungry. He stared at the first serving woman. He knew he had seen her before. She was one of the women standing behind the wounded leader. She was small and looked to be no more than eighteen. Her long hair was piled on her head and held there with patties of mud. She gave Troyes a small wooden bowl, patted his head, ran her finger through his wavy hair, and picked out crisp, brown morsels for him. Then she gave Brett a bowl and held the tray out to the chief, so he could pick out the morsels he preferred. The young woman touched Madoc's arm and pointed to what looked like a pile of oysters. She pointed to other strange things on her tray and finally to something that looked like tiny boiled onions. She touched the onions and let her head fall to her shoulders, her eyes closed, and her tongue hung out. She opened her eyes and smiled. Madoc saw the chief avoided the onion things. The woman kept looking at Madoc as she handed out the small, empty bowls.

The chief threw bits of food in four directions. Food morsels landed on guests or on the dirt floor and were quickly picked up.

"He feeds little people!" whispered Brett. " 'Tis a good sign. Huh?"

"He may be honoring his gods for the goodness that has been provided this day," said Caradoc.

"More important, what was that lass trying to say?" asked Conlaf.

"We are not to eat the things that look like onions," said Madoc. "They will make you sleep."

"Maybe Mud Patties has more to say, but she has to be careful," said Conlaf. "Hope you figured her words right. I do not know what to say. Does she know 'thank you'?"

"You do not have to say anything. Keep your lips sealed, listen and think," said Madoc as the food plate was passed under his nose. He studied it for a moment then said, "I spy smoked oysters. A delicacy in any language." He took one and popped it into his mouth, leaving his bowl empty.

Nearby the barbarians stopped talking. They were astonished that a man would be so discourteous. They elbowed one another and tittered about the weird actions of the stranger.

Madoc expected the boneless meat of an oyster. Instead his mouth was filled with a tiny bird, defeathered and boiled in spiced oil. He saw the barbarians watching him and was

not about to lose face by spitting out the bony, bitter mouthful. He chewed innards, crunched bird bones, swallowed,
and turned to Caradoc. "I be glad these barbarians have
gods, otherwise I would give them the trickster that let me
eat a whole little bird. I think it was a wren," he said. " 'Tis
making me ill."

"With the smile I give them, I be saying 'tis impolite to
laugh at a man who is so hungry he wolfs anything resembling food," said Conlaf. He drew his lips back from his
teeth in a mocking smile.

Madoc, truly feeling unsettled, wondered how Conlaf
could act so reckless when he, himself, felt so precarious.
He thought, *the stench of them and the stink of us mixed
together under the same roof is sickening. I can not possibly eat anything more.*

Brett said he thought some of the meat was dog and
eating it would be a Welsh *geis*, something prohibited.

Madoc said it was also a geis to refuse to eat if you were
a guest in another man's home. So, when the plate was
again passed, he filled his bowl with pieces of flat bread
and put a hunk of some kind of meat on top so it would
look as though he had heaped the bowl full of meat.

The other druids followed his suit, picking out the
squash from unidentifiable vegetables and separating
shrimp, scallops, and clams from the mystery seafood that
was tough as leather.

Brett said, "If I eat barbarian food, I could be poisoned
and die. That is what the lass said." He shuddered and
looked at Madoc.

Madoc said, "Do not eat the onions." He hoped that
Conlaf kept his mouth full and would not comment about
the dark, lukewarm drink. But his hope was futile.

After one sip, Conlaf said, "I never before drank black
tea that tasted like poisoned horse piss."

The barbarians wiped their greasy hands in their straight,
dark hair and went outside. Madoc was appalled at their
gross behavior. He and his men followed Chief Wren who,
with Brett and Troyes ahead of him, went outside.

The afternoon was humid and warm. More clouds now
showed in the northwest.

Madoc thought if they left one by one no one would

notice until it was too late. He was careful not to frighten Brett and gently took his hand. He nodded to the others to get Troyes and walk away with no unusual fuss.

Quick as a flash, Rabbit was beside Madoc and softly touching his shoulder. His brown eyes were gentle, yet sad beyond description. Madoc was dumbfounded when Rabbit pointed to Brett, put his hands together, and lay his head on them to indicate sleep. He wanted Brett to stay all night! Madoc shook his head, nay.

Rabbit growled, put his hands under Brett's arms, and lifted him in the air.

Madoc had no idea what Rabbit was doing, but whatever it was, he did not like it. He stared at him and tried to will him to put the boy down.

Rabbit put Brett down, put his hand on the small of his back, and forced himself to stand straight. His face was flushed and shone with perspiration.

Madoc exhaled. His heart raced. He believed his thoughts had forced Rabbit to release the boy. He put his hands together and lay his head on them to show that he would fain stay the night in place of Brett.

Rabbit rubbed his cramped back muscle, looked put out, stamped his foot, and shook his head. He pushed Madoc aside like dry tumbleweed, took Brett's hand, and walked away.

Brett jerked his arm. "Let me go!" he croaked, hoarse as a raven. Saliva bubbled from his mouth.

Troyes pulled his right fist back and let it fly into Rabbit's solar plexus. Rabbit stumbled. Troyes grabbed Brett and darted between groups of barbarians.

"Run!" yelled Madoc.

The barbarians were fast. They left Madoc gaping as they surrounded Troyes and Brett. Madoc had a glimpse of Rabbit holding a bone knife between Troyes's ribs.

The chief limped to Madoc, gave him a black look, and said several words that resembled thunder.

Madoc said that he got the message and that he and his men were going to stay until Troyes and Brett were set free, if it took all night.

The chief slipped his bent arm like an iron band around Brett's chest and his good arm around Troyes's. He hissed between his teeth, and his face looked harsh as stone.

"What do you intend to do?" shouted Madoc, shaking his finger so close to the chief's mouth that it could have been bitten off. "I be through poking at a hornet's nest. We are outnumbered and do not want to be stung. We can make hand signs and grimaces, negotiate with one another. I wish I understood your tongue."

The chief's face became a stubborn mask. He did not flinch or lower his eyes.

Madoc said, "What do you say?" Still the chief's face remained hard and silent as a stone. Madoc thought, *At least he has not flatly refused.* Tense, Madoc and his men followed the limping, groaning chief, who held on to Brett and Troyes as if they could be blown away by a sudden blast of wind.

Conlaf talked about using physician's knives to cut the scar tissue on the chief's legs and bent arm to relieve his pain and limp, in exchange for Brett and Troyes. "I do not know if this buzzard would hold still for us to mess with his legs," he said. "These people seem to think it an honor, not a disgrace, to have their flesh scarred, looks worse than druid honor-marks. 'Tis like Welsh crofters meeting up with a bunch of French fishermen who can not understand one another. Only this is worse because these barbarians have long-sloped foreheads and wear the skimpiest of clothing. Did you see the women in short skirts and tiny vests of bird feathers? Our women would never, in a hundred years, wear something like that."

" 'Tis a pity!" said Conlaf.

"For once forget about women!" said Madoc. "Your reworking-the-scars idea might work. By now the chief knows we want Brett."

"These people are not so different from us," said Conlaf. "Rabbit tries to imitate our words. I suspect he wants to understand us."

The chief led them to a muddy, swamplike pond below the village courtyard. Madoc could think of nothing but the clash of cultures. He thought, *Yea, we people are similar, but our habits and speech are different. What brings people close together besides men and women? Food? Kindness? Conlaf's idea of medical aid to the king just might bring*

us together and initiate an understanding. Of most impor-
tance, however, will the barbarians give up Brett and
Troyes? He half wished he had taken Clare's advice and
brought a couple of stinkballs to give these people a smell
of Hell: burning brimstone. Then he thought of their fierce,
gamey food, their pungent body odor, and decided no smell
would faze them. He prayed that the time between now and
the middle of the night passed quickly. Four undernour-
ished horses might put awe and fear in their hearts. Time
was on his side. Be patient, he told himself.

XVIII
The Crane's Spirit

The carved cypress artifact [a crane's head], known as the
Thomasson figurehead, was found near the Florida pineland
Site after a storm in 1971. There were nine drilled holes in
the figurehead, probably used to tie it to a costume or to
manipulate the lower and upper beaks.... Two toggles,
hanging at the waist and connected to the figurehead by way
of cords passing through the tall panel, permitted two oper-
ations. By pulling one toggle, the dancer clacked the beak
shut and, with the other, pulled the neck up against the backing panel. When the toggles were released, as when imitating
a crane's wing display, the beak opened and the neck
stretched forward.

> —William H. Marquardt, "From Out of the Darkness
> Comes Great Crane Spirit," *Calusa News*

The pond's banks were crowded. This was some kind of
celebration. The whole village was there and then some.
Troyes and Brett were placed between half a dozen women
for safekeeping. Among the women was the one that Madoc had recognized earlier during the feasting. She was the
one who let him know it would not be wise to eat the little
onions. The chief, wearing only Conlaf's tattered shirt,
went to the center of the pond where the brackish, brown
water was thigh high. Rabbit and several other important
men, wearing small aprons, waded in.

Madoc kept his eyes on Brett and Troyes. He motioned
for his companions to stay among a group of trees that
looked like common lindens to him. The trees had a delightful honeyed fragrance, and bees were busy visiting
each yellow, star-shaped flower. The flowers dangled in
clusters of six from a stem that came out of the center of

a leaf that looked like a stiff, green ribbon. Madoc remembered how the flowers turned into round, hard nuts the size of peas, and he had a sudden nostalgia for a summer day in Wales. He wanted no more scratching with gar teeth. He made his eyes rove slowly over the crowd and said, "There are at least two hundred men here. Have we walked into a trap?"

"Not yet," said Caradoc. "Methinks 'tis a holy day. Be patient, see what spells they perform."

"Look at that!" Riryd could not suppress his laughter. "The women have Brett dressed in feathers like a big white bird! A crane! They are making quite a fuss over him!"

"Maybe they think he is some kind of doll to dress up," said Dewi. "They do not have many male children of their own. All I see are lassies. He is their number-one exhibit."

"Exhibit?" said Madoc.

"Aye, see how he struts around the pond?" said Riryd. "Watch."

The druids stayed inside the cover of the trees, but moved slowly behind the women who clustered around Troyes. They washed and combed his long hair. Madoc called out to Troyes and asked what was going on.

Troyes was not sure, and said he did not care if the woman daubed mud on seashells to decorate his hair, but he wanted no costume stuff. He said he felt better with the druids close by. He pointed toward Brett.

Madoc was astonished to see a second boy dressed like a big white crane beside Brett. The boy clucked and hopped on one skinny leg then the other. He knew just what to do. On his bare feet were strapped oversized stork feet. He kept the back toe of the stork feet elevated, in the manner of the crane. His long, wooden, yellow bill opened, his neck extended down, and he pretended to peck at scraps thrown on the ground.

Brett was embarrassed to have a feathered cape with a tail tied on his shoulders. He wore a tiny male apron made of black-tipped white feathers. On his own neck and head he wore the long neck and head of the crane carved in wood and held on with some kind of close-fitting cap. He was awkward and did not know how to manipulate the strings that caused the wooden beak to open and close. He had to be prodded to move about by someone dressed in a black, feathered cape and a cap with a yellow bill, like a blackbird.

Another man, with a wolf-robe over his shoulders and a ferocious mask with pointed ears and gar teeth in the open muzzle, chased the two lads. Blackbird jabbed Brett with a stick so he would run. It looked like the stick moved by itself behind Brett while Blackbird stood perfectly still.

" 'Tis a magic spell," said Thurs.

"Nay, 'tis only a trick," said Conlaf waving his hands against mosquitoes. "Blackbird is a healer. He rubbed salve on the king's legs."

They smelled the burning feathers as a group of women singed the white breast feathers from a pile of dead cranes with thin black legs and part-naked heads.

Madoc listened to the women gobble and clack whenever they picked up a dead bird. "Are the women talking to each bird's spirit?"

"Common cranes are probably sacred here!" said Conlaf, betting that there would be a feast before the day was over.

Caradoc told them to listen to the drumming. "Tum-tum-boom! Tum-tum-boom! Means something." More sloped-headed men came out of the trees, shucked off their clothes, and went naked into the pond.

"Look at that!" whispered Dewi, pointing to Blackbird, who chewed a piece of bull-thistle root. When the root was mush, he smeared it on the scratches he inflicted on a line of younger men.

Wolf played a three-note dirge on a willow stick. Madoc said that the index finger of Wolf's right hand was missing, and when he raised his arms while playing the flute, one could see crisscross scars on his chest. "He is the one who put the red-ocher handprints on Brett. He looks like a war leader."

"Look at the young men lining up on the bank, like a flock of gulls facing into the wind, waiting for their initiation and scarification," said Conlaf.

Troyes heard the druids and said, "These bloody barbarians think the more scars, the more invincible a man is. The men scratch each other with gar teeth or a comb made from a splintered bird leg-bone tied onto a quill frame that stings like fire. The men never cry out, which proves their bravery." He held up his arm that had been scratched and then he pointed to the shells daubed with mud stuck in his hair.

"You look like a bloody barbarian!" said Madoc, swatting mosquitoes, and showing his scratches.

"Sshh!" warned Conlaf.

Chief Wren sucked on the handle of the beaker Brett had given him. Smoke came out of his nostrils, making him look like a fire-breathing dragon. His important men made a noise in their throats that sounded like clacking cranes.

Women with water flowers in their hair handed out tiny clay beakers of black soup. After drinking it, the men made disgusting noises, passed stinking gas, and ran for the tallest marsh grass, hawking and spitting while squatting.

Madoc thought the marshland would not support their weight, but the waterlogged sand looked surprisingly springy. "What are they doing?"

"They make water, squat, and heave their insides out," said Troyes. "The black drink makes them sick. Afterwards they run into the pond and splash like dogs thrown into a creek."

"It makes my stomach curdle," said Riryd.

" 'Tis a purge," whispered Conlaf. "They clean their bodies inside and out."

Blackbird took off his costume and handed it to a young woman with bare breasts and long legs. She ran the tip of her pink tongue against his cheeks and lumpy neck. Her hands caressed his sagging hams. Madoc gasped as the woman swayed her hips and pulled Blackbird's apron to one side. She massaged his loins with a piece of slippery bark. Her hands cupped his stick and made it bob out of the water like the head of a snake.

All eyes were on the center of the pond where another bare-breasted young woman caressed the chief. His stick was up. He put his hands on the lass's undulating hips, arched his back, and sprayed like a waterspout.

"Can you beat that?" said Riryd, wide-eyed. "In front of the gods and everyone! I could never perform before a crowd."

"Oh? Just look at the front of you!" teased Conlaf. " 'Tis

like a live squirrel trying to see daylight." He poked his fist
into Riryd's belly.

Madoc put a hand over his mouth to keep them quiet
and pointed to a line of bare-breasted beauties with white
flowers in their hair. They stood in front of a line of young
men freshly scarified. Lines of blood slid down the arms
and legs of some, the backs and breasts of others. The
young women stroked the men's thighs with little pieces of
slippery bark and in no time each man's stick stood up like
a flagpole. Their climaxes took place like a row of foun-
tains. Their seed floated in little white masses, converged
in front of the king and Blackbird for two or three heartbeats, then disappeared. The sticks fell like trees blown
down during a hurricane.

The druids looked crosswise at each other, not knowing
whether to make some ribald remark on the near-perfect
timing.

The lasses at the edge of the pond trilled their tongues,
stamped their feet, and churned the water to a spray. The
spray produced miniature rainbows when the sun peeked
from behind white clouds. Hands reached out as if trying
to touch the rainbows.

"Well-a-way!" said Conlaf, letting the air out of his
lungs as if someone had squeezed his chest. "I never—! I
was right! Purged of everything! Clean inside and outside!"

Madoc pointed to Blackbird shivering in the water. He
looked old as the hills, with lumps the size of hazelnuts on
the front of his neck and under his arms. A young woman
took him by the hand, led him to the embankment, and
replaced his cape and cap. He stood, blue lipped, between
Wolf and Chief Wren. He wrung water out of his skimpy
apron. The newly scarified men lined up two by two behind
Wolf. He paraded them around the shore and took them to
the trail that led to the village. Some of the men made a
low rumbling in their throats, keeping time to drum beats
and flutelike notes by jabbing the chief with pointed sticks
to make him limp along faster.

Young women, little girls, and dogs followed. The dogs
spread out, sniffed and yipped at Madoc's men, who forced
themselves to stand quietly until the dogs were used to their
smell.

Two women pushed Troyes so he too limped along the path. He called to the druids, "Lord God, I be glad Brett did not see that—that holy ceremony!"

"Where is he?" said Madoc.

"With the women and children," said Troyes.

"Come on!" said Madoc. "Let's follow the women and children."

The natives strutted like birds in loops and spirals as they went through the village to the courtyard. In the center of the yard were two poles about three-ells long set into the ground one and a half ells apart. Another pole was placed between the two and tied horizontally half an ell above the ground. A fourth pole was placed across the top so a square frame was formed and tied with braided-grass rope. The chief, Troyes, and Blackbird stood in front of the frame. Wolf, still wearing the hideous mask, and Rabbit stood in back of the frame. The young men formed a circle around them with women and female children forming a circle around the young men.

Madoc and his companions quietly moved into the women's circle, looked for Brett, and tried to be inconspicuous behind several bunches of little girls who chased the scrawny, yellow dogs.

A dog growled. Madoc petted it and it snapped at his hand. That made the little girls cackle and run around the dogs.

Troyes was beside a short post with a chunk of ice that did not melt. Madoc looked harder and saw that it was really the biggest, clearest rock crystal he had ever seen. It was bigger than a man's head. Sunlight was drawn inside it, and when the light escaped, it separated into rays of many colors, like the rainbows at the pond. The barbarians made a guttural chant and extended their hands through the rainbow. They touched Troyes when the drums beat like thunder.

Madoc was uneasy and searched for Brett. His hand enfolded the tiny crystal that had stayed in his pocket since the time Annesta gave it to him. That long-ago time seemed related to another age. He could not recall details of Annesta's face. He remembered the clean fragrance of her hair.

He forced himself to concentrate on the future and to leave the past behind. He thought about the four horses that would come and dazzle these people into giving up their hold on Brett and Troyes. Time was the savior. His tight feeling did not go away. He was not at all certain what was going to happen before this day was over.

Suddenly, two reed cages appeared on either side of Troyes. Barbarians pushed and shoved one another to stand close to the cages. Madoc leaned one way, then another. He could not see what was in the cages, so he handed the scepter to Conlaf and asked Dewi to boost him up.

Dewi bent so that Madoc could sit on his shoulders, then stood up while holding onto Madoc's ankles.

"Aawwk!" Madoc cried through clenched teeth. "There is a big crane in each basket!" A dog growled and Dewi rocked from side to side. Madoc hunched down and said, "Hold still!" through his teeth.

"A bloody dog is chewing my leg!" whispered Dewi. When he shook his leg, his shoulders moved back and forth. He felt Madoc clinging to his hair.

"Hit the bloody beast!" said Madoc.

Conlaf hit the wolfish dog with the scepter. It yipped and ran, with its tail between its legs, in and out among the women. The women kicked it, making it yip louder. The little girls squealed with delight and with small bare feet kicked to make the dog yip.

Madoc's stomach constricted. "Suppose they are having a gathering here to mete out some kind of punishment?" he said. "Like the baskets of the old, annual law court in Wales?" A tingling started at the back of his neck and traveled down his spine.

"Memories are like corks left out of the bottle," said Caradoc. "They swell with time and no longer fit. We be far away from Wales."

Madoc's foreboding grew. "Suppose Brett or Troyes heedlessly breaks a barbarian code?"

"Just tell us what the chief is doing," said Caradoc.

"Opening a basket and pulling out the crane," said Madoc. "Oh Lugh! 'Tis Brett! From here I can see his feathered cape and tail. The laddie's legs are scratched bloody, like he has been in the briars. His skin was made black with ash mixed in grease." The barbarians' chanting became so loud that Madoc could no longer be heard while sitting on Dewi's shoulders. Dewi squatted down. Madoc slid from his back. "Separate and move to the men's line," he said. "Keep your eyes open."

They moved between the women, up from one circle to the next. Little girls laughed and swatted the druids with sticks. The women bared their teeth, hissed, and pinched them. When Madoc was in the circle of old men, his feet were stepped on. He looked between the shoulders of the younger men.

Troyes was tied to the post holding the crystal. He managed to pull his sash free and waved it above his head. Brett's head bobbed and a smile lighted his face. At the same time the sun came from under a cloud and sent a rainbow through the crystal. Troyes's wavy dark hair shone between the mud and shells. The drums beat with the shifting changes in light and caused the crowd to hush. Madoc had a fleeting urge to hold his little crystal in the sun to free its rainbow.

A young woman brought Brett a small gourd of dirty-looking soup. He swallowed, once, twice, made a face, and refused to drink more. The woman's words turned to hissing. She held Brett's head in one hand and his nose in the other. Another woman poured the soup into his open mouth. He swallowed and yelled. His face became red. The crowd murmured.

"Ye be poisoning him!" yelled Troyes.

"You saw the king and his men drink that black liquid," said Madoc.

The gourd was taken to the second youth dressed as a crane. He drank eagerly. The crowd chanted. Then the gourd was filled and taken to the men in the first circle. Each man took a sip and passed it on until it needed refilling and went to the next row. Flatulent sounds and smells filled the air.

Madoc moved into the first circle to see what was going on. His hand holding the scepter was gouged with something sharp. The man next to him grinned and held his own arms out. They had long, red scratch marks. The man on Madoc's other side was scratching his own chest with gar's teeth. Drops of blood appeared in the scratch grooves. He rubbed the blood across his chest and made a red handprint on the bare back of the man beside him and raked his gar's teeth across it. The scratched man did not cry out or move. Madoc was perplexed by the indifference to pain.

Suddenly he was jostled. He thought Rabbit was next to him, but he was behind him. In the blink of an eye his shirt was gone. "What the—?" He was astounded that his shirt could be lifted from his back without seeming to go over his head or off his arms. The men on either side smiled but otherwise little attention was paid to him.

The gourd of dark liquid was in his hands and he hesitated, until the man beside him flashed a set of gar's teeth. He held his breath and gulped. The liquid stung his mouth and throat. It was an astringent that tasted like green walnut husks soaked in pinesap and fermented turnips. For a moment he thought he was going to be ill. He took a deep breath to calm his stomach that grumbled with gas. He forced himself to remain passive, to center his thoughts inside himself and to minimize the wave of nausea in the pit of his stomach. Rabbit scratched his back. He felt no pain and knew it was the magic of the drink. He thought his eyesight was heightened when he saw Brett's nostrils flare as the chief took a step toward him.

Brett's skinny leg stuck out and tripped Chief Wren so that he fell facedown on a stone. Blood trickled from his nose that lay on the side of his face, broken. His hands opened and closed. There was no sound, except the wind moving through the grass and the palm fronds. A woman helped the chief wipe his face with cattail down. It was the same woman Madoc had recognized earlier. She looked at him and started to say something, then closed her mouth, rubbed her hands together, and made a noise that sounded like a crackling fire. It meant naught to Madoc so he watched the chief, whose mouth was open. With narrowed eyes he glared at Brett, whose mouth twitched upwards, and his arms shook making the crane's beak open and close.

Madoc saw this as his opportunity. He told his men to create a rumpus, frighten the women so they would scream, then he would crown Wolf, Blackbird, and Rabbit with the scepter. Amid all that commotion he would rescue Brett and Troyes.

Before Madoc's grand plans were firm, the chief raised his hands and yelled, *"Anestsa!"*

Madoc was stunned. He could not move or speak. The unexpected word, so close to his beloved dead wife's name, paralyzed him.

Women and little girls ran to the grassy terrace on the left of the field. Rabbit freed Troyes's arms and ankles and disappeared. Troyes shouted, "Run! Run for your life!" The druids ran after him.

Madoc came to his senses when two men blocked his way. One grabbed his arm. The other held a bone dagger to his chest. A rumble of thunder spoke to him. The gods were on his side. He swung the scepter and hit the jaw of the man holding his arm. The man loosened his grip. Madoc hit him again. He did not think what he was doing, only that he was the one to rescue Brett, and he hit the other man so hard that the scepter left a red mark on his chest before it slipped out of his hand.

Brett screamed from inside the basket in a high, loonlike voice. "For troth, they will hurt ye, not me. They will not kill a dumb water crane. Run, Master Madoc!"

Madoc's left hand pulled the thin-edged dagger out of his soft flesh just below his right ribs. He did not feel the flesh wound nor the blood running under his tunic, but he was dizzy, something was eating his stamina. He turned and almost tripped because Troyes was so close, with his mouth open, his left arm bloody, and a bone knife in his right hand.

Madoc gasped, pushed Troyes to the ground, and reached to pull Brett out of harm's way. Brett was not there and neither were the baskets! He could not believe his eyes and swore. Someone in a blue Welsh shirt lifted Troyes to his feet. Madoc yelled, "Run! Run to the ships!"

Madoc's five men disappeared into the crowd. He willed himself to stay on his feet and not falter. He told himself to wait a moment so that he could get his second wind. He did not know how long he stood still. When he felt better, he would swing his balled fists into the first man that came near.

The man was Rabbit and, for a moment, it looked like they held each other upright. Rabbit pulled back one hand and reached inside his skimpy breechclout. Madoc thought he was going to be slashed again for a certainty. He swung his fist, hit Rabbit's neck, and felt something slam into his chest. His hands reached up to grab Rabbit's shiny black hair. Instead he grabbed a leather pouch.

Rabbit's sorrowful, scarred face was close, his fists wiped across his eyes, and his tear-wet hands slid down Madoc's cheeks, like an apology. He pointed to the baskets holding the boys and clasped his hands across his chest. Then he melted into the crowd like goose grease into a hot biscuit.

For a moment Madoc was stunned with an overpowering feeling of sadness and ignorance because Rabbit had tried to tell him something that he could not figure out. His thoughts spun around and around. *What caused the man to cry? Loss? Of what? A wife, a child? Had Rabbit lost a child? Was the other child dressed as a crane Rabbit's child? Was he going to be sacrificed to some barbarian god? Or was Brett going to be sacrificed? Or both of them? No! That could not be true. So, how did Rabbit father a small boy, when there did not seem to be any other boys around, only girls? What made Rabbit special? Was he born with a defect, something thought sacred?* It was a puzzle, and Madoc was almost too tired to think on it. He slouched against a gray boulder and thought of himself inside the boulder where there was only silence and darkness.

Poof! Like dandelions' seeds blown away by the wind, everyone was gone except Conlaf, who was doping Madoc's waist, the flesh wound, with salve. " 'Twill heal," said Conlaf. "Where is your shirt?"

"Rabbit took it."

"Well, mine is gone, too," said Conlaf, swiping a hand across the gar scratches on his chest. "These people have a trick of taking what they want."

"Aye, right off a person's back," said Madoc. He got to his feet and was shaky. He told himself the weakness would pass. "Someone in a blue shirt took Troyes to the ships," said Madoc. "Did you see his bloody arm?"

"I never saw him. My itchy right side was scratched

good, and I lost my shirt to that bloody chief," said Conlaf. "I cannot remember how he took it off." He rubbed his side and wiped his arm across his forehead. "You say Troyes got away and went to the ships?"

"Ya," said Madoc. "I thought he did, but I be not certes. He was with someone in a blue shirt. Maybe it was your shirt. Maybe he is with Brett."

"Dewi said you pushed Troyes to the ground; the barbarians thought he was dead, left him, and went after Brett."

"Lugh! Where is that lad?"

"With the chief."

"Doing what?"

Conlaf looked perplexed. "Brett said he would be all right."

Madoc remembered that he was going to rescue Brett and Troyes and be a hero. He groaned.

"I saw you fight two barbarians. Good for thee."

"Fighting is not for me," Madoc said and shivered. "Did you see Rabbit take my shirt? How did he do it? Is he wearing my shirt? Do you trust him?" He felt mysterious, barbaric spells in the humid air and shivered again.

" 'Tis a trick, that is all," said Conlaf.

"Where is your shirt?" asked Madoc again.

"I told you. I lost it a while back," said Conlaf. "I put it on the wounded woman. I drank the damn, bloody, black brew and it stole my memory. I hung on to my healer's bag, so no scolds."

"I will not scold you. Horses are our trick," said Madoc. He watched the dark clouds swirling in from the west. He wondered if they were bringing wind or rain for the night. He prayed for both. The sooner darkness came, the sooner the horses would come and astonish the barbarians right out of their scars. He heard the distant rumble of thunder and shoved the leather bag Rabbit had left him into his tunic pocket. There was time to examine the bag later. It smelled like it held a dead rat.

Madoc and Conlaf followed the noisy barbarians to the grassy steps alongside the courtyard, not unlike a Welsh jousting field.

Some men waved bone knives at them. Conlaf whispered that he had stones hidden inside his tunic to use if necessary.

Madoc said that fighting had failed. "Throw away the stones and remember we are druids. I will talk to the barbarians."

"You cannot speak in their tongue."

"There are other ways to speak."

"I honor your intelligence, but you are lost in the fog," said Conlaf. "These men are barbarians! They would as soon slice off your head as slice an apple in half."

Madoc bit his tongue, knowing that he could not afford an argument right now.

"Smooth the way so I can heal the chief's legs and bent arm." Conlaf met Madoc's eyes. " 'Tis our last chance."

"You forgot the horses," said Madoc. "Time is on our side."

Conlaf surveyed the darkening sky. "You forget the swinging bridge in a wind storm."

The crowd hushed as two basketlike cages were brought out and boys, with faces painted white and dressed as cranes, crawled out and stood by the upright poles of the open rectangle. Bare-breasted women added rows of feathered bracelets, anklets, and a pearl neckband to one of the crane costumes. The boy smiled, and his crane neck extended forward. A woman fluffed the feathers on the second crane's cape. He was quiet and did not move his arms or legs. His white face made him unrecognizable.

"That one is Brett," said Madoc. "The laddie is scared stiff as a log."

The women paraded the cranes in front of both terraces packed with people. Madoc wondered if the amount of hissing or applause decided which crane was favored. If applause was good, Brett was out, because he drew hisses. He stumbled over his feet and acted dumb, like he did not know where to walk. The barbarian boy held up his head to show off his pearls.

The boys' white faces were covered with masks made to look like white breast feathers. Three-toed feet made of black hide were tied onto their bare feet. The boys tried to avoid stepping on their black hide feet as they turned here and there and strutted around the field. With their feet covered and masks that hid even their necks, Madoc could not tell which boy was Brett. He kept asking, "Which one?"

Conlaf would hesitate and point to the one with no pearl necklace.

Madoc was not convinced. Not knowing which crane was Brett made Madoc panicky. "I be going to talk with the chief. He can tell me which is Brett."

"I will go with you," said Conlaf.

Madoc thought there was a chance that he could make it clear they were not warlike and then it would easily follow that Conlaf could barter his healing skills for Brett. He thought of the barbarian women and decided to keep quiet about their female hostage. He did not have to tell everything he had to bargain with. He stood up. Barbarians' eyes were on him. Their hands were ready to grab on to knife handles. Madoc carried the scepter as if it were the most holy of crosiers. A sultry breeze kicked up dust and caused the scepter's feathers to stand straight out as though held up by an unseen string.

Conlaf walked behind Madoc. The two men did not hesitate, but went with their heads up past a line of hissing young men who were waving stone knives, as though it was part of the ceremony. When the two men were face to face with the chief, the barbarians held their breath. They had not expected that two strangers would be so bold as to approach their headman.

From the corner of his eye Madoc watched the dark clouds overhead. The storm was close. He looked into the glinting black eyes of the chief, whose broken nose was red and swollen. He took a long slow breath. He made himself speak slowly in a clear voice to explain his proposal as though the chief and his people could understand every word he said. He glanced at the two big cranes. Each stood quiet, except the one on the right dipped his beak up and down once in a while. Madoc thought that was a sure sign from Brett. He pointed to the head-bobbing crane and then to himself. He said that his healer, he pointed to Conlaf, who held up a delicate, thin, leaf-shaped metal knife and a vial of black salve, would relieve the thick scars on the backs of the chief's knees and take away the pain. Conlaf rubbed the back of his own knees, walked around the chief,

and touched his scarred legs with his fingertips. He danced
a little jig, flexed his legs, and pointed to the chief's stiff
legs. He grimaced as though in pain, rubbed his legs, smiled
and took a deep breath, and pointed to his straight legs as
though he felt just fine. Then he pointed to the chief's bent
arm and waved his arm in the air showing how flexible an
arm could be. The silence was heavy. He pointed to the
crane he figured was Brett and crossed his arms across his
chest. *Maybe that fool chief will think the boy is mine*, he
thought. *That would be right! The lad is mine more than
his!*

The chief looked puzzled, breathed through his mouth,
and pointed to the puckery scars on the back of his legs,
then he pointed to Madoc's smooth, hairy legs. He limped
around Madoc, squinted one eye, and pointed to Conlaf.

Conlaf pulled up his trousers to show his unblemished
legs. He bent his knees and kept them stiff as he limped
like the king. He mimed the cutting of the scar tissue and
applying a healing salve. Then he held his breath, pointed
to Brett, opened the physician's box, and held his palm out
to the chief.

Nearby, Rabbit opened his mouth and said, "Aahh!" as
though he understood all of it, but he said nothing, only
looked like he had a bellyache.

Conlaf let out his breath as the chief picked up one of
the small steel knives and tested the sharp edge with his
thumb. The skin parted in an instant and a bead of blood
grew on the chief's thumb.

Conlaf drew in his breath and did his best to keep the
open box steady. One swipe of the chief's hand could cut
the throats of both himself and Madoc. The chief's black,
beady eyes were wide. He pricked his other thumb. Thunder rumbled so loud that the earth seemed to vibrate. He
smiled and pressed his thumb against Conlaf's forehead,
leaving a round, red print. He turned his back to the two
men and had a conversation with Rabbit, who crossed his
arms on his chest like Madoc had done. His face turned
sad, and he pointed to Madoc, and then to himself, then to
each of the boy cranes. The chief looked disgusted and
slashed his hand through the air as though cutting off the
conversation.

Madoc, fearing that the chief was going to limp away, drew moist air into his lungs, jigged here and there, and said in a clear, loud voice, "Brett! Hop like this, so we know 'tis you! Be quick!" The crane on the right bobbed its head. Two breaths later, the crane on the left hopped, and right away they were both jigging. Madoc smiled and his heart danced. The crane that bobbed its head was Brett. He just knew it. He looked around the green court for a place to escape. Time was short.

The chief turned and his eyes glistened. He tried to grin, but his broken nose was too painful. He cackled and pressed his bloody thumb against Madoc's forehead. His knees were bent, but still he towered above Madoc. He pointed to the crane on the right who was now clacking his wooden beak. Madoc put his index finger alongside the chief's and together they marked the air above the right crane. Lightning flashed pink and thunder rumbled loud. The chief lurched backwards and opened his hand to expose one small, metal-bladed knife taken from Conlaf's surgical box, kept in his leather bag. The knife dropped as if his hand had run into a patch of nettles. His palm was cut and bleeding. He marked the mask of the bobbing crane with his bloody hand and led the boy to the grassy seats, where he pointed out that Madoc and Conlaf were to be seated with their boy crane. He went back, picked up the knife, and handed it to Conlaf as if it were part of a rehearsed performance.

The crowd remained dead quiet because this was something new. The chief held his hurting nose, breathed through his mouth, and with his bloody hand waving in the air, gave a loud howl. It was the signal for the ceremony to begin. The crowd exploded with hand-clapping approval.

Feeling lighthearted, Madoc pushed the crane down between himself and Conlaf on the wide, grassy seats. Conlaf put the precious little knife back in the box. He could not remember the chief taking it, or even noticing it was gone. *That is a first class thief*, he thought.

Madoc grimaced at the bloodied feather mask Brett wore and whispered that he was proud to be next to someone who acted like a man, even while encased in feathers. Brett did not laugh. "This is life," said Madoc. "No matter how

bad times become, they are not so bad as they might be."
Brett's beak opened and closed. Madoc's heart soared and
he smiled. He told Brett he would be plucked as soon as
they hit the trail for the ships. Brett made a guttural sound,
and Madoc said, "You do not have to act like a big crane
with us." He exchanged a glance with Conlaf and put his
arm across the boy's shoulder.

XIX
Brett

The fate of captives among the Southeastern Indians varied immensely. Sometimes they were adopted and treated exactly as blood kinsmen, sometimes they were put in a precarious and uncertain position of a "slave," and sometimes they were tortured to death in a most horrible manner. . . . The Calusas [Gulf coast to Florida] are reported to have sacrificially killed one prisoner each year as a "propitiatory" offering.
—Charles Hudson, *The Southeastern Indians*

Cougar thought, *I might be crazy, but not necessarily stupid. I am not afraid. I am in the shelter of Pale Hair, and he is going to bring Nohold here. What then? I do not even know what is happening in my old village. What will Chief Wren do when he finds I am here, alive? He is the person I fear. What will he do when he finds Little Mother? What will happen to her? Who will take care of her?*

The questions without answers were overwhelming and endless. She felt the texture of the blankets that surrounded her. They were soft and light, easier to lie under than hides or woven strips of plant fiber. She felt the pallet underneath and discovered that inside the covering were many dried leaves, wider and thinner than reeds. She liked the smell of them and the way they rustled when she moved. Her eyes closed, and she wondered where Little Mother and Ibis had gone. She could see Chief Wren wandering over the sandy place after the dagger had flown into her back. She was thankful that it was not covered with fish poison. The Calusa used poison to kill fish, not people. However, things were different now that Wren was chief. He did not always do things the Calusa way. He had copied the Tequesta and

filed his front teeth into sharp points and taught the men to
believe face, limb, and body mutilations were beautiful. He
killed the baby boys for fear one or more of them could
eventually take his powerful authority away.

*He kicked me, believing I was dead and intending to
leave my body to the crows and scavengers. Has he come
back to look for my body and found it gone? Did he remember he had given it to the Dark Hair? Did he think
Dark Hair was a scavenger? Well, he is wrong. Dark Hair
tended my wound as gentle as a woman healer and gave
me a place to sleep. Dark Hair has a funny, dark, furry
face. He speaks in breezy whispers. I listened to him carefully and found out the names of things. I already know
Pale Hair is called Madoc, which sounds like two branches
scraping together in the wind. Is Chief Wren angry with
Little Mother and Ibis? Did he plan to bury me deep inside
the earth or cut my body in little pieces and give them to
the ever-hungry Sacred Fire to eat? The questions are endless.*

She opened her eyes and wondered why she did not
show the strangers how to mound up the earth to look like
a fresh grave. Wren would not look for her if he thought
she was in a grave. She sat up. The man who had come to
look after her was gone. She pushed the blankets together
to look as though she was still sleeping and climbed over
the side of the ship. The rope ladder did not reach the water
at low tide, so she jumped. She hoped no one saw the
splash. She swam ashore then ran to the place where she
was certain she had fallen with the dagger between her
shoulders. Quickly she pushed sand over the seagrass and
made a large mound. She put stones around the outside of
the mound and pink-and-white shells over the top. She sat
quietly a moment, listened, and heard only the swish of the
sea. She was certain Little Mother had not followed Ibis
home to Wren. She thought she knew where Little Mother
would go. Fog was beginning to roll off the sea to the land.
It was hard to see around Nohold's lodge.

She called softly. No one answered and she went inside.
The room felt larger than before. No, that could not be.
There was hardly anything left in the room, only the
smooth, dirt floor. There were coals glowing in the central

fire and a scattering of driftwood. "Yu!" She stubbed her
toes on a couple of logs against the wall. She poked the
fire with a stick to stir up a flame and looked around. There
were no pallets for sleeping, no clothing hanging on the
sticks woven into the grass-lined walls. A couple of empty
food bags hung in their place, but nothing else. *Nohold had
moved out. Where did he go? So, was Little Mother with
him? Where was Ibis?*

Outside she smelled damp earth and crushed grass in the
fog. She shivered and wondered who or what crushed the
grass. She tried to see what was moving in the darkness.
She heard whisperings and smelled smoke. Or was it the
smell of Dark Hair's blankets that still clung to her? No, it
was live smoke from wood and grass. Something was burning! She saw orange, hungry flames coming through the
walls at the front of Nohold's place.

*Good Spirits! Help me! Believe me! I did not start a fire
inside Nohold's place when I stirred the ash. I saw no
sparks spread to the scattered drift. Oh, I should have put
the drift in a pile against the wall!*

She turned to go back inside. She stopped when she
heard someone cough and looked around for a place to
hide. There was only grass close to the lodge. The fire was
spreading from the small poles in the walls to the grass
roof.

She ran into a small buttonwood whose branches were
asymmetrical. She grabbed a branch thick enough to hold
her weight. It was cold, damp, and peeling, but solid. She
pulled herself up and almost cried out because of the sharp
pain between her shoulders. She tried to ignore the pain in
her frenzy to climb higher. She tried not to imagine how
the wound had opened and was probably gushing with
blood. She grasped the next branch to pull herself higher,
but it swung down with her weight. She felt for another
branch and found one covered with twigs full of leaves.
She clambered onto it and lay on her belly. She was in a
perfect position to watch the ground under the tree. She
inched backwards until she felt the tree's trunk. She pushed
herself up so that she could either straddle the branch or
pull her feet up and sit with her shoulder against the trunk.
Sparks rose from the roof of the lodge, but with no wind

there was no reason to worry that the tree would be in trouble. She looked above and saw the dark crisscross of branches. Beyond them tiny orange sparks flew up and died in the darkness. Clinging to the trunk with one hand, she leaned forward and felt her back. Satisfied that the bandage was in place and dry, she gritted her teeth and sat back, wishing the terrible pain to go away. Something crawled across her bare foot. She thought of beetles, spiders, and scorpions. She wiggled her foot, drew it up, and slapped at whatever was there. She rubbed her cold foot and pulled up the other foot to rub. Her legs felt better when they were perched on the branch for a while. To keep from falling, she hung tight to the tree trunk. She heard the snapping of twigs in the brush away from the lodge. She imagined the noises were Chief Wren and a couple of his subchiefs who had come earlier to get Nohold and anyone else asleep in the lodge. Wren would be angry when he found the lodge cleaned out, so he would destroy it with fire.

How fortunate I am that Chief Wren did not find me, she thought and lifted one corner of her mouth into a smile.

The bright, hungry flames crackled, shrieked, crashed, roared, and hissed as they licked their way through Nohold's place. The roof fell, roaring louder than a waterfall. The noise startled her and made her cling tighter to the tree. She marveled at the beauty of the sparks that spewed into the air looking like fireflies. She closed her eyes and could see the sparks for a long time behind her lids. Maybe she dozed a little. After that, all she saw was a low circle of fire and heard the hissing it made as it crept along damp grass.

She thought Wren was hiding in the grass hoping that Nohold would come back when it was daylight. She imagined he was hiding and laughing at the surprise he had for Nohold. She thought she could hear him laugh. Then she thought, *What if Wren cleaned out the lodge after he took Nohold, Little Mother, and Ibis away? Where would he take them? What would he do with them?* It was the last question that she did not want to think about. She moved her leg and wondered if she could get out of the tree without making any noise. She sat back, shivered and ached, and berated herself for leaving Pale Hair's lodge. She imagined what could have happened to her if she had stayed. She leaned forward trying to see better. *Did I see someone go inside?* she asked herself. No, there was no one near. She asked herself if she had stayed in Madoc's lodge, would her back be so painful? She told herself no, and she would have learned who Pale Hair was and where he and his people came from. *I would have learned a handful of his strange words. It would have been my opportunity to get away from Wren but now I have missed it by worrying so much about Nohold and Little Mother. Should I be worrying about Ibis? Of course, I should. Wren might hurt her. Have I been wrong to leave my safe place with the strangers?*

If I could do it over, I would do the same, she thought. *My friends are in trouble. I have to help!* She closed her eyes and tried to relax, Her legs cramped and her back and arms were stiff. She thought she heard someone, something in the brush. The dripping fog brushed her cheeks and mixed with her tears. Her hair was wet. It was too dark to see anything but the dying flames around the perimeter of the lodge. Now everything was dead quiet. The swish-swash of the incoming tide was subdued by the low, heavy fog.

When the flames died to a rhythmic glow inside a few coals, they looked as if they were breathing. She slid over the branch she sat on and put her feet down on the next branch. She leaned over slowly, hanging on to the bottom branch, and began lowering herself to the ground, one leg at a time. She slipped, tumbled, skinned her knees and the heels of her hands, and twisted her back. Her legs trembled when she stood. She hung on to the tree. Light drizzle was falling, but it did not bother her because she had more important things to look after.

Nohold's lodge was dead. No flames were inside, only the red, hot coals. A couple of tongues of orange strong enough to survive the drizzle's mist flicked outside in the grass. She kicked sand on the flames. In the center of the lodge floor over the fire pit were two crossed hickory logs, black, smoking, and hot enough to burn her flesh. Someone had put them there after she had left! So, maybe she had heard someone. The hickories were the crossed logs of a Sacred Fire, which is started in order to eat the ghostly soul out of a haunted lodge. No smell, sight, or sound of the lodge's ghost would be left after a Sacred Fire. *Nohold would do that to his lodge to distract Wren!* she told herself. *So, he had been here!* She wanted to run through the smoke and hot ash to find him and ask about Little Mother and Ibis. She wanted to cry out, but she calmed herself and walked slowly around the blackened edge of the lodge and through the singed, wet grass. When her feet were really wet, she went over the edge and through the inside ash that was already cooling with the dampness on top, but still fiercely hot underneath. She kicked hot, little ash heaps, but uncovered nothing. She hurried to cool her blackened bare feet in the wet grass. The fire had left nothing. Only the crossed logs, hunks of charcoal, and ash showed that this lodge had once been a living thing.

Gone, same as my past, she thought. *Sandpoint is so changed that it has nothing of Grandmother, Egret, or Otter. The first part of my life is ended, wiped out.* The black, acrid fumes of the ash were distasteful and she coughed. *When Chief Wren and his men do come to rout out Nohold and kill whoever is hiding with him, they will find no one. Yu! I would like to see the looks on their faces,* she thought. She walked back to the space where the lodge had been.

The space seemed much smaller than when it had high walls. Shivering and aching, she could not make herself step through the hot ash again. She could not withhold a cry and let it spill out in a hoarse whisper. "Nohold! Nohold!" she said over and over. Her back hurt, so she lay on the damp grass. She tucked her legs up tight against her belly and held her arms against her chest, her fingers clasped the multicolored bead necklace around her neck. She meant to rest only a moment. Behind closed eyes she saw herself running to Pale Hair's lodge on the water.

She thought of Grandmother poking through the huge pile of drift. It was now gone to make way for a stone with the likeness of Chief Wren carved on its face. Grandmother took home a strange baby girl she found under the drift. It was always a comfort to be with Grandmother and later to learn they were truly related. She wept for the love and security Grandmother had given her. She thanked Grandmother every day for not forcing her head on a cradleboard.

Grandmother had not lain in a cradleboard either, so their heads were not misshapen. She thought, *If the Calusa really looked at the pale-faced strangers, they would see how handsome people could be without sloped foreheads.* She wept for the lessons and knowledge she had learned from Egret, the finest grandfather she knew. She wept for Little Mother, her unborn child, and Otter, who had had no chance to become a man. He would have been as fine a man as Egret if he had lived. She wept for Hyacinth and Owl, who would not let themselves believe that she was their true daughter. In their mind their daughter was still a baby, two summers old. She wept for Healer, the only kin left who loved and accepted her as herself. She wept for Ibis, who knew not the delights and wonders of living in the old Sandpoint, before Wren became a murderous, dictatorial chief. She wept from pain, exhaustion, and the knowledge that nothing would be the same the moment she stood up or a new day dawned.

The sound of voices awakened her. The sun had not come up from the horizon yet, but the night sky was fading and showed only a thin layer of fog. She was stiff and her back still ached. She remembered she did not want to be found by Wren and made into a sacrifice to some needy god. She crouched in the grass.

She saw Nohold. He no longer wore the woman's skirt she had given him. He wore moccasins and leather breeches and a shirt made of the same kind of soft material she had felt in Black Hair's blankets. Nohold looked to be a younger, stronger person. He was scraping sand to put out a little fire that ran through the grass. Little Mother, Ibis, and two strange men also scraped sand on small patches of fire. She understood what they were doing. They wanted to stop the fire from spreading to the Sandpoint village. *Yu! Good!* They had burned the lodge so that Chief Wren would look no farther for his wife, Ibis, and Nohold. *So, where were they going to go? Of course! They would go to Pale Hair's lodge with her.*

Ibis saw her. "Why are you here? Is your back healed?"

"I came to get all of you to come with me to Pale Hair's lodge," said Cougar.

"I like you," said Ibis. "I will remember all of you. You have not seen me. I am sleeping in my lodge, waiting for my man to tell me it is time to get the morning fire started." She put her arms around Cougar. "Oh, you smell like smoke! Me, too! I shall start the morning fire so my man will scold and call me stupid for squatting in the smoke. I came to warn Nohold that Chief Wren was going to burn his lodge. When I found Nohold, he had already started his own fire, and I found Little Mother with him. Then the three of us found these two men, called Conn and Clare, who were looking for Nohold's place because you told them to bring him to you. Cougar, when you came, things really got mixed up around here. I tried to warn the Pale Haired one, during our Celebration of Blessings for Health, but he may not have understood. I believe what you said, that he is good. Go with him. Take care of Nohold and Little Mother. You have to leave before sunup, before the village awakens. Wren will come here first thing." Ibis turned and left without making a sound as she ran barefoot through the wet grass.

Cougar put her arms around Little Mother. Then she went to Nohold, took his pine stick with a thick branch of needles on the end, and swept around the back side of the burned area and under the buttonwood. "Ibis is right," she whispered. "We have to hurry. Wren will be here looking for you as soon as the sun shows his face. Let Wren think we are all ghosts." She showed Clare how to sweep the sand to wipe out their footprints and then throw the stick among the pines so that it looked like ordinary windfall.

Clare thought that Cougar was a real spunky girl and smiled while shaking his finger at her. She knew he would not scold her with his funny-sounding talk, like the sound of wind whistling through the tall trees.

Clare took Nohold and Cougar in his coracle. Conn took Little Mother in his coracle, saying she was really the same as two. She understood his meaning and smiled. He twirled the little craft around and around, and she clung to the sides as if she was in a water spout that was going to rise out of the sea any moment. When they reached the ship, Conn and Clare learned that no one had left with the four horses Madoc had asked for. The men were afraid the horses were not strong enough to carry them, and they were still debating what to do.

Little Mother was afraid to go up the ladder, climb over the gunwale, and slip to the deck. The smell caused her to hold her nose. When she saw more men with round heads, beards, and the skinny cows, she screamed, thinking they were all ferocious beasts that never cleaned themselves. Nohold stood stiff, afraid to move in front of the strange beasts. Cougar tried to tell them not to mind the smell. The beasts were enclosed so they would not hurt anyone. "They do look funny, but not ferocious." She said the round-headed men with hair on their faces were all right. They just had no women to pull the hair out for them. Little Mother wanted to start removing the beards right away. She thought it was something the men expected the women to do. The men ignored her babbling. Instead, she and Nohold were given pallets to sleep on. Cougar pulled her pallet close to her friends and assured them that everything was all right. When Little Mother and Nohold saw her calm and fearless attitude, they felt better and were asleep in a few minutes.

Gerard from the *Gray Wolf* called to Kabyle on the *Vestri* and told him that his horses were ready to go to Madoc and Conlaf as soon as possible. "Lead the poor, weak, underfed beasts. No man can ride them! 'Twill take someone who weighs next to naught to ride any one." In his mind he thought of the small, barbarian lass he had heard was on Madoc's ship.

On Madoc's ship, Brian and another messmate had their dark heads bent over the sleeping barbarians to have a better look. They argued between themselves about all three being women. No one seemed muscular enough to be a man. One extremely thin person had a bony face, large feet, only one hand, and a wide jaw that seemed out of place for a woman. This person wore strange leather trousers and a tattered linen shirt. When Brian reached out to push the hair from the bony face, Nohold put his one hand across his mouth and made a funny, deep-throated, crying sound and looked around like a frightened animal. He did not like these ghostly, pale, dark-haired youths peering down at him. He said something the boys did not get, waved his stumpy arm with no hand, and looked at Clare.

Clare said, "Lads, where is your judgment? Stand back. No one likes to be stared at."

Brian said, "We do not have any judgment about her. We just wanted more information."

"*Her* is a *him*, wearing my shirt because he was cold in the rain," said Clare. "He suffers from lack of food and may be related to the wounded lass. He has made signs to indicate that the wounded lass fed him. But look at him. Starvation is his middle name. Your job is to put some fat under his skin. The lass, bulging with child, is the wife of the village king, whose name is Wren. She is afraid of Wren, her husband. I know not why. What I know is that we have stepped in the middle of a family quarrel. I pray these three people are kept safe, and no barbarian comes aboard awarring. We might learn something new from these three."

Clare had understood Little Mother's distaste for the cow pen and cleaned it out after he made sure that Cougar's bandage was still tight and not bleeding. While shoveling the dung off the deck, he asked Cougar, with hand signs, why she was not afraid of him or the other men.

She told him that through her dreams she knew Pale Hair and his people were good. She seemed to think they were ghostly spirits. Her words and hand signs puzzled Clare. How could she already know Madoc and believe he was some kind of spirit? To find out what she was talking about, he had to learn her language. He sat on the pallet beside Cougar and asked if she had ever ridden horseback. She did not understand; she had never seen a horse. He took her to the beach and showed her four thin, gangly horses. She held her breath when he got on the back of one. When he got off, he asked if she would like to ride one. If he could, she thought she could, but it was a scary thing to do. She had never seen anyone ride on the back of a beast with four legs. Clare hung onto the rope that he put around the horse's neck and walked it slowly along the damp sand on the beach. After a while, Cougar had more confidence and Clare gave Cougar the end of the rope. She seemed delighted and dug her bare heels into the horse's sides so that it began to walk in circles. "Good!" cried Clare. "You learn fast! Madoc will like that."

"Good!" cried Cougar with delight. "Yu!"

Clare talked to Kabyle, who stood in awe watching this good-looking barbarian lass ride a horse for the first time in her life. She was no longer afraid, but was unabashed and having a good time. "She will be the best help we can send Madoc," said Kabyle. "She can talk to those people for him and bring Brett and Troyes back. Allah is on our side this night." He stood beside the horse and patted its nose as he tried to tell her that she was going to bring the man and boy back here where they belonged.

She understood that Madoc and Dark Hair, called Conlaf, were trying to bring back the boy with the fiery hair and the man with black waves in his hair. She was going to explain to the chief that the two were not gifts. She tried to tell this man, who made his head look big by wrapping it in a pink cloud, that the chief had tried to kill her, and she did not want to talk to him.

"Talk to him while sitting on the back of the horse," said Kabyle. "That will scare your chief. You show him who is boss!"

Cougar asked about that word, *boss*. Kabyle explained it was the person with the best words, the power.

"Aye! And so, I am boss," she said, "Wren hears me. Wren gives back his gifts. Wren is a bloody thief! Madoc is smiling."

Clare found some warm clothing for the girl to wear.

The drizzle held the dust in place when the breeze came in gusts. The gathered barbarians set up a cacophony of squawking. Madoc scarcely heard the noise or saw that the second crane's three-toed feet were tied to the bottom two corners of the pole frame, and his little, painted-white hands were tied around the top corners of the frame. Madoc was filled with thanksgiving, because Brett was sitting beside him and not spread out on the pole frame.

The puny arms of the crane on the frame were covered with feathered bracelets. The fine misty rain plastered the bracelets and feathered anklets against his skinny limbs. The wind blew his cape open, showing a thin, scratched-raw, red chest and the pearl necklace. Madoc wanted to take the barbarian lad off that flimsy wood frame, but this was a different place with different people with different ideas. He remembered what he had learned from Llieu when he was a small boy: "The story of mankind is half about education and half about catastrophe." He could not figure out the knowledge these people had or the catastrophic mistakes they were making. And he dared not make his feelings known. The incoming fog and light drizzle depressed him. He wished he had his rain gear when the mist collected and ran down his neck. He looked at Brett and wondered if his feathers were mildewing next to his skin. He looked for the bloody hand print on the mask and decided the misty rain had washed it off.

The palsied subchief, Blackbird, ruffled the feathers on the bracelets, anklets, and cap so that the framed crane looked like some grand prize.

A scantily dressed young woman gave Chief Wren a staff with a long-beaked bird carved on the head. The staff's shank was unusually wide at the bottom. Chief Wren leaned on the staff for a while with his head bowed, his mouth open, and his nose dripping blood. The broken nose was giving him a lot of pain. He finally minced around the spread-eagled crane and ruefully handed the staff to Wolf, another subchief, who gave it to Blackbird.

Madoc's uneasiness refused to be shaken off. He thought about the healing trial that Conlaf had proposed. He wished it were done.

Conlaf asked, "What are the barbarians up to?"

Madoc shook his head.

Chief Wren stood behind the wet, bedraggled crane and held the staff over its head.

"Is he casting charms?" said Madoc uncertainly. "I wish that boy crane was not there. Are he and Brett the only young boys around? There is something spooky about the way Rabbit, the long-eared subchief, hangs around the lad on the frame. I be inclined to believe the lad is his son, who has been saved for this special purpose, whatever it may be. Do you think we are seeing some kind of annual ritual? Something to pacify one of their gods or what?"

A piercing cry flew from Rabbit's throat as Chief Wren

brought the staff down on the head of the boy crane. The blow sounded like a large gourd being thrown against a flat rock. "Placht!" The crane's feather mask lay in pieces on the wet ground. The crane's head lay over the left, crushed shoulder. One jaw was pushed up beside his bloody nose, giving him a grisly smile. Wolf walked around the frame and kicked the boy on the back, making his head bounce crazily. The crowd went mad with screams.

Madoc's stomach became upset. He had to turn away before the nausea became so great that he would have to heave in front of Brett. He could not believe the brutality. Druid logic told him that these people believed in living above pain. It was unseemly to show pain. But this was an appalling show of sacrificial violence by a man to a child. It was so far beyond brutality that it had no name.

Chief Wren's face was hard as stone, but the expression in his eyes was triumphant when he gave the staff to Blackbird and put his hands on the mangled shoulders of the sacrificial lad. The drumbeat was slow and muted. Chief Wren held cupped hands out to the misty rain. He licked the cool water, and his wet face showed satisfaction as if a terrible thirst had been slacked, or he felt the rain god was happy.

Madoc imagined the child was the yearly gift that propitiated the rainmaker, who sent the refreshing water when most needed, at the end of the long winter. The rhythm of the seasons was crucial to all living things. He saw the agony on Rabbit's wet face and thought, *What does the lad's mother feel?*

Chief Wren held his face to the gray sky to catch the mist. He was more bulky than he had been in his youth, and the bulk was held together with thick sinew and muscle. His scarred face was rough and dark as tree bark. His eyes were brown and hard as hickory nuts.

Blackbird whacked the lad's mangled face once more, spreading droplets of blood, brains, and broken bones on himself. He wiped a hand over his face, laid the bloody club on the bloody, wet earth, and gave the chief, who had proved himself strong enough to make the first death-strike, a long-suffering look of pity.

The staccato drumbeat was louder. The barbarians

whooped and hollered. They swarmed like ants on a bucket of honey. They were all over the center square, pushing and shoving in their scramble to get near the dead lad. They clawed and tore at his stained feathers, as if they were some kind of sacred relics. They elbowed the chief, who tried to stay his ground, a necessity to show who was stronger. In the tough and tumble scuffle, the chief was pushed down and his hand covered his throbbing nose. His head was kicked and his legs walked on. The villagers' voices became louder, seeming to indicate that the village was stronger than the chief. To Madoc it looked like the villagers had one and only one thought in mind now, to grab a feather from the costume of the sacrificed lad. Wolf stood over the pitiful body peeling the bloody skin inside out, up over the head and down the broken jawbone.

Both Madoc and Conlaf were sickened by the sounds they called *primitive* and sights they named *horrible* and *too violent* for civilized beings. It was a working up of a people's spirit and had no meaning for them except revulsion. Madoc turned away again and shielded Brett from the savage spectacle. The chanting village men followed Blackbird, who carried his bloody trophy, the sacrificed lad's feet, into the village's main hall, the council hut.

The drumming ceased and the silence was deafening.

Dozens of women and children surrounded the grisly dead lad. They poked pointed sticks at the body, the peeled head, and skinless face. They made gouges in the red flesh. They grabbed at the remaining straggly feathers.

A couple of women wiped raindrops and blood spatters off their children's faces, then swatted them, and grabbed for their sticks to whack at dogs that nipped at the dead youth's fly-covered flesh.

Madoc spied the forgotten Chief Wren, facedown on the muddy ground. He took Brett's hand. They pushed their way past the women and children. Conlaf followed, kicked a mangy dog, and knelt beside the bruised and forgotten chief.

Conlaf saw more dark clouds on the horizon and said, "Get this man to his house. More rain is coming." He pulled Chief Wren to his feet so that he could hobble between himself and Madoc.

Chief Wren gritted his teeth, determined not to show these strangers that he felt any kind of physical pain.

Brett seemed to know his way around the village and took them to a grassy lodge, pushed aside the door-flap, and went down the earthen steps to the one large room.

When Madoc's eyes became accustomed to the darkness, he nodded to two women sitting together on a fur-covered bench, eating and sewing. They jumped up, embarrassed to be caught eating in front of men. Madoc again recognized one of the women when she smoothed the furs on a sleeping bench. She was the one he had seen first behind the woman who was wounded, and seen again when they were given food. He nodded and she said, "Madoc," as clear as a blue sky.

Brett made a slashing motion with his thumb. The women put their hands over their mouths and fled outside with Brett following them. Madoc called and motioned for Brett to come back, but he sat on the steps and did not come down to the floor. "Wait right there for us," said Madoc. "Who is the lass that spoke my name? I want to talk with her." He waved his hands toward the door-flap.

Brett shrugged.

"Where are the others that were with her when the woman was hit with the dagger?"

Brett shrugged.

Madoc was distracted by fresh flames flickering in a stone-lined firepit in the center of the dirt floor. Opposite the door was a split-log bench covered with fur robes where the chief lay moaning softly with his mouth open gulping in air. Skin and feather clothes hung on wooden pegs above the bench.

Conlaf wiped rain from his face, hands, and arms on his shirt then wiped the chief's face. "First fix the broken nose," he said, pulling a leather pouch from his physician's bag tied to his waist. He told Madoc to heat water for tea. Madoc could not find a kettle or pot. Brett went outside and brought in the woman Madoc had said he wanted to talk with.

She pointed to a clay bowl beside the stones at the fire-pit. Madoc gave her the pouch containing dried leaves.

She smelled the leaves, understood, and went outside with the bowl.

When she opened the door-flap, there was enough light for Madoc to see a naked baby girl tied immobile to a cradleboard on the other sleeping bench. The baby's head was held in a triangular space made by boards that kept her forehead flattened. Her eyes were pushed to the sides of her face, like a horse.

That made Madoc wonder if his men with the horses would find the right trail. He was sure that Brett would tell him if anything unusual came up the brow of the hill. Anyway, it was not dark yet.

The woman came back. Her dark hair was in wet strings from a drizzly rain shower, and the bowl was full of water. She set it on a warm stone, pulled wood from a basket, and built up the fire. Her eyes glinted in the firelight, and she put a pinch of the dried-leaf mix into the water. After a few moments, she stirred it with her finger, licked the finger, and added another pinch of mix. She smiled, pointed to herself, and drew a picture of a long-legged water bird with a slender, curved bill.

"Ibis," said Madoc, thinking about the curved bill on that water bird, which made it distinctive. She smiled and he felt a tingle up and down his backbone. *Maybe I can communicate with these people. Maybe we can get along.* He wondered what was similar in the barbarians' superstition and the druids' truth. He motioned for her to help him move the chief's bench closer to the door and for her to fasten the door-flap open so that Conlaf could see better.

Conlaf rummaged through the wood basket and found two tiny sticks that suited him. He put a salve along both sides of the chief's nose, placed the sticks on the sticky salve, and pushed. There was a grating sound and then the nose was back in its original shape.

The chief kept his eyes closed and groaned.

Madoc pointed to the chief, and Ibis drew a small bird in the dirt.

"Wren," said Madoc.

"Wren," said Ibis. She pointed to Conlaf.

"Physician," said Conlaf.

"Fizz-ish-on," said Ibis.

Madoc laughed and said, "Conlaf, the Healer."

"Conlaf," said Ibis, breathing through her mouth and making guttural sounds. Then she drew three stick figures in the earth. There were two women, one with a large belly, and one man. Around the figures she drew a ship with a sail that looked like a lone wing.

Madoc studied the picture for a long time figuring what it might mean. "I think she is telling me that we have three barbarians on board the *Gwennan Gorn,*" he said finally.

There was talking outside the door. Ibis erased the drawing with her bare foot and stood next to Conlaf as if interested in what he was doing to the chief.

The other woman, who was there when the chief came in, came back and stood beside Ibis. Wolf and Blackbird hobbled through the hide-door, showing they were old friends. Wolf flailed his arms and struck at the unnamed women with his fists so that he alone could stand close to Conlaf to see what was happening.

Ibis put two fingers together to show that they were man and woman, husband and wife. Then she pointed to Chief Wren and put two fingers together.

So, Ibis is Chief Wren's wife, Madoc thought and with loud words he told Wolf not to strike any woman, even if she was his wife, and to stand back because the physician needed more room.

Wolf hung his head over Conlaf's shoulder. Conlaf winked at Madoc and raised his shoulder quickly. Wolf's teeth knocked together so that he bit his tongue. Madoc held his breath, thinking there would be a confrontation, but Wolf picked up his baby girl and made gurgling noises close to her ear while he stood well away from Conlaf, who whistled between his teeth to ease his nervousness.

The women smiled behind their hands, and Ibis whispered, "Fuzz-on Conlaf."

Conlaf packed wadmal over the sticks around the chief's nose. He put a piece of thin hide across the nose to hold the sticks and wadmal in place, pulled it over and under the ears, and with Madoc's help tied it securely in the back of the chief's head.

Blackbird watched every move.

Conlaf was sure that Blackbird was a healer. He held

some tea in a little beaker to the chief's lips. Blackbird stepped in and took the beaker and sipped first, then nodded his head to the women who took turns sipping and smacking their lips. Finally the chief raised himself, took the clay beaker of tea, and emptied it. Conlaf said, "Get them out of here! There will not be enough tea to keep this man groggy while I repair his legs!"

Madoc stepped back and looked around to give himself time to think. He held his nose and pointed to the baby.

The women put their hands over their mouths as if to cover their embarrassment. One of them cuffed the baby, so she cried, for soiling the cradle board. Ibis pulled the cradle board off the bench, buzzed and clucked as she fussed over the clean up.

Conlaf fed the chief a few more sips of tea. The two women took the baby out of the cradle board and put her in the big clay bowl and carried her outdoors. They were gone for some time. When they came back, the baby's fingernails were blue and she was shivering, but clean. They put clean moss in the bottom of the cradle board, tied her back inside, and the women took turns nursing her. When she cried, they pinched her lips together so that she had to breathe through her nose and could not suck in enough air to cry, only mewl.

Conlaf gave more tea to the chief and a little clay cup of salve to Blackbird to hold while he rolled the chief over on his belly. Madoc held the chief's head to the side, so he would not lie on his broken nose. Conlaf rubbed salve over the chief's scarred left leg. He held the blade of one of the metal knives above the pink, puckered flesh and pressed down. He used his thumb on the bone handle to control the cutting depth.

Conlaf said he needed water. Madoc waved his hand to attract attention. He pointed to the big bowl the baby had been in and made pouring motions with his hands. Ibis nodded and took the bowl outside. Soon she was back with cold water. Conlaf took his shirt off the chief, soaked it in the water, wrung it out, and soaked up oozing blood from the chief's leg. The chief moaned and his eyes opened and crossed. Madoc had to put his knees on the chief's arms to keep them from whipping here and there. Wolf put his knee on the chief's left leg. When the chief moaned again, Blackbird said, "Yu," pushed Madoc out of the way, and rubbed some of the salve he held on the chief's right leg before Conlaf cut through the scar tissue.

Blackbird leered at Madoc, pushed at a slight bulge in his leather shirt, and thrust out his lower lip. Impulsively, Madoc put his hand inside Blackbird's shirt. He prayed he would not touch something wet and slimy or put his hand in the mouth of a snake. He pulled out his own linen shirt. "Yahoo!" he said and thumped Blackbird on the back.

"Tear your shirt into strips, put astringent on the bleeding, then salve, push the flesh together, and wrap the strips tight around the right leg," said Conlaf.

Madoc tore his shirt into strips. Blackbird took off his feather cap, put it on the chief's head, scratched his head with one finger, and pulled his lips back into a grin.

"Keep the bloody feathers out of here!" yelled Conlaf. "Lugh's luck will have these legs healed. But feathers can take the luck out of healing!" He threw the cap across the room.

"Yu!" said Wolf.

Blackbird held his sides and shouted, "Lugh!"

The women grinned.

It was almost dark outside, and Conlaf said something about no light.

Madoc made a torch with a couple of sticks of wood and a hunk of tar he found in Conlaf's leather bag. He kept it away from the walls and roof of the hut, but held it where it would help Conlaf see to finish the operation.

Blackbird smiled when Conlaf again gave him the salve to hold while he straightened both the chief's legs and had Wolf hold them flat. Conlaf rubbed an astringent on the left leg to stop the bleeding. He put more salve on the fresh cut, pushed the flesh together, and bandaged the leg tightly. He tried to explain to Blackbird and Wolf that the chief would walk without a limp in a few weeks, but he was not sure the men understood his words or gestures. Madoc turned the chief over on his back. Conlaf cut the scarred tissue on the chief's bent arm, straightened the arm, treated it with astringent and salve, and tied it against the chief's side. He reached for the salve to put in his bag. Blackbird held the clay cup to his chest and would not give it back.

"Leave him be," said Madoc. "He is the healer for his village. He will tell his people that he is the one that holds the magic that made their chief walk without a limp, straightened his arm, and put his nose together. He will be important. He does not want to lose favor to us, the strangers."

Conlaf understood.

Blackbird scratched the lumps on his neck and put his hand into the physician's box. When his hand came out, it held the lid to the clay cup. He stuck his tongue out for emphasis, pulled his bone knife from the waist of his breechclout, and whacked it into the earthen floor, barely missing Conlaf's foot.

The women again were taking turns nursing the baby, who was covered with a square of soft leather. They grinned and put their hands over their eyes.

" 'Tis time to get out of here," said Madoc. "You cannot leave any understandable instructions. You will have to believe you did something decent for a barbarian."

Conlaf cleaned his knives in the bowl of bloody water, wiped them on scraps from Madoc's shirt, and put them in the box. The chief moaned. Conlaf motioned for Blackbird to give him another cup of tea.

Blackbird drank half the tea himself and gave the rest to Wolf.

"Both men will soon be too sleepy to look after the chief," whispered Conlaf. "That will get them out of the way so the women can care for their chief." He pointed to the women, to the tea, and to the chief.

The women giggled. Ibis put a fistful of tea leaves in her hand.

Conlaf found his damp, bloody shirt in Wolf's hands and left it.

Brett was not on the steps. Outside there was a feeling of heaviness in the cool air. It had been a long day. Both men were worn down to a dull, aching fatigue. There was fog in the lowland where the lake was, and Conlaf remarked about its beauty.

Madoc thought it mysterious and disturbing and preferred to look at the stars and quarter moon between the moving bunches of ground fog. He listened for the sound of horses' hoofs or familiar singing along the trail. He heard the whirring of countless insects and the croaking of pond frogs. He looked for Brett to come running after them. He was put out with the lad for not staying on the steps. Where could he be? He worried about the lad's safety.

The two men walked behind the council hall to the trail leading downhill looking for Brett. The grassy square in back of the hall was empty and quiet. Madoc suddenly had a queasy feeling in the pit of his stomach. He had no reason for his fear, but it was as menacing as uncouth savagery. Perhaps it was only that these people were so different in their customs, or perhaps the two of them were being watched. These villagers' way of life disturbed him. On the other hand, he and his men were the first people from the other side of the sea to disturb these inhabitants. He was too exhausted to say anything and knew Conlaf felt the same.

They walked back up the hill. The earth was muddy from the rain. There was enough starlight to see that a few women stood around the square frame. The mangled body of the dead lad was gone. But held out toward the two men, between two giggling women, was a big, shabby crane jumping up and down on muddy three-toes, with the hind toe elevated.

"Lugh's blood!" said Madoc, running. "Brett, what happened? You look awful!" He looked at Conlaf and back at Brett. His heart skipped a beat. The women made clucking noises.

Brett's ugly mask and crane's cap were gone. When he jumped up and down, his red hair bounced from side to side.

For a moment Madoc wondered why his red hair was not wet like the women's, then he decided that the cap and mask had probably kept it dry. Brett's legs were no longer covered by feathered anklets. They were black with mud, rain streaked, and long red scars were visible. His face looked lopsided, but it was Brett's short, upturned nose. He grinned.

Madoc felt as if he had been in that dark hut with the

chief for days. He embraced the lad, who stood stiff as a board. He stared at the backs of Brett's brown hands that were scarred with healed white grooves. He pulled away and stared into unfamiliar dark, glinting eyes, full lips, and a high sloping forehead that did not belong to Brett at all. His heart jammed his throat.

The barbarian lad wore Brett's freckled facial skin like a tight mask. Brett's ears were cut out, and the holes were looped over the barbarian's ears. Brett's scalp of thick red hair was pulled over the barbarian's head and tied to his own dark hair. He made a hideous sound, and his clumsy bird feet squished in the mud. He held on to the feather apron and strutted.

Conlaf was stunned. He could not believe what his eyes told him. He shook the lad. "Brett, talk to me, lad! Do not play games," he said, feeling angry and foolish. The lad swaggered back to the grinning women.

"Oh, Lugh! What have I done?" Madoc's cry was anguish from a shattered heart turning to wild anger.

XX
Black Bog

Burial customs—the use of red ocher [hematite, anhydrous iron oxide, Fe_2O_3] . . . with the corpse, and the intentional breaking of grave goods—existed in the Southeast throughout the prehistoric period.
　　　　　　　　　—Charles Hudson, *The Southeastern Indians*

Madoc and Conlaf walked single file away from the sleeping village. Each man mulled through his own thoughts and sifted them through broken hearts. They went over and over the scenes of the two boy cranes and each time knew each would always have chosen the boy who bobbed his head. The boy nodded in the manner they each remembered Brett would do. That boy had to be Brett! Did the villagers know the difference between the two boys? Did Chief Wren know? Probably.

Madoc wondered what it was that Rabbit had tried to tell him. That moment when he seemed so sad—what did it mean? *Brett brought us hope, made us sing, gave us strength. He was so young. His death was vicious, grisly, and hideous beyond description, and for what purpose?* A breeze blew in his face cooling the sweat, making him cold and shivery.

"Brett was as brave as the bravest," said Conlaf and the fast-moving dark clouds rumbled their agreement.

"I want to kick, punch, and wring the neck of every barbarian," said Madoc. "I want to battle them until they are bloody dead!"

"When he died, he saved the life of the barbarian lad," said Conlaf. " 'Tis something a druid would do."

"How can you compare a barbarian to one of us?" Madoc was incredulous. "They do not think, nor talk like us. They believe in treachery. They scarify themselves."

"I think you know a human life, no matter who it belongs to, is the most magnificent creation ever created," said Conlaf. "If we had grown up here, we would think as the barbarians think. We misunderstand them and instead of body scars, we have blue markings, called honor marks, on our skin. We are proud of our honor marks, and they are proud of their scarification."

On the outskirts of the village the distraught men stumbled upon two old crones sitting around a cook-fire. Madoc was thirsty and pointed to a water bowl, then to his mouth. Both women shrugged their shoulders, went about their business of grappling red hot stones with two sticks, and dropping them into a large, finely woven basket that held water. He saw there were chunks of raw meat in the steaming water. Suddenly he cringed and pointed to a small, pale foot poling out of the basket. It had four toes. He had to turn away. His head swirled with nausea and his stomach rumbled.

The women smiled, looked at the dark sky, and pointed to a cluster of stars peeking out between broken clouds. They pointed to the unusual foot as if it was a gift from heaven, or—a gift to heaven.

" 'Tis something highly prized," said Conlaf with a controlled, unnatural calm. " 'Tis to be a gift to the rainmaker, who lives in the sky, in exchange for today's showers and more to come."

Madoc could not speak.

One of the women poked the foot into the steaming water with a peeled stick. The other picked cooked flesh off and lay it in a pile on a piece of hide.

Madoc put his hand over his mouth and ran to the tall grass. When the spasms subsided, he straightened and looked over the hill to the trail that led back to the ships. In the sand at the bottom of the hill he saw the wheel-like circles built on seven mounds. One circle had seven open spokes lined with sprinkles of red ocher, as though waiting for the bodies of the dead to fill them. There were already broken pottery vessels and beads in a couple of the graves. A chill began in the pit of his stomach and radiated out to his arms and legs, so that he trembled like the cottonwood leaves. These people spread red ocher on their dead the same as the Welsh druids. Why? Did they also believe the hematite powder would protect the bones so if needed they could be used in an afterlife? This was the age-old custom, from beyond remembering, that continued with the druids. The misty rain came and Madoc, with his fists clenched into tight balls, stood quietly beside his friend.

Conlaf said, "Brett worried about something bad happening to him. He felt his luck running out. Did we and the gods forsake him? We should demand his bones from the old women!"

"I remember we left a land of treachery and brutality behind," said Madoc. "We did not come here looking for barbarians to kill our laddie and put his bones in one of the spokes of a circular burial mound!"

"Maybe the gods warned him, and he did not know what to do about it," said Conlaf. "We should burn down their huts while they sleep! They deserve it."

"We have to think before we act," said Madoc. "Usually none of us know when, but death and ill luck come to all of us. We appeared, and the barbarians took Brett because he was something unusual, special. They honored him and offered him as a gift to appease their gods. You said that! Human sacrifice is acceptable here. Ages ago, the Celts came to our land and made sacrifice acceptable to druids in Britain. Thus druids have a history of human sacrifice. Later the Romans and Normans came, and they mixed with Celtic druids and later became Irish and Welsh people. That is all. The barbarians did not deceive us. We can understand their ceremonies because our people have lived through and beyond that kind of behavior. I did not expect this, but we were not deceived. So, let the bones be. They do Brett no good now anyway."

"I say we were deceived! If not by barbarians, by whom?" said Conlaf.

"By ourselves. Deceived by our perception of the barbarians and their acts," said Madoc. "Brett had faith that we would rescue him. He believed in us, and it gave him the strength of an oak. We betrayed him."

"Nay, 'twas our perception that beguiled us," said Conlaf. "For a short time we honestly believed that we saved Brett. We did not know we had the wrong lad. Our hearts were right. We felt good."

"We should have used reason, not heart's feeling," said Madoc, rubbing his eyes. "Barbarians are as devious as us when in a tight spot. We should have expected them to act like they did."

" 'Tis hindsight," said Conlaf. "My question is: Where did these barbarians come from?"

"Who was here when they came?" said Madoc.

The misty drizzle stopped, and Madoc pointed to the tall buttonwood trees at the head of the sloughlike pond. The diameter of their trunks was as wide as the length of two men, if they were laid one after the other, head to foot. Growing on the upper branches were little balls dangling on stringlike stems. The bottom asymmetrical branches were strung with silver skeins of thin, curly moss that danced in the breeze.

"Reminds me of Conn's wispy beard," Madoc said. The breezes stopped, and it seemed there was not a breath of air. The clouds mirrored themselves in the pond along with a few bright stars that peeked between those clouds. The muddy water looked dark and formidable. Myriads of birds were in the pond. White birds with long, yellow legs fed among cattails. Something disturbed a bunch of pink-breasted birds that were feeding on the pond's scummy shore.

It was the two crones. From the ratty-looking hide they threw bits of flesh into the water. The birds fought for every scrap. The pelicans came first, then the herons thrust their beaks into the water catching bits of flesh, jerked their heads upwards, and swallowed in a dancelike rhythm.

Madoc's stomach cramped again. He turned away and said, "I certes hope Troyes is safe. If he is not with the ships, I do not want to imagine what the barbarians might have in mind for him."

"So, you think he is with the barbarians?"

"I have that feeling," said Madoc. "When we meet the horsebackers, we will know if he made it back to the ship or if he is here with the barbarians."

Halfway through the stand of buttonwoods Conlaf

wanted to rest. "We could wait for the men with the horses."

"Keep moving," said Madoc. "When we meet the horsebackers, we rest." After a little while Madoc stopped and sniffed the air. "I smell dust and horse sweat!" He listened to the breeze and clapped Conlaf's shoulder. "Well-away! What took them so long?" He put on a good face to greet his men and hurried past the thick plants that were hard to see in the dark and whose slender leaves were sharp as needles.

Four people with four horses waited on the far side of the swinging bridge.

"Lugh's britches! What were you waiting for?" called Madoc.

"The lass learned to ride a horse," said Clare. "She is on our side and pretends to have nerves of iron. Treat her well. It was Kabyle's idea that she ride a horse into the barbarians' village."

"But the bloody horses refuse to cross a flimsy bridge," hollered Erlendson.

"Have you seen Troyes?" asked Madoc.

"We thought he was with you," said Einon. "The others, Caradoc, Thurs, Riryd, and Dewi are back at the ships."

Madoc's good face was short lived. "There was a confused struggle," he said. "Someone in a blue tunic pulled Troyes to his feet and walked him away."

"Not me," said Einon. "I have not seen the Frenchman since this morning."

Madoc pressed his thumbs against his temples, then banged a fist on Conlaf's chest, and said, "Tell me again, what happened to your shirt. Think!"

Conlaf's neck turned red. "Chief Wren took it. But first someone took my tunic. For troth I do not recall. Mayhap Rabbit pulled it off when I was in a fog from the black soup."

"What color was your tunic?"

"You bloody well know 'twas blue," Conlaf hung his head.

"Where was Rabbit when you cut on the chief's legs?"

Conlaf shook his head and asked how was he to know. " 'Tis bad enough to make me admit in front of everyone that I know not where I lost my tunic. You know I cannot remember. My shirt—the chief wore it. I used it to soak up blood and left it with Wolf. You know that!" He rubbed his bare chest and then his scaly, scabby, right side.

"Troyes was taken by one of the barbarians wearing your shirt," said Madoc. "If the horses will not go across the bridge, we have to carry them. Two, three men to a horse. We will take two horses across. And send the other two back."

"But you asked for four horses!" said Einon.

"Stop!" said Cougar, surprising everyone and leading her mare to the bridge. "You fuss same as small boys. I am leader. I ride beast or lead beast. No one carries beast across bucking bridge!"

Madoc could not believe that the barbarian girl was there, sitting on top of a horse, telling him and his men what to do. Conlaf thought the situation was ludicrous and began to laugh. Madoc looked at him and chuckled deep inside his chest, but he saw the wisdom. This young woman could talk with the barbarians. She knew her way around. And she was riding a horse! *She speaks so I understand.* He stood beside her. "Follow me. I will show you how to lead the horse so it will follow you across the bridge. Go slow, sing a little, not too loud. I be glad to see you."

"Help me stand on ground," she said, swinging her legs together and sliding down the side of a little black-and-white spotted mare into Madoc's outstretched arms. "Horse is like riding canoe in storm, breath-catching." She clung to Madoc a moment. Her mouth smiled and her eyes were wide with excitement. "I can show you around village in dark, but on horseback I—I feel big butterflies inside me."

"Do not go into that village ready to start a war in the middle of the night!" said Conlaf, shaking his finger.

"War is not going to happen," said Madoc. "The lass will tell the chief what I say. We have horses and words, no other weapons. If the barbarians do not listen to logic, they will be persuaded by fear of something they have never seen before and do not understand."

Madoc chose a spindle-shanked, brown stallion that seemed stronger than the others and least skittish. He led it with makeshift reins slowly across the swinging bridge. All the time he talked, cajoled, and waited until the bridge's swaying settled, then again inched forward. "Come on, 'tis like the deck of a sailing ship. Slide your feet. You can cross. Step easy. Come. Come. Good. Yu." Between his words he heard the men behind him whispering. He knew they thought that each step would be the stallion's last, that it would bolt and tumble into the canyon. There was no moon, but here and there stars twinkled between clouds. Madoc slid his feet so that he knew at all times he was on the bridge. On the other side, he sighed, rubbed his hand on the tense muscles in the back of his neck, and hollered, "We made it!"

"Where is Brett?" Einon called.

The question stabbed like an icicle into Madoc's heart. He took his time, breathed deeply, and answered, "On the Otherside. Center your thoughts and sing to cheer his spirit in Sid. Conlaf can tell you about the lad's bravery."

"I be staying with you," called Conlaf.

"Nay, you are important. You are a physician," said Madoc. "The barbarian lass and I will do this."

"Troyes is a physician," said Conlaf.

"Go back," said Madoc. "Ten sails full of men cannot have too many healers. 'Tis better. Go back, everyone!"

"But you are the chief shipmaster, the leader," hollered Conlaf.

"So—follow my orders!" said Madoc. "I go with Cougar, not alone." He heard her speaking softly to the mare and sliding her bare feet across the boards on the bridge. He heard the men whispering and for a short moment he knew exactly how Cougar felt. He doubted that he was qualified to be a leader of any kind. He did not stand up well against the barbarians, and his latest blunder was leaving Troyes with them. He was angry with himself. He did not think like a barbarian and thus did not know what they might do. It was this unknown that made mush inside his head and made him clamp his teeth together stubbornly as he motioned Cougar to come off the bridge and helped her mount her horse. Then he rode the stallion without looking behind him. He prayed they would find Troyes safe.

There was no visible firelight around the barbarians' village. He stopped and saw two men walking back and forth across the path. He guessed they were night guards for the village. Cougar caught up with him and whispered, "Yu. Madoc."

She wore a cape whose ends were tied around her waist with some kind of string. She pulled the cape over her head like a cowl and tied the string around her neck. It was hard to see her face. She wore a moss skirt underneath a kind of breechclout. She touched his arm, startling him. She smiled and repeated her grunt, "yu," which meant *good*. She put her fingers to her lips, pointed to the two men ahead, and put her hands in front of her face. Madoc thought she was telling him that they were guards. He pointed to her and said, "Name?" She leaned close and said, "Name Madoc, name Clare, name Kabyle. Me Cougar."

Oh ho, he thought, *Clare has been teaching her*. "Good, Cougar," he said, nudged the stallion, and they rode forward. He could hear her whisper, "Good."

The guards moved out of the way and were too flabbergasted to stop whatever it was they saw or thought they saw. A scene of a man and woman growing out of the backs of two unknown, four-legged beasts was so unthinkable that neither man could speak words out loud about what they had seen. There was no name for such a two-headed beast.

A couple of dozen dogs barked and followed the horses. When the horses nickered, Cougar laughed, and the dogs dropped back and growled.

Madoc had no idea which hut Rabbit occupied. He stopped and held his hands straight up against the sides of his head and said, "Rabbit."

Cougar answered, but Madoc was not sure if she said, "good" or "come." He followed her. The nighttime air was cool and made his mind feel like wool.

She stopped at a hut on the outer rim of the village. He dismounted, held the reins, and helped Cougar dismount. She gave him her reins, scratched on the door-flap, and swatted at unseen, biting insects.

A sleepy woman, with a fur robe over her bare shoulders, answered. It was so dark that she did not see the horses at first, but she sniffed suspiciously.

Madoc put his hands close to his head with the palms

up. Then he pointed to his arm, where Rabbit had the rabbitlike tattoo.

The woman sniffed again, puzzled by the strange smell of fresh horse dung, pointed to the center of the village, and held up four fingers. She meant that Rabbit was in the fourth hut from the council hall, which was in the center. Madoc did not know which side of the center.

Cougar knew. "Come," she said, letting Madoc boost her on the mare's back and nudging it with her bare heels.

Madoc mounted the stallion and heard the woman scream as they galloped away. He was certain she would wake her neighbors and cause enough noise to make the welkin ring.

Cougar looked for the place where she thought Grandmother's hut used to be. Everything was rebuilt; nothing was recognizable. She stopped, and he helped her dismount. He took the horses' reins, so she could lead the way. She scratched on the woven withie door-flap. There was no sound from inside.

Madoc moved his horse closer to the lodge, dismounted, and said, "Troyes, come out." They heard footsteps, then nothing. Cougar said something. The door opened and Rabbit in a blue tunic, Troyes's tan trousers, and brogues said, "Ma-tuck!"

Behind him Troyes squatted on his haunches in the middle of the lodge with a boy about Brett's age. They were by a tiny orange fire in the center of the dirt floor. Troyes and the boy wore trousers that were two pieces, one for each leg; a tiny apron hung from their waists in front and back. In their mud-daubed hair was a dried lizard. Troyes's swollen face was scratched with double lines filled with dots. He looked entirely barbarian, with his muscular arms, his black hair and dark eyes.

Cougar said that the young boy was Rabbit's son, who had been kept alive for this year's sacrificial ceremony. But because of a lucky circumstance Rabbit had his son alive for at least one more year. These people used the strangers' innocent lad instead of one of their own. She turned back to Rabbit and asked him a question. Madoc was certain she asked if they would sacrifice Troyes next year? Rabbit nodded as if that was the plan.

Cougar scowled, went inside, and sat between Troyes and the boy. Rabbit, whose arms were scratched with parallel lines, pushed the door-flap higher and Madoc went in. Rabbit motioned for him to sit in the place of honor, opposite the door-flap at the back wall. The dagger wound on Rabbit's left arm was bandaged between elbow and shoulder with leaves tied with strings of vine.

Madoc told Cougar to tell Rabbit that Troyes belonged to the men who came in the ships that were beached on the sand. She spoke softly to Rabbit and then she pushed Troyes and the boy outside. The boy yelled. Rabbit ran outside and stopped when he saw the two horses munching the dry, salt grass.

Cougar waved her hands trying to tell Troyes to get up on the stallion. Finally she gave him the reins. She pulled herself onto the back of the mare by holding on to the mane.

Madoc noticed that Troyes wore shoes that were made of one piece of hide sewn up the back and tied with thong around the ankle. Over the toes the leather was sewn in a pucker. For a moment he wondered if Cougar had traded Troyes for him and that he would be expected to stay with the barbarians. But she gave him the reins to her horse and told him to lead the way.

Rabbit's copper earbobs swung back and forth. He was afraid to get too close. He told Cougar that the ghostlike strangers, with strange beasts larger than dogs, were more powerful than his people.

Cougar told him that Chief Wren was more dangerous than any big beast.

Rabbit looked startled. He could not believe a young woman had come to his lodge at night, on the back of a strange four-legged beast, with enough courage to slander the chief. Something unheard of had happened in the village of Sandpoint this night. He held his son close to his side.

By this time, curious men, women, and little girls stood in their doorway to see what was going on. They were awed and frightened by the big, skinny, shambling, four-legged beasts that nibbled the straw hanging loose on the outside wall of a lodge. None of them ever dreamed that anyone, let alone this young woman who had been away for several years, would be so bold as to talk like a chief and ride a beast larger than a dog. The villagers did not have the courage to venture past their door-flaps and Madoc was relieved. The stallion snorted to rid its nose of the biting insects. Women and small girls screamed and ran inside, milling dogs yipped and grumbled, like a council of timid men who could not decide on a plan of action.

Rabbit smiled nervously as his boy ran back into their hut.

Madoc patted the stallion's flank.

Rabbit's son came back and handed Madoc something wrapped in leaves. It smelled like smoked meat. The boy spoke to Madoc. Madoc asked Cougar what he said.

"He so sorry about your child," said Cougar. "He liked him, a friend."

The words brought tears to Madoc's eyes. "Thank you, Friend," he said and touched the boy's forehead.

Rabbit gingerly touched the stallion's flank and drew his hand back as if it was scalded. The neighbors laughed behind their hands, but would not come outside near the two beasts.

Madoc bowed four times, grabbed a handful of mane, and pulled himself up in front of Troyes. "Ride like lightning!" he said.

Troyes hollered, "Well-a-way!"

Cougar yelled, "Col-Uza!" and they were over the berm and out of sight before anyone thought about using a slingshot or knew if what they saw was real or some mass dream.

Madoc pulled the stallion up near some brush and gave the reins and the leaf-wrapped package to Troyes. "Hold these," he said. "I will not be gone long. I have a job to do to set myself right with these people and with my own. I need Cougar to translate a few words."

He had seen the chief's hut and figured if he could go around the back, past the guards, he could give that bloody chief something to talk about the rest of his life. He took the reins of the little mare from Cougar's hands and talked to her softly so that she would know what he wanted her to do. Then he walked bravely up to the lodge, scratched on the door-flap, and held it open so he and Cougar could see with the help of starlight before they went inside. The center fire was small, flickering flames. Two women lay on a pallet with the baby in a cradleboard hung on the wall above them. Wolf was still there curled up on the dirt floor with his back against a log. The chief was under a coverlet of small animal skins sewn together, making a buzzing sound as he drew in each breath through his mouth. Cougar awoke the startled women and told Ibis to boil water for tea. She rubbed her eyes and followed directions without question. Afterwards, Ibis and Blackbird's wife woke Wolf, who seemed surprised but pleased to see Madoc.

Wolf's muscles rippled when he stretched his arms over his head. He sat up, and Madoc saw Blackbird on the floor behind him; his bare chest looked broad as a well-fed horse's. Madoc half-wished he had brought the horse inside right away. But that would have frightened the stuffing out of everyone and they would not listen to what he had to say. He pulled Wolf to his feet and said, "You knew all along the boy you sacrificed was ours. Bloody crafty of you! And bad manners!" Madoc lifted his brow, honked like a goose, and waddled around so that there would be no question that he was talking about the boy that was sacrificed. He pointed to the baby asleep in the cradleboard and looked at Wolf, then at his woman. "How would you like it if someone skinned your lassie and hung her out for the birds to peck her eyes out?"

Cougar's face turned pale, but she translated the best she could. Then she told Madoc to talk slow.

Wolf blinked. He pointed to Chief Wren who was still sleeping.

Blackbird got up and spat on the chief.

"This is not all the fault of your bloody chief! You did not stop him from killing the village's male children and mistreating women! I do not care if Chief Wren awakens and hollers because he is in pain. You barbarians are going to learn a bloody lesson. Do not ever again lay a hand on any of our people! You do not use any of us in your murderous, sacred sacrificing." He felt his anger rise and his heart pound. He stopped a moment while Cougar spoke and told himself to speak slower and with a calmer tone. He wanted these men to be his friends. "It is time for you to think for yourselves!" He pointed to his forehead and pounded the top of his head for emphasis. "Chief Wren will destroy all of you the way he destroys your baby boys and tells your wives what to do." He held his arms out like he was rocking a small child. "Choose another leader! It is time to trade more with other tribes. See where you people fit into civilization. Do you understand me? Get rid of your chief. No more Chief Wren! Give Wren a fishnet, a canoe and paddle, and bid him good-bye."

Blackbird pulled his lips back from yellowed, uneven teeth. It was no smile. He could not think clearly, tried to get up, but was unsteady on his feet. Madoc knew it was the effect of the tea Blackbird had drunk earlier.

Madoc preferred talking whenever there was a confrontation. He stepped back with his hands in his pockets. "Rabbit and his son would like to work with you to set this village on its feet, the way it was several years ago when your people knew right behavior from wrong. You decide, but I believe Rabbit would make a decent chief after Wren leaves."

He turned to Cougar and said, "Be sure they understand what I say. Tell them two or three times if you have to."

Then he again looked at Blackbird and Wolf. "So then, in the morning go to see Rabbit and talk things over. While Wren cannot get off his pallet, go talk to the other folks. Think about it. We have come from a long way across the Western Sea, and we want to be friends." He crossed his hands over his heart. "We look for a place to build a village. When it is done, we invite you to visit us. You will be welcome; friends." Wolf closed his eyes and Madoc thought he was sleeping. Talking to these people seemed impossible, but it was the only course he saw available. When Cougar finished telling them what he had said, Madoc told her to go outside, grab the mare's mane, and pull herself onto its back. He would hold the door-flap open for her.

When she left, Wolf's woman followed her outside.

Madoc swore under his breath.

The muscles in Wolf's jaw moved up and down. Madoc thought he was called an ugly name. He did not care. He could do as well, especially when Cougar was not translating. "You are two yellow-livered, goddamned barbarians. That is worse than pagans and no better than mongrel dogs," he said and was agile enough to step aside to avoid Wolf's first punch. But the second one took his breath away and made him double over. He hunched over as far as he could and waited for his breath to come back and then he raised up, bumping into Blackbird's chin with his head, and his elbow hit Wolf's nose. Blackbird bit his tongue and spat blood. Wolf's nose bled like a mountain spring after a good snowfall and warm weather.

Wolf's woman came back with water, built up the fire, and put the clay jar full of cold water on a stone near the flame. She looked at the baby. Satisfied, she sat on their pallet, looked at the three men, and put her hands over her mouth and giggled like their bumping each other was the funniest thing she had ever seen in her life.

The two men smiled and held out bloody hands. Madoc grabbed both of them and said, "Friends." He rubbed a bloody hand across his forehead, then across Blackbird's and Wolf's forehead, leaving a wide, red line behind. He felt light-headed, heard the snort of a horse, and held the door-flap to one side. Everyone gasped when they saw the head of a huge beast with Cougar sitting astradle holding the reins tight so the horse would not move forward. "Madoc is leader of a group of powerful spirit men," she said, "who do not give their boy children to the gods. They say no matter what you do, the rains come and go."

Chief Wren let out a high-pitched cry and sat up with his legs straight out in front and one fist squeezed into a ball the size of a large turnip. Wren's eyes were wide open with a gleam of pure madness. He was ready to get into what he thought was a battle, but he could not get his legs to move, because they were bound so tightly.

"Lugh's lungs!" said Madoc. "Ibis, give the chief more tea." His anger was gone. "We need to get out of here. My job is done."

"Bloody well-done," said Cougar.

Wren looked like he had seen a fire-breathing dragon and gave out another blood-curdling yell. His upper lip curled, and he said something that sounded like cursing.

Later, Cougar told Madoc that Chief Wren said as soon as he was on his feet, he would kill her again, even if she had become a ghost. Then she said Chief Wren was a lying snake, with no more backbone than a snail. She rode the mare away. Madoc followed on foot, as Blackbird, Wolf, and the two women watched from the front of the lodge.

Years and years afterwards the Calusa tribes had a legend about the pale men who drifted into their territory in floating, winged lodges to bring them the gift of the sacred mug and a sacrificial male child with flaming hair. The Calusa believed these men were ghosts during the day and half-men, half–terrible four-leggeds at night. They said that one of the men put Chief Wren's broken nose back together. With a magic knife the same man cut the back of Wren's legs and inside the elbow of one of his arms. After a handful of days he could walk without a limp. In another handful of days his legs did not hurt unless it was about to rain. With pride in their voices, the Calusa said that Rabbit, Wren, Blackbird, and a powerful, ghostlike man with a strange voice and hair the color of sun-dried grass, became brothers. Other ghostlike men took with them the ghosts of Chief Wren's pregnant woman, Little Mother, the round-headed woman known as Cougar, and the one-handed trader called Nohold. They rode tall four-leggeds, which snorted and switched long, hairy tails that were plenty much longer than a dog's tail. After a couple of days, the ghost-like men left and rode their lodges on the sea.

There was a ghost with dark, wavy hair whom Rabbit had hoped to keep as a son. This ghost limped around Rabbit's lodge without a whimper and would have made a truly brave war-chief. Like the other ghosts, Wavy Hair flew away on the back of one of the four-leggeds, leaving behind a silver cloud that settled in the sand. Chief Rabbit celebrated the ghost's memory once a year and did away with human sacrifice to the gods, and the rains still came to wet the earth.

Troyes never knew he was to be groomed as a war-chief, but he knew he was never so thankful to see anyone as he

was to see the barbarian lass and Madoc outside the doorway of Rabbit's hut that night.

On the way through the oaks they scared a raccoon eating
a mouse, and Madoc took it as a sign to tell Troyes and
Cougar about Brett. He was not sure if Cougar understood
because she seemed to be as surprised about the description
of the square frame, where Brett was tied, as Troyes. She
believed it was something Chief Wren had seen others,
maybe an Ais tribe, do. She thought he had brought the
ceremony back as something he could use to impress the
god of rain with, the power he possessed over his own
people. He would show his people he was as strong as any
rain god. So, he had all the boys under twelve summers
killed. Little Mother had told her that the massacre was
something the Sandpoint Calusas would never forget.
Surely, the people had thought, that year there would be so
much water in the rainy season that the whole village would
have to move to higher ground. But the rain came and went
the same as always. "I think the people of Sandpoint have
begun to think for themselves," she said.

Madoc only understood that Cougar was saying something about the fat, over-hungry rain god and the people in
Sandpoint beginning to think for themselves.

Troyes thought she talked about the next big rain. He
was upset about the death of Brett and did not question her.
A couple times he pushed tears from his eyes. When they
reached the plants with sharp needlelike leaves, he said, "I
loved that laddie like a small brother. I confess that each
time I find a friend, my heart becomes a target. This time
the bloody barbarians found the target and destroyed it."

Madoc saw that Cougar was so tired she swayed back
and forth with the gait of the mare. He stopped the horses
at the bridge. He was disappointed that men and fresh
horses were not there waiting for them. He said that the
men probably became tired of waiting and went back to
the ships. Their two horses were breathing hard and sweating. Troyes rubbed them with grass and tried to lead the
stallion across the bridge. It balked, and Cougar took the
reins, talking softly, and led it easily. The little mare that
she had ridden started across with Madoc as he talked to

it. Each time the bridge swung, the mare stood still. When the bridge was calm, the mare went on. " 'Twas easier than I thought," he said. "And so these barbarians saw their first horses this day."

"Night," said Cougar with a little swagger to show that a horse did not frighten her; however, every time the horses nickered, she jumped.

He asked with hand signs if her back was hurting.

She said, "No." Then surprised him by saying, "Need sleep," and closed her eyes.

He and Troyes put her on the stallion in front of Madoc so that he could hang onto her. Troyes was glad to be given a chance to ride by himself. As they rode, Cougar slept and Troyes told how Blackbird had cut open a fleshy plant with little sharp points along the edges of the thick leaves and smeared the slimy juice on his dagger wound. "It did not hurt or sting," Troyes said. "Blackbird bound my wound tight with a cloth of woven plant fiber so the edges of skin overlapped. I do not want to be left with an ugly scar."

Madoc said Conlaf or Llieu could pull the flesh apart so the edges would heal flat.

Troyes said, "When Rabbit was asleep, I sat in the darkest corner and pulled the flesh apart. I clamped my tongue between my teeth so I would not yell with hurt. The skin was already knit. I am telling you that we need some of that healing plant."

"If you know how it looks, you will find it," said Madoc.

Going over the high ground that was lined with stones, Troyes's horse stumbled on a large rock. He dismounted and looked at the mare's leg. Cougar woke and she and Madoc climbed down. They found no bones broken, but decided not to ride until they were certain that the mare's leg was all right.

They came to a large bog and saw gourd plants twining around each other among the sumpweed. The waterlogged sandy soil was surprisingly springy around the edge of the bog's dark water. Madoc took the opportunity to wash the blood off his arms and face, thinking that it attracted the tiny, whining insects that choked the air and bit any exposed flesh. He liked the pleasant fragrance of the bog's white flowers, like honeysuckle, but he despised the biting insects.

Troyes slapped and scratched and pointed to rough logs that lay like dark tree trunks. One of the trunks rose up out of the thick, murky water in the bog's center, showing yellow skin on the underside. Yellow-green eyes sat deep under warty brows. The men were dumbfounded, half-afraid, yet curious. Cougar seemed unconcerned and told them to stay high above the water and then closed her eyes to sleep.

Madoc said he had never seen logs that had an open snout with rows of daggerlike teeth. They could not thoroughly examine the forbidding loglike beast, because the middle of the bog became black muck that was so soft they sank to their ankles. The horses sank farther and Madoc said they had to get on drier ground fast. Madoc's heart leaped when two of the scaly logs slid up on a muddy bank and lumbered off into the ferns on stubby legs with wicked claws, dragging thick-barked, polelike tails. One log opened its long snout to show spiky teeth and closed it with a loud crack.

Troyes grabbed Madoc and both men put their hands over their mouths so they would not cry out like a couple of scared lassies. Their laughing woke Cougar, who laughed with them.

Madoc said he did not remember this part of the trail and wondered if he was going in the right direction. "Hey, it is dark and the landmarks look different. We can rest until there is more light."

When the morning's first dim light appeared, Troyes woke the others by becoming excited about a couple of snakes writhing like sticks about finger-thick in the bog. He wanted to be out of the bog and on solid terrain. He pointed to his soft shoes that the muddy sand threatened to suck from his feet.

"Your shoes are like pampooties. A snake can poke its sharp fangs clean through," Madoc said. "Would you rather be aback the horse?" Troyes climbed on the stallion and felt much better for it. Madoc helped Cougar on the smaller mare, and the sky brightened. When the sun was over the horizon, it was hard to see the difference between green water plants and green mossy ground. It was all the same texture and color. Madoc led the horses down a little slope, slipping and snorting. The front legs of the mare buckled, straightened, and then buckled again. The half-starved beast was a worn-out beast, and she screamed and lunged, trying to get a solid purchase under her feet.

Cougar slid off. Madoc took the reins and was shocked to find the mare would not move. She could not move but was being dragged slowly downwards through black ooze and green plants. Her eyes rolled back and her ears lay forward. She rolled her head from side to side so that she seemed to be lying in a verdant meadow. She stretched out her neck and dashed her head against the dark green surface, splashing soupy, black mud.

Cougar looked about for something solid. She called out for a long stick. Madoc threw her the chief's scepter, and she tied the reins to it and laid it behind a half-submerged tree trunk. Troyes gathered more sticks. Madoc pulled on the reins trying to help the mare, but it was no use. She wheezed, foundered, and sank deeper. "She drinks and breathes muck every time she swings her head," said Madoc, up to his waist and sinking deeper in the weedy bog.

"I think you two should get out of there," said Troyes.

"My legs will not move," said Madoc. "I need you to pull me out."

"I cannot find a stick long enough to reach either of you," said Troyes.

Madoc looked at Cougar who had her hand out to him. He stretched his arm out and clasped Cougar's hand. She was almost pulled off the log. She handed the scepter to Madoc, and he used it to go hand over hand until he was near the mare that neighed, sputtered, and frantically flopped her head.

"I do not know what to do," said Troyes.

"If the bloody little horse would be still, I think I could get on her back," said Madoc. "How do we make her stop thrashing about? She is half drowned and her legs are already useless."

"Dagger," said Cougar, holding out her hand.

Madoc felt at his waist and pulled out the bone dagger. He tossed it to her and at the same time let go the reins. They fell on top of a bunch of weeds.

Cougar caught the dagger by the handle and pulled at the pile of reins until she found the scepter. She lay on the log and pushed the scepter under her belly so it would not slide off the log. She spoke softly to the little mare and held her head between her muddy arms. Tears stung her eyes. She blinked and with one strong thrust of the dagger cut the horse's throat. The mare looked startled and shook her head from side to side, then she stopped thrashing.

Both Madoc and Troyes were surprised at the dagger's sharpness. Cougar had done something they did not have the heart to do. Her action was both good and sad. She was surprised at the warmth of the spurting blood. It felt comforting on her hands. The mare's head was heavy in her arms. The bog covered the mare's chest. She threw the scepter, still tied to the mare's reins, back toward Madoc. He caught it and slowly he pulled himself to the horse. Then little by little his knees and feet came up and finally he lay on the back of the horse, like Cougar lay on the log.

All the while Cougar kept watch for the big jaws with sharp teeth that she knew would come seeking the source of the salty blood that painted the green weeds red.

Madoc's arms ached. He was afraid the mare would go under before he was out of the water and able to crawl over the spongy ground. He wanted to yell at Cougar for killing the mare, but he could not. She had done the right thing. He knew if he stayed on the back of the dead horse, he could find a way to get to the shore without sinking in the bog again. She had traded the mare's life for his and saved him. He heard Troyes yell for him to grab the horse's mane so he would not fall off. He heard the stallion switch his tail against the hordes of biting flies, and he heard the stinking bubbles break as they came to the surface. Then he felt Cougar's hand nudge him. She held up the mangy-looking scepter. It was not tied to the stallion's reins. For a moment she lay her head against Madoc's leg, then she pulled back and threw the bloody scepter so that Troyes had to wade in, pick it up, and run back to safe ground before being sucked into the sand. She told Troyes to use the stallion to pull out the carcass of the mare. Then she put both her arms around Madoc's leg and said, "Yu!"

Troyes was surprised that she had watched the horses

close enough to know that they could pull heavy loads. He looked at her with more respect and tied the reins of both horses together. He hooked the scepter around the front leg of the stallion and pulled and pulled. The stallion moved a step or two forward. Troyes prayed that the scepter would hold and the dead horse would come loose. The stallion was exhausted and refused to pull hard. Finally he held the mare's reins and pulled. When Madoc was close enough to the spongy shore, Cougar told him to slip off and lie full length in the muck.

Cougar slid off the log and told Madoc to use his hands to pull himself through the weeds and past the snakes to safe ground. Gracefully she moved hand over hand until she lay in ankle-deep water to catch her breath.

Troyes crouched at the edge of the bog and saw the little mare go under the water and not come back to the surface. He reached for Cougar, then for Madoc.

Cougar said, "Bog wanted a taste of the beast more than us. Bloodthirsty thing!"

Madoc shook his fist at the bog and thanked Cougar for her bravery. "For a tiny person you have a big heart."

Cougar laughed and waved the bone dagger in the direction of the old log she had used. "Yu," she said.

Pure exhaustion caused Madoc and Troyes to think it a great joke Cougar had played on the bog. She had cheated it out of swallowing a man and given it a poor, skinny mare instead. Troyes wiped tears from his eyes. "I thought you both were goners, and I was really scared," he said.

Cougar answered by waving the flies off the smoked meat that Madoc had been given by Rabbit's son. A whole venison ham lay in the middle of the green leaves she had pulled away from it. She cut four tiny slices, threw them in the four directions, and then cut three much larger pieces. She popped one piece in her mouth and wiped her hands on her muddy skirt.

"What the hell," said Madoc, with his mouth full and his stomach growling from hunger. "I believe the little mare's spirit wants us to live! I thank the laddie for giving us this smoked deer meat. I thank the two of you and the mare and the stallion, because I owe my life to every one of you." He closed his eyes. When he opened them, loglike bodies with big, long mouths were thrashing the water as they bit and tore at horseflesh beneath the surface.

"I owe my life to the two of you," said Troyes. "I be forever grateful."

"Madoc! Troyes!" said Cougar, making a contented, purring sound in her chest.

After a while the bog water was smooth and held the mirror image of the sky. In the center of the bog the weeds were torn and still red with blood and pink with bits of flesh. The edges of the bog were green and soft with algae. Madoc imagined it full of life: snakes, logs with long snouts, wiggly, unknown, slimy things feeding on each other in a heartless manner that was perfectly natural. The air was moist and held dozens of scents from the earth. A woodpecker's loud drilling startled them. It was time to move on. Cougar carried the smoked meat, and Madoc, with the scepter, walked in front. Cougar said she would find the trail to the seashore and the floating huts. Behind them, Troyes led the tired stallion.

They came to an open space where the sun had dried the mud into a chaos of patterns. They heard faint crackling noises as gases escaped through the cracks. Cougar held her nose against the rotten smell. Madoc shivered, stopped a moment, jabbed the butt-end of the scepter into a little puddle of black, soupy muck, and shattered the reflection of the white clouds. "Keep it," he said to the bog and hurried away without looking back.

Madoc felt good walking beside Cougar. She was someone who knew how to live in this land. She was intelligent and a fast learner. Already she knew a few dozen of his words and was almost fearless. She could ride a horse. She would kill a horse to save a man's life. She was a wonderful friend. He reached over and took her hand. She said something that ended with his name. It made him feel good. He said, "Friends."

She repeated the word and squeezed his hand.

They were indifferent to the blood and mud caked on their clothing. Together they looked back at Troyes who was also mud from head to foot. "You look like a bog spirit," said Madoc.

"Master Madoc, look in the next basin of clear water.

There be three bog spirits," said Troyes. "Our shipmates will take us all for barbarians."

They climbed over downed trees and pushed their way through the pine woods. Every muscle ached. Madoc was glad he was not leading the drooping horse that seemed more tired than the three humans. When they came out on the sandy shore, there was not a ship in sight.

"Have our mates sailed without us?" asked Troyes.

"Ask only, do we go upshore or downshore?" said Madoc.

"First we sit," said Cougar.

"Pray that our eyes and ears will give us the answer," said Troyes. He listened to the whisper of the wind in the pines. He strained to hear a sigh that would tell him where the ten sails had gone. He was too tired to decipher the wind's sighs.

Madoc made a small fire with driftwood in a scooped-out hole in the sand. He laid the big smoked venison ham on two narrow sticks. When the meat was warmed through, he cut off four small bits and threw one to each of the four directions.

Cougar nodded approval and thought it the best venison she had ever tasted when Madoc fed her a chunk. After eating the rest of the meat, they felt better, and the men taught Cougar more words, like *grass, shells, wood, fire, smoke, work, run* and *laugh.* She examined the hands of both men and compared the palm lines to her own. They slept in the tall grass behind a dune, and when they woke, the sun had passed its zenith, and they heard pounding, like a hammer on wood. They moved toward the sound, hoping it was not a woodpecker. They found the ships sitting downshore from where they were. They brushed the dried mud off their clothing, forgot the dried mud on legs and arms, and hurried to be counted for the evening meal.

Cougar watched Madoc's arms swing from broad shoulders as he walked. He had that hard-muscled look of a man who was used to hard work. She imagined him stripped down to his breechclout, building a lodge. She pictured him pulling in a full net of fish with his faded-looking, pale yellow hair flying over his forehead in the breeze. His wide, competent hand brushed the soft curls out of the way so he could see. He turned and looked behind. His teeth flashed in the waning sunlight when he smiled. He was rugged, but not in a rough, muscle-bound way. His eyes were inquisitive, sympathetic, intelligent, and so startlingly blue that they took her breath away when she looked at them. They reminded her of a bit of liquid blue paint sitting in perfectly white, round seashells. "Yu," she said. The spirits had put the best man they had in her path, and she was grateful.

XXI
Riryd

"Aber-Kerrik-Guignon:
non sunt
Guigon Gorn, Madauc,
Pedr Sant, † Riryd, **filius**
Quenti Gueneti
an, 1171."

The late Rector of Iden, in Kent, the Reverend E. F. Synnott, made a remarkable discovery in a sale-room at Rye in Sussex several years ago. . . . The manuscripts . . . appeared to be some form of port records for the twelfth and thirteenth centuries, compiled partly in Latin and partly in broken English . . . a list of ships lost, or unaccounted for in various ports of England and Wales. On the document there were no marks against the name of Madoc's ship, but against that of *Pedr Sant* was the sign of the Cross . . . [which] may have indicated that this ship was sunk.

—Richard Deacon, *Madoc and the Discovery of America*

When Riryd saw his brother, his anger boiled over before anyone could greet the three properly. Riryd shook his fist and shouted, "Brother, you look barbaric, like one of them! We shall rally, with sharp cane staves, stink bombs, and march into the barbarians' camp this very day or night! They will pay dearly for taking Brett's life. That is fair balance!"

Without washing his bloody face and hands, Madoc reminded him that they would be outnumbered. " 'Tis foolish to start an unbalanced battle. You are no coward, but do you want to sacrifice another man? Look, we lost Brett to

the barbarians, but we have Troyes, and we have three barbarians as friends. I lost the little mare in a black bog. We
did not come to fight. Look, we can leave—sail to a place
where no people claim the land." His whole body felt as
though it had been dragged through the sand and trampled
on by well-fed horses. He was beginning to regret going
back to give Blackbird and Wolf the words they deserved
in order to make them think. Maybe it would have been
better to leave them alone. Why did he ever think that good
leadership or pride and integrity were worth such agony?

"You look," said Riryd, "Einon, Willem, and I talked it
over and we, your kin, believe you, our leader, should show
your respect for Brett by taking revenge on the barbarians'
leader!"

"So, who are the barbarians? We do not yet know," said
Madoc. "The New Religionists' sacred book says the Lord
God created man in His image. How and where was man
created? Was mankind created in Britain, in the land of the
Northmen, or here? Or—was there more than a single cre-
ation? Is the sacred book wrong? So, who are these people?
Have you talked with them?"

"Of course not!" snapped Riryd. "But I know who they
are! They are cannibalistic barbarians!"

"Let it go!" said Madoc. "I never saw them eat raw flesh.
I never saw them eat human flesh. Conlaf and I saw some
old women cleaning bones. They may have been Brett's.
We saw a—a four-toed foot. That is all. They dumped the
offal into the pond for the blackbirds and herons. Troyes
thinks they will put Brett's bones in a place of great
honor—in one of those boxes in their council hall, and after
a time in their seven-spoked mounds lined with ochre. Druids use ochre in their graves. Brett's spirit will like that.
He will feel at home, close to his folks."

Riryd would not let it go. "We ought to show the barbarians which of us is the greater! We are hawks. They are
buzzards!"

Madoc pulled from his muddy tunic pocket the mud encased, stinking leather bag that Rabbit had thrown against
his chest. Was that yesterday or three days ago? It felt like
another age. "A gift the buzzards left," he said and held it

away from his nose so all could see what he might shake out. It was heavy, and he expected it might be a dead lizard or hairy spider stuffed with stones. Instead it was a copper cube the size of the palm of his hand. Four sides were pecked to make a stylized picture of a freckle-faced lad wearing feathers with a high crane headdress. His left foot had four toes!

" 'Tis Brett!" said Troyes, scratching through the mud in his dark hair.

In the bottom of the bag was the pearl neckband Rabbit's son had worn as part of his decoration. "We may talk differently, but we communicated!" choked Madoc. "Rabbit and even his son recognized we loved our laddie."

"Then why did they permit Brett to be sacrificed?" said Troyes. He stared at Cougar, hoping she might shed some light on this horrible act.

Her eyes filled with tears. "Man and woman love baby," she said, fingering the string of small, multicolored precious stones she wore around her neck. She was thinking that babies were loved by their mother and father. Parents would do anything for babies, but when full-grown they were on their own and parents did not even recognize them, let alone go out of their way for them. It still hurt to remember her own experience with her true parents.

" 'Twas not Rabbit who chose which crane-boy to be skinned," whispered Madoc, throwing down the wide pearl neckband as if it was blighted. "It was Chief Wren. Do you know I could have broken his nose again? Instead I walked away! I left a piece of my mind with Blackbird and Wolf. I lectured them as if they were my brothers. Cougar told them my words in their language. We ended friends. Cougar scared the piss out of Chief Wren by coming into the lodge on top of the little mare. He thought she was some four-legged beast from the spirit world. So then, the two sides are even."

Conlaf picked up the pearls. "These are worth a sailing ship in Wales!"

"Aye, 'tis Brett's legacy," said Madoc, rubbing his head. "This is all we have of him, besides his brave spirit." He put the pearls into the bag with the copper cube. "Physicians have seen pestilence lay low all sorts of folk. Is pestilence greater than the folk it slew? And how can one measure? We have ships to sail toward another place. When we find *our* land, we shall make markers to help us not only remember Brett, but the other men who gave their lives so that the rest of us might have peace."

Riryd continued to spill his thoughts of war. "I be thinking we could use thorns to work us into battle. The barbarians will face a sea of troubles from us."

Madoc sneezed and felt as if a hot iron sizzled inside his soul. He understood how his brother felt. He, too, had reacted with rage about Brett's terrible death. "So. You truly believe a fight will settle something?"

"Aye!" Riryd shook his fist in the air. " 'Twill end the barbarians' cannibalism!"

"I told you, we did not see the women eat flesh." Madoc was agitated with his brother's stubbornness, his inability to see things his way. "There is no end to humans' fighting. We saw that in Wales. These barbarians have lived by their own rules far longer than we know. We cannot yet speak their tongue. No wise man fights." He paced and ran his hands through his unruly curls. "Do you fight the sea when it drowns a friend?" No one answered, and he wished Conlaf would say something to finish the conversation. He was sick from that ball of fury that lay in his heart. A wall of grief rose inside that made him stagger. He stopped walking, looked into Riryd's eyes, and collected his thoughts. "In every experience is the beginning of wisdom," he said. "Think this: Let us go forward wiser than before." He sneezed, his head throbbed, his throat ached, and his heart grieved.

He put his hand on Riryd's shoulder. "And what about you and my other brothers?" he said in a thick voice. "Do you understand love and loyalty among us and our fellow men? Do you know the great responsibility we have to the three barbarians that are now on my ship? We were underdogs trampled by ignorance. In our land we left a war among lords and peasants that reached out to break hearts far beyond relatives and friends. Will we start awarring here? Nay, we are druids and have more useful things to do. We shall find a place where we can all live without warring. We shall leave the majority of the barbarians and study the stars that seem to us to be dislocated in this land. There are strange plants and strange animals to know. The three barbarians will teach us their knowledge of our new place. In exchange we will teach them our wisdom. We will anchor in the bay for the night and leave for our un-proved land at the first hint of morning light. Nights in this land do not cool much; they are twice as humid as days."

Riryd took his brother's hand and said, "I am certain it is right to leave these bloody barbarians to themselves; on the other hand, we must take three of them with us or they will lose their lives. We have seen the same kind of killing among our own people. So they come with us. We share and they share. 'Tis a good exchange. I love thee, *Cymro*."

Madoc went abroad the *Gwennan Gorn* and asked Con-laf to look at Cougar's old wound between her shoulder blades. "The lass behaves as if she has known us for years." he said. "She has no fear or prejudice. She tells me what to do. She is a born leader. She learns our language faster than I can separate her words, which sound to me like water sloshing in a gourd. I cannot sleep for thinking where she would be if she had grown up Welsh or Irish. She might be an archdruidess, or lord of a large province, or more likely head of a school for runaway children. She has a big, kind heart toward those in trouble."

"Do not go soft over one small, intelligent, barbarian lass. No womanizer are thee," said Conlaf as he rummaged through packets and salves in his leather case. He smiled when he saw that Cougar's dagger wound was a healthy pink and the skin was knitting together well.

More clouds moved in and covered the stars. Gwalchmai sang a praise-song for Madoc for bringing Troyes back safely. Conlaf sang a praise-song of satire to the gods who caused Madoc to choose the wrong crane-boy and then helped Madoc lose his way and lose a good horse in the bog. He sang another song about the mysterious fluids he called humors that were out of balance in Madoc's body. He said, "Yours is the disease of all wise men; you give your heart away at the wrong time. From now on your every act is scrutinized by the gods and us sailors."

"You cannot do that," said Madoc, sneezing.

* * *

That night nine ships anchored in a circle around the *Gwennan Gorn*, so that the messmates could talk to one another. Madoc made up his own satire song. It was the kind of singing that was common with the Welsh when they felt ill and perverse. Everyone thought Madoc was emotionally spent, not too wise, and not thinking like himself at all when he sang, "Are you, my best friend, Conlaf, punishing me with my choice of cranes, when my head is heavy as stone? The gods have not finished punishing me. I cannot breathe. My heart is gone. There is Shipmaster Troyes who made up his mind to live with the barbarians. He even wore their clothes. His boots were so soft they fell off his feet so he had to become a horsebacker. He followed us home and never said a word about being on the wrong trail when we went through a black bog. He stood on the bank and wrung his hands while I floundered in the muck and nearly drowned. Oh, Troyes was a brave fellow, but the barbarians scared the good sense out of him. I imagine he and his men are talking of mutiny, and I do not blame them. They are the ones that believe they can live with the barbarians." Madoc coughed and wished he could be in a feather bed with hot stones at his feet.

"Water," sang Conlaf. "Drink water. Rest before you catch your death."

"I be not about to catch my death," sang Madoc. "I will stay a long ways behind it." He thought he had something else to sing, but could not remember it. He wished he had hot mead to drink. It would ease his throat.

Conlaf gave Madoc a pinch of valerian root.

Madoc put the little bit of root under his tongue. He felt too miserable to go to his own sleeping pallet, so he lay on the boards close to Cougar and the two other barbarians. "I be sick as a bear coming out of hibernation," he said. "What is wrong with me?"

Cougar took his head in her lap and stroked his forehead, his jaws, and his neck. She rubbed his shoulders and his back. When he was asleep, the drizzle came. She curled herself around him like a mother protecting her child.

The rain stopped with the first light of dawn. Troyes brought his ship close to the *Gwennan Gorn* and said that he was going to sail the *Un Ty* and her men back to Wales, and he would be pleased to have other ships follow. "We shall be sailing against the sun from west to north to east and mayhap run into ill fortune or death," he said. "I would just as leave drown in the sea as be cut apart by barbarians or a blast of satire from the chief shipmaster."

Madoc gave a whispered shriek. He was having a cold sweat and was stiff in every joint. He lowered a coracle and paddled to the *Un Ty*, climbed aboard, and spoke with a dry throat as best he could about responsibility and commitment. He reminded the men that sooner or later they would all die, and if they had stayed in Wales, they would most probably already be in the land of Sid. He was short tempered. This was his fight. He said there was nothing in France for Troyes or in Wales for any of them. "Yesterday Conn said that the wheel of fortune revolves, and once again the cup of hope has been dashed from our hands. I be the one responsible for this blemish, not you. Today I say, with no thought of satire, that the new land holds surprises, but eventually we will hold the cup. If we have a true enemy, we shall give him no rest. We will hit him with powerful words, emphasized by hand gestures, when he least expects it and convince him that warring, even on the ground of his choosing, is a losing game for both sides. Sail with us. 'Tis our destiny to build a free and peaceful colony. Brett, who one day was to be honored with his first woad-markings, would expect that much of you."

Troyes bowed his head and held his hand against his aching arm. A single sob rumbled from his chest. "If it gives his death meaning, I will live on unproved land and civilize bloody barbarians. I be with you."

"We be with you," said the other men on the *Un Ty*.

Encouraged by the change of heart, Madoc asked for the *Un Ty*'s sail to be raised and to follow the *Gwennan Gorn* along with the other eight ships.

The sailors sailed upwind and found it impossible to do anything but wedge to leeward and hang on. With every sixth or seventh wave, the decks were awash in swirling, bubbling green water. The severe wind blew all night.

Madoc tied Little Mother, Nohold and Cougar to the gunwale close to himself. "You people have a job to stay alive," he said. "My job is to keep the ships safe so my men survive. 'Tis all the same. *Survive!* That is the word to remember!"

The shipmasters never knew how close Chief Wren's barbarians had been to them when they left that morning. When the sun climbed the horizon and shone on the smoldering ashes of Nohold's place, hordes of barbarians, painted for war, armed with slingshots and bows and arrows, came out of the sandy depression where they had slept. Wolf, the War Leader, stretched his sore muscles, gingerly rubbed his swollen eyes, and talked about going into one of the houses that could float on water. He made up stories about the wondrous sights that would be inside the houses, which included the giant dogs that these men rode or led around by a rope tied to the beast's neck. While rubbing the sleep from their eyes and circling their small morning fires, the barbarians were dead certain the pale strangers were on shore. Some were truly surprised when they saw that the floating houses and strange beasts had disappeared from the bay. War Chief Wolf, Blackbird, and Rabbit exchanged satisfied smiles. They had told Chief Wren, before leaving him on his pallet in the care of the women, that the pale spirit men would never go to war with them. They promised Wren that these strange men were fair and honest traders, who thought about problems, then talked them through in a friendly way.

"We are friends with them," said Rabbit.

"No! You can not be!" shouted Wren. "They are ghosts. We can never be friends."

By evening the windstorm was over. Madoc and his men were beached on white sand. They sang mourning and honoring songs for Brett as they mended the ships' sails and their clothing and fished from the coracles before they supped.

The next morning Cougar and Little Mother showed the messmates how the Calusa gathered oysters and dug for clams. Nohold showed the messmates how to make traps for the river otter, which gave them the softest fur to make moccasins that could be worn aboard the ships. The two barbarian women showed the men how to harvest the large, wild, morning-glory root, boil it, and add other vegetables, such as ground nuts to make an edible soup. The vegetables had a salty taste, which made them very palatable. Madoc recognized that the mistletoe in this new land was similar to the Welsh sacred mistletoe. Its roots grew in the bark of a tree or shrub. Cougar told him that is why the Calusa say that, "it is partnered," meaning, "it is married." Madoc translated the Calusa word for the delicate lady's-slipper flower to "partridge moccasin." Cougar told him that the common fern was called "the bear lies on it," because bears like to sleep in the fern beds.

Four days were long enough to lie around on the white beach. During a morning's high tide, the ten ships sailed west into unusually warm water that was bluer than any sea-water seen before. This warm water was clear and unusually salty. By afternoon the air was moist, heavy, and oppressive. The men sulked, were ill tempered, and the shipmasters were grumpy. Conlaf sneezed and broke out in a cold sweat that did not evaporate. His pulse was faster than usual, and he was growly.

Madoc wondered if there was any land that would suit most of his men. He imagined he heard the gods laughing at him because perhaps there was no such thing as *suitable land*. He wondered if he really wanted to find suitable land or just sail the sea and explore strange sights. He wondered if he was terrified of what he might find on suitable land. The barbarians, unexpected people, puzzled him most of all. Nohold was a likeable, hard-working man. Even with one hand he could manage most anything. He looked after the young woman called Little Mother with a tenderness that was refreshing. Madoc admitted only to himself that he was drawn to Cougar because she was intelligent, kind, thoughtful, cute, funny, and courageous. Her dark beauty struck him as so natural and refreshing that he never tired of watching her.

At twilight a bank of purple-green clouds rolled overhead. Madoc could not remember ever having seen such a cloud. He asked Cougar what a purple cloud meant.

"Luck bad," she said, touching his right hand that was curled around the steering oar.

The squall started mild enough, and the men put on rain

gear. Madoc made a mental note to grease his leaking canvas raincoat on the next clear day. The thick air brought out all the stinking body odors and rotten fish-oil odors of the ship. He made a mental note to have a swim in the warm water on the very next clear day. He noticed that the tear in the sail had not been mended and decided not to gripe about it, but to ask Cougar to mend it.

The needle seemed dull as he showed her how to force it through two layers of linen sailcloth flapping in the wind. He pushed the heel of the needle on the boom with all his might and had it half through the cloth when it ran into the palm of his right hand and broke off. The imbedded point hurt when he rubbed his hand. "I be a damned bloody fool!" he said. "Lugh, I be clumsy! You do it!"

Cougar had no trouble with the steel needles. They were much sharper than the bone needles she was used to. The sail was mended while Conlaf cut into Madoc's palm with one of his little steel knives to probe the needle tip. He coughed and could not get it out. Cougar asked to try probing for the needle tip, but Conlaf feared she would force it deeper. She asked Conlaf to put a dab of herbal ointment on Madoc's hand and wrap it with the strip of wadmal.

Madoc had one of the men hoist the sail and tried to forget about his aching hand. By midnight his hand was swollen, but he had no time to lie down to sleep or to worry about the tormenting pain. When the wind pressure on the sail was too great, he had to pull the sail down. He damned Conlaf for leaving the bloody lines tangled, and he told him to grope hand over hand for the lines, straightening them out, and bring the sail down. His hand ached as he watched Conlaf bundle the sailcloth and stow it away.

Conlaf was feverish when he brought willow bark for Madoc to chew to deaden the pain.

As a curling wave broke over the ship which stood with her prow in the air, Madoc and Conlaf hunched over, hanging on to the sail and boom. If they had tried to walk, it would have been like climbing the face of a smooth cliff. Everyone was tense waiting for each new crush of water. Little Mother cried, and Nohold pulled her against his chest, even though she was tied onto the gunwale as Madoc instructed. Cougar's face was white, but her mouth was clamped shut as she leaned herself close to Madoc and watched him brace himself and hang tight to the steering oar.

The *Gwennan Gorn*'s cows had survived starvation and every other storm, but this night one scrawny cow was choked to death with its tether rope. The other cow mooed mournfully, and Madoc hollered to Conlaf to choke it. Conlaf chuckled and said, "Madoc, you have to learn how to give orders you truly want carried out when you yell to this bloody bunch of sailors."

Madoc told him to keep his head up, and his eyes and ears open, and to make sure there were two men on bailing-watch working the bilges. Madoc told Cougar to take care of Little Mother, and he untied Nohold from the gunwale and showed him how to check and recheck the lashings on the coracles. Nohold proved that he could tie the lashings using one hand and the stump at the end of his other arm as well as most two-handed men. Madoc explained to him that if the storm continued, the ship could crack in half, so it was good to keep his eyes on the inside-wall seams where the sea hit as hard as handfuls of thrown gravel. He pointed to the little coracles that might save some of them.

Madoc coughed so hard it was hard to show Nohold how to hang a torch on the stern and keep it lit. Nohold showed him how to build a triangular shield with three boards so the torch would not blow out. But it did blow out. The occasional stars that appeared between the clouds seemed below their feet. Time after time the ship hovered a moment and then fell forward in slow motion into deep troughs that seemed to have no bottom. Madoc stood beside the steering oar naked. This had become the sailors' practice so that their clothing would not be whipped to rags with wind and salt water. It was so dark only the whitecaps close against the ship could be seen. The waves billowed. Madoc shivered and the rain slid off his back. He imagined he heard the surf pounding on rocks, and thought of being shattered into tiny chips of wood, bone, and flesh. He cursed the first light of day because it was late. When the ship fell, the water seemed to splatter into thousands of flying white birds. Some fell back into Madoc's mouth and tasted salty, and most fell back into the sea and disappeared like bits of ice in hot water.

By morning's full light the wind did not seem so strong as it hummed in the sail's lashings. The sky lightened to show gray-green clouds. The sea was steely black. Dewi stood leeward beside Madoc and Conlaf. "I have seen green clouds bring wind," he said. Then he pointed. "Lord God! A waterspout!" The wind snatched away his last words. The clouds came down to a slim point, and the sea rushed up in dark ribbons to meet it. Then the dark, wild nixe that was born of that violent mating swayed and danced in a powerful whirligig that moved across the sea so fast that it gave off a deafening roar. It headed in the direction of the *Gwennan Gorn*'s bow.

"We will be sucked into the middle of the spout!" said Conlaf. The air was too warm, and he was sweating.

"Grab oars!" said Madoc. "Move!" His knuckles clamped the oar and he steered away from the vicious, hanging, dark arm of the cloud.

"We shall end downside up in the sea!" yelled Dewi. His hair flew from side to side in spikey peaks.

The waterspout bobbed along faster and seemed to grow larger. The ship fought against swells that moved counter to the main current. Dewi pulled hard on his oar. Conlaf and Tipper groaned and moaned at their oars and swore at the angry seagods.

Seabirds made frightful squawks and fell with spread wings into the trough of the waves. They lay quiet as though they had given up their life force in the face of something more powerful: the wind.

Madoc was as gray-white as the faded, rolled sail in the bottom of the ship. One hand gripped the rudder that was out of the water, and the other, white knuckled, clung to the gunwale. He did not look at the line of ships following him, but prayed for guidance and never took his eyes off the spout. He made the ship slide down into the trough of a large swell, knowing full well the danger. In the trough, he had no control over his ship, but it was his only way to avoid being hit straight on.

"We are all going to drown!" yelled Tipper as the ship heeled over, her gunwale almost level with the water. "This is what comes of having a woman aboard! We have two and that is double trouble!"

Two men bailed the ship's bilge as fast as their arms permitted.

Madoc cried, "Stop! Bailers! Up the mast. Lift her up. 'Tis our only chance. Lugh! Move! Everyone else lay amidship."

There was some yelling between the bailers. One said the bloody shipmaster was moonstruck. "Tie yourselves to the gunwales!" he hollered.

Madoc saw Cougar was tied, but she lay on the deck with one leg and one arm over Little Mother. She held her tight and spoke softly to her friend. She shook her fist at Madoc. He could hear his name come back to his ears on the heavy wind, and for an instant he wondered what she was saying about him in this terrible moment. He guessed the women were blaming him for the rough seas. Being on board a ship in a storm must be frightening as death to barbarian lasses. The next instant his voice came in urgent gasps over the wind to yell to the men who were not at the oars or bailing tins. "Do not stand bleating! Up mast! Lift! Get your heads down. Move sharp. Push the mast across the gunwale. Good. Move as fast as you can, as far as you can. Move it into the side of the spout when 'tis close. Understand? Hang on! Get set. Ready? Heave!"

He thought it was impossible to break the spout, but he had to keep the men busy, to try something before it spun into the ship splintering it into a million pieces and flinging every man holus-bolus into the sea.

The ship sailed so close to the spout that the roar was deafening. The steering oar was again out of the water. From the corner of his eye Madoc saw Nohold helping Conlaf and Dewi push the end of the mast into the center of a whirling spiral of water. Then the mast and broken hunks of crystal splashed and clattered onto the deck, leaving fish, birds, and driftwood to pour back into the sea. Madoc hung on to the steering oar and prayed no one would be washed overboard. The heaving ship's crew had bloodied hands, knees, elbows, and smashed fingers and toes. It wallowed and pitched but stayed upright. Madoc was proud of her. She was part of him and he was part of her. No one on his ship had gone overboard. He loved the *Gwennan Gorn* because she had saved not only his life but others, even three barbarians, from the cruelties of the people living on land and the storms that take over the sea. So, that was the purpose of the ten-ship fleet: survival.

The gray-green clouds seemed to wait until the *Gwennan Gorn* was directly beneath before opening up and spilling sheets of rain. The bailing watch went back to work. The rain turned to hailstones the size of hazelnuts, which hurt when they hit exposed flesh and left dents in soft pine-wood kegs.

Amidship was a span of ice pellets. Madoc asked two of the messmates to scoop the hail into cooking pots and buckets to use as fresh water. "Cannot be too much salt water in it," he said.

The clouds moved away, and the men sang a song of victory when the sun shone through the huge multicolored rainbow. The gunwales and every wood plank steamed in the hot sunlight as if a fire had been set underneath. Madoc felt sweat collect on his brow as he spread blankets to dry on ropes.

For the main meal that evening, each person broke open a large nut, drank the sweet juice, and gnawed on the rich, white meat. The messmates spent the rest of daylight throwing out everything damaged by seawater, drying the rest, and reorganizing the stores.

After sup, Madoc paced the deck and scanned east, west, north, and south for the other nine ships. He did not feel totally whole without the sight of the nine ships behind him or in a circle around him. On the starboard there was low, flat land of sand and dunes stretching as far as he could see. He guessed that his ship had made little headway during the storm. A few moments later he called from the bow, "Sand bar ahead!" he ordered the oars out. As the *Gwennan Gorn* moved closer to the long, narrow sand bar, Madoc saw that on its other side was a wide gap and a cluster of planked ships as safe as babes in a mother's arms. He felt as though a weight fell from his chest. He smiled.

Conlaf, feeling much better, called, "Ships ahead— seven, maybe, eight!"

Madoc rounded the sandbar and then saw an island

about three-and-a-half leagues wide. On the seaside of the island was a wide strip of seaweed. It looked like a strip of solid land, but there could be dozens of ells of water beneath the greenery. Madoc's smile disappeared and his chest tightened. It was hard to tell, but the green weeds seemed to surround pieces of planking—ship's planking. He decided the other ships were so busy following one another out of the rough sea into the refuge of a bay that was protected by hills in the background that they had probably missed seeing what might be a sunken ship. He did not want to follow his last thought with the knowledge that only eight ships followed him. It was hard to ask the question: *Where is the ninth ship?*

Finally, he told himself that he had never seen barbarians with a planked ship. There was only one logical conclusion. A lump formed in his throat. The planking in the weeds was from a ship of his own fleet. He signaled the eight ships to go beyond the bay and anchor on the shore. He was going to explore the bed of seaweed. Before sundown he beached the *Gwennan Gorn* on the sandbar and took to the sea alone in a coracle.

Sitting in the coracle, Madoc poked in the seaweed and debris with his paddle. He pounded on the cracked and broken hull of the overturned ship. Her mast floated beside the wreckage, and there was no sign of life. At first Madoc refused to recognize the ship. He sat and stared at the wreckage for a long time wondering how it got there.

Conlaf came to him in another coracle and said, "The sea was awfully high. I believe they all drowned. 'Tis a pity, because we are so close to finding a place for a new colony. They would have liked to have seen our new land, to have been a part of finding it."

Maybe they will see it, if we find them, thought Madoc, probing a soggy gray mass, which he did not recognize as anything significant. He imagined the men from the *Pedr Sant* alive and floating somewhere.

" 'Tis the swollen carcass of a damnable sheep," said Conlaf. "The *White Crane* and *Pedr Sant* are the only ships with sheep."

"The *Crane*, with its white bird in the stern, is anchored

in the bay." Madoc's voice was low and sad. "So, this is all that is left of *Pedr Sant* and—and her crew? Nay! Riryd is a fine shipmaster. His men know what to do in a storm."

In his mind's eye, Madoc saw the dark hair and bright lively eyes of his brother. Freckles always danced on Riryd's nose as he talked with that Irish brogue. In his head Madoc heard his brother say, "I love thee, Cymro." In his head he saw his half-brother Einon's serious face and ruddy nose. He stood up, shook his paddle toward the horizon, rocked his coracle so it shipped water, and in one breath railed, "Lugh! Did you do this? Did you cause the death of the *Pedr Sant*, including my brothers and my sailors? If you did, I be not going to speak to you again. Ever!" He dropped his paddle with a splash. *How could I pray to a god that lets so many good men die?* He thought.

Conlaf plucked up the paddle and slipped it into Madoc's coracle.

Madoc sat motionless, not minding the water. He drew up his knees and held them tight with his arms. His eyes were dry; his head lowered. He stared at the peeled sticks forming the bottom of the little boat. Suddenly he looked up. He felt himself driven by that unfathomable energy of grief. He was determined to pull what was left of the *Pedr Sant* from her watery grave. The hide of the sheep would make someone warm boots or a coverlet. Her planks could be used to mend the other ships. The spirits of her thirty-two men seemed to energize Madoc. He fastened the carved claw of his paddle onto Conlaf's coracle and pulled floating planks into both coracles. They worked as a team to pull the mast and whatever else could be salvaged from the sea into their two coracles. When they unloaded on the island, they came back for more. When it was finished, Madoc sat in his beached coracle with his head bowed. He was exhausted. He heard, saw, and felt nothing from the outside. All of him, his physical organs and the thoughts swirling around in his brain, were enclosed inside a strong bony skeleton and held together by a tough skin covering.

"Leave the shipmaster be," said Conlaf to Madoc's crew. "His spirit is seeking its own peace. We will spend the night here. In the morning I will rub his arms and legs with sweet oil. You shall see before tomorrow's end Chief Shipmaster

Madoc will be striding about shouting more orders at us. He will tell us to bring all these wooden planks to the mainland! 'Twas one brother of his blood, his half-brother, thirty brothers of his heart, and six sheep that he—that we lost to the sea this time. 'Tis more than the barbarians took! Why do we have to fight so hard for peace? In the end, are we caught in our own storm?" His voice broke; he could not go on.

Tipper said, "We knew if we stayed in Wales we would be killed for our beliefs. We knew unproved land in unknown seas might mean death. We chose the unknown. We were not coerced. We vowed to build a settlement of freedom, peace, and understanding. This we will do no matter what happens. We do this for love of our fellow druids and the Old Religion."

"Aye, aye!" shouted Madoc's crew.

The two women and Nohold were busy scraping the flesh from a sheep's hide. Cougar promised Little Mother she would make the softest hide blanket ever seen for her coming baby girl. "Soft, white fur—fine for a girl," she said.

"Big girl," said Little Mother with her hands on the top of her large, full-blown belly.

The next morning the planking and mast from the *Pedr Sant* was loaded on the *Gwennan Gorn*'s deck. Then Madoc sailed into the bay, which was about ten leagues wide at the entrance, bowl shaped, and excellent protection from storms. He scouted around the bay's shoreline before beaching with the other eight ships. For the next few days he sent two or three ships at a time to look for men clinging to floating debris or coracles from the *Pedr Sant*. Nothing was found. Neither did the men see barbarians' fires along the curved beach in the evenings. There was no sign of other humans, only themselves.

Madoc said they would camp on the fine, dry white sand that reminded him of Aberffraw. He hunkered down and looked across the calm bay. He saw nothing to put fear in his heart. This place was paradise compared to the bogs and insects the men had seen. The sides of the bay were well protected by hills that circled his ships like a mother's protective arms around her children. It felt familiar and warm, a safe place. He stood alone with his eyes shut and his hands at his side for a long time, thinking of the people close to him that he had lost in his lifetime.

My foster parents, Dornoll and Seth, and my sister, Wyn, gave me a chance to learn about the stars and navigation. My true father, Owain, gave me the opportunity to travel, to learn about people. My beloved wife, Annesta, gave me a daughter and a sense of honor. Brett gave me a sense of humor and made my heart light. My brother, Riryd, and half-brother, Einon, gave me direction. The more he thought about these dear people now on the Otherside, the more he realized how much he owed them. *I can never pay them back. How could I?* At that moment he believed he heard Riryd's voice on the gentle wind saying, "I found this place, but could not get inside the safe harbor before the storm took us. 'Tis a gift for thee, Cymro."

He opened his eyes and saw a meadow of wild flowers and a herd of white-tailed deer crossing a shallow river. Beauty, fresh water, and game—what more could his men want? "*Diolch*," he said aloud in Welsh. "Thanks." Suddenly he became aware that one of the cows had died in the storm and still lay in the pen giving off an overpowering rotten stench.

Tipper, with tongue in cheek, asked if they could land and have a roast.

Madoc frowned, held his breath in the fetid air, helped Tipper cut the putrefying cow loose, and together they lowered it overboard. He suddenly noticed that his sore hand did not throb with every heartbeat. He pulled off the dirty wadmal. The palm was red, the swelling down, and Conlaf's knife cut lay open. On top of the wound, shining in the sunlight, as long as Madoc's thumbnail and thin as a splinter, was the needle's tip. He showed Cougar and said, "You were right, it was bad luck, but remember this: seawater from a spout is the best medicine for festered needle points."

She smiled and did not laugh when she saw Madoc's hand was much better. She asked if women were bad luck on a sailing ship as big as a lodge.

"That is said sometimes among our men, but what does

it matter? I know 'tis not true. Women are good luck, not bad luck. Dead cows are bad luck," said Madoc, laughing and thinking how well he felt. His fever was gone. His sore throat was no more. He and everyone on his ship had worked with reason against the waterspout, and the gods were on his side. The wheel of fortune had spun and most of their cups had been spared.

In the morning he examined the head of the bay and discovered what appeared to be two rivers flowing down from some vast area in the north. In the distance were hazy, blue hills. By afternoon the messmates caught pigeons, large as chickens, by throwing nets into the air when the birds swooped low. Each was baked in a coating of mud that cracked and peeled off along with feathers and fatty skin. After a delicious meal, the men talked about taking the ships further up one arm of the muddy estuary to see what was there.

Madoc took his ship up one of the arms of the mighty drainage basin to get above brackish water and the tides. The water became shallow, and there were trees instead of swamp grass on either side of the river's bank. At noon the ship was anchored as close to a high-cut bank as possible. Nohold and a few men in coracles explored further upstream. They found that the waterway was divided into many channels by large grassy islands. On the islands were rabbits, big birds, possum, and snakes. There was no sign of human habitation, no sign of flesh-eating cannibals, and Nohold did what he could to let the men know he had never been there before and never heard of any traders who had been. He felt certain the land belonged to no one but the wild game.

That evening Madoc announced to all of the men, "This is the place! The *Dre!*" He told them that the ships could navigate easily upstream to the high cutbank and there, where the view was like standing on top of the world, they would build a village.

The men shouted, "Hooray!" and ran up and down the low dunes singing ballads like children.

Even though still grief stricken, Madoc laughed when Cougar's foot sank as high as her thigh in the fine sand just over the crest of a wide dune, where the grains were deposited in the wind's shadow and built up to a slope of increasing steepness. She pulled her foot up, stepped down again, and started an avalanche. At the same time a strange and startling booming began that built to a roar as the tongues of flowing sand slid down the slipface. In no time there were a dozen men strung out on the breezy top of the wide dune. Cougar showed how she put her foot over on the lee side, away from the sea where there was no breeze, and let it sink into the sand. "Dead men with us," she said to Madoc. "Have laugh." She pushed the sand with her foot and started another slab of sand gliding downward, and the booming began again.

This phenomenon was so unexpected and so delightful to Madoc and his men that they put their grief behind and were like young boys playing with a new toy. Some climbed other dunes and discovered that if the angle of repose was as high as the first dune, they could invariably make the booming roar as sand was pushed into the downwind slope. No one tried to explain the phenomenon. They just enjoyed making the sand roar.

Caradoc said he had once heard that there were dunes on Anglesey that made the sound of tolling bells on warm summer evenings, if the wind was just right. Before nightfall the *Gwennan Gorn* led eight sails to the ideal campsite of high land, with the river running around three sides. It was like ideal hilltop fortifications in Wales. The beach was wide enough, when the dense willows were cut back, for the ships to be brought onto it by rollers. The top grassland could be reached by digging footholds in the cutbank. Nohold suggested that they cut steps and lay rock on the earth to hold the steps' shape, and he showed how easy that was to do.

Madoc remembered the fiber ladder he had seen with Brett and suggested they use withie ladders that could be hauled up in case of a barbarian invasion from the water. Llieu reminded him that a stairway was much easier to carry things from the beach to the top. Then he said, "It is skill with weapons, in our case, words, that determines the outcome of a battle, not so much the type of fortification, even though no way of climbing to the top where the huts would be, might hold an enemy for a time.

Nohold, a trader, learned the language easily and surprised Madoc by saying, "If you plan on peace, first thing, plan on strategy with words and actions; other weapons may be necessary, but secondary."

Madoc realized there was much to learn and listened to everything. He noticed that Cougar also was listening and repeating words.

The wide grassy land was above the flood plain and gave a fine view in all four directions. On the fourth side, behind the hilltop, was a forest of long-needled pine trees. The riverbanks were thick with willows and birds. It would be easy to erect willow palisades for protection against marauders of any kind, animal or human.

"Huzza! This is the place," repeated Madoc. "*Cymru Newydd,* New Wales. Let us give thanks to the Chief Lord God for bringing us to this place."

The men clasped hands and stood in a huge circle around Madoc. He reached behind the circle and brought Cougar and Little Mother in, next to Nohold. "Every one same?" asked Cougar.

"Aye!" said Madoc. "Everyone is the same in this place."

"Yu!" said Cougar.

Madoc closed his eyes and cleared his mind of stray thoughts in an effort to bring the spirit of every man who had lost his life on the journey back among the living. Cougar had said, "Dead men with us." He wanted those men to know the joy the living felt. He tilted his face to the sky and thought about the thin veil that separated the spirits of the living and dead. Wind sighed through the pines. He stood perfectly still and breathed the warm, humid air in and out. The druids softly chanted their thanksgiving and circled sunwise then counter sunwise around their leader.

In his mind Madoc saw the dark green trees standing watch over unfamiliar, bearded faces chanting around, not him, but a roaring fire. The picture faded and the trees watched over others sitting in a circle around a single tree and singing. He felt that the spirits of Brett and Riryd were near. They had shown him that a succession of people, through the ages, occupied this place. He truly thought he could feel the presence of spirits. The druids' chanting became louder than the wind swishing through the treetops, then stopped. He inhaled deeply and exhaled slowly. He held out his hands to embrace the God of gods. His right hand tingled, as though touched by something soft and gauzy. He opened his eyes as the last rays of the sun bathed the circle of extraordinary people in its golden glow. He closed the prayer by saying, "We have given our thanks and now we ask that the gods bless our *Llan Newydd* with a sign."

A lone eagle lazily glided overhead and perched in a treetop as if to watch over the newcomers. At Madoc's feet lay a gold-brown feather, a gift.

XXII
Earth and Sky

Women . . . drink a glass of water containing a teaspoonful of Queen Anne's Lace seeds immediately after intercourse to prevent pregnancy. And women . . . chew dry seeds of Queen Anne's Lace to reduce fertility. Both practices were known to women 2,000 years ago.
—John M. Riddle, J. Worth Estes, and Josiah C. Russell, "Birth Control in the Ancient World," *Archaeology*

Madoc fastened the eagle's feather into the right side of his lean-to where everyone could see it and know that it was a sign their endeavor would flourish.

Some of the druids sat in their lean-tos and studied the barbarians' fishing spears. Nohold showed the men how they were made, with the ends similar to the feathers on an arrow. Each spear's plume was taken from the same bird-wing in order to get the correct spin.

Madoc found that cattail, plantain, beach grass, willow, oaks, wild rose, pink clover, witch hazel, and giant thistle were similar to those plants in Wales. The finger-sized branches of the unfamiliar, crooked little trees with exposed roots were excellent for bows when peeled and smoked over a cool fire. The wood was not soft like pine, and not brittle like oak.

One morning, while hacking off some long finger-sized branches to make himself a bow, he heard Cougar and Little Mother talking. Cougar seemed excited about something. At first Madoc thought it was just the way two women talk when they find something special, and he expected Cougar would ask him to come see what they had found. Maybe it would be some fleshy, sweet-tasting berry. He was hungry for something sweet. When they did not come near him, he went to them and looked at the sorrel they were picking. "What are you going to do with this?" he asked, picking up a scaly little bulb.

"Soup," said Cougar. She picked up several little three-leafed stems and said, "Tea."

Little Mother began to moan and held her hands against her distended belly. Water ran down her bare legs. "Oh, yu!" she said, bending over.

Cougar looked under Little Mother's skirt and told her to lie with her back on the ground, under the pines where it was cool. She touched Madoc and pointed to the ground.

He did not want to stay. He wanted to find Conlaf or Troyes or Llieu, and he said he would get a healer.

Cougar put her hands behind his knees so that he bent his legs and sat on the ground next to Little Mother. She put his hand on Little Mother's big belly. Something underneath the skin was moving, twisting, turning ever so slowly, and suddenly her belly was hard as stone. He jerked his hand away, stood up, and said he would get help.

Cougar grabbed his hands. "Cougar is healer," she said. "Needs you. Stay."

Little Mother's face contorted with pain. When her face relaxed, she took short breaths and beads of perspiration dotted her forehead like drops of rain.

Madoc squatted on his haunches, wiped Little Mother's forehead, and wiped his hand on the fallen pine needles. His eyes were frantic when he looked at Cougar. "Honest, I know naught about birthing, except a dog having pups. This is the same, huh?" He sat down. "This will be over in a minute. Then I can get my friend Conlaf, the best healer I know."

She thought, *I like this man, who knows all about men. He has no fear of what they think. He can talk to their heart and to their mind and make them see what he is thinking. He can be sad with them or joyful with them. They are willing to follow him any place, because they love him. He is honorable and knows he is obligated to his men. Certainly he had a mother. He had a wife. Still, he does not know much about women. So, he is not complete in his knowing. Imagine a grown man, who does not know his opposite side. I will teach him.*

She pulled her hair back and tied it behind her ears with a thick stem of grass. She sat beside him and put his hand on Little Mother's belly again. Under her breath she said, "Yu," as if she were telling him, "Good. This is the thing that you have to do. Help me and I will help you know women."

He saw Little Mother's breasts looking at the sky like two huge eyes with purple-brown aureoles and he wanted to yell, "Help!" He thought about what would happen in Wales or Ireland. His culture never let men hang around during the birthing process. A midwife would be present; if not, the mother was on her own. It was believed that delivering a baby was a natural event, like a dog having puppies, and needed no advice from a male physician, unless there was a problem.

Cougar took Little Mother's moss skirt off and laid it aside. She dumped the sorrel bulbs from a large pot and took it to the stream. While she was gone, Madoc saw, with fascination, that Little Mother's swollen belly contained a visible force, a real creature that exerted its own energy inside Little Mother's protesting body. This creature's activity caused so much pain that Little Mother was indifferent to and isolated from anything else around her. He pushed hair away from her eyes and said, "Everything will be all right. You are not the first mother in the world."

He thought of his boyhood and the limited number of days he had studied medicine. Archdruid Llieu knew early on that he was never going to be a healer, because all he ever dreamed about was sailing. Those days were nothing like this. He wondered if either Llieu or Conlaf had seen a real woman in the throes of a normal birthing. Troyes once told him that he knew what to give women to abort their fetus, rusty wheat, but even in Paris, he had never attended a human birth. He began to feel pleased that Cougar wanted him to stay, yet his feelings were mixed with trepidation. He had no idea what to do.

Little Mother was no help. She paid no attention to him. She let him stare at her nakedness and looked only inside her own head where she saw a precious baby girl struggling to get out, to walk on the earth, and look at the blue sky.

She knew from experience that she was subject to the will of the unknown creature inside her, a will that was stronger than hers. From now on it did not matter what Little Mother wanted; this girl baby's wants came first.

Madoc took Little Mother's hands, and she squeezed so hard that he could feel the sharp bite of her short nails. She opened her mouth and, without embarrassment, growled deep inside her throat and then screamed like an animal caught in a vicious trap.

Cougar came back and talked in soothing whispers. She dribbled water from the clay pot on Little Mother's lips as they pulled back from her teeth. The water spilled from the corners of her mouth. Cougar told her she was doing fine. "It will be over soon. The man with the pale hair is beside me. He knows things you and I never heard of, but he missed knowing the feelings of a mother bringing forth a new life. You will teach him something so wonderful that he will never forget. I tell you that to touch his hand makes my arm tingle. He gives me butterflies in my belly. He came to help us save your baby."

Little Mother grimaced and growled. Her eyes closed and popped open.

Cougar lay her ear against the mountainous belly and said, "bit-a-bit, bit-a-bit. Yu."

Madoc wanted to lay his ear against that huge belly and listen to the bit-a-bit sound, but he knew he dared not. He looked at Cougar's small hands and long narrow fingers. His eyes moved up her arms to her shoulders and neck. She was evenly proportioned, beautiful. Her face was calm as she pushed Little Mother's legs apart. She placed Little Mother's feet solidly on the ground so her knees formed the top of a tent. She lowered her head and squinted at the dark, red place in the middle where the legs were attached to the body.

She put two fingers inside the dark, red hole for an instant, then tried three fingers. Afterwards she wiped off the slimy stuff on the grass and sat on the other side of Little Mother. She put her hand over Madoc's that was on Little Mother's belly and sang a short three-note song over and over. Madoc asked what the words were, and she explained so that Madoc sang with her. "Come. Come little baby. I will show you the earth and the sky."

Little Mother pushed out a low growl from the back of her throat when another hard contraction slammed into her midsection. Cougar pushed on Madoc's hand. He was certain that Little Mother would tear herself in two if it were necessary to push out the small creature. This terrible, wonderful ability was a natural thing with women. He admitted to himself that he did not understand why women ever let men lie with them. But men had always had their way with women. Was that the ultimate weakness of women? It did not make sense. He got up, went to the stream, and cut the bark from a couple of young willow branches. He cut them in small pieces and told Little Mother to bite on them. "Ease pain," he said.

The sun dropped lower in the sky. Madoc felt a chill in the air. Little Mother perspired. Her face had lost its healthy brown color and was a kind of blotched sandy color. Cougar made grunting sounds trying to get Little Mother to push more. She held her hand up to indicate that the cervix had spread more than her three fingers. Madoc held Little Mother's hands, and they were no longer squeezing hard. During each contraction, Cougar pushed below the breastbone with her small hands trying to force the creature out.

Cougar found it hard to sit still. She paced around Little Mother and looked at the top of her legs to see if anything was being forced out besides the bloody water. She muttered to herself.

Little Mother looked worn out. Her face was dun colored and flat, a mask covering her nearly unbearable pain. She was a wounded animal, breathing from the mouth, staring at nothing, and screaming at the pain given to her by an offspring leaving the womb and beginning to unfold its tiny arms and legs. The earth and sky were quiet, waiting, absorbing this worldwide, primitive drama.

Madoc thought Cougar looked too young to be a healer, not the way he imagined a midwife would be, watching the struggle between mother and child. The force of the next contraction made him shudder. Both women moaned and growled as the pain rolled out. Madoc stood, took a few steps, and said he was going after a healer.

Cougar pointed to herself. She knew that the only healers he had with him were men. It was obvious that they had little or no practice with births. "Please sit," she said.

He smiled at her. She looked at him for a moment and held his gaze momentarily, then he lowered his eyes.

She saw that her scrutiny made him uneasy, and she was glad because it showed her that he realized there was something building between them. She held his hand and ran her other hand up and down his arm.

The sensation gave him goose bumps. His heart began to race. This woman had magic in her fingers.

Little Mother's contractions came closer, harder and faster, leaving no time for her to take a deep breath between muscle compressions. Now her noises were nothing like screams. They were deep, violent, primordial sounds heard during the formation of the universe. They were as old as the breaking apart and coming together of stars. They were as old as the rising up of mountains, the cracking of ice-jammed rivers, the bursting of tightening tree-bark, and the first howling of a newborn just out of his protective water-filled cocoon.

Madoc sat down. Cougar gave him a drink of water and what was left over she held to Little Mother's lips, whose throat was so tight that she could not swallow. Instead she narrowed her eyes and grunted deep inside her chest.

Madoc did not believe anyone could stand so much pain. He wondered if all that energy was worthwhile. He thought, *No human can survive this much pain.*

"Soon," said Cougar, looking at the top of Little Mother's legs. She continued to add her own howls and grunts of encouragement.

Lugh, do not let this mother die, Madoc thought.

Cougar took his arm and placed it lengthwise, from hand to elbow, below Little Mother's breasts. "Uuargh!" she said. "Push!"

He got up on his knees and when he heard the anguished little growly cries and felt the tired muscles tighten, he pushed gently, slowly, with his forearm against the bulging flesh. He was afraid to push hard. He did not want to hurt Little Mother. What if he pushed on the neck of the creature inside? Could he choke it? He pushed a little harder and felt the muscles flex and relax. He heard Cougar let out her breath. He stopped pushing.

Cougar squatted down, and they both looked at the top of Little Mother's legs. Suddenly, a shiny wet, black arc of hair was visible, but when the contraction relaxed, the dark arc disappeared. He looked at Cougar as if to say she was right when she said, "soon."

She looked disgusted. "Push!" she said, and her bent arm, from the elbow down, punched into Madoc's middle. "Uugh!" Air expelled. He bent over and stayed that way for several moments. She bent over him. He felt her breath falling soft against his cheek. Her eyelashes fluttered against his cheek. She spread her hand across his chest and moved downward to his breastbone. When her hand was under the breastbone, she pushed. There was no question what she wanted him to do. This time he would do it right.

She picked up the empty pot and went for more water.

He placed his arm back in position on the distended belly. Little Mother grabbed on to his arm like it was a safety bar. She held her breath, and he felt her muscles tighten. He heard mewly sounds, and he pushed hard. Little Mother's hands tightened. He leaned across her and put his other arm across the bottom of her abdomen and the hand flat on the ground so he had better leverage. He imagined that he could feel the creature inside slide down a little. He pushed harder and thought it was like gripping on to the steering oar in stormy weather, when his hands became fused to the wood. He imagined seeing two tiny legs flex and kick back against his arm. There was the sound of a plop, like a tiny frog jumping into a pond. He held his breath and hoped the creature would not shoot out like an arrow from a bow. He did not want to disappoint Cougar, and so, he would not let up the pressure until Little Mother gasped for air. He pulled one arm back, sat up on his haunches, and let his pushing-arm rest under the warm, heaving breasts.

Cougar's cool fingers pulled his arm back. She smelled of yellow rue. She showed him the strong-scented, bitter-tasting leaves she had found by the stream. "Use later. Stops bleeding," she said, kneeling beside him with her cool face against his hot face. He could feel the trickle of her tears, taste their salt on his lips, and he breathed deep. He was ready to push again if she asked him. Instead, she surprised him and held up two fingers. "Babies," she said, pushing her fist fast past the fingers of her other hand.

The big pot was half-full of water, and a pile of green sphagnum moss was beside a handful of rue and plantain. He asked if he should build a fire to warm the water. She shook her head, laughed, and shoved half of the moss under Little Mother's blood-messy buttocks. Suddenly, a slippery, warm, round, dark arc became a whole ball, and a head slipped out. She put her fingers over the top of the little head, stroked a tiny ear, and twisted the head so that he could see the face, calm as death. The creature's eyes were closed. It slipped further and exposed a tiny shoulder. Cougar's hand went over the shoulder and under the arm. She pulled with a steady pressure, like pulling on something sinking in quicksand. The creature fell into her hands. It curled into a ball, with its knees pulled up against its arms. It was covered with slime and blood, and its purple little face was wrinkled like a shrunken old man. Between its crinkled thighs was a short, wormlike penis. She lay him on Little Mother's gray, moss skirt so his face was close to the ground. A flexible, narrow tube stretched tight from the middle of his belly back inside Little Mother, who moaned. Cougar fed her tea made from dried trillium leaves and root. She drank but did not open her eyes. Next to that tube another ball of dark hair slipped out. Cougar was surprised, but knew exactly what to do. She held the second head in one hand and turned the face up toward the sky. She held the tiny jaw in the other hand and jerked so that the neck stretched out and a shoulder appeared, then an arm and another arm. The second baby slid out with his legs curled up against his belly so that his penis was easily seen. He too had a dark, purple cord attached to his belly. Cougar gave the second baby to Madoc to hold while she bit off the cord of the first baby close to its belly. A few drops of blood oozed out, and she folded the cord over and wrapped a thread of her hair around it to hold it in place, until it dried and dropped off by itself. She put the first baby in the pot of water, so his head leaned on the edge, and gave Little Mother more of the trillium potion. Madoc gave her the second baby so she could bite off his cord.

Squatting against the pot, he washed the first baby using a pad of moss to scrub it clean. It took time to clean off the slimy mess. The baby looked at the sky, shivered, drew a breath, and gave a lusty cry. He held the baby out, away from his body, in the palm of his hand, and it sprinkled the seagrass. Then he wrapped it in the moss skirt.

Cougar hummed softly and put the second baby in the pot of bloody water for Madoc to wash after she had secured his cord with a long thread of her hair. After washing, Madoc patted him dry with green moss. The baby opened his eyes, sucked in several long breaths, and waved his arms. Madoc turned him on his belly. He looked at the earth, sprinkled, and then he cried loud and dry. He had no tears. Madoc wrapped him in his shirt.

Cougar would not let Madoc throw out the bloody water but put the pot next to Little Mother's legs. Squatting next to Little Mother with the second baby in his arms, he rocked back and forth and spoke softly.

The baby stopped crying and closed his eyes. His small face was flat and looked like the face on a little girl's leather doll.

Madoc laid the twin babies on Little Mother's chest. She touched her babies, looked at them for only a moment, then closed her eyes. In a disappointed voice she said she had expected a girl. Madoc told her two boys were a special prize. She did not know the word *prize* and gritted her teeth and tightened her stomach muscles into a push. A rounded bunch of purple-red flesh, zigzagged with blue veins and held together inside a transparent membrane, slid from the torn, bloody hole at the top of her legs.

Madoc was startled and picked up the babies. He had forgotten about afterbirth.

Cougar scooped up the placenta as if she had been waiting for it and set it aside. She gave Little Mother a handful of plantain leaves to chew to stop the bleeding. Little Mother shivered and licked her blue lips. Cougar washed her with bloody water and packed crushed plantain and moss tightly against the top of her legs so that it could be held in place with a female belt. She pulled a string at her waist, stepped out of her moss skirt, and tucked it around her friend.

When the first baby cried, the second baby cried. Madoc held both of them. He stared at the first baby wrapped in the gray, moss skirt and the second baby wrapped in his soft, linen shirt. He paced back and forth and hummed. He felt elated. He had seen these babies take their first breath and their hard-laboring mother live through all of it. "Lugh, we thank you for strong mothers," he said softly.

Cougar put the afterbirth in the pot with the bloody water, went to a sandy place beside a large stone, and buried it deep enough to keep animals and bad spirits away. She wiped out the pot with leaves and sand and left it in the sun to dry and purify.

Madoc let the first baby's mouth enclose his finger. He was surprised that the infant did not know how to suck. He sat beside Little Mother so she could see her twin sons and smile. He could tell she had forgotten her disappointment that the babies were not a girl, nor two girls. Even with her eyes closed, she smiled. *She is glad the babies are out and the work is over*, he thought. He had never heard a mother complain about carrying a load of babies in her belly or being afraid of the birth process. He thought it must be something a mother puts up with, to have such a wonderful thing as a new tiny person, or two tiny persons. He suddenly thought of his wife, Annesta, who had delivered her baby—their baby—without him, but of course his mother was there, and she knew exactly what to do. Brenda would like Cougar. With the twins cuddled in his arms, he looked at Cougar and said, "See Earth, wrapped in your skirt. See Sky wrapped in my shirt. I be thankful you knew what to do. You are a fine healer; I thank you."

She repeated the *thank you* words. Then slowly and carefully told him that Little Mother, her twin boys, she and Nohold could never go back to their village and remain alive. Chief Wren would kill them. She believed the twins were a special sign from the spirits, a kind of double power. She thought both babies were meant to live. When grown, they might be a protection against the chief of Sandpoint. Every Calusa woman knew that the weaker of the twins was usually left overnight near the nearest alligator bog. If the infant was alive the next morning, it was kept. She explained with a few words, hand signs, and facial expressions that today's Sandpoint alligators were well fed because Chief Wren allowed no newborn boys to live for fear they would one day get together and take his chief-power away. If a mother hid her baby boy and he was found later, he was sacrificed to the rain spirit by throwing him to the logs with big jaws and sharp teeth, the alligators. "Rabbit's son was hidden. When he was found, he was kept to act in the Crane Ceremony as a special gift to the rain spirit. So then, next year he will probably be sacrificed, unless Rabbit takes him away or something happens to Wren."

Madoc was astounded. It was hard to believe that the barbarians reacted to power much like English kings. He tried to tell her. But he was not certain she understood about English kings or his Welsh half-brother, King Dafydd. He lay the babies naked on Little Mother's chest, so she could look them over.

She immediately enclosed them in her arms, combed their soft, dark hair languidly with her fingers, and let the tears slide down the sides of her face. "Oh! Tee hee!" she giggled, when showered by both baby boys. "Ooo! Tee hee!" Cougar and Madoc joined her laughter. It had turned into a fine day.

"Hey, I kept the skirt and shirt dry," said Madoc. Still laughing, he rewrapped the babies, hoping there was a better way to tell them apart than from their wrappings.

Cougar smiled like she had read his mind, pushed him aside, and rubbed a pinch of sorrel greens on the ankle of Earth, who then had an unmistakable, round, green-purple spot on his leg.

All smiles, Cougar put her juicy fingers on Madoc's lips, then wrapped her arms around him. She rubbed her face on his arm, then on his face. For a moment the world closed in on only the two of them, and he truly believed they had done something wonderful together. It was indescribable. She tightened herself against him so he could feel the softness of her tiny breasts. She pulled his buttocks in so close that he could feel the bones on either side of her pelvis. His exhaustion was swept away. He wanted to hold her like this for a long time. He was aroused and wanted to lie on the mossy stream bank with her. He took a deep breath and chided himself and was glad that he had not lost his mind. He gently pulled himself away. He could not take advantage of this beautiful young woman he hardly knew. He only happened to be there to help out in a birth. Cougar knew what to do. Surely she had seen many births before. *Is she a midwife or a general healer? Who taught her? Her dead grandmother? I do not know who she is, except intensely interesting and exciting. She is a barbarian. She has made me see the world in a wild, primitive new way.*

He told her he wanted to name the babies Earth and Sky. She pointed to Little Mother. Of course, he would ask her when she was awake.

Two days later, before the stars came out, Madoc went to find Conlaf. He was worried about Little Mother, who had not awakened enough to sit up, and she smelled funny. "Smells like the dead cow," he told Conlaf. "Is that normal after birthing? Is it?"

Conlaf, the Healer, had never seen parturition, because it was a woman's thing. He wanted to tease Madoc about being a midwife, but after feeling Little Mother's face and arms, he said she was too warm. She had a fever, and he could treat that with tea from sassafras root. He asked Clare and Tipper to make a sling to carry Little Mother back to the camp where she could be kept in blankets, have her face cooled with a wet cloth, drink Conlaf's sassafras tea and Cougar's plantain and comfrey tea.

Nohold was all smiles, as if the babies were his. The third day Little Mother awoke, and he brought her water, rubbed her back and shoulders, and talked with her. She told him that Madoc wanted to name her babies and what the words meant. He said the names over and over to himself, "Earth. Sky." Finally, after the evening meal, he came to Madoc, smiled, repeated the names, and said, "Yu. Good."

Madoc went back with him to see how the babies were doing or what Cougar was doing; he was not sure. Little Mother was feeling better, and her skin was not so warm to the touch. She and Cougar were squatted together on the deck of the *Gwennan Gorn*. Each had a baby, coaxing it to her breast. The babies groped and bobbed. Madoc was taken aback. What in the world was Cougar doing acting like a barbarian? She was not a mother. Madoc slumped to the deck and chewed on a yellow stem of seagrass.

"No milk," explained Nohold. "Babies learning." He made sucking sounds.

Madoc could not stop laughing until Conlaf asked what was so funny about such a bizarre sight. Conlaf repeated Nohold's words and said, "They are training the laddies to suck. In a day or two when Little Mother has milk, the babies will know what to do. 'Tis a wonderful thing. Our young mothers could learn something here."

"If you say so," said Madoc. He was put out that he had not thought of that. He was put out because Cougar was exposing her beautiful, firm little breasts in front of these men. It did not seem proper. Of course it was all right for Little Mother—those were her babies and they needed to be fed. But Cougar was a beautiful girl by anybody's standards. He felt his face grow warm. He had to stop feeling this way. He drew a deep breath. He had no business to be so foolish. He was the chief shipmaster and had taken a pledge not to consort with the barbarians.

Well, of course, I knew that. But one could learn a lot about this new land through friendship. Nohold could teach the men many things. He is an honest, hard worker, and it is easy to see he is fond of Little Mother and her brood. He is not as sickly as when we first found him. I like him.

In a couple of days Nohold built a shelter for himself, Little Mother, her babies, and Cougar. Then he offered to help the men build their shelters. He learned to talk easily with them, and they learned more of his words. He confessed that the babies cried a lot. He asked Conlaf and Archdruid Llieu to look at them. Llieu said it was all right for small babies to cry, not to worry. Conlaf said he thought the babies were not gaining weight. They were not eating enough. He experimented with his little finger, and they sucked all right. They were more powerful than the warm-water bloodsuckers that ate the infection out of pus-filled wounds. He sought out Little Mother who was grinding the heads of wild grains into flour. She sat with her back against a pine and ground slowly. Conlaf thought she still smelled sickish and remembered what Madoc had said about her smelling like the dead cow. At first he had dismissed the smell, thinking she was bleeding. Most women smelled unhealthy during their period. He sat beside her. Her arms shook. He put a hand on one of them. She was hot as a stone sitting in the afternoon sun. Her face was shiny. Her eyes glistened. He looked down her throat and saw nothing unusual. He asked if she had any boils or wounds. She shook her head. He asked if she was still bleeding.

"Little," she said.

"Can I see?"

"No," she said. "You not my man. Shame!"

He called Cougar and told her he did not believe Little Mother was healing properly and asked her to look at the top of her legs and tell him what she saw. "When was the last time she had intercourse?"

Cougar looked at Conlaf, turned her head, and spit to show that the question was unnecessary. "She no do that until babies old enough to eat mush." She put her ear on Little Mother's chest and listened and said, "Bist, breath—bit-a-bit, bit-a-bit. Bist, breath—"

Conlaf said, "Bist?"

"*Bist* comes when she breathes."

"All right," Conlaf said. "I understand. Let us have a look."

Cougar told Little Mother to lie on the ground with her knees up.

Conlaf went down on his hands and knees and smelled the infection immediately. He could see the vulva was dark red and swollen. He saw where it had torn during the birth. Cougar said she was packing Little Mother with crushed plantain leaves each morning after she stood waist deep in the stream to clean herself. She did not know anything else to do. Conlaf said Little Mother was to stay on her pallet for the next couple of days. No standing in the stream. Nohold could not come near while she was unclean. He wrinkled his face while thinking that childbirth fever was something he knew about, but he had never worked with a patient who suffered from it. Midwives treated it and dreaded it. It was common and fatal where he came from.

Cougar said she thought standing in the cold water every day had dried up Little Mother's milk. "So, babies are hungry."

Conlaf thought she was more astute than he had expected. He said to repack the patient with fresh plantain each day. Little Mother was not to nurse the babies until he said so, but she could drink all the comfrey tea she wanted.

"Not nurse! Babies will die!" said Cougar, looking at Conlaf like he was the dumbest healer she had ever spoken with.

"Babies will live," said Conlaf. "Your friend, Madoc, will show you how to feed them. He can do wonders with a hunk of wool, a clay flask, and warm, dilute, goat's milk. 'Tis something he learned years ago on a trip from Iceland."

She did not understand. She was lost in Conlaf's words, but she heard *Madoc* and knew there was nothing to worry about. Madoc would help her with the babies.

Later she was astonished that Madoc could get babies to suck on wool and draw milk from a flask. She could not believe he knew so much about babies and so little about women. Handsome Pale Yellow Hair was an enigma.

Periodically the hunters went out before daybreak to wait at the river for the little deer to come for their morning drink. These men had never seen so many small-sized deer congregate in one place to push and jostle for a drink in the muddied shallows. Standing downwind, with a bow and arrows ready, they killed six deer before frightening the rest away. At sunset the men went back to the watering hole for another kill.

Clare and five others dried and smoked the venison. They were certain the land would keep them supplied with food and clothing for the rest of their lives. In the New Land, as in Wales, they utilized the whole animal, even pulverizing the bone to use as thickener in soups. The horns and hooves were boiled for glue used on bows and to hold tight the feathers and stone points of arrows.

Gerard, with his long dark hair tied to the back of his

neck with a leather thong, searched upstream for shell mounds but found none. Instead he found an outcropping of a white rock that looked similar to a chalky mineral he had used in Wales to loosen unwanted hair from hides. The powdered ore was heated in kettles, poured in a hole dug in the ground, and mixed with seawater. Hides were laid flat to soak in the holes or vats, hair-side down. The hair cells inflated and fell off. The hides were scraped clean of fat. Hides to be tanned were immersed for several days in water containing pounded oak bark in a second hole in the ground. Tanned hides were used for brogues, tunics, and trousers. Hair was left on hide of poor quality, which was hung as doors, like the cottage doors of Welsh crofters.

When summer was more than half over, Conn and a half a dozen shipbuilders replaced the temporary lean-tos with more durable cottages made of woven willow withies plastered with river mud mixed with dried grass. Five cottages occupied each side of a square, two men to a cottage, thirty-two men around a square. Each of six squares had a wide, flat-stone walkway in front of the cottages.

Gwalchmai, the old court bard, became grouchy and asked to live alone so that he could rest or recite poems whenever he wished without disturbing someone else. The unoccupied cottages were used as shelters to carry on with necessary village crafts during the time of rain or fierce wind. Other empty cottages were used for storage. Conn hung dried and smoked venison, stored in coarse linen bags, in an airy cottage. Sun-dried fish, stored in another cottage, lay on flat stones covered with a layer of dry sea sand, a layer of fish, and more sand. The salts in the sand tended to flavor the fish, and the sand pulled out the moisture and kept the meat dry and free of contamination. Conn made holding-pens from woven willows for the sheep, goats, one cow, and the remaining horse.

Conn kept one eye on Nohold, who began to build a large, regular barbarian cottage that would house himself, the two women, and two babies away from the main village but closer to the fresh-water stream. He started digging a large hole so that the cottage would be half underground and shielded from strong winds. To Conn the place looked like a catch basin for water in a heavy rain. He talked to

Nohold and after that several men came to help work his cottage. The hole was refilled, and the cottage was built like the druids', on top of the ground so that rainwater ran off. The inside walls were plastered white with the slurried residue of powdered white rock and hair from the tanning vats. Both Cougar and Little Mother thought they had the most beautiful cottage on earth.

Little Mother spent more and more time inside. She said the breezes made her nervous, and the babies kept her awake at night. She said she was worn out from afterbirth pains and wanted to sleep. Cougar collected handfuls of bird feathers and burned them with yellow pine splints. Little Mother breathed the smoke, but her pains would not go away. At night she kept the door-flap open because she said it was too hot inside. For days Cougar made certain she was drinking the comfrey tea. Then she added chokecherry juice and powdered root mallow and baneberry to the tea. Cougar often asked if she was feeling all right. Little Mother always said that she was fine. But she became thin and spitless.

"I guess it takes a long time to recover from having two babies," said Cougar, feeding Sky goat's milk while Earth howled. She wanted Little Mother to feed Earth, but did not have the heart to ask her to leave her pallet. *Maybe she does need rest*, she thought. When Sky was asleep, she picked up howling Earth, ran her fingers across the baby's face, and patted his back before feeding him. His lips were dry and cracked, and his soft skin was dry and hot. He sucked unevenly, like his mouth or throat hurt.

Cougar sat on the pallet thinking how to tell Little Mother that Earth was feverish when Little Mother opened her dull eyes and asked where her babies were. Sky slept beside her, and Earth was howling next to her ear. "Right here," said Cougar. "Earth is bawling. One or the other boy is always crying hungry." She rocked Earth, but his crying did not stop. She walked around and around the cottage. She cleaned his bottom and put fresh moss inside his diaper strap.

Nohold came in. He spoke to Little Mother and went back outside.

"He hopes the babies sleep tonight. He thinks I should be feeding them," said Little Mother.

Cougar uncovered Little Mother and felt her hot breasts. She knew the milk from fevered breasts was certain to give the baby stomach cramps. "Do not worry," said Cougar, biting her tongue. "Some babies have a hard time nursing at first. Baby Earth will be fine in a day or two."

She put a little cold comfrey tea in Earth's flask. He drank it quickly, so she gave him warmed goat's milk, and he started screaming again, with his dry eyes squeezed shut. He hardly stopped yelling long enough to suck more than a couple of drops at a time. His face was red, his mouth was a wide-open circle, and his tongue jumped nervously. His wails filled her with despair. She wanted to shake the screams out of him, but she held him tight to her chest and patted his little back. She sang in his ear. She gave him cold, watery goat's milk, and he began to suck. "So you like cold food!" she said. "I wish you had told me." She nuzzled the baby, who was sweaty and sour. It was hard work nursing through a bit of sheep's wool. She took a deep breath and began to think like a healer. Baby Earth was feeling better; his fever had broken. This was a turning point. She looked at Baby Sky sleeping peacefully and prayed he stayed well. She pulled the blanket Madoc had given her higher around Little Mother's hot shoulders. All of a sudden the nauseating smell hit her. It was worse than before. Little Mother was not getting better. She made a poultice from the spore mass of a puffball and applied it to Little Mother's vulva.

She told Madoc there was trouble. He took her to Llieu and together they tried to explain the situation to him. Llieu found it hard to believe that Madoc had truly stayed to help in the birth of twins. When Madoc was young, he could hardly stomach watching puppies being born. Llieu followed Madoc and Cougar back to Little Mother, who coughed and said that she could not sleep because both babies were crying. Llieu looked at the sleeping babies.

Llieu had one sniff of the sickening smell and shook his gray head. "I know not what is best to give her," he said. "Dried brown cakes made from the milky-white juice of wild lettuce turns brown in air, but never mind that, it is good for agues and fevers, and helps one sleep. Try it."

Little Mother coughed and held her hands on her chest.

"From now on dream of being well and cuddling those two babies of yours," said Llieu, putting his cool hand on her cheek. "You are such a little thing. 'Tis hard to believe you have had two previous children. Perhaps these new ones will help fill the sad hole of your loss."

"Who told you?" whispered Little Mother.

"Cougar told me about your fine son, Otter, and your sweet little boy, Hummer."

For Llieu Little Mother swallowed the bitter-tasting brown stuff he pushed between her teeth. In a little while she thought she felt better. The pain went away, and she let her eyes close. Then Llieu showed Cougar how to make a poultice of pounded anise seed mixed with lanolin, the oil from sheep's wool, of which he still had a good supply. He warmed it over a glowing coal in the central firehold, put it on a pad of dry moss, and told Cougar to replace the pad between Little Mother's legs with this new one. "Do that once a day, in the morning." Holding his breath, he examined the stinking pad Cougar wanted to discard quickly. He gave it back, shook his head, and arranged his face so it was solemn, calm, and not frightening. He left her a good supply of lanolin and powdered anise seeds and a little brown cake. "Your friend is very ill. The infection from childbirth we can heal, but the sickness in her lungs is harder. Hear the funny breathing when you put your ear on her chest? There is a sickness in her lungs. Have her stay in bed, no bathing in the cold stream. She can drink all the comfrey tea she wants, day and night. The only excuse for her to get up is to relieve herself. If you missed any of my words, ask the young fellow called Madoc. He seems to have a way of talking to you. Also, he will not tell you this, but I will. Do not play with his heart. He is not going to open it for you." He turned his head, not wishing to see the hurt in Cougar's eyes, nor the anger in Madoc's.

For days afterwards Madoc would not speak to Llieu for inserting himself into something that was not his business. He told Conlaf that Llieu was getting to be a busybody, trying to run other people's lives. Each morning Madoc went to Nohold's place with goat's milk for the babies. Already she was putting powdered meal and berries in the milk, diluting it with cold water from the stream. The babies grew and were more awake during the day. Sky slept through the night, and Earth only woke once and howled for his feeding. Madoc taught her to scrub the milk vials with sand and water and leave them in the sun to dry. She washed the lamb's wool with water and dried it in the sun. They worried about Little Mother.

Nohold hovered over her pallet and did not want to leave for the work of felling trees to prepare a clear space for planting grains in the spring. He wanted Little Mother well so that they could be husband and wife.

The words brought tears to Little Mother's eyes.

Cougar told him he was out of his head. "You cannot marry her. She is already married to the chief of Sandpoint. Wren will break your neck," she said.

"No, he will not look for me. I am dead to him," said Nohold. "Little Mother needs help raising twin boys. We are a family. I like her. She is a good friend and companion. When older, the boys can help me if I go back to being a trader."

"I like her, too," said Cougar. "But none of us are making her better."

"I will bring a turtle," said Nohold. "Cooked right, it will give her strength."

The druids had kept the grains for planting dry in sacks covered by an oiled canvas. Brian had become friends with another messmate, Roi, from a different ship. They were both about the same size, with dark hair, freckles across their noses, and flashy brown eyes. Madoc put the two of them in charge of planting, tilling, and harvesting. They spread offal from butchering on the fields and asked Gerard for leftover animal droppings not used in hide vats. Gerard scowled and cried, "If I hear of anyone calling me a fancy name because of my turd-hunting occupation, I will—I will make him eat one of the wild sausages!"

Shipbuilders dug a ditch a yard wide and a yard deep around the entire village. Three sides were protected from unexpected invaders by the high river cliffs. On the fourth side, facing the forest, Dewi and a handful of men built a palisade wall from a row of pointed pine stakes close-set on the inside berm of the ditch. They learned to spare their metal tools and use them only when it was absolutely necessary by building other tools from bone and stones as early Welsh crofters had done, which was similar to the methods Nohold had recently taught them. Once Madoc told him that his ways were similar to his old people's far across the western sea. "I think your people are like us, only a century or two behind us." Nohold did not know what a century was.

Madoc's men, who worked from sunup to sundown, looked as brown as the barbarians. For comfort, in a land of heat and humidity, they wore only boots and trousers. Often they lay abed at night with aching muscles, but none complained of hunger pangs or whined about biting insects. A breeze blew over the village, keeping the insects away and cooling the late summer sunshine.

Before autumn was over, the last horse died, maybe from the heartbreak of not having another of his kind for company or, maybe, from disease. His intestines were filled with worms, the same thready worms that were found in deer intestines. Llieu admitted to Madoc that he could not read the auguries from wormy intestines, except to say, "Predictions from a few worms in intestines of a large horse are not of much consequence. 'Tis like looking at the Snowdons in January and noting that in a hole at the bottom of one mountain is a warm nest of tiny field mice, then pronouncing that the mountains are warm in winter."

Blind Efyn, the alchemist, who lived with Rhan, heard Llieu talking to Madoc and made a noise in his throat. "The smallest thing is important to any mystery, whether it be to foretell the future or used for a natural beauty aid," he said. "And speaking of beauty aids, if you desire to change the color of your gray hair to black, I can make a concoction of a single leech set to corrupt in vinegar for sixty days in a leaden vessel. The preparation is so strong that you must hold oil in your mouth while the dye is on your head or your teeth will turn black. I found a cube of lead near the barbarians' salt-making pans."

Madoc looked surprised, "Salt making? Here?" he said.

"Aye. I was just walking high on the beach one morning, and I found the pans sitting in the sun with hot coals underneath them to evaporate the water quickly. I bent down to examine them and picked up this polished lead cube. Feel it. See, it is the oily feel of smooth lead. What a surprise to find it in this new land, huh? I have wanted to show it to you. Lead is the magic to make that black dye. I learned the dye trick from an alchemist in Dubh Linn. Have you ever seen a barbarian with gray hair? No. They all have black hair. You are the only one around here with gray hair, except Gwalchmai. Can there be alchemists here?"

"Well, I do not know," said Llieu, surprised that the blind man knew his hair was gray. "Gray becomes me. I want no black hair. But I think you are right about minuscule things. Spontaneous generation is a good example of not seeing anything strange or untoward for days, then overnight a sublimation can be crawling with mites. Surely you have heard of such." Knowing Efyn could not see, Llieu made a circular motion with his index finger around his own right ear to signify he thought himself becoming as eccentric as the alchemist, who carried vials and flasks in the pockets of his tunic. Llieu had seen one of Efyn's clay pots with a winged staff marked on the side and knew that he had brought quicksilver to the new land.

Madoc asked Llieu if the dead horseflesh was safe to eat.

Llieu sat down and closed his eyes. His chin rested in one cupped hand. The other hand covered one ear.

"Is the horseflesh usable?" Madoc said again. When Llieu did not answer he said, "Do you hear me?"

Llieu's dark eyes opened. He smiled and said, "The day you say that you have found the primordial material from which everything is made, I will listen with both ears. Right now you will be glad to know that horsemeat looks clean, like the venison. No worms. Messmates can dry it over smoke or roast it."

"If we find worms in the men, we will have something to worry about," said Madoc.

"What would you do if the men had worms?" asked Llieu.

"I would have you, Conlaf, and Troyes try one herbal infusion after another until you found the specific quintessence."

"I wish we could communicate better with barbarians," said Llieu. "I bet my mildewed boots that little thing, Cougar, knows plenty. She will tell you if you can understand her. I bet she has seen intestinal worms in the local deer same as we. We need some of her wisdom and knowledge to live in this place."

Madoc bit the inside of his mouth then said, "Lately, I have begun to wonder if the way to wisdom is not so much sitting at the feet of the teacher, but through observation of actual situations by the pupil. I told you everything I remembered about the birth of one baby after another. I learned by being there, watching, listening, and helping. Cougar takes care of Little Mother like she is a true Healer. Little Mother has lived longer under her care than you thought possible. You are right, she is wise in many things we know nothing about."

"You are a thinker, my son," said Llieu. "You see that the barbarians have knowledge of things that are foreign to us. Different groups of people grow in knowledge at their own pace."

"Think of the different things we have seen and done since leaving Wales," said Madoc. "My knowledge has increased, but has my wisdom? I be not the same person who left Abergele, or am I?"

"Man grows, man changes," said Llieu. He cleaned the dead horse's pen. He hauled the old manure, crawling with tiny worms, on a crude wooden sled across the tall grass to a place between the village and the marked-off planting area. He spread it so the sun could purify it. He moved the horse's split-barrel water trough to the sheep pen and used the logs around the horse's pen as supports to make a wattled roof to protect the sheep and goats from sun and rain.

In the evening the men joined around the central fires in various cottages for a game of *tawlbwrdd*, storytelling, or music with harps, zithers, and *crwths*.

Madoc noticed that Finn, the good storyteller, and his friends never asked anyone else inside their cottages. But he was too preoccupied with setting up a snug, workable colony to let such a small matter prey on his mind. Every day he gave thanks to the gods that he and his men were free from threats on their lives, free to sing, to make music, to argue, or recite poetry. This was a good place. He congratulated himself on his success. He drew closer to these men whenever they met to discuss their problems. He tried to be courteous to each one, to avoid being overbearing with his authority. He felt beloved because each man could look him in the eye, express affection with a frown followed by a smile, if they disagreed, or with laughter and an impromptu song if they agreed. No one ever left a council meeting in a huff. For weeks he was content. Then gradually he began to ask himself if this was all there was to a good life. He began to berate himself for not bringing women. He blamed the gods for his overprotection of them. Now in retrospect, he was sure they would have fared as well on the sea voyage as any of the men. He missed having women about the village. He missed their chatter and singing. It was not natural to have a village of only men. He decided to go and see how Nohold was doing, to invite him and Cougar to hear the zither music and some Welsh songs that night. Maybe Cougar would sing a couple of her songs. He was going to ask her.

XXIII
Samhain

In importance down the ages is the observance of Samhain,
Hallow E'en, the beginning of winter when the powers of
darkness are threatening to obliterate for ever the life-giving
rays of the fertilizing sun. As, in old Celtic tradition, the gods
were particularly hostile and dangerous at this time, playing
cruel tricks on their worshippers, propitiated by sacrifice—
human in pagan times—so in the surviving practices the festival is marked once more by fire, violence, the demand on
the part of the young men for gifts from those at whose homes
they clamour for entry and the subsequent vandalism which
ensued when hospitality was refused. Again, as in ancient
times, hints of sexual license and temporary release from the
normal conventions are commonplace.

—Anne Ross, "Material Culture, Myth and Folk Memory,"
The Celtic Consciousness

When Madoc got close to the cottage, he saw someone
sitting outside on the ground holding the twins. He thought
it was Little Mother and was relieved to see that she was
feeling well enough to sit outside. But as he got nearer, he
saw it was Cougar and she was crying. He picked up Baby
Earth, who smiled at him and tried to grab his chin. Cougar
pointed to the inside of the cottage. Inside Nohold sat by
the fire-pit with Little Mother's head and shoulders in his
lap. The rest of her body was curled around him. He was
rocking and singing one of those three-note songs. It
sounded forlorn, like the call of geese in the fall when they
migrate to a warmer climate.

Nohold nodded and asked if Madoc knew what would
bring someone back from a long sleep.

Madoc looked more closely at Little Mother. He pushed

her hair off her forehead and said her skin felt as cold as the stones outside the door. Her round eyes stared at the small flickering fire, but did not blink. "When did she go to the Otherside?" he asked.

"I do not know," Nohold said. "In the middle of the night the women were arguing. Little Mother wanted to nurse the babies, but Cougar said she could not until her fever went away. Little Mother said she was cold, and her breasts were so swollen they hurt. She wanted to feed the babies. Cougar said her breasts were lumpy and hot, and the milk would make her babies sick. When they were quiet, Little Mother came to my pallet. We lay close together like a man and woman. She wept and said the tears were for me because I loved her. I was happy thinking Little Mother was going to be well, and I would have a real family. Cougar was first to get up. She built up the fire, fed the babies, cleaned them, and packed their bottoms with clean moss. Then she cried and said that Little Mother was cold and had no pulse. I thought I could feel her pulse, and I was sure I could feel my woman's breath. Where she lay against me she was warm. I told Cougar she did not know what she was talking about and to leave. I did not want to hear her snuffling. When she left, she took the babies. I brought Little Mother close to the fire for warmth, and now I wait for her eyes to open." Tears fell down his cheeks.

"They are not going to open," said Madoc. He let Nohold be by himself for a few moments, then he softly told him that he would see that Little Mother's spirit was sent to the Otherside with a fine celebration. In Wales, it was harvest time and the time to prepare for winter by starting with the Samhain celebration. "We will wrap Little Mother in a blanket and lay her in the ground with a scattering of red ocher. There will be funeral music and songs such as you have never heard before. Afterwards there will be a feast with horsemeat."

"Burial and celebration is the Calusa way," said Nohold. He laid Little Mother on her pallet and dug a hole the same size as the pallet beyond Little Mother's head. Before putting her in the earth, he fixed her hair around her face and pulled her skirt around her legs that were pulled up under her chin, then covered her, except her face, with a hide. Her arranged her arms on top of the hide. "She said that she was pleased with the way Cougar and I cared for her fat babies. She said that she wanted another hide of one of those woolly sheep to wrap each of her babies in something warm and soft. I told her I would talk to you. She reminded me that boys grow fast, then she laid her head on my chest and closed her eyes. I went to sleep careful not to move or disturb her. I dreamed of things we were going to do together, while living close to good men, who would help us when trouble came. I dreamed of good times together. When I woke up, her head was still on my chest, and her face was blue and cold. I want her comfortable. Do not sit her up."

Madoc told his men that Little Mother was dead, and it was the desire of Nohold to let her body stay on the sleeping pallet when she was buried in the floor of her cottage.

Gwalchmai stood balancing himself on a cane and said, "This is the time that the earth takes its path under a Scorpio sky. It is a time for cleansing. I propose this is a good time to reenact the old Samhain Cleansing-by-Fire. We have all done and said things we are not proud of. Now is the time we cleanse ourselves of our weaknesses and begin anew in this new land. The ancient legislative druids punished unrepentant criminals by burning them in giant wicker forms, like effigies. We can vindicate our own jealousies and angers with an Effigy-Fire built to the nines, with no human sacrifices."

Madoc, delighted with the idea said, "Huzza! You be in charge of the fire."

Before the Samhain celebration, Erlendson made willow nets and strung them across the river to catch fish. He also found a grove of wonderful-smelling cedar trees and asked Madoc if it would be appropriate to use them for a Sacred Circle. "They are not stones, but their red heartwood is decay-proof. Caradoc is studying the alignment of the stars in this place. He will mark sunrise and sunset before and after Samhain for exact placing of the king post and heel post." Madoc said Erlendson could cut down nine of the largest trees, and after debarking them, he might carve a few lines in old Runic code on each.

When they were set in the ground to form a circle, Madoc asked if every man's name could go on the posts to make it a real memorial. "Rub the names of the dead with red clay."

Erlendson said it would take more than his lifetime to carve every man's name on the posts, but he would carve the names of the dead. The names of the living he would mark on pieces of hide, put them in greased pouches, and bury them in white quartz pebbles under each of the nine posts.

"After each name of our men on the Otherside, add something special," said Madoc. "Attention must be paid to our ghosts."

"Done," said Erlendson. "Short remembrances, one or two words." He could tell Madoc had more on his mind, and waited.

Finally Madoc said, " 'Tis a waste to lose a total of thirty-nine men to storms, starvation, and ship wrecks, and one to the barbarians! I damned Lugh for the loss of our men. Now I confess I was wrong."

"So, you admit you are not perfect," said Erlendson chuckling. "Once I swore I would never sail with you. I confess, I, also, was wrong. However, there is one fault *you* continue to carry."

"What?"

"You expect too much of your men, and you expect even more of yourself. Where is your confidence, Shipmaster Madoc?"

"My confidence comes from the confidence of the men."

"Look close, the men put their trust in you. The gods rejoiced the day we sailed with you. We have seen unbelievable things. We have made history."

Madoc blushed from praise he was not used to.

That evening Caradoc told the men that now was the time to mark themselves as explorers and no better way than to give each other a small tattoo. "All of us shall wear the chief shipmaster's name on his left thigh," he said. The men agreed and tattooed each other with Madoc's name under the small triangle on top of a half circle: a single sailing ship, the symbol for Madoc.

Clare suggested that they build a rath, or hill of piled stone, along the riverbank. Gerard wanted to build an outdoor deck from debarked pine logs where the men could sit in the cool evening breezes. Caradoc wanted to continue the study of the movement of the stars and simply set the time of summer and winter solstice in their new land with the layout of the circle of nine cedar posts.

Samhain, the first of *Tachwedd*, November, was the perfect time to thank the gods for guiding them to this warm, fertile river land. It was time to commemorate all of those who lost their lives. Llieu said he would recite the praise and satire poems. Other men planned to bring the six nondruids, Kabyle, Erlendson, Bjorko, Camin, Brian and Troyes, into the druid's circle. Nohold and Cougar were asked to say a few words in praise of Little Mother. Nohold choked up and could say nothing. Instead he lit a pine branch, and when it flared, he doused it in a bucket of water to show how fast the life had gone from Little Mother. Cougar said she had been worried for some time that Little Mother would not live. The yellow orchids had blossomed out of season this year, before spring began. "The early blossoms were a sign," she said so everyone could understand, "that someone's early death was close. This morning I knew Little Mother's spirit had crawled inside me when I broke wind. It had the smell of her breath. I believe she wants to see how you men-spirits celebrate the last days at the edge of winter. That is not everything. Her spirit wants to be certain I care for her babies. So, I expect to break foul wind while she is with me for a few days."

No one dared open his mouth after Cougar's eulogy.

The next day, the eve of Samhain, the six nondruids were brought to the deck of pine logs. They were invited inside the druids' circle. Kabyle was highly honored when asked to become a druid, but said that his own religion served him well, and in most respects was not much different than what the druids believed when it came to knowledge and secrets of the Omnipotent. But he was not too impressed by tattoos around fingernails. He said with a shy smile, "If it would please you druids, I will partake of the initiation, but continue to call on Allah to keep me out of trouble. And I would like to have a large ship, like the *Vestri*, with a billowing sail tattooed on my chest."

Llieu was pleased with the iconoclast and made the ceremony special by tattooing Kabyle first. Sigurd did the chanting and afterwards said he put the initiated men into a hypnotic trance, so the embedding of the woad dye mixed with animal grease was not overly painful. When the ceremony was near its end, Llieu, dressed in his long gray robe and rainbow sash, asked Madoc, who was seated in a place of honor at the top of the mystic circle, to come forward.

After more of Sigurd's chanting, Conlaf held a firebrand so that Llieu could see to prick the outline of a dolphin, with its head below Madoc's left knee, and its tail touching his ankle. This was the symbol for a master of the sea. Madoc recalled that his father carried the same honor and wondered about mysteries in a man's life that are destroyed by death.

Sigurd said, "This night we leave our door-flaps open so that the spirits of our fellow seamen can enter and see how we fare."

Near dawn, the lone cow, even though she no longer gave milk, along with two goats, two kids, six sheep, and four lambs, were driven through the smoke from the purifying Samhain bonfire to keep them healthy through the coming year.

Afterwards Tipper suggested that the cow be butchered for the feast for giving thanks to the gods. "There is only one of her species, so she is never going to calf. Next year her meat will be too tough to enjoy. Master Madoc says he does not want to be more special than any one of us. But I think it appropriate that his cottage have the distinction of being different with a cowskin door instead of the ordinary deerskin."

Madoc was in half a mind to reject the cowhide along with the miserable memories of that bloody beast aboard his ship. Then he came to his senses and reconsidered his small-minded notion. Instead he asked if he might also have the cow's horns to make a couple pibgorns, a sort of flute with a cow's horn at the end. He said he had willow wood that was the proper size for two flutes.

Dewi did the butchering that night. No one was surprised when he found worms in the cow's intestine. Her meat appeared to be free from parasites. He buried her entrails before moonset. He buried them deep in the pine forest to ward off the *Tylwyth Teg*, who were believed to be powerful, minuscule Welsh beings, unpredictable and oftentimes vindictive. He had never seen one and so far there was no proof that little people lived in the new land, but it behooved him to take no chances nor to let them spread worms to the men.

Long before sunrise the cow was impaled on a spit over the bonfire. The men stopped smacking their lips and pulling meat from the bones and began singing when the sun came flashing red against Caradoc's temporary cedar king-post in the wood henge. They sang a welcome to the new day in the new land. The heelpost would be placed in line with the Samhain sunset. The other post had been temporarily set in the circle to mark moonrise, moonset, and the alignment of important stars. When Caradoc's testing and retesting satisfied him, the posts were solidly set in the earth.

Early in the morning on Samhain, Madoc played one of the new pibgorns. He looked like an unabashed, overgrown youngster learning to control the squeals and creaks of a new dogcart. He was so delighted with his homemade instrument that he played during the noon meal. Afterward he laid aside the pibgorn and said, "We are incomers who occupy a new Wales, *Cymru Newydd*. We are no longer *y Cymry,* Welsh people, we are Drudion, the Brave people, the Mighty People. Our chief Bard, Gwalchmai, will make a song, a poem about what we have done. The song will tell those who come after us who we were. 'Twill be of greater importance than history—if 'tis told right. When he has it finished, he will tell us. I suppose it might take him some days before he has it composed."

Gwalchmai did not stand, but crossed his hands over his chest to show his love for his fellow druids, nodded, and smiled broadly. This was a great honor for him.

Llieu stood and began the Praise-Ceremony by saying, "Madoc, I prize you as one of my most pigheaded pupils. We are not all brave and mighty. Look at me. I be scared of the black, hairy spiders and yellow snakes that come into my cottage. Since leaving *Cymru*, my mighty size has shrunk, leaving me wrinkles and little breath. I agree, we are a circle of *druids*. We are connectors between the old land and the new. We are the druid connection. Thus, with a clear conscience, I salute my former pupil as Master Leader Madoc in the New Land, *Llan Newydd*."

The men cheered and sang in heartfelt harmony as Gwalchmai, looking pale and sickly, sat and played accompaniment on his precious harp. Madoc was expecting Llieu's satire, but not so much praise. He held his head high and his hands together so that no one could see he was flustered. It was decided on the day after Samhain that they would continue to call themselves druids, their village simply *Llan Newydd*, and Madoc was again voted Leader.

Nohold could not stay in the place where Little Mother's body lay cold and unresponsive under the earth. He could not watch the pale-faced men celebrate something he did not understand. He was devastated. All his plans were gone. He was left with two babies that were not his. He wanted to die. Little Mother's eyes were closed under red-colored stones, and she could not look at the sky. Nohold led Madoc around the open grave while Cougar held the twins, hummed softly, wiped tears from her eyes, and sprinkled the rusty-red ocher over the body.

Kabyle looked handsome in his freshly washed pink head wrapping. Cougar gave Nohold the old hide to lay over Little Mother's body. She had painted twining green leaves and small animal faces on it, thinking it would have pleased Little Mother to sleep under a colorful hide. Madoc was surprised at the beauty of the painting as he pushed earth over it. Nohold stamped the earth down tight and laid stones over the top so no animals would get into the grave.

Cougar tried to talk to Nohold, but he walked outside. She followed and sat against a pine holding the babies in her lap. The smell of the roasting horsemeat on the top of the mesa made her stomach turn so she did not go with

Nohold and Madoc to join the feast. She also would not go into the cottage where Little Mother was buried. That night she had stayed outside holding the babies close to keep them warm.

In the afternoon she needed more goat's milk so she went to the village to find Madoc. All along the main street were huge figures that Finn and his friends had made for the Effigy-Fire. Actually they had spent weeks inside Finn's place quietly making them in secret to celebrate Samhain. Now everyone walked along the street admiring them and waiting to see what was going to happen next.

The first effigy, with puffballs tied around its neck and under its arms, left no doubt in Cougar's mind that it represented Blackbird. The next, with an ear missing and bandages around one arm and with two stiff legs, was, of course, Chief Wren. The most peculiar of the effigies resembled the roly-poly, plant-eating sea monster the men called a sea cow. Cougar noticed its flippers were made from the abundant, fan-shaped palm leaves and a sea grapevine tail. There were other effigies made from long yellow grass and rushes that represented some of the pale men. She stopped beside a straw man with his arm around the shoulder of a straw woman holding straw twins. It caught her by surprise and brought tears to her eyes. All these straw-and-wicker forms were made to celebrate Little Mother's spirit that had gone to live with the ghosts. The kindness and good will of these men, who certainly must be from the spirit world, were overwhelming.

Clare came up beside her and admired the twins. "They are growing so fast that the next thing I know they will be running up and down our streets," he said. That made Cougar smile so he asked her where Nohold was. She wiped the heel of one hand across her face and said that he had been grieving off and on, but she was sure he would be back today. By then others were crowding around Cougar and passing Earth and Sky from one to another. The men talked about their own children and found it a good time to say how much they missed them. Troyes turned and ran from the effigies with Sky under his arm. Cougar called to him, just as old Gwalchmai screamed and pointed.

Someone, without thought, had leaned a lighted torch

against the snout of the sea cow. It flared, exploded, and engulfed the whole figure. The fire snapped, popped, and spread through the ground leaves and pine needles to the other figures, causing druids to step back from the roaring heat and licking flames.

A sudden breeze blew sparks into dried grass and turned it into a leaping, luminous finger pointing to the pines that swayed and sighed beyond the village. Cougar was caught in the crowd. The babies were nowhere in sight. The druids crowded around one another, got in each other's way, and tried to smother the fire with stomping feet and green deer hides. The breathing and coughing from the smoke was loud. The tall orange flames broke into dozens of fiery fingers headed in the same direction, down the high plateau to the next flat level where Nohold's cottage stood with its welcoming door-flap wide open. The fire pushed on, and Cougar ran to stamp the tall, dry grass around Nohold's cottage. She went around the back and found his shovel, made by fastening a pelvis bone of a doe to a straight pole handle. She scraped away the dried grass from the cottage until she noticed that the fire was moving under the soft, dry ground from root clump to root clump. She stood still. *Let it burn*, she thought. Not to see Little Mother in everything he looked at was what Nohold wanted.

Madoc came down the hill with a bucket of water. She would not let him use it. "No!" she cried. "Let the fire eat it." She turned her face so she could not see. Madoc put the bucket down and held her in his arms. He gently released her and pointed up toward the village. He had the bone shovel in one hand and took the bucket's bail in the other. She put her hand on the other side of the bucket's bail and was surprised how it cut into her hand. She grabbed a handful of grass and made a padding.

Madoc said, "Yu," and did the same.

Underground fingers of fire changed direction and circled two squares of cottages. Forty cottages, including those of Finn and his friends, were fire damaged even though soaked with buckets of drinking water. Orange fingers broke again and again into an ever-widening bank of flames, sparks, and smoke. The fire went on without stopping, no matter how many druids swarmed, stomped, and shoveled.

Cougar found Brian by the stream sitting with the babies, who were sound asleep on the green moss.

"I like them," he said. "They remind me of my small sisters."

She scooped more water in the bucket and carried it to the sweaty and thirsty men.

Madoc chopped burning trees and pushed piles of burning brush onto open ground. He thought of the creation of dazzling effigies that made his skin tingle with approval, but now his attitude had turned upside down. His skin burned as if singed, and his thoughts were hot and ready to be expressed out loud. How could these wise men be so careless, so thoughtless? Was something happening to their minds? He hesitated opening his mouth for fear the words would scorch whomever was close enough to hear.

The men worked frantically beating the top of the ground, but their efforts only pushed the fire underground inside the thick layer of dried needles at the edge of the forest. The fire moved on toward several acres of dry pines that were girdled with rings cut into their bark and left to die so that the field could be cleared for planting in spring.

That evening, among the blackened rubble of Nohold's cottage, Cougar found the clay vials that held the babies' milk. She tried to scrub the black off the outside, but it seemed useless. She asked Madoc for more wool and a clay jar of goat's milk. He went with her to free Brian from his job as baby-sitter. They found him walking back and forth with two crying babies and whistling at the top of his lungs. "My baby sisters liked my whistling, but these boys only want to eat," he said. "I put fresh moss in their diaper strap." His face reddened. "I—I made a twin carrier out of some heavy bark and strips of hide I grabbed out of Nohold's place before they were ruined. The babies will be easier to carry on your back, one at each shoulder." He put it on his back to show how it fit over his shoulders. "I can tool designs in the leather, and you can brighten it with paint. You know, like you did on that little piece of skin that covered your dead friend. That was such a pretty thing."

"A pretty thing," she said, smiling at the wide, handsome cradle board. He already had it packed with moss so that inside it was a soft bed for the babies. Cougar was delighted the way it fit the twins. She told Brian the twins would grow to have round heads, like him. "Round better than flat, like stepped on."

Madoc told Brian what a nice thing he had done and sent him to get his supper and to bring something to Cougar and himself before dark. Brian slicked back his unruly blond hair and brought them roasted horsemeat and biscuits. The horsemeat was tough and bitter, not sweet like venison. Cougar had never tasted biscuits. She told Madoc they were light as eating dandelion fluff and smacked her lips. Madoc nodded and ate with his fingers the same as she.

There was no place to sleep for some of the men but on their ships. Madoc was put out with Nohold for leaving Cougar alone, so he stayed with her on the mossy bank of the stream.

In the middle of the night it was cold, and she got up to build a fire. "No!" he yelled. "We do not need more fire! Put the firestones away!" He saw the frightened look on her face and smiled, "I will get us a blanket. I should not have yelled at you."

"You thought I started the big fire?"

"Of course not." When he came back, she was cuddled around the babies. He lay down against her back and pulled the blanket over the two of them. She wanted to tell him about her dreams before he had come. He could not understand how she could possibly know him—see him in dreams before he was there. He put his hands on her face and felt the tears. He pulled her closer and let his hands settle at her waist. He kissed the back of her neck and smelled smoke in her hair.

A kiss was something new. It lit a spark in the middle of Cougar's stomach. The feeling was like the time she let Otter have his way with her. She was puzzled how a man, who was a spirit, could make her feel this way. She took his hand and put her mouth on it. The feeling was still there. Her eyes closed, and she felt herself drift into his warmth.

The babies cried and she got up to feed them. It was still dark. Everything smelled of smoke. A little breeze stirred up some ash in the middle of the nearby burned cottage. She thought she saw a movement among the trees, but it did not happen again. She thought it was just the breeze in the branches. She made certain the babies were wrapped well, and she crawled back under the blanket with Madoc. This time his back was against her front. Her hands moved along his spine and around his sides. He turned and wrapped his big hands around her. Her lips parted and his lips covered hers. They were demanding yet gentle. She did not know what it was called, but it was so dizzying that she forgot everything. She pressed herself close to him. He was the man she had longed for.

Madoc put his hands around her face, pulled away, and took a deep breath. "I do not know who you are," he said. "I like you—oh, I do, so much. But it is not fair to you. You do not know me. I am a Welsh druid. I took an oath not to fraternize with barbarians."

She moved away from him not understanding his words. Then she put two fingers over his mouth and moved closer so that her bare breasts touched his bare chest, and let her hand move down his stomach. She put her mouth on his.

He ran his tongue around her lips and took her hands in his. "That was before I met you." He smiled. "No kissing, while I try to tell you something."

"Kissing," she said and pouted with her lips together. She thought about getting up and finding somewhere else to sleep, but she did not want to. She wanted to be close to him, to feel his hands on her, to let him feel her most sensitive place, to be inside of her. Aye, she wanted him to take her, like a man takes a woman. She wanted to be his. She was free to do as she wanted. Her friends were gone, all but Healer. They could go and live with Healer. She would love him. Her parents did not want her. Nohold walked away from her. This was the thing to do. This was her way now.

"I wish I had some mead," he said.

"Mead?" she asked, perplexed.

"A drink that can make one feel warm and bubbly."

"I be bubbly," she said. "I want. . . ."

"You will find out people do not always get what they want," he said. "Sometimes what they want is not good for them."

His words had a sting and she sat up. "You are good for me," she said.

"No—you are not thinking straight," he said.

"I am ugly to you?"

"No! You are beautiful to me. You are the most attractive woman I have seen since we left Lundy Island and waved to my old friend Blackberries. In fact you look a little like her."

"I look like your other woman?" she said and threw a blackened stick at him. "You are not so attracted to me!"

"No! Now, this is what I mean. We come from different cultures. I was raised as a fosterling. I did not really know my parents until I was a half-grown boy. My father was a leader, a chief, a prince of a province. My mother is a wise woman, a healer. A brother killed my wife. When we boarded ten sailing ships, my spirits rose even though I became responsible for all those men. We left our country to save a way of thinking more than our necks."

"Well," said Cougar, "my father is a priest for the head man of all the Calusa. My mother takes care of children; readies them for the Sacred Sacrifice to the god of sun or rain. Neither believes I am their daughter, who, they believe, drowned as a baby. If I were still two summers old, they might believe me. The old Healer believes, but she lives far away at the Big Lake. Nohold is so full of grief that he does not see me. Little Mother is dead, same as Otter, Hummer, Egret, and my wise grandmother, who taught me her songs. In good times and bad I have her music in my head. I miss her the most. She believed in the dreams I had about you and your spirit followers coming here in floating lodges. I believed the spirits were bringing you to me. And so, why? Why do you not belong to me?"

"Whoa back! Maybe we both come from interesting places," he said. "What else do we have in common? Loneliness for our family. Does that mean I be yours or you are mine? I do not think so." He had a note of amusement in his voice, and it made her frown.

"You want your stick inside me? You, me, close together."

His eyebrows shot close together. No woman had ever been so blunt, so innocent and to the point with him before. Her talk was enough to arouse a man. "Yes," he said, "and no! I be too old for you. I mean—you are like a daughter. I want to take care of you."

She scowled and her skin felt hot.

"You are most like a sister. I care for you and I want to be your friend. Come sit down where 'tis warm. We can talk about this."

She wanted to do just that, but at the moment she hated the daughter-sister concept and needed to think. She missed Nohold and desperately wished he were here. Where was he? Was he all right? He could not go away and die like the others. She told herself she could not stand that. She would fall apart. She could not allow herself to fall apart; the twins needed her. In most clans if a woman had two babies at the same time, the weaker was left out all night. If he survived, he was kept. Neither of these babies had been left out. Both were healthy and needed constant care. Would Madoc care for them? She was not so sure. It was her job. She had to keep herself together and not think of Nohold or anyone else. She picked up the babies and, without looking back, moved further down the bank of the stream, where there was cold, damp sand and gravel to sleep on and no blanket to sleep under. It was a long time before she fell asleep.

The next morning when Madoc awoke, he was exhausted. Most of his men were exhausted. The sunrise was blood red. Behind Llan Newydd village the beautiful pine forest was transformed into ugly, smoldering black sticks, and the ground was covered with dirty-gray ash. Among the burned trees were a few green ones. They were heavy with fragrant resin, saved by some inexplicable miracle, air currents or low fog. Smoke rose to meet scattered clouds. The sun remained angry-red, until two days later when dark clouds covered its face. The Cleansing-by-Fire cleared the land marked for planting quicker than the druids ever anticipated.

Madoc could not think of a good reason to reprimand or punish Finn and his friends. They were already filled with remorse. They were eager to restore the damaged cottages. They removed burned willow sticks, wove in new ones, and covered the outside with fresh mud. It took nine days to restore them.

When the cottages were repaired, Conlaf said, "I believe those barbarians got back at us by having their spirits bring on the fire. Their spirits are stronger than ours."

"You mean they have lived under every kind of adversity you can think of and still go on?" asked Madoc. "On the other hand, you cannot be sure if our big fire was naught more than a careless mistake by Finn and his bloody friends. Or destiny?"

"You mean fate?" said Conlaf.

"What men commonly call fate is mostly their own foolishness," snorted Madoc. He put his hand on the top of his head. Something wet had fallen there. He looked, half expecting to see a bird. Before the fire, large gulls came in clouds to darken the sky and roost in the pine trees. There had been so many that some of the tree limbs broke under their weight. The men had used torches to blind them and long poles to knock them from their nighttime perches. That day the sky was dark, but not with gulls. The wind rose and swirled ash and smoke into the village. The raindrops were big and close together. It was the first good rain since building the village. The men hurried inside their cottages to rekindle small fires in each fire-pit so that the warm updraft prevented rain from pouring through the smoke hole. Before long the men came out to dig trenches around the cottages and extend them to the middle of the street to carry the rainwater to the ditch surrounding the village. That day Madoc noticed that Cougar sat outside the lean-to she had made for herself. Nohold was not around. Madoc wondered if he had left again, but he did not go down and speak to Cougar.

Nine days later Nohold came back and said his private grieving was over. He began to build a lodge for himself and a separate place for Cougar and the babies. For days after that Madoc watched Cougar from a distance, but did not go down to see how she was doing. Some of the other men went with Clare to help Nohold. When they came back, they said the babies were fat and cute as a lamb's ears.

XXIV
Llan Newydd

Mariners of the Eleventh Century were familiar with the compass although it was only a magnetized needle, floating upon a cork or reed, which pointed roughly toward the north.
—Zella Armstrong,
Who Discovered America? The Amazing Story of Madoc

Finn and his friends rebuilt the great hall, so that it was a long, all-purpose cottage that had a fire-pit down the center of the trodden earth floor and a long table on one side. Two parallel lines of hewn tree trunks supported the roof. *Cruck trusses*, or large branches that curved inwards, were left near the top of the trunks. A straight piece of timber was placed on the top of the crucks, and the roof frame was built onto this support. Afterwards the walls and roof were wattled and thatched. The covered hall gave the men a place to eat together, enjoy entertainment, and to talk no matter what the weather. Madoc tied a golden-brown eagle's feather above the door-flap.

The day Finn and his friends replaced the palisade wall and one side of the burned sheep's pen, they found one of the lambs missing. That same day Conlaf made himself a new pallet, which was a stack of pine boughs under deer-skins covered with frayed blankets. He lay down saying his stomach was on fire.

Madoc went to Llieu, and he brought back a beaker of strong willow-bark tea to stop the gnawing fire in Conlaf's midsection. Llieu had advised Conlaf not to eat anything solid for the next couple of days.

A couple of days later Conlaf felt better, and he told Madoc about his plan for planting the blackened land behind the burned palisade. "For every bad thing there is a good thing," Conlaf said. "Think about it. The fire was a blessing. It burned all the deadwood and litter on the forest floor. Now no fire can be started by lightning or even by barbarians who might sneak into Llan Newydd. What is more, the fire covered the ground with ash, which makes new grass thick and healthy and brings edible mushrooms. Look at how much of the forest has been cleared behind our village. We could not have done all that in six years! We can see who and what is moving on the cleared land. With no trees or underbrush, the land is open meadow for the big birds and deer to browse. Good balances bad. We will remember the fire of the year 1171 as good."

"Plant the fruit and nut trees we brought between the crops," said Madoc. "They have been lying in the ground to keep them alive. It is time for them to put their roots down."

That night the wind became strong across the tops of the river cliffs and blew over some of the blackened trees that stood like naked skeletons. After three days of rain, despite a nagging stomach ache, Conlaf took six men out to stack burned logs in neat rectangles around the perimeter of designated fields, not unlike stones stacked around the meadows in Wales. When the men were covered with black soot, ash, and soil, Madoc told them to build wide steps down to the river so they could wash. He told them all their water would come from the river from now on. The little stream was for Nohold and Cougar to use. He felt he was learning to be a good leader, one who lived above the emotions of his men and kept his own emotions under control.

Herds of deer did not come back to the charred area. Gulls and passenger pigeons made dark clouds overhead, but never stopped to roost on the piles of black stocks. Each day an eagle glided on the thermals above the village and each night perched on an isolated, tall green pine like a lone sentinel. Madoc found a black, brown, and white wing feather and kept it, thinking it was a gift from the eagle.

The autumn days were warm and the night cool. It was not as cold as it was in Wales at this time of year. The druids learned to tell the difference between low clouds and fog that came in from the sea during the night. Fog usually left by midday. There was no hint of snow in the gray clouds, only warm misty fog for a day or two, then days and days of rain.

The day before December 30, 1171, Madoc said he felt as though the sun had abandoned them.

That evening in the great hall the men noisily ate roast gulls and a dried, orange fruit that contained twin flat seeds. Conn led them in a Welsh song that asked the sun to show its face so the crofters would know the sun was still a good friend. His gray hair straggled outward and touched his shoulders. He wore newly made leather shoes that resembled high-top pampooties rather than brogues. He was the resident bard, since Gwalchmai had become too ill to leave his pallet.

Madoc thanked the singers, sat beside Conn, and said, "Visit Gwalchmai and catch the words he sings. As long as he is pouring forth words for the song of Llan Newydd, he will live. He sees death as an adventure that is too large to begin right now."

"Until we have more vellum, I will keep his words on bark and in my head," said Conn. He hesitated a moment and looked at Madoc sitting inert as stone. He laid his hands on Madoc's slumped shoulders, let them wait, heavy and patient, until Madoc turned to face him. "Master, I can see you are sad from an old sorrow. Do you want to talk about it?"

"You see too much," said Madoc. "But you are correct, I have felt melancholy and sentimental for days, like the mist before the rain. I keep recalling the death of my father two years ago. I did not know him well. My ties of affection are many times stronger with my foster fathers. You would think the death of my wife, or Brett, or another man would be uppermost, but I seem to have put them aside. I do not know why his memory plagues me. Today is the worst. I imagine him as a ruler of men in the Otherside, meeting important personages such as Thomas of London." His face turned pale and he stuttered, "It—it is ridiculous of me. Owain is dead and Thomas of London—I do not know where Thomas is. He was a good friend of my father. Sing something frivolous so that my thoughts lighten."

"Your ghosts are begging attention," said Conn. His eyes

danced above his wide grin. He rummaged among a pile of furs against the wall and brought out his harp. "Listen." For a few moments he strummed a tune he had learned at the Dubh Linn shipyard. When he had some words in mind, he stood on a split-log bench, strummed softly, and announced that the evening's entertainment would be in honor of the mighty prince of Gwynedd, Owain, son of Gruffudd. He said he was certain that the prince knew and approved of their journey to find a land where a man could sleep at night without fearing death from soldiers, neighbors, or next of kin. "One thing Prince Owain might not understand is why we have no horses or women. He loved both. I can see him wagging his finger at us.

"How can you haul a cart without a horse?
Your village will be short lived.
All the knowledge and mysteries of the Old
    Religion may as well be dead;
There are no children for you to teach.
I pity you bloody pagans."

The great hall was quiet except for the crackling of the fire in the trench. The men looked at each other knowing Conn was right. Yet none was prepared to hitch a cart to a sheep and expect it to carry a load of sod, nor to bring a barbarian woman into his hut for the sole purpose of populating a nursery. The thoughts that came to mind made the men uncomfortable. They shrugged their shoulders and laughed nervously. Conn hummed, stepped onto the slab table, felt warm air around his head, closed his eyes, and sang more.

"We thought you just and honorable on earth,
    Owain ap Gruffudd.
Are you a respectable ruler in the Sid?
Do not ask us to trade places! Lugh forbid!
Here we have found peace to work our land
    and never mind the mud."

Conn's words stayed stubbornly in Madoc's mind. He closed his eyes and right away he thought about Cougar.

To survive one generation after another, this village of men indeed needed women.

Cougar awoke to refresh the fire and feed the babies a cereal made from pounded grains and water. She saw through the open door-flap that Nohold was asleep on his pallet. She prayed that he was back for good. A person could only mourn so long for someone before mourning became a kind of sickness. She stood close to his pallet and wondered if he had been to see Madoc. She thought of Madoc constantly. She closed her eyes and saw Madoc's face with the sky-blue eyes ringed with curls, like autumn's golden, curly, long grass. His hair was soft as thistledown, even his whiskers were soft. Each night she longed to feel his big, gentle hands on either side of her face. She wished he were curled tight against her back, talking with her. She wanted to tell him that she never thought of him as a brother. During the cool fall days she watched him busy with his men. She knew that old Gray-Hair, who made soft music plucking on strings, had worm disease. She remembered the day she told Conlaf, the Healer, the dark-haired one with soft, brown eyes, to give Gwalchmai tea made from pulverized pinkroot or stinkweed. But Conlaf thought he knew best and gave the old Gray-Hair wormseed root. It did not rid him of worms. She had told Madoc, but his mind had been filled with other things a good leader worries about. *Maybe I should go to see Madoc*, she thought. *That is exactly what I want to do. But he was the foolish one who said I was like a sister. He needs to come to me. I will show him I can be much better than a sister. He and I together.* She smiled.

"I believe Cougar got back at me for saying she was like a sister," said Madoc. "You know, she believes we are spirit people. She believes we do not have as much need for the lambs as she, a living person. She wants me to give her a lamb. She wants the hide to make another bunting for one of the babies. Women! This one does not even know what lambs are or how to care for them."

"And so, she does not want to be your sister?" said Conlaf. "Lugh! Man, have you forgotten how women think?"

"Of course not!" said Madoc. "How can I forget, when I never knew! It is not right to get mixed up with a b-barbarian. She is so attractive, a pretty little thing by anyone's standards, and she has learned to speak our language quite well. Listen, she thinks I am some kind of god and wants to claim me as her special kind of god. Ah—she is a delight."

"Of course, she is telling you she wants to be your woman!" Conlaf snorted. "Sounds like a woman in heat to me. I can not believe you are telling me this. Most of the men I know would like to be in your boots. They would tell you how lucky you are. Hey, are you diddling her?"

"Hey, what?" said Madoc. "Diddling? What do you think I be? I took the druidic oath to keep our colony, our village, pure from outside blood. If I want a woman, I will go back to Wales for one!"

"Is Cougar safe with all these men?"

"Of course she is safe. She lives with Nohold. He takes care of her. Our men are honorable. They are druids. They took the oath, same as you and I."

"And so, maybe you ought to talk to her about the lamb that is missing. Put your mind at ease; see if she knows where it is. Is she sewing a lambskin bunting?"

"I will do that," said Madoc, disconcerted by Conlaf's suggestion that Cougar might have taken the lamb. "I will ask her about the lamb, then I will ask her for a barbarian potation to stop your bellyache."

"Hey, before you go, I have a question. If we had Welsh women here, would you seriously think twice about Cougar?"

Madoc started to shrug and change the subject back to Conlaf's illness. He was put out with Conlaf's words about Cougar. What did he know about her? He was tired of being interrogated about what he thought about women in general and Cougar in particular.

"Would thee?"

"Hey, no more questions," said Madoc, annoyed and thinking he would feel better if he told his best friend how he really felt. Maybe then he would leave him alone. "Just between us. Aye. I would, if I truly allowed myself. You irritate me, but she makes me feel wonderful. At the same time she drives me crazy. You know bloody well what I mean. I like her."

"Ya, I know, you imagine you are in love, you bonehead."

All winter Madoc stayed close to the men to oversee their various divisions of work. He set up a method for bartering goods from one group to another.

One day the blackened grass seemed suddenly washed clean by the persistent rain, and the very next morning there were gray rings from three-to-six hands in diameter here and there on the wet, new green grass. Tipper said they were fairy rings for certain, just as he had seen in the Welsh meadows. He was convinced that the little people had found them and were living comfortably under rocks and piles of brush. "*Gogoniant!* Glory for the little people that come out in the middle of the night and dance in circles!"

Sigurd said, "This place is more and more like *Fychan Cymru*, Little Wales."

Someone else thought it would be a good idea to plant a staff with some kind of banner at the edge of the cliff so that when the men came up or down the river, they could see it and know they were approaching their home peninsula.

Druids had never had a banner. If they did, no one knew of it because it was so secret. Erlendson said that the Viking flag was a black raven, with its wings outspread, on a white background. Dewi said that in honor of the *Pedr Sant*, Shipmaster Riryd, and his crew, the Irish flag made of three vertical strips, green, white, and orange might be nice. In the end they planted the only banner anyone had, a red dragon painted by the artist, Glyn, on a rectangle of leather. It was fastened to a peeled pole that was held straight in a deep hole with sand and white quartz gravel. Llan Newydd began to feel like home.

A week of continuous rain caused the river to rise at the end of January so that the ships had to be tied to tree trunks growing at the edge of the cliffs. One night of high winds battered the little ship, *Ystwyth*, to kindling between *Gray Wolf* and *Buck Deer*. The next day Madoc had all movable things taken off the unharmed ships, taken several leagues upstream, put on rollers, and pulled to higher ground. The coracles, used for fishing, were kept inside the village. Conlaf turned a coracle upside down on his cottage's smoke hole to keep the continuous rain out. He had to keep the door-flap open to let the smoke out.

Madoc brought his vellum journal from the *Gwennan Gorn*'s forecastle and put it on the wood shelf in his cottage. He wanted to keep track of the winter's floodwaters and the time deemed right for planting peas, barley, and oats. He would soon have to have a new journal for such recordings. He hoped that the few sheep would multiply so that it would be all right to eat one and make thin vellum out of its skin. Deerskin could not be scraped as thin and fine as lambskin. He set out Wyn's clay figures on his shelf and was filled with wonder at the beauty and feeling of movement in the little beasts. A lump came into his throat as he stroked a little rabbit and spoke to it the way children speak to their toys. He promised to keep it from harm, murmuring childhood sayings that became truth through the force of remembered love. He thought what his dear foster sister might have accomplished had she lived. He turned the iron kettle, which had held the little clay animals, upside down for a stool. He sat with the soft aura of the firelight around his figure and stared at the row of animals that seemed to dance in the firelight.

The next day Madoc again worried about his friend Conlaf, who had become so tired that he stayed on his pallet and complained of more belly cramps. "I will sit with you for a while. 'Twill be a break from all the work of getting this colony up and running."

"I appreciate your company," said Conlaf. He had never complained about the fiery, red scratches the barbarians left on his right side. Underneath the healed, pale scratches, his leprosy appeared to be contained in knots much like a tangle of yarn. He put a hand on his midsection and repeated four times a magical charm to quiet a sour stomach. "I catch you under my hand. Lo, the heat from my hand has power against all internal demons. Be mindful of the heat and settle into a peaceful rest with no malice against he who houses you."

Madoc closed his eyes and willed Cougar to come and relieve Conlaf's stomach pains. Cougar did not hear his plea; if she did, she ignored it. After a while, he prayed that the spring sunshine would restore his friend's health. If Conlaf were gone, he would surely fall apart. Everything in his body would turn to dust, except the outpouring tears. He could not hold that much dust together with tears.

The druids remembered *Imbole*, the second day in February. It was the time in Wales when the first stirrings of spring began deep within the belly of the frozen mother earth. Winter weather had been gray and drizzly, not cold enough to snow. The men celebrated with songs to guide the sunlight back to the Earth. They smiled because Woodchuck was not frightened by his shadow this day. The Welsh said Woodchuck was out searching for food and a female. The druids looked for familiar woodchuck signs. What they saw was an unfamiliar water-dwelling rodent with webbed feet and a long hairless tail.

In March the rains ceased. The burned area behind the village was green with grass and bright with red and yellow flowers, a meadow. The black skeletons of burned pines were softened with a covering of moss. Gorlyn found familiar, edible mushrooms, like tiny sponges near the stumps of burned trees. The men ate them with greens until they balked at seeing another little sponge on their wooden supper trenchers. Those complaining loudest were shown how to tie the mushrooms upside down with woven grass to dry for use at a later time.

On this diet color returned to Conlaf's cheeks, and he would not stay inside his cottage. He was up early exploring the New Land. He walked through the canebrakes, broke finely tatted webs sparkling with dew, and snacked on blackberries. Among the trees strung with long strands of silver-gray moss, he saw the rattlers with diamondbacks that glided in search of rodents through the fern.

Nights were chilly and humid; days were warm and humid. While the men staked out with twine several large square patches of earth for planting, the warblers flitted through the branches and the pileated woodpeckers hammered. The topsoil was turned over with primitive bone shovels so it became clods with grass growing out of them upside down. With sticks, they broke the clods that were lashed together by sinuous roots, then smoothed the soil with heavy rakes made from a pole attached to a short wooden board with pieces of bone pushed into a row of holes. Oats and barley seedlings thrived in the sandy soil. Peas grew tall and leggy. Some thought the peas should have been planted sooner when the time was auspicious with a waxing moon. Others said they needed to be planted away from the shade trees that had escaped from the fire.

Sigurd said he was no crofter, but he wondered why the men did not collect seeds from native plants and cultivate them. "I have seen that done in Ireland, and the cultivated plant is larger than the wild one."

Efyn, the alchemist, said he knew something about grafting, and he could use his knowledge to make the branch of a Welsh apple tree grow on a native hickory tree. "That would impress the barbarians with our magic!"

One day Madoc wrote the suggestions in his journal, thinking some would be worth a try. He favored collecting seeds from the wild grains in the fall to plant the following spring. He sat against a warm gray stone in the shade, closed his eyes, and felt infinite calm. This was a new beginning. He believed he had everything he wanted or needed until something tickled his nose. He opened his eyes, and Cougar stood in front of him holding a long stem of wild grass.

"Nohold is watching the twins," she said. "I came to show you how to catch a bunch of fish." Under one arm she carried a wadded net made of twisted plant fibers. She told him to bring the egg-shell, meaning the round coracle. "I bring food for us and for the fish."

Madoc put his journal away and carried a two-man coracle over his head. They followed a game trail close to the river and went over several rises. At the wide place, where the river flowed into the sea, they lowered the coracle, pushed it into chest high water, and got in. Sitting back to back, Madoc paddled until Cougar said it was the place she had seen blue crabs bottom-feeding two days before. She waded ashore, found a large rock, tied a fiber rope around it, dropped it near the coracle for an anchor, climbed inside, and tied the other end of the rope to an inside rib.

She pulled open the casting net, took out a good-sized leather box that held a couple of handfuls of green grasshoppers, tied one onto a single, braided-fiber line, and handed the baited line to Madoc. "Hold it in the shallows, and when crab takes grasshopper, pull up gently and put crab in here." She shoved a huge, loosely woven basket toward his feet. Madoc easily learned to catch crabs and was ready to go home with a full basket to show off their catch. "No home," said Cougar, pulling a string at the top of the basket so the crabs would not crawl out. "Fish now."

Madoc heard loud popping and thought it was some kind of shorebird hunting minnows.

She chuckled and pointed where the tide had ebbed, exposing the dark, slick rocks, piles of broken oyster shells, and broad flats of purple-brown pluff mud to the sun. Gases trapped in the greasy mud expanded and burst through the surface, leaving little wells behind. She pointed and told Madoc to paddle to the place where the river lay quiet in a round, deep, green hole surrounded by cypress knees. There the channel was nearly imperceptible. She smiled, made a happy sound in her throat, and showed him a bulge in the water where a large-sized fish swam.

She shook out the big, awkward net to make certain its top was wide open, and held one end of its drawstring in her left hand. She gathered some of the top in the same hand. With her right hand, she grasped one of the stone weights tied to the bottom. She astonished Madoc by rotating her hips and shoulders back to the left and then swinging to the right, leading with her right hand and swirling the net out. The net spun open and landed with a splash where they had seen the bulge in the water. After a few minutes, she pulled in the closed net containing half a dozen mullet and a few shrimp. "Yu!" she said and handed the net to Madoc as she picked up the flopping fish and shoved them onto a forked willow stick. The shrimp went into the empty grasshopper box.

Madoc forgot to let go the stone weight on the first cast, and the net fell in a tangled bunch at the side of the coracle. Cougar showed him again and brought in more shrimp and so many mullet that they had to eat the lunch of hard, flat bread Cougar had brought. They then used the larger, leather lunch box for the mullet and the shrimp went in the grasshopper box. A couple more times Cougar cast the net and then let Madoc try again. They filled the boxes and lined the bottom of the coracle with shrimp and mullet.

Madoc was enthusiastic with barbarian-type fishing. The next time he cast the net it thrashed around in the water and was so heavy he hollered that he was afraid he was going to lose it. Cougar told him to sit still or he would tip the coracle, and she bent double with laughter. Together they hauled the net to the surface, and Madoc gave one huge heave and raised it into the coracle.

"Yu Lugh!" shouted Cougar as a shark with a mouth full of sharp teeth flopped around on the mullet and shrimp near their bare feet and legs.

It took only seconds for both of them to climb out of the coracle into the chest-deep water. The shark bit his way out of the net, attacked the shrimp, and went after Madoc's boots. Madoc hit him over the head with the paddle three or four times. When it was stunned into a coma, they cautiously got back into the coracle.

Cougar used a bone knife to cut its head off, which she threw far out into the water, hitting a cypress knee. "Would bite us, right through our wrapping," she said, pointing to her clothing and flesh. "Enough fish for one day."

To carry their catch home, Madoc took the front end of the coracle and Cougar took the back. Madoc felt awkward and clumsy and did not say much on the way back. He wondered why he felt confused and could not think of anything to say. He turned and looked at Cougar. She looked up. Her smile was lopsided, distant, and she did not meet his eyes. *She knows something I do not*, he thought.

That evening, while Cougar, Clare, and Conn cleaned the fish, Madoc went to get Nohold and the twins to come to a fish, crab, and shrimp supper at the Llan Newydd great hall. Cougar could no longer hold on to the story of Madoc's shark. Afterwards, the men held their sides laughing. Before the evening was over, one fish story matched another until everyone that had a story was heard.

Hesitating for the right words, Nohold told the story of one cold winter when he was a boy. The cold lowered the temperature of the shallow water so quickly that the trout were stunned and immobilized. "Too cold to swim," he said. The people of his village scooped up the fish in all baskets they could find. They had a grand feast with enough left over to have smoked fish well into spring.

Conn promised to make up a song that would make the fish that lived in the shallow part of the river proud.

On the first day in April, Madoc directed several men to scrape moss and mildew from the outside of the *Gwennan Gorn.* Tipper stepped beside him in the ship's shade and said, "The deer came back. I saw some in the grassy park made by the fire. Come hunting with some of us tomorrow. Ask Nohold, he might like to go."

"Thanks," said Madoc. "I will ask him. Do you remember he promised to show us how to surround a small herd of deer and drive them over the cliff to the riverbank? That would be easier than trying to get close enough to spear one or two, or to shoot arrows. We can butcher beside the river and bring the meat and hides up the steps. What do you think?"

"I think I can get about twenty men for one of those surrounds," said Tipper. "And wonder of wonders! I saw the lost lamb you are looking for. You could catch her with a fishnet."

"You are not just a singing bird who thinks he saw a lost lamb?" said Madoc, picking up Tipper's scraper.

"If you think me a bird singing, I will show you wool caught on a brush pile a half a league away in a patch of stinkweed." Tipper pulled a hunk of wool out of his tunic pocket.

"Hell's fire! I owe Cougar an apology," said Madoc, putting the scraper on the ship's deck where Tipper could find it. "I honestly thought she took the lamb and skinned it days ago. She longs for another bunting for the little laddie who has none."

Madoc stopped at the stream first and cupped the cool water in his hands for a drink, then he held his wet hands to his face. It felt good. At his feet the stream ran deep and still. The overhanging ferns hardly moved. Iridescent wings carrying a dragonfly stirred the ferns and passed over Madoc's head. The water under the big log swirled into a whirlpool with bubbles full of their kind of talk. It had been a while since he had really talked with Cougar. Had he missed those talks? Oh, yes, he had. A dozen times since they had fished he had almost gone to see her. *I wanted to sit by the fire on chilly days and talk with her,* he thought. His ears cocked. He thought he had heard the babies cry. They would be big by now. Babies grow fast. Suddenly he was as anxious to see the twins as he was to see Cougar. He was short of breath and his heart pounded. He had not seen the inside of her new cottage. Would it reflect her? Would it take on some of the magic enchantment that she emanated? He fingered the rough bark of a pine tree and felt where the now-hardened pitch had spilled out from a broken branch, like crystalline tears.

"Madoc! How long have you been here?"

"What?" He jumped as though he had been bee stung as Cougar's voice penetrated his thoughts.

"Not long," he said. "I was looking to see if that big log was still across your stream. I can move it for you, cut it up, and you can use it for firewood and get to your water hole easier."

"Sometimes I walk across the stream on it or sit and listen to the stream gurgle. Leave it alone. I like it. What I need is another blanket of lamb's wool," she said, laying the twins down on the soft moss. "I let them crawl out here. It is easier on their knees than the dirt floor of the big lodge. But I have to watch. They like to get into the water."

"One of our lambs ran away," said Madoc. "Do you know anything about it?"

"No. Could I help you look for Lamb?" she said.

"I be going to send Conlaf after it," he said, feeling awkward. "Maybe I will go with him. Actually, I came to apologize because, for troth, I thought you had stolen—aw, taken, our lamb. Honestly, I knew you would not take it, but I could not imagine who else wanted it—really wanted it."

"Thanks for thinking of me. I am glad about that. But you are right, if someone had taken that lamb, I might have been the one." She gave him a quirky smile. "I promise, if

I ever do, I will leave a thank you—like you explained your barter system. You give me something I want. I give you something you want. Come see our big lodge."

"Big lodge?" said Madoc.

"Aye. We live in the big lodge. It is warmer in winter and cooler in summer. Easier to take care of the babies and to cook when two people do the work at the same time. Nohold enjoys these boys as much as if they were his own."

Madoc ran across the moss to pick up Sky who was about to crawl into the stream's shallow pool with the tadpoles. Earth was behind him, saying, "Da, da!" He put Earth under his other arm and looked up at Cougar who was laughing as both babies squirmed to get down on the ground again.

"Come on up and see Nohold. He would not want to miss you," said Cougar.

"So you live here with Nohold?" He felt foolish asking. "You and he—"

Sky let out a squeal of delight as he caught hold of Madoc's beard.

"Oh yes. He and I—It has worked out." She stopped, stared at him, then started again. "Madoc, you and I will always be—friends, like you said, yes? I have thought about it. I think about you. I dream of you. But I cannot live with a spirit. One day you will go back to your spirit world across the sea, and maybe I will go back to my grandmother, the Healer, close to the Big Lake." Her face was sober and her dark eyes gentle. "Your face, the sound of your voice, the touch of your hands, something of you will live in my heart forever, next to Grandmother's songs. They are mine to think about whenever I want."

"You would miss me? I mean, would you ever want to come to see me because the ache in your heart was so great?"

"This past winter, when my heart really ached, I almost came a dozen times. Yes, I missed you so much, I thought my heart was broken in little pieces. I was certain it would never heal. I missed talking with you. I missed seeing you. And so, instead of seeing you, I made myself look at those precious babies, and I took care of them. When we went fishing, I realized in a roundabout way the twins were a gift from you. They are alive because of you. Both Nohold and I owe you our lives. Mayhap this is what you came to our land for. Like you explained, it is destiny. I understand what destiny is now."

Madoc drew in a breath. He wanted to pull her close and feel her breath on his cheek.

"I missed you touching me most," she said. "But you were right. You could not leave all those men who depend on you. Nohold and I are man and woman, and you are our good friend." She wiped her tears quickly. "Nohold is right for me; he knows who I am. I know who he is. We are a family. You know I always wanted a family. And so, I thank you and your gods and ghostlike spirits every day."

"Ya, same as I thank the little people that live under the rocks for letting us stay here peacefully in both freedom and security. Did you know the deer have come back?" said Madoc, feeling uncomfortable. "The little people forgave us about the fire, and they sing and dance every night in the fairy circles. When you sit on that log over the stream, you can hear them if you listen carefully."

"Fairies? I do not know them," said Cougar.

Nohold came out of the big lodge and smiled at Madoc. "Come inside and see what Cougar has done."

There were shelves all around the lime-washed sides of the cottage and wooden pegs for clothing, but the clothing lay in heaps here and there. On two sides of the lodge, where there might be openings or windows in Madoc's cottage, there were paintings which brought the outdoors inside. Cougar stepped over a heap of clothing to show Madoc one of the paintings that was of the stream and the log that lay across it. In the painting a gull was perched on the log and ferns grew around the base where the roots were exposed. There was another painting of two smiling babies swinging in their cradle board tied to the big tree growing beside the lodge. The paints were made from fine-ground ore or powdered, dried plants mixed with gulls' egg-whites. For a brush she used rabbit's fur. Cougar told Madoc she tried many things, like goose grease and pine pitch, before she found that whites of eggs would dry smooth and rabbit's hairs carried the colors better than anything.

Madoc thought her paintings were better than anything

he had seen in Wales or even in places outside of Wales. They brought a lump to his throat, and he did not know what to say. Women in his country did not do painting. They sewed, embroidering pictures. He suspected women in this country tried to keep the lodge neat and clean. He could see that Cougar had better things to do than hang up clothing and fold bedding. He was sure, if taught, or if Cougar had colored threads, that she could do as well or probably better than most.

"It took her many, many days. But no one could have done better than my woman," Nohold said with pride.

Madoc nodded his agreement as he let Nohold's words, "my woman," bounce around in his head. Finally he told Nohold about the deer hunt. Nohold agreed to be ready to go at the village gate at dawn.

Both babies began to holler. They were standing, holding on to a large lidded basket. Cougar sat them on the earthen floor. "They crawl, they stand, but are not sure how to walk—yet," she said. "They are so determined. They want to walk. When they do—you will hear me scream for help. They will be everywhere, into everything."

When he left, Cougar put her arms around him and kissed him. "Good to kiss a friend," she said.

Madoc's heart pounded. He took Nohold's good hand and said, "Aye, friends forever."

In the morning Conlaf did not have to tell Madoc that he was ill. Madoc saw his gray skin color and told him to stay on his pallet. "I am going to bring Cougar up the hill to see you."

"Aw, I talked to her once, and she said I had worms, same as Gwalchmai. I told her she was only hoping I had worms. Do you have to get her? Let Troyes or Llieu come see me."

"First I have to beg off the deer hunt. You and I are not going."

"Aaww," said Conlaf.

Cougar came to look at Conlaf's pallor. He was pale as a ghost, his tongue was covered with a white coat, and his hands and feet were puffy. She put a hand on his belly and let her fingers push. He yelled that it hurt. She told him again, "You have worm disease."

He admitted he had passed a few white, thready things, but said he would be better once the sun was back. She said the sun had been back for a month. She told him that sheep with worms have no tender bellies because they ate stinkweed, the scruffy-leafed plant that appears sprinkled with ash. She said she watched the horse and cow shy away from stinkweed in favor of tender shoots of green grass, and they had tender bellies and lots of worms.

"How do you know that?" asked skeptical Conlaf.

"I pet the animals and talk to them. I get to know them," she said. "I learn things, by seeing and listening."

"So, I see why Madoc loves you," said Conlaf. "He thinks you might be a druid."

"I think a druid is a ghost or a spirit," she said. "I be not ready to come into your ghost world." Her eyes became soft, and blinked to hold back tears. "Drink tea made from stinkweed's leaves and spiky, yellow-green flowers. Your cramps will disappear, and your color will come back. There is a quintessence in stinkweed that kills the worms."

"Anyone who talks like that is for certes a druid," said Conlaf, feeling better already knowing he could be cured. "You are already with us. You talk like Madoc."

"No! You are teasing. I learned from listening," she said. "You have worms and there could be others. Madoc and Clare, for instance. Everyone in your village drink stinkweed tea for a while."

Conlaf promised her to have stinkweed tea with all the men at every meal. Miraculously, after a week Conlaf's old stomach ache disappeared, and Madoc felt a heaviness lift from his shoulders. Others who felt weak as watery soup, gained color and strength and were able to go about their jobs with enthusiasm and energy.

Madoc visited the ailing Gwalchmai, who was thin as a pole, weak as a chick in a thunderstorm, and coughed so much it was a chore to talk. Gwalchmai said he had no aching belly, but would fain like to see the copper cube Rabbit gave Madoc. The next time Madoc visited, he put the cube and pearl neckband in Gwalchmai's hands.

"Give it to Brett's family," Gwalchmai said. "Tell them of his bravery." He coughed, closed his eyes, and said, "The neckband, use it to buy another sail."

"How am I going to do that?" said Madoc. "We are here, and Brett's family and shipbuilders, if alive, are on the other side of the sea in Wales."

"Do it," insisted Gwalchmai, coughing. "My life string is worn out. The coughing sickness eats my strength. Death creeps up whether I want it or not." He closed his eyes and Madoc left.

In the morning Gwalchmai lay peacefully quiet. His breath was gone.

With heavy hearts the druids dressed him in his newest tanned-skin tunic and trousers. He was uncommonly light as they laid him on a wooden raft and sent his burning body out to sea at sunset, as was the sacred ritual at the end of an archdruid's life.

Finn recited Gwalchmai's greatest deeds and those of his kin for nine generations back. At the end he said, "Every morning for weeks I thought my friend, Gwalchmai, was dead, but he was sleeping. This morning he lay so peaceful I thought him sleeping, but he was dead."

The next morning Tipper told Madoc that he and twenty men were leaving for the deer hunt. Madoc said he and Conlaf were well enough to go along part way and bring home the lost lamb.

"I know Cougar wants the lamb's skin to make a bunting for one of her babies, and you want the skin to make vellum!" chided Conlaf. "I am going to protect the life of that lamb!"

Tipper had his men and Nohold at the village gate when Madoc and Conlaf got there. They found eight deer browsing in new grass close to the river. The hunters, with bunches of river-willow tied to their clothing as camouflage, made a downwind U-formation and slowly pushed the herd further and further up the hill to a rocky ledge. Close to the ledge the grass was sparse, and the deer became nervous and darted from one side of the U to the other. The hunters closed their line and rushed the deer over the edge. The sounds of hooves sliding, rocks tumbling, and deer screaming was deafening. The hunters clung to rocks and weeds so they would not fall with the deer.

When the dust settled, the men looked over the edge and saw a mass of squirming, broken bodies. Tipper was first to rush down the hill and along the river's edge. He called for others to come and pick out their catch, then he held his bow taut and let an arrow fly into the lungs of a buck. He tied a fiber rope around three of the deer's legs, dragged it away from the others, peeled the hide, and butchered it. The river ran red along the shore where others butchered their deer.

Madoc and Conlaf waved their arms to keep the pesky yellowjackets away. Someone brought a wooden sled that had hauled sod across slippery grass. The loaded sled was too heavy to haul up the hill, and the men had to use their backs to carry meat and hides. Madoc heard grudging remarks about not having horses to carry the loads of meat. Another man talked about women and how nice it would be to have a fair face to help with the butchering.

Madoc and Conlaf went downriver to a little grove of trees untouched by the fire, where the lamb was last seen. Madoc carried a fishnet over his shoulder. He said he was hungry and wished the hunters had built a fire to roast some of their catch by the river.

"I am tired of drinking bitter-as-gall stinkweed tea," said Conlaf and put his fingers to his lips. He pulled aside a bush and uncovered a bed of white flowers that resembled tiny bells. "Lugh, I thought it was the fool lamb," he whispered. He let the bush swish into place.

A couple of jays flew from one bush to another. A raven croaked a harsh statement from a protruding stone and lifted one greasy wing to probe for lice. A little flock of nervous wrens flitted about, rode the breeze, and came back to hide in the bushes.

"I be sailing to Wales for horses and women," Madoc said in his best matter-of-fact tone. "Mayhap I will bring back a couple of dogs, loveable dogs, not wild like the barbarians have."

Conlaf stood still. "My God, you mean it," he said. "You cannot. What about leaving Cougar? The twins are growing faster than a windstorm. We all need you here!"

"Kabyle can keep everything orderly," said Madoc. "No-hold takes good care of Cougar and the twins. For some time I have been thinking about it. The men are right. We need women and horses to make a permanent settlement. The Northmen realized that when they settled Greenland. I will go with two ships. The other ships will stay in case the village needs to move for any reason or their lumber can be used for more permanent buildings. I can buy one or two new ships and will come back with three or four ships. I will bring Llorfa, if she will come. What do you say?"

"I do not know what to say," said Conlaf. "I thought you would stay several years to prove this land. Coins? You need coins in Wales!"

"I have Brett's pearl neckband, and if I need more, I will see Thomas, Archbishop of Canterbury. He will be surprised!"

"Oh, Lord God!" Conlaf's eyes clouded. "You are fooling with me. You are not serious? Too many things can happen. How long will you be gone? Are you tempting the gods to rearrange your life?"

"I can do it! I have to, or else our village will last only as long as the man with the most years to live! I did not fight cross currents coming around the east side of the dog's tail for naught. That warm current is strong enough to take me north. When my sailing intuition tells me I have gone far enough, I will look at my magnetized floating needle and go east until I find Ireland. There is nothing to it!"

"It cannot be easy going against the sun's path. 'Tis counter to sane sailing. You have lost your wits!" said Conlaf.

"Nay. I have sailed from west to north to east and naught terrible happened. If my idea of a proven Welsh colony is to work, I have to go back for women this spring, while the weather is good."

"I wish there was another way."

"There is," said Madoc in a whisper so low that Conlaf turned his head to hear. "You want a barbarian woman or Llorfa?"

"That is no choice for me," said Conlaf, and he closed

his eyes. "I think you and Cougar could be a pair if you had not taken a vow of no intimacy with barbarians."

"Ya, well then wish me Lugh's luck or a god's speed."

Conlaf's eyes popped open. "Look! That bloody lamb is just standing there. Shhh! You will frighten it. Give me your net. I can get it." He shoved Madoc aside, kept his eyes on the lamb, and threw the net.

The lamb squirmed, tangled itself, and bleated. It took in quick breaths.

Madoc saw its sides heave and heard Conlaf shout, "Hooray! Huzza! I got it!" He also heard a rattle like dry seedpods. There was no breeze to rattle dry pods.

Conlaf stepped forward to scoop the lamb in his arms. His right foot slipped into a hollow under a rotting log. He sat down, pulled his knees up to his chest, and held his right leg. "Feels like the sting of a thousand yellow jackets where my boot and leather leg wrappings do not meet."

From the corner of his eye Madoc saw the dusty snake slide past. It had deep depressions on either side of its snout, between eye and nostril. It rustled like dry bones knocking together and disappeared in the brush. He scooped the kicking lamb into his arms.

Conlaf rocked back and forth, breathed deeply trying not to faint, and said, "Jahoo! Do not—do not put that lamb in my lap. Tie her in the net, then look at my leg!"

The lamb bleated but could not move with the net wound around her body. Madoc looked at Conlaf's right leg and said, " 'Twas a bloody snake."

The leg was already swollen above the ankle, so that the skin was tight and shiny. Two red marks showed where the fangs had sunk into the flesh. Conlaf pushed the flesh around the fang marks. He was able to squeeze out a few watery drops of blood. He squeezed more. He let the bright red blood ooze down to the ground. He had never treated snakebite before, but he knew in the physician's box there was a ten-year-old theriac made from powdered viper and opium mixed in honey that Llieu used against poisons. He lay inert on the ground. His leg continued to swell. He groaned and fluttered his eyes. His mouth was so dry he could not speak.

Madoc pulled out a handful of lamb's wool and took it

to the river to saturate with water. He lay the wet wool on Conlaf's leg. He was frustrated with his lack of knowledge of medicines. Here was his best friend, who, moments ago, was in splendid spirits. Now his friend lay in agony with a spiking fever and a swelling leg, and he could die. Madoc had to think of something. "I am going after Cougar," he said. "She lives in this bloody land and will know what to do."

"No! No!" said Conlaf. "We have to learn ourselves what to do if we are going to live here. Plantain leaves will take the heat out."

Madoc pulled his boot off, filled it with water, mashed some plantain leaves, wet them, and placed half of them over the red marks. With his finger he managed to get the rest of the green slurry between Conlaf's lips. He dribbled water in the dirt and rolled the wadded wool in the mud. He patted it like a poultice over the crushed leaves and around Conlaf's swollen leg. The foot and ankle were so swollen the boot would not budge. Madoc swore and cut it off with the steel daggerlike knife he wore tied to his belt.

Conlaf's eyes stayed closed even when he vomited. He would not say another word. Once in a while he came out of his stupor, groaned, and tried to take his shirt off. Madoc felt his forehead, chest, and arms. His skin was hot and dry and scaly rough under his right arm.

Madoc loosened his own shirt and laid it over Conlaf. He longed to go for Cougar, but he dared not leave Conlaf alone because there were wolves. He had heard them bay at night. Maybe there were panthers. He had not seen any, but Kabyle had. He splashed water on Conlaf's head and hands. He prayed to Lugh and made promises to the water god if he would pull his friend through. He put his mouth close to Conlaf's ear and said out loud, "You are going to Wales with me, my friend. Only Lugh knows what would happen if you do not go with me. You are so clumsy. Lord Lugh! Why did you put your leg against a snake? Why did you leave off your leg wrappings above your boot? Why? Why?"

He went to the river for more water. The lamb bleated as if it wanted a drink. He did not look at it, but said, "Lady Lamb, 'tis your fault. If you had stayed with the rest of your band, we would not have come looking for you. If Conlaf dies, I will kill you. I swear it. Crack! I will break your neck and make vellum from your miserable hide."

The lamb stopped bleating and dozed off. Towards evening the lamb woke up and said, "Baaa." Madoc let it lick water from his boot before he limped with one boot on, one off, down to the river for more water. He was hungry and pulled a handful of wild onions, washed them, stuffed them in his mouth, and felt guilty because Conlaf could not eat. He spat out the tiny bulbs and filled his boot with more water.

He used his knife to make feathery chips from some dead twigs. He created sparks by scraping two granite stones together as fast as he could. The sparks did not always touch the dry chips, and when they did, they died. The fire took a long time to begin. His wrists ached with the effort. The first flame burnt the hairs off the back of his fingers. He licked them to ease the sting. He was so exhausted that he lay down beside Conlaf and slept. He dreamt that he backed away when he saw the leper's mark, the ugly, rough, white patch with the little nodules under Conlaf's right arm. He saw Conlaf's spirit step through the veil, as easy as going through a spider's web, to the Otherside. He took the *Gwennan Gorn* back to Wales and told Llorfa that Conlaf lived in Sid. She cried and he put his hands over his ears. A cooing dove wakened him. He was cold, crampy, and stiff.

Conlaf moved! He sat up! He sang a seaman's ditty! He wiped his mouth on the back of his hand and pointed to Madoc's boot. "Say, I drank water from that? No wonder it tasted like dirty-foot jam."

Madoc jumped up. "Thank Lugh, you evil son of a jackal, you are alive! You are all right! God, I love you! Your bad humors are in balance and your soul is light."

"What did I do that was evil?" said Conlaf. He tried to stand and found he was weak as watered mush.

"You did not say if you would sail to Wales with me," said Madoc. "You need me to take care of you in case you break your leg—or I need you to take care of me in case I run into that trifler, Robert. Remember him?"

"I had almost forgotten. 'Tis Llorfa I cannot wait to see.

Let Llieu, Troyes, and Cougar be Llan Newydd's physicians. You will need me on the homebound ships with all those beautiful women. Zowie! If you do not take me, I will decide to develop a terrible longing, which only a barbarian woman can satisfy. What would you say if you came back and found a barbarian female sleeping on my pallet, cleaning my cottage, and sewing my trousers?"

"Conlaf! You cannot feel that way." Madoc pretended shock. "Not ever. We be druids, not a barbarian's mate!" He stopped, laughed. "Maybe we will develop some kind of trade among the barbarians, if they have something we need. If not, we will find our own food, make clothing, split logs for cottages, and teach our children to be thinkers and use the knowledge that gives us our good life. We will build a nation on New Land."

"*Cyfraith,* Madoc! A nation with laws according to Madoc," snorted Conlaf. He stood; his leg hurt, and he sat down. He pushed on the flesh on his leg. The dimple he made disappeared fast. The swelling was receding.

"You have sore places, little lumps, under your right arm. I remember it used to itch," said Madoc. "I had a dream about it and believe you have leprosy."

"I told you it was the leprosy. That is all I will say about it. I try to think 'tis naught but scabies, a skin infestation made from the itch mite."

"A couple of years ago you carried a sick child, somewhere near Paris. Has it always itched since then?"

"Llieu looked at it and said it was scabies," said Conlaf. "The barbarians scratched it and made a hellish sore. I bathed it with juniper-wood water, and it healed, but now these nodules have appeared. Why do you raise your eyebrows at me?"

"Has Llieu ever seen leprosy?"

"The nodules will go away in a few weeks," said Conlaf. "I can take care of it. 'Twas only a dream you had, naught more." He bit his tongue. He could not bring himself to name again the actual cause of those white scales, sores, and lumps under his arm where once he had held a leprous child and later he had held a festering, leprous leg while scraping away putrid flesh. He had tried to tell Llieu, but in his heart he knew that the old physician did not know what he was talking about. He knew what it was, and he wanted to ignore it. He wanted to tell Madoc that during the great fire he had discovered that he had lost sensation in his right hand. But if he went to Wales, there was hope that an antidote for leprosy had been found. With hope there was no need to tell anyone anything. Hope!

Madoc worried about Conlaf as he prepared for the homeward trip. He, too, secretly hoped that there were physicians in Britain who now had a specific for scales, nodules, weeping sores, and the dreaded leprosy. He hoped that going back to Wales would help him push Cougar out of his thoughts. But honestly, he feared it would not. This woman was the most interesting he had met in a long time. She learned and remembered everything he said. He was certain she knew much more than he would ever learn about the barbarians. He loved listening to her. He was learning her language and thought it more musical than his. He loved watching her move gracefully, without a thought of shyness. Her skin was unblemished; her hair was silky clean and smelled like the sea, the land, the flowers all rolled into one. She was trusting, an experimenter, a childlike risk taker, and so happy caring for the twins that he felt a sharp stab of jealousy. How could a man really forget a woman like that?

Erlendson was honored to be the other shipmaster and suggested that both their ships be fitted with a metal cleat with three indentations facing obliquely forward to secure a taking-spar in three different positions when the wind was abeam to port or across the port bow. He oversaw the placing of new weatherboards on each ship. The *Gwennan Gorn* and the *White Crane* were fitted with pine reinforcements over the broad, rounded bilge. The forward and aft half-decks were extended so there would be more room to carry horses, cows, dogs, and women.

Madoc promised the druids axes, knives, daggers, pitchforks, grindstones, hammers, beetle and wedges, brushscythes, sickles, weeding hooks, hay forks, rakes, skuttles, shearing-shears, scales, weights, and carpenter's crave. He appointed Llieu the Chief Physician, Caradoc the Keeper of the Laws, and Kabyle in charge of the colony's crafts.

Kabyle told him not to bother about bringing swine back, because he would take it as a deep insult to be appointed Keeper of the Pigsty, and he would never touch one forkful of pork. "Do not waste your time with them. Bring back some good sheep dogs and Allah will praise you."

On the morning Madoc and Erlendson were to sail downriver to the sea, the archdruids were up before dawn to perform a special ritual to give the two shipmasters and their crew of five men apiece, good fortune and gods' speed back to Llan Newydd.

Ten druids gathered between the ring of nine cedar posts facing the rising sun and chanted a greeting to the new day. They declared that Madoc was the master leader of their community so long as he lived. They promised to keep the abandoned cottages in good repair, using them only as storage until their owners returned. The rising sun warmed their faces. Birds twittered and whirled in gregarious flocks from one tuft of grass to the next. The doves made plaintive calls, "Hi ho, here we go, go." Then from across the village came an answer, "Oh no, you cannot go, go." Later, some said it was not another dove answering the first, but Cougar's plaintive cry.

Before leaving, Madoc wrapped Wyn's precious clay animals in soft doeskin and placed them in the iron kettle in the center of his plank table, and told himself that they were in the place of honor in his cottage. On impulse he pocketed the clay rabbit as a gift to his daughter. They were his most-prized possession besides the House of Gwynedd signet ring he wore on a thong around his neck. He had the copper cube and pearl neckband in his bundle of clothing. He thrilled with the notion of bringing his foster father, Sein, his mother, Brenda, and his young daughter, Gwenllian, to Llan Newydd. He took a bundle of fresh-cured deer hides to his ship before Conlaf caught him daydreaming. The hides were to convince Welshwomen there was a land of plenty across the sea.

On the way he stopped beside the sheep pen to say farewell to Lost, the little female lamb. All of a sudden he heard the familiar, dry, rattling sound. The lamb lay on the ground. He put the hides down, climbed the fence, and felt the lamb's neck. When he bent over, he saw the snake, with deep depressions on either side of its snoutlike mouth, back away and curl itself around a clacking, rattling tail. It was like the snake that bit Conlaf. The lamb's pulse was faint, then gone. In anger he lay her woolly body on a post and looked for something to beat the rattler to death. From under a pile of wood, a yellow-brown snake glided toward the rattler whose black tongue flicked in and out. Madoc watched the rattler's head weave back and forth. The whirring never stopped. The yellow-brown snake glided away the instant the rattler struck. On the ground where the venom spilled was a small, dark stain. The rattler relaxed a moment with its head down, its eyes mere slits. The yellow-brown snake, its jaws wide open, moved and swallowed the rattler, making itself look fatter, inch by inch.

Madoc ran fast downhill to Nohold's cottage. He pulled the thong with the signet ring over his head and pushed it into his closed fist. He told himself he was going to have Cougar take care of the bucket of little clay animals for him. She could look once a week to see if they were still on his table and make certain every one of the men was well. Would the men enjoy seeing her and the twins? Of course! Maybe one of the men would teach the twins to speak in Welsh. He hoped so. He wanted Nohold to take the best care of Cougar while he was gone. He would always thank her for teaching him to be sensitive about people's feelings. He was grateful she had let him help with the twins' birth. Not many women would want a man around, but she wanted him to learn about fishing, birthing; about women. He would tell her that he would always remember her. He knew he would think of her often—every day.

Nohold was hunting a bear for its hide, so he had to talk with Cougar first thing. He opened his hand and showed her the signet ring. " 'Tis something special to me," he said. "It says that I come from a place across the sea called Gwynedd. You keep it. I am leaving a part of myself here with you."

"Yu," she said with tears in her eyes. She put the thong

over her head and held the ring in one hand until it felt warm, then she untied the string of rainbow stones and took them from her neck. She looked at Madoc who was looking at the sleeping babies. "You wear this; it will keep you safe. I have worn it since before the time I can remember. When I become a ghost, I will look for you, the ghost wearing rainbow beads."

"I will see you before you become a ghost. After the rainy season, I will be back with many women. You will like them, and they will bring you embroidery thread. You will learn how to sew designs as colorful as your painting."

"Embroidery?" Her face squinched into a smile, and she wiped the tears on the backs of her hands. She stood close to Madoc and put her hands around his neck to tie the necklace. She kissed him. He held her close so he could feel her heart beating with his own. He told her about the clay animals in the bucket on his table. They were the link between the women in his life. Across the great distances were women who cast feelings in his belly. Each was special—different, but special. Annesta had a spirit like Wyn. Surely Cougar has that same spirit in this unknown land. "You have a real good spirit," he said, letting his arms fall to his sides.

"You love me, a barbarian, and I love you, a ghost. What is real?"

"The spirits cannot be touched."

"Come back, you have my heart!" said Cougar. "I do not like those ghostly women you will bring here. Dump them and fill your boat with little lambs with soft fur."

"Clashes in life give us thrills and love," he said. "They are good. I be gone."

Madoc hurried back up the hillside. His hand felt the precious colored beads around his neck. He vaulted the fence, picked up the hides, and hurried down the hillside's stone steps to tell Conlaf that the lamb and rattler were dead.

Kabyle overheard and said, "I will have vellum made for thee from that skin. 'Twill be waiting for your return. Praise Allah for yellow snakes!"

"I cannot wait so long. Give the hide to Cougar. She

will give you a kiss in exchange." Madoc handed the hides to Conlaf and took Kabyle's arm. "It has struck me that we, animals and us, must help one another live together. All creatures are bound in some mysterious way. Do you believe that?"

"Aye. Allah told you that," said Kabyle. He stood close to Madoc and whispered, "I be a ninny running at the mouth. I, who am staying, am frightened as much as you, who are leaving. You leave us alone in an unfamiliar land. Shove off before Llieu puts his arm around you. If that old man weeps, I will not be able to hold back my own tears."

Madoc backed away, ran his hand over Kabyle's shoulder, and said, "Go see Nohold often. He and Cougar will help you with unfamiliar things in this land. You can trust them. They will do what they say." He saw that Erlendson was already standing on the deck of the *White Crane*, and Conlaf was motioning to him from the *Gwennan Gorn*. Madoc called out reassurance to his fellow druids gathered on the riverbank. "We will bring horses to pull the plows that you will build in our absence."

Erlendson said, "As far as the horses and cows and dogs go, you can purchase them from us with goods or labor."

"I will make you new boots if you give me a young pup," said Caradoc.

Thurs said, "Bring cabbage seed! 'Twill grow in the rainy season."

Jorge said, "Are you certes that you can bring us enough women on two or three ships?"

Erlendson said, "We will come back in more ships if we get more women to come with us. We can teach the women to be messmates and sailors. But mind, each man can only choose one woman!"

Llieu said, "We do look forward to seeing comely faces in place of ragged beards. I will keep in mind that the women will have a say in our lives and laws!"

Madoc said, "Choose governors, set bartering prices, and make laws while we are gone."

"Hurry back," said Sigurd.

"We pray the gods be with you," said Willem. "Bring back my dear wife, Goeral, your sister."

"Watch for mermaids!" said someone. "Avoid the storms!" said someone else.

Madoc's hands were sweaty. He watched Conlaf scratch at the healing snake bite on his leg, then scratch the scaly stuff under his right arm. Suddenly it occurred to him that the druids standing on the shore were truly afraid the sea would swallow the two ships going or coming. They would never see each other again. Madoc called, "I know how you feel. I also have a knot in the pit of my stomach. We will be back! You can bet your best wool stockings on it!"

"We will consult the stars!" said Liam.

Madoc fairly snorted. "Stars determine naught, incline naught, suggest naught about a man's comings and goings. You are free men, free from the dictates of your birth land, free from movement of the stars, free to study and work as you see proper."

Each man wanted to call out something special. No one knew quite what to say. Their words seemed trite and inappropriate. They waved and sang rounds, and finally Conn led them singing their special song, Gwalchmai's poem about the trials and joys of finding their New Land. He sang the old archdruid's final song about Madoc going fishing and netting a man-eating shark that was so large, when fried it fed all the men for sup. The oars dipped into the brown river-water and pulled the ships midstream where the fast current flowed to the sea.

There was no thunder, no rainbow, no eclipse, no passing comet when the two sails met the sea, only the sun beating hot through humid air. The warm, blue, northern current was in place to carry the *Gwennan Gorn* and the *White Crane* back to Gwynedd's culture of brother warring against brother.

When the two ships were out of sight, Kabyle turned and walked to the sheep pen to pick up the dead lamb before it was discovered by a buzzard or hawk. At first he was puzzled, then he was shocked because the lamb was not there. He looked at the exact spot where it had lain. Gone! Draped over the fence post, as if for payment for the white lamb, was a large, furry, brown bear carcass—the first bear the druids had seen in Llan Newydd.

"America has been discovered before,
but it has always been hushed up."
—Oscar Wilde (1854–1900)

Epilogue
Madoc Legend: Myth, Fact or Fiction?

It must not be forgotten that numerous legends were also current amongst . . . the Bretons and the Welsh, to the effect that a great foreign country lay across the sea in the far west. This popular tradition was so strong that an expedition put to sea from Bristol as late as 1480 to seek for this remote western continent. It was inspired by information contained in two ancient MSS, from the Abbeys of Strata Florida (the Welsh Caron Uwch Clawdd) and Conway, relating to a great expedition launched by King [sic] Madoc of North Wales in the year 1170. Sailing round the south of Ireland, he and his many companions discovered vast tracts of land beyond the western sea. According to these ancient chronicles Madoc returned to Wales to enlist fresh colonists, having left a hundred and twenty settlers behind him. He then re-embarked with ten ships and several hundred passengers. This was the last that was heard of Madoc or those who accompanied him. So much for the MSS. The negative conclusion of their account does not, of course, necessarily imply that Madoc failed to reach his objective. As is proved by the Norsemen's voyages to America a hundred and fifty years later, it is by no means impossible that the ocean was crossed several times at about this period.

—Paul Herrmann, *Conquest by Man*

History affirms that Madoc, bastard son of Prince Owain Gwynedd, lived from the middle of the twelfth century to near its end. Exact dates cannot be agreed upon. Old bardic poems tell us that Madoc, weary of war, sailed with about two hundred men in ten ships, soon after his father's death on December 31, 1169, hoping to find freedom in unproven land. Did Madoc discover America? No—the Vikings and perhaps others were there before him. Did Madoc settle somewhere in America? I cannot say for certain, maybe yes, maybe no. So, what do I know? One of the last American legends to obtain widespread publicity is that of the Welsh Madoc (Madog ab Owain Gwynedd). Late medieval Welsh poets had characterized Madoc as a sea rover. Between 1578 and 1584, Queen Elizabeth's astrologer, John Dee, and the writer on explorations, Richard Hakluyt, resurrected Madoc, by now a mythical figure, and concocted a story that he had discovered America long before Columbus. At that time Francis Drake and Walter Raleigh were staking a claim to North America; Madoc's story lent an air of legitimacy to English territorial ambitions.

According to Richard Deacon's (pen name for G. D. McCormick) well-researched book, *Madoc and the Discovery of America,* Owain Gwynedd, Madoc's father, died a year before Thomas Becket and was buried in consecrated ground in the Lady Chapel of Bangor Cathedral amid much controversy. Baldwyn, Archbishop of Canterbury after Becket's death, advised that Owain's body be removed from the cathedral. The local bishop had his own ideas about the treatment of a Welsh hero and had a passage made from the vault through the south wall of the chapel, and deposited Owain's remains outside the cathedral, but still in consecrated ground. A visitor to the cathedral today will find the reputed tomb of Owain Gwynedd in the Lady Chapel.

Prince Owain had nine children by his two wives, according to Arthur Davies, in "Prince Madoc and the Discovery of America in 1477." Davies said that Owain "left behind him many children gotten upon divers women." The various children, mostly males, fought among themselves for leadership of the northern Welsh.

From various other accounts of the genealogy of the house of Gwynedd, Owain is credited with as few as fourteen to as many as twenty-seven illegitimate children. I used the genealogy by John Edwards Griffith, compiled in 1914, found in the County Archives, Caernarfon, Wales, which lists Madoc as one of Owain's nineteen sons.

Arthur Rhys, in his pamphlet *Did Prince Madoc Discover America?* names Madoc's mother as Brenda, an Irish lady, and Riryd as Madoc's older full brother and Goreal as his full sister. *The Annals of Conway Abbey* show that Madoc married Annesta, a maid to Christiannt, who was Owain's first cousin and his second wife. Madoc and Annesta had a daughter, Gwenllian, who married Meredydd, son of Llowarch ap Bran, Lord of Menai, and they had a son, Meredydd of Bodorgan. From Gwenllian the genealogy was traced by Kathleen O'Loughlin in her *Madoc ap Owain Gwynedd* to Llewelyn ap Heylin, who may have fought Bosworth for Henry Tudor. This relationship is not confirmed by all historians. Some believe it may have been an attempt to prove the Tudors were descended from Madoc.

Prince Owain's bard, Llywarch, *Prydydd y Moch,* recited an ode about a Madoc in 1169, which was later written down. However, the Madoc he spoke about may have been different from the legendary Madoc of this writing. Gwalchmai, also one of Owain's household bards, sang:

> "Madoc kindly apportioned gifts;
> He did more to please than offend me. . . ."

Historians point out that Giraldus Cambrensis, the ablest historian of twelfth century Wales, did not mention Madoc, even though he was familiar with affairs in the court of Owain Gwynedd. Other historians say that Giraldus was only twenty-four and completing his education at the University of Paris from 1166 to 1172 when Madoc sailed westward, so he would not have written about him.

Bards, at that time, memorized history for nine generations back for members of their household and orally passed on songs and odes. In 1450, Maredudd ap Rhys, a clergyman who called himself Chief Bard, wrote several odes about Madoc, "Son of Owain Gwynedd who loved the sea." Also, around this time the Cardiganshire poet-priest, Deio an Ieun Du, wrote that Madoc was a renowned sailor, patron saint of fishermen, and a well-known legendary figure; "knight of the mead, fair peacock, son of Owain Gwynedd."

On November 6, 1493, Peter Martyr, a scholar of An-
ghiera, and chaplain for Ferdinand and Isabella of Spain,
was invited to the Spanish court when Columbus, fresh
from his first voyage, described his findings. Afterwards
Martyr wrote in his *Decades, Ex-Hispania Curia,* "That
some of the inhabitants of the islands honoreth the memory
of one Matec when Columbus arrived on the coast." He
wrote that Columbus referred to one stretch of the Sargasso
as *Questo de Mar di Cambrio,* "These are Welsh waters,"
and he labeled an eastern bay on the Gulf of Mexico, now
called Mobile Bay, *Tierra Los Gales,* "land of the Welsh."

A Russian historian, Professor Isypernick, of the Uzbec
Academy, found a letter in 1959 written by Columbus to
Queen Isabella. The letter revealed that Columbus was well
aware of the existence of the West Indies when he set out
on his first expedition. The letter referred to the Sargasso
Sea as "Welsh Waters" and the land around Mobile Bay as
"Land of the Welsh." This proves Columbus had maps of
the West Indies provided by earlier navigators, even before
Martyr published his *Decades.* Columbus did not arrive in
America by chance.

In his 1984 publication, Arthur Davies shows that a
Welshman, John Lloyd or John Scolvus (the Skillful), explored the North American coast as far as Maryland in
1477, using information from Madoc's twelfth-century voyages. Lloyd's exploration was fifteen years before Columbus and the 1492 discovery of the West Indies.

In 1540 Hernando de Soto landed in a sheltered bay
(Mobile Bay, Alabama, with Dauphin Island). He found
remains of fortifications, which he believed could not be
works of Indians, but built by men from Britain. His findings led many to believe the stone fortifications were built
by Welshmen, chiefly Madoc and his companions.

A French map of the 1600s had the names "Saint Brendan?" and "Matec?" written beside the Azores. In the corner of the map is a note after the words, "Matec, Voyez
Guillaume P-B et Jacob van Maerlant." Guillaume, P-B was
Willem, the Minstrel, who is thought to be the translator of
Madoc's story for the Flemings. The Flemings were
brought to Britain by Henry I and settled on the borders of

England, Wales, and in Pembrokeshire to be used as mercenaries against the Welsh. However, many Flemish moved to the side of the Welsh and were attached to the armies of Madoc's father, Prince Owain Gwynedd, and fought against Henry I's army. Jacob van Maerlant, a Dutch writer, wrote in his *Spiegel Historical* about "Madoc's dream" to sail the western sea in search of new land.

There were more accounts of Madoc after printing was available. For instance, in *The Historie of Cambria, Now Called Wales*, by Caradoc of Llancarfan, edited in English by David Powel, D. D., Madoc was listed as one of Prince Owain's sons, "Loved by many, but caring nothing for power," who "left the land in contention between his brethren and prepared certain ships with men and munitions and sought adventure by seas, sailing west." Madoc left Wales from the old stone pier beside the Afon Ganol and landed at what is now Mobile Bay, Alabama, to begin a Welsh colony. Today scholars argue about the reliability of this work.

B. B. Woodward, in his *History of Wales*, also believed that Madoc left Gwynedd by sea to search for a new homeland. *The Dictionary of National Biography of Wales* listed Madoc in its "Lives of Distinguished People," saying that Madoc was the "reputed son of Owain Gwynedd and he discovered America."

There is evidence that Spaniards were perturbed that America was discovered before Columbus by someone from Europe, either the Vikings, the Irish, or the Welsh. Spanish archives show that in 1526 the Spaniards sent out three expeditions, one to the West Indies in search of Madoc's legend and two to the Canaries (Fortunate Isles) in search of St. Brendan's tale.

Letters exchanged between the King of Spain and Luis de Rojas, Governor of Florida, between 1624 and 1627 state that expeditions were made to search for people of British origin in the areas from which reports of Madoc's landing had come: Florida, Alabama, Georgia, and Mexico. Allegedly, Spain was anxious to prevent claims by England or anyone else of landing in the New World before Columbus.

In 1858, in Llangollen, Wales, the Eisteddfod offered a prize for the best essay on Madoc's discovery of America. Six essays were submitted and five authors took the story of Madoc for historical truth. The sixth author, Thomas Stephens, a self-educated pharmacist, denounced as unproven the "historical facts" about Madoc. Stephens suggested that the lost colonists of Roanoke, some of whom were Welsh, may have intermingled with the local natives and, if so, that would explain the Welsh-speaking Indians in the North Carolina area. Since the essay was on the non-discovery, the judges disqualified his effort. This made Stephens extremely angry, and he protested loudly—but the Eisteddfod Committee held fast. His "debunking the facts" essay was published posthumously in 1893. Some historians applauded it, but others were skeptical, and Madoc's legend continued to live.

The work of Zella Armstrong seemed to make Madoc's legend a distinct possibility. As a direct consequence of her work, on November 10, 1953, the Virginia Cavalier Chapter of the Daughters of the American Revolution erected a memorial tablet at Fort Morgan, Mobile Bay, Alabama, bearing these words:

> *"In memory of Prince Madoc, a Welsh explorer,*
> *who landed on the shores of Mobile Bay in 1170*
> *and left behind, with the Indians, the Welsh*
> *language."*

In 1969 G. D. McCormick tested the theory of Madoc crossing the Atlantic in a shallow, open vessel by sailing across in a small, American-built, flat-bottomed landing craft. He was told his craft would never finish the trip, but it did. That gave McCormick the impetus to face ridicule and discouragement from many historians and complete his task of compiling documents on the Madoc legend. "On the purely literary side there are endless disputes about the correct translations of ancient odes, the authenticity of sources, and the countless foreign references to Madoc. Notably the almost unknown, sublimely romantic, yet factually based narrative about Madoc came from the elusive Willem, the Minstrel of Holland," McCormick wrote, using the pseudonym, Richard Deacon. He researched, examined, and discussed references that are factual and those that are pure hoaxes.

Bernard Knight wrote his famous adventure story of Madoc based on historical facts, *Madoc, Prince of America*. Armstrong, McCormick, and Knight restored credence to the legend of Madoc.

Gwyn A. Williams, Professor of History at the University College, Cardiff, Wales, did his best to shoot down the facts surrounding Madoc with his book titled *Madoc, The Making of a Myth*. Williams showed how people used the Madoc myth to make history. He wrote what every historian, writer, reader, and politician knows: ". . . ideas, no matter how fanciful or utopian or even lunatic, can become material force."

John D. Fair published an article in *The Alabama Review* about a man called Hatchett Chandler, who became overseer of Fort Morgan in 1945 and later the fort's museum curator. Chandler was a self-educated, colorful character. He published a well-received pamphlet of stories about Mobile Bay in 1950. A year later the Gulf Shores Lion's Club named him "Outstanding Citizen of South Baldwin County." In 1955, the State Park Board tried to remove Chandler as curator, because instead of being on the job, he toured the state of Alabama to give talks on the history of Mobile Bay. In 1960 he was given the title, Honorary Historian of the State of Alabama. A year later Chandler published a pamphlet titled *Little Gems from Fort Morgan*. One of the gems was the story of Madoc, in which he drew heavily from the works of Armstrong and McCormick.

According to John Fair, Chandler became "an enemy of the state bureaucrats," "spiteful in his writings," and made "gross distortions of reality. . . . The serious and inevitable consequence of displaying a legend so emphatically was that a generation of visitors to Fort Morgan accepted it [Chandler's Madoc story] as truth . . . Chandler ignored the fact that some of his information had never been proved as historical fact and that his own sources and reasoning were specious." Chandler died in 1967 and was buried 1,300 feet southwest of Fort Morgan.

My husband, Bill, and I went to Mobile in March 1988 to investigate the story of Madoc starting his first colony near the shore of Mobile Bay. I was disappointed not to find the memorial tablet that had been erected by the Daughters of the American Revolution. After a lot of hemming and hawing, the young man behind the museum desk said that the marker had blown down during Hurricane Helena in 1985, and was now locked in the tractor barn. He said, "At least one couple a month comes to Fort Morgan asking to see the Madoc marker, but no one can see it at present. A man from Wales came in February, 1988 and was given permission to photograph the marker in the barn."

In 1973, a Welsh community in New York State commissioned a bronze likeness of Madoc to be placed in the History Museum at Mobile. I asked about the statue at both the History Museum and the Public Library in Mobile, but no one had heard of it. Museum personnel, library people, and even bookstore employees in Mobile seemed embarrassed to talk about the Madoc legend, and they shied away from discussing it.

I believe these people feel chagrined, victimized, and taken-in because for many years one of their own, Hatchett Chandler, misled them (don't confuse me with proven facts) into believing all of the Madoc legends were gospel truth. The people of Mobile have nothing to be ashamed of. History is sometimes based on supposition and slanted by the particular beliefs of authors and the age in which the writing takes place. "History is an outgrowth of the tendency for historians to identify with the groups about whom they write, so that a mingling of truth and falsehood, blending history with ideology, result," said John Fair, quoting the Alabama historian W. H. McNeill.

The American end of the Madoc myth is elusive, at times whimsical, and has little substantial, historical evidence to back it up. Would that it were not so. These tales are full of adventure, romance, and human interest. They tempt and seduce storytellers to make use of them, so that the Madoc myth continues to live, fueled by the retelling, the oral tradition of the bards.

Years ago I became enticed and peeled back the legends layer by layer and found a few historical scraps. I tied those scraps together with the popular myths, and my own imagination arising from researched, twelfth-century background material, and wrote my own version of the Madoc story. My seduction, however, is not complete, because my research of stories about Madoc and his kin is unfinished. Eventually, I shall bring my readers from the twelfth century to the nineteenth century and introduce them to the unusual, blue-eyed Mandan Indians of North Dakota.

Anna Lee Waldo

The extensive historical notes supporting *Circle of Stars* may be obtained from the author by writing to Hope Dellon, Executive Editor, at St. Martin's Press, 175 Fifth Avenue, New York, NY 10010, or by logging onto the website: www.annaleewaldo.com.

Acknowledgments

I am indebted to my late father, Lee William Van Artsdale, who piqued my interest in history when I was old enough to paddle a canoe. He was the first to tell me the story of Madoc, whom he said arrived in North America after the Vikings and nearly three hundred years before Columbus landed in the Bahamas, or West Indies. He said Madoc and his crew settled along Mobile Bay before de Soto ascended the Mississippi, before Marquette ascended the Missouri, and Madoc's followers eventually, by intermarriage, became the Mandan Indians of North Dakota.

I thank Bill, my husband, who does not complain, within my hearing, about the stacks of papers he must walk around to find me at my desk. He does not complain, too loudly, about late meals if my spirit is not ready to come back to the twenty-first century. Bill and our five children have always urged me to go on when there have been dark days. I love them for that, plus all the other wonderful qualities that they have.

I am grateful to all the people in Wales who were so kind and helpful, especially to Miss Ann Thomas, Senior Assistant Archivist, and Mrs. Catherine Hughes, Archives Assistant at the County Archives, Caernarfon, Wales. They helped me with the "Pedigree of the kings and princes of Wales" and the "Tribe of Owen Gwynedd."

I give thanks to Blanton Blankenship, park manager, Fort Morgan, Mobile, Alabama Historical Commission, Gulf Shores, Alabama. He understood my quest but believes the Madoc legend is pure myth perpetuated by the British to promote the idea that they were among the first to colonize America, after the Spanish gave credit to Columbus for finding a wealthy new land.

Fred Steele told me that the pole star is invisible in the high latitudes in summer. He explained that the stars Arcturus or Anares remained stationary and were bright enough to have their height measured above the horizon during the hours of dusk and dawn by early navigators. He explained that Venus, the third brightest object in the sky, orbits greatly among the stars, sometimes even backing up in a peculiar manner (retrograde motion), so that it was not used by ancient mariners. I thank him for letting me use his *Pilot Charts* to study the Atlantic's surface currents and climate conditions during various months of the year.

I thank the librarians of the California Polytechnic State University and San Luis Obispo Public Library who submitted many interlibrary book and manuscript loans for me. I am indebted to the late Oscar Collier for his never-ending belief in this project. I am forever grateful to my agent, Jean Naggar, for her wise advice, understanding, and invaluable expertise. I owe my editor, Hope Dellon, special gratitude for convincing me that the Madoc story needed a strong woman. The consequence of Hope's insistence gave my Madoc story a new character, Cougar, a Calusa Indian girl, for old world–new world contrast of twelfth-century clash of cultures.

I thank all the copyright owners, authors, publishers, and people who gave me permission to use quotations from their books, pamphlets, and magazine and journal articles. The epigraphs and notes give proof that Madoc was a leader of great courage. He brought a group of brave men in ten small ships, with single sails, from Abergele, Wales, across the Atlantic to a place we call Mobile Bay. He then directed a colony to be established and afterwards followed the Gulf Stream back to Wales to add women and horses to his thriving colony. Of course, there were unpredictable hardships and adventures in sailing ships filled with women and children. There was more excitement when these druidic men and women found the original colony empty and discovered scattered villages of strange people living on the vast, unfamiliar, western land.

Bibliography

Circle of Stars is a historical novel based upon the following sources:

CELTS:

Foss, Michael, *Celtic Myths and Legends* (Barnes & Noble Books, New York, 1995)

Fox, Charlotte Milligan, *Annals of the Irish Harpers* (London, 1911)

Green, Miranda J., *The Celtic World* (Routledge, London, 1996)

Hubbell, Sue, "There's No Toppin' Hoppin' John," *Smithsonian* (Vol. 24, No. 9, Dec. 1993)

Hubert, Henri, *The Greatness and Decline of the Celts* (Dorset Press, New York, 1995)

James, Simon, *The World of the Celts* (Thames and Hudson, New York, 1993)

Kershaw, Nora, *Celtic Britain,* vol. 34 (Thames and Hudson, London, 1964)

Matthews, John, ed., *A Celtic Reader* (The Aquarian Press, Northampton, England, 1991)

Oakeshott, Ewart, *The Archaeology of Weapons* (Barnes & Noble Books, New York, 1960)

O'Driscoll, Robert, ed., *The Celtic Consciousness* (Braziller, New York, 1982)

Rees, Alwyn and Brinley Rees, *Celtic Heritage* (Thames and Hudson, New York, 1978)

Sharkey, John, *Celtic Mysteries* (Thames and Hudson, New York, 1979)

DRUIDS:

Daniel, Sir John, *Philosophy of Ancient Britain* (Williams and Norgate Ltd., London, 1927)

Ellis, Peter Berresford, *The Druids* (William B. Eerdmans Pub. Co., Grand Rapids, 1995)

Hamilton, Edith, *Mythology* (New American Library Inc., New York, 1969)

Herbert, A., *An Essay on Neodruidic Heresy in Britannia* (H. G. Bohn, London, 1838)

Higgins, Godfrey, *The Celtic Druids* (Rowland Hunter, Ridgeway & Sons, Piccadilly, London, 1829)

Kendrick, Thomas Downing, *The Druids, Keltic Prehistory* (Mathuen, London, 1927)

Llywelyn, Morgan, *Druids* (Wm. Morrow and Co., Inc., New York, 1991) An historical novel from the druid perspective of Caesar's campaign in Gaul.

Morganwg, Iolo, compiler, 1801, *The Triads of Britain* (Wildwood House, London, 1977)

Owan, A., *The Famous Druids* (Clarendon Press, Oxford, 1962)

Pflugh, Harttung J., "The Druids of Ireland," *Royal Hist. Soc. Transactions* (Vol. 7, 1893)

Spence, Lewis, *Druids, Their Origins and History* (Barnes & Noble Books, New York, 1995)

GENEALOGY:

Bartrum, P. C., "Hen Lwythau Gwynedd A'R Mars; Fifteen Tribes of Gwynedd," *National Library of Wales Journal*, 201–235 (Vol XII, No. 3, Summer 1962)

Lloyd, John Edward, *The History of Wales from the Earliest Times to the Edwardian Conquest*, vol. II, chap. XIV, "Owain Gwynedd," 487–535, "Genealogical Tables," 766 (Longmans, Green and Co., London, 1911)

O'Laughlin, Kathleen, *A Few Notes on Madoc ap Owen Gwynedd Including His Genealogy* (St. Catharines, Ontario, Canada, 1947)

Lundy:

Chanter, John Roberts, "History of Lundy Island," *Transactions of the Devonshire Association* (Vol. VI, 1871)

Kidson, Clarence, "Lundy," *Encyclopaedia Britannica* (Vol. 14, William Benton, Publisher, Chicago, 1965)

Madoc:

"Afon Ganol Wall Fragments," *Transactions of Caenarvonshire Hist. Soc.* (1956)

Armstrong, Zella, *Who Discovered America? The Amazing Story of Madoc* (The Lookout Pub. Co., Chattanooga, 1950)

Caradoc of Llancarfan, *The Historie of Cambria, Now Called Wales* (transl. into English by Humphrey Llwyd, ed. David Powel, D. D., London, 1584)

Chandler, Hatchett, "Gem 23, Prince Madoc," *Little Gems from Fort Morgan, The Cradle of American History* (The Christopher Publishing House, Boston, 1961)

Chapman, Paul H., *The Man Who Led Columbus to America* (Judson Press, Atlanta, 1973)

Davies, Arthur, "Prince Madoc and the Discovery of North America in 1477," *Jour. of the Royal Geographical Soc. Engl.* (Vol. 150, No. 3, Nov. 1984)

Deacon, Richard, *Madoc and the Discovery of America* (Braziller, New York, 1966) Contains much good research.

Fair, John D., "Hatchett Chandler and the Quest for Native Tradition at Fort Morgan," *The Alabama Review* (A quarterly journal of the Alabama Hist. Soc., vol. XL, no. 3, July 1987)

Hakluyt, Richard, *The Voyages, Navigations, Traffiques and Discoverees of the English Nation*, vol. 3 (Bishop, Newberrie and Barker, London, 1600)

Knight, Bernard, *Madoc, Prince of America* (Robert Hale Ltd., London; St. Martin's Press, Inc., New York, 1977)

A novel that has Madoc leaving from Lundy Island to find new land.

O'Laughlin, K., *Madoc ap Owain Gwynedd* (St. Catharines, Ontario, Canada, 1947) Also see: *Wele Madoc Dewr Ei Fron* (St. Catharines, Ontario, 1942)

Pohl, Frederick J., *Atlantic Crossing before Columbus* (W. W. Norton and Co., Inc., New York, 1961)

Pugh, Ellen, *Brave His Soul; The Story of Prince Madoq of Wales and His Discovery of America in 1170* (Dodd Mead, New York, 1970)

Ratcliffe, Michael, "Madoc Fever," *Ninnau, The North American Welsh Newspaper* (Vol 14, No. 1, Nov. 1, 1990)

Rea, Robert R., "Madagwys Forever! The Present State of the Madoc Controversy," *Alabama Hist. Quarterly* (Vol. XXX, Spring 1968)

Rhys, A., *Did Prince Madoc Discover America?* (A pamphlet, Chicago, 1938)

Southey, Robert, *Madoc* (Monroe and Francis, Boston, 1805), also *Madoc, An Epic Poem* (Longman, Hurst, London, 1805)

Stephens, Thomas, "Madoc, an essay on the discovery of America by Madoc ab Owain Gwynedd," *Llangollan Eisteddfod,* 1858 (Longmans, Green and Co., 1893)

Thom, James Alexander, The Children of First Man (Fawcett Gold Medal, New York, 1994)

Williams, Gwyn A., *Madoc, The Making of a Myth* (Eyre Methuen, London, 1979)

Williams, John, *An Enquiry into the Truth of the Tradition Concerning the Discovery of America by Prince Madoc ab Owain Gwynedd* (J. Brown, London, 1791)

Winter, Pat, *Madoc* (Bantam Books, New York, 1990)

MEDIEVAL MEDICINE:

Buchman, Dian Dincin, *Herbal Medicine* (Random House, Wings Books, New York, 1980)

Lee, Hugh B., "Letters to the Editor," *The Wall Street Journal* (June 20, 2000)

Richards, Peter, *The Medieval Leper* (Barnes & Noble, Inc., New York, 1977)

Riddle, John M., J. Worth Estes, and Josiah C. Russell, "Birth Control in the Ancient World," *Archaeology* (Vol. 17, No. 2, March/April 1994)

Vogel, Virgil J., *American Indian Medicine* (Ballantine Books, New York, 1973; Univ. of Oklahoma Press, 1970)

Welcome, Sir H. D., "Ancient Cymric Medicine," *Meeting of British Med. Assoc. at Swansea* (B. Wellcome and Co., 1903)

Wulff, Robert M., *Village of the Outcasts* (Doubleday and Co., Inc., New York, 1966)

SAILING SHIPS:

Broecker, Wallace S., "The Once and Future Climate," *Natural History* (Vol. 105, No. 9, Sept. 1996)

Contreras, Carlos A., "Navigation of St. Brendan and the Discovery of America," *Medieval Assoc. of the Pacific* (Univ. of California, Irvine, Feb. 22, 1992)

General Surface Current Chart of the World, Jan., Feb., & Mar. (Pilot Chart, Defense Mapping Agency, Hydrologic Center; Pub. By George E. Butler Co., San Francisco, 1976). Courtesy of Fred Steele.

General Surface Current Chart of the World, July, Aug., & Sept. (Pilot Chart, US Naval Oceanographic Office, Dept. of the Navy and by the Environmental Data Service, Natl. Oceanic and Atmospheric Adm. of the Dept. of Commerce; pub. by the Defense Mapping Agency Hydrographic Center, Washington D.C., 1976 and Jan., Feb., & Mar., 1949). Courtesy of Fred Steele.

Goetzmann, William H. and Glyndwr Williams, *The Atlas of North American Exploration* (Prentice Hall General Reference, New York, 1992; Swanston Pub. Ltd., London, 1992)

Hamilton, Edith, *Mythology* (New American Library Inc., New York, 1969)

Herrmann, Paul, *Conquest by Man*, trans. Michael Bullock (Harper & Brothers, New York, 1954)

Heyerdahl, Thor, *Early Man and the Ocean* (Doubleday, New York, 1979)

Jastrow, Robert and Malcolm H. Thompson. *Astronomy: Fundamentals and Frontiers* (John Wiley and Sons, New York, 1977)

Lemonick, Michael D. and Andrea Dorfman, "The Amazing Vikings," *Time* (May 8, 2000)

MacLeish, William H., "The Blue God, Tracking the Gulf Stream," *Smithsonian*, 44 (Vol. 19, No. 11, 1989)

Marcus, G. J., *The Conquest of the North Atlantic* (The Boydell Press, Suffolk, England, 1980) Excellent descriptions aboard open ships and experiences of early explorers.

Ocean Passages (Pub. by The Admiralty, London, Dec. 6, 1950). Descriptions of the ocean passages from Wales, to the Canaries, then west to Cuba to Mobile Bay. From Mobile Bay around Florida, past Charleston, Chesapeake Bay toward Ireland. Courtesy of Fred Steele.

Richardson, Sarah, "Vanished Vikings," *Discover* (Vol. 21, No. 3, March 2000)

Stowe, Keith, *Ocean Science* (John Wiley & Sons, Inc., New York, 1983.)

Vesilind, Priit J., "In Search of Vikings," *National Geographic* (Vol. 197, No. 5, May 2000)

Vitullo-Martin, Julia, "Columbus's Circle," *The Wall Street Journal* (October 8, 1999)

World Climatic Sheet 1, Jan.: Sheet 2, July (Pub. by The Admiralty under Superintendance of Vice-Admiral Sir John Edgell, E.B.E., C.B., F.R.S., Hydrographer, 1943). Courtesy of Fred Steele.

PLANTAGENET ENGLAND:

Barber, Richard, *Henry Plantagenet, 1133–1189* (Barnes & Noble Books, New York, 1993)

Barlow, Frank, *Thomas Becket* (Univ. of California Press, Berkeley, 1986)

Jack, R. Ian, *Medieval Wales* (Cornell Univ. Press, Ithaca, 1972)

Knowles, D., "Archbishop Thomas Becket; A Character

Study," *Proc. of the British Academy* (Vol. 35, 1949)

Taylor, Ernest, "Grand Jury System Used for Centuries," *San Luis Obispo County Telegram-Tribune* (Tues., Oct. 8, 1996)

Warren, W. L., *King John, 1167–1216* (Univ. of Calif. Press, Berkeley 1961; Barnes & Noble, Inc., New York, 1996)

PREHISTORIC FLORIDA AND GULF COAST:

Blanchard, Charles E., *New Words, Old Songs* (Inst. of Archaeology and Paleoenvironmental Studies, Univ. of Florida, Gainesville, 1995)

Bodtker, Michael B., private correspondence, May 11, 2000.

Brown, Jan, "The Past Revisited: Calusa Indians Leave a Legacy of an Empire," *Gulfcoast Living* (April 1987)

Davis, Dave D., ed., *Perspectives on Gulf Coast Prehistory* (Univ. Presses of Florida, Gainesville, 1984)

Edic, Robert F., *Fisherfolk of Charlotte Harbor, Florida* (Inst. of Archaeology and Paleoenvironmental Studies, Univ. of Florida, Gainesville, 1996)

"Federal Writer's Project of the Work Projects Administration for the State of Florida," *Florida, A Guide to the Southernmost State* (Oxford Univ. Press, New York, 1956)

Hudson, Charles, *The Southeastern Indians* (Univ. of Tenn. Press, Knoxville, 1987)

Larson, Lewis H., *Aboriginal Subsistence Technology on the Southeastern Coastal Plain During the Late Prehistoric Period* (Univ. Presses of Florida, Gainesville, 1980)

Marquardt, William H. and Claudine Payne, eds., *Culture and Environment in the Domain of the Calusa* (Inst. of Archaeology and Paleoenvironmental Studies, Univ. of Florida, Gainesville, Monograph No. 1, 1992)

Middleton, Harry, "Gulf Stream," *Southern Living* (Vol. 24, No. 7, July 1989)

Neuman, Robert W., *An Introduction of Louisiana Archaeology* (Louisiana State Univ. Press, Baton Rouge, 1984)

Stowe, Keith, *Ocean Science* (John Wiley & Sons, Ind., New York, 1983)

Waller, Karen J. and William H. Marquardt, "The Discovery of Pineland's First 1,500 Years," *Calusa News* (Inst. of Archaeology and Paleoenvironmental Studies, Florida Museum of Natural History, No. 7, Dec. 1993)

Walthall, John A., *Prehistoric Indians of the Southeast* (Univ. of Alabama Press, Tuscaloosa, 1980)

WALES:

Berman, Bob, "Millennium Dance," *Discover* (Vol. 20, No. 12, Dec. 1999)

Hartley, Dorothy, *Lost Country Life* (Pantheon Books, New York, 1979)

Houlder, Christopher Howard, *Wales, An Archeological Guide and Early Medieval Field Monuments* (Faber and Faber, London, 1974)

Jones, Pierce T., "Medieval Settlement in Anglesey," *Anglesey Antiquarian Soc. Transactions* (1951)

Lloyd, J., *A History of Wales from the Earliest Time to the Edwardian Conquest*, 2 vols. (Cymmrodorion, London, 1939)

Miles, John, *Gerald of Wales, Geraldus Cambrensis* (Gomer Press, London, 1974)

Morris, Jan, *The Matter of Wales* (Oxford Univ. Press, New York, 1984)

Simmonds, L. A., *Welsh Legends and Folklore* (James Pike Ltd., St. Ives, Cornwall, Engl., 1975)

Tomes, John, ed., *Blue Guide: Wales and the Marches* (Ernest Benn Ltd., London, 1979)

Williams, Gwyn A., *The Land Remembers, A View of Wales* (Futura Publications Ltd., London, 1977)

Woodward, B. B., *History of Wales* (Virtue and Co., London, 1953)